THE MAMMOTH BOOK OF
BEST NEW HORROR

VOLUME 23

Edited and with an Introduction by
STEPHEN JONES

ROBINSON

RUNNING PRESS
PHILADELPHIA · LONDON

Constable & Robinson Ltd
55–56 Russell Square
London WC1B 4HP
www.constablerobinson.com

First published in the UK by Robinson,
an imprint of Constable & Robinson, 2012

A copy of the British Library Cataloguing in Publication
Data is available from the British Library

UK ISBN 978-1-78033-090-7 (paperback)
UK ISBN 978-1-78033-091-4 (ebook)

1 3 5 7 9 10 8 6 4 2

First published in the United States in 2012 by Running Press Book Publishers,
A Member of the Perseus Books Group

Books published by Running Press are available at special discounts for bulk
purchases in the United States by corporations, institutions, and other organizations.
For more information, please contact the Special Markets Department at the
Perseus Books Group, 2300 Chestnut Street, Suite 200, Philadelphia, PA 19103,
or call (800) 810-4145, ext. 5000, or email special.markets@perseusbooks.com.

US ISBN: 978-0-7624-4597-4
US Library of Congress Control Number: 2011939126

10 9 8 7 6 5 4 3 2 1
Digit on the right indicates the number of this printing

Running Press Book Publishers
2300 Chestnut Street
Philadelphia, PA 19103-4371

Visit us on the web!
www.runningpress.com

Printed and bound in the UK

CONTENTS

ix
Acknowledgements

1
Introduction: Horror in 2011

89
Holding the Light
RAMSEY CAMPBELL

104
Lantern Jack
CHRISTOPHER FOWLER

111
Rag and Bone
PAUL KANE

125
Some Kind of Light Shines from Your Face
GEMMA FILES

142
Midnight Flight
JOEL LANE

152
Trick of the Light
TIM LEBBON

169
But None Shall Sing for Me
GREGORY NICOLL

189
About the Dark
ALISON LITTLEWOOD

203
The Photographer's Tale
DANIEL MILLS

220
The Tower
MARK SAMUELS

231
Dancing Like We're Dumb
PETER ATKINS

245
An Indelible Stain Upon the Sky
SIMON STRANTZAS

258
Hair
JOAN AIKEN

266
Miri
STEVE RASNIC TEM

281
Corbeaux Bay
GEETA ROOPNARINE

286
Sad, Dark Thing
MICHAEL MARSHALL SMITH

301
Smithers and the Ghosts of the Thar
ROBERT SILVERBERG

324
Quieta Non Movere
REGGIE OLIVER

342
The Crawling Sky
JOE R. LANSDALE

369
Wait
CONRAD WILLIAMS

390
The Ocean Grand, North West Coast
SIMON KURT UNSWORTH

424
They That Have Wings
EVANGELINE WALTON

446
White Roses, Bloody Silk
THANA NIVEAU

461
The Music of Bengt Karlsson, Murderer
JOHN AJVIDE LINDQVIST

496
Passing Through Peacehaven
RAMSEY CAMPBELL

510
Holiday Home
DAVID BUCHAN

511
Necrology: 2011
STEPHEN JONES & KIM NEWMAN

577
Useful Addresses

ACKNOWLEDGEMENTS

I would like to thank David Barraclough, Kim Newman, Vincent Chong, Mandy Slater, Amanda Foubister, Rodger Turner and Wayne MacLaurin (*sfsite.com*), Peter Crowther and Nicky Crowther, Ray Russell and Rosalie Parker, Gordon Van Gelder, Andy Cox, Joe Morey, Ellen Datlow, Charles Black, Debra L. Hammond, Douglas A. Anderson, Gavin Grant, Nicholas Royle, Val and Les Edwards, Sandra Ferguson, Johnny Mains, Brian Mooney, Andrew I. Porter, Philip Harbottle, Conrad Williams and, especially, Duncan Proudfoot, Max Burnell and Dorothy Lumley for all their help and support. Special thanks are also due to *Locus*, *Ansible*, *Entertainment Weekly* and all the other sources that were used for reference in the Introduction and the Necrology.

MIDNIGHT FLIGHT copyright © Joel Lane 2011. Originally published in *The Horror Anthology of Horror Anthologies*. Reprinted by permission of the author.

TRICK OF THE LIGHT copyright © Tim Lebbon 2011. Originally published in *House of Fear: Nineteen New Stories of Haunted Houses and Spectral Encounters*. Reprinted by permission of the author.

BUT NONE SHALL SING FOR ME copyright © Gregory Nicoll 2011. Originally published in *Zombiesque*. Reprinted by permission of the author.

ABOUT THE DARK copyright © Alison Littlewood 2011. Originally published in *Black Static*, Issue 25, November 2011. Reprinted by permission of the author.

THE PHOTOGRAPHER'S TALE copyright © Daniel Mills 2011. Originally published in *Theaker's Quarterly Fiction*, Issue 36, Spring 2011. Reprinted by permission of the author.

THE TOWER copyright © Mark Samuels 2011. Originally published in *The Man Who Collected Machen and Other Weird Tales*. Reprinted by permission of the author.

DANCING LIKE WE'RE DUMB copyright © Peter Atkins 2011. Originally published in *Rumours of the Marvellous*. Reprinted by permission of the author.

AN INDELIBLE STAIN UPON THE SKY copyright © Simon Strantzas 2011. Originally published in *Nightingale Songs*. Reprinted by permission of the author.

HAIR copyright © Joan Aiken Estate 2011. Originally published in *The Monkey's Wedding and Other Stories* and *The Magazine of Fantasy & Science Fiction* No. 696, July/August 2011. Reprinted by permission of Small Beer Press and the author's estate.

MIRI copyright © Steve Rasnic Tem 2011. Originally published in *Blood and Other Cravings*. Reprinted by permission of the author.

In memory of

RAY BRADBURY
(1920–2012)

To the dust returned

INTRODUCTION

Horror in 2011

IN JANUARY, HarperCollins US changed the name of its genre imprint Eos to Harper Voyager, to bring the list in line with the publisher's UK and Australian sister companies to create a global brand.

America's second-largest bookstore chain, Borders, filed for Chapter 11 bankruptcy protection in February with debts totalling $1.29 billion and assets of $1.275 billion. Despite closing more than 200 stores over the following few months, Borders eventually announced it was going into liquidation in July after no bidders for the troubled chain came forward. The remaining stores finally closed their doors in September.

February also saw the surprise collapse of Canada's largest book distributor, H. B. Fenn & Company, when the company filed for bankruptcy with liabilities of around $25.6 million. The company's entire workforce of more than 125 employees was laid off immediately.

REDgroup Retail, Australia and New Zealand's largest bookseller with such chains as Angus & Robertson and Borders (no connection to the US bookstore), was also placed into voluntary administration the same month, with debts of around A$51.8 million.

In better news, the struggling HMV sold British bookshop chain Waterstone's to Russian billionaire Alexander Mamut for £57 million. Bookseller James Daunt, owner of six independent Daunt Bookshops in London, was named as managing director and announced that he wanted the 296-branch chain "to feel like your local bookstore".

A year after putting itself up for sale, America's biggest bookseller, Barnes & Noble, received an injection of $204 million in August when conglomerate Liberty Media purchased a stake in the company, but declined to buy the company outright.

In October, Amazon Publishing announced that it would be launching 47North, a new science fiction, fantasy and horror imprint edited by Alex Carr. The new imprint was named after the latitude co-ordinates in Seattle where Amazon is based. Titles would be available in print, audio and, of course, Kindle formats.

At the beginning of the year it was revealed that a new American edition of Mark Twain's classic 1884 novel *The Adventures of Huckleberry Finn* had replaced the use of the racially offensive word "nigger" with "slave", to make it more acceptable to modern readers. However, some critics complained that the censored version was "cultural vandalism" and was at odds with the anti-racist theme that Twain was writing about. *The Adventures of Huckleberry Finn* is reportedly the fourth most-banned book in US schools.

In May, a survey amongst secondary school English teachers in the UK found that they were ditching classic novels and Shakespeare from their curriculum because boys aged eleven to fourteen said they lost interest if the book they were studying was longer than 200 pages.

That same month, an investigation by the *London Evening Standard* newspaper discovered that one in three children in the city did not own a single book, one in four schoolchildren aged eleven could not read or write properly, and one in five school leavers was unable to read confidently.

Meanwhile, in December the results of a survey conducted by the UK's National Literacy Trust revealed that around 3.8 million children in the country did not own a book. This meant that almost a third of all British children did not have any reading material, with boys again being the most likely to be missing out.

In Stephen King's *11/22/63*, a man dying of cancer travelled back through a wormhole in a Maine diner to a specific day in 1958 and attempted to prevent the assassination of President John F. Kennedy by Lee Harvey Oswald five years later. Curiously, the book was retitled *11.22.63* in the UK, but *not 22.11.63*!

The paperback edition of King's *Full Dark, No Stars* added a new short story, "Under the Weather", to the original four novellas.

J. K. Rowling planned to start exclusively selling the e-book versions of all seven of her *Harry Potter* novels via her new Pottermore.com website, which was supposed to launch in October but suffered from technical delays. Once fully operational, the free site would also offer other Potter-related material, including interactive games.

Meanwhile, the estate of a man claiming that *Harry Potter and the Goblet of Fire* was plagiarised from the 1987 book, *Willy the Wizard: Number 1: Livid Land*, finally had its case dismissed in the UK after seven years when the plaintiff failed to start paying a £1.5 million deposit ordered by the Chancery Division of the High Court to cover costs.

Rowling also left her long-time literary agent, Christopher Little, and went to a new agency set up by Little's business partner, Neil Blair.

Arabat: Absolute Midnight was the third volume in the projected five-book fantasy series written and extensively illustrated by Clive Barker, which began in 2002.

Miniaturised humans battled against giant-seeming insects in *Micro*, which Richard Preston completed from an unfinished draft by the late Michael Crichton.

The Burning Soul by John Connolly was the tenth in the "Charlie Parker" series, while *Samuel Johnson vs. the Devil: Hell's Bells* (aka *The Infernals*) from the same author was a sequel to his YA novel *The Gates*.

Narrated by its murdered protagonist, *Ghost Story* was the thirteenth volume in Jim Butcher's best-selling "Dresden Files" series.

Dean Koontz's horror novel *77 Shadow Street* was about a cursed apartment building. Bantam supported the book's release with an online "360-degree immersive experience".

The trade paperback of *What the Night Knows*, a supernatural serial killer novel from the busy Mr Koontz, also included a related novella originally published as an e-book, while *Frankenstein: The Dead Town* was the fifth and final book in the series from the same author.

Richard Matheson's latest novel, *Other Kingdoms*, was about witchcraft and magic in a rural English village, as told by an ageing horror writer.

When a couple of ageing musicians discovered an abandoned baby girl in the woods, they set in motion a chain of horrific events in John Ajvide Lindqvist's fourth novel, *Little Star*.

Family Storms and *Cloudburst* were the first volumes in a new series by the still long-dead V. C. Andrews®.

A couple buried in an avalanche emerged to discover a world apparently devoid of anyone but themselves in Graham Joyce's *The Silent Land*. Stephen King described it as "Scary *Twilight Zone* stuff, but also a sensitive exploration of love's redemptive power."

A man found that his life had been "modified" out of his control in *Killer Move* by Michael Marshall (Smith).

Inspired by the Hammer Films tradition, Christopher Fowler's *Hell Train* was set on a locomotive travelling through Eastern Europe during the First World War.

As a companion to its series of new *Sherlock Holmes* adventures, Titan Books issued Kim Newman's novel *Professor Moriarty: The Hound of the D'Urbervilles*, which continued the exploits of "the Napoleon of Crime" and his debauched henchman, Colonel Sebastian Moran.

Meanwhile, John O'Connell's novella *The Baskerville Legacy* focused on the relationship between Sir Arthur Conan Doyle and real-life journalist Bertram Fletcher Robinson, who some claim came up with the idea for *The Hound of the Baskervilles*.

The Dark at the End was reportedly the final volume in F. Paul Wilson's long-running "Repairman Jack" series, while *Out of Oz* marked the end of Gregory Maguire's best-selling "Wicked" series (at least for now).

In Adam Nevill's *The Ritual*, a group of four campers encountered monsters both human and supernatural in an ancient Scandinavian forest.

A former airline pilot searched for his missing girlfriend in a strange coastal village in *Loss of Separation* by Conrad Williams, and a man believed he had discovered a map to the city of his dreams in Nicholas Royle's novel *Regicide*, an expanded version of the author's story "Night Shift Sister".

The Shadow of the Soul was the second book in Sarah Pinborough's "Dog-Faced Gods" series, as detective inspector Cassius "Cass" Jones continued his investigations into the sinister activities of the immortal "Network".

Ghost of a Smile was the second in Simon R. Green's "Ghost Finders" series about agents working for the Carnacki Institute.

A gate in an urban housing project led to a world of ghosts and monsters in Gary McMahon's *The Concrete Grove*, the first volume in a new trilogy, while *Dead Bad Things* from the same author was about a reluctant psychic and included a bonus short story.

The dead were restless in *Graveminder*, the first adult novel by best-selling YA author Melissa Marr, and a seventeen-year-old girl uncovered her family's dark secrets in Essie Fox's Victorian Gothic mystery *The Somnambulist*.

Aloha from Hell: A Sandman Slim Novel was a sequel to *Kill the Dead* and *Sandman Slim*, as Richard Kadrey's anti-hero took on an insane serial killer who was mounting a war against both Heaven and Hell.

Joseph Nassise's *Eyes to See* was the first in a trilogy about a man with the ability to see ghosts, and a survivor of a terrorist attack could hear the voices of who perished in Robert J. King's *Death's Disciples*.

A woman could tell when men were about to die in Michael Koryta's *The Cypress House*, while an ancient evil infected an island lighthouse and a big cat sanctuary in *The Ridge*, from the same author.

Something huge and tentacled emerged *Out of the Waters*, the second in David Drake's "Books of the Elements" quartet.

People started turning into cannibalistic monsters in *Vacation* by Matthew Costello, and a woman's New York apartment was infested with insects no one else could see in Ben H. Winters' *Bedbugs*.

Fired Up by Jayne Ann Krentz was the first book in the "Dreamlight" series and the seventh in the "Arcane Society" series.

Diabolical was Hank Schwaeble's sequel to *Damnable*, while *I Don't Want to Kill You* was the third book in the humorous serial killer trilogy by Dan Wells about sociopath John Wayne Cleaver.

Skinners: The Breaking and *Skinners: Extinction Agenda* were the fifth and sixth books, respectively, in the series about monster-hunters by Marcus Pelegrimas.

Former Leisure executive editor Don D'Auria moved to small press/e-book imprint Samhain Publishing, where he launched a new horror line in October with no less than five books from Ramsey Campbell, including the new novel *The Seven Days of Cain*.

Other titles from the same publisher included *Angel Board* by Kristopher Rufty, *Borealis* by Ronald Malfi, *Wolf's Edge* by W. D. Gagliani, *Forest of Shadows* by Hunter Shea, *Dead of Winter* by Brian Moreland, *Dark Inspirations* by Russell James, *Catching Hell* by Greg F. Gifune, and *The Lamplighters* by Frazer Lee.

Steve Hockensmith's *Pride and Prejudice and Zombies: Dreadfully Ever After*, illustrated by Patrick Arrasmith, was the third in the trilogy that started with Seth Grahame-Smith's best-selling pastiche and continued with Hockensmith's prequel.

Derived from the same source material, *Mr Darcy's Bite* was a werewolf novel by Mary Lydon Simonsen, *Jane Goes Batty* was the second book in Thomas Michael Ford's series about a vampire Jane Austen in the present day, and *Jane Austen: Blood Persuasion* was the second in the humorous vampire series by Janet Mullany.

And still the dross kept coming with such literary "mash-ups" as *Alice in Zombieland* "by" Lewis Carroll and Nickolas Cook, and *The Twilight of Lake Woebegotten* by "Harrison Geillor".

In *Grave Expectations* credited to Charles Dickens and Sherri Browning Erwin, young Pip was a werewolf and Miss Havisham a vampire, while *A Vampire Christmas: Ebenezer Scrooge,*

Vampire Slayer by Sarah Gray (Colleen Faulkner) pretty much spoke for itself.

Oscar Wilde teamed up with Arthur Conan Doyle and Bram Stoker to investigate some bizarre killings in Gyles Brandreth's *Oscar Wilde and the Vampire Murders*, while *The Damned Highway: Fear and Loathing in Arkham* was a gonzo mash-up of H. P. Lovecraft and Hunter S. Thompson by Brian Keene and Nick Mamatas.

Gregor Samsa transformed into a kitten instead of a cockroach in *The Meowmorphosis* by Franz Kafka (who should be spinning in his grave) and the pseudonymous "Coleridge Cook".

Maureen McGowan's *Sleeping Beauty: Vampire Slayer* was a YA novel in the "Twisted Tales" series, but perhaps the year's most interesting mash-up came from author Cecily von Ziegesar, who reworked her popular 2002 novel as *Gossip Girl: Psycho Killer*.

Charlaine Harris' eleventh "Sookie Stackhouse" novel, *Dead Reckoning*, involved the telepathic waitress in the firebombing of Merlotte's bar and a plot by her lover Eric to destroy his new vampire master.

In *Hit List*, the twentieth volume in Laurell K. Hamilton's best-selling "Anita Blake" series, the vampire hunter found herself battling with the Mother of All Darkness once again for possession of her body.

The titular lawman's job was to control the blood-drinking "Sunless" who lived in ghetto areas of London in James Lovegrove's *Redlaw*, and a woman investigated her uncle's murder in Piper Maitland's *Acquainted with the Night*.

Although Trevor O. Munson's *Angel of Vengeance* was the inspiration for the short-lived CBS-TV series *Moonlight* (2007–08), featuring an undead private investigator, the novel had never been published before.

In S. M. Stirling's *The Council of Shadows*, a follow-up to *A Taint in the Blood*, reluctant "Shadowspawn" Adrian Brézé embraced his dark heritage to save his kidnapped lover.

Jacqueline Lepora's *Immortal with a Kiss* was a sequel *to Descent Into Dust* and again featured vampire-hunter Emma Andrews, while *Vampire Federation: The Cross* was the second book in the mystery series by Scott G. Mariani (Sean McCabe).

The Moonlight Brigade by Sarah Jane Stratford was the second in the "Millennial" series about vampires fighting the Nazis in World War II.

Following on from *The Strain* and *The Fall*, *The Night Eternal* was the final volume in the vampire virus trilogy by Guillermo del Toro and Chuck Hogan.

Set in nineteenth century Russia, *The Third Section* was the third book in Jasper Kent's historical "Danilov Quintet".

Hateful Heart was the fourth volume in Sam Stone's "Vampire Gene" series and involved time-travelling vampires and the last remnants of the Knights Templar.

Memories We Fear was the fourth in the "Vampire Memories" series by Barb Hendee, and *Crossroads* was the seventh book by Jeanne C. Stein to feature vampire Anna Strong.

Set in seventeenth century Bohemia, *An Embarrassment of Riches* was the twenty-third novel in Chelsea Quinn Yarbro's "Count Saint-Germain" historical vampire series.

Stay-at-home father Simon experienced some disturbing physical changes when he met a group of playground dads in Jason Starr's *The Pack*, and the last known lycanthrope tried to evade capture from vampire monster hunters sanctioned by the Vatican in Glenn Duncan's *The Last Werewolf*.

Wolf Tales 12 was the final volume in the erotic shape-shifter series by Kate Douglas.

2011 was definitely the year of the zombie. Film director Tobe Hooper collaborated with Alan Goldsher on the zombie horror novel *Midnight Movie*, which was based around a supposedly "lost" movie made by Hooper.

Acknowledgeing its debt to George Romero's 1968 movie *Night of the Living Dead*, Daryl Gregory's *Raising Stony Mayhall* detailed the life of the eponymous zombie narrator in an alternate world where the walking dead regained rational thought.

Set in the aftermath of the zombie apocalypse, the titular bookseller's blog formed the basis of *Allison Hewitt is Trapped* by Madeleine Roux, while Colson Whitehead's satirical novel *Zone One* looked at the repercussions of a zombie plague in a near-future New York.

Scavengers by Christopher Fulbright and Angeline Hawkes was a zombie novel from Elder Signs Press.

Steven Saknussemm's debut novel *The Zombie Autopsies* was presented in the form of a series of scientific journals and other research documents, while Ray Wallace's *Escape from Zombie City* had the format of a choose-your-own adventure.

A woman realised that she had become a zombie in Sophie Littlefield's *Aftertime*, while a girl found she had the power to create zombies in *Unforsaken*, a YA novel from the same author.

K. Bennett's *Pay Me in Flesh* was the first in the "Mallory Caine, Zombie at Law" series. No, really.

Dead of Night was a zombie novel by Jonathan Maberry, while *Dust & Decay* was a sequel to the author's post-apocalyptic zombie novel *Rot & Ruin*.

Having been forced to kill his sister in *Feed*, future blogger Shaun Mason tried to discover who deliberately infected her with the zombie virus in *Deadline*, the second book in the "Newsflesh" trilogy by Mira Grant (Seanan McGuire).

A girl was the only survivor in her town of the "Feeding Plague" in *Frail* by Joan Frances Turner (Hilary Hall), the sequel to the post-apocalyptic *Dust*.

Originally published online for free in 2003 and in the UK in 2005, David Moody's zombie novels *Autumn: The City*, *Autumn: Purification* and *Autumn: Disintegration* finally received their first American print editions from St. Martin's Griffin. From the same author, *Them or Us* was the final book in the "Hater" trilogy.

Flip This Zombie and *Eat Slay Love* were the second and third books in Jesse Petersen's humorous "Living with the Dead" series which began with *Married with Zombies*.

Xombies: Apocalypso was the third book in the series by Walter Greatshell, as was James Knapp's *Element Zero* in the SF/zombie series which began with *State of Decay*.

Featuring zombie detective Matt Richter, *Dark War* was the third in the "Nekropolis" series by Tim Waggoner.

Abaddon Books' *Tomes of the Dead* series continued with Chuck Wendig's *Double Dead* and Tony Venables debut novel *Viking Dead*.

* * *

There was a touch of Bradbury about Erin Morgenstern's debut novel *The Night Circus*, which concerned a pair of rival 19th century illusionists and a mysterious circus where magic really worked.

In Deborah Harkness' debut *A Discovery of Witches*, the first in a planned trilogy, a woman with powers she had long denied teamed up with a 1,500-year-old vampire to solve a series of mysteries.

In *The Taker* by former CIA intelligence analyst Alma Katsu, an ER doctor encountered a mysterious woman who claimed to be 200 years old.

Saw screenwriters Patrick Melton and Marcus Dunstan teamed up with Stephen Romano for their debut novel, *Black Light*, about a private investigator/exorcist who found himself working on a case that might finally solve the mystery of what destroyed his family.

An ex-soldier and narcotics dealer hunted a serial child-killer through the ugly alleys of Low Town in Daniel Polansky's first novel, *The Straight Razor Cure*.

When a First World War veteran inherited his family's old Georgian plantation, he encountered an evil that had been patiently waiting for his return in poet and playwright Christopher Buehlman's debut, *Those Across the River*.

Two sisters sent to stay with their elderly aunt uncovered an evil that had lain hidden for years in Lindsey Barraclough's *Long Lankin*, which was inspired by an old English folk ballad.

In *Outpost* by former gravedigger and film projectionist Adam Baker, the skeleton crew on a derelict refinery platform in the Arctic Ocean discovered that the outside world had been devastated by a global pandemic.

After eating a teenager's brain, a zombie decided to rescue the boy's girlfriend in *Warm Bodies*, a first novel by Isaac Marion, and a college professor was transformed into an intelligent zombie in Scott Kenemore's debut, *Zombie, Ohio*.

Beloved of the Fallen was a romantic angel thriller that marked the novel debut of "Savannah Kline" (Kelly Dunn).

A forensic psychologist was obsessed by the legend of Elizabeth Bathory in Holly Luhning's *Quiver*, while a college freshman found herself in a battle between vampires and werewolves in Jennifer Knight's debut *Blood on the Moon*.

Will Hill's debut, *Department 19*, was a young adult first novel about a secret government organization descended from Van Helsing that hunted vampires, and a fragile teenager began to remember why her friends died after experimenting with an Ouija board in Michelle Hodkin's YA debut, *The Unbecoming of Mara Dyer*.

Chuck Palahniuk's blackly comic *Damned* was about a spoiled teenager trapped in Hell with people she wouldn't be seen dead with.

An African-American professor set out to find the lost world described in Edgar Allan Poe's story "The Narrative of Arthur Gordon Pym of Nantucket" in Mat Johnson's novel *Pym*.

An Uncertain Place, the seventh crime novel in the series featuring Commissaire Adamsberg by Fred Vargas (medieval archaeologist Frédérique Audoin-Rouzeau), took the French police chief and his colleague Danglard from a collection of severed feet outside London's Highgate Cemetery to the hunt for a possible vampire in Serbia.

Steve Mosby's *Black Flowers* was another crime-crossover, which began when a little girl mysteriously appeared on a seaside promenade with a disturbing story to tell.

Anthony Horowitz's "missing story" pastiche, *The House of Silk*, found Sherlock Holmes and Dr Watson investigating the disappearance of four Constable paintings along with the establishment of the title. It was the first spin-off book to be officially endorsed by the estate of Sir Arthur Conan Doyle.

New Random House imprint Vintage Classics, dedicated to publishing classic science fiction and horror novels, was launched in April with a series of anaglyphic 3-D covers and red-and-blue glasses included in each volume.

The initial five titles were *Planet of the Apes* by Pierre Boulle, *Twenty Thousand Leagues Under the Sea* and *Journey to the Centre of the Earth* by Jules Verne, *The Lost World* by Arthur Conan Doyle and *The Call of Cthulhu and Other Weird Tales* by H. P. Lovecraft.

Edited with an Introduction and notes by S. T. Joshi, *The White People and Other Weird Stories* collected eleven stories by Arthur Machen, along with a Foreword by film director Guillermo del Toro.

Steampunk: Poe was a young adult collection of seven stories and six poems by Edgar Allan Poe, illustrated in steampunk-style by Zdenko Basic and Manuel Sumberac.

Tales of Mystery and Imagination from Barnes & Noble included twenty-nine stories by Poe, along with colour plates by Harry Clarke and an Introduction by Neil Gaiman, while the author's *The Raven and Other Poems* was a companion volume collecting fifty-seven poems with the original colour illustrations by Edmund Dulac. An attractive illustrated tie-in book bag was also available.

Unfortunately, in February it was announced that the city of Baltimore was cutting its funding to the Edgar Allan Poe House and Museum, and that the popular tourist attraction would have to become self-sustaining or it would close.

From Barnes & Noble's bargain Fall River imprint, *The Body Snatcher and Other Classic Ghost Stories* edited by "Michael Kelahan" (Stefan R. Dziemianowicz) contained twenty-nine tales by M. R. James, Charles Dickens, Edith Wharton and others.

Also edited under the "Kelahan" name from the same imprint, *M is For Monster* was an anthology of twenty-six stories arranged alphabetically by monster, from "Alien" to "Zombie".

"Kelahan" also contributed an Introduction to *H. P. Lovecraft Goes to the Movies*, a collection of fifteen stories that were made into films (or at least inspired them), while Dziemianowicz himself introduced Robert Louis Stevenson's *The Strange Case of Dr Jekyll and Mr Hyde and Other Terrifying Tales*, which included the title novel and eight short stories.

Published as part of the Barnes & Noble Library of Essential Reading with an Introduction by Jeffrey Andrew Weintock, *The Call of Cthulhu and Other Dark Tales* was an attractive hard-cover collection of fifteen tales that included notes and story introductions by S. T. Joshi.

From Creation Oneiros, *The Dream-Quest of Unknown Kadath and Other Oneiric Tales* contained the title novella and fifteen stories by Lovecraft, with an Introduction by D. M. Mitchell.

Meanwhile, *Eldritch Tales: A Miscellany of the Macabre* was a companion volume to the earlier Lovecraft collection, *Necronomicon* (2008), once again edited with an Afterword by Stephen Jones and illustrated throughout by Les Edwards. The leather-bound volume contained fifty-four stories and poems, including the complete "Fungi from Yuggoth" cycle, along with the author's seminal essay, "Supernatural Horror in Literature".

From the same editor/illustrator team of Jones and Edwards, copies of *Conan's Brethren* were actually produced in 2009, but distribution was delayed for more than a year over a legal wrangle concerning copyright in the works of Robert E. Howard, who died in 1936.

The 40th Anniversary edition of William Peter Blatty's 1971 novel *The Exorcist* was slightly revised with a scene added.

Originally published in 1992, Kim Newman's classic Victorian vampire fantasy *Anno Dracula* was re-issued by Titan Books as a classy-looking trade paperback that included plenty of additional material by the author.

A thirteen-year-old was told three stories of loss and grief by a walking tree in Patrick Ness' powerful young adult novel *A Monster Calls*, inspired by an idea by the late children's author Siobhan Dowd and illustrated by Jim Kay.

Eddie: The Lost Youth of Edgar Allan Poe was a novel about the misadventures of the author as a young man, written and beautifully illustrated by Scott Gustafson.

A young girl from Louisiana travelled to a London boarding school, where she became involved in a series of murders apparently inspired by Jack the Ripper in *The Name of the Star*, the first in Maureen Johnson's "Shades of London" trilogy.

The offspring of a serial killer discovered a doorway to another place in *Slice of Cherry* by Dia Reeves.

Children sent to camp to overcome their phobias began to change ominously in Patrick Carman's *Dark Eden*, which was also available in a multimedia app version.

In the near-future, a girl looked for her past in a New Orleans cut-off from the rest of the US and inhabited by supernatural creatures in Kelly Keaton's *Darkness Becomes Her*.

In *The Iron Thorn* by Caitlin Kittredge, a teenager living in the city of Lovecraft in an alternate 1950s tried to avoid going mad, as the rest of her family had done, when she turned sixteen.

A girl became obsessed with the objects she discovered in her family's new home in Jennifer Archer's ghostly novel *Through Her Eyes*.

While they were staying at an old lake house, a girl's boyfriend started acting strangely in Emma Carlson Berne's *Still Waters*, and *The Hunting Ground* was another haunted house novel by Cliff McNish.

A teenager could hear the voices of his missing school-friends in *Cryer's Cross* by Lisa McMann.

Two sisters encountered a powerful ghost in *Texas Gothic* by Rosemary Clement-Moore, the daughter of a fake Victorian medium could see a real ghost in *Haunting Violet* by Alyxandra Harvey, and a girl could see ghosts during a visit to the English city of York in *Dark Souls* by Paula Morris.

A ghost tried to solve her own murder in *Ghost of a Chance* by Rhiannon Lassiter, while a ghost watched as his former girl-friend and best friend got involved with each other in *Wherever You Go* by Heather Davis.

And a dead teen tried to discover what happened to her with the help of another spirit in *Between* by Jessica Warman.

Seventeen-year-old Cas and his Wiccan mother travelled to Ontario to destroy the ghost of a murdered 1950s high school teen in *Anna Dressed in Blood* by Kendare Blake.

A family of witches kept their powers secret in *Witches of East End* (aka *Witches of the East*), the first in the "Beauchamp Family" series by best-selling author Melissa de la Cruz.

Crave was the first book in a trilogy by Melissa Darnell about a war between witches and vampires.

The Cellar by A. J. Whitten (Shirley Jump and Amanda Jump) was a YA horror novel inspired by *Romeo and Juliet*, while Stacey Jay's *Juliet Immortal* found Shakespeare's lovers on opposite sides in the battle between Good and Evil.

Jackson Pearce's *Sweetly* was a dark twist on the "Hansel and Gretel" story, and *This Dark Endeavor* by Kenneth Ogiwara was a prequel to Mary Shelley's *Frankenstein*, about Victor Frankenstein and his dying twin brother Konrad. Chris Priestley's *Mister Creecher* was based on the same source novel.

Two teenagers found themselves staring at death after a car wreck in *August* by New Zealand writer Bernard Beckett, while three teens living a New Zealand town discovered the secret behind the suspicious deaths of their brothers in *The Shattering* by Karen Healey.

Death Watch was the first in the "Undertaken" trilogy by Ari Berk.

Illustrated by Coleman Polhemus, *Return to Daemon Hall: Evil Roots* was the second volume in the series by Andrew Nance, and *From Bad to Cursed* was the second title in Katie Alender's "Bad Girls Don't Die" series.

A girl was torn between her living and ghostly boyfriends in *Shift*, the sequel to Jeri Smith-Ready's *Shade*, while *The Waking: Spirits of the Noh* was the second book in a Japan-set trilogy by "Thomas Randall" (Christopher Golden).

Ocean of Blood and *Palace of the Damned* were the second and third volumes in the "The Saga of Larten Crepsley" vampire spin-off series by "Darren Shan" (Darren O'Shaughnessy).

Lisi Harrison's *Monster High 2: The Ghoul Next Door* and *Monster High 3: Where There's a Wolf There's a Way* were the second and third volumes in a series of YA tie-in novels based on a series of dolls.

Set in a haunted boarding school, *The Screaming Session* was the third book in Nancy Holder's "Possessions" series. The busy author also teamed up with Debbie Viguié for *Damned*, the second in the "Wicked" spin-off series, "Crusade", and *Unleashed*, the first volume in the "Wolf Springs Chronicles".

The Isle of Blood was the third in Rick Yancy's "Monstrumologist" series about an apprentice monster-hunter.

Everfound was the final book in Neal Shusterman's supernatural "Skinjacker" trilogy, while *The Hidden* was the third and final book in Jessica Verday's trilogy set in Sleepy Hollow.

The Spook's Destiny (aka *The Last Apprentice: Rage of the Fallen*) was the eighth in Joseph Delaney's series about an apprentice ghost-buster, illustrated by Patrick Arrasmith.

A young girl had a strange reaction to a vampire's bite in R. A. Nelson's *Throat*, and *Jane Jones: Worst Vampire Ever* was a humorous novel about a nerdy undead teenager by Caissie St. Onge.

The Slayer Chronicles: First Kill was the first in a spin-off series from "The Chronicles of Vladimir Tod" by Heather Brewer, while *By Midnight* was the first volume in Mia James' "Ravenwood" vampire mystery series. It was followed by *Darkness Falls*.

Catlyn Youngblood, a descendant of Abraham Van Helsing, unknowingly fell in love with a vampire in *After Midnight*, the first volume in the "Youngbloods" series by "Lynn Viehl" (Sheila Kelly, who writes under a variety of pseudonyms).

Jason Henderson's *Alex Van Helsing: Voice of the Undead* was the second book about another teenage vampire-hunter, and *The President's Vampire* was the second book in a series by Christopher Farnsworth.

The Vampire Diaries: The Return Vol.3: Midnight was the seventh volume in the overall series by L. J. Smith, while *The Vampire Diaries: Stefan's Diaries Vol.3: The Craving* and *Vol.4: The Ripper* were the third and fourth volumes in the uncredited spin-off series based on Smith's books and TV series. The author was also only credited as "creator" on *Vampire Diaries: Hunters: Phantom*.

Thirst No.4: The Shadow of Death was the latest volume in the YA "Last Vampire" series by Christopher Pike, and *Afterlife* was the fourth book in the vampire school series by "Claudia Gray" (Amy Vincent).

Waking Nightmares was the fifth in Christopher Golden's "Shadow Saga" series about Christopher Octavian.

Blood Ties by Mari Mancusi was the sixth in the "Blood Coven Vampire" series, and Melissa de la Cruz's *Bloody Valentine* and *Lost in Time* were the latest titles in the prolific author's "Blue Bloods" series.

Awakened and *Destined* were the eighth and ninth volumes, respectively, in the "House of Night" vampire series by P. C. Cast and Kristin Cast.

After an electromagnetic pulse wiped out technology, a sixteen-year-old girl and her friends attempted to evade the flesh-eating "Changed" of a post-apocalyptic world in *Ashes*, the first in a new trilogy by Ilsa J. Bick.

In Ty Drago's *The Undertakers: Rise of the Corpses*, a boy discovered that he could see that many of the people around him were actually the walking dead.

The Fear by Charlie Higson was the third in the author's zombie series that began with *The Enemy* and *The Dead*, and following on from *The Forest of Hands and Teeth* and *The Dead-Tossed Waves*, *The Dark and Hollow Places* was the final volume in Carrie Ryan's post-apocalyptic zombie trilogy.

Wereworld: Rise of the Wolf was the first in a new YA series by Curtis Jobling, while *Fateful* was a werewolf romance set on the *Titanic* by "Claudia Gray" (Amy Vincent).

Christine Johnson's werewolf novel *Nocturne* was a sequel to *Claire de Lune*, Karen Kincy's *Bloodborn* was the second novel about a shape-shifting teen in the "Others" series, and *Trial by Fire* was the second volume in Jennifer Lynn Barnes' "Raised by Wolves" series about human Were-pack alpha Bryn.

The Abused Werewolf Rescue Group was Australian writer Catherin Jinks' follow-up to the humorous *The Reformed Vampire Support Group*, as a teenage werewolf received help from an unexpected source.

Changeling: Zombie Dawn was the fifth and final volume about a teenage werewolf by Steve Feasey.

R. L. Stine, Margaret Mahy and Nina Kiriki Hoffman were amongst the contributors to the young adult anthology *Bones: Terrifying Tales to Haunt Your Dreams*.

The Doll: The Lost Short Stories was a collection of thirteen "forgotten" short stories (not all genre) by Daphne du Maurier, mostly written between 1926–32, eight of which were re-discovered online by a bookseller in Cornwall. Cemetery Dance published a limited hardcover edition.

Steel and Other Stories was a collection of fifteen stories by Richard Matheson, published to coincide with the release of the movie *Real Steel*, which was based on the title story.

Give Me Your Heart: Tales of Mystery and Suspense collected ten reprint stories by Joyce Carol Oates.

*   *   *

Ellen Datlow's *Supernatural Noir* featured sixteen original dark fantasy stories with a *noir* sensibility by Lucius Shepard, Jeffrey Ford, Caitlín R. Kiernan, Joe R. Lansdale, Melanie Tem, John Langan and others, while *Naked City: Tales of Urban Fantasy* from the same editor contained twenty contributions from, amongst others, Shepard, Ford, Kiernan, Jim Butcher, Peter S. Beagle, Christopher Fowler, John Crowley and Pat Cadigan.

Datlow's *Blood and Other Cravings* was about different kinds of vampirism and featured seventeen (two reprint) mostly horror-lite stories by Reggie Oliver, Steve Duffy, Melanie Tem, Lisa Tuttle, Barbara Roden, Kathe Koja, Steve Rasnic Tem, Carol Emshwiller and Margo Lanagan.

Co-edited by Ellen Datlow and Terri Windling, *Teeth* contained seventeen YA vampire stories by Garth Nix, Kathe Koja, Lucius Shepard and others, along with a poem and the lyrics to a song.

Edited by George R. R. Martin and Gardner Dozois, *Down These Mean Streets: All-New Stories of Urban Fantasy* collected sixteen tales by Charlaine Harris (whose name was bigger than everybody else's on the cover), Joe R. Lansdale, Simon R. Green, S. M. Sterling, Carrie Vaughn and others.

Ghosts by Gaslight: Stories of Steampunk and Supernatural Suspense edited by Jack Dann and Nick Gevers brought together seventeen original stories by Lucius Shepard, Robert Silverberg, Garth Nix, Gene Wolfe, Margo Lanagan, Peter S. Beagle, James Morrow, Terry Dowling and others. Unfortunately, most were more steampunk than supernatural.

One of the first titles to be published by the new Jo Fletcher Books imprint from Quercus was *A Book of Horrors*, edited by Stephen Jones. The original anthology contained fourteen alternating novellas and short stories by Stephen King, Peter Crowther, Angela Slatter, Dennis Etchison, John Adjvide Lindqvist, Ramsey Campbell, Michael Marshall Smith, Elizabeth Hand and others.

To mark the launch of the imprint, JFB also produced a paperback sampler that included contributions from, amongst others, Tom Fletcher, Charlaine Harris and Christopher Golden, Alison Littlewood, Sarah Pinborough, Tom Pollock and Michael Marshall Smith, as well as a useful ring-bound notebook.

Edited by Jonathan Oliver, *House of Fear: Nineteen New Stories of Haunted Houses and Spectral Encounters* included original fiction by Lisa Tuttle, Terry Lamsley, Robert Shearman, Christopher Fowler, Nicholas Royle, Tim Lebbon, Joe R. Lansdale and others, along with more irritating story introductions by the editor.

There were more ghosts to be found in *Haunts: Reliquaries of the Dead* edited by Stephen Jones. However, these revenants haunted specific items, locations and people in twenty-four stories (ten original) and a poem by such authors as Ramsey Campbell, Neil Gaiman, M. R. James, Tanith Lee, Richard Matheson, Robert Silverberg and Michael Marshall Smith.

From Virago, *Something Was There . . . Asham Award-Winning Ghost Stories* edited by Kate Pullinger featured sixteen stories, including the winner of the 2011 writing award for women and a recently discovered new tale by Daphne du Maurier.

With *Vampires, Zombies, Werewolves, and Ghosts: 25 Classic Stories of the Supernatural*, editors Barbara H. Solomon and Eileen Panetta covered all their bases with stories by Stephen King, Ray Bradbury, Ramsey Campbell, H. P. Lovecraft and, er . . . Woody Allen.

Edited by John Skipp, *Demons: Encounters with the Devil and His Minions, Fallen Angels, and the Possessed* was another catch-all anthology of thirty-five stories, two novel excerpts and two essays by Neil Gaiman, Kim Harrison, W. W. Jacobs and others.

The Monster's Corner edited by Christopher Golden contained nineteen stories (one reprint) told from the monster's point-of-view by Kelley Armstrong, Michael Marshall Smith, Kevin J. Anderson, Simon R. Green, Sarah Pinborough and others.

In the Shadow of Dracula from IDW Publishing contained twenty-one classic vampire stories from 1816–1914, edited with story introductions by Leslie S. Klinger.

From Skyhorse Publishing, *Vintage Vampire Stories* edited by Robert Eighteen-Bisang and Richard Dalby included thirteen rare vampire stories, along with two novel excerpts, notes for an early draft of Bram Stoker's *Dracula*, and a historical essay.

Mike Ashley edited and introduced *Vampires: Classic Tales* that included twelve stories, mostly written before Stoker's novel, but also featuring contributions by Brian Stableford, Nancy Holder and Tanith Lee.

A new edition of *The Mammoth Book of Dracula* edited by Stephen Jones added a reprint "Sookie Stackhouse" story by Charlaine Harris.

Harris and Toni L. P. Kellner edited *Home Improvement: Undead Edition*, which contained fourteen stories about horrific house renovations, including a new "Sookie Stackhouse" tale about an old murder and a ghost.

Zombies! Zombies! Zombies! edited with an Introduction by Otto Penzler was a huge anthology about (mostly) . . . zombies. It contained fifty-seven stories by Stephen King, Ramsey Campbell, Robert R. McCammon, Theodore Sturgeon, Henry Kuttner, Manly Wade Wellman, H. P. Lovecraft and others.

Zombiesque, edited with Stephen L. Antczak, James C. Bassett and Martin H. Greenberg, featured sixteen original stories told from the walking dead's point of view by Nancy Collins, Tim Waggoner, Gregory Nicoll, Nancy Holder, Wendy Webb and others.

Ellen Datlow's *The Best Horror of the Year: Volume Three* featured twenty-one stories, Stephen Jones' *The Mammoth Book of Best New Horror 22* contained twenty-three, and Paula Guran's *The Year's Best Dark Fantasy & Horror: 2011 Edition* collected thirty-one.

The Datlow and Jones volumes overlapped with six stories (by John Langan, Brian Hodge, Norman Partridge, Karina Sumner-Smith, Mark Morris and Christopher Fowler) and one author (Joe R. Lansdale). The Jones and Guran books each contained the same stories by Caitlín R. Kiernan and Partridge, and different stories by Lansdale and Angela Slatter, while the Datlow and Guran anthologies shared just the Partridge story and authors Laird Barron, Stephen Graham Jones and Tanith Lee.

"Lesser Demons" by Norman Partridge was the only story to appear in all three "Year's Best" horror volumes.

From new print-on-demand imprint Dark Continents Publishing, *Quiet Houses* was a portmanteau collection of seven haunted house stories by Simon Kurt Unsworth, loosely linked together by paranormal researcher Richard Nakata. The author also helpfully supplied a guide to his inspirations for the buildings concerned.

Paul Kane's novel *Pain Cages* from Books of the Dead Press came with an Introduction by Stephen Volk.

We Live Inside You from Swallowdown Press collected nineteen stories by Jeremy Robert Johnson and featured glowing cover quotes from Jack Ketchum, John Skipp, Cody Goodfellow and Chuck Palahniuk.

From Mythos Books, *Dreams* collected fourteen stories (four original) by Richard A. Lupoff with notes on each by the author.

Florida's Distillations Press issued *These Strange Worlds: Fourteen Dark Tales* by Daniel Powell, seven of which were original to the collection, while *Eyeballs Growing All Over Me . . . Again* contained twenty-three short short stories by Tony Rauch, available as a trade paperback from Eraserhead Press.

Weird Horror Tales from Cornerstone Books/Airship 27 Productions was a collection of seventeen Lovecraftian horror stories and three poems by Michael Vance, based around the small town of Lights End, Maine. Earl Geier supplied the illustrations.

From Miskatonic River Press, Scott David Aniolowski "selected and edited" the Lovecraftian-themed anthology *Horror for the Holidays*. Featuring twenty-five stories (three reprints) and a poem based around different holidays during the year, contributors included H. P. Lovecraft, Ramsey Campbell, Thomas Ligotti, Will Marray, Donald R. Burleson, Robert M. Price, W. H. Pugmire, Don Webb, William Meikle and Cody Goodfellow.

Edited by S. T. Joshi for the same PoD imprint, *Dissecting Cthulhu: Essays on the Cthulhu Mythos* contained twenty-one articles by such well-known Lovecraftians as Richard L. Tierney, Dirk W. Mosig, David E. Schultz, Simon MacCulloch, Robert M. Price, Will Murray and Stefan Dziemianowicz, amongst others.

The Undying Thing and Others from Hippocampus Press collected twenty-six stories by Barry Pain, with an Introduction by Joshi.

The Man Who Collected Machen and Other Weird Tales from Chômu Press reprinted Mark Samuels' 2009 collection with four additional stories (one original). From the same publisher, Daniel Mills' *Revenants* was a historical novel about a cursed New England village, while the undead hero of Michael Cisco's *The Great Lover* resisted the white-noise forces of Vampirism.

Originally published as an e-book, *Spore* by John Skipp and Cody Goodfellow was yet another zombie novel, available as a print-on-demand title from Dorchester.

A girl was mysteriously drawn to her grandmother's unusual house in Tanith Lee's *Greyglass*, from Immanion Press, and an ancient evil returned to a Massachusetts town in Brendan P. Myers' *Applewood*, available from By Light Unseen Media.

From LCR Books, *The Fourth Fog: A Horror Novel for the Ages* by Chris Daniels was about the breakdown of society and killer flies.

Frankenstein in London was the third in Brian Stableford's "The Empire of the Necromancers" series from PoD publisher Black Coat Press.

For the same imprint, Stableford also translated and supplied the Introductions for *The Vampire Lord Ruthwen* (*Lord Ruthwen, ou les Vampires*), an 1820 sequel to Polidori's *The Vampyre* by French writer Cyprien Bénard, and the 1824 novel *The Virgin Vampire* (*La Vampire, ou la vierge de Hongrie*) by Etienne-Léon de Lamothe-Langdon.

Christopher Fulbright's novella *The Bone Tree* was set in a Civil War graveyard and was available from PoD imprint Bad Moon Books. From the same publisher, Bill Gauthier's *Alice on the Shelf* was a twisted novella inspired by the classic children's book, while *The Templar* contained three horror novels by Joseph Nassise, two original.

Terror Tales of the Lake District from Gray Friar Press was an original anthology of thirteen stories (two reprints and another revised) inspired by the old Fontana Books series of the 1970s. The solid line-up of contributors included Adam L. G. Nevill, Simon Clark, Simon Bestwick, Peter Crowther, Ramsey Campbell, Gary McMahon, Reggie Oliver and editor Paul Finch, who also interlaced the fiction with accounts of myths and legends of the area.

As usual selected by Charles Black for Mortbury Press, *The Eighth Black Book of Horror* featured a strong line-up of names, with thirteen original stories by Reggie Oliver, David A. Riley, Gary Fry, Mark Samuels, Paul Finch, John Llewellyn Probert and Thana Niveau, amongst others.

Edited by website founder Jeani Rector for Imajiin Books, *What Fears Become: An Anthology from the Horror Zine* contained thirty-three stories (including two by the editor, plus nine reprints), along with poetry and artwork. Contributors included Bentley Little, Graham Masterton, Ramsey Campbell, Joe R. Lansdale, Elizabeth Massie, Melanie Tem, Scott Nicholson, Piers Anthony, Richard Hill and Conrad Williams. Simon Clark supplied the Foreword.

Published by Rainstorm Press, *Mutation Nation: Tales of Genetic Mishaps, Monsters and Madness* was edited by Kelly Dunn and included eleven original stories by Roberta Lannes, Maria Alexander, Barbie Wilde, Stephen Woodworth, Wendy Rathbone and others.

Editor Peter Mark May dedicated *Alt-Dead: The Alternative Dead Anthology* to "the independent writers and authors in the horror genre that don't always get the breaks and the big deals". Available on-demand from Hersham Horror Books, it contained sixteen original stories by Stephen Bacon, Stuart Young, Gary McMahon, Jan Edwards, Stuart Hughes, Johnny Mains and others, including a collaboration between Steven Savile and Steve Lockley.

Karen A. Romanko edited and introduced *Jack-o'-Spec: Tales of Halloween and Fantasy* for PoD imprint Raven Electrick Ink. The trade paperback featured twenty-six stories and poems by Bruce Boston, Geoffrey A. Landis, James S. Dorr, Marge Simon and others, including the editor.

James Ward Kirk edited *Indiana Horror Anthology 2011*, which included poetry, flash fiction and short stories by Matt Cowan, James S. Dorr, Lee Forsythe and other writers living in the south-western state.

Published by Stumar Press, *Derby Scribes 2011* was an anthology of eleven stories (one reprint), written by members of the eponymous writing group and edited by Stuart Hughes. Contributors included Simon Clark, Alison J. Hill, Conrad Williams and the editor himself, while group founder Alex Davis supplied the Introduction.

Edited by Asa Merritt for Phoenix Pick/Arc Manor Publishers, more than half of the print-on-demand *First Blood: Birth of the Vampire* was taken up with a moderately annotated reprinting of Bram Stoker's *Dracula*. The rest of the book included five obscure precedents to Stoker's novel, plus "The Vampyre: A Tale" by John William Polidori and "Carmilla" by J. Sheridan Le Fanu, along with selected chapters from John William Rymer's *Varney the Vampire: Or, the Feast of Blood*.

Edited by publisher Russell B. Farr for Ticonderoga Publications, *Dead Red Heart: Australian Vampire Stories* was a bumper anthology of thirty-three stories about different kinds of vampires. From the same imprint, editor Liz Grzyb's *More Scary Kisses* contained seventeen paranormal romance stories.

Bluegrass Symphony by Lisa L. Hannett was a debut collection of twelve dark fantasy stories (one reprint), with an Introduction by Ann VanderMeer and an Afterword by the author.

Also published by Ticonderoga, *The Year's Best Australian Fantasy and Horror 2010* edited by Grzyb and Talie Helene contained thirty-two stories and a poem.

Dead But Dreaming 2 was an on-demand Cthulhu anthology from Miskatonic River Press. Edited with a Foreword by Kevin Ross, it featured twenty-two original stories by William Meikle, Don Webb, Darrell Schweitzer, W. H. Pugmire, Rick Hautala, Donald R. Burleson, Cody Goodfellow and Will Murray, amongst others.

After a hiatus of fifteen years, editor Doug Ellis finally published the fourteenth issue of *Pulp Vault* through Tattered Pages Press/Black Dog Books as a substantial softcover volume. Boasting a previously unpublished cover painting by Virgil Finlay, it featured many fascinating articles and classic pulp fiction by, amongst others, Bob Weinberg, Will Murray, D. H. Olsen, Donald Wandrei, Hugh B. Cave, Otto Binder, Doug Klauba, Tom Roberts and Mike Ashley.

Only nine months after the launch of the Kindle, Amazon.co.uk announced that e-books were now outstripping the sale of hardcover books by two-to-one on its site in the UK. However, the online retailer also added that hardback sales were continuing to grow. In America, e-books reportedly sold more than all the paperback and hardcover copies put together.

Figures released by the Association of American Publishers in June confirmed that revenues for print books had decreased dramatically, while the income from e-books jumped 161 per cent from $30 million to $181.3 million in just one year.

In the UK, e-books accounted for up to 10 per cent of total book sales after a rise of 600 per cent in the first half of the year, resulting in a total revenue of £25 million.

As a result of these dramatic increases, it was also revealed that e-book piracy had become a huge problem, with many hundreds of recorded books being offered illegally for free downloads.

Penguin announced in November that it would withhold editions of its e-books from British and American libraries amid "concerns about security". The publisher said that it was also considering withdrawing its electronic books from Amazon's lending service for the Kindle e-reader. Penguin joined Simon & Schuster and Hachette Book Group, who already had a similar ban in place, while HarperCollins restricted the number of times a library book could be loaned out digitally.

Amazon.com announced that Charlaine Harris became the first genre author to sell more than a million books for the Kindle e-reader, putting her alongside other "Kindle Million Club" members Stieg Larsson, James Patterson and Nora Roberts/J. D. Robb. She was soon followed by Michael Connelly, Suzanne Collins, Lee Child and George R. R. Martin.

BlackBerry launched its compact PlayBook in June as a direct rival to Apple's hugely successful iPad, despite complaints about a lack of available software.

Brian Keene was one of a number of disgruntled authors, including Tim Waggoner, Craig Spector and Mary SanGiovanni, who called for a boycott of the troubled Dorchester Publishing for reportedly selling e-books of various titles after the rights had been reverted.

In September, Gollancz launched its SF Gateway digital library with plans to have around 5,000 back-list titles available as e-books in three years' time.

Stephen King's original story *Mile 81*, about a mysterious mud-splattered station wagon that lured its victims to their doom, was available as an e-book in September. It also included a teaser excerpt from the author's novel *11/22/63*.

The Ghost Story Megapack from Wildside Press was a cheap e-book compilation of twenty-five out-of-copyright stories by Mary Elizabeth Braddon, Bram Stoker, Rudyard Kipling, E. F. Benson, Wilkie Collins and others. The publisher also offered various other electronic "Megapacks", including *The Horror Megapack*.

Available exclusively on Kindle, *The Odd Ghosts* was a collection of eight original stories by Maynard Sims (L. H. Maynard and M. P. N. Sims).

Edited by Jeani Rector, *The Horror Zine* was published online every month, and produced a special Joe R. Lansdale issue in October.

Trevor Denyer's *Midnight Street* was available as a PDF download for a suggested donation, while editor Joe Vaz's *Something Wicked* magazine became a digital-only publication starting with issue #11.

After interviewing a psychic on his show, a radio presenter was menaced as he attempted to solve the mystery of a missing girl in Ramsey Campbell's paranoid chiller *Ghosts Know*, available from PS Publishing.

For fans of the author's earlier work, PS also reprinted Campbell's first book as the properly titled *The Inhabitant of the Lake & Other Unwelcome Tenants*. First published in 1964 by Arkham House, each of the ten Lovecraftian stories was beautifully illustrated by Randy Broecker, and the collection also contained the original versions of seven stories, notes on the first drafts, reproduced correspondence between the author and August Derleth, and an extensive and entertaining Afterword explaining how the book came about.

Ian R. MacLeod's *Wake Up and Dream* was set in an alternate Hollywood of 1940 and involved one-time actor and unlicensed private eye Clark Gable and the mystery of a device that changed the world of entertainment forever.

Edited by Conrad Williams, *Gutshot: Weird West Stories* was an anthology of twenty original tales by Michael Moorcock, Thomas Tessier, Joe R. Lansdale, Christopher Fowler, Peter

Atkins, Adam Nevill, Joel Lane and other dangerous desperados.

PS published two short story collections by Christopher Fowler back-to-back in a single volume in the style of an old Ace Double. *Red Gloves: Devilry* contained fourteen stories (three original) comprising "The London Horrors", while *Red Gloves: Infernal* featured thirteen tales (two original) of "The World Horrors".

Carol Emshwiller's *In the Time of War and Other Stories of Conflict/Master of the Road to Nowhere and Other Tales of the Fantastic* followed the same double format, with covers by Ed Emshwiller and Introductions by Ursula K. Le Guin and Phyllis Eisenstein, respectively.

Edited with an Introduction by Stephen Jones, *Scream Quietly: The Best of Charles L. Grant* collected thirty-two stories by the late writer of "quiet horror", along with a Foreword by Stephen King, commentary by Peter Straub, Kim Newman, Thomas F. Monteleone and Nancy Holder, an interview with the author by Nancy Kilpatrick, and interior illustrations by Andrew Smith. Former *Weird Tales* artist Jon Arfstrom painted the stunning cover art.

After being widowed at no less than three previous publishers, Mark Morris' collection *Long Shadows, Nightmare Light* finally saw publication from PS with an Introduction by Christopher Golden. It contained fifteen stories (two original).

James Lovegrove's second collection, *Diversifications*, contained sixteen reprint stories and an Afterword by the author, while *The Butterfly Man and Other Stories* was a retrospective collection of eighteen horror stories (five original) by Paul Kane with another Introduction by Christopher Golden. The author's first accepted story from 1998 was included as a special bonus.

As part of its ongoing "PS Showcase" series, *The Emperor's Toy Chest* collected fifteen stories (four original) by Tobias Seamon, and *Dark Dreams, Pale Horses* contained six stories (three original) by Rio Youers with an Introduction by Brian Keene.

PS also published new novels by Chaz Brenchley (*Rotten Row*) and Lavie Tidhar (*Osama: A Novel*), along with James Cooper's horror novella *Terra Damnata*.

Most PS books were available as 100 signed copies and also in a non-jacketed trade edition.

Graced with an attractive dust-wrapper painting by the legendary Ed Emshwiller, *The New and Perfect Man* was volume 24/25 of *PostScripts* edited by Peter Crowther and Nick Gevers. The always-eclectic hardcover anthology contained twenty-eight stories by Carol Emshwiller, Michael Kelly, Ramsey Campbell, Thomas Tessier, T. M. Wright, Christopher Fowler, Rio Youers, Jay Lake and many others.

The titular rock band was menaced by a deranged Afghanistan war veteran and other forces of darkness in Robert McCammon's *The Five*, while *The Hunter from the Woods* was a collection of six linked stories featuring the secret agent protagonist of the author's 1989 wartime werewolf novel *The Wolf's Hour*. Both books were available in signed and also traycased ($250.00) editions from Subterranean Press.

Baal was a reprint of McCammon's first novel, originally published in 1978, with a 1988 Afterword by the author. It was available in a 1,000-copy signed edition and a traycased, leather-bound deluxe edition of fifty-two copies ($250.00).

Set 150 years after the world ended, a clan of subterranean survivors had to evade the eponymous vampire-creatures while crossing a radioactive wasteland in *The Fly-by-Nights* by Brian Lumley. The novel was available from Subterranean Press in both a trade edition and a 250-copy deluxe edition with a different dust-jacket, illustrated by Bob Eggleton.

Limited to 750 copies from Subterranean, *Mortality Bridge* was a deal-with-the-Devil novel by Steven R. Boyett.

Edited by publisher William Schafer, *Subterranean: Tales of Dark Fantasy 2* contained eleven original stories by Joe Hill, Kelley Armstrong, Norman Partridge, Caitlín R. Kiernan and others. A signed and slipcased edition ($150.00) came with extra illustrations and a chapbook by Joe R. Lansdale.

Two Worlds and In Between: The Best of Caitlín Kiernan (Volume One) collected twenty-six stories (one a collaboration with Poppy Z. Brite), dating from 1993–2004, most of which had been significantly revised. It was also available in a 600-copy signed edition with sixteen pages of illustrations by various artists and an extra chapbook.

Forever Azathoth collected sixteen Lovecraftian stories (one original) by Peter Cannon and was published in a signed edition of 350 copies, while *Amberjack* contained twelve stories and thirteen poems by Terry Dowling, with an Introduction by Jack Vance. It was published in a signed edition limited to 750 copies.

Grimscribe: His Lives and Work was a revised and "definitive" edition of Thomas Ligotti's 1991 collection of fourteen stories, which was also available in a signed leatherbound edition.

Subterranean also reissued *The Horror Stories of Robert E. Howard*, illustrated by Greg Staples, as both a limited slipcased edition ($150.00) and a fifty-copy leatherbound deluxe edition ($400.00).

With an Introduction by Norman Partridge, *Yours Truly, Jack the Ripper* contained Robert Bloch's classic story along with the novel *The Night of the Ripper*, the *Star Trek* teleplay *Wolf in the Fold*, and Bloch's Foreword to the anthology *Ripper!*.

The Juniper Tree and Other Blue Rose Stories contained four loosely connected stories by Peter Straub, plus an interview with the author by Bill Sheehan. It was available in a regular hardcover edition and as a 250-copy leatherbound, signed edition.

The Ballad of Ballard and Sandrine was a surreal novella from the same author, published in a deluxe hardcover edition by Subterranean Press at the very end of the year.

Cemetery Dance Publications re-issued Stephen King's collection *Full Dark, No Stars* in a two-colour edition illustrated by Jill Bauman, Glenn Chadbourne, Vincent Chong and Alan M. Clark. It was published in a slipcased edition ($75.00), a leatherbound traycased edition signed by the author ($360.00) and a fifty-two copy traycased lettered edition signed by King and the artists ($1,500.00).

King and CD also teamed up for a special 25th anniversary edition of the author's novel *It*. The exclusive oversized deluxe edition include the complete text, a new Afterword by the author, nearly thirty interior illustrations by Alan M. Clark and Erin Wells, and a wrap-around dust-jacket painting by Glem Orbik.

The author and publisher also issued *The Secretary of Dreams (Volume Two)* as an exclusive slipcased edition in a very limited print-run. Not available in stores, the hardcover collected more of King's classic tales, illustrated by Glenn Chadbourne.

The Century's Best Horror Fiction was published by Cemetery Dance in two huge volumes, covering the years *1901–1950* and *1951–2000*. Editor John Pelan selected one representative story for every year of the twentieth century.

As if Pelan's volumes were not enough of a treat for horror fans, CD also brought out *The Horror Hall of Fame: The Stoker Winners* edited with an Introduction by Joe R. Lansdale. Covering the first decade of the HWA's annual award, which began in 1988, the volume featured contributions from George R. R. Martin, Alan Rodgers, Elizabeth Massie, David B. Silva, Nancy Holder, David Morrell, Robert Bloch, Thomas Ligotti, Harlan Ellison and others, including the editor himself. Each story was illustrated by the busy Glenn Chadbourne.

Edited by Kelly Laymon, Steve Gerlach and Richard Chizmar, *Laymon's Terms* was a large anthology of forty tribute stories and forty-five appreciations to the late Richard Laymon, along with various pieces by Laymon from his own files, including six stories and four poems. It was available in trade edition ($50.00), a 400-copy slipcased edition signed by most of the contributors ($150.00) and a fifty-two copy lettered and traycased edition ($400.00).

Illustrated by Vincent Chong, Jay Bonansinga's futuristic Lovecraftian novelette *The Miniaturist* was the eighth volume in the "Cemetery Dance Signature" series, limited to a 550-copy signed edition and twenty-six traycased, leatherbound lettered copies.

Picking the Bones collected seventeen stories (three original) by Brian Hodge, while the long-delayed *Stories from the Plague Years* collected nine long stories (two original) by Michael Marano, illustrated by Gabrielle Faust. John Shirley supplied the Introduction.

Kin was a serial killer novel by Kealan Patrick Burke, available in an edition of 750 signed copies, and CD also reprinted Simon Clark's 1997 novel *King Blood* and Edward Lee's 2008 novel *Bride of the Impaler* in 1,000-copy signed editions and limited traycased, leatherbound editions.

Cemetery Dance also issued an omnibus of William Peter Blatty's novels *The Exorcist* and *Legion*, illustrated by Keith Minnion and featuring an interview with the author by Brian

Freeman. The book was available in a 750-copy signed edition and a lettered, traycased and leatherbound edition of fifty-two copies ($400.00).

Richard Matheson's *Nightmare at 20,000 Feet* from Gauntlet Press collected the original story along with scripts for the *Twilight Zone* TV version and the movie adaptation, illustrated with storyboards and photos. Contributors included William Shatner, Richard Donner, Carol Serling and Richard Christian Matheson, amongst others, and the book was available in a bewildering number of different editions, ranging from $50.00 up to a signed deluxe version priced at $1,000.00.

Dawn to Dust included two unproduced screenplays, two drafts of a teleplay and a previously unpublished short story by Ray Bradbury, along with various ephemeral material and an Introduction by the author. Edited with a Preface by Donn Albright, the book was available in three states, with the lettered and traycased edition ($250.00) also containing unused sketches and fragments from *The Illustrated Man*.

Also from Gauntlet, *J. N. Williamson's Illustrated Masques*, edited by Mort Castle and David Campiti, presented graphic adaptations of eight stories that originally appeared in the late Williamson's *Masques* anthologies by Stephen King, Robert R. McCammon, Robert Weinberg, F. Paul Wilson, Paul Dale Anderson, Wayne Allen Sallee and two by co-editor Castle, who also supplied a Preface. A fifty-two copy lettered and signed edition cost $1,500.00.

Earthling Publications produced *The Very Best of Best New Horror: A Twenty-Year Celebration* edited by Stephen Jones in 300 numbered copies signed by the editor, and a 200-copy slip-cased edition ($250.00) signed by all the contributors, including Stephen King, Peter Straub, Harlan Ellison, Clive Barker, Neil Gaiman and Joe Hill.

Peter Crowther's *By Wizard Oak* was a Halloween novel from Earthling with an Introduction by Rick Hautala.

From new imprint Flying Fox Publishers, *Portents*, edited with an Introduction by Al Sarrantonio, was inspired by the "quiet horror" of Charles L. Grant's *Shadows* series. The anthology was limited to 1,000 numbered hardcovers and featured nineteen original stories by Joe R. Lansdale, Gene Wolfe, Kim

Newman, Brian Keene, Elizabeth Massie, Ramsey Campbell, Steve Rasnic Tem, Joyce Carol Oates, Christopher Fowler and others, along with a Foreword by Stephen Jones.

John Hornor Jacobs' debut novel *Southern Gods*, from Night Shade Books, involved the search for a legendary bluesman, Ramblin' John Hastur, whose music reputedly sent men mad and caused the dead to rise.

Jonathan Wood's *No Hero* was another debut novel, about an Oxford police detective recruited to battle tentacled Lovecraftian horrors.

On the same theme, editor Ross E. Lockhart's *The Book of Cthulhu* collected twenty-seven tales (two original) by Ramsey Campbell, David Drake, Caitlín R. Kiernan, Thomas Ligotti, Joe R. Lansdale, Cherie Priest, Bruce Sterling, Gene Wolfe and other, more surprising, contributors to the Mythos.

The Panama Laugh was a zombie novel by Thomas S. Roche, while J. M. Lassen edited the YA anthology *Z: Zombie Stories* containing eleven stories (one original) by Kelly Link, Nina Kiriki Hoffman and Scott Nicholson, amongst others.

The Miscellaneous Fictions of Clark Ashton Smith from Night Shade collected eighteen peripheral stories (two original), a poem and a play, along with a Foreword by editors Scott Connors and Ron Hilger and an essay by Donald Sidney-Fryer.

Published by Tartarus Press, Reggie Oliver's fifth collection, *Mrs Midnight and Other Stories*, quickly sold out of its 400-copy hardcover printing. The book contained thirteen stories (four original) and also included some delightful heading illustrations by the author.

Michael Reynier made a fine debut with his collection *Five Degrees of Latitude*, which contained five novellas written in the classic tradition, while *Frankenstein's Prescription* by Tim Lees was an impressive novel about the search for eternal life that also involved Mary Shelley's sympathetic creature.

Also from Tartarus, *Dark Entries*, *Powers of Darkness* and *Cold Hand in Mine* reprinted the stories by Robert Aickman (1914–81), while *We Are the Dark* was a reprint of the 1964 collection of collaborations between Aickman and Elizabeth Jane Howard. The new edition was officially launched at the Halifax Ghost Story Festival.

From Side Real Press, *Delicate Toxins: An Anthology Inspired by Hanns Heinz Ewers* was a beautifully-crafted hardcover edited and introduced by John Hirschhorn-Smith. It contained eighteen original tales inspired by the German author of "strange" fiction (1871–1943) by such writers as Richard Gavin, R. B. Russell, Mark Valentine, Reggie Oliver, Michael Chislett, Mark Samuels and Thana Niveau. Limited to 350 numbered copies and priced at a very reasonable £30.00, copies purchased directly from the publisher came with a unique signed bookplate.

Paul Kane's *Shadow Writer* from MHB Press was a beautifully-produced volume containing the contents of the author's first two collections, *Alone (In the Dark)* (2001) and *Touching the Flame* (2002), along with four previously uncollected tales (two original), poetry, a graphic novel script, story notes and an Introduction by Simon Clark. The special signed edition was limited to a 150-copy numbered Collector's Edition, a seventy-five copy Deluxe Edition numbered in roman numerals, and twenty-six copies lettered A–Z.

Clark also supplied the Introduction to Paul Kane's third collection of the year, *The Adventures of Dalton Quayle* from Mundania Press, which contained seven comedic reprints featuring the eponymous psychic investigator.

Rumours of the Marvellous collected fourteen stories (one original) by Peter Atkins, with an Introduction by Glen Hirshberg. It was published by Alchemy Press/Airgedlámh in a signed and numbered hardcover edition of just 250 copies.

From Screaming Dreams, *Hunter's Moon* was a debut novella by Charlotte Bond, about four university friends who discovered that dark forces awaited them on holiday in a quiet French village.

Everyone's Just So So Special was a collection of twenty-one tales "of the comic and the macabre" (fourteen original) by Robert Shearman, published in teeny-tiny type by Big Finish Productions.

Published in pocket-size by Borderlands Press, *A Little Gold Book of Ghastly Stuff* collected obscure fiction, introductions, essays, speeches and poetry by Neil Gaiman.

Edited by D. F. Lewis, *The Horror Anthology of Horror Anthologies* from Megazanthus Press was a clever idea for an anthology, even though not all of the twenty original stories stuck strictly to the theme. Contributors included Rhys Hughes, Joel Lane, E. Michael Lewis, Mike O'Driscoll, Reggie Oliver, Mark Valentine and D. P. Watt.

Published in an edition of just 100 copies to coincide with a special exhibition of artist John Martin's work at London's Tate Britain gallery, *Pandemonium: Stories of the Apocalypse* was edited by Anne C. Perry and Jared Shurin and contained eighteen original stories by Lauren Beukes, Jon Courtney Grimwood, Lou Morgan, Jonathan Oliver and others, along with an Introduction by Tom Hunter. The hardcover was sold exclusively through Tate Britain, although an e-book edition was also available.

The revived Sarob Press issued Mark Nicholls' collection of classical ghost stories, *Dark Shadows Fall*, while *Flame & Other Enigmatic Tales* contained four short stories (one reprint) and two novellas by the conjoined Maynard Sims, illustrated by Paul Lowe.

From Small Beer Press, *The Monkey's Wedding and Other Stories* was a posthumous collection of nineteen delightful stories (seven original) by Joan Aiken (1924–2004), mostly written in the 1950s and 1960s. The book also included a 1995 Introduction by the author and a new piece by her daughter, Lizza Aiken.

Maureen F. McHugh's *After the Apocalypse: Stories* collected nine contemporary tales (three original).

Edited by Eduardo Jiménez Mayo and Chris N. Brown for Small Beer, *Three Messages and a Warning: Contemporary Mexican Short Stories of the Fantastic* contained thirty-four quite short tales with an Introduction by Bruce Sterling.

Published in trade paperback by Two Ravens Press ("the most remote literary publisher in the UK", situated on the Isle of Lewis, in the Outer Hebrides), *Murmurations: An Anthology of Uncanny Stories About Birds* was edited by Nicholas Royle and contained thirty stories (sixteen original) by, among others, Joel Lane, Russell Hoban, Tom Fletcher, Jack Trevor Story, Mark Valentine, Conrad Williams, R. B. Russell, Michael Kelly, Daphne du Maurier, and the editor himself. Featuring a Foreword by Angelica Michelis, all royalties and fees were donated to The Royal Society for the Protection of Birds.

Bite Sized Horror: The Obverse Quarterly: Book One was edited with an Introduction by Johnny Mains for Obverse Books. The slim anthology featured original stories by Reggie Oliver, Paul Kane, David A. Riley, Marie O'Regan, Conrad Williams and the editor himself.

Herbert van Thal's "lost" 1933 collection *Child Performer* was reprinted by Noose & Gibbet Publishing as *The Mask and Other Stories*. The author's only collection of short stories, written when he was in his twenties, the slender hardback was bulked out with a new Introduction by Johnny Mains, van Thals' 1945 essay "Recipe for Reading" (originally written for his two godsons), and various Introductions by the author. The 100-copy edition sold out in under a month.

The stated ethos of new imprint Dark Minds Press was to publish projects that were "produced to the best standards of production achievable". Unfortunately, the anthology *Dark Minds: An Anthology of Dark Fiction*, "selected and prepared for publication" by Ross Warren, featured far too many basic design and typographical errors. Gary McMahon and Stephen Bacon were the best-known of the twelve contributors, while Will Jacques contributed some squiggly interior art.

David J. Howe's Telos Publishing imprint issued a collection of his own writings, *Talespinning*, that included short stories (five original), a pair of unfinished novels, two 100-word *Doctor Who* drabbles and a couple of DVD scripts.

From the same imprint, *Zombies in New York and Other Bloody Jottings* collected thirteen stories (ten original) and six poems (five original) by Sam Stone, along with a Foreword by Graham Masterton, and half-page Afterword by actor Frazer Hines, and copious commentary by the author. Russell Morgan supplied the interior art.

The Bible Repairman and Other Stories from Tachyon Publications collected six ghostly stories by Tim Powers, including a sequel novella to *The Stress of Her Regard*.

Edited with an Introduction by Joe R. Lansdale, *Crucified Dreams: Tales of Urban Horror* included nineteen reprint stories by Stephen King, Harlan Ellison, Lucius Shepard, Michael Bishop, Joe Haldeman, Lewis Shiner, Norman Partridge and the editor himself.

Lansdale was also co-editor of *The Urban Fantasy Anthology* with Peter S. Beagle. It contained twenty reprint stories broken down into "Mythic Fiction", "Paranormal Romance" and "Noir Fantasy" by, amongst others, Charles de Lint, Neil Gaiman, Kelley Armstrong, Suzy McKee Charnas, Thomas M. Disch, Holly Black, Tim Powers and the two editors. The book also included new Introductions by Beagle, Lansdale, de Lint and Paula Guran.

Also from Tachyon, *Kafkaesque: Stories Inspired by Franz Kafka* edited with an Introduction by John Kessel and James Patrick Kelly contained seventeen reprint stories by Kafka, J. G. Ballard, Jorge Luis Borges, Carol Emshwiller, Damon Knight, Rudy Rucker and others, along with a comic strip illustrated by Robert Crumb.

From Centipede Press, *Deadfall Hotel* was a new novel by Steve Rasnic Tem about a haunted hotel, illustrated by John Kenn Martensen. Limited to 300 signed copies, the book also included an Afterword by the author and a new short story.

Published as part of the imprint's oversized "Masters of the Weird Tale" series, *Old Time Weird Tales & Quality Horror Stories* collected thirty-eight stories and novellas by Karl Edward Wagner. Edited with an Introduction by Stephen Jones, the massive tome also included reprint pieces by Peter Straub, David Drake and the late author, along with a new Afterword by Laird Barron. The book was illustrated in colour by J. K. Potter and also featured many rare photographs.

In the same series, *Henry Kuttner* collected twenty-nine horror and supernatural tales by the pulp author with an Introduction by editors Stefan Dziemianowicz and Robert Morrish. Once again, J. K. Potter supplied the frontispiece and endpapers artwork. Both books were limited to 200 signed copies ($295.00 apiece).

Haffner Press' *Terror in the House: The Early Kuttner Volume One* collected author's first forty stories, most of them taken from the pages of *Weird Tales* and such "shudder pulps" as *Thrilling Mystery* and *Spicy Mystery*. Edited by Stephen Haffner, the hefty hardcover included a Preface by Richard Matheson and an Introduction by Gary G. Roberts Ph.D.

The Corn Maiden and Other Nightmares from Mysterious Press contained seven macabre tales by Joyce Carol Oates, mostly reprinted from non-genre sources.

Edited by Bill Breedlove and John Everson, *Swallowed by the Cracks* from Dark Arts Books featured sixteen original and reprint stories about "the spaces between" by Lee Thomas, Gary McMahon, S. G. Browne and Michael Marshall Smith.

The indefatigable Joe Morey continued to produce a range of attractive trade paperback under his Dark Regions Press imprint. William Ollie's *Fifteen Minutes* concerned a centuries-old ring that had the power to transform its wearer, while *Pitch* from the same author was a Halloween novel set in the 1960s.

Something deadly came out of the ocean near a quaint fishing village in Shaun Jeffrey's *Fangtooth*.

Nightingale Songs was a third collection from Canadian writer Simon Strantzas, containing twelve stories (four original) along with an Introduction by John Langan, while *The Gaki and Other Hungry Spirits* collected seventeen stories (six original) by Stephen Mark Rainey.

A huge seismic disturbance in North Korea had global consequences for a biomedical engineer in Michael McBride's novella *Blindspot*, and a woman continued to suffer from a childhood trauma in Paul Melniczek's novella *The Watching*.

The Engines of Sacrifice contained four new Lovecraftian novellas by James Chambers, and W. H. Pugmire's *Gathered Dust and Others* collected eighteen Lovecraft-inspired stories (four original) and an Introduction by editor Jeffrey Thomas.

Beautiful Hell was another entry in Thomas' own demonic "Hades" series, reprinted from a 2007 volume. A twenty-six copy leatherbound and slipcased edition quickly sold out.

The Invasion and *The Valley* formed a "Dark Regions Double" by William Meikle, and the publisher also issued the authorised pastiche *Sherlock Holmes: Revenant* by the same author in a special signed and numbered trade paperback edition, limited to just 125 copies.

From companion imprint Ghost House, Meikle's *Carnacki: Heaven and Hell* was a collection of ten original stories based on the character originally created by an uncredited William Hope Hodgson, nicely illustrated by Wayne Miller.

Most Dark Regions/Ghost House titles were available in various print editions as well as ebook format.

Edited by Jason V. Brock and William F. Nolan, *The Devil's Coattails: More Dispatches from the Dark Frontier* was a follow-up to the co-editors' previous anthology, *The Bleeding Edge*, also from Cycatrix Press. The heavily-illustrated volume contained new fiction, poetry and a even a teleplay by Ramsey Campbell, the late Dan O'Bannon, John Shirley, Melanie Tem, the late Norman Corwin, Steve Rasnic Tem, Richard Christian Matheson, Earl Hammer Jr., Nancy Kilpatrick, Marc Scott Zicree, Gary A. Braunbeck and others, including both editors. Limited to 500 trade hardcovers, there was also a fifty-two copy signed and lettered edition for $194.95.

Jeffrey Thomas' *Blood Society* from Necro Publications was about an immortal criminal.

For Aeon Press Books, John Kenny edited *Box of Delights*, and anthology of sixteen original stories that included Steve Rasnic Tem, Kristine Kathryn Rusch, Mike Resnick and Don D'Ammassa.

Edited by Adam Bradley for Morpheus Tales, *13 Tales of Dark Fiction* included contributions from, amongst others, Eric S. Brown, Joseph D'Lacey, Gary Fry, Andrew Hook, Shaun Jeffrey and Gary McMahon.

The ubiquitous McMahon also had a new collection of stories out from Gary Fry's Gray Friar Press, limited to 100 signed hardcover copies. *I Know Where You Live: Tales of Modern Unease* contained sixteen stories (two reprints) along with a Foreword and story notes by the author.

A group of TV ghost-hunters investigated an abandoned summer house in David L. Golemon's *The Supernaturals* from Seven Realms Publishing.

Vampires: The Recent Undead from Prime Books was an anthology edited with an Introduction by Paula Guran. It collected twenty-five stories from the first decade of the twenty-first century by Charlaine Harris, Kim Newman, Michael Marshall Smith and others.

For the same imprint, Guran also edited *Halloween*, which contained thirty stories and three poems by Peter Straub, Ray Bradbury, Esther M. Friesner and others, and *New Cthulhu: The*

Recent Weird, which featured twenty-seven stories by, amongst others, Neil Gaiman, Michael Marshall Smith and Caitlín R. Kiernan.

Edited by John Langan and Paul Tremblay, *Creatures: Thirty Years of Monsters* contained twenty-six stories by Clive Barker, Joe R. Lansdale, Kelly Link and others.

The cleverly-titled *Bewere the Night*, edited by Ekaterina Sedia for Prime, contained twenty-nine stories about shape-shifters (seventeen original).

Limited to just 100 copies from Moshassuck Press, *Lovecraft's Pillow and Other Strange Stories* collected seventeen tales (seven original) by Kenneth W. Faig, Jr., most of then taken from amateur press association publications.

From gaming-related imprint Chaosium, *Cthulhu's Dark Cults* edited by David Conyers contained ten stories (one reprint) inspired by H. P. Lovecraft's Mythos.

Lois Gresh's collection *Eldritch Evolutions* from the same publisher contained twenty-six Lovecraftian stories (nine original) with an Introduction by Robert Weinberg.

Age-old horrors returned to the small town of Parr's Landing in Michael Rowe's 1970s-set horror novel *Enter, Night*, published by Canada's ChiZine Publications.

From the same imprint, a despondent man made his way across an unsettling American landscape in Tom Piccirilli's novella *Every Shallow Cut*, while a wealthy industrialist attempted to create a perfect community amongst a race of shape-shifters in David Nickle's *Eutopia: A Novel of Terrible Optimism*.

A Rope of Thorns was the second novel in Gemma Files' "Hexslinger" weird Western series.

Most ChiZine books were available in signed hardcover editions only by pre-order.

Chilling Tales, somewhat obliquely subtitled *Evil Did I Dwell: Lewd I Did Live*, was the first in an original horror anthology series edited with an Introduction by Michael Kelly and published in trade paperback by Canadian imprint Edge Science Fiction and Fantasy Publishing. The eighteen contributors included Richard Gavin, Barbara Roden, Simon Strantzas, Nancy Kilpatrick, David Nickle, Brett Alexander Savory, Sandra

Kasturi, Gemma Files and others, while the cover was by the distinctly non-Canadian Les Edwards.

Gaslight Arcanum: Uncanny Tales of Sherlock Holmes was the third in a series of supernatural Sherlockian anthologies edited by J. R. Campbell and Charles Prepolec. It contained twelve stories (one reprint) by Stephen Volk, Christopher Fowler, Fred Saberhagen, Simon Kurt Unsworth, Simon Clark, Paul Kane, Tony Richards, Kim Newman and others, with artwork by Dave Elsey, Mike Mignola and Luke Eidenschink.

Edited by Nancy Kilpatrick, *Evolve Two: Vampire Stories of the Future Undead* contained twenty-two new stories about how bloodsuckers and humans might co-exist after a future apocalypse. Contributors included Kelley Armstrong, William Meikle, John Shirley, Bev Vincent, Thomas Roche, Tanith Lee and Sandra Kasturi.

From Edge's Hades Publications imprint, *Rigor Amortis* was an anthology of zombie erotica edited by Jaym Gates and Erika Holt which featured thirty-three stories and two poems, while *Those Who Fight Monsters: Tales of Occult Detectives* edited by Justin Gustainis contained fourteen "urban fantasy" stories by Carrie Vaughn, Tanya Huff, Lilith Saintcrow, Simon R. Green, T. A. Pratt and others, including the editor.

From PS Publishing's poetry imprint, Stanza Press, *A Woman of Mars: The Poems of an Early Homesteader* collected thirty-three poems about the red planet by Australian writer Helen Patrice. It was limited to 300 hardcovers signed by the poet and illustrator Bob Eggleton.

Blood Wallah and Other Poems from Dark Regions Press collected forty-three poems (fifteen original) by Robert Borski, illustrated by Marge Simon.

From Australian PoD imprint P'rea Press, *The Land of Bad Dreams* edited by Charles Lovecraft featured twenty-eight poems by Kyla Lee Ward, who also supplied the black and white illustrations.

PS Publishing also launched its first issue of the "PS Quickies" chapbook series with Ramsey Campbell's original short story *Holding the Light*.

Hector Douglas Makes a Sale was another slim chapbook from PS that contained a missing section from Ian R. MacLeod's alternate-world novel *Wake Up and Dream*, the reasons for which were explained by the author in an extensive Afterword.

From Nicholas Royle's chapbook imprint Nightjar Press came *Remains* by Ga Pickin, *Sullom Hill* by Christopher Kenworthy, *Lexicon* by Christopher Burns and *Field* by Tom Fletcher. Each title was limited to 200 signed and numbered copies.

Simon Marshall-Jones' similar Spectral Press imprint was launched with the chapbook *What They Hear in the Dark*, a haunted house story by Gary McMahon. It was followed by *King Death* by Paul Finch, *Nowhere Hall* by Cate Gardner and *Abolisher* of Roses by Gary Fry. Each slim volume was limited to only 100 signed and numbered copies apiece.

From Bedabbled's B! imprint, *Three Demonic Tales* by Michel Parry contained two reprints (originally published in the 1970s under the pseudonym "Roland Caine") and an original story. It was limited to just fifty signed copies.

Mysterious Islands was a selection of nautical nightmares (including H. P. Lovecraft's "Call of Cthulhu") and other horrors by artist Gary Gianni. The chapbook was limited to 1,000 signed and numbered copies from Flesk Publications.

There was a touch of the *memento mori* hanging over *The Magazine of Fantasy & Science Fiction*, which put out its usual six bumper issues featuring fiction by Kate Wilhelm, Albert E. Cowdrey, Richard A. Lupoff, Alan Dean Foster, Paul Di Filippo, Chet Williamson, Don Webb, Scott Bradfield, Steve Saylor, Peter S. Beagle, Esther M. Friesner, Geoff Ryman, Sarah Langan, M. Rickert, Tim Sullivan, and the deceased Joan Aiken, Alan Peter Ryan and Evangeline Walton, among others.

David Langford, Paul Di Filippo, Paul Dellinger and the late F. Gwynplaine MacIntyre contributed to the "Curiosities" column, and editor Gordon Van Gelder wrote a fascinating editorial in the May/June issue about the strange life and even stranger death of "Froggy" MacIntyre.

A free Kindle version of *F&SF* was also launched that included various columns and a sample short story.

Andy Cox's *Black Static* turned out six colourful issues with the usual news, reviews and opinion columns by Peter Tennant, Tony Lee, Stephen Volk, Christopher Fowler and Mike O'Driscoll. Maura McHugh, James Cooper, Simon Kurt Unsworth, Joel Lane, Simon Bestwick, Ramsey Campbell, Alison Littlewood, Christopher Fowler, Gary McMahon and Andrew Hook were amongst those who contributed stories, and there were interviews with Angela Slatter, Steven Pirie, Tim Lees, Tom Fletcher, Kaaron Warren and D. F. Lewis.

Black Static's sister SF publication, *Interzone*, also produced six attractive-looking issues.

The two issues of the magazine that continued to call itself *Weird Tales* was filled with the usual whimsical nonsense, along with interviews with writer Caitlín R. Kiernan, Angry Robot publisher Marc Gascoigne and artist Carrie Ann Baade.

Thankfully, in August, editor Ann VanderMeer announced in a surprisingly self-congratulatory press release that publisher John Betancourt of Wildside Press was selling the magazine to author/editor Marvin Kaye. However, as a result of the change in ownership, VanderMeer – who had been reading fiction for the magazine for five years – and her all-female management staff would be let go.

The new owners of *Weird Tales*, Nth Dimension Media, Inc., brought out a special electronic issue in time for the 2011 World Fantasy Convention that featured stories by Meg Opperman, Jean Paiva, Parke Godwin, Tanith Lee and Christian Endres.

The second annual issue of editor Michael Kelly's *Shadows & Tall Trees* from Undertow Publications retained its trade paperback format with eight original stories of "quiet, literary horror" by Steve Rasnic Tem, Ian Rogers, Alison J. Littlewood and others.

The first perfect-bound issue of David Memmott's ambitious literary journal *Phantom Drift: A Journal of New Fabulism* included eleven stories (one reprint), eight poems, two essays and two artist features. Contributors included Brian Evenson and Ray Vukcevich.

For the third time in recent years, it was announced that *Realms of Fantasy* magazine was being closed down, with the October edition being the final issue from the current publisher.

Meanwhile, editor John Joseph Adams purchased both *Fantasy* and *Lightspeed* magazines from Prime Books and announced plans to combine them into a single ebook.

The April issue of *Suspense Magazine* included an interview with Jack Ketchum.

Issue #117 of *Granta: The Magazine of New Writing* was a special devoted to "Horror" that included contributions from Paul Auster, Don DeLillo, Will Self and Stephen King.

In the first issue of the year, King announced that he was giving up his column "The Pop of King" in *Entertainment Weekly* after seven years. However, the author did contribute a "Summer Reading List" to the magazine's special June issue that featured Robert McCammon's *The Five*, Graham Joyce's *The Silent Land* and Michael Koryta's *The Cypress House*, and he was back in December with a list of the year's "Pop Culture Favourites" that included Justin Evans' ghost novel *The White Devil*.

The 28 October edition of the magazine also featured an exclusive excerpt from the author's new novel, *11/22/63*.

Canada's *Rue Morgue* produced eleven high-quality issues featuring interviews with filmmakers John Waters, Alejandro Jodorowsky, Tom Holland and Guillermo Del Toro, veteran actress Carla Laemmle, singer Alice Cooper, authors Michael Louis Calvillo, John Shirley and John Landis, and editors Ellen Datlow, Christopher Golden and S. T. Joshi.

The bumper 14th Anniversary Halloween Issue celebrated twenty-five years of *The Fly* with interviews with director David Cronenberg and cast and crew members of both the original trilogy and the remake.

The May/June issue of the revived *Famous Monsters of Filmland* was a H. P. Lovecraft special, featuring articles on the author and the movie adaptations. Bob Eggleton produced covers for that issue and the following one, a special Japanese monsters (*Kaiju*) edition, which confusingly resurrected the *Monster World* logo on one version of the magazine. The artist also contributed an article about his connection with Godzilla.

The six issues of Tim Lucas' *Video WatcHDog* included an overview of the *Friday the 13th* series, a tribute to French director Jean Rollin, an extensive look at the career of actor Eddie

Constantine and interviews with actresses June Lockhart and Mimsy Farmer, along with all the usual reviews and columns.

To celebrate the opening of the British Library's science fiction exhibition "Out of This World", the *Guardian* newspaper's *Review* section on 14 May was a "SF Special Issue", in which some of the world's leading SF writers were asked to choose their favourite author or novel in the genre. Russell Hoban chose H. P. Lovecraft, Liz Jensen picked *The Day of the Triffids* and China Miéville went for *The Island of Doctor Moreau*. The supplement also included a "My Hero" piece on Gene Wolfe by Neil Gaiman.

In January, *Locus* celebrated its 600th issue with a special feature on digital publishing that featured contributions from Neil Gaiman, Cory Doctorow and Charles Stross, amongst others. That same month, the magazine launched a new digital edition, which was initially offered free to overseas subscribers.

Throughout the year *Locus* featured interviews with Robert J. Sawyer, Gene Wolfe, Oscar-winning artist Shaun Tan, Jay Lake, Margo Lanagan, Geoff Ryman, Andy Duncan, Charles Stross, Gemma Files and a lot of new writers that most readers had probably never heard of.

Now published by Centipede Press, the first edition of *Allen K's Inhuman Magazine* for a couple of years was a bumper one. Issue No. 5 included twenty-three stories (five reprints) and three poems by, amongst others, Donald R. Burleson, David Gerrold, Cody Goodfellow, Barry N. Malzberg, James A. Moore, Lisa Morton, Darrell Schweitzer, Michael Shea and Tim Waggoner. Although, as usual, editor Allen Koszwoski illustrated all the stories, there was also a Lovecraftian art gallery featuring work by Dave Carson, Jill Bauman, Bob Eggleton, Randy Broecker and others.

Centipede also brought out the second issue of *The Weird Fiction Review* edited by S. T. Joshi. The annual trade paperback journal included eight stories (by Caitlín R. Kiernan, Simon Strantzas, Donald R. Burleson and others), seven poems, six essays and an artist's gallery by Alexander Binder.

With its two 2011 issues, Rosemary Pardoe's *The Ghosts & Scholars M. R. James Newsletter* reached its twentieth edition.

Contents included Jamesian fiction from Christopher Harman and C. E. Ward, articles by Mark Valentine and the editor, plus news, letters and reviews, along with the first publication of a 1888 supernatural poem by M. R. James.

David Longhorn's *Supernatural Tales* reached its twentieth issue with six stories by Daniel Mills, Katherine Haynes, Michael Chislett and others, along with a brief reviews section.

Published both online and in print, the four issues of *Theaker's Quarterly Fiction* featured some impressive stories along with the book reviews. Edited by Stephen Theaker and John Greenwood, contributors included Rhys Hughes, Alison Littlewood, Maura McHugh and Daniel Mills.

The August issue of *Lady Churchill's Rosebud Wristlet* included fiction by Carol Emshwiller and an obscure reprint by the late Joan Aiken.

The three issues of Hildy Silverman's *Space and Time: The Magazine of Fantasy, Horror, and Science Fiction* included fiction and poetry by Adam Corbin Fusco, Michael Kelly, Don Webb, Josepha Sherman, Don D'Ammassa, Kim Antieau, Forrest Aguirre, Darrell Schweitzer, Kurt Newton, James S. Dorr and others, along with interviews with Ben Bova and Harry Turtledove, and some excellent black and white illustrations.

The four attractive-looking issues Terry Martin's *Murky Depths: The Quarterly Anthology of Graphically Dark Speculative Fiction* featured a number of comic strips (including continuing series by Richard Calder and Lavie Tidhar), plus short stories and artist interviews.

The four issues of *Morpheus Tales* were packed with the usual fan fiction, while the fortieth edition of Ireland's perfect-bound *Albedo One* was a bumper 100-page issue that included twelve stories and interviews with James Patrick Kelly and the late Colin Harvey.

After a bonus-sized 65,000-word issue #13, the following edition marked the final publication of R. Scott McCoy's *Necrotic Tissue: The Horror Writers' Magazine* from Stygian Publications. It featured the usual mix of fiction and 100-word shorts, along with an interview with writer John P. McCann.

The two issues of James R. Beach's *Dark Discoveries* included interviews with Sir Christopher Lee, Bruce Campbell, F. Paul

Wilson and Allen Koszowski; articles on the *Weird Tales* artists, *giallo* cinema and the history of splatterpunk, and fiction and poetry from Gene O'Neill, Joe R. Lansdale, Nick Mamatas, Edward Lee and the late Richard Laymon, among others.

The Winter issue of *Machenalia: The Newsletter of The Friends of Arthur Machen* was a thin one, mostly devoted to a 2010 Australian stage production of *The Great God Pan*.

Issues #18 and #19 of *The Paperback Fanatic* included interviews with authors Basil Copper and David Case, fascinating articles by Ramsey Campbell (on Solomon Kane), Lionel Fanthorpe, Bill Pronzini and Graham Andrews (on J. G. Ballard's US editions), a tribute to artist Jeff Jones, and an always-lively letter column.

The second issue of Martin Jones' *Bedabbled!*, devoted to British horror and cult cinema, was a "Cult of Satan" edition that included informative articles on such films as *Virgin Witch*, *Satan's Slave*, *The Devil's Men* and *Nothing But the Night*, along with interviews with director Norman J. Warren and film-maker/anthologist Michel Parry.

The delayed Winter 2010 *BFS Journal*, published by The British Fantasy Society, turned out to be a somewhat haphazard hardcover omnibus of *New Horizons*, *Prism* and *Dark Horizons*, edited by Andrew Hook, David A. Riley, and Sam Stone and Ian Hunter, respectively. Along with fourteen stories and six poems, the book also contained columns by Ramsey Campbell, Mark Morris, John Llewellyn Probert (on R. Chetwynd-Hayes) and Mike Barrett (on Fritz Leiber), plus interviews with Mark Samuels and Kari Spelling.

The subsequent four issues settled down as a trade paperback, with Peter Coleborn replacing Sam Stone as editor of *Dark Horizons*. Fiction and poetry authors included Allen Ashley, Mike Chinn, Sam Stone, Michael Kelly, Storm Constantine and Joel Lane; Rod Rees, Mary Danby, Jo Fletcher and Peter Crowther were interviewed, and Mike Barrett contributed a fascinating series of articles on lesser-known Arkham House writers.

However, with the Winter 2011/2012 edition it was all change again, as Lou Morgan replaced David Riley and *New Horizons* was dropped from the now fully-integrated line-up.

Amongst his many other responsibilities to the Society, Chairman David J. Howe not only served as Editorial Consultant on the above editions of the *BFS Journal*, but he also found time to edit a huge celebratory anthology, *Full Fathom Forty: British Fantasy Society 40th Anniversary*. Boasting a Cthulhu cover by Bob Eggleton, the nearly 500-page volume featured forty stories (thirteen original) by, among others, Conrad Williams, Christopher Fowler, Jasper Kent, Robert Shearman, Paul Finch, Stephen Gallagher, Simon Clark, Kim Newman, Ramsey Campbell, Graham Masterton, Stephen Laws, Sam Stone and Jonathan Carroll.

Midnight Echo was an attractive-looking magazine put out by the Australian Horror Writers Association. Edited by Leigh Blackmore, the perfect-bound fifth issue included numerous short stories and poetry by Terry Dowling, Rick Kennett, Bryce Stevens, Charles Lovecraft, Kyla Ward and others, along with interviews with Jeff Lindsay and Chris Mars.

Patrick McAleer's *The Writing Family of Stephen King: A Critical Study of the Fiction of Tabitha King, Joe Hill and Owen King* from McFarland & Co looked at the literary careers of the author's wife and two sons.

From the same imprint, Rocky Wood's *A Literary Stephen King Companion* was a handy guide to the best-selling author's fiction and films, including entries about the characters and settings.

In *Becoming Ray Bradbury* from the University of Illinois Press, Jonathan R. Eller took a look at the author's early life through to 1953. The biographical study also included sixteen pages of photos.

Edited with an Introduction by Phil and Sarah Stokes, *Clive Barker: The Painter, the Creature, and the Father of Lies: 30 Years of Non-Fiction Writings* from Earthling Publications collected Barker's articles, introductions, reviews and artwork, along with a new Foreword by the author. As well as a trade hardcover, it was also available in a signed, slipcased leather-bound edition of 250 copies ($125.00), and a twenty-six copy traycased lettered edition containing an original sketch by Barker ($750.00).

Published by the Stokes themselves, *Beneath the Surface of Clive Barker's Abarat Volume 1* was a handsome, full-colour illustrated guide to the book series that included a glossary and an interview with the author.

"It's easy to be smart, later" was one of the many epithetical sayings quoted in *bugf#ck: The Useless Wit & Wisdom of Harlan Ellison*®, a delightful pocket-sized hardcover from Edgeworks Abbey/Spectrum Fantastic Arts, edited by Arnie Fenner.

Nested Scrolls: A Writer's Life was a typically idiosyncratic memoir by "transrealism" writer/software designer Rudy Rucker. Along with the trade edition, it was also available from PS Publishing in 100 signed and slipcased copies that came with a CD-Rom containing thirteen sets of book-writing notes in a one million-word file entitled *Twenty Years of Writing*.

From Tartarus Press, *Time, A Falconer: A Study of Sarban* was Mark Valentine's biography of the writer (a pseudonym for career diplomat John William Wall), limited to 400 copies.

Lest You Should Suffer Nightmares: A Biography of Herbert van Thal was an expanded version of Johnny Mains' Afterword to his 2010 anthology *Back From the Dead*. The slim hardcover also included a selection of letter reproductions, a van Thal checklist, an article reprinted from *SFX*, and reminiscences by various contributors to the *Pan Book of Horror Stories* series, including Conrad Hill, David A. Riley, David Case and John Burke. It was published by Screaming Dreams in an edition of just 100 copies signed by the author and Les Edwards, who did the stunning cover portrait.

Massimo Berruti's *Dim-Remembered Stories: A Critical Study of R. H. Barlow* from Hippocampus Press looked at the career of the troubled young man who became H. P. Lovecraft's literary executor, with a Foreword by S. T. Joshi.

With David E. Schultz, Joshi also edited *An Epicure in the Terrible: A Centennial Anthology of Essays in Honor of H. P. Lovecraft* for the same PoD imprint. Some of the thirteen essays had been updated.

Also from Hippocampus, *A Monster of Voices: Speaking for H. P. Lovecraft* collected thirteen essays and a poem by Robert H. Waugh.

Edited by S. T. Joshi, *Encyclopedia of the Vampire: The Living Dead in Myth, Legend, and Popular Culture* from Greenwood/ABC-CLIO contained numerous critical essays on authors, characters and vampires in literature and the media by Stefan Dziemianowicz, Paula Guran, Melissa Mia Hall, Stephen Jones, John Langan, Barbara Roden, Christopher Roden, Brian Stableford, Bev Vincent and many others, as well as a general bibliography.

Joshi also supplied the Foreword for Scarecrow Press' *21st-Century Gothic: Great Gothic Novels Since 2000* edited by English professor Danel Olson. The book contained fifty-three essays by, amongst others, Steve Rasnic Tem, Nancy A. Collins, Adam L. G. Nevill, Don D'Ammassa, Lisa Tuttle, Robert Hood, Darrell Schweitzer, Nicholas Royle, Lucy Taylor, Graham Joyce and Reggie Oliver, along with extensive appendices.

Zombies! An Illustrated History of the Undead was put together by former *Rue Morgue* editor Jovanka Vuckovic and covered the *walking dead* ("undead" refers to vampires) in films and fiction.

The Sookie Stackhouse Companion included a new novella by Charlaine Harris, various lists, synopses and trivia, and an exclusive interview with *True Blood* creator Alan Ball, while *Vampire Academy: The Ultimate Guide* was an in-depth look at the YA series by Michelle Rowen and Richelle Mead.

Edited by Jamey Heit, *Vader, Voldemort and Other Villains: Essays on Evil in Popular Culture* was published by McFarland & Co.

From the same publisher, *Seduced by Twilight: The Allure and Contradictory Messages of the Popular Saga* was a look at Stephenie Meyer's anaemic YA series by Natalie Wilson. *Theorizing Twilight: Critical Essays on What's at Stake in a Post-Vampire World*, also edited by Wilson with Maggie Parke, explored the influence of Meyer's books and films on popular culture in fifteen essays.

Stephenie Meyer's *The Twilight Saga: The Official Illustrated Guide* was aimed at the young adult market and included illustrations by various artists along with an extensive interview with the author.

Cory Doctorow, Jules Feiffer, Stephen King and Tabitha King were among the fourteen authors who contributed stories to *The Chronicles of Harris Burdick*, based around the illustrations of Chris Van Allsburg. Lemony Snicket supplied the Introduction.

Written by Adam-Troy Castro, *V is for Vampire: An Illustrated Alphabet of the Undead* was embellished with two-colour illustrations by Johnny Atomic. The same team was also responsible for *Z is for Zombie*.

Edited by Arnie Fenner and Cathy Fenner, *Spectrum 18: The Best in Contemporary Fantastic Art* from Underwood Books collected work from more than 300 artists, including Grand Master Award recipient Ralph McQuarrie.

Chamber of Chills Volume One was the first in the sumptuous "Harvey Horrors Collected Works" series from PS Artbooks. Collecting seven full-colour reprints of the 1950s pre-Code horror comic, with a gonzo Foreword by Joe Hill and an informative article by Peter Normanton on the career of artist Al Avison, the book came in three states: a bookshop edition, a slipcased edition with a print signed by Hill, and a twenty-six copy deluxe lettered traycased edition (£249.99) that included a print signed by both Hill and artist Glenn Chadbourne.

It was followed by *Witches Tales Volume One*, with an Introduction by Ramsey Campbell and art print by Bryan Talbot, and *Tomb of Terror Volume One* with an Introduction by Stephen Jones and art print by Randy Broecker.

As if that wasn't enough, PS Artbooks also launched a series of glorious full-colour reprints of such ACG (American Comics Group) titles as *Adventures Into the Unknown*, with an Introduction by Barry Forshaw, and *Forbidden Worlds*, with an Introduction by Stan Nicholls. Artists Glenn Chadbourne and Edward Miller, respectively, contributed a "re-imagined" covers to each volume.

DC Comics: The Art of Modern Mythmaking from Taschen Books celebrated the comics publisher's seventy-fifth anniversary and featured more than 2,000 images over more than 700 pages.

After almost a decade, Steve Niles' *30 Days of Night* became a regular monthly comic from IDW.

Joe R. Lansdale scripted the four-part *30 Days of Night: Night, Again* and a four-part contemporary version of *H. P. Lovecraft's The Dunwich Horror*, while the writer teamed up with his son John L. Lansdale for the three-part *Robert Bloch's That Hellbound Train*, all from IDW.

Clive Barker and Christopher Monfette went back to the beginning for their new *Hellraiser* comic from BOOM! Studios, while *Dark Shadows* from Dynamite did the same for the 1960s TV series.

It Came from Beneath the Sea . . . Again from Bluewater was a sequel to the 1955 Ray Harryhausen movie, and BOOM!'s *Planet of the Apes* picked up from where the last film in the original series, *Battle for the Planet of the Apes*, left off.

Let Me In was a prequel series to the Hammer version of John Ajvide Lindqvist's vampire novel, while *The Thing: The Northman Nightmare* was a prequel to the recent movie prequel, both from Dark Horse. *The Strain* from the same publisher was adapted from the trilogy of novels by Guillermo Del Toro and Chuck Hogan.

John Saul Presents The Blackstone Chronicles from Bluewater was based on the author's serialised novel, and *The Martian Chronicles* and *Something Wicked This Way Comes* were graphic adaptations of Ray Bradbury's books by Dennis Calero and Ron Wimberly, respectively, with new Introductions by the author.

Anita Blake, Vampire Hunter: Circus of the Damned Book 1: The Charmer and *Book 2: The Ingenue* each collected five issues of the Marvel comic book based on the novel by Laurell K. Hamilton, adapted by Jess Ruffner and illustrated by Ron Lim.

Illustrated by Alberto Dose, *Killing the Cobra: Chinatown Trollop* was a vampire mystery from IDW, based on the "PI Felix Gomez" series by Mario Acevedo, who contributed a new story to the graphic novel.

For all those who wanted their walking dead in four colours, they could choose from *Daybreak*, *Battle for the Planet of the Living Dead*, *Fail of the Dead*, *iZombie: Dead to the World*, *Marvel Zombies Supreme*, *Night of the Living Dead: Death Valley*, *Zombie Chuck* and many other zombie comics titles too numerous to mention.

In September, DC Comics completely rebooted its most popular titles, including *Batman*, *Superman* and *Wonder Woman*, restarting the numbering with issue #1. It was hoped that the younger, more human characters would appeal to a greater number of casual readers.

In March, a near-mint copy of Marvel's *Amazing Fantasy* #15 – featuring the first appearance of Spider-Man in 1962 – sold for a record $1.1 million (£680,000) in an online auction.

The following month, a 9.6 copy of Marvel's *X-Men* #1 sold for $200,000 (£123,184) in a private sale conducted by Metropolis Comics/ComicConnect.com. The transaction set a new price record for 1963 debut issue.

A year-and-a-half after a previous edition of *Action Comics* #1 (June 1938) – which featured the first appearance of Superman – sold at auction for a reported $1.5 million (£950,000), another copy went under the hammer in November and broke *that* record, selling for $2.2 million (£1.4 million). The issue, which belonged to Hollywood actor Nicolas Cage, had been stolen in a 2000 burglary from a storage locker and was only recovered in April. The name of the buyer of the "mint" condition comic was not revealed.

The year's clutch of movie tie-in editions included *Conan* by Michael A. Stackpole, *Transformers: Dark of the Moon* by Peter David and *Cowboys and Aliens* by Joan D. Vinge.

Sarah Blakley-Cartwright wrote the young adult tie-in to *Red Riding Hood*, which came with an Introduction from the film's director, Catherine Hardwicke. The book was published without the final chapter, which only became available after the release of the movie.

Don't Be Afraid of the Dark: Blackwood's Guide to Dangerous Fairies, credited to Guillermo del Toro and Christopher Golden, was an epistolary prequel to the movie, set 100 years earlier. Troy Nixey supplied the illustrations.

Conan the Barbarian was a collection of six of Robert E. Howard's original stories with a tie-in cover to the disappointing movie, while Susan Hill's slim 1983 novel *The Woman in Black* was reissued in a tie-in edition to the forthcoming Hammer production.

The revived Hammer Films announced that it had done a deal with Random House UK to publish novelisations and new books based on the classic films under the Arrow Books imprint.

The first two titles to be released were Francis Cottam's novelisation of the Hilary Swank thriller *The Resident* and a re-issue of *The Witches* (aka *The Devil's Own*) by "Peter Curtis" (Nora Lofts). Cyril Frankel, director of the 1966 movie version, contributed a new Foreword to the latter.

The series properly kicked off later in the year with Guy Adams' novelisation of *Kronos* (with a Foreword by writer/director Brian Clemens), Shaun Hutson's *Twins of Evil* (with a Foreword by director John Hough) and K. A. John's *Wake Wood*.

More mystifying were re-issues of Graham Masterton's *The Pariah*, *Family Portrait* and *Mirror*, also published under the Hammer banner.

Enjoying its first US publication from DreamHaven Books, *Creature from the Black Lagoon* was an official hardcover reprint of the super-rare 1954 British movie tie-in by "Vargo Statten" (John Russell Fearn) which came with a new Introduction by David J. Schow, and Afterword about the author by Philip Harbottle, a selection of uncommon production and behind-the-scenes stills, and a cover painting by Bob Eggleton. The 250-copy Limited Edition was signed by actress Julie Adams and stuntman/swimmer Ricou Browning.

TV show tie-ins included *Warehouse 13: A Touch of Fever* by Greg Cox, and *Supernatural: One Year Gone* by Rebecca Dessertine and *Supernatural: Night Terror* by John Passarella. *The Walking Dead: Rise of the Governor* was credited to the comic series creator Robert Kirkman and Jay Bonansinga.

The Coming of the Terraphiles was a *Doctor Who* tie-in by none other than Michael Moorcock, while Paul Finch authored *Doctor Who: Hunter's Moon*.

To tie-in to the spin-off series, Sarah Pinborough wrote *Torchwood: Long Time Dead*, while *Torchwood: The Man Who Sold the World* was by Guy Adams.

Tim Waggoner teamed up with Jason Hawes and Grant Wilson, the stars of the Syfy reality TV show *Ghost Hunters*, for the novel *Ghost Trackers*.

Mark Morris' *Dead Island* and B. K. Evenson's *Dead Space: Martyr* were both based on the video games. The tie-in to the post-apocalyptic *Rage* was written by Matthew Costello, who also contributed to the development of the video game it was based upon.

Arkham Horror: Dance of the Damned was the first volume in Alan Bligh's "Lord of Nightmares" trilogy, a gaming tie-in inspired by the work of H. P. Lovecraft. From the same author, *Arkham Horror: Ghouls of the Miskatonic* was the first book in the "Dark Waters" series.

Nightmare Movies: Horror on Screen Since the 1960s was a welcome reissue of Kim Newman's encyclopaedic 1988 volume, totally re-written, revised and updated.

Covering much of the same ground, Jason Zinoman's *Shock Value* looked at the genre filmmakers of the 1960s and 1970s.

Bob McCabe's *Harry Potter: Page to Screen* weighed in at a hefty 540 pages.

The first volume in the "Deep Focus" series of film criticism books from Counterpoints/Soft Skull Press was *They Live*, a look at the 1988 John Carpenter film by Jonathan Lethem.

Triumph of the Walking Dead: Robert Kirkman's Zombie Epic on Page and Screen was an unauthorised guide to the comic book and TV series, edited with an Introduction by James Lowder. The book included fifteen essays by Lisa Morton, Kim Paffenroth and Jay Bonansinga, amongst others, along with a Foreword by Joe R. Lansdale.

Supernatural: Bobby Singer's Guide to Hunting was a tie-in to the TV series by David Reed.

The Gothic Imagination: Conversations on Fantasy, Horror, and Science Fiction in the Media featured interviews between John C. Tibbetts and such writers as Stephen King, Ray Bradbury, Gahan Wilson, Robert Bloch, Ramsey Campbell, Brian Aldiss and others.

Attendance figures at the US box-office hit a sixteen-year-low in 2011, with a drop of approximately 3.6 per cent on revenues from the previous year. The reason for this could be that films are available on an increasing number of platforms, which no longer means that you have to go to your neighbourhood movie theatre to see them.

History also has a tendency to repeat itself, so it was no surprise that the 3-D "revolution" in films and TV looked ready to stall in 2011 – just like it had done previously in the 1930s, 1950s and 1980s. At the cinema, audiences proved reluctant to pay extra just for the (often shoddy) 3-D experience, while 3-D television sets were still prohibitively expensive for most people, not helped by a lack of product to show on them.

Still, that didn't stop Warner Bros. from releasing the eighth movie in the *Harry Potter* series in 3-D, the first to be shown in the process. Despite the final film in the franchise being something of a disappointment after the solid storytelling of the previous entries, *Harry Potter and the Deathly Hallows Part 2* smashed all records before it, clocking up the highest-grossing opening weekend ever ($168.55 million) in July, beating *The Dark Knight*, *Spider-Man 3*, *The Twilight Saga: New Moon* and *Pirates of the Caribbean: Dead Man's Chest*. The film went on to pass the $200 million point in just five days, and achieved a world-wide take of $900 million ten days after that.

In the UK, the film broke box-office records by taking £23 million over its opening weekend, beating the previous entry's £18.32 million, and the eight *Harry Potter* movies are now officially the highest-grossing film franchise ever.

"Inspired" by Tim Powers' superior novel, Rob Marshall's 3-D *Pirates of the Caribbean: On Stranger Tides*, the entertaining fourth instalment in the Disney franchise, involved zombified sailors and murderous mermaids as Johnny Depp's increasingly silly pirate Jack Sparrow joined Ian McShane's sorcerous Blackbeard and his duplicitous daughter (Penélope Cruz) in a race to find the fabled Fountain of Youth.

Matt Damon's New York politician was warned by Terence Stamp's mysterious man in black that his life was destined along a different path in *The Adjustment Bureau*, based on a story by Philip K. Dick.

Dick could just as well have been the inspiration for Neil Burger's *Limitless*, in which Robert De Niro's ruthless businessman wanted the secret of the "smart pill" that allowed Bradley Cooper's struggling novelist to access the unused areas of his brain.

Jake Gyllenhaal found himself living two separate lives in Duncan Jones' *Source Code*, which bore more than a passing resemblance to *Deja Vu* (2006), while Justin Timberlake was living on borrowed time in the near-futuristic *In Time*. The latter movie was briefly the subject of a lawsuit by Harlan Ellison, who claimed that the film infringed upon his story "'Repent, Harlequin!' Said the Ticktockman".

Gwyneth Paltrow was the first victim of a viral epidemic in Stephen Soderbergh's *Contagion*, an all-star version of the kind of disaster films regularly churned out by the Syfy channel. Made for a fraction of that film's budget, *Perfect Sense* featured Eva Green and Ewan McGregor's characters falling in love as a world-wide epidemic robbed people of their sensory perceptions.

2011 was certainly the year for alien invasions at the cinema. Based on a comic book, Jon Favreau's $163 million *Cowboys & Aliens* was executive produced by Steven Spielberg but it failed to deliver the thrills, despite teaming Daniel Craig and Harrison Ford against alien invaders in the Wild West.

J. J. Abrams' $50 million homage to producer Spielberg, *Super 8*, was a summer movie about a group of school friends who witnessed a spectacular train crash and became involved with an escaped extraterrestrial who just wanted to go home.

Aaron Eckhart's military veteran led a platoon of soldiers and some jittery camerawork against an alien invasion in the noisy *Battle: Los Angeles*, while a group of young people were trapped in a Moscow invaded by aliens through the power supply in *The Darkest Hour*.

British sci-fi nerds Simon Pegg and Nick Frost picked up the eponymous alien escapee (voiced by a potty-mouthed Seth Rogen) in Greg Mottola's likeable comedy *Paul*, which also featured Jason Bateman, Jane Lynch, Blythe Danner and Sigourney Weaver.

Nick Frost also turned up as a laid-back drug dealer in Joe Cornish's inventive *Attack the Block*, which mixed its laughs with scares as toothy alien balls of fur met their match at the hands of a gang of urban teenagers on a South London estate.

Shia LaBeouf's hapless hero Sam Witwicky teamed up with Victoria's Secret model Rosie Huntington-Whiteley to battle the evil Decepticons in Michael Bay's 3-D second sequel, *Transformers: Dark of the Moon*. Patrick Dempsey, Frances McDormand, John Turturro, John Malkovich, Buzz Aldrin and Leonard Nimoy (as the voice of "Sentinel Prime") were lost amongst the special effects mayhem.

Hugh Jackman's washed-up fighter trained a boxing robot in Shawn Levy's *Real Steel*, based on the story by Richard Matheson, and five scantily-clad women used their fantasies to escape from a mental institution in Zack Snyder's *Sucker Punch*.

In Dominic Sena's ludicrously entertaining *Season of the Witch*, a pair of disillusioned fourteenth century Crusaders (Nicolas Cage and Ron Perlman) were forced by Christopher Lee's plague-ridden Cardinal to escort a suspected witch (Claire Foy) to a remote monastery. After being attacked by wolves and zombie monks, they discovered an even greater evil awaited them at their destination.

Cage also starred as a vengeful escapee from Hell on the trail of an evil satanic cult leader in Patrick Lussier's 3-D *Drive Angry*, which, despite the non-stop action, flopped at the box-office.

Based on another graphic novel series, Paul Bettany's futuristic vampire-hunter had to rescue his kidnapped niece in the 3-D *Priest*, while Anthony Hopkins' ageing exorcist teamed up with a young priest (Colin O'Donoghue) to banish a demon possessing a pregnant Italian teenager in *The Rite*.

Director Guy Ritchie and actors Robert Downey Jr. and Jude Law were reunited for *Sherlock Holmes: A Game of Shadows*, a sequel to the 2009 film, as the Great Detective tried to prevent a devious Professor Moriarty (Jared Harris) from starting the First World War.

After eleven years, Neve Campbell, Courteney Cox and David Arquette returned for Wes Craven's *Scr4am*, which updated its scares for a new generation who couldn't care less. Despite featuring TV heroines Anna Paquin, Kristen Bell and Hayden Panettiere, it became the lowest grossing entry yet in the spoof slasher series.

Tony Todd returned to the series as a creepy coroner in *Final Destination 5*, in which the survivors of a bridge collapse met their graphic demises in gore-drenched 3-D.

Colin Farrell was the vampire that moved-in next door in the surprisingly good 3-D remake of the 1985 comedy-horror film *Fright Night*, which also featured David Tennant in the original Roddy McDowall role.

Rebecca De Mornay's mad matriarch dominated her sadistic sons in *Mother's Day*, a remake of the 1980 slasher film of the same name, while Leighton Meester's crazed stalker put a kitten in a clothes dryer just to make her point in *The Roommate*, a risible PG-13 rip-off of *Single White Female* (1992).

A belated prequel to Tim Burton's 2001 remake, Rupert Wyatt's *Rise of the Planet of the Apes* was a surprise box-office hit, opening at #1 in America.

Paul W. S. Anderson directed a silly 3-D steampunk version of *The Three Musketeers* starring his wife, Milla Jovovich, who criticised Summit Entertainment on Twitter for failing to market the movie properly.

Mary Elizabeth Winstead was part of a Norwegian team that discovered something under the Antarctic ice in *The Thing*, a belated and pointless prequel/remake of John Carpenter's 1982 movie (which itself was a remake).

Meanwhile, Carpenter himself directed *The Ward*, in which Amber Heard's teenage pyromaniac ended up in a spooky 1960s insane asylum.

Husband and wife stars Daniel Craig and Rachel Weisz refused to promote the final cut of Jim Sheridan's *Dream House*, which gave away all its surprises in the trailer and quickly sank without trace on both sides of the Atlantic.

In America, Hammer's psychological thriller *The Resident* went directly to DVD, despite starring Hilary Swank, Jeffrey Dean Morgan and Christopher Lee. At least it received a negligible cinema release in the UK, as did the pagan thriller *Wake Wood*, another Hammer production that had been sitting on the shelf for a few years.

Co-scripted by Stephen Volk and director Nick Murphy, *The Awakening* was an atmospheric low-budget period ghost film set in a haunted boarding school.

Given its slightly more than $1 million budget, James Wan's *Insidious* turned out to be one of the most profitable films of the year, taking more than $53 million at the US box-office. Produced by the team behind the terrible *Paranormal Activity* franchise and written and directed by the creators of the *Saw* series, it was an intentionally old-fashioned ghost story about parents fighting for the soul of their son.

Two sisters discovered footage of themselves from 1988 that proved they had always been a magnet for the supernatural in *Paranormal Activity 3*. Made for just $5 million, the prequel opened in the US at #1 with a gross of $52.6 million – the biggest horror film and best October opening ever.

Shark Night 3D served up college co-eds as chum, while a group of foxhunters became the hunted in *Blooded*. *Apollo 18* was another "found footage" flick, this time set on the Moon.

A brother and sister wandered around a forest investigating the paranormal in the Spanish-made *Atrocious*, while the Norwegian *Troll Hunter* was like *The Blair Witch Project* with giant furry trolls.

Guillermo Del Toro produced *Julia's Eyes*, Guillem Morales' Spanish supernatural thriller in which Belén Rueda's Hitchcockian heroine investigated the death of her blind twin sister. Del Toro also produced and co-scripted *Don't Be Afraid of the Dark*, a loose remake of a 1973 TV movie, about an old manor house haunted by little evil critters.

Pedro Almodóvar's *The Skin I Live In* starred Antonio Banderas as an obsessed plastic surgeon in an art house homage to Georges Franju's *Les yeux sans visage* (aka *Eyes Without a Face*).

Gustavo Hernández's Spanish thriller *The Silent House* played out in real time and was based on a true murder mystery that happened in 1940s Uruguay.

Louise Bourgoin was the female Indiana Jones battling mad scientists, dinosaurs and reanimated Egyptian mummies in Luc Besson's comic book-inspired *The Extraordinary Adventures of Adele Blanc-Sec*.

Kirsten Dunst and Alexander Skarsgård were unlucky enough to schedule their nuptials for the same day as a rogue planet was about to crash into the Earth in Lars von Trier's *Melancholia*, which debuted in America on video-on-demand.

Mike Cahill's *Another Earth* was another indie feature, in which a woman (Brit Marling) won a trip to an identical planet orbiting her own world.

The Dead was a low budget zombie film shot in Africa, and the bargain budget zombie apocalypse continued in the British-made *The World of the Dead: The Zombie Diaries*.

The horror comedy *Dylan Dog: Dead of Night*, which starred Brandon Routh as a paranormal investigator, took under $1 million during its opening week in the US.

A pair of assassins discovered that there was more to their latest job than they expected in Ben Wheatley's *Kill List*. *Tucker & Dale vs. Evil* was a low budget spoof on backwoods slasher films, while Jason Bateman and Ryan Reynolds swapped bodies in the comedy *The Change-Up*.

More tragedy than Greek, Theseus (future "Superman" Henry Cavill) led his Olympian chums against Mickey Rourke's evil King Hyperion in Tarsem Singh's overblown *Immortals*, released in "epic 3-D".

Your Highness was a witless fantasy spoof that somehow managed to feature James Franco, Natalie Portman and Charles Dance in its cast.

Despite Jason Momoa's solid Hyborian warrior, and Ron Perlman as his father, the 3-D *Conan the Barbarian* was a disappointing origin story of Robert E. Howard's sword-wielding hero.

Audiences were colour-blind to the 3-D *The Green Hornet*, in which Seth Rogen's mugging millionaire became a crime-fighter with the aid of Jay Chou's far more intelligent Kato, and Ryan Reynolds made a lightweight *Green Lantern* in Martin Campbell's disappointing origin story of the DC Comics superhero.

James McAvoy and Michael Fassbender played the younger incarnations of Professor X and Magneto, respectively, in Matthew Vaughn's better-than-expected "preboot" of the Marvel Comics franchise, *X-Men: First Class*.

Marvel continued to build towards its multi-hero *Avengers* epic in 2012 with the release of Kenneth Branagh's mighty 3-D *Thor*, which introduced the planet Asgard's God of Thunder (Chris Hemsworth), exiled to Earth by his father Odin (Anthony Hopkins). Meanwhile, Chris Evans' wartime weakling became *Captain America: The First Avenger* in Joe Johnston's nicely old-fashioned 3-D adventure, which pitted the all-American hero against Nazi villain the Red Skull (Hugo Weaving).

Comedian Rainn Wilson became low-rent hero "The Crimson Bolt" in *Super*, which also featured Ellen Page, Liv Tyler, Kevin Bacon and Nathan Fillion.

Based on Kazuo Ishiguro's 2005 novel about teenage cloning, *Never Let Me Go* starred Carey Mulligan, Andrew Garfield and Keira Knightley, while Alex Pettyfer's stranded alien might just as well have been another *Twilight* vampire in the teen romance *I Am Number Four*, produced by Michael Bay.

The less said about Bill Condon's *The Twilight Saga: Breaking Dawn – Part 1* the better, as Bella and Edward got married, moped around and had a vampire baby.

Directed by Catherine Hardwicke, who was responsible for the first *Twilight* movie, *Red Riding Hood* put a werewolf spin on the same basic premise.

A young Parisian orphan (Asa Butterfield) befriended forgotten cinema pioneer Georges Méliès (Ben Kingsley) in *Hugo*, Martin Scorsese's 3-D paean to the movies, which also featured Sacha Baron Cohen, Ray Winstone, Emily Mortimer, Jude Law, Richard Griffiths and Christopher Lee.

Maybe because it was released in "4-D Aroma-scope", but Robert Rodriguez's *Spy Kids: All the Time in the World* was a box-office stinker.

Despite being directed by Steven Spielberg, the 3-D motion-capture used in *The Adventures of Tintin: The Secret of the Unicorn* just made the comic strip characters look creepy.

One of the biggest box-office bombs of the year was Walt Disney's *Mars Needs Moms*. Estimated to have cost around $150 million, the 3-D motion-capture comedy took just $6.9 million in the US during its opening weekend. However, *Hoodwinked Too!: Hood vs. Evil* actually had the worst opening ever for a 3-D movie, grossing just $4.1 million at 1,500 movie theatres.

At the Orange British Academy Film Awards on 13 February, director Tim Burton presented eighty-eight-year-old Sir Christopher Lee with the Academy Fellowship – the highest accolade given out by BAFTA for contribution to film. Previous recipients included Alfred Hitchcock, Steven Spielberg, Charlie Chaplin, Elizabeth Taylor and Sean Connery.

The 83rd Annual Academy Awards were announced in Hollywood on 27 February. Natalie Portman won the Best

Actress award for her portrayal of a crazed ballet dancer in *Black Swan*, and *Toy Story 3* picked up the awards for Best Animated Feature Film and Original Song ("We Belong Together"). *Inception* scooped up a quartet of technical awards for Cinematography, Sound Mixing, Sound Editing and Visual Effects. The Art Direction and Costume Design awards went to *Alice in Wonderland*, and *The Wolfman* was the winner of Best Makeup. Co-directed by Australian genre artist Shaun Tan, *The Lost Thing* won for Best Short Film, Animated.

The highlight of the evening was when ninety-four-year-old Hollywood legend Kirk Douglas presented the award for Best Actress in a Supporting Role.

On 12 November, Honorary Academy Awards for lifetime achievement were presented to actor James Earl Jones (the voice of "Darth Vader" in the *Star Wars* movies) and veteran make-up artist Dick Smith (*The Exorcist*).

Before Warner Bros. began pulling all eight Potter DVDs from retail shelves at the end of December in preparation for future upgrades, the Blu-ray release of *Harry Potter and the Deathly Hallows Part 2* included an in-depth conversation between J. K. Rowling and Daniel Radcliffe, along with an interactive option. The Potter franchise has already generated around $51 billion for the studio's Home Entertainment division – on top of the $7 billion earned during the films' theatrical release.

Following complaints in the press by Dutch director Tom Six, in October, the British Board of Film Classification lifted its ban on *The Human Centipede 2 (Full Sequence)*, giving the controversial body-horror movie an "18" certificate on DVD after two-and-a-half minutes were cut from the original running time.

Scott Spiegel's *Hostel: Part III* found its natural home after being released directly to DVD, as did Victor Garcia's Mexican-set *Hellraiser: Revelation*, the ninth film in the franchise and the first not to feature Doug Bradley as "Pinhead".

Danny Trejo, Ving Rhames and the busy Sean Bean starred in *Death Race 2*, a DVD prequel to the 2008 remake.

A couple were trapped in their island home by a washed-up soldier in Carl Tibbetts' debut *Retreat* which, despite starring

Thandie Newton, Cillian Murphy and Jamie Bell, also went straight to DVD.

Released on DVD as an "After Dark Original", *The Task* was about a reality TV show recorded on a haunted prison ship.

Skin Eating Jungle Vampires from Chemical Burn Entertainment had all the quality of a bad home video. The same was true of *The Stone: No Soul Unturned* and the terrifically titled (but ultimately disappointing) *Fast Zombies with Guns*, from the same distributor.

Survivors of a terrorist bomb attack had to also escape the walking dead in *Zombie Undead*.

The Blu-ray of David Lynch's *Blue Velvet* (1986) featured more than fifty minutes of "newly discovered" scenes never included in the finished film.

The Complete 50th Anniversary Collection of the 1960s TV series *The Avengers* was issued by Optimum as a limited edition thirty-nine disc set that featured every episode digitally restored and more than thirty hours of bonus material.

The Complete Sherlock Holmes Collection was a five-disc Blu-ray set containing all fourteen of Basil Rathbone's Holmes films, dating from 1939–46.

Guillermo del Toro, John Landis and Roger Corman were among those who were commenting on the horrors of the past on the DVD compilation *Trailers from Hell! Volume 2*.

1980s stars Kristy Swanson, D. B. Sweeney and Robert Davi turned up in the entertaining Syfy channel movie *Swamp Shark*, John Schneider was slumming in *Super Shark*, and Robert Picardo had a cameo in *Mega Shark vs Crocosaurus*.

Syfy also revived the careers of 1980s pop rivals Deborah (Debbie) Gibson and Tiffany, who teamed up for Mary Lambert's *Mega Python vs. Gatoroid*, which also featured former Monkee Micky Dolenz as himself.

Brian Krause and C. Thomas Howell battled arachnids from Afghanistan in Jim Wynorski's dire *Camel Spiders*; Robert Patrick was involved in a civil war on Mars in the videogame-based *Red Faction: Origins*, and Lance Henriksen made a brief appearance in *Scream of the Banshee*.

A giant monster nearly destroyed the entire planet in *Behemoth*, a mutated root system threatened to tear apart the Earth in *The Terror Beneath* (aka *Seeds of Destruction*), and a proofreader and an archaeologist teamed up to prevent the end of the world in *Doomsday Prophecy*.

A volcano under Yellowstone Park exploded in a *Super Eruption*, while Stacy Keach's mad meteorologist used a weather weapon to destroy his enemies in *Storm War*.

Danny Glover's obsessed Captain Ahab wanted revenge on a Great White . . . er, Dragon, in the Syfy "original" movie *Age of the Dragons*, a medieval reworking of Herman Melville's *Moby Dick*.

H. G. Wells was no doubt spinning in his grave as mutated monsters travelled back in time in *Morlocks*, and Ray Harryhausen would have been equally disappointed by the bargain-basement *Sinbad and the Minotaur*.

Meanwhile, an unrecognisable Richard Grieco played the evil Loki in *Almighty Thor*, another cheap knock-off from The Asylum, who would also have you believe that its low budget alien invasion movie *Battle of Los Angeles* was in no way similar to the bigger budget *Battle: Los Angeles*.

Alien bacteria animated an eighteen-foot golem in *Iron Invader* (aka *Metal Shifters*), and alien technology created a terrorist weapon in *Cold Fusion*.

The Syfy's channel's two-part *Neverland* was yet another version of the *Peter Pan* story, with Rhys Ifans as the future Captain Hook, Anna Friel as his pirate lover, and Keira Knightley as the voice of a CGI Tinkerbell.

A modern-day Dorothy Gale (Paulie Rojas) discovered that the best-selling books she had written were based on her suppressed childhood memories in Syfy's two-part *The Witches of Oz*. The supporting cast included Billy Boyd, Lance Henriksen, Jeffrey Combs, Mia Sara, Sean Astin and Christopher Lloyd.

Pierce Brosnan's best-selling novelist investigated the death of his wife (Annabeth Gish) in Mick Garris' two-part, four-hour supernatural mini-series of Stephen King's *Bag of Bones* on A&E, which also featured genre veteran William Schallert.

Based on a comic book, the unfortunately titled *Steve Niles' Remains* was yet another reworking of *Night of the Living Dead* and was the first original movie produced by the Chiller cable TV channel.

Housewife Halloween movies included Lifetime's *Possessing Piper Rose* starring Rebecca Romijn, and Hallmark's *The Good Witch's Family* starring Catherine Bell. Martin Mull's titular phantom attempted to scare away a family who moved into his house in *Oliver's Ghost* for the same network.

Eddie Izzard portrayed a mysterious stranger who turned up on Christmas Eve in the BBC-TV movie *Lost Christmas*, while *The Borrowers* was yet another version of Mary Norton's classic children's books. It featured Christopher Eccleston, Victoria Wood and Stephen Fry, and was also broadcast by the BBC at Christmas.

Lifetime's unauthorised biopic *Magic Beyond Words: The J. K. Rowling Story* featured Poppy Montgomery as the struggling young *Harry Potter* writer and proved, if there was any doubt, just how boring being an author really is.

For the first time since its 2005 revival, the BBC's *Doctor Who* totally lost the plot (literally) under new show-runner Steven Moffat. Matt Smith's increasingly annoying time traveller faced his "final" days as he and his various companions bumbled their way through thirteen episodes that culminated in a ludicrously complicated finale that totally failed to deliver a satisfying conclusion to the season's multiple plots.

Neil Gaiman, Mark Gattis and Toby Whithouse scripted episodes, and guest stars included Frances Barber, Hugh Bonneville, Lily Cole, James Corden, Ian McNeice, Simon Callow, Mark Gattis, David Walliams, and Alex Kingston as the no-longer-enigmatic River Song.

As usual, the Christmas special, *The Doctor, the Widow and the Wardrobe*, was also a disappointment, as the Doctor whisked a wartime widow (the excellent Claire Skinner) and her two children off to a Narnia-like winter wonderland filled with menace. Guest stars Bill Bailey, Arabella Weir and Alexander Armstrong were completely wasted, thanks to Moffat's lacklustre script.

Earlier in the year, viewers of the children's show *Blue Peter* took part in a competition to design a new version of the central console of the TARDIS.

Despite an injection of cash from America's Starz network, the BBC's ten-part mini-series *Torchwood: Miracle Day*, in which the usually immortal Captain Jack Harkness (John Barrowman) was the last man in the world who could die, was ultimately disappointing, despite solid support from series regular Eve Myles and new team members Mekhl Phifer and Alexa Havins. The impressive list of US guest-stars included Bill Pullman (as a creepy paedophile-murder), Lauren Ambrose, Wayne Knight, C. Thomas Howell, Ernie Hudson, John de Lancie, Nana Visitor and Frances Fisher.

Angela Pleasence popped up as a psychic bag lady, Peter Bowles played an old newspaper editor, and the intrepid reporter adopted an alien daughter in the BBC's fifth and sadly final series of *The Sarah Jane Adventures*, which only ran for three two-part episodes in October due to the death of its star, Elisabeth Sladen.

Although ostensibly aimed at young adults, BBC 3's six-part *The Fades* was one of the best and darkest supernatural shows of the year as teenage outsider Paul (Ian de Caestecker) discovered that he was really one of a group of "Angelics" that could see the cannibalistic dead, who were returning in corporeal form to wreak revenge upon the living and bring about an apocalyptic future. Daniel Kaluuya as Paul's geeky friend Mac managed to keep the tone of Jack Thorne's superior series from getting too dark.

At the beginning of February British TV came up with not just one, but two haunted house series. Based on an unproduced 2008 pilot for an American show called *The Oaks*, ITV's *Marchlands* was about three families living in the same rambling old house in 1968, 1987 and 2010, who were all connected by the restless spirit of a drowned eight-year-old girl. Atmospherically told over five one-hour episodes, the increasingly spooky series featured Jodie Whittaker, Alex Kingston, Dean Andrews, Denis Lawson and Anne Reid amongst its impressive ensemble cast.

Less impressive was *Bedlam*, the first original drama commission from cable TV channel Sky Living, in which no horror cliché was left unturned by its three soap opera creators. Over six episodes, former mental illness patient Jed Harper (Theo James), who could see ghosts and how they died, and his only likeable flatmate Ryan McAllister (*Pop Idol* winner Will Young) investigated multiple hauntings in Bedlam Heights, a creepy apartment block converted from an old insane asylum. Coincidentally, the first episode also involved the vengeful ghost of a drowning victim.

Neither show was as outright ludicrous as FX's thirteen-part *American Horror Story*, but what would you expect from the people who brought you *Nip/Tuck* and *Glee*? Connie Britton, Dylan McDermot and Taissa Farmiga were the dysfunctional Harmon family who moved into an old Los Angeles mansion, only to discover that it was not only haunted by the world's most dysfunctional ghosts, but that they had also inherited the neighbour from hell (a scene-stealing Jessica Lange). A two-part Halloween episode introduced Zachary Quinto and Teddy Sears as a deceased gay couple, Mena Suvari guest-starred as the 1940s "The Black Dahlia" murder victim, and pretty much everybody ended up dead (if not gone) at the end.

The second season of Reece Shearsmith and Steve Pemberton's gruesome six-part comedy horror series *Psychoville* from the BBC saw the return of embittered clown Mr Jelly (Shearsmith) and Imelda Staunton's mysterious company director Grace Andrews, and the introduction of obsessive librarian Jeremy Goode (Shearsmith again), who was haunted by a Silent Singer (also Shearsmith). Christopher Biggins and American director John Landis both had cameos in the second episode.

More soap opera than science fiction, the BBC's eight-part *Outcasts* followed the trials and tribulations of a group of bickering Earth settlers trying to build a new future on a distant planet called Carpathia. Unfortunately, despite an ensemble cast that included Liam Cunningham, Hermoine Norris, Daniel Mays, Eric Mabius and Jamie Bamber (whose character was killed-off in the first episode), not only was the show a dull reworking of the 1994–95 series *Earth 2*, but the central mystery also owed much to Ray Bradbury's *The Martian Chronicles*. The series was quickly moved to another time-slot because of disappointing viewing figures.

Despite occasional flashes of welcome humour, the third season of the BBC's *Being Human* was a grim affair as vampire Mitchell (Aidan Turner) rescued ghost Annie (Lenora Crichlow) from Purgatory and was forced to face the consequences of his bloody massacre of a passenger train in the previous series.

While werewolves George (Russell Tovey) and Nina (Sinead Keenan) found themselves expecting a baby, unexpected visitors dropping by the housemates' new Barry Island home included teenage vampire Adam (Craig Roberts), who was really forty-six years old; party-loving zombie girl Sasha (Alexandra Roach); werewolf traveller McNair (Robson Green) and his son Tom (Michael Socha); stressed-out social worker Wendy (Nicola Walker); persistent policewoman Nancy Reid (Erin Richards), and mysteriously resurrected vampire Herrick (Jason Watkins), who claimed to have lost his memory.

An eight-part spin-off show, *Becoming Human*, was available on the BBC website (and subsequently edited-together as a TV special). It involved schoolboy vampire Adam (Roberts again) teaming up with a werewolf (Leila Mimmack) and a human (Josh Brown) to solve a mystery.

Relocated to Boston, an American version of *Being Human* starred Sam Witwer as vampire Aidan, Meaghan Rath as ghost Sally and Sam Huntington as werewolf Josh. The first season aired over thirteen episodes on the Syfy channel.

In the second season of Syfy's *Haven*, loosely based on a Stephen King story, all the main protagonists discovered that there were secrets in their past they never knew about.

Bi-sexual succubus Bo (Anna Silk) learned to work with the Fae, despite the new Ash (Vincent Walsh), while werewolf detective Dyson (Kris Holden-Ried) sacrificed his ability to love in the second season of Syfy's *Lost Girl*.

The third season of the channel's enjoyable *Warehouse 13* saw the return of Jaime Murray's terrific H. G. Wells, while *Eureka*'s Douglas Fargo (Neil Grayson) made a return visit to the Warehouse, which was apparently destroyed in the season finale. Kate Mulgrew, Anthony Michael Hall and Aaron Ashmore joined the cast as semi-regulars.

The third series of Syfy's *Sanctuary* ended with the inhabitants from Hidden Earth coming to the surface, and the fourth season kicked off with Dr Helen Magnus (Amanda Tapping) travelling back in time to Victorian London to prevent Adam Worth from changing history. In the two-part finale, Magnus put her long-term plans for the Sanctuary network into action, as Caleb (Gil Bellows) plotted to turn the human race into Abnormals.

Syfy's likeable *Eureka* (aka *A Town Called Eureka*) ended its fourth season with an accidental spaceship launch, but it was back three months later with a Christmas special in which everyone was turned into cartoon characters.

Based on the series of dark and gory high fantasy novels by George R. R. Martin, HBO's terrific ten-part *Game of Thrones* was, quite simply, one of the year's best TV dramas in *any* genre. The superlative cast included Sean Bean (whose lead character was surprisingly killed off in the penultimate episode), a scene-stealing Peter Dinklage, Mark Addy, Lena Headey and Jason Momoa.

With its fourth season, HBO's *True Blood* finally inherited the mantle of 1960s daytime soap opera *Dark Shadows* as Sookie (Anna Paquin) returned from fairyland to find that Fiona Shaw's possessed witch had cast a spell over Eric (Alexander Skarsgård), causing him to lose much of his memory.

In a major departure from the original books, a leading character was surprisingly killed off by Skarsgård's vampire, and the season finale featured the shocking deaths of three, or possibly four, other major characters. Veterans William Schallert and Katherine Helmond turned up in nice cameos.

The sixth season of Showtime's *Dexter* jumped ahead a year as Michael C. Hall's killer-with-a-code encountered a pair of religious "Doomsday Killers" (Edward James Olmos and Colin Hanks), a reformed Brother Sam (rapper-actor Mos Def), a septuagenarian serial killer (veteran Ronny Cox) and his own dead brother (Christian Camargo).

With its delayed fourth and fifth seasons filmed in Ireland, ITV's always bonkers *Primeval* returned in January for seven episodes as Connor (Andrew-Lee Potts) and Abby (Hannah Spearitt) escaped the Cretaceous Period only to find that the ARC (Anomaly Research Centre) had been rebuilt and was now controlled by mysterious magnate Philip Burton (Alexander Siddig), who had his own secret agenda. Despite the introduction of a new team of dinosaur-hunters, previous cast members Lucy Brown and Jason Flemyng returned for an episode apiece.

The series was back with a further six shows in May, and included an episode in which a velociraptor was accidentally sent back to 1868 London, where it gave rise to the legend of "Spring-heeled Jack".

There were more CGI dinosaurs in Fox's much-delayed *Terra Nova*, executive produced by Steven Spielberg, in which the annoying Shannon family (led by Jason O'Mara and Shelley Conn) travelled back from a dystopian future to 85 million years in the past to make a new life for themselves in what was basically a thirteen-part reworking of *Land of the Lost* with added rebel factions and conspiracy sub-plots.

Not content with boring audiences rigid with the family values of *Terra Nova*, Steven Spielberg also executive produced TNT's tedious *War of the Worlds*-inspired *Falling Skies*, in which a history professor (*E.R.*'s Noah Wyle) and a rag-tag group of resistance fighters mostly talked their way through yet another alien invasion of Earth.

If *Terra Nova* and *Falling Skies* could make dinosaurs and alien invasions dull, then AMC's increasingly pointless *The Walking Dead* was guilty of doing the same thing with zombies, as the ever-dwindling band of survivors (led by Andrew Lincoln's cuckold Sheriff) took refuge on a seemingly-tranquil rural farm until they went and looked at what was kept in the barn. It was perhaps no surprise that creator and executive producer Frank Darabont stepped down as showrunner after just a few episodes into the second season.

Despite its lethargic pacing, the show still managed to rank as the top-rated cable TV drama amongst young adults in the US, with average viewing numbers of nine million.

Sam (Jared Padalecki) returned from Hell without a soul, and angel Castiel (Misha Collins) went off the rails in the disappointing sixth series of The CW's *Supernatural*. In the best episode of the season, Sam and Dean (Jensen Ackles) were transported to an alternate reality, where they were actors in a TV series called . . . *Supernatural*.

The seventh season kicked off with the brothers trying to find a way to stop a power-mad Castiel, and *Buffy* cast members Charisma Carpenter and James Marsters turned up as a pair of bickering married witches.

The third season of The CW's unwatchably awful *The Vampire Diaries* was joined by the equally turgid teen witch series, *The Secret Circle*, also based on a bunch of books by L. J. Smith and executive produced by Kevin Williamson. At least Natasha Henstridge was on hand in the latter show to chew up the scenery as a scheming older witch.

Looking as if it was filmed on a $5.00-per-episode budget, *Brighter in Darkness* was an amateurish half-hour gay vampire soap opera filmed in and around Wales that ran for eight interminable episodes on a cut-price UK cable TV channel.

Michael Emerson's billionaire scientist and Jim Caviezel's former CIA hitman teamed up to prevent crimes before they happened with the help of a handy gizmo in CBS' *Person of Interest*, executive produced by J. J. Abrams.

NBC's *Grimm* featured David Giuntoli as a homicide detective, the descendant of the eponymous clan of supernatural hunters, who discovered that the fairy tales were based on fact. Silas Weir Mitchell's reluctant werewolf sidekick was the best thing about the show.

Fairy tale characters inhabited two different worlds in ABC's *Once Upon a Time*, which debuted with an impressive 12.8 million viewers and became the highest-rated new drama amongst adults in the US.

Meanwhile, the parallel universes merged in the fourth season of Fox's underrated *Fringe*, where for a while it seemed as if Peter Bishop (Joshua Jackson) had never existed.

Xander Berkeley played a mysterious patron who sat in a diner and helped people solve their problems in Hulu's five-part series *The Booth at the End*, which was also available as webisodes.

MTV's reboot of the 1980s movie franchise *Teen Wolf* was an entertaining and edgy twelve-part series aimed at young adults. Tyler Posey's likeable high school student Scott McCall found himself turning into a werewolf just as he discovered that the girl of his dreams (Crystal Reed) came from a long line of werewolf hunters. Unfortunately, the show premiered in a graveyard slot in the US.

Death Valley was a spoof mockumentary series on MTV about the LAPD's Undead Task Force dealing with criminal vampires, werewolves, zombies and other supernatural creatures while being trailed around by a camera crew.

Stoner metalhead Todd Smith (Alex House) and his high school friends continued to search for the Satanic book of spells in the half-hour Fear Net comedy series *Todd & the Book of Pure Evil*.

A supposedly dead cop (David Lyons) donned the superhero outfit and teamed up with an investigative blogger named Orwell (Summer Glau) to bring down her father's evil corporate company in NBC's enjoyable superhero series *The Cape*, which ran for only ten episodes.

Over at Syfy, Glau also guest-starred on the eleven-part *Alphas*, a dropped ABC pilot in which David Strathairn's scientist was the leader of a group of five ordinary people with extraordinary abilities who battled to save the world from a secret terrorist organisation called Red Flag.

In the third series of the E4's eight-part *Misfits*, the gang of super-powered young offenders decided to change their powers and had to deal with an alternate reality involving time-travelling Nazis. Meanwhile Seth (Matthew McNulty) used his resurrection power to bring his former girlfriend back from the grave as a bloodthirsty zombie, and the gang ended up encountering a fake medium who had the power to call their fallen foes back from the dead.

ABC Family's *The Nine Lives of Chloe King* was about a sixteen-year-old girl (Syler Samuels) who found out that she was descended from an ancient race of half-humans with feline powers.

Following an hour-long opener, Nickelodeon's *House of Anubis* was shown in forty-five daily ten-minute instalments and involved a group of eight students investigating mysterious disappearances at an English boarding school. It averaged almost three million viewers in the US and was also available online.

In the six-part *The Sparticle Mystery*, a group of children discovered that everybody on Earth over the age of fifteen had been transported to a parallel dimension when an experiment went wrong.

Nathaniel Parker joined the fourth season of the BBC's increasingly impressive *Merlin* as Arthur's duplicitous uncle, Agravaine. The thirteen-part series featured Lancelot (Santiago Cabrera) sacrificing himself and then returning from the dead;

the discovery of the last remaining dragon's egg; an encounter with a vampire-like Lamia; the possessive spirit of murdered Druid child; the introduction of Tristan and Isolde, and an epic two-part finale in which the evil Morgana (Katie McGrath) led a full-on assault upon Camelot.

Eva Green's far sexier "Morgan" also took over Arthur's fabled city in the otherwise redundant ten-part Starz series *Camelot*, which also featured Joseph Fiennes as an older and dirtier version of Merlin.

The Simpsons Treehouse of Horror XXII on Fox included lame spoofs of *Dexter* and *Avatar*, while Mike Judge's animated *Beavis and Butt-Head* returned to MTV in October with an episode in which the two stupid-smart buffoons poked fun at the *Twilight* movies as the dumb duo tried to get themselves bitten by a werewolf so they could attract girls.

Liam Neeson and Peter Mayhew voiced their characters Qui-Gon Jinn and Chewbacca, respectively, in different episodes of the Cartoon Network's *Star Wars: The Clone Wars*.

Wolverine and *Iron Man* both got *anime* makeovers, while 1980s cartoon *Thundercats* was revived for a new generation of potential toy consumers.

James Roday and Dulé Hill's comedy investigators went undercover as Tom Cruise's Lestat and William Marshall's Blacula, respectively, in a vampire-themed Halloween episode of USA Network's *Psych*, while Castle (Nathan Fillion) and Beckett (Stana Katic) investigated the death of a TV ghost-hunter in a supposedly haunted mansion in the Halloween episode of ABC's *Castle*.

The recent publication of Bram Stoker's *Dracula* resulted in a number of apparent vampire attacks at an exclusive girl's school in a fourth season episode of Canada's *Murdoch Mysteries*. In another episode, the uptight detective (Yannick Bisson) investigated what seemed to be a case of demonic possession.

For its special Super Bowl episode in February, Fox's *Glee* included a performance of Michael Jackson's "Thriller", complete with a zombie football team.

In January, ABC's *V* reboot returned for ten episodes before it was finally put out of everybody's misery. Original star Marc Singer turned up in the final episode while Jane Badler, who reprised her role as the evil "Diana" from the original 1983 show, turned out to be alien leader Anna's (Morena Baccarin) estranged mother.

Medium finally also reached the end of its seven-year run on NBC in January. The final episode flash-forwarded forty years into the future.

Chuck played out its fifth and final season on the same network, as Zachery Levi's character created his own spy agency. Mark Hamill guest-starred in the first episode.

The CW's *Smallville* ended after ten seasons with a satisfying two-part finale that finally saw the return of Michael Rosenbaum's Lex Luthor.

The Syfy channel finally aired the remaining nine episodes of its overblown *Battlestar Galactica* prequel, *Caprica*, which ended on a virtual reality teaser for a second series that never happened.

NBC's meandering *The Event* was also justifiably cancelled, as was Syfy's *SGU Stargate Universe* after only two seasons.

As part of Turner Classic Movies's "Lost and Found" series, in April the station showcased a rare print of the 1976 Spanish film *The Mysterious House of Dr C* (aka *Dr Coppelius*), while two months later the "Drive-In Double Features" series presented a number of 1950s "Monsters, Mutants and Martians". In August, the channel programmed a day of Lon Chaney, Sr. films, including *The Monster*, *Mockery*, *The Unknown*, *West of Zanzibar* and both the silent and sound versions of *The Unholy Three*.

On October 3, TCM premiered *A Night at the Movies: The Horrors of Stephen King*, an hour-long documentary in which the author traced the history of the genre through personal recollections and film clips.

Appropriately, director John Carpenter was the TCM's Guest Programmer for the month, and his picks included *The Thing from Another World*, *It! The Terror from Beyond Space* and *The Curse of Frankenstein*.

Rex Appeal was an hour-long BBC4 documentary about dinosaurs in the movies.

William Shatner, Leonard Nimoy, Nichelle Michols, Billy Mumy, Angela Carter and Marta Kristen were amongst those who recalled the golden age of TV science fiction and the sometimes rivalry between Rod Serling, Gene Roddenberry and Irwin Allen in an episode of PBS' *Pioneers of Television*.

Ridley Scott executive produced the Science channel's eight-part *Prophets of Science Fiction* docu-series, which began its run with an episode about Mary Shelley (played by Mara King in the re-enactments).

Broadcast by BBC3 from Kirkstall Abbey on 19 March, *Frankenstein's Wedding: Live in Leeds* was a muddled musical retelling of Shelley's classic novel. Andrew Gower played Dr Victor Frankenstein, while David Harewood was his sympathetic Creature.

During the summer, actress Joanna Lumley joined an online petition of those opposed to BBC Radio 4 controller Gwyneth Williams' plans to cut the broadcaster's short story output in favour of more news coverage.

To tie-in with the launch of the mini-series *Torchwood: Miracle Day* in July, Radio 4's *Afternoon Play* presented *Torchwood: The Lost Files*. Broadcast in three forty-five minute episodes, John Barrowman, Eve Myles, Gareth David-Lloyd and Kai Owen recreated their original TV roles alongside Martin Jarvis, Juliet Mills and Rosalind Ayres.

All the Dark Corners featured three spooky tales by Andrew Readman, Paul Cornell and Rosemary Kay and was broadcast over three successive days in the *Afternoon Play* slot, while *The Shining Guest* was written and narrated by Paul Evans and used real-life sound recordings to tell the story of a puzzling ancient corpse discovered in the Welsh hills. It was produced by the same team that created *The Ditch* in 2010.

Other editions of the *Afternoon Play* featured Kim Newman's *Cry Babies*, about busy couple's genetically enhanced daughter; Sally Griffiths' *Haunted*, in which a professional illusionist and a spiritualist medium teamed up for a television show with unexpected results, and *A Time to Dance*, directed by Julian Simpson, in which a mysterious plague affected London's South Bank.

Joan Aiken's *Black Hearts of Battersea* was adapted over two days in the same slot at Christmas.

Julian Simpson's *Bad Memories* for Radio 4's *The Friday Play* slot involved the macabre disappearance of a family from their remote country home in 2004, and the discovery six years later in the cellar of five bodies apparently dating back to 1926. The hour-long drama made use of digital audio files to unlock the key to the time-travel mystery.

David Robb starred as Professor Challenger in Chris Harrald's two-part dramatisation of Arthur Conan Doyle's *The Lost World* as part of the radio station's *Classic Serial* series.

Wilkie Collins' 1868 macabre mystery *The Moonstone* was adapted into four one-hour episodes on Radio 4 starring Kenneth Cranham, Eleanor Bron and Bill Paterson, and Cranham also portrayed carnival owner Mr Dark in Diana Griffiths' hour-long adaptation of Ray Bradbury's *Something Wicked This Way Comes*, broadcast as *The Saturday Play* on 29 October.

The following month, Robert Powell starred in an hour-long adaptation of Alan Garner's *The Weirdstone of Brisingamen* in the same slot.

The crew of a spaceship retrieving a valuable ore from an abandoned mining operation on a mysterious planet encountered an intelligent life form in Mike Walker's hour-long *The Saturday Play: Landfall.*

Radio 4's *Weird Tales* returned for four new episodes, while *Beasts on the Lawn: Saki 2011* featured updated dramatisations of five stories by Edwardian author Saki (H. H. Munro), set in a gated community and linked by security guard Clovis (Pippa Haywood).

Filmed twice by director George Slulzer, *The Vanishing* was an hour-long radio dramatisation in July of Tim Krabbe's *The Golden Egg*, about a man attempting to discover what happened to his missing girlfriend.

Dramatised by Brian Sibley in six one-hour episodes to celebrate the 100th anniversary of the birth of Mervyn Peake, *The History of Titus Groan* encompassed the entire *Gormenghast* trilogy and the epilogue written by his widow, with a cast that included David Warner, Miranda Richardson, Tamsin Greig and William Gaunt.

As part of the morning fifteen-minute *Woman's Hour Drama* slot, *Kiss Kiss* presented five macabre stories by Roald Dahl, dramatised by Stephen Sheridan. Each episode starred Charles Dance, supported by a cast that included Celia Imrie, Ronald Pickup and John Baddeley.

In May, *The Doll: Short Stories by Daphne du Maurier* featured abridged readings of three stories by the author of *The Birds*, while *Summer Ghosts* in August presented readings of three fifteen-minute spooky tales set in daylight written by Sophie Hannah, Louise Welsh and Adam Thorpe.

David Tennant returned to Radio 4's *Book at Bedtime* with *A Night with a Vampire 2*, for which he read fifteen minute adaptations of "The Lady of the House of Love" by Angela Carter, "The Girl with the Hungry Eyes" by Fritz Leiber, "Bewitched" by Edith Wharton, "Drink My Blood" by Richard Matheson and "A Lot of Mince Pies" by Robert Swindells.

In the same slot, Derek Jacobi read Anthony Horowitz's Sherlock Holmes pastiche *The House of Silk* over ten nights in early November. Meanwhile, James Fleet played Inspector Lestrade, who introduced four half-hour episodes of *The Rivals*, featuring other fictional detectives of the period. The weekly series kicked off with an adaptation of Edgar Allan Poe's "The Murders in the Rue Morgue" starring Andrew Scott as C. Auguste Dupin.

In April, BBC Radio 7 was re-branded BBC Radio 4 Extra. Jonathan Morris' four-part *Doctor Who: Cobwebs* reunited fifth Doctor Peter Davison with companions Turlough, Tegan and Nyssa in an abandoned gene-tech facility, and their adventures continued in Stephen Cole's *Doctor Who: The Whispering Forest* and Marc Platt's *Doctor Who: The Cradle of the Snake*.

Meanwhile, *Doctor Who: The Hornet's Nest* featured fourth Doctor Tom Baker in three two-part adventures ("The Stuff of Nightmares", "The Dead Shoes" and "The Circus of Doom") scripted by Paul Magrs.

The Horror at Bly was Neville Teller's response to Henry James' *The Turn of the Screw*, while actor Richard Coyle read H. P. Lovecraft's *At the Mountains of Madness* over five half-hour episodes on successive nights in June.

Don Webb's four-part dramatisation of *Elidor* updated Alan Garner's 1965 novel for a new audience of younger listeners.

In mid-September, Radio 4 Extra broadcast half-hour productions of "The Captain of the Polestar" by Arthur Conan Doyle, "Olalia" by Robert Louis Stevenson and "The Brownie of the

Black Haggs" by James Hogg under the umbrella title *The Darker Side of the Border*.

Mark Gattis returned to introduce new half-hour episodes of *The Man in Black* on the same station in October, including "Lights Out" by Christopher Golden and Amber Benson.

Radio 4 Extra celebrated Halloween with a selection of Gothic tales from the archive that included an adaptation of Loren D. Estleman's *Sherlock Holmes v Dracula*, a reading of Oscar Wilde's *The Canterville Ghost*, a reading of Tanya Huff's "Quid Pro Quo" as part of *A Short History of Vampires*, and a forty-five minute adaptation of Sheridan Le Fanu's *Carmilla* starring Anne-Marie Duff, Celia Imrie, David Warner and Brana Bajic in the title role.

Each evening during the same week, *Haunting Women* presented five fifteen-minute supernatural tales by Dermot Bolger, while Benjamin Whitrow read *Ghost Stories by M. R. James*.

Christopher Lee's Fireside Tales was a fifteen-minute series broadcast over Christmas in which the veteran actor read Edgar Allan Poe's "The Black Cat", Jerome K. Jerome's "The Man of Science", E. Nesbit's "John Charrington's Wedding", Ambrose Bierce's "The Man and the Snake" and W. W. Jacobs' "The Monkey's Paw".

In October, BBC Radio 3's *Opera on 3* broadcast Opera North's new version of Tchaikovsky's *The Queen of Spades*, featuring soprano Dame Josephine Barstow as the mysterious old Countess.

BBC Radio 2 celebrated the twenty-fifth anniversary of the musical *Phantom of the Opera* with *The Phantom Phenomenon* in November. Lyricist Don Black talked to composer Andrew Lloyd Webber and others about their involvement in the longest-running Broadway musical of all time, which is estimated to have grossed $5.6 billion to date around the world.

Described as a "historical-shtetl-magic-realist-feminist-musical audio drama", *The Witches of Lublin* premiered on New York radio stations WBAI and WNYC in April. Co-scripted and introduced by Ellen Kushner, the broadcast included Neil Gaiman amongst the voice cast.

Broadcast on Radio 4 in February, *The Priest, the Badger and the Little Green Men from Mars* was Rob Alexander's half-hour profile of prolific genre writer-turned-reverend [Robert] Lionel Fanthorpe, who contributed readings from his own work.

Comedy broadcaster Natalie Haynes investigated the modern fascination with blood-drinkers and the walking dead in Radio 4's half-hour *Vampires v Zombies*, while in the two-part *Cat Women of the Moon* on the same station, novelist Sarah Hook looked at how the SF genre pushes the boundaries of sex with the help of China Miéville, Iain Banks, Nicola Griffith and Robert Winston.

Hosted by *The League of Gentlemen* writer and actor Jeremy Dyson, *The Unsettled Dust: The Strange Stories of Robert Aickman* was a half-hour reappraisal of the author's work, broadcast on Radio 4 in December.

The CD box set of *Tales from Beyond the Pale: Season 1* was hosted by Larry Fessenden and included audio plays featuring Vincent D'Onofrio and Ron Perlman.

The "curse of Spider-Man" continued when actress T. V. Carpio, who took over the role of the evil Arachne after the original actress suffered a concussion, was forced to pull out of the $65 million Broadway show *Spider-Man: Turn Off the Dark* in March following an injury sustained during an on-stage battle.

Following a series of accidents, multiple missed opening dates and a critical lambasting, controversial director and co-writer Julie Taymor was relieved of her day-to-day duties by producers the same month, and the troubled production shut down for more than three weeks as a new team was brought in to re-imagine the show. It finally opened in June to mostly unenthusiastic reviews.

Five months later, former director Taymor reportedly sued the producers of the show for $1 million compensation, claiming they had "violated her creative rights".

Benedict Cumberbatch and Johnny Lee Miller alternated as Frankenstein and his Creature in Nick Dear's new adaptation of *Frankenstein* for director Danny Boyle, which premiered at London's National Theatre's Olivier in February.

Anita Dobson and Greta Scacchi portrayed Joan Crawford and Bette Davis, respectively, during the making of the 1962 movie *What Ever Happened to Baby Jane?* in Anton Burge's *Bette and Joan,* which opened at London's Arts Theatre in May.

That same month, Terry Gilliam directed Hector Berlioz's opera *The Damnation of Faust* at the Coliseum, while Arthur Darvill portrayed a melancholy Mephistopheles in Matthew Dunster's revival of Christopher Marlowe's *Doctor Faustus* at Shakespeare's Globe in June.

Adapted by Bruce Joel Rubin from his 1990 movie, *Ghost The Musical* opened in July at London's Piccadilly Theatre.

Despite a much-hyped revamp in November 2010 and a subtle title change to *Phantom: Love Never Dies,* Andrew Lloyd Webber's musical sequel still closed its London run at the end of August after just seventeen months. Although a Broadway transfer for the show was delayed, the new version received rave reviews when it opened in Melbourne, Australia, in the summer.

Meanwhile, Lloyd Webber's production of *The Wizard of Oz* opened at the London Palladium in March. Michael Crawford starred in the titular role.

Following his stage success with *Ghost Stories,* the *League of Gentlemen*'s Jeremy Dyson adapted three classic tales for *Roald Dahl's Twisted Tales.* Polly Findlay's production ran for a month from the end of January at London's Lyric Hammersmith theatre.

Actress Judi Bowker (who played "Mina" in the 1977 BBC version of *Count Dracula*) starred in Harry Meacher's stage play *Mist "After Dracula",* which ran for three nights at the end of February at the Rosslyn Hill Unitarian Chapel in London's Hampstead area. Meacher himself portrayed Van Helsing in the play, which was set ten years after the Count's death.

Based on his 1985 cult movie, Stuart Gordon directed *Re-Animator The Musical,* adapted from H. P. Lovecraft's story. With music and lyrics by Mark Nutter and starring Graham Skipper as crazed medical student Herbert West, the critically-acclaimed stage show ran from March until August at The Steve Allen Theater in Los Angeles.

In July, The 2nd H. P. Lovecraft Festival was held at St. Marks Theater, New York City. Written and directed by Dan Bianchi, performance art company Radiotheatre! performed stage versions of "Reanimator" and "The Call of Cthulhu".

Meanwhile, from its usual venue in Portland, Oregon, the H. P. Lovecraft Film Festival expanded to Los Angeles in September. Along with screenings of short films and rarities (including a new version of *The Whisperer in Darkness*), the event featured appearances by directors Roger Corman and Guillermo Del Toro and readings by Michael Shea, Cody Goodfellow and Jenna Pitman.

Alison Steadman, Hermione Norris, Robert Bathurst and Ruthie Henshall starred in a revival of Noël Coward's *Blithe Spirit* at London's Apollo Theatre, while Michael Ball and Imelda Staunton were the stars of Jonathan Kent's critically-acclaimed revival of Stephen Sondheim's macabre musical *Sweeney Todd*, which made its debut at the Chichester Festival Theatre.

Ralph Fiennes starred as a tortured Prospero in Trevor Nunn's sold-out revival of William Shakespeare's *The Tempest*, which ran at London's Theatre Royal, Haymarket, over nine weeks in September and October. The production took more than £1 million in advance ticket sales.

In early summer, the Regent's Park Open Air Theatre staged an outdoor production of William Golding's *Lord of the Flies*.

The Veil, playwright and director Conor McPherson's first piece in five years, dealt with secrets and spiritualism in 1822 Ireland, while a revival of Alan Ayckbourn's 1994 play *Haunting Julia* was said to have caused the show to be stopped six times after audience members collapsed at the Garrick Theatre in Lichfield.

The Caped Crusader battled his greatest foes, including the Joker, the Penguin, the Riddler and Catwoman in the musical extravaganza *Batman Live*, which kicked off a world arena tour at the O_2 in London in August.

The following month, Somtow Sucharitkul's ghost opera *Opera Siam: Mae Naak* premiered at the Bloomsbury Theatre.

In December, London's Southwark Playhouse mounted a production of the late Diana Wynne Jones' novel *Howl's Moving Castle*, narrated by Stephen Fry.

Throughout the year, the organisers of *2.8 Hours Later* transformed areas of British cities into giant urban chase games in which participants assumed the role of zombie attack survivors trying to reach a final sanctuary before they were "infected" by the walking dead.

John Carpenter and Steve Niles were brought in by Warner Bros. to work on the first-person shooter game *F.E.A.R. 3*, which featured the return of devil child Alma.

An idyllic getaway was overrun by an invasion of zombies in the survival game *Dead Island*, while *Resident Evil: The Mercenaries 3D*, released for the new Nintendo 3DS handset, was basically a reworking of episodes from previous games in the franchise.

Players of the challenging *Dark Souls*, an unofficial follow-up to the equally difficult *Demon's Souls*, were among the dead trying to regain their mortal lives in a world where evil had triumphed.

In the near-future, a global conspiracy to create cyborgs was at the heart of *Deus Ex: Human Revolution*, while the eagerly awaited *Dead Space 2* quickly became one of the most popular electronic games of the year.

Despite the success of the movie, *Harry Potter and the Deathly Hallows Part 2* was as disappointing as all the other games in the movie tie-in series. At least *Captain America: Super Soldier* was somewhat better.

The Caped Crusader attempted to bring order to the urban chaos that was *Batman: Arkham City*, an even better sequel to the excellent *Arkham Asylum*.

The successful *Dead Space* game franchise was reconfigured for mobile use on iPhone and iTouch, so that the touch-screen player could use their finger to slice off limbs, and *Call of Duty: Black Ops Zombies* was available as an app for download onto iPads and iPhones.

Featuring the voice of actor Benedict Cumberbatch, *The Nightjar* was a creepy SF game sponsored by Wrigley's chewing gum for free download onto iPhone.

For fans of H. P. Lovecraft, the Cthulhu Waterglobe was inscribed with the author's famous couplet from the *Necronomicon*, or you could create your own eldritch lore with the Lovecraftian Letters magnetic words, which came in a metal tin containing more than 500 pieces.

The first issue of 2011 by Britain's Royal Mail, "FAB: The Genius of Gerry Anderson", featured six stamps honouring the TV creator's five decades of work with *Supercar*, *Fireball XL5*, *Stingray*, *Thunderbirds*, *Captain Scarlet* and *Joe 90*. The set also included the UK's first-ever lenticular set that depicted the "4-3-2-1" opening sequence of *Thunderbirds* when the stamps were tilted back and forth.

In March, the Royal Mail issued a set of eight stamps celebrating "Magical Realms" with two images each from the *Harry Potter* movies, Terry Pratchett's "Discworld" books, C. S. Lewis' "Chronicles of Narnia" series and Arthurian Legend. The special presentation pack included an essay by Kim Newman about British magical fantasy.

In July, an insert poster for the 1936 Universal movie *Werewolf of London* sold for $47,800 (including 19.5 per cent Buyer's Premium) at auction, and five months later, Orson Welles' 1942 Oscar for Best Screenplay for *Citizen Kane* sold for $861,542 to an anonymous bidder.

Universal Studios added a "King Kong 360/3-D Ride" to its Hollywood amusement park. Created by Peter Jackson, the ride was promoted as the "world's largest 3-D experience".

Meanwhile, over at Disney World and Disneyland, a new 3-D *Star Wars* motion-simulator ride offered a different combination of more than fifty story elements, making every trip a unique experience.

An historic 1925 carousel in the George F. Johnson Recreation Park in Binghamton, New York, was refurbished in August with various scenes from *The Twilight Zone* painted by Cortlandt Hull. Rod Serling, the creator of the show, rode the same carousel as a boy and used it as the basis of a 1959 episode entitled "Walking Distance".

The 2011 World Horror Convention was held in Austin, Texas, over 28 April–1 May. Guests of Honour were authors Jack Ketchum (Dallas Mayr), Joe Hill and Sarah Langan, ChiZine editors Brett Alexander Savory and Sandra Kasturi, British artist Vincent Chong, and media writer Steve Niles.

Brian Keene and bookseller Del Howison were Special Guests, and Joe R. Lansdale was Toastmaster. Jack Ketchum was given the convention's Grand Master Award in a ceremony on the Friday night.

The winners of the Horror Writers of America 2010 Bram Stoker Awards for Superior Achievement were announced at the Stoker Awards Weekend in Uniondale, New York, on 19 June.

In a whole raft of announcements, the Silver Hammer Award for outstanding service to the HWA was presented to Angel Leigh McCoy, The President's Richard Laymon Service Award went to Michael Colangelo, and Joe Morey of Dark Regions Press received the award for Specialty Press.

The Poetry Collection award went to Bruce Boston for *Dark Matters*, Gary A. Braunbeck's *To Each Their Darkness* received Non-Fiction, and Stephen King's *Full Dark No Stars* picked up Collection. The Anthology award was given to *Haunted Legends* edited by Ellen Datlow and Nick Mamatas, while Joe R. Lansdale's story "The Folding Man" from the same book received the Short Fiction award. Long Fiction was given to Norman Prentiss for *Invisible Fences*, the First Novel award was a tie between *Black and Orange* by Benjamin Kane Ethridge and *Castle of Los Angeles* by Lisa Morton, and Peter Straub was presented with the Superior Achievement in a Novel award for *A Dark Matter*.

It had been previously announced that Ellen Datlow and veteran EC artist Al Feldstein each received Life Achievement Awards.

Celebrating the thirty-fifth British Fantasy Convention, FantasyCon 2011 was held in Brighton, England, over 30 September–2 October. Guests of Honour were Gwyneth Jones, John Ajvide Lindqvist, Peter Atkins and Joe Abercrombie. Brian Aldiss and Christopher Paolini were Special Guests and Sarah Pinborough was Mistress of Ceremonies.

The British Fantasy Awards were presented at a banquet on the Sunday afternoon. The awards for Best Film and Best Television went to Christopher Nolan's *Inception* and the BBC's *Sherlock*, respectively. Best Graphic Novel was *At the Mountains of Madness: A Graphic Novel* by I. N. J. Culbard, Best Magazine was Andy Cox's *Black Static*, and the Best Small Press award went to Telos Publishing for the second year running.

Vincent Chong won Best Artist, and his book *Altered Visions: The Art of Vincent Chong* also picked up the Best Non-Fiction award. *Back from the Dead: The Legacy of the Pan Book of Horror Stories* edited by Johnny Mains was awarded Best Anthology, and Stephen King's *Full Dark, No Stars* was announced Best Collection. Best Novella was presented to *Humpty's Bones* by Simon Clark, while Sam Stone collected Best Short Story for "Fool's Gold" (from *The Bitten Word*) and The August Derleth Award for Best Novel for *Demon Dance*, the third volume in the "Vampire Gene" series.

The Sydney J. Bounds Award for Best Newcomer went to Robert Jackson Bennett for his novel *Mr Shivers*, and Terry Pratchett was announced as the recipient of the Karl Edward Wagner Special Award.

Following the presentation of the awards, there was almost instant condemnation from many people in the audience who quickly realised that at least four of the winners were directly connected to the small press imprint run by the British Fantasy Society's current Chairman/Awards Administrator/Co-Presenter (making it the most successful publisher in the forty-year history of the awards), while both the Best Short Story and Best Novel awards had gone to his partner.

While there was no evidence of any wrongdoing on anyone's part, the subsequent online controversy, which also made the national press in Britain, resulted in the formation of an interim BFS committee and the entire voting process being made far more transparent in future.

Held in San Diego, California, over 26–30 October, World Fantasy Convention 2011 stuck rigorously to its somewhat watery theme of "Sailing on the Seas of Imagination", thereby leaving Guests of Honour Jo Fletcher, Neil Gaiman, Parke Godwin, editor Shawna McCarthy and artist Ruth Sanderson, along with Toastmaster Connie Willis, a little becalmed.

As usual, the World Fantasy Award winners were announced at the banquet on the Sunday afternoon. The Special Award, Non-Professional Award went to Alisa Krasnostein for Twelfth Planet Press, and Marc Gascoigne received the Special Award, Professional for his Angry Robot imprint.

Best Artist was Kinuko Y. Craft, Karen Joy Fowler's *What I Didn't See and Other Stories* won Best Collection, and *My Mother She Killed Me, My Father He Ate Me* edited by Kate Bernheimer was awarded Best Anthology.

The Best Short Story Award went to Joyce Carol Oates' "Fossil-Figures" (from *Stories: All-New Tales*) and Elizabeth Hand's "The Maiden Flight of McCauley's Bellerophon" (from the same anthology) won Best Novella. In a surprisingly feminist list of winners, the Best Novel Award went to *Who Fears Death* by Nnedi Okorafor, who subsequently complained about the award being in the form of a bust of H. P. Lovecraft, because she considered the author "a talented racist". Her reaction was mostly based on a poem Lovecraft wrote almost a century earlier, when he was in his early twenties.

Peter S. Beagle and Angélica Gorodischer had previously been announced as the recipients of Life Achievement Awards for having demonstrated outstanding service to the fantasy field.

I've talked about integrity and the validity of awards in these pages before, and I don't plan to go into the controversy surrounding the 2011 British Fantasy Awards any more than I have already done so elsewhere, other to say that I believe that people know when they really do or do not deserve to win an award, and they have to live with their actions – and the consequences of those actions – for the rest of their lives.

I'm not sure how worthwhile any award is if you know that you have actively campaigned to win it.

I would also not be surprised if many readers are now scratching their heads at some of the winners of the World Fantasy Awards above and asking themselves "Who?"

You may also have noticed that with this volume, the editorial matter is shorter than in recent editions of this series. This is because, according to my publishers (and a handful of "reviewers" on Amazon), the non-fiction elements are superfluous to the rest of the book, and they have ordered me to cut this material, despite the fact that it costs them nothing extra in editorial fees to include.

On a more positive note, I am delighted to announce that with this twenty-third volume, *The Mammoth Book of Best New*

Horror has surpassed both Ellen Datlow's *The Year's Best Fantasy and Horror* (twenty volumes) and Karl Edward Wagner's *The Year's Best Horror Stories* (twenty-two volumes) as the longest-running "Year's Best" horror anthology series of all time!

We could not have done it without the authors, readers and booksellers who have continued to support these volumes for more than twenty years. Thank you all, and special thanks to Nick Robinson and my current editor, Duncan Proudfoot, for their continued belief in me and this series.

See you all in volume twenty-four!

The Editor
May, 2012

RAMSEY CAMPBELL

Holding the Light

RAMSEY CAMPBELL WAS BORN in Liverpool, where he still lives with his wife Jenny. His first book, a collection of stories entitled *The Inhabitant of the Lake and Less Welcome Tenants*, was published by August Derleth's legendary Arkham House imprint in 1964, since when his novels have included *The Doll Who Ate His Mother*, *The Face That Must Die*, *The Nameless*, *Incarnate*, *The Hungry Moon*, *Ancient Images*, *The Count of Eleven*, *The Long Lost*, *Pact of the Fathers*, *The Darkest Part of the Woods*, *The Grin of the Dark*, *Thieving Fear*, *Creatures of the Pool*, *The Seven Days of Cain* and the movie tie-in *Solomon Kane*.

His short fiction has been collected in such volumes as *Demons by Daylight*, *The Height of the Scream*, *Dark Companions*, *Scared Stiff*, *Waking Nightmares*, *Cold Print*, *Alone with the Horrors*, *Ghosts and Grisly Things*, *Told by the Dead*, and *Just Behind You*. He has also edited a number of anthologies, including *New Terrors*, *New Tales of the Cthulhu Mythos*, *Fine Frights: Stories That Scared Me*, *Uncanny Banquet*, *Meddling with Ghosts*, and *Gathering the Bones: Original Stories from the World's Masters of Horror* (with Dennis Etchison and Jack Dann).

"'Holding the Light' came out of an experience in Rhodes two years ago, at Epta Piges ('Seven Springs')," recalls the author. "During the occupation, Italians constructed an irrigation tunnel there, 180 metres long and very much like the one that figures in my tale. It's a favourite stop on guided tours and turned up on two that we took. You won't be surprised that I was delighted to go through it both times, though others in the party stayed out.

"Pete Crowther had mentioned a Hallowe'en chapbook he wanted to publish, including several new tales. Sadly, the event he wanted to build it around didn't work out, but by that time I'd written my contribution, and he published it as a singleton.

"As soon as I went through the Epta Piges tunnel the first time I knew I had a tale for him."

A s HIS COUSIN followed him into the Frugoplex lobby Tom saw two girls from school. Out of uniform and in startlingly short skirts they looked several years older. He hoped his leather jacket performed that trick for him, in contrast to the duffle coat Lucas was wearing. Since the girls were giggling at the cinema staff dressed as Hallowe'en characters, he let them see him laugh too. "Hey, Lezly," he said in his deepest voice. "Hey, Dianne."

"Don't come near us if you've got a cold," Lezly protested, waving a hand that was bony with rings in front of her face.

"It's just how boys his age talk," Dianne said far too much like a sympathetic adult and blinked her sparkly purple eyelids. "Who's your friend, Tom?"

"It's my cousin Lucas."

"Hey, Luke."

Lezly said it too and held out her skull-ringed hand, at which Lucas stared as if it were an inappropriate present. "He's like that," Tom mumbled but refrained from pointing at his own head. "Don't mind him."

"Maybe he doesn't want to give you his germs, Lezly." To the boys Dianne said "What are you going to see?"

"*Vampire Dating Agency*," Lucas said before Tom could make a choice.

"That's for kids," Lezly objected. "We're not seeing any films with them."

"We don't have to either, do we, Lucas?" Tom said in a bid to stop his face from growing hotter. "What are you two seeing?"

"*Cheerleaders with Guts*," Dianne said with another quick glittery blink.

"We can't," Lucas informed everyone. "Nobody under fifteen's allowed."

Tom glared at him as the girls did. At least none of the staff dealing with the noisy queues appeared to have heard the remark. Until that moment Tom had been able to prefer visiting the cinema to any of the other activities their parents had arranged for the boys over the years – begging for sweets at neighbours' houses, ducking for apples and a noseful of water, carving pumpkins when Lucas's received most of the praise despite being so grotesque only out of clumsiness. Now that the parents had reluctantly let them outgrow all this Tom seemed to be expected to take even more care of his cousin. Perhaps Lucas sensed his resentment for once, because he said "We don't have to go to a film."

"Who doesn't?" said Dianne.

Tom wanted to say her and Lezly too, but first he had to learn "Where, then?"

"The haunted place." When nobody admitted to recognising it Lucas said "Grinfields."

"Where the boy and girl killed themselves together, you mean," Lezly said.

"No, he did first," Dianne said, "and she couldn't live without him."

It was clear that Lucas wasn't interested in these details, and he barely let her finish. "My mum and dad say they did it because they watched films you aren't supposed to watch."

"My parents heard they were always shopping," Tom made haste to contribute. "Them and their families spent lots of money they didn't have and all it did was leave them thinking nothing was worth anything."

That was his father's version. Perhaps it sounded more like a gibe at the girls than he was afraid Lucas's comment had. "Why do you want us to go there, Luke?" Dianne said.

"Who's Luke?"

"I told you," Tom said in some desperation, "he's like that."

"No I'm not, I'm like Lucas."

At such times Tom understood all too well why his cousin was bullied at school. There was also the way Lucas stared at anybody unfamiliar as if they had to wait for him to make up his mind about them, and just now his pasty face – far spottier than Tom's and topped with unruly red hair – was a further drawback. Nevertheless Dianne said "Are you sure you don't want to see our film?"

She was speaking to Tom, but Lucas responded. "We can't. We've been told."

"I haven't," Tom muttered. He watched the girls join the queue for the ticket desk manned by a tastefully drooling vampire in a cloak, and then he turned on Lucas. "We need to switch our phones off. We're in the cinema."

Accuracy mattered most to Lucas. Once he'd done as he was told Tom said "Let's go, and not to the kids' film either."

A frown creased Lucas's pudgy forehead. "Which one, then?"

"None of them. We'll go where you wanted," Tom said, leading the way out into the Frugall retail park.

More vehicles than he thought he could count in a weekend were lined up beneath towering lamps as white as the moon. In that light people's faces looked as pallid as Lucas's, but took on colour once they reached the shops, half a mile of which surrounded the perimeter. As Tom came abreast of a Frugelectric store he said "We'll need a light."

Lucas peered at the lanky lamps, and yet again Tom wondered what went on inside his cousin's head. "A torch," he resented having to elucidate.

"There's one at home."

"That's too far." Before Lucas could suspect he didn't want their parents learning where the boys would be Tom said "You'll have to buy one."

He was determined his cousin would pay, not least for putting the girls off. He watched Lucas select the cheapest flashlight and load it with batteries, then drop a ten-pound note beside the till so as to avoid touching the checkout girl's hand. He made her place his change there for him to scoop up while Tom took the flashlight wrapped in a flimsy plastic bag. "That's mine. I bought it," Lucas said at once.

"You hold it then, baby." Tom stopped just short of uttering the last word, though his face was hot again. "Look after it," he said and stalked out of the shop.

They were on the far side of Frugall from their houses and the school. An alley between a Frugranary baker's and a Frugolé tapas bar led to a path around the perimeter. A twelve-foot wall behind the shops and restaurants cut off most of the light and the blurred vague clamour of the retail park. The path was deserted apart from a few misshapen skeletal loiterers nuzzling the wall or propped against the chain-link fence alongside Grinfields Woods. They were abandoned shopping trolleys, and the only sound apart from the boys' padded footsteps was the rustle of the plastic bag.

Tom thought they might have to follow the path all the way to the housing estate between Grinfields and the retail park, but soon they came to a gap in the fence. Lucas dodged through it so fast that he might have forgotten he wasn't alone. As Tom followed he saw his own shadow emerge from a block of darkness fringed with outlines of wire mesh. The elongated shadows of trees were reaching for the larger dark. By the time the boys found the official path through the woods they were almost beyond the glare from the retail park, and Lucas switched on the flashlight. "That isn't scary," he declared as Tom's shadow brandished its arms.

Tom was simply frustrated that Lucas hadn't bothered to remove the flashlight from the bag. He watched his cousin peer both ways along the dim path like a child showing how much care he took about crossing a road, and then head along the stretch that vanished into darkness. The sight of Lucas swaggering off as though he didn't care whether he was followed did away with any qualms Tom might have over scaring him more than he would like. He tramped after Lucas through the woods that looked as if the dark had formed itself into a cage, and almost collided with him as the blurred jerky light swerved off the path to flutter across the trees to the left. "What's pulling something along?" Lucas seemed to feel entitled to be told.

"It's got a rope," Tom said, but didn't want to scare Lucas too much too soon. "No, it's only water."

He'd located it in the dried-up channel out of sight below the slope beyond the trees. It must be a lingering trickle of rain, which had stopped before dark, unless it was an animal or bird among the fallen leaves. "Make your mind up," Lucas complained and swung the light back to the path.

The noise ceased as Tom tramped after him. Perhaps it had gone underground through the abandoned irrigation channel. Without warning – certainly with none from Lucas – the flashlight beam sprang off the ragged stony path and flew into the treetops. "Is it laughing at us?" Lucas said.

Tom gave the harsh shrill sound somewhere ahead time to make itself heard. "What do you think?"

"Of course it's not," Lucas said as if his cousin needed to be put right. "Birds can't laugh."

Once more Tom suspected Lucas wasn't quite as odd as he liked everyone to think, although that was odd in itself. When the darkness creaked again he said "That's not a bird, it's a tree."

Lucas might have been challenging someone by striding up the path to jab the beam at the treetops. As he disappeared over a ridge the creaking of the solitary branch fell silent. Though he'd taken the light with him, Tom wasn't about to be driven to chase it. He hadn't quite reached the top of the path when he said "No wonder aunt and uncle say you can't make any friends."

He hadn't necessarily intended his cousin to hear, but Lucas retorted "I've got one."

Tom was tempted to suggest that Lucas should have brought this unlikely person instead of him. His cousin was taking the light away as though to punish Tom for his remark. Having left the path, he halted under an outstretched branch. "You can see where they did it," he said.

The flashlight beam plunged into the earth – into a circular shaft that led down to the middle of the irrigation tunnel. At some point the entrance had been boarded over, but now the rotten wood was strewn among the trees. Tom peered into the opening, from which a rusty ladder descended into utter darkness. "You can't see if you don't take the bag off."

As darkness raced up the ladder, chasing the light out of the shaft, Lucas said "What do you think is laughing now?"

"Maybe you should go down and find out."

Another hollow liquid giggle rose out of the unlit depths, and Tom thought of convincing his cousin it wasn't water they were hearing. Lucas crumpled the bag in his hand and sent the light down the shaft again. The beam just reached the foot of the ladder, below which Tom seemed to glimpse a dim sinuous movement before Lucas snatched the beam out of the shaft and aimed it at the branch overhead. "He hung himself on that, didn't he, and then she threw herself down there."

He sounded little more than distantly interested, which wasn't enough for Tom. "Aren't you going down, then? I thought you wanted a Halloween adventure."

The glowing leafless branch went out as Lucas swung the light back to the path. "All right," he said and made for the opposite side of the ridge.

Did he really need absolute precision or just demand it? As Tom trudged after him he heard a rustling somewhere near the open shaft. "I thought you never left litter," he called. "How about that bag?"

"It's here," Lucas said and tugged it half out of his trouser pocket before stuffing it back in.

When Tom glanced behind him the Frugall floodlights glared in his eyes, and he couldn't locate what he'd heard – perhaps leaves stirring in a wind, although he hadn't felt one. Of course there must be wildlife in the woods, even if he'd yet to see any. He followed Lucas down the increasingly steep path and saw the flashlight beam snag on the curve of a stone arch protruding from the earth beside the track. It was the end of the tunnel, which had once helped irrigate the fields beyond the ridge. Now the fields were overgrown and the tunnel was barricaded, or rather it had been until somebody tore the boards down. As Lucas poked the flashlight beam into the entrance he said "Where's the bell?"

Tom thought the slow dull metallic notes came from a car radio in the distance, but said "Is it in the tunnel?"

Lucas stooped under the arch, which wasn't quite as tall as either of the boys. "Listen," he said. "That's where."

Tom heard a last reverberation as he stepped off the path. Surely it was just his cousin's gaze that made him wonder if the noise had indeed come from the tunnel, unless someone was playing a Halloween joke. Suppose the girls had followed them from the cinema and were sending the sound down from the ridge? In his hopelessly limited experience this didn't seem the kind of thing girls did, especially while keeping quiet as well. The thought of them revived his discontent, and he said "Better go and see."

Lucas advanced into the tunnel at once. His silhouette blotted out most of the way ahead, the stone floor scattered with sodden leaves, the walls and curved roof glistening with moss, a few weeds drooping out of cracks. The low passage was barely wider than his elbows as he held them at his sides – so narrow that the flashlight bumped against one wall with a soft moist thud as he turned to point the beam at Tom. "What are you doing?"

"Get that out of my face, can you?" As the light sank into the cramped space between them Tom said "I'm coming too."

"I don't want you to."

Tom backed out, almost scraping his scalp on the arch. "Now you've got what you want as usual. Just you remember you did."

"It won't be scary if we both go in." This might have been an effort to placate his cousin – as much of one as Lucas was likely to make – but Tom suspected it was just a stubborn statement of fact. "I'm not scared yet," Lucas complained. "It's Halloween."

"Want me to make sure?"

"I know it is." Before Tom could explain, if simply out of frustration, Lucas said "You've got nothing to do."

He sounded intolerably like a teacher rebuking an idle pupil. As Tom vowed to prove him wrong in ways his cousin wouldn't care for, Lucas ducked out of the tunnel and thrust the flashlight at him. "You can hold this while I'm in there."

Tom sent the beam along the tunnel. It fell short of the ladder, which was a couple of hundred yards in. Once Lucas returned to the tunnel the light wouldn't even reach past him. Tom was waiting to watch his reaction to this when Lucas said "I don't mean here."

He might have been criticising Tom's ability to understand, a notion that was close to more than Tom could take. "Where?" he demanded without at all wanting to know.

"Go up and shine it down the hole, then I can see where half-way is. Shout when you get to the hole."

"And you answer." In case this wasn't plain enough Tom added "So I can hear."

"Course I will."

Tom could have done without the haughtiness. He made off with the flashlight, swinging it from side to side of the deserted woods. As he reached the top of the path the lights above the distant retail park glared in his eyes, and he had a momentary impression that a rounded object was protruding just above the shaft at the midpoint of the tunnel. He squeezed his eyes shut, widening them as he stepped onto the ridge. Perhaps he'd seen an exposed root beyond the shaft, but he couldn't see it now. He marched to the opening and sent the beam down to the tunnel, where he seemed to glimpse movement – a dim shape like a scrawny limb or an even thinner item retreating at speed into the dark. It must have been a shadow cast by the ladder. "Come on," he called. "I'm here."

"I'm coming."

Tom was disconcerted to hear his cousin's shout resound along the tunnel while it also came from beyond the ridge. Despite straining his eyes he couldn't judge how far the flashlight beam reached; the glare from the retail park was still hindering his vision. He dodged around the shaft to turn his back on the problem, and saw that the beam of the cheap flashlight fell short of illuminating the tunnel itself. "Can you see the light?" he called.

"I see something."

Tom found this wilfully vague. "What?" he yelled.

"Must be you."

This was vaguer still, particularly for Lucas. Was he trying to unnerve his cousin? Tom peered into the shaft, waiting for Lucas to dart into view in a feeble attempt to alarm him. Or did Lucas mean to worry him by staying out of sight? Tom vowed not to call out again, but he was on the edge of yielding to the compulsion when an ill-defined figure appeared at the bottom of the shaft. He didn't really need it to turn its dim face upwards to show it was Lucas. "What am I doing now?" Tom grudged having to ask.

"Holding the light."

"I'm saying," Tom said more bitterly still, "what do you want me to do?"

"Stay there till I say," Lucas told him and stooped into the other section of the tunnel.

Tom tried to listen to his receding footsteps but soon could hear nothing at all – or rather, just the sound he'd previously ascribed to plastic. Perhaps the bag in his cousin's pocket was brushing against the wall, except that Tom seemed to hear the noise behind him. Had Lucas sneaked out of the far end of the tunnel to creep up and pounce on him? Surely his shadow would give him away, and when Tom swung around, only the trees were silhouetted against the glare from the retail park. He'd kept the flashlight beam trained down the shaft on the basis that he might have misjudged Lucas, but how long would he have to wait to hear from him? He had a sudden furious idea that, having left the tunnel, Lucas was on his way home. "Where are you now?" he shouted.

"Here," Lucas declared, appearing at the foot of the shaft.

So he'd been playing a different trick – staying out of sight until Tom grew nervous. "Finished with the light?" Tom only just bothered to ask.

"Go and meet me at the end," Lucas said before ducking into the dark.

Tom felt juvenile for using the flashlight to search among the trees around him – he wasn't the one who was meant to be scared – and switched it off as he hurried down the path. He was waiting at the mouth of the tunnel by the time his cousin emerged. Lucas looked dully untroubled, unless the darkness was obscuring his expression, and Tom wished he'd hidden long enough to make his cousin nervous. "What's it like?" he tried asking.

"Like I wasn't alone."

"You weren't."

"That's scary."

Tom thought he'd been more than sufficiently clear. He was feeling heavy with resentment when Lucas said "Now it's your turn."

As Tom switched on the flashlight, darkness shrank into the tunnel. "You can't do that," Lucas protested. "I'm supposed to go on top with it so you'll be in the dark."

Was he planning some trick of the kind Tom had spared him? When Tom hesitated while the unsteady shadows of weeds fingered the moss on the walls of the tunnel, Lucas said "I have to say what we do with it. It's mine."

Tom was so disgusted that he almost dropped the flashlight because of his haste to be rid of it. "I'll have to shout," Lucas told him. "You won't see."

He hadn't extinguished the light, which scrambled up the path ahead of him, leaving Tom to wonder if Lucas was uneasy after all. Suppose that distracted him from keeping the beam down the shaft? Once his cousin vanished over the ridge Tom peered along the tunnel, but it might as well have been stuffed with earth. He hadn't distinguished even a hint of light when Lucas called "It's waiting."

His voice was in more than one place again – somewhere down the tunnel and on the ridge as well. It occurred to Tom that he should have extracted a promise, and he cupped his hands around his mouth to yell "Say you'll wait there for me."

"That's what I'm doing."

Tom could have fancied he was hearing another voice imitate Lucas. "Say you will," he insisted, "as long as I want the light."

"I will as long as you want the light."

This had to be precise enough, and surely Lucas was incapable of acting other than he'd said he would. Wasn't his saying it in more than one voice like a double promise? Tom had no reason to hesitate, even if he wished Dianne were with him to be scared and then comforted. He wouldn't be comforting Lucas, and he ducked into the tunnel.

The darkness fastened on his eyes at once. They felt coated with it, a substance like the blackest paint. It hindered his feet too, as if they had to wade through it, shuffling forward an inch at a time, which was all he felt able to risk. He extended his arms in front of him to avoid touching the slimy walls, though he could have imagined his fingertips were about to bump into the dark. Of course there was nothing solid in front of him. Lucas hadn't switched off the flashlight and sneaked down the ladder to stand in the blackness until Tom's outstretched fingers found him. Just the same, the thought made Tom bring his hands back and lower his arms. "Are you really up there?" he shouted.

"You'll see."

His cousin's voice was somewhere ahead and above the tunnel. Otherwise the exchange didn't reassure Tom as much as he would have hoped if he'd needed reassurance. It wasn't simply that his shout had been boxed in by the walls and the roof that forced his head down; his voice had seemed muffled by some obstacle in front of him. Was he about to see it? There appeared to be a hint of pallor in the blackness, if that wasn't just an effect of straining his eyes or of hoping to locate the flashlight beam. When he edged forward the impression didn't shift, and he kept his gaze fixed on the promise of light until his foot nudged an object on the floor of the tunnel.

He heard it stir and then subside. He had no room to sidle around it, and he didn't care to turn his back. By resting his foot on it and trampling on it he deduced that it was a mass of twigs and dead leaves. He trod hard on it on his way past, and worked out that the material must have fallen down the shaft, which was just visible ahead by the light that nearly reached down to the tunnel roof. He could scarcely believe how long he'd taken to walk halfway; it felt as if the darkness had weighed down the passing of time. A few waterlogged leaves slithered underfoot as he reached the shaft and was able to raise his head. "See me?" he called.

Lucas was an indefinite silhouette against the night sky beyond the flashlight, which almost blinded Tom even though the beam on the wall opposite the ladder was so dim. "You were a long time," Lucas protested.

An acoustic quirk made versions of his voice mutter in both sections of the tunnel. Before Tom could reply, less irately than the complaint deserved, Lucas said "When you've been through the rest you have to come back this way."

That he had needn't mean Tom should. Lucas wasn't frightened yet, which was among the reasons why Tom intended to leave the tunnel by the far end so as to tiptoe up behind him. He shut his eyes to ready them for the darkness as far as he could. He hadn't opened them when Lucas enraged him by calling "Are you scared to go in?"

Tom lowered his head as if he meant to butt the dark and advanced into the tunnel. He wouldn't have believed the blackness could grow thicker, but now it didn't just smother his eyes – it filled them to the limit. He'd taken a very few steps, which felt shackled by his wariness, when his foot collided with another heap of leaves. He heard twigs if not small branches snap as he trod several times on the yielding heap, which must be almost as long as he was tall. Once he was past it the floor seemed clear, but how far did he have to shuffle to catch his first glimpse of the night outside? It couldn't be so dark out there that it was indistinguishable from the underground passage. He was stretching his eyes wide, which only served to let more of the darkness into them, when his foot struck a hindrance more solid than leaves – an object that his groping fingers found to be as high and wide as the tunnel. The entrance was boarded up.

So Lucas hadn't just been setting out the rules of the game. Perhaps he'd believed he was making it plain that Tom couldn't leave the tunnel at this end. Tom thumped the boards with his fists and tried a few kicks as well, but the barrier didn't give. When he turned away at last he had to touch the cold fur of the wall with his knuckles to be certain he was facing down the tunnel. He shuffled forward as if he were being dragged by his bent head, and his blacked-out eyes were straining to find the light when his toe poked the mass of leaves and wood on the floor. If he was so close to the shaft, why couldn't he make out even a hint of the flashlight beam? "What are you playing at?" he shouted.

There was no response of any kind. Perhaps Lucas had decided to alarm him. He dealt the supine heap a kick, but it held more or less together. He tramped on it a number of times while edging forward. It was behind him, though not far, when something moved under his feet – a large worm, he thought, or a snake. As he stumbled clear of it he heard scattered leaves rustle with its movement, and recognised the sound he'd attributed to plastic on his way to the tunnel. He needn't think about it further – he only wanted to reach the light. That still wasn't visible, and he wasn't eager to shout into the dark again, surely just because Lucas might think he was scared. He had no idea how many timid paces he'd taken before he was able to lift his head.

For a moment this felt like nothing but relief, and then he saw that the top of the shaft was deserted. "Lucas," he yelled. "Lucas." He was trying just to feel furious, but the repetition unnerved him – it seemed too close to doing his best to ensure that only his cousin would respond. He was about to call once more when Lucas appeared above him, at least fifty feet away, and sent the flashlight beam down the highest rungs of the ladder. Tom would have shouted at him except for being assailed by a sudden unwelcome thought. He knew why he'd seemed to take too long to return to the shaft: because the supine mass on which he'd trodden was further from it than before. While he'd been trying to find his way out, it had crawled after him in the dark.

He twisted around to peer behind him, but the blackness was impenetrable. Although he was afraid to see, not seeing might be worse. "Lucas," he blurted, and then forced himself to raise his voice. "Send the light down here."

The response was a noise very much like one he'd previously heard – a clang like the note of a dull bell. Now he realised it had been the sound of an object swinging against the ladder, repeatedly colliding with the upper rungs. This time the flashlight was making the noise, and struck another rung as it plummeted down the shaft. The lens smashed on the tunnel floor, and the light went out at once.

"What have you done now," Tom almost screamed, "you stupid useless retard?" He dropped into a crouch that felt as if a pain in his guts had doubled him over. His fingers groped over the cold wet stone and eventually closed around the flashlight. He pushed the switch back and forth, but the bulb must be broken too. When he jerked his head back to yell at Lucas he saw that the dim round hole at the top of the shaft was empty once more. He staggered to his feet and threw out a hand to help him keep his balance, and clutched an object that was dangling beside him in the tunnel. It was the rope he'd wanted to think was a worm or a snake.

A mindless panic made him haul at the bedraggled rope, and an object nuzzled the back of his hand. It was a face, though not much of one, and as he recoiled with a cry he felt it sag away from the bone. He was backing away so fast he almost overbalanced when he heard sounds in the other section of the tunnel. Between him and the way out, someone was running through the absolute blackness as if they had no need of light – as if they welcomed its absence.

For a moment that seemed endless Tom felt the darkness claim him, and then he shied the flashlight in the direction of the sodden flopping footsteps. He clutched at the ladder and hauled himself desperately upwards. He mustn't think about climbing towards the outstretched branch that had creaked as the boys made for the ridge. Perhaps nobody had killed themselves – perhaps that was just a story made up by adults to scare children away from any danger. He could no longer hear the loose footsteps for all the noise he was making on the shaky ladder. Lucas must be waiting by the shaft – he'd promised to – and of course he'd turned the light away when he'd heard Tom thumping the boards that blocked the tunnel. The thought gave Tom the chance to realise who the friend Lucas said he had must be. "I'm still your friend," he called, surely not too late, as he clambered up the rusty ladder. He didn't dare to look down, and he was just a few rungs from the top when he lost his footing. His foot flailed in the air and then trod on the head of whatever was climbing after him.

It moved under his foot – moved more than any scalp ought to be able – as he kicked it away. He was terrified what else he might tread on, but he only found the rung again. His head was nearly level with the exit from the shaft before a pulpy grasp closed around his ankle. However soft they were, the swollen fingers felt capable of dragging him down into the blackness to share it with its residents. He thrust his free hand above the shaft in a desperate appeal. Surely Lucas hadn't felt so insulted that he'd abandoned his cousin – surely only he was out there. "Get hold of me," Tom pleaded, and at once he had his answer.

CHRISTOPHER FOWLER

Lantern Jack

CHRISTOPHER FOWLER WAS BORN in Greenwich, London. He is the award-winning author of more than thirty novels and twelve short story collections, including *Roofworld*, *Spanky*, *Psychoville*, *Calabash*, *Hell Train* and ten "Bryant & May" mystery novels.

His memoir *Paperboy* won the Green Carnation award. He has written comedy and drama for the BBC, has a weekly column in the *Independent on Sunday*, is the Crime Reviewer for the *Financial Times*, and has written for such newspapers and magazines as *The Times*, *Telegraph*, *Guardian*, *Daily Mail*, *Time Out*, *Black Static* and many others.

He recently wrote the *War of the Worlds* video game for Paramount, featuring the voice of Sir Patrick Stewart, and his two-volume collection, *Red Gloves* from PS Publishing, features twenty-five new stories to mark his twenty-five years in horror.

"This story came about because I needed something for Hallowe'en," explains Fowler. "I was doing a gig at the London Metropolitan Archive, and figured I'd be on stage for fifteen minutes, tops.

"When I arrived, I found a wing-backed armchair on the stage and the organiser told me I had an hour to fill. I had no other stories on me.

"Desperate, I looked into the audience and found one of my fans there, who had another of my tales on him. I had written

'Lantern Jack' to be read aloud, and it saved the day, partly because I thesped it to the max and discovered my inner Olivier that night."

No, PLEASE, YOU were before me. Age before beauty, ha ha. I'm in no rush to be served. The barmaid knows me, she'll get around to looking after me soon enough. This is my local. I'm always in here on special evenings. Well, there's never anything on the telly and at least you meet interesting people here. There's always someone new passing through.

I don't come in on a Saturday night because they have a DJ now and the music's too loud for me. You'd probably enjoy it, being young. I haven't seen you in here before. This place? Yes, it's unusual to find a traditional pub like this. The Jack O' Lantern has an interesting history. Well, if you're sure I'm not boring you. I like your Hallowe'en outfit; sexy witch, very original. This place is a bit of a pet subject of mine.

We're on the site of an ancient peat bog. The strange phenomenon of gas flickering over it was called *ignis fatuus*, from which we get the flickering of the Jack O' Lantern. They built a coaching inn on the marsh in 1720. Not a good idea. Even now, there's still water seeping through the basement walls. Later it became a gin palace. That burned down, and it was rebuilt as a pub called The Duke of Wellington. Being on the corner of Southwark Street and Leather Lane, the pub was caught between two districts, one of elegant town houses and the other of terrible, reeking slums.

See this counter? It's part of the original bar. Solid teak, brass fittings. It was curved in a great horseshoe that took in all three rooms, the public, the snug and the saloon. But the Jack was caught between two worlds. The drunken poor came in on that side in order to drown their miseries in cheap ale, and the fine gentlemen ventured in to swig down their port while visiting the brothels nearby. Oh yes, there were dozens in the back streets. The area was notorious back then. It's all gentrified now. Urban professionals. They don't drink in here. Not posh enough for them. They'll be the first to scream when it's gone. Not that the area will ever really change. You don't change London, London changes you.

Of course, there was always trouble in here on All Hallows Eve, right from when it first opened. One time, close to midnight, two of the king's horsemen came in and proceeded to get drunk. They mocked one of the poor ostlers who stood at the other side of the bar, and brought him over for their amusement. They challenged him to prove that he had not been born a bastard. When he couldn't do so, they told him that if he could win a game of wits, they would give him five gold sovereigns.

They placed a white swan feather on one of the tables and seated themselves on either side of it. Then they produced a meat cleaver that belonged to the cook, sharpened it and challenged him to drop the feather into his lap before they could bring down the cleaver on his hand.

The ostler knew that the king's horsemen were employed for their strength and speed, and feared that they would cut off his fingers even though they were drunk, but once the bet had been made he couldn't refuse to go through with it. You never went back on a bet in those days.

They splayed his fingers on the table, six inches from the feather. As one of the men raised the cleaver high above his head, the other counted down from five. The ostler held his hand flat and lowered his head to the level of the table, studying the feather. Then, as the countdown ended and the cleaver swooped, the ostler sucked the feather into his mouth and spat it into his lap. He won the bet. Unfortunately, the king's men were so angered that they took him outside and cut off his nose with their swords. The nose remained on the wall here for, oh, decades.

During World War II no one was much in the mood to celebrate Hallowe'en. No female could come in alone, because it was considered immoral in those days. Well, so many men were off fighting, and most of the women around here were left behind. If they entered the pub by themselves it meant they were available, see. But there was one attractive married lady, a redhead, Marjorie somebody, who came in regularly and drank alone. None of the accompanied women would talk to her – they cut her dead. This Marjorie took no notice, just sat at the bar enjoying her drink.

But the whispering campaign took its toll. The other women said she was a tart, sitting there drinking gin and French while her husband was flying on dangerous missions over Germany. The pointed remarks grew louder, until they were directly addressed to her. Finally, Marjorie couldn't sit there any longer without answering back. She told the others that her husband had been shot down during the first weeks of the war, and that was why she came in alone, because it was his favourite place and she missed him so much.

The other women were chastened by this and felt sorry for her, but in time they became disapproving again, saying that a young widow should show remorse and respect for the dead. People were very judgemental in those days.

Then on 31 October 1944, when she'd been at the bar longer than usual, a handsome young airman came into the pub towards the end of the evening and kissed her passionately without even introducing himself. Everyone professed to be shocked. The women said it was disgusting for her to make such a spectacle, but their disapproval turned to outrage because she slid from her stool, put her arm around his waist and went off into the foggy night with him.

It wasn't until the barman was cleaning up that night that he found the photograph of Marjorie's husband lying on the counter. And of course, it was the young airman. He'd come back to find her on All Hallows Eve. Had he survived being shot down after all, or had the power of her love called him back from the other side, to be with her again? They never returned to the pub, so I don't suppose we'll ever know.

In the 1960s they changed the name of the pub again. It became "The Groove". Psychedelic, it was, very druggy. All crimson-painted walls and rotating oil lights. Let's see, then it was "Swingers", a purple plastic seventies pick-up joint, then in the eighties it was a gay leather bar called "The Anvil", then it became "The Frog 'n' Firkin", then it was a black-light techno club called "ZeeQ", then it was a French-themed gastropub, "La Petite Maison", and now it's back to being "The Jack O' Lantern" again. Always on the same site, always changing identities. But the nature of the place never changed, always the rich rubbing against the poor, the dead disturbing the living, the marsh rising up towards midnight.

See the pumpkin flickering above the bar? It's lit all year round, not just tonight. If you look carefully, it looks like you can see a skull behind the smile. It was put there one All Hallows Eve in the sixties. For months a sad-looking young man and his sick father would come and sit in that corner over there. The young man wanted to move in with his girlfriend, but her life was in Sheffield, and being with her meant moving away from his father. I would sit here and listen to the old man complaining about his illnesses, watching as his son got torn up inside about the decision he knew would soon have to make.

His father would sit there and cough and complain, and would catalogue the debilitating diseases from which he was suffering, but the funny thing was that he looked better with each passing week, while his son looked sicker and sicker.

I could see what was going to happen. The young man had to make a choice, and his decision coincided with his father's worst attack, although nobody knew what was wrong with him. The old man still managed to make it to the pub every night. The son made up his mind to leave, but he couldn't desert his father, even though Papa was slowly draining his life away. Finally he broke off with his girlfriend to look after his father, who looked so well in his hour of triumph that even the son became suspicious.

I heard the girl quickly married someone else. We didn't see the boy for a while, but when he finally came back in, he sat on that stool alone. It seemed the old man had fallen down the coal cellar steps at midnight on Hallowe'en, and had twisted his head right round. The son put the Jack O' Lantern up there that very night. It even looks like the old man . . .

The bar stool didn't stay empty for long. It was taken by a vivacious young woman who turned the head of every man as she pushed open the crimson curtains into the pub. Everyone loved her, the way she laughed and enjoyed the company of men so openly, without a care in the world. She came in every evening at eight o'clock. She drank a little too much and never had any money, but being in her presence made you feel like you'd won a prize.

She wanted to fall in love with a man who would bring some order to her chaotic life, and then one day she met such a man at a party. He held a senior post in the American Embassy, and gave her everything she ever wanted, a beautiful house, nice clothes, money, stability. She stopped her drinking, bore him a son and became a model wife. His only stipulation was she should never again come into the pub. One evening he came home and found her hanging from a beam in their farmhouse. I think you can guess what night that was.

Of course, everyone in here has a story. There was a woman who used to come in once a month and get completely legless, but the landlord never banned her. I asked him why, and he told me that she was an actress hired to play drunk in bars for the Alcohol Licensing Board. They used to collect data on how often drunks were served liquor, and she came here to practise her act. The stress of her job got to her, though. One evening, she decided to have a real drink and got genuinely plastered, but the landlord thought she was just acting again. On the way home, she drove her car into a lamp-post and was beheaded. Hallowe'en again.

Look, it's like the lantern's laughing now, isn't it?

You think this pub has endured more than its fair share of tragedy? I knew them all, and I'm still here. I sit here drinking while the tragedies of others unfold around me, and I can do nothing for them, any more than they can change me. And which of us is the main character in the story? Perhaps we only ever belong at the edges of someone else's tale. We suffer, we cry, we die unnoticed, and the people we consider unimportant fail to sense our suffering because to them we are merely background colours, minor characters in their story.

Of course, I could add my own story to the list of peripheral tales. I could tell you about the bizarre death of my wife, and what happened when the newspapers discovered where I had buried—oh, but that was so long ago.

Who am I? They call me Lantern Jack. I suppose I'm the pub mascot. Only here one night a year. And only ever seen by special people.

What's that? You can see me?

Yes dear, and I'll tell you why.

Come closer.

Closer.

Let me whisper in your ear.

It means you join me tonight.

Well, I should let you get on. I shouldn't have taken up so much of your time. I'm sure you must have many important things to do before midnight.

Cheers!

PAUL KANE

Rag and Bone

PAUL KANE IS AN award-winning writer and editor based in Derbyshire, England. His short story collections are *Alone (In the Dark)*, *Touching the Flame*, *FunnyBones*, *Peripheral Visions*, *Shadow Writer*, *The Adventures of Dalton Quayle* and *The Butterfly Man and Other Stories*.

He is the author of such novellas as *Signs of Life*, *The Lazarus Condition*, *RED* and *Pain Cages*, and his novels include *Of Darkness and Light*, *The Gemini Factor*, *Lunar* and the best-selling "Arrowhead" trilogy (*Arrowhead*, *Broken Arrow* and *Arrowland*).

With his wife Marie O'Regan, Kane is co-editor of the anthologies *Hellbound Hearts* (stories based around the Clive Barker mythology that spawned *Hellraiser*) and *The Mammoth Book of Body Horror*. He is also co-editor (with Charles Prepolec) of the forthcoming *Beyond Rue Morgue* from Titan Books.

His non-fiction volumes are *The Hellraiser Films and Their Legacy* and *Voices in the Dark*, while his zombie story "Dead Time" was turned into an episode of the NBC-TV series *Fear Itself*.

"The Rag and Bone man's cry was a familiar one to me growing up on a council estate in the 1970s and 1980s," recalls the author, "but for some reason they stopped coming around when I was in my teens.

"Then I was visiting my parents a few years ago, and I heard it again. Looking out of the window, I saw a scrap truck rather than the original wagon, but it set me thinking about how a profession like that has been going for so long and will never really die out.

"I'm also one of those people who likes to find out the origins of words and names, so I did a little digging into the history of Rag and Bone men – the results of which are included in the story.

"I was also very consciously trying to create my own bogey-man, having been influenced by the likes of Michael, Freddy, Jason, Pinhead and Candyman over the years. Hopefully I succeeded, or at the very least caused some readers a few sleep-less nights."

WHEN TED OPENED his eyes, he realised he was hanging in a room, surrounded by corpses.

Not hanging, as in hanging out – but in the literal sense. Suspended by the wrists, feet dangling with no sense of the floor below them. It was quite dark, and he was only able to see the dead people because of the moonlight, filtering in from a small grilled window to the left. The angle of that moon told him he was underground.

Ted blinked a few times, taking in the shapes of the suspended bodies. They were hung, just as he was, like meat in a freezer. He could see the wounds that had been inflicted on some of them: cuts, savage and unforgiving – the blood now dried in the slits. Some were naked, some wore scraps of clothing, torn away during whatever struggle had ensued before their deaths, or perhaps even afterwards? Some had been so brutally attacked, that he could see bone poking through in places: at the knee in one case, the forearm in another, ribs in a third.

Ted squinted, attempting to make out more, but it was impos-sible. Some had their backs to him, some were further away, some in corners. The ones closest appeared to be female, that much he could tell. One's shapely legs were in view, and anoth-er's breasts were exposed – were it not for the fact they both had jagged slashes across them, he might have been quite aroused by the sight.

Jesus, he told himself, *not now, and definitely not here.* Wherever "here" was. But he couldn't help himself. It had always been his weakness. If the average man thought about sex every seven seconds, then Ted was so far above average it was ridiculous. It was a wonder he could concentrate on work half the time.

Concentrate now, though. Try to figure out what you're doing here. Or, more importantly, how to escape.

He struggled to pull himself up, maybe try and work his wrists free of the bonds holding him, but it was too difficult. For one thing he didn't feel like he had any energy, perhaps an effect of being in this position for too long? A torturer's potential victim. Because he'd seen this pose before in TV shows and movies, hadn't he. They always did this to the people they'd captured, usually questioning them for information in thrillers. Was that it, was this work related? Some old business enemy, of which admittedly there were many.

That didn't make sense. Why all the others? Maybe he was the subject of a serial killer. They did the same thing sometimes, stringing up folk like animals, cutting off skin to use for God knows what purposes. It would certainly fit with the corpses who had been mutilated. He tried not to think about it.

Ted attempted again to pull free. Maybe he was still feeling the after-effects of whatever drug had been used to incapacitate him?

He remembered that much: whoever had done this had come up behind him in the car park, silent and deadly. By the time he'd known there was someone there, it was already too late – he'd felt the prick of a needle in his neck and it was all over. Blackness, that's all he could remember . . . until this. And part of him now wished he was still unconscious.

He closed his eyes, perhaps to pretend, but all he could see were those cuts. Ted could imagine the pain, putting himself in the dead people's places – could feel what he was surely about to experience, when whoever had done this returned.

Ted heard a sound and snapped himself out of his thoughts. A voice. Dear Christ, the killer was coming back already, before he'd even had a chance to formulate a plan of action. But no, it wasn't that at all. Someone was speaking, yes, but it wasn't in the assured voice of a murderer. Someone in control of the situation, without compassion – someone who could do the things that had been done in this slaughterhouse.

This was more like a whimper, a groan. "Help me," it said. Then there was movement. One of the "corpses" nearest to him shifted position, spinning round on the rope that was holding it . . . her. Because as Ted could see, this was a woman too; the blouse and skirt, as ragged as they were, gave it away. Her face caught the light from the moon and he almost gasped in horror at what had been done to it. Part of the woman's cheek had been ripped away, a large flap of skin peeled off, revealing cheekbone and teeth. The edge of her lip had been torn as well, leaving her with a permanent frown on one side – like a person who'd suffered a severe stroke. No wonder she was having trouble speaking.

Her hair – it appeared silver, but then that was probably just the effect of the light . . . more probably blonde – looked like it had been hacked at as well: one side cut short, possibly with a knife, while the other was still long and fell over her left shoulder. That too was exposed and horribly scarred. Her head was tilted, and to be honest she still *looked* dead, but she was moving, and she was speaking. "H-Help . . . Help me," repeated the woman, and this time Ted saw a saliva bubble form in that ruined cheek, popping as she spoke her next word, "P-Please."

What could *he* do? Ted was in no position to help anyone, even if they were gazing at him like that – so pleadingly. It was all he could do to even look at the poor wretch, her appearance so far removed from the usual beauties he liked to associate with. He said nothing, merely attempted a half-hearted shrug.

"*P-Please,*" came the voice again, filled with such agony Ted felt compelled to finally say something.

He'd opened his mouth, but before any words could emerge something else moved in the darkness. Something silent and deadly. The something that had come up behind him in the car park, hidden in the shadows all this time. A figure, which sidled up behind *her* now, grabbing the woman's neck and jerking it backwards, so the cords there were standing proud. Ted wanted to look away, but it all happened so fast. The large knife was suddenly up and being drawn over the woman's throat, like a cellist with a bow. Except the only music that emerged were the deep grunts and chokes of someone trying to breathe. A concerto in death minor. It took just moments for the noise to stop, but it seemed like hours to Ted – must have seemed like *years* to the woman with the ruined face.

The figure still held back behind the hanging body, for now it *was* a body and nothing more. That final bit of life had been extinguished, such as it was. Ted wanted to ask who this person was, but couldn't get a word out now through fear. Blood was pouring from the slit in the blonde woman's throat, spilling over her shredded blouse. Ted caught a flash of eyes looking at him, the killer's wild stare sending chills through his body. When the figure revealed itself, he did gasp.

Audrey? No, it couldn't be!

Ted took in the sight before him, the small woman dressed in dark clothes, almost like she was in mourning: black top, black trousers . . . black gloves. It matched her raven-coloured hair, which, unlike the dead blonde woman's, had been styled by a professional. Even after all that excitement there was barely a curl out of place, the mark of an expert hairdresser. An expensive one, at that.

Ted could do nothing but gaze at her, that knife still in her hand, dripping with the blood from her fresh kill. Audrey? *His* Audrey. She was no murderer. She wouldn't even let him kill spiders in the bath.

His mind flashed back to their first meeting, at that club in the city. She'd been with a couple of friends, he'd been alone and had zeroed in on her, flashing that confident, charming smile, guaranteed to work. Her friends had giggled at his jokes, Audrey had told him she wasn't interested, that she even had a boyfriend – he hadn't lasted long once Ted was on the scene – but by the end of the night he'd secured her phone number.

On their first date, he'd picked her up in his Corvette ZR1 and impressed her with talk about his business ventures. He found out that she was very family orientated – devoted to her father, because he'd brought her up when her mother had died in childbirth.

"I feel so comfortable telling you all this," Audrey had said. "Don't know why."

"I do," Ted replied, grinning.

It hadn't been long before he'd become a permanent fixture in her life . . . and her bed. Soon after, they were dividing their time between his place and her apartment. Not long after that, she'd taken Ted to meet her father, Frank, at the family home – a huge house just outside the capital. It was far enough away to pretend it was the countryside, but just close enough to smell the exhaust fumes from the cars. Here Frank lived, all alone – retired due to ill health, but content. Ted had done the same with her silver-haired father, charming him as they drank wine out in the garden, finding out more about the family business.

Frank had made his money through scrap over the past few decades, but the trade went back a long way. "I can remember doing the rounds with my dad as a kid, collecting all kinds of stuff in a horse-drawn cart on the streets, ringing the bell. Nowadays it's all in trucks and vans," he laughed. "You know, a lot of people think that Rag and Bone men only go back a couple of hundred years, but some say it's further. To the middle ages, or maybe even before that."

"That's fascinating," Ted told him, stifling the yawn that was building.

"They got their name because they'd even collect rags, which could be sold to paper-makers and weavers, and the bones from meat. That could be turned into bone char, bone ash, bone carver . . . even glue!"

Ted listened, humoured the man, but he didn't care about *how* Frank had come by his cash – the heritage obviously important to the guy. He was only interested in the fact that Audrey would come by it one day. Less than a week later, and with Frank's approval, Ted proposed and was delighted when Audrey said yes. They were happy, both of them, and went on that way for a good year or more—

So why was she doing this? He felt like asking her, then hesitated, still seeing that crazed look in her eyes. Something had changed. She was no longer the woman he knew as his fiancée. She was something else – something *unhinged*.

His eyes were at least adjusting to the light better, and he could see more of his surroundings. More of the corpses that filled this place, although he still didn't recognise it.

"There, that's better," Audrey said, stepping away from the dead woman, her voice cold and hard. "Another one of your whores silenced."

Ted frowned. What was she talking about? His eyes flitted from the psychopathic Audrey to the dead woman. Did he know her? Forget about the scarred face and body, the blood; take all that away and did she look familiar? Ted still couldn't see it. He looked around at the other bodies nearby, and beyond Audrey. Yes, they were *all* female, he could see that. But—

Another one of your whores . . .

He tried to swallow, but was having difficulty. He'd never known their names, any of them, but yes, the more he looked, the more his eyes adjusted to the light in here . . . *Jesus*, he said to himself. He thought he'd been so careful.

It stood to reason, no one woman was ever going to satisfy *him*. That wasn't how he was made. He loved Audrey, in his own way, and the others were just conquests – to keep his hand in. Sex, nothing more. Plus which, they all knew he was engaged: he'd told them and they hadn't seemed to mind. If anything, some of them found this a turn-on.

The more he focused, forcing himself to see the walls of that room, the more he could make out the evidence of those encounters he couldn't resist. No, that made it sound like they seduced him, when it was so obviously the other way around.

All those nights working late, at conferences or attending business meetings, when actually he was on the prowl again, on the hunt. The photos were there, tacked up on those walls: large, grainy, black and white prints. Some of him and women at bars, at hotels, at clubs like the one where he met Audrey. Some were even worse. Snapshots of the hot, frenzied couplings, rutting like animals – through windows, and some from inside the room itself (a professional then, some kind of PI . . . so Audrey hadn't been as naïve as he thought; it explained why she'd stalled over the wedding).

Ted looked from the pictures of those women alive, to the dead bodies hanging in that basement lair. And, God help him, he was able to match them up. Well, most of them. Some were beyond even his identification.

Ted could imagine the pain Audrey had felt when she'd seen some of those photographs. Pain that might tip you over the edge. Pain he now saw in her look – along with revenge. She'd been on her very own hunting trip and now that she'd punished the women who'd slept with him, Ted was next. What was the betting she'd saved the most brutal tortures for last?

He was about to plead with her, but knew that would do no good. Once Audrey had made her mind up about something, that was it. But as she approached, still wielding the knife, he found himself whimpering, "Please, *no*."

When she continued on anyway, he gritted his teeth, the real Ted emerging. "You'll never get away with this, Audrey. I'm telling you. What the fuck do you think you're going to do with all these bodies anyway?"

She paused, as if contemplating this – maybe the first time she'd even considered it during this whole spree. But Ted should have known better. Just as she'd been clever enough to hire the snoop, she'd had her endgame figured out well in advance. Audrey leaned in, too quick for him to flinch, and whispered, "He knows what you've done, and he's coming for you."

What? What the fuck did that mean? Ted braced himself for Audrey to strike, to begin slashing him with the knife. But she didn't. Instead she pulled back, grinning (it reminded him of his grin, that – the satisfied one he couldn't help whenever he'd scored). She was stepping away, leaving him alone. *Don't question it,* he told himself, *it at least buys you some time.*

Then he heard the sound. At first it seemed a long way off, that bell. Then the call followed it, equally distant. "*Rag and Bone!*" it went.

Ted cocked an ear. There it came again. The bell, and the cry: "*Rag and Bone!*"

Audrey's grin widened and she moved over to the side of the room, climbing some steps. At first Ted thought she might be ascending to an upper floor, but then she reached above her and undid a latch. Audrey flung open the doors – cellar doors that led to the outside.

His first thoughts were: I can use that to escape, if only I can get free of these bloody ropes. His next thoughts, when the light from the moon illuminated more of that place, were about those wine bottles at the back of the cellar. Ted knew where he was now, even though he'd never been down here. Had only been to the place itself on a handful of occasions.

It was the wine cellar in the family house: a hobby of Frank's and perfect for something like this. No one would hear the screams. And they were far enough away from civilisation that nobody would hear the cry drawing closer and closer, louder and louder.

"*Rag and Bone!*"

It was a strange call, like the person shouting it couldn't quite say the words. It reminded Ted of how newspaper sellers on street corners shout out the names of the tabloids.

"Audrey," Ted began, but she was taking no notice. She was too busy looking out through the trap door. Ted heard the sound of hooves next, accompanying the bell and the cries.

Jesus, what was going on here? One of her dad's old mates drafted in to help? It made sense. Like Audrey, they really wouldn't have been too happy if they knew the truth.

"*He knows what you've done, and he's coming for you.*"

But what had he done, really? All Ted had suggested was that Audrey invest in a few of his ventures – she had the money now, and it would really help him out (his flashy cars and dinners a front for covering how badly he'd got into debt). Selling the family business wasn't asking too much, was it? Her father had been the one hanging on to the past; why should she?

And she'd done it, even though she was doing other things behind his back (he could talk), hiring that PI for example. Audrey had sold up because she loved him.

The scrap business scrapped, Ted bailed out.

He saw the horse's feet now, pulling up outside; the cart behind. And from this angle, Ted could also see the boots when they jumped down – big, hobnailed ones, crunching the gravel round the back of the house. A faint whistle drifted down into the cellar, echoing throughout.

Audrey pulled back, waving a hand and inviting the newcomer in. The larger figure descended. Bulky, wearing some kind of long coat, he also sported a cap that was pulled down low on his head. His frame virtually blocked out any light from above, leaving the figure in silhouette as he glanced at Audrey – awaiting orders, it seemed. She pointed to the bodies and the man nodded, stomping over to the first. He hefted it onto his shoulder like it weighed nothing, whistling happily.

So that was the plan? thought Ted. *Get this bastard to dispose of the evidence of Audrey's sick and twisted exploits?* He said nothing as, one by one, the corpses were carried up the steps and – though he couldn't see properly – he assumed, dumped into whatever cart was up there. Why a cart, he had no idea. Why not a van or truck? Was he some kind of purist or something? Not even Frank had been that bad.

Frank . . . Ted thought about the old man now, and about what he'd done.

He shook his head; there wasn't time for that. He was in *real* trouble. As the last of the women were carried and loaded up, Audrey pointed towards Ted. She obviously couldn't bring herself to do anything to her lover. Instead, she'd shown him what she'd done to his "whores" and was now leaving Ted to the attentions of this nutter. He didn't know which was worse. At least he might stand a chance of talking Audrey round. Possibly. Maybe.

But there was no chance of that now, because the collector was next to him, whistling, shouldering Ted and cutting the rope attached to the ceiling. Ted groaned as he was given the fireman's lift, the rotten stench of the man like garbage. It was only when he was being carried that Ted noticed the shabby clothes the man was wearing, the state of the coat not dissimilar to the dress of Audrey's victims; the man's trousers scuffed and tatty.

Then Ted was being hauled up into the night air. He tried to struggle, but again it was either the position he'd been in or the after-effects of the drugs that prevented him – he had hardly any strength at all. So, when he was thrown in the back of that cart, an old-fashioned wooden one just like those Frank had described, he couldn't fight back.

"Audrey?" he just about managed, as the Rag and Bone man left him, skirting round to the driver's seat at the front.

But Ted's fiancée simply stared after them. Then, as the transportation set off, Ted saw her retreat back down into the cellar – no doubt to clean up – leaving him to his fate.

The ride wasn't a comfortable one. Apart from the stench, some of it from the bodies, most of it from the cart and the man driving it, there were the jolts as it went over rocks or uneven terrain.

On one particular bump, Ted found himself rolling over to face a girl who'd had her eyes plucked out, the black sockets staring back at him (what had been her name? Jackie, Debra, Sandra? Who the Hell knew?). He couldn't even muster a scream and was thankful when the next jolt came and righted him again.

They seemed to be travelling quite fast though, hardly enough time for Ted to worry about where this guy would be dumping them: burying them in a wood, weighing them down in a lake perhaps? In a deserted quarry?

He was wrong on all counts, because when the cart eventually arrived at its destination, the Rag and Bone Man had returned to his home (one of Audrey's dad's old places perhaps? Had this bloke bought it?). Ted took in the yard when they rode through the gates – a typical scrap merchant's, with bits of old bicycles, worn-out beds, washing machines and every other bit of discarded detritus you could imagine piled on every side. It wouldn't be hard to lose a few bodies in that lot. The perfect place, in fact.

The man pulled his horses to a standstill and clambered down. The moon was slipping behind a cloud so Ted still couldn't get a good look at the man's face as he began to unload the contents of his cart. He needed to see him, for when he got away – he'd need to describe him to the police. Audrey first. Then this guy. The cops would throw the book at them both.

(Oh yes, and what happens when they go digging around in *your* past? What happens when they find out about Frank?)

The huge figure began picking up the corpses again, putting them over his shoulder. He whistled once more as he worked, which made what he was doing all the more disturbing. He tossed them on the heaps of rubbish as if he was flinging old tyres.

Ted tried to twist away, to get his legs and arms moving, to climb out and get free of this place. Run, find a phone and—

But he was going nowhere. They were down to the last few women in the cart, which didn't take the man long to clear.

"Look ... Hey, I have money," Ted managed. (*Oh yeah, whose?*)

The man ignored him, heaving the last of the scrawny bodies onto a pile of trash.

He turned and began making his way back towards Ted.

"Can't we at least talk about it, please?"

"Help me. P-Please!" The words of that woman back in the cellar rattled around in his head.

The man was drawing nearer. "Please, I don't want to die!" shouted Ted, with more force than he'd been able to muster since he woke.

His captor paused then, lingering as if mulling something over. Then he began to walk off to one side.

Yes! I've got through to him, thought Ted. *Maybe I should offer him some money again?* He frowned, though, as he watched the man rooting around in the rubbish there, fishing something out. As the large figure turned, Ted saw he was holding up a cracked mirror.

And, as the guy came back, the moon passed from behind those clouds at the same time as the Rag and Bone Man lifted his head. Ted just about had time to register those features – and realise just how appropriate his name was – before the mirror was lifted.

Then it all fell into place. Flashes of the man's face, so similar to Frank's, something he himself had inherited through a bloodline and profession that went back so far. (*A lot of people think that Rag and Bone men only go back a couple of hundred years, but some say it's further. To the middle ages, or maybe even before that . . .*)

A trade plied during plague times, when they would carry the dead away from infected areas? You don't, you *can't*, do something like that without being granted some kind of immunity by Death himself. They were His helpers, in effect: some even changing to resemble their master.

The rags and bones, all that was left of the dead, were collected by them. By people who were little more than rag and bones themselves. It was a bloodline that had been broken when Ted came along – not simply persuading Audrey to sell up, but engineering the little "accident" that would take Frank's life and provide the means for her to do so.

Frank was an old man, his heart weak: it wasn't that hard to sneak inside the house and give him a little . . . scare.

Just like Ted was scared now. Because not only was he seeing something he really didn't want to in the mirror, he was also remembering. That it hadn't been the first time he'd woken up back there in the cellar, that Audrey had already done things to him which made the others look like she was just getting started. Pain so intense he'd blocked it out, kept alive – barely – while he watched her cut up the women.

But not kept alive long enough.

The image, the face – or what was left of it – staring back at Ted was barely recognisable as his own. It had been shredded, along with the rest of him: skin flayed from his body so that you couldn't tell where his clothes ended and his flesh began. Ted recalled the whipping now with some kind of cat o' nine tails, spiked ends digging deep with each swipe. He howled then, just as he had when Audrey had done her worst, finally getting up close and personal, pulling off his finger- and toe-nails, doing hideous things to his privates that meant he'd never be capable of cheating on anyone again.

Ted looked away and the Rag and Bone Man dropped the mirror. His charge had seen enough obviously, but things were only just getting started.

Ted looked past the skeletal figure, whose coat could no longer conceal its ribcage, open to the air. This representation of everything Frank held so dear, this figure that was all the Rag and Bone Men there'd ever been rolled into one, had made its home in a fittingly nightmarish place.

Because the more Ted looked, the more he saw of the yard, filled not only with ordinary rubbish, but the more specific junk of human waste. Bones, organs, scraps of clothing, all plugged the gaps where he'd dared not look before.

Ironically, Ted felt like laughing. He'd been pleading for his life when all along there was no life to spare. No wonder Audrey had been ignoring him – had he really been speaking at all? Had any of this actually been happening? It certainly felt real to him, but that didn't mean anything.

Somehow Ted knew he would soon fill the spaces here, just like those women who wronged Audrey, who'd wronged the line. Trapped in their own private Hell. (For a moment, Ted wondered if they were seeing this, or something else entirely; perhaps this little treat had been reserved only for him?)

But it was time, he saw. When the Rag and Bone Man came for him now, Ted surrendered without protest.

To be carried over to the pile of junk, of scrap human life.

To join the walls of organs, body parts and muscle.

To join . . . no, finally to *become* the rag . . .

. . . and the bone.

GEMMA FILES

Some Kind of Light Shines from Your Face

GEMMA FILES IS A former film critic/film history teacher. She is now probably best-known for either her 1999 International Horror Guild Best Short Fiction Award-winning story "The Emperor's Old Bones", or her Weird Western "Hexslinger Series" trilogy (*A Book of Tongues*, *A Rope of Thorns* and *A Tree of Bones*) from ChiZine Publications.

She has stories upcoming in the anthologies *Magic*, *A Season in Carcosa* and *A Mountain Walked*, and is currently hard at work on what she hopes will be her first contemporary horror novel.

"I wrote this piece very quickly," explains the author, "in a sort of frenzy, while deep in the middle of putting together my second novel. I'd agreed to contribute something to Conrad Williams' anthology *Gutshot*, a collection of 'weird west' tales from PS Publishing, and this was what came out.

"At the time, I wasn't entirely sure if it fit the bill, but Conrad liked it enough to pick it up, so who am I to say?

"As for influences: I've been a Greek mythology buff from childhood on, so I'd always wanted to do something about Medusa and her sisters, the Gorgonae.

"I'm also a huge fan of HBO's sadly defunct Dustbowl Gothic series *Carnivàle*, which probably shows, but there's some input there as well from Robert Jackson Bennett's first novel, *Mr*

Shivers, and even Peter Crowther's Depression-era werewolf tale 'Bindlestiff', which I read in his collection *The Longest Single Note*.

"I also stole the title from a line in a Barbra Streisand song, 'Prisoner (Theme from *Eyes of Laura Mars*)'."

It is immediately obvious that the Gorgons are not really three but one plus two. The two unslain sisters are mere appendages due to custom; the real Gorgon is Medusa.
—Jane Ellen Harrison

COOCH'S THE ONE *thing always plays*, Miz Forza told me, right from the start. And damn if I didn't come pretty quick to believe her 'bout that, just like I did 'bout so much else: Better than freaks, better than tricks, safer and more sure by far than creatures that required twice the feed of a grown man, not to mention a whole heap of mother-lorn care lest they catch ill and shit 'emselves to death, run wild and kill the rubes, or just bite at their own bellies 'til their guts fell out on the road.

Not that anything was really *safe* back then, in them dustbowl days of endless dirt and roaming; it was our stock in trade to hook folks in and get 'em riled up, after all, then see how much money we could pull from between their starving teeth before the inevitable backlash. The whole damn world was a half-stuffed firecracker, just as like to fizzle as it was to take your face off, and waiting on the spark – or maybe a mine dug deep in the mud of *La Belle France* of the kind Half-Face Joe used to tell tales on, a-whistling into Skinless Jenny's ear and flapping his flippered hands along for accompaniment, as though he was making shadow-dogs bark on Hell's own wall. After which Jenny would translate, her own uncertain voice sweet and slow as stoppered honey, while the lamplight flickered so bad it looked like every one of her Thousand and Ten Tattoos was dancing the low-down shimmy with each other.

Joe'd been a handsome young man once, 'fore them Europe kings and such got to squabbling with each other. Now he took tickets with a bag over his head 'til it was time to stump up on-stage and exhibit himself, making women and kids squeal and grown-ass men half-faint with his flesh's horrid ruin. In an odd way, he made a perfect palate-cleanser for the cooch show, too . . . always boiled the crowd off a bit, sent the ladies scurrying, leaving their menfolk ready to pay big for a bit of sweet after all that sour.

Them gaiety-gals was the real stars of the show, though, for all they came and went right quick – got picked up in one shithole town, dropped off again three more over, and never seen since. I didn't ever tend to look too hard at their faces, myself – why bother? Be it on-stage or off-, wasn't a one of us didn't know how with them, all true interest began to build strictly beneath the neck.

Five gals on either side, one in the middle. Ones on either side did their Little Egypt harem dance, the classic shake and grind, in outfits that flashed their hips, thighs, the fake jewels in their belly-cups, 'fore popping their front-closed brassieres apart to let their boobies sway free. One in the middle, though, whoever she might be that week – she was the real deal, the star attraction. The one who risked the full blow-off and lifted her split skirt high, let the rubes gape at the hidden-most part of herself while up above the Mask of Fear nodded and grinned, all pallid skin and bruisy eyes and dead snake hair hung in clusters like poison vine, adding a very particular sting indeed to *her* all-too-naked tail.

"I don't suppose you even know what this is," Miz Forza said to me, the first night I turned up shivering at their campfire with my hand half-out, half-not, just in case they took a notion to whip me for it. She had it hung up on a stand, like for wigs, and was stroking it all over with some foul-smelling stuff meant to keep it supple; the other gals all just sort of looked 'round it, shoving Miz Farwander's stew inside as fast as it'd go, like they was trying to forget how one of 'em would have to stick her head inside 'fore the next work-a-day was done.

What the Mask was made of I didn't know then, and didn't want to – but I sure did want me some of what else they had. So I squinted hard, then back up at the caravan's walls, which were covered in similar figures, their paint weather-worn yet still somehow bright, like fever.

"Looks like the Medusa, to me," I said, finally. "That old hag-lady with hissers for locks, who could turn men t'stone with one look-over. Some Greek fella cut her head off for her, hung it on his shield, an' used it to get him a princess t'marry. And then a horse with wings come out her neck, if I don't misremember."

The Mizes exchanged a glance at that, near to surprised as I'd ever seen 'em come. From the start, they read like sisters to me, though their names was different: Miz Forza was the smaller, dressed like a fortune-teller in a hundred trailing skirts and scarves, all a-riot with colour; Miz Farwander was tall as some men and tougher than most, never wore nothing more elaborate than a pair of bib overalls and a greasy pair of cowboy boots, with her hair crammed down inside an old newsboy's cap so tight she might as well be bald. Come to think, they neither of 'em liked to show their hair none – Miz Forza's was wrapped like rest of her in a scarf the colour of money, wound 'round with a string of old pewter coins. And she wore gloves, too, right up to her elbows, while Miz Farwander's hands were covered so deep in grime and such it was like they'd been dyed – black and grey, with no easy way to tell their fronts from their backs, except by what she was doing at the time.

And: "That's good," she said, approvingly, and grinned at me wide, so's I could see her teeth were all capped and shod in metal from east to west – metal of every sort: Silver, tin, steel, bronze, and even a hint or two of gold. "Ain't it, sister? Most don't know the old tales, not anymore."

Miz Forza nodded back. "That's right, that's right; they do *not*, sad to say." To me: "And who was it taught you the right way of things, dear? Your mother, maybe? Grandmother?"

"That'd be my Ma. She loved all that old stuff."

"But you don't have no true Greek in you, do you, even so? Not by the shape of your face, or the colour of your eyes . . ."

I blushed a bit at that, though I tried not to, for I'd been twitted over these things often enough, in previous days.

"Don't rightly know," I said, shortly. "Don't rightly care too much, either . . . not 'less it'll get me a job, or some of that stew you're ladlin' out there. 'Cause if it will—"

Miz Farwander laughed. "If it *will*, then you're Greek through and through, ain't you – both sides for a hundred generations, all the way back to Deucalion's mother's bones? Aw, you don't have to answer, child; I can see you need feedin', sure as sin. And the storm-bringer Himself knows we got enough to go 'round."

Miz Forza cast eyes at her, sidelong, as though to warn her not to speak so free. But Miz Farwander just shrugged, so she turned back to me instead, asking—

"And what might your name be, gal? If you don't mind me askin'."

"Persia," I said. "Persia Leitner."

"That German?"

"For all's I know."

"Your Ma might be able to tell us."

"Might, if she was here," I allowed, the pain of that old wound seeping up through me once more. "But . . ."

Miz Forza nodded as though she'd heard all this before, which she probably had. "And you don't know your Pa either, I s'pose," she suggested, without any malice.

I grit my teeth. "S'pose not," I answered. "But I sure ain't the only one like that, 'round these parts."

"Oh, no, no, no. No, Persia . . . you surely ain't." A pause. "Sounds a bit like 'lightning', though, that name. Don't it?"

I'd never thought so, but that smell was making my mouth water hard, so I nodded. The gals all murmured amongst 'emselves, like a flock of cooing doves. And:

"It *does*, yes, now you mention," Miz Farwander told Miz Forza, musingly, as she passed the last cup they had on over – and even as I sunk my face in it, through one more glance back and forth again right overtop me, like I wasn't even there. "It certainly does, at that."

You'll recall the pictures, no doubt – migrant mothers, carts jam-packed with Okies bound to pick or beg, Hoover camps in every mud-field and vacant lot. Houses buried window-deep in sand and milk-starved babies buried shameful shallow, or not even buried at all. They look like a bad dream now, or even lies, but they sure wasn't; I saw it all. Hell, I *lived* it.

When the crops dried and the dust come down to scour us clear, it was like every drop of colour just went out of the world – drained slow, like a man can die from one little cut alone, he only gets caught the exact wrong way. Like we was all of us being poisoned by coal-dust, or tin, or cheap nickel coating boiled off of pot-bottoms along with our daily mush, and didn't even know it. Oh, there was symptoms and that, which we mainly put down to hunger, a powerful thing; hunger will make your head ache and give you double vision, sure enough, under any circumstances.

But I can't think it was hunger alone that drove my Ma stark crazy, always following things from the corners of her eyes that simply weren't there to any other person's reckoning – not that, nor having no money, doing things with all manner of men that weren't none of 'em my Pa, always living hand to mouth, chased from town to town like dogs and thrown rocks at for grappling at scraps.

My Ma said my Pa was some gangster in Kansas City, and she'd had to run from him – or maybe it was *her* Pa she'd run from, who'd paid men to cram her in a car's trunk and dump her far from her home, to fend off the shame of her falling to ruin. But then again, sometimes she said my Pa was a wolf, or a burst of lightning, or the wind. Said he'd come winding through sunlight-wise under her window-shade one day, and fell head-long into her lap like a shower of gold.

He made me shiver, she told me. *Made me bow down, like Heaven's king himself. Persia, don't ever forget . . . he made you.*

I learned to hate just about every person I saw, during those days. While my Ma grew more and more tired, more and more silent, 'til the morning came she wouldn't say nothing at all, wouldn't even open her eyes. Wouldn't even call after me when I left her there by the roadside, sleeping under a tree like King Minos' daughter after the wine-god told old Theseus he wanted her for himself, so's he and his had better cut and run 'fore she woke up to complain about it.

I was glad she'd told me stories like that one, eventually; they gave me different ways to look at things and bright scenes to play out inside my head when I sore needed 'em – like radio-music to most, I guess, or those Motion Picture shows I never had a coin worth wasting on. Helped me make my mind up, and told me how one day I'd know I was right to do her like I did. But the further I got from her side, I found, they didn't give me no damn comfort at all.

It was on down that same road a spell I first met with the two Mizes, though, once Momma's face had faded into the same dust as everything else that ever fell behind me. And it was only 'cause of them yarns of hers I knew what-all tale them paintings on their caravan's side spelled out, which (like I told you) soon proved to at least count for something, in their eyes. With that one conversation, I gained what few keys to the kingdom they ever seemed like to dole out: The knowledge while this was their show, in the end, we at least had open invitation to try and keep up with it, for exactly so long as it suited them both that we should.

Miz Forza and Miz Farwander offered an open hand and a shut mouth, which was a hell of a lot more'n most; they didn't care where you'd been or where you was bound for, and they neither of 'em seemed to count the straight law as a friend. Hard work spent setting up and tearing down got you a share in whatever food might come their way, a part of the day's take and the right to sling your bed-roll near their fire.

"Depression", they called it, and that was the God's own truth. You felt it in your empty gut, your equal-empty chest, as though it was you who'd died instead of everybody else and all this living on you'd done was only a cruel trick, a walking ghost's delusion. Made your days so bone-weary it was like you was still dreaming – and not a good dream, either, nor yet a bad; nothing so easy. Most like them awful dreams you have where you work all day, then muse on doing the exact same thing all night, back-aching and useless: Ones you wake up from spent as ever, but with nothing to show for all your toil.

So the cooch, with its tinsel and soft light, its sway, its trailing crinolines . . . the curve of a woman's flesh barely wrapped, then peeled free by stages . . . that was a show worth the seeking out, for most men. And at the end of it all they went knees-down for a glimpse of that ultimate holy mystery, some girl's secretest parts shining like a rose on fire, exposed at the tangle crook of two thighs and framed in stocking-tops and musk.

Under the Mask or not, working cooch was fast cash that left almost no taste of sin behind. Unlikely as hell any of 'em would find herself recognised once she chose to move on, and we didn't truck with private viewing parties after the lights went down, either – not like most others did. Not unless someone pressed too hard for Half-Face Joe to handle, wouldn't resign himself to take "no" for an answer. And even then—

—well, we didn't tend to see those men again, no matter how short a time 'fore we swung back by their town, in future. And nobody, to my knowledge, ever did ask the two Mizes why.

Yeah, I saw how the cooch made fools and kings of men both at the same time, how it drew one common sigh wept out from twenty different mouths at once. Saw how it made 'em throw down pennies they couldn't afford, or stuff worn-soft bills they should've fed their kids with into the girls' garters with lust-shaking hands.

And I ain't too proud to admit it, either: After so much toil and sorrow, I wanted me a piece of that, cut big and steaming. Wanted it *bad*.

Lewis Boll I met in Miz Forza and Miz Farwander's service, too. He was twice my height but a third of my weight, lanky as a giraffe's colt, with squint blue eyes and a lick of too-long black hair that always fell down to brush his brows by noon, no matter how hard he slicked it back of a morning. He had stubble on his stubble, a shadow that started well before four o'clock and ran 'til right you could see exactly where his beard would go, if he just let it. And half-grown or not, he was the first boyfriend I ever had that seemed like a man.

Lewis was a genuine Okie from way back in the Bowl, last left standing in a clan that'd once been thirty or so strong; he liked money far more'n he liked his liquor, so we had that in common. Right now he worked roustabout, wrangling ropes and poles for the cooch show tent, but his grand ambition was to either rob banks like Pretty Boy Floyd or get himself in my pants, which-ever came first; sounded a deal nicer, the way he used to say it. But fine talk or not, he did get a tad nasty when I told him straight out which one it wasn't likeliest to be.

"What you savin' it for, Persia?" he demanded. "I'm gonna be rich – hell, we both are. What's mine'll be your'n, you just wait a while . . ."

"Uh-huh. Well, holler back at me when you already got some-thin' to swap me for it – 'cause right now, what you 'n' me both got's 'bout the exact same amount of nothin' much. And that ain't enough to make me drop my drawers on-stage, let alone off-."

Lewis coloured a bit at the choice of words, since he well knew where *my* ambitions lay: Up on that same podium with the rubes all panting up at me like begging dogs, and the Mask of Fear stuck fast to my kisser.

But: "You got your blood yet, Persia?" was all Miz Farwander asked me, back when I made my first play for the position. "No? Then you'll just have to wait, my darlin'. 'Cause we won't take no gal ain't bled yet."

"No indeed," Miz Forza chimed in from her crocheting in the caravan's corner, nodding right along. "No gal ain't bled can wear *her* face, for us, or elsewise."

"She" was what they both called the Mask, though damn if I knew why – what everyone called it, even the gals who'd put it on, none of whom got to keep it for long. Like I said, they came and went; went faster than came, if I'd stopped to think on it. And the one time I collared one to quiz her on how it felt to be inside, she'd only shook her head, as though there weren't words enough to answer my question in the short span of time she had 'fore the next show rolled out.

"You just sort of have to be there," she said, finally. "Be *in* it. That then . . . *that*'s when you'll know."

But being hungry makes a gal apt to stay maiden far longer than if she's well-fed, as I'd long since found out and hitherto been grateful for, seeing how it meant no matter what-all might occur along the road, I wasn't too like to catch myself a child from it. So all I could do 'til my courses came was sit there and watch Miz Forza handle the Mask of nights, curing its slack white face like leather with delicate strokes of that awful-stinking salve. Sometimes she'd raise it up so they was eye-to-eye and contemplate it a spell, mouth pursed and sad-set, like she ached to kiss it. Then Miz Farwander might brush by and pat Miz Forza's dainty-gloved fingers with her own grease-black ones, delicate enough to not even leave a smudge behind.

"Courage, my dear one," she'd murmur. "Her time will come again, and ours with it."

And: "I don't see how," Lewis said, from the other side of the fire. "That Greek fella of Persia's did for her way back when, ain't that so? Took a sword to her, and sawed her neck right through. Cut the head off a snake, what the body does after don't matter none; it's dead 'nough from then on, all the same."

Miz Farwander shot him a dark look. But Miz Forza just give a light little laugh, suitable to polite dining-room conversation.

"Oh, men do like to think that," she replied, to no one in particular. "But a woman like Her – She's right hard to kill, just like that serpent with a hundred heads: Strike off one, two grow back out, twice as poisonous. Cut off the head, more monsters just leak out; *new* monsters, maybe. Maybe even worse."

Agreed Miz Farwander: "A woman like that can strike every man alive blind, deaf and dumb without even tryin', root him to the spot and make him stand stock-still forever. That's why cooch plays so well, in the end; they say all's we are is pussy, but what comes from pussy, exactly? Blood, and dirt, and salt, and wet . . . poison like wine, fit to turn both heads on any man ain't queer. *Any* man, at all."

Lewis give a disgusted look, and spit hard.

"You bitches is somethin' else," he announced, probably aiming it my way, as much as theirs. But I'd still been following that last thought along, which was why I suddenly heard myself come out with—

"Well . . . *everything* does, don't it? Everything."

Miz Farwander grinned her too-sharp grin at that, all those metal fangs a-glint in the firelight, like scales on a skittering lizard.

"Reckon you got the right of it there, Persia. So don't you let no one tell you you ain't smart enough to keep up, not when it really counts."

That night Lewis took me up into the midst of a fallow corn-field to show me the gun he'd won in a card-game two nights back, and I let him kiss me 'til I was wet and panting, slip my shirt off my shoulders so's my titties could feel the night on 'em while up above a storm came rolling in, fast as Noah's Deluge. Don't rightly know why myself, but I wanted to, even if it wouldn't go no further; good enough reason for that night, at the very least.

But then ball-lightning started to roll back and forth 'cross the sky, snapping at the clouds like some big invisible body was riled near to bursting by the idea of what we were doing – and when he pushed his hand down under my skirt it come up dark red, copper-smelling, with proof of my sin come upon me at last smeared all the way up his palm to the wrist.

"Finally!" I blurted out. "Very first chance I get to run Miz Forza down, that damn-almighty Mask is mine!"

Lewis looked at me like I'd grew another head, then, and that made me angry – angry so much, I hardly couldn't speak.

"Don't want that for you," was all he said, shaking his head.

"What should I care what you *want*, Lewis Boll, 'for' me or elsewise? You ain't my damn Pa."

His eyes sparked. "That's 'cause you ain't got no Pa, Persia Leitner, nor no Ma neither; you *did*, maybe you wouldn't be 'spirin' to flash your trim at every Jack Henry got the fare. That stuff leaves a stain, gal, deep and deeper. Just 'cause it don't show on the *face*—"

"Oh, go on and shout it, preacher's boy! I'll have Her head to hide me, you fool; won't no one know me from Adam's house-cat, once that thing's fit on."

"'That '*thing*' is right. Horrible goddamned . . .'"

"It's a mask, is all. All of it! All of *this*. It's just a damn *mask*."

A mask. *The* Mask. Both, and neither.

I guess he thought we'd made promises to each other; he'd made 'em to me, anyways, that was true enough. But I never said a thing of the same sort back to him, and that's the fact, 'cause going by my Ma's experience alone I already knew better than to trust some snake-in-pants with my one and only future, no matter how much I liked him or how good his lips felt on mine. Any man made me *shiver* or want to *bow down*, that wasn't exactly a recommendation; quite the opposite.

So I left him there with his pecker out and I walked away stiff-backed, buttoning up my front again as I went, straight to the two Mizes' caravan. And when I made 'em my offer again, this time—

—they took it.

*   *   *

I remembered what my Ma said about that old hag-woman, Medusa. How she'd been young and pretty once, and her sisters alongside of her. How she'd been took up and played rough with by yet one more of them horny old god-Devils – the one who ruled the seas, might be? Him with his trident? And because he'd made sport of her in the temple of some goddess she served, it was *her* who had to bear the brunt of things when the goddess got angry, though only on her own behalf . . . Medusa who ended up getting cursed to monsterhood while the one who'd stole her virtue swum free, and the goddess she'd vowed her life to left her to weep in the ashes.

It was her sisters who stood by her then, and them only – they who were immortal, while she could be killed. They who took on the same monstrous form, and spun a spell so's that she could protect herself by turning any man fool enough to try and approach her to lifeless rock with her naked eyes alone, a human statue fit only to crack and crumble into dust.

But that one Greek fella who cut her down, he used a trick to 'scape her wrath – taught to him by the same goddess who'd took against her for all time, back when the sea-god had his way. He was a god's son himself, the cause of much unhappiness on his Ma's part, when her Pa saw what'd come to pass. And his name, his name . . .

. . . damn if his name wasn't almost same as mine, now I come to think.

But it took me a long time to recall that, afterwards. And by the time I did, at last . . . it truly didn't matter none.

No God but the one, down here where I was raised. And not too much of Him, neither, when things really counted.

Skinless Jenny helped me fit the Mask of Fear on that very night while the two Mizes watched, holding hands, and Half-Face Joe extolled my charms out front, racking up the take. I hadn't seen Lewis Boll all day, though the tent sure got itself up on time; thought maybe he'd finally run off to find himself a bank to knock over, and told myself I didn't much care.

I'd worried over my state, too, knowing what-all I was going to have to do in order to earn my money that night. But Miz Forza simply smiled, and called that last gal over – she gave me her Dutch Cap, all fresh-boiled and cleanly, to cram up inside myself. "Works just as well t'keep things in as it does t'keep 'em out," she confided, and I chose to believe her.

I barely recognised my own body in the dim bronze mirror hung up at the back, to make the tent seem bigger – so smoothed and plucked and powdered, legs shaved and wild half-whatever hair tamed to a fare-thee-well, pinned up under the Mask's slippery cap. I was a creature of myth, of legend, and where I moved I cast a net far wider than my gauze and crinolines alone could swing. My high heels clicked onto the stage like talons.

"Oh, you're a *demigoddess* like that, my sweet Persia," Miz Forza told me, admiring. "I always knew it, always. Didn't we, dear?"

"Yes indeed," Miz Farwander chimed back, nodding her head, her grin curling up on either side to show even more teeth than was usual. "Always. Right from when she told us what they called her."

And I saw her tongue poke out to touch her bottom lip, a bit too quick to notice, 'less you were looking at her straight-on – so long and red, so thin, a flickering spear. Almost as though it'd been sharpened.

Up above, the dregs of last night's storm still roiled, and the Mask felt hot and heavy against my sweating face. Behind one curtain, Skinless Jenny struck up on her dulcimer, hammers flying, skittering out trails of extra music while the gramophone ground on: Some mean old moanin' blues tune I half-remembered from earlier days when I'd heard my Ma humming it, leant up 'gainst the sill in some lousy little coal-town hostel—

> *Black mountain people, bad as they can be*
> *I said black mountain people, they bad as they can be*
> *They even uses gunpowder . . . to sweeten they tea . . .*

While out from behind the other, meanwhile, my fellow cooch-gal handmaidens come trooping heel-to-toe, white arms waving languid as twister-shucked branches after the real wind's already blown by. Their palms were stained with henna and lip-rouge, a kiss pressed full-on at the centre of every one right where those lines that are supposed to map out love and marriage split apart

– like they split apart now, so's the rubes (who were standing ass-to-elbow by that point) could catch their first glimpse of me in full regalia, with everything I had 'neath my jaw-line hanging out on display.

Oh, and I heard 'em make that single almighty *gasp*, too, as they did; Jesus, if it wasn't enough to make my own head swim same's if I'd been punched, under the Mask's brutal weight. Like a shot of that same rot-gut I'd been proud to never touch a drop of, sped straight through 'tween my breasts and into my beating heart.

I let my own arms drift up, slow as parting black water. Let my own hot hands cup together 'neath Her face and made with a vampish pose, like I was Theda Bara. There in the spot's single bright column, I shook back both our heads together, and let them snaky locks fall where they may – up, down, to either side, so's my nipples rose up and peeped out like two new red eyes through a dreadful forest's wall of vines. Took my cue from Miz Farwander and stuck my tongue through Her slack mouth – far as it'd go and farther still, 'til it ached right to root – to lick Her bluish-purple lips.

And as I thrust the Mask open 'round me, forcing myself inside, it was as though I felt myself crack open too, somehow. Felt Her enter into me, through every pore, at the very same time . . .

Which, of course, was right about the moment I finally noticed Lewis Boll standing in the third row back, with that gun of his already drawn and cocked the Two Mizes' raptly attendant way.

They can't see him, I thought. *Light's in their eyes – no way, no-how. Oh, goddamn him and goddamn me too. He's gonna go 'head and ruin every damn thing.*

"Gun!" one of the rubes yelled out, which let loose with a general back-stumble, a crash and rip and the racket of thirty men with two feet apiece set off running flat-out, not caring who they might plough into, so long's they ended up out of range. The gals did much the same, scattering like mice when the kitchen door slams open. I saw Joe grab Jenny by the arm and haul her clear in mid hammer-fall, putting paid to the music half; one kick did for the other, as the gramophone needle skipped and tore 'cross the whole of the record at once.

An empty tent with the back half tore down and rain falling in – just me, Lewis and the Mizes, with me froze in place mother-naked and masked, sweat drying on my goose-pimpled everything. As he looked me right in the eye, or close enough, with his finger never straying from the trigger – stood there with his hat-brim dripping into his collar and *told* me, like it was some sorta damn foregone conclusion—

"Persia . . . you're comin' with me now, gal. Gonna leaves these two witches to their own damnation. We'll git married, have us some young'uns, live high; Law won't never catch us, not if we start out runnin' fast enough. Won't that be fine?"

And: *Might have been, for some,* was what I thought, but didn't say; *might still be, for you, with someone else. 'Cause . . . I just ain't that gal you're thinkin' of, Lewis Boll. Never was. Never will be.*

I looked at him, past him. Saw the dim bronze shadow of myself in Miz Farwander's mirror, looming over Lewis like an angry spectre, for all you could see the full range and extent of my shame. And as I kept on looking, I saw one of Her snakes – *my* snakes – start to move its slick green head, to rise and keep on rising like it planned to strike, flickering its impossible tongue out like a kindling flame.

And Lewis . . .

(oh, Lewis)

. . . for all he didn't see it too – for all he couldn't've – he went rigid, went grey, went heavy, went dead. Stood there while the stone spread fast all over him like mould does on cheese or a blush follows a slap, 'til Miz Forza stepped forward lightsome as always, took him by the elbow and pushed him off-balance, to shatter on impact with the raw dirt floor.

"There," she said, clapping her gloved hands. "That's that. And now we're alone again at last – just the three of us."

Upstairs, the thunder crashed, like God Himself was breaking rocks. But Miz Farwander simply shrugged her shoulders at it with a brisk little *tut-tut* noise, flicking her too-long tongue against her metal teeth, and told the sky above her:

"Oh, go on and howl all you want to, father-killer – you had *your* chance 'fore you let yourself get old, let the white Christ take half the whole world over and some host of no-name one-gods take the rest, with barely even a fight. But you still had to keep spillin' your seed hither and yon, didn't you, where we could get to it? And now it's done. We're three once more, whole and perfect, with nothing at all left to stop us."

She put one hand on my right arm as Miz Forza took my left, and the two of 'em drew me away – cooed at me, stroked me, told me to keep my eyes down 'til we was inside the caravan itself, for fear of any further accidents. And when we got inside they sat me down easy with my feet up, to give me some time to settle in and come to terms with what had happened; Miz Farwander made tea, while Miz Forza tipped a bottle of something into it – that salve she'd used to keep the Mask good-looking? I hoped not, but it sure to hell did stink almost the same—

I was shaking as I sipped, watching her slip off her gloves, so's I could see her hands clear for the first time ever: Black like Miz Farwander's, from tips to wrist. Exactly like.

They knit their four black hands together tight and rocked together, like they was almost about to cry. And I saw—

—I realised—

—remembering those sisters of Hers, who lived forever and took on Her ugliness, who made monsters of 'emselves even though they didn't have to, just so's She'd never have to be alone—

—that all their fingers were nails, and all those nails were claws. That their tongues were equal long and sharp, just as their teeth (metal or no) were fangs. That their hair was snakes too, come seeking out now from under cap and scarves alike, to say hello to mine.

For it was like Miz Farwander'd told my no-'count Pa, that ranting lightning-strike voice lost behind the thunder: We *was* all the same again, all three, at long last. Just like 'fore my head was cut off, and my spilt blood birthed out a horse with wings, in and amongst so many other equal-awful creatures.

I wear the Mask of Fear at all times now, shows notwithstanding, and am worn in turn: She is my face, I her body. To even try taking it off would rip us both apart and force the two Mizes to start over – something I could never countenance, even for my own comfort; I owe them so much, after all. And thus together we hold pride of place while Miz Forza sets at my right hand, Miz Farwander at my left, looking up at me with a swoony mutual love that I can't feel, startling-keen as any knife slid fast and sure 'tween the ribs.

We eat well, and plenty. I freeze 'em in their tracks, they knock 'em down. And the caravan moves on, moves on, through this new world with its ancient tides, the ebb and flow of inhumanity. Dustbowl's just a word to most, near nine decades gone, all but forgotten. Yet you only fool yourselves to think it's over, for though hunger may be better-hid, it is never far behind.

That's why cooch still plays, now as ever. Like it always did.

I take the stage nightly, hard and proud and cold, a dead light shining from my rigid face; I live always in company but always alone, obdurate, untouched, imperturbable. As though I too was turned to stone that night, so long past – me, Persia Leitner, who am now called by many other names: *Sister, Dread Lady, Queen of Snakes, Mask of Fear. Poseidon's whore, Athena's injustice, Perseus' victim. Zeus' bane.*

Medusa.

Next show starts right soon, rubes. C'mon inside, look up. Look hard. No, *harder*.

And now . . .

. . . let me show you somethin'.

JOEL LANE

Midnight Flight

JOEL LANE'S PUBLICATIONS IN the supernatural horror genre include three short story collections: *The Earth Wire*, *The Lost District* and *The Terrible Changes*, while a collection of his supernatural crime stories, *Where Furnaces Burn*, is forthcoming.

He is also the author of two mainstream novels, *From Blue to Black* and *The Blue Mask*; three poetry collections, *The Edge of the Screen*, *Trouble in the Heartland* and *The Autumn Myth*; a chapbook, *Black Country*; a booklet of crime stories, *Do Not Pass Go*, and a pamphlet of erotic poems, *Instinct*. His articles on great weird fiction writers have appeared in *Wormwood* and elsewhere.

Current projects include a collection of ghost stories, *The Anniversary of Never*.

"'Midnight Flight' was written for *The Horror Anthology of Horror Anthologies*, edited by D. F. Lewis," explains Lane. "It's a tribute to the classic weird fiction anthologies I read before my teens, and to the libraries – now shut down or severely depleted – where I found them.

"That led naturally into a story about the loss of memory, and how memory might not want to be lost."

PAUL COOKSEY REMEMBERED the book's title on the same day that he forgot where he lived. As his bus neared the Hockley Flyover and the tall buildings on either side receded, he had a momentary sensation of flying on wings of concrete. Night was falling, but the street-lamps hadn't yet come on. Cars streamed past on the outside lane. He closed his eyes, and a name he'd been trying to recall for months came back to him as naturally as if he'd never lost it. *Midnight Flight.*

The editor's name continued to elude him, and it wasn't any of the usual suspects. The book had been in the school library, quite battered when he'd read it in . . . 1956 it must have been, when he was twelve. The first book of horror stories he'd read, unless you counted the children's versions of Norse and Greek myths and *Beowulf*, which you probably should.

As the bus crawled through heavy traffic on the Soho Road, the teenagers shouting into their mobiles and headphones leaking beats drove the book from his mind. But now he'd remembered the title, maybe he'd be able to track down a copy. It might even have the original cover. He couldn't see through the murky windows to identify his stop, and the chanting around him was getting louder as if the reception was better at this point. Paul rose to his feet and cautiously pushed his thin body past the standing youngsters. Nobody moved to let him through.

Midnight Flight. There was a story about a lonely boy who collected moths and was drained of blood by a vengeful giant moth with skulls on its wings. And a story about a dead lake haunted by a terrible black moth. There were other kinds of winged creature in the book, including one that could only fly in utter darkness because it came from outer space, but it was the moth ones he remembered most clearly. For years he'd dreamt of flying through the night on fragile wings.

"Get out the fucking way!" A boy on a racing bike narrowly missed him on the pavement. The cold air transmitted the near-impact. Paul looked around in confusion. He must have taken a wrong turning: there were no familiar landmarks in sight. A woman with a pram was approaching; he'd better ask her.

"Excuse me," he said as she drew level with him. "Do you know the way to . . ." *What was the name of the road?* He shook his head. "Shit."

"Even my daughter knows that." The woman smiled. "Where are you trying to get to?"

"My flat. Just can't . . ." Blood rose to his face, silencing him.

"Have you got a bus pass?"

"I can walk, it's not far." Though he was no longer sure of that.

The woman touched his arm. "For your address."

Doubtful, Paul pulled out his wallet and checked. His address in Victoria Road was there. He'd never been good with women's names. "Thank you," he said, breathless with relief.

"No worries." He watched her continue up the road, weaving to negotiate the shattered paving stones. The sky overhead was fully dark; a helicopter's light moved slowly above the rooftops. Paul replaced his wallet and buttoned up his coat. He wasn't convinced the face in the bus pass photo was him, but you couldn't be sure of everything.

Three days later, he remembered the editor's name. It happened in the Black Eagle, while he was trying to read the new menu. The lines were too close together, blurring like ripples on still water. He folded the card and put it down, trying to recall what he'd last eaten here. At the next table, a middle-aged man with a beard was being tugged from side to side by headphones plugged into some round, black device that looked about to crawl away. He raised his arms above his head. Paul looked back down at the menu card and immediately saw the words: *Thom Creighton Parr*. He adjusted his glasses and read: *Torn chicken pasta*. But he was sure it was the right name. When he closed his eyes he could see it under the book's title, superimposed on an image of blurred wings against the night. Black on dark blue.

The pasta was too expensive, so he opted for pie and chips, which didn't remind him of anything. It didn't taste of anything either. The bearded man played invisible drums in the air. The sound of voices arguing at another table rose to a violent pitch, though Paul couldn't see any movement. He left his pint unfinished. On the way out, a grey-haired woman turned her head towards him and smiled. "How's it going?" He didn't recognise her; she must be speaking to someone else. But she looked disappointed when he didn't stop. Embarrassment made him head for the door as quickly as his shaky legs would go. Was it possible that every memory he regained had to be paid for with another one?

A grey dawn was filtering through the curtains, turning his bed to concrete. Paul sat up and gripped the sides of his head to absorb the dull throbbing before it could break free. His throat was dry. Flakes of dead skin drifted from his fingertips. Was that what old age meant, that the layers of skin went deeper so that less and less of you was alive? He reached out to the bedside table, switched on the lamp and picked up a second-hand book. A detective story. But his eyes were too tired: the lines of print crept across the yellowing paper. When he couldn't read, why was he convinced that *Midnight Flight* would release him from pain and loneliness? Was it just because it had done that for him as a child?

Perhaps the local library could help him. Not that it would have the book, or any book published in the last century. But the computers whose blank screens had frozen him out might hold some answers. Paul washed and dressed a little faster than his usual lethargic morning pace, putting on his favourite cardigan despite the holes he noticed in its left shoulder and arm. *Midnight Flight* was out there, nestling on a wooden shelf, its pages waiting to be turned again. Maybe the same copy he'd read and re-read all those years ago.

The library's few bookshelves were mostly taken up with standard reference works and large print volumes – which Paul, for the first time, wondered if he ought to borrow one of. A few newspapers were scattered on the tables between the long ranks of computers.

The librarian, a short middle-aged man with an oddly boyish expression, looked up *Midnight Flight* on his desk terminal. "No copies in the library system any more," he said. "There'd be one at the British Library, of course, but that's in London. Have you tried ABE Books?" He didn't know what that was. The librarian checked his ticket, then found him a computer and showed him how to search. No second-hand copy seemed to be available online. The librarian left him to further searches. "Good luck, Mr Cooksey." Paul wondered who he was talking to. He had to look back at his own ticket to see that was his name.

A search for Thom Creighton Parr yielded seven links. Three of them were to listings of second-hand copies of his book on bowling, *Green Pastures*, while two more were bowling society websites that cited the same book. Another was a Wikipedia entry that gave Parr's birth date as 1923, but no death date. It mentioned *Midnight Flight*, but only to describe it as a "long-forgotten horror anthology" with only one edition, in 1954.

The final link was to a website called Crypt of Cobwebs, dedicated to British and American horror fiction. Paul hadn't read much in that genre since *Midnight Flight*. He'd tried a few other anthologies in the 1960s and '70s but had given up, nauseated by severed heads and vats of acid. The linked passage was in an article on British horror anthologies before 1980. It said:

> One of weird fiction's great "lost books" is *Midnight Flight* edited by Thom Creighton Parr (Acheron Press, 1964), which is thought to have included tales by Lovecraft and Jacobi. All the stories involve winged nocturnal creatures. A reviewer called the book "too disturbing to read", and it was never reprinted – though of course, true weird fiction stood little chance of being appreciated in the Marxist 1960s. Copies are hard to track down. It's rumoured that copyright problems led to copies of the book being recalled. Or maybe they just flew away.

The article was by Niall Verde. Working back through the Crypt's elaborate structure, which seemed to extend under a broad church, Paul found topics ranging from an early Gothic novel to a recent erotic vampire thriller. Verde was among the most frequent posters. His comments, always made in the early hours of the morning, were mostly concerned with how little "the herd" understood about "true weird fiction". In the course of a bitter argument with another insomniac, he remarked that "visionary" works such as his own collection *The Veil of Fail* were doomed to oblivion because "writers who care more about creating great fiction than self-promotion will always be passed over." There was a link to Verde's personal website, but Paul had seen enough. He cleared the screen, then tried a search for Acheron Press. Much to his surprise, the imprint still existed. He wrote down the address, which was in Stafford.

The train shuddered as it lost and gained speed, pausing between stations in a landscape of shut-down factories and empty fields. The view had been sprayed white and called morning, but he could see the night sky underneath. Then the young man sitting in front of him pulled down the grey curtain so he could read his phone. Paul closed his eyes and shivered. He didn't want to be alone with his memories, because they couldn't be relied on. The gaps were spreading, a ragged pattern of darkness like the wings on the cover of *Midnight Flight*.

He'd written to Acheron Press, and a typed letter had come back with a shaky signature. The original publisher was still alive, though a decade older than Paul, and said he still got occasional queries about *Midnight Flight*. Their stock had been destroyed in a fire in 1971. There'd been some ex-library copies in circulation for a while. They'd never considered reprinting the book because, after the fire, they'd switched to publishing nonfiction – mostly natural history and Egyptology. The business was steadily winding down, though a few local societies and museums supported it.

What had made Paul buy the train ticket was the news that Parr was still alive. The Acheron publisher still sent him occasional royalties for some entomology books he'd provided photographs for. Since 2006 he'd been living at a nursing home in Stoke-on-Trent. The publisher had commented: "He and I used to keep in touch, but these days I'm afraid he's hardly there."

The train ground to a halt. Paul wiped his eyes with a hand that felt dry as paper. Surely this was the fool's errand to end them all. A man losing his memory on a quest to find a man who'd already lost his own. He wanted to believe that Parr could help him find the book – or even tell him, from further down the road, where his own journey into darkness was heading. Perhaps this happened to everyone who'd read the book.

Last night he'd sat by the phone, trying to remember his sister's number or the number of anyone he knew. His address book had flown away months ago. Paul had lived alone since his teens. Hadn't slept with a woman in thirty years, still missed it though he doubted much would happen if he got the chance. All in all, he'd rather miss things than forget what they were like. Hence the ticket.

On the platform at Stoke, Paul was surprised how unsteady his legs were. As if not just the two-hour journey but the change of scene had affected his connection with the ground. He bought an A–Z map in the station newsagent, but couldn't make out the street names.

Outside the station everywhere seemed to be boarded up. He'd never find the way. It was hard enough with places he knew. Behind the derelict buildings, the illusion of daylight seemed more fragile than ever. He waved down a black cab and asked the driver for the Tyton Retirement Home.

"Been away, have you?" the driver asked as Paul settled himself awkwardly in the back.

"Yes." Why not let him think that? If he said he didn't live here, there would be questions he couldn't answer. The cab swerved around potholes in the road, passed the grey skeletons of buildings. This might as well be his home: a town that had lost its sense of identity. He belonged here. The driver stopped at a traffic light; a young woman crossed the road, a phone pressed to the side of her face.

The nursing home was a few miles out of town, where the dereliction was softened by the flame and rust of autumn trees. Dead leaves marked the road with an incomplete pattern. The cab's wheels crunched on the gravel driveway. The building had a new white frontage, though its side was rotting grey brick. Paul paid the driver; it was almost all the cash he had.

The young male nurse who answered the door stared at Paul as if trying to remember who he was. Paul knew how the lad felt. He said, "I've come to visit Mr Parr. Is he in?"

The nurse nodded. "You'll find him in room 17, ground floor." As Paul moved towards the door, he added: "Have you booked?"

"Sorry, no. I wasn't sure when I'd get here." The nurse looked like he was considering blocking the way, but then stepped aside at the last moment.

The interior of the home was poorly lit and smelled like an old-fashioned dry cleaner. Mothballs, that was it. Pipes vibrated behind the walls. The dirt in the cracked floor-tiles suggested a partly-erased image. Most of the doors were shut, but the open ones leaked other smells: antiseptic, stale urine, bacon. A cry echoed through the narrow corridor, more like a seagull than a human voice.

Room 17 was on the right, a long way into the building. Paul had to touch the raised number to make sure of it. The door was open by a crack. He pressed his shoulder to it and stepped through. A small room with a table and a few chairs, a bookcase, a TV set with the picture on but no sound. A flickering mercury light. Two shrunken figures in armchairs, not watching the TV. Neither of them moved as Paul entered the room.

"Is Thom Parr in here?"

The two men looked at each other. Then one of them pointed back over his shoulder. Paul realised there was a side room, or an alcove, with a vague shape just visible against a creased black curtain. "Thank you," he said, and walked through.

The stuttering of the light made it hard to understand what was there. The curtain was just random streaks of damp in the wall. The man seated in the chair, or rather held by it in a sitting position, was wrapped below the neck in a lace blanket. He was almost bald. His eyes were sunk so far into his narrow face that it took Paul a while to see that they were open.

"Mr Parr? Hello?" The face didn't stir. Paul looked closer. He could have been looking in a cracked and grimy mirror. "I'm a reader," he said, and blushed with shame at the uselessness of that. "Are you okay?"

There was no sound of breath. The old man's lips trembled, but perhaps that was just the light. Paul reached out slowly and touched the side of his throat, where the pulse should be. The flesh was cold. He brushed a fingertip against the dry lips: no air movement. He wondered what he might have to do to be sure that Parr was dead. Maybe the problem was in himself.

He reported the death back at the reception desk. They didn't seem either surprised or upset. He asked if there was anyone who needed to be informed, and was told that Parr had no relatives and no property. Everything he owned had been sold to pay for his place at the retirement home.

When Paul left, the daylight was fading. He felt drained by the effort of reporting the death, as if he'd used up his clarity of mind for the day. He'd better get back to the station, but that didn't seem possible until he got his bearings. The still face drifted in front of him, shedding flakes of skin like dead leaves. His legs ached, but he couldn't stop walking until the white building was out of sight. Then he walked on, looking for a sign.

Woodland, reminding him of childhood walks with his parents. Later, with girlfriends, he'd stayed in the city, maybe walked hand in hand along the canal towpath. Never made love out of doors. But the smell of decaying leaves excited him for some reason he couldn't explain. If only he could find the book, he could become Parr, not have to go home to a city he didn't know any more.

Not only his legs but his lungs ached, his hands were losing sensation, his throat was raw. But he couldn't stop. As if there were wings at his back. Night was falling, crossing out the errors of daylight. Burning the page.

At the edge of the wood, he reached a derelict house. Its doorway and windows were boarded up. Had Parr tried to sell it? He dimly remembered going into a derelict house on one of those childhood walks, finding a butterfly brooch, giving it to his mother. Black or dark blue. Had that happened, or was it a dream?

Behind the house was a patch of waste ground. He couldn't see where it ended, though he could hear running water. And a faint pulse, like the beating of wings. He could just make out a few dead trees in the half-light around him, with no leaves to shed. Had this been a garden? Was his real life coming to an end, as well as the false life in a city whose name he couldn't remember? The ground was as cold as the thin face he'd touched. The pulsing of wings made him flatten himself against the dead grass and fragments of stone, the pattern he couldn't see.

Then the wings were above him, beating slowly in the dark, their edges brushing his face. The pages turning. The dark covers shutting out the town's distant light. A clear memory came back to him: lying with his first girlfriend on a narrow bed, pinning back her wings of flesh with his tongue. Their hands locked together. And then the book folded around his body, and its dry pages gave the dust of their stories back to him.

TIM LEBBON

Trick of the Light

TIM LEBBON IS A *New York Times* best-selling writer from South Wales. He has had thirty novels published to date, as well as dozens of novellas and hundreds of short stories.

His latest novels include *Coldbrook* from Hammer/Arrow, *The Heretic Land* from Orbit, and *London Eye: Toxic City Book One*, the first in a new YA trilogy from Pyr. Other recent books include *The Secret Journeys of Jack London* series (co-authored with Christopher Golden), *Echo City* and *The Cabin in the Woods* movie novelisation.

The Secret Journeys of Jack London is in development with 20th Century Fox. Several other projects are also at varying stages of movie development, and he is working on new screenplays, solo and in collaboration.

Lebbon has won four British Fantasy Awards, a Bram Stoker Award and a Scribe Award, and he has been a finalist for the World Fantasy, International Horror Guild and Shirley Jackson Awards.

"I often think the spookiest thing about a ghost story is the setting," reveals the author. "So when I was asked by Jonathan Oliver at Solaris to write a haunted house story, I found myself dwelling more on the house than the ghost.

"Buildings are home to histories, but is it our imaginations that project them? Or are they really there, in the fabric of the building, its dust-sheened floors, its still air?

"Approach this from the viewpoint of a character already confused and on edge about where she is, and why, and 'Trick of the Light' is the result. I'm very pleased with the story, and delighted and proud to see it included herein.

"It spooked me a little when I was writing it . . . and surely that's a good sign."

I̶T WAS THE longest drive she had ever made on her own, and she so wanted the house to feel like home. But when she turned up the short driveway from the narrow country road, and the place revealed itself behind a riot of trees and bushes, Penny stopped the car and looked down into her lap.

"Oh, Peter," she said. In her mind's eye he was smiling. But in his eyes there was no humour. Only a gentle mockery.

I should never have come. I don't belong here. Peter would have loved it, but I should be back at home in our nice little house, coffee brewing, patio doors open to the garden I made my own, and which sometimes he would sit in with a map book open on his lap, pretending to be with me but never quite there. I should never . . .

Penny's hands were clasped in her lap. She forced them apart and reached for the ignition, turning the keys and silencing the car's grumble. It, like her, had never come so far.

She looked up slowly at the house, trembling with a subdued fear of elsewhere that had been with her forever, but also a little excited too. This was her taking control. Her heart hurried, her stomach felt low and heavy, and she thought perhaps she might never be able to move her legs again. The mass of the house drew her with a gravity she had never been able to understand, but which now she so wanted to. For Peter's memory, and for the short time she had left, she so wanted to understand.

She had bought it because of its uniqueness. While it had a traditional-enough lower two levels – tall bay windows, stone walls, an inset oak front door, sandstone quoins – a tower rose a further two storeys, ending in a small circular room with a coni-cal roof and dark windows.

The estate agent had told her that an old boss of the coal mines had used the tower to oversee work in the valleys. The mines were long gone and the valleys changed, but Penny quite liked the grounding of this story. It gave the building a solid history, and that was good. Mystery had always troubled her.

Beyond photographs, this was her first time seeing the house. Her first time being here, in her new home. She knew that Peter would have been impressed.

"I think you'll like it here," she said, and as she reached for the door handle, a movement caught her eye. She leaned forward and looked up at the tower's upper windows. Squinting against sunlight glaring from the windscreen, holding up one hand, she saw the smudge of a face pressed against the glass.

"Oh!" Penny gasped. She leaned left and right, trying to change her angle of sight through the windscreen, but the face remained. It was pale and blurred by dust. She was too far away to see expression or distinctive features, but she had the impression that the mouth was open.

Shouting, perhaps.

Penny shoved the car door open and stood, shoes crunching on the gravel driveway, fully expecting the face to have vanished as she emerged from the vehicle's warm protection. But it was still there.

"Ah, Mrs Summers," a voice said. A tall, thin man emerged from the front porch, and though she had not met him, she recognised her solicitor's smooth manner and gentle voice. "Is there . . .?" He rushed to her, his concern almost comical.

Dust, she thought. The shape was much less solid now.

"Hello, Mr Gough." She only glanced at him as she held out her hand, and he shook her hand whilst looking up at the tower.

"A problem?" he asked. "Broken windows? A bird's nest in the aerial?"

"No," Penny said. *I did not see a face at the window.* "No problem. Just a trick of the light."

Mr Gough's affected concern vanished instantly, and his smile and smoothness returned. "It is a beautiful sunny day, isn't it?"

Penny did not reply. She approached her new home, and already she could hear the phone inside ringing.

*   *   *

Peter moves his food around the plate. Pork chops, boiled potatoes, carrots, cauliflower. He's eaten some of the meat, and picks at where shreds are trapped between his teeth.

"Fuck's sake," he says.

"Peter, *please* don't talk to me like that," Penny says. Sometimes she thinks she would prefer outright anger, but Peter rarely loses his temper in front of her, and he has never touched her. Not in anger. And recently, not in any other way either.

"It's just . . ." He trails off, and she knows what he has to say.

"It doesn't appeal to me," she says. "The heat, for one. Flies, midges, the diseases they carry. The toilets out there, and you know me and my stomach. The water . . . you can't drink the water. And the sun is so strong. I burn just *thinking* about going out in the sun."

"All those things seem big to you now," Peter says. She can hear his desperation and impatience. They have been through this so many times before.

"I can't help how I feel," she says. It makes her sad, this gulf between them. It has always been present, but there were bridges – their love, the passion, and Peter sometimes going off on his own. But he says he cannot do that anymore. Says he needs her with him, now that he's getting older. Just because he has changed, doesn't mean she must too. The bridges are failing.

"Just a week," he says. "The food is amazing, and there's this one place in the hills that is just perfect for watching the sunset."

"The food here is good," Penny says, glancing down at his plate.

"This crap?" He shoves his plate across the table. It knocks over a glass of water, and Penny shifts back on her chair to avoid getting soaked. He'll apologise, she thinks, but something subtle has changed. "You just want to stay here in your little house, cooking the same food, watching TV, letting the world go by and watching . . . watching the sun set over the roof of your neighbours' houses."

"*Our* neighbours," she corrects him.

"Fuck's sake," he says again. "It's always been you living here, Penny. I just exist."

"I can't help it if you want to—" she says, but Peter has already turned around and walked from the room. She hears him storming upstairs, opening and closing cupboards, and when he comes down again he is wearing his walking boots, trousers, and a fleece.

"Where are you going?"

"Somewhere," he says. The gentle way he closes the front door is worse than a slam.

Penny sits for a while, sad, analysing what has passed between them. Then she clears the table, makes a cup of tea, and turns on the TV in time for *EastEnders*.

"I *worry* about you," Belinda said.

"I'm fine."

"Mum, you don't sound fine."

"It was a long drive, that's all, dear. And you know me, I haven't driven that long in . . ." *Ever*, Penny thought. *I'm further from home than I've ever been.* She felt suddenly sick, and sat gently on the second stair.

Take a rest, Peter says, tough voice soothing. *Take the weight off.*

A shadow filled the doorway and Mr Gough paused, as if waiting for her permission. She waved without looking, and the shadow entered her house.

"So the house?" Belinda asked.

"Is beautiful. He'll love it." There was an awkward silence.

"Russ and I will bring Flynn down for a visit next weekend. See if you're settled all right, look around. Russ says to make a list of any jobs that need doing."

"I won't have it that he's dead," Penny said. "You know that."

"Mum, it's been over seven years. He's been declared—"

"I don't care what some strangers declare about my husband. I'd know if he was dead, and I say he isn't. He's . . . gone somewhere, that's all."

"What, for a long walk?"

"Belinda."

"Sorry, Mum. But don't talk as if you and Dad had some kind of special bond. We both know that isn't really true, is it?"

"It'll be lovely to see Flynn," Penny said. "The garden's big enough to kick his football around. And can you ask Russ to bring some stuff for cleaning windows?"

"I will, Mum." Belinda's voice was heavy with concern and frustration, but Penny was here now. She had made the break. Left her own home, bought somewhere unusual, twelve miles from the nearest town and without bringing her TV with her. The furniture was coming the following day, but she had brought with her everything she would need for her new life – walking boots, coat, and a map.

"It's not much, dear," Penny said. "I know that. It's not Cancun, or China, or an Antarctic cruise, or the Northern Lights, or any of those things he always wanted to do with me. But it's something. It's a small step on a longer journey. He'd be very surprised of me and . . . proud, I think."

She glanced up at Mr Gough, listening and trying to appear distracted. And then she looked around the large hallway, three doors leading off into new rooms, timber floor scuffed, ceiling lined with old beams. "He'll love it here."

"Okay, Mum. Just . . . call me if you need anything. Will you do that?"

"Of course. Give my love to Russ and little Flynn."

"Love you, Mum. Really."

Belinda hung up first, and Penny could tell that her daughter had been starting to cry.

"Would you like a tour?" Mr Gough said.

Penny shook her head. "Just the keys, please."

"But you really should look at the tower, it's a remarkable feature, makes the house—"

"Really, I'm fine. Very tired." Penny stood, wincing at the pain in her hips from the long drive.

"Okay, then," the solicitor said. Smile painted on, now. He handed her a set of keys, then a smaller set. "Spares." He glanced around. "Lovely old place. You're very lucky, Mrs Summers."

As he turned to leave, a sense of such profound terror and isolation struck Penny that she slumped back against the stair banister, grabbing hold as the house swam around her. She tried to call out, but her mouth was too dry. *Help me!* she thought, feeling a great weight of foreboding bearing down upon her. *Up there, there's something above, a terrible thing that is pressing down on me now I'm inside. Dusty windows, a trick of the light, but I can hear it up there, I can almost smell it, and I wish I was back in my garden with the roses and rhododendrons.*

Then the feeling started to filter away, and she knew that this was an important moment. She could give in to the terror and run. Or she could remain in her new home.

There, there, Peter says, his rough working-man's fingers stroking her cheek with infinite care and softness. *Come on, my little rose. Don't be afraid. You never have to be afraid when you're with me.* He has not spoken to her like this since they were in their twenties, madly in love and obsessed only with each other. *I'll never let anyone or anything hurt you.*

"Thank you, Mr Gough," she whispered. The departing solicitor waved a hand without turning around, indicating that he must have heard.

As he climbed into his Jeep, he glanced back at the house just once. Not at Penny. At the tower. His constant smile had vanished.

She gave herself a tour of the house and wondered what she had done.

The fear had settled ever since she had reached a decision to sell the family home and move here. Belinda and Russ had been stunned, but increasingly supportive, as Penny had stuck to her guns and insisted that this was just what she wanted.

"Maybe your father is right and I am just stuck in my ways," she said, and the worry niggled at her that this was hardly a big step. Moving from the home she had shared with Peter for forty years, out into the country, into a hamlet where there were fewer than a hundred people living, the house Grade II listed and an architectural oddity that occasionally attracted visitors . . . it was nothing, really. The sort of change some people welcomed every couple of years of their lives.

But to Penny, it was the world.

The house was incredibly quiet. So much so that as she strolled through its corridors and rooms, she heard a high, lonely aircraft passing over the landscape outside. *You'll never get me on one of those*, she'd said to Peter when he suggested a simple flight to the Channel Islands to get her used to flying.

Penny opened the back door and paused, head tilted. She smiled. "One step at a time," she said.

The garden was wild and overgrown, awaiting her attention. The rooms inside were not decorated to her taste, but neither were they worn enough to require immediate redecoration. There was wooden flooring throughout – it would take her some time to get used to that, as she was more at home with patterned carpets. The house smelled unusual, and the sounds were strange – creaks, groans, taps – and she had no real sense of its shape and the space it occupied. It was nowhere near home, and she felt something like an intruder.

When the furniture and boxes arrive tomorrow everything will change, she thought. But the idea of seeing her belongings transported here and dropped in place by sweaty removal men suddenly hit home. Everything she had ever owned was packed in a lorry somewhere right now, ready to be transported across the country and deposited in this strange place.

Home is where you are, she'd said to Peter once, but he'd scoffed and gone into a quiet sulk. Later, he'd said, *You're rarely where I am*.

"Everything I have will be here, apart from him," Penny said. Her voice was loud. A bird sang somewhere in the garden, as if in response.

A steady *tap*, *tap*, *tap* came from somewhere that did not feel like part of the house.

Penny walked from the kitchen to the hallway, unconsciously matching the rhythm with her own footsteps. She paused at the staircase, one hand on the banister, looking up. The sound was more distant than the bedrooms or bathroom on the first floor. More hollow, and sadder. She knew the sound.

Peter, sat in his armchair with a glass of whiskey in one hand and his eyes distant, while she sat on the sofa and watched the next episode of some TV series she was already losing interest in, and his foot would tap against the wooden leg of his chair. Just a gentle impact, as if he were ticking away the seconds of his life. She would hear, but had never, ever said anything. He was always like this after an argument – a screwed up travel brochure beside his chair, and a dead dream floating in his glass.

He would usually go anyway, but never with his wife.

Tap, tap, tap . . .

"Peter," Penny breathed. The noise ceased. She held her breath.

Keys in hand, Penny walked slowly upstairs. Each tread had its own feel and sound, and probably its own memories as well. This one, a child sitting playing with toy cars. This one, a man tripping and spilling a tray of breakfast he'd been carrying for his wife. And this, someone kneeling and crying, perhaps in dread, perhaps ecstasy.

Spooking yourself, Peter says. *You always worry too much, my rose*.

Penny reached the landing and stood before the doorway that led to the tower. She had not looked inside on her first walk around the house. Had passed it by, truth be told, because it had felt like the last place she wanted to see. *Too dusty up there*, she'd thought, and she decided that was the one place she'd send Russ when he and Belinda came over the following weekend. Up into the tower, to clean those windows and see what else was there.

"Silly," she said. She reached for the door.

"You're just stuck here," Peter says. "Don't you see that?"

"But I like it here."

"You used to enjoy travelling. All those weekends we spent down in Cornwall when we were courting. The tour of Scotland in the motor home. Don't you want to do all that again?"

It always goes the same way.

So Peter packs a bag and leaves. He says he is going hiking for a weekend in the Lake District, but he never comes back. His body is never found.

Penny insists that Peter is still alive somewhere, and that drives a rift between her and her daughter. Because there was never any tension between Belinda and her father, and if he *is* still alive, she says, he would contact her.

"No," Penny says whenever the subject is brought up. "He's not gone. Not Peter. He's out there somewhere, waiting for me to join him. And one day, I will."

Belinda never believed that she would. In truth, neither did Penny. But discovering that she only had months to live had changed something fundamental about the way she viewed the world. Before, she had felt safe and secure in her own small bubble of existence. Now, she already sensed that everything else was moving on. Leaving her behind. She was a dead woman walking, and she had one more chance.

She paused with her hand on the door handle. It was metal, curved, and vaguely warm, as if someone gripped it on the other side. It was only a tower, and a room. Perhaps there was a chair up there, and she could sit and look out over the landscape, watching the sunset over a hillside instead of her neighbours' rooftops for the first time in—

Tap, tap, tap.

The sound was closer. Beyond the door, up whatever staircase might have been built within the tower. Peter, tapping his foot impatiently against the chair's leg.

Penny gripped the handle tighter, but was suddenly certain that there was someone directly on the other side of the door, holding the handle, ear pressed to the wood, smiling expectantly as they waited for her decision.

My little rose, Peter says, *sometimes you're so scared of the smallest things, so fragile and sensitive. It's a hard world, hardy and impartial. But I'll look after you. Sweet Penny.*

She let go of the handle and took two steps back until she nudged the landing balustrade. The tapping had stopped, but the silence was worse.

"Stupid woman!" she berated herself, and she started singing to fill the space. Still singing, she searched through the set of keys until she found one that locked the tower door. She paused again then, listening for movement on the other side. But there was none.

"Of course not," she said. "Just an empty room, and dust."

Hungry, thirsty, a little angry with herself for being so easily scared, Penny went down to the kitchen and switched on the kettle. She'd brought everything she needed to make tea and cook a simple meal, but as the kettle boiled she opened the back door and looked out onto the wild garden again.

Water bubbling and steaming behind her, she walked outside, fiddled with the key ring until she had removed the key to the tower door. She threw it as far as she could into the garden, turning away so that she did not even see where it landed.

"There," she said. "That settles it. The house is way big enough for me anyway." She entered the house again, not once looking up.

And not looking up meant that she felt watched.

Penny ate her fried egg sandwich. She'd speckled it with cayenne pepper, because Peter used to like that, and so spent the next half an hour sipping milk from the bottle and trying to lick the burn from her lips. And she tried to make sense of the house around her as the light outside changed.

She missed her little three-bedroom house. Living room, kitchen, dining room, spacious hallway, stairs, three bedrooms, bathroom, she had always known where she was in that house in relation to every other room. Her awareness had always filled the entire place, when Peter was there with her and, later, when he was gone. It had been more than a home, and sometimes she'd forgotten where she ended and the house began.

She wasn't like one of those strange people who never liked to go out. She went out plenty, to the shops and garden centre and to the chip shop on a Friday. But she always looked forward to returning home.

Now, the new house hung around her like something waiting to pounce. There was no sense of equilibrium here. The first floor felt as though it sought to crush the ground floor. The kitchen was too large, crushing out the dining room, storage room, and pushing into the corner of the quirky living room.

Penny felt vaguely dizzy, as if some part of the house was constantly moving, just slightly. Even when she closed her eyes and hung onto the table, the feeling persisted. Perhaps it was the landscape moving, and the house remained still.

And above it all, the tower.

Maybe Belinda is right, she thought, squeezing her eyes against the idea. But it could not be shunned. *Maybe he is lying dead out there somewhere, gone to bones and dust. Worms in him. And he'd have died alone, perhaps with a broken leg or a heart attack, under lonely skies without me to be there with him. Without me* . . . She opened her eyes when she felt the first tears squeezing out.

"Don't be soft, Penny," Peter says, and for an instant she looked around, certain that she actually heard those words spoken. The natural direction for her to look is up. "I'm fine. You know I am. Fine now that you've made the break, and taken the risk. And how does it feel, my rose? How does it feel?"

"I'm not sure yet," Penny said. Even the way her words echoed was unfamiliar. "I'm a little bit afraid."

"Don't be, my darling," Peter says. Penny had not heard such love in his voice for many years.

Dusk approached. In the valley, it was a wild time. The breeze increased, rustling the trees along the edge of Penny's new garden. Dogs barked from somewhere far off. Birds flitted overhead and, sitting out in the garden, Penny watched them circling the tower. None seemed to land. She could not blame them. There was something so intrinsically wrong there, but she was doing her best to steer her attention away from its upright bulk. To give in to the tower would be to admit defeat.

"I might just as well go home," she said. The overgrown garden dampened her voice, and her words quickly faded to memory. This was going to be her home for now on.

She walked around the garden with a glass of wine. She had never usually drunk wine except on Friday evenings, and then only a glass or two after eight o'clock. Now it was Tuesday, barely six-thirty, and she loved the feel of the glass in her hand, the fruity taste of wine on her lips.

The garden was larger than she had thought at first. Either that, or the boundaries were poorly marked and she was strolling across open hillside. She always felt the bulk of the house to her left, but most of her attention was directed downwards, at the twisted vegetations, long grass, and exposed tree roots that sought to trip her. She stepped over and around

obstructions, and thought perhaps tomorrow she would walk
further into the hills. There was a famous trail up on the ridge,
so Mr Gough had told her. Popular with walkers. Peter had
been a walker.

"I was a sitter," she spoke to the garden. "A not-doer. A nothing. A . . . waste of space." She hated the term, because Peter had
used it referring to her on more than one occasion. "Waste of
space." She looked across at the house, the looming tower, and
realised that she now stood in its shadow.

The sun touched the hillside beyond, and cast a palette of
reds and oranges around the tower's stark lines. The glazed
room on top was exposed to the sunset. There was a solid
shadow within, as if a shape was standing in the centre of the
room. And Penny wondered what would change were she to
suddenly disappear, and what would fill the space she had left
behind.

She began to cry. It was dislocation and fear, but also a growing sense that time had passed her by. She had never, ever
thought like this before, even when Peter had angrily insisted
that he only had one life, and he would not let it fritter away
waiting for her.

Penny thought that moving here had opened up her view on
things, and she could see a mile along the valley to the ridge
behind which the sun hid for the night.

"Don't be sad," Peter says. His voice is stronger than the
breeze, brighter than the sunset, and more meant for her than the
hushing trees and calling birds. "You've done well, my sweet
rose. You know not to waste any more time, or time will waste
you."

"Are you coming back to me?" she asked.

"You think I ever left?"

Penny stares up at the tower room, convinced that she will see
movement there, or a face, or a sign that this new home is more
than just her own. But still it exudes a weight of wrongness, as if
the tower and room had been built onto the house long after it
had first been constructed. Or, perhaps, the house had been built
around the much older tower.

"I'm not going there," she said. "The house is plenty big
enough without me ever having to go there." No one replies, and

she sees that her glass is empty. She does not even remember drinking the wine.

Back in the kitchen, the bottle is empty as well. Penny sits on an old stool and rests her arms on the worktops, her head on her arms. She closes her eyes.

Tap, tap, tap . . .

"You never call me rose anymore," she says.

"Huh."

"What does that mean?"

Peter looks across at her from the driver's seat. They are stuck in traffic on the way home from the supermarket. She bought food, he bought a CD and a book about Eastern European cuisine and a cheap one-man tent light enough to carry on a hike or a bike. "That was a long time ago," he says.

"So much just fades away," Penny says sadly.

"Huh." The car pulls forward some more, and Penny watches her husband driving. He remains silent, stern. She wishes he would just throw her a glance, a smile, a cheeky, *My rose never fades*. But the rot has set in years before, and now they are simply playing the game.

She opened her eyes to darkness, and a cruel throbbing against her skull. The house sat around her, quiet, still, and she felt that it was observing her pained waking. The weight of above pressed down against her, almost crushing her into the stool and worktop.

How could the tower have not tumbled long before now? How could it stand, so heavy and dense?

Even though she could no longer hear the tapping sound, she could feel it through her hands and feet. Transmitted through the body of the house like a secret message from one room to another. *All about me*, she thought, and she slipped from the stool to the kitchen floor.

She unrolled the sleeping mat and sleeping bag, climbed in, ignoring the pressure on her bladder, the need for a drink of water, the fear of what else might be sharing the floor with her in the darkness. She had not been this drunk in decades, but today she welcomed it.

Her world swayed. She was protected by numbness, and still feeling that *tap*, *tap*, *tap* touching delicately against the flagstone floor, she was pulled back into unconsciousness.

Dawn, and she had dreamed of Peter sitting upright on a chair in the room at the top of the tower. There was no other furniture. Just Peter, seven years older than when she had last seen him, walking boots and trousers and waterproof jacket still on, day pack propped by his side with the flask open and cup steaming coffee, sandwich box balanced on one knee. *So you came?* he had asked, not sounding surprised. He had always known that Penny, his rose, would follow.

"I have to see," Penny said. She glanced around the kitchen until she saw the set of keys, remembered throwing the tower key outside. Then recalled the spares Mr Gough had given her. She emptied her bag on the worktop and snatched up the key ring.

Her head throbbed with each stair she climbed. Her heartbeat matched her footfalls, reverberating through the house. She wondered whether her presence here would become an echo for whoever might own the building after her, but she did not like thinking that he would become only an echo. Peter was much more than that, wherever he was. A man so alive could, would always be more.

At the door to the tower, she touched the handle again. It was cool. It took a while to find the key that fitted the lock, and as she tried she looked around the landing, at all those closed doors. She had been into each room yesterday, but did not own any of them.

The key turned, and the lock tumbled open.

"Are you there?" she asked, expecting the tap, tap, tap. But there was nothing. She pushed the door open.

The tower structure was square, the staircase circular, made of cast iron and probably worth a small fortune. It did not make a sound as she climbed. She passed two windows out onto her garden, but it felt as though she was looking onto a world she had never visited. She saw places she had been, recognising none of them.

The stairs ended on a narrow landing with a single door. It was dusty and cobwebbed. She touched the door handle and it was warm, but she did not wait to think about why. She unlocked it with another key, wondering only vaguely why the tower room should be locked away behind two doors.

"Open the door, my little rose," she said, imagining the words on her husband's lips, and she turned the handle. Peter was waiting for her inside, and soon she would hear his voice again.

As Penny pushed the door open she saw something flash across the small room beyond, dashing for cover, terrified of being seen. She gasped, hand pressed to her chest. Her heart matched the tap, tap, tap she no longer heard, and as its thunderous beat transferred through her hand to the door, she saw a smear of light shivering in the room's opposite corner. A window-shaped reflection, brought to life by her fear. She shoved the door a little more, and the reflection disappeared.

She entered the room. There was nothing there. The dusty windows caught the sun's early light and filtered it, casting dust-shadows against the floor and one wall.

The door was closing behind her, and Penny turned to see herself in the mirror hung on the back of the door. Through the haze of old dust covering the glass, she looked nebulous, almost not there.

Also not there, Peter. There was no chair, no husband. The room contained old, old dust, and stale air, heavy with the aromas of age and seclusion.

"I'm here," she said. "I'm here!" Louder. Dust floated down from the ceiling and flitted in pale sunbeams, like tiny flies startled at her presence.

A broken wooden blind hung down across one window, and one end tapped gently against the panelled wall. There were no broken panes, no breeze. Penny closed her eyes and felt a slight dizziness not connected to her hangover. The tower moved, or the world. Now that she was here it did not matter which.

Penny began to understand. She had not come here to die. Neither had she come to try and make amends to her absent husband, or to prove to herself that she was not as he had always portrayed her. She had come because this was another place where she belonged. This empty, barren room was her home, not the house down below. And there was no way she could leave here again, because everywhere else felt so terrible, threatening, and a million miles away from where she needed to be.

She pressed her face to a glass pane. At least with dust on the windows, she was shielded from some of the distance.

Soon, she would lock the door, prise a window open a crack, and drop the keys outside. Belinda and her family were not visiting for ten days, so there was plenty of time. Because hers was the face at the window. And she was a trick of the light.

GREGORY NICOLL

But None Shall Sing for Me

GREGORY NICOLL'S SHORT FICTION has appeared in dozens of anthologies since the 1980s, including *Ripper!*, *Confederacy of the Dead*, *Still Dead: Book of the Dead 2*, *Cthulhu's Heirs*, *100 Vicious Little Vampire Stories*, *Freak Show*, *It Came from the Drive-In*, *Gahan Wilson's The Ultimate Haunted House* and *Mondo Zombie*.

However, after witnessing a profoundly disturbing act of real-life violence in 1999, the author avoided the horror genre for nearly a decade. Many of his best tales were reprinted in the 2004 collection *Underground Atlanta*, and more recently he penned a dark mystery for a book of New Hampshire-based thrillers entitled *Live Free or Die Die Die*, as well as a steam-punk novelette for the anthology *Clockwork Fables*.

About the story reprinted in this volume, Nicoll says, "It was being asked to create a tale for *Zombiesque*, a book of zombie stories told exclusively from the zombies' point of view, which finally lured me back into writing horror.

"I'd previously done some savagely gory zombie stories for John Skipp's anthologies, but that's the last thing I want to do this time. Instead I thought, hey, what about an eerie, mystical *voodoo* zombie story that takes place on a south sea island? After all, George Romero had *nothing* on Val Lewton.

"Of course, what nearly did me in was not realising how diffi-cult it would be to write a zombie's-point-of-view story set in a real place that was so exotic and unfamiliar to me. I had to keep stopping over and over to research history, culture, folklore, religion, and geography. I even stopped and read the entire memoirs of an African slaver.

"This dragged the process on for several months and almost caused me to miss the deadline but, as a result, the finished short story is woven with a novel's worth of details."

WARM CARIBBEAN SEAWATER splashed gently over his bare brown ankles, clawing at the soft crystalline sand under his feet as it glided back into the foamy surf, beckoning him toward the ocean depths, urging him to join its turbulent blue-green mysteries.

He stood firm, unmoving, resolutely upright and solidly ashore, ignoring the siren calls of the waves. Many decades before, his long-ago mothers and long-ago fathers had crossed that great ocean in the belly of the slave ship *Brillante*, each of them rationed just one pint of unsalted water per day, their dry and piteous cries answered only by the sting of the slaver's cat o' nine tails.

His people still spoke of the cruelty of Captain Homans who, on one infamous voyage, rather than allow his illegal human cargo to be captured by the policing British frigates, had dragged every dark-skinned man, woman, and child from the hold of his ship and cast them into those waters, with the iron shackles still fastened tightly about their legs. It was whispered that the echoes of their voices could still be heard, crying out from those depths, their horror at this fate mixed with joy that their suffering was finally at its end.

Tonight, for a moment, he thought he could hear them.

Though his eyes were huge and white, bulging on his face like two eggs taken from the nest of a goose, his unblinking grey pupils revealed little to him beyond indistinct variations of light and shadows. Instead, whenever and wherever he walked, his steps were guided by the more potent signals of sound and smell. Unable to distinguish morning from twilight, he determined the hour of the day by feeling the ocean's tides. Now, as the white waves crashed against the high, jagged black horns of rock on St Sebastian's coastline, he knew that evening had finally come.

In the distance, from across the sugar cane fields, came the forlorn call of a huge horn made from the great curled shell of a conch, a voice from the sea displaced far inland. It was the signal for which he had been waiting, the summons for the faithful to gather at the *hounfour*, where tonight they would conduct a ceremony with a blood sacrifice.

He had a duty to perform there. A potentially deadly duty. Yet he had no fear of death.

He had been dead himself for years.

He was called Carrefour, named for the moonlit crossroads where he stood guard.

Nearly seven feet high, he was a human statue with skin darker and drier than the husks of over-ripening cane that grew around him on every side. The strong, warm tropical winds blew and shook those rain-starved stalks violently, but Carrefour did not move. Nor was there the slightest flutter among the close, tight curls of woolly hair which clung to his scalp. His great muscular brown chest was bare. Carrefour's only clothing was his loose pair of blackened sackcloth trousers, so old and so stiff that even the wind could not bestir them.

As if frustrated by its inability to ruffle Carrefour, the night breeze swirled toward a large ceramic jar which hung some distance away, suspended by hemp ropes from a crude scaffold made of driftwood. The jar had been carefully pierced with irregular holes in several places, like a whistle, so that the air would howl when passing through. Its tone was low and mournful.

From the place of worship, just a short distance away through the cane fields, came the steadily pounding rhythm of the *tamboulas* and the frantic rattling of instruments made from bones and gourds. The dancers had begun to move and chant, singing and crying out, raising small offerings as they asked the serpent-spirit Dumballah Wedo to bring rain to these thirsty fields.

Carrefour smelled blood.

The rich, fragrant red liquid dripped thickly and steadily from the carcasses of a white she-goat and a black he-goat as they dangled from the branches of a nearby tree. The animals' life essence had been drained to satisfy the thirst of the *loa* whose presence was expected at tonight's ceremony. Their bodies now swayed in the wind, grisly fruit that no living man would pick.

The musk of the dead animals was strong, almost overpowering, yet Carrefour's widened nostrils picked up another scent behind it in the wind tonight. It was faint at first, a vague hint of something less natural to these fields than the carcasses and the cane. It was a faraway aroma of silks and soaps. The strange scent hovered ghostlike in the distance, but slowly drew nearer.

Woman, he thought. *The healer.*

The scents reminded him of an encounter he had observed earlier, during the daytime, in the village where he concealed himself from the burning afternoon sun. There were two strangers in the market, a man and a woman, both white and both smelling of alcohol. The man stank of the rum distilled from this island's own cane. He spoke loudly, his words distorted by the strong drink. The woman smelled sweetly of a very different alcohol, the kind Carrefour knew was used in the medicine rooms of the island's Great White Mother.

He had seen the rum-soaked man before, out in the cane fields. Carrefour recognised him as the brother of the planter who owned these fields. Those two men lived together near the coast, in the old Fort Holland, a sombre stone mansion whose central courtyard was infamously decorated with a massive wooden figurehead salvaged from the wreckage of the slave ship *Estrella*.

The woman who had accompanied him, however, was completely unknown to Carrefour.

These two white strangers had sat together in the café across the market. Their faces were a mere blur to Carrefour's unblinking eyes, but from their different scents and their differing words, he detected a tension between them. The rum-soaked man was in great need of healing. The medicine-woman was a healer. Yet Carrefour sensed that the rum-soaked man's need was simply too great. He was broken. He was already lost. The medicine-woman's words were soft and caring, but they came too late.

The man had done something evil and selfish, something so foul to the eyes of God that its infamy had inspired their village's calypso troubadour to compose a ballad about it. Carrefour had heard the song, but had never seen its subject until that moment.

As he had tried to remember the words of the ballad, the troubadour had appeared there in the street, as if lured by Carrefour's thoughts, and had begun to sing the song from the next corner. That round little fellow with his sad guitar had strummed the song quite mournfully, singing of the sorrow and shame brought to the rum-soaked man's family.

The drunken man's crime was familiar to Carrefour. Once, long ago, he too had lusted after his own brother's wife . . .

A strange light gleamed through the cane stalks.

It is she who walks toward me, Carrefour observed, *the healer-woman.*

The small spot of light moved along the ground, blazing from a silver cylinder clasped in the healing-woman's hand, its beam guiding her across the uneven terrain. As her gentle footsteps tentatively approached the wind-swept crossroads where he stood guard, Carrefour's senses were at full alert. He saw her now through his murky eyes, the same female stranger from the village, drawing cautiously closer in the moonlight. The faint perfume of the medicine-alcohol still lingered about her. She wore a white gown, over which she had pulled tightly a dark wool shawl. She moved in the direction of the ceremony, following the sound of the drums.

Carrefour knew she could not go there.

I must not let her pass.

Accompanying the medicine-woman was another white female. This one moved more slowly, but with a strangely regular rhythm. Though Carrefour could not discern the features of her face, he noticed the strong line of her eyebrows, arching gracefully like the countenance of a white owl. There was something curiously *regal* in how she bore herself, as if she were the exalted lady of a great estate. No sooner had the thought formed in his mind than Carrefour knew she was the one, the wife of the plantation owner, and the object of the damning passions of that planter's brother.

This woman was dressed only in ivory-hued silks, as if she had just risen from her bed. She smelled strongly of oils and powders, along with something else . . .

And then he knew.

She is one like me.

The second woman was, like himself, a zombie.

There was no stink of the grave about her. Unlike Carrefour, this one had never lain immobile with her heart stopped by the strange paralysis of the island magic, nor had she felt the first shovel full of earth tossed onto her chest, followed by another and another, until it seemed the weight of the whole island was atop her.

Neither had she known, some nights later, the sudden horrid jolt of awakening to an unholy and maddening afterlife, bringing with it the strength to claw oneself up from beneath the thick carpet of dark, wormy earth, through thick yellow roots and heavy veils of rough, tooth-like rocks and, finally, to walk once again in the moonlight.

This one's fate had clearly been much different. Doubtless her passage had taken place in a big house, on a soft bed, with palm fans and silken curtains. But she was just as dead. And, sadly, just as alive.

Is it I alone who see this?

Carrefour stepped forward. The healer's light beam illuminated his face, causing her to stop short. She gasped and covered her mouth in horror at the sight of him, stifling a scream; but her silent white companion remained expressionless and unmoved.

Since the night of his resurrection, Carrefour had been assigned many tasks by the *houngan* priest and even by the Great White Mother, but all these chores had involved only the use of his massive size and matching strength. None had required thought and reasoning. Tonight's task was simple, to guard the crossroads and let only the faithful pass by. These two were *not* of the faith, and by the command with which he had been charged, he should drive them away. Yet there was a purpose driving them here, a purpose which was not his to deny.

The planter's wife wore a small patch pinned to her gown, indicating she had been approved to attend the *hounfour* tonight, but the healer did not.

Carrefour hesitated only briefly before stepping aside.

The healer will see, at the hounfour, *and tonight she will learn of our ways . . .*

They moved past him, the healer giving one nervous glance back, her expression a strange mix of fear and gratitude, before pressing on toward the sound of the ritual drums.

Carrefour stood for a moment, alone in the crossroads, listening to the wind howl through the holes in the dangling ceramic jar.

Then, slowly, he turned and followed them.

Flickering torchlight reflected off the long, gleaming steel blade as the *sabreur* danced to the hammering of drums within the sacred circle. The air was hot and musky despite the wind, for the *hounfour* was hidden down in the low ground, its edges ringed by tall benu trees whose branches were heavy with fruit. The faithful watched the *sabreur*'s sacred dance, enraptured, from the periphery of the circle. The whiteness of their fine linen suits and cotton gowns contrasted starkly against their dark faces, black skin sparkling with perspiration.

The two white women emerged from the darkness and stood at the edge of the circle. The healer nervously beheld the scene, but her companion was expressionless and unmoved. Carrefour stopped a short distance behind them, concealing himself back in the shadows.

Many of the worshippers clutched offerings of live hens and wicker baskets of eggs which they brought as offerings to the serpent-spirit Dumballah Wedo. Others had already placed their gifts around the central post, beside the tall black top hat and the cigarettes that had been laid out for the exclusive use of Papa Ghede, brother to the Patron Spirit of the Farmers, should he care to make his appearance tonight. Nearby stood a tall clear glass bottle filled with first-distillation rum, into which a dozen large red-orange Cuban peppers had been inserted, crushed, and mixed. One sip from this vessel would sear a mortal man's throat and force his eyes to close shut in choking agony.

It was Ghede's favourite drink.

The *sabreur* slung his huge sword left and right, and then stopped and held it proudly aloft as the faithful cried out joyfully. The drummers increased the speed of their rhythmic pounding on the *tamboulas*, and a row of dancers strutted into the circle. They were half a dozen young women of the island, chosen for their beauty and the magnificence of their swelling bosoms, which they bared proudly as they danced. Smiling, they leapt in unison left and right, necklaces of bead and bone swinging to and fro between their naked breasts while, down below, their white skirts twirled to the rise and fall of the drummers' beat.

From a group of faithful seated near the two strangers, a small dark-skinned boy suddenly leapt into the circle. His arms flailed as if he were a marionette shaken on its strings, and it was immediately evident to Carrefour that the little one's mind was not his own. Less than ten years in age, this child was now the helpless puppet of a *loa*, come to join the festivities.

The boy lurched to a stop at the central post. Quickly donning Papa Ghede's black silk hat, which would have slipped down and covered his head completely if not for his wide ears blocking its descent, the child poked several cigarettes between his lips and lit them all almost simultaneously with the flame from a dripping crimson wax candle. Puffing pungent white smoke, he hoisted the rum bottle and flicked the cork from its aperture before darting into the line of dancers.

The drummers quickened the pace of their rhythm yet again, excited to have such a prominent *loa* here in their midst, even if the human body he had chosen to inhabit was hardly much larger than a monkey. The worshippers applauded and swayed eagerly with the music, confident that if Papa Ghede had joined their ceremony, the spirits of Zaka and Dumballah must be nearby as well. This would bode well for their harvest.

Hopping about and then undulating as if engaged in intense copulation, the small boy passed down along the row of dancers. He briskly pinched each one on her buttocks as her skirt rose with the beat. After leaving his mark in this manner upon the whole company, he stopped at the far end of the circle and, taking the cigarettes from his mouth, threw his head back and opened his jaw wide.

How the oversized top hat remained atop his head through this was impossible to determine, but even more astonishing was what followed. The possessed child tilted the bottle of fiery pepper-infused rum and poured nearly a quarter of it straight into his mouth, gulping it down eagerly and without pause. Even from the far side of the circle, the stinging aroma of that fiery spiced rum burned at Carrefour's nostrils.

Carrefour noticed the healer-woman react to this event, reflexively turning to the planter's wife in alarm. Seeing that her silent companion was still unmoved, the healer moved forward as if to intercede between the boy and the bottle. Carrefour extended one arm and held her back, restraining her from entering the circle.

Her shawl was soft under the coarse husk of his hand, her body warm and yielding beneath it. Briefly, a dim vision of his own long-ago woman flickered somewhere in the fading grey pools of memory inside Carrefour's mind.

He released the healer. She turned and looked up at him with an expression he was unable to interpret as either terror or relief.

The drums continued their relentless pounding. At the edge of the circle, the possessed boy laughed shrilly and began to dance in place, again joyfully following the beat. His high-kicking steps never faltered as he alternated each long drag on his smouldering cigarettes with a deep gulp from his incendiary bottle. When all the rum was drained from it, he cast it aside and jumped to the centre of the circle, throwing his arms upward with a swift, violent move which brought the entire dance to halt.

After one final savage flourish, the drums fell silent.

The *sabreur* stepped forward, raising his sword. He then lowered it slowly, extending its hilt to the child. The boy seized the huge blade, its edge nearly as long as his own entire body, and turned toward the two white visitors. He pointed the tip of the sword at the planter's wife.

The circle was completely silent. The only sound was the howl of the wind through the cane and dangling whistles.

Back behind the *sabreur*, on the wicker and cane-husk wall of the *hounfour*, a small door swung inward, its crude wooden frame creaking weakly. The possessed boy passed the sword back to its bearer, marched forward, and stepped through this portal. The door creaked shut behind him.

Silently, a small procession of the faithful advanced and began forming a line outside the door, awaiting their own opportunities to speak with the wise *houngan* within, to ask him to interpret the ways of the spirits for them and to advise them on their prayers. The healer-woman stepped forward to join them, glancing back briefly at Carrefour as if to ask his permission.

He made no move to stop her.

The healer stepped aside briefly to pick up the discarded rum bottle. She raised it toward her nostrils as if to sample its scent, but dropped it before it reached her face. Her lips curled and she grimaced in open disgust at the potent smell wafting from its uncorked end.

In a moment, the door of the *hounfour* swung open again and the boy emerged. He no longer wore the black hat of Papa Ghede. He walked normally, as if nothing out of the ordinary had happened. When the faithful reached down to rub his shoulders or to pat him on the head as he passed down the waiting queue, he looked up with genuine surprise, baffled by their excessive attentions.

The healer woman knelt before him and, in a soft voice which Carrefour could not clearly hear, asked him some questions. The child shook his head and smiled. She leaned forward more closely and whiffed the boy's breath. Her forehead creased with confusion. Clearly she was puzzled, for the boy did not reek in even the slightest way of the cigarettes or of the fiery rum which the whole circle had watched him consume.

A native woman now stepped to the door of the *hounfour* and whispered a question for the priest inside it. He answered her in a deep voice which reached Carrefour's ears as a low rumble, like great wooden wheels rolling over cobblestones. The woman nodded, accepting the holy man's answer, and stepped away. Another worshipper, who had waited in the queue behind her, beckoned for the healer to take her place. The white visitor accepted gratefully, but when the healer reached the door, it opened. She was ushered briskly inside and the door creaked shut behind her.

A low murmur grew steadily among the faithful waiting for the *houngan*. They gestured at where Carrefour stood. For a moment he imagined that they were staring and pointing at him, but he soon realised that their attentions were focused on the planter's wife. She remained near the edge of the circle, unmoving and unmoved, where she had stood throughout the entire ceremony. The *sabreur* walked slowly up to her, extending the tip of his sword. He pressed it against the bare flesh of her left arm and drew its edge down purposefully, finishing the stroke with a quick and forceful turn which spun her slightly on her heels, so that Carrefour could now see her face. A longitudinal wound, nearly four inches across, opened in the white woman's arm. The skin on either side parted like a pair of thin, pale lips opening to speak.

But no blood flowed forth.

The murmuring of the crowd rose to a tumult.

"Ghost," one voice hoarsely whispered.

"Living dead," another gasped.

"Zombie!" someone shouted.

The door of the *hounfour* creaked open again and the healer-woman dashed out. Close behind her followed the island's Great White Mother, and then the *houngan* himself. The healer looked in horror at the bloodless wound and, grasping the planter's wife by the arm, led her quickly from the circle. The *houngan* and the Great White Mother spoke to the worshippers, calming them and asking that they resume the service.

Carrefour watched the scene carefully through his dull, milky eyes. He saw the Great White Mother turn and steal a curious, lingering glance after the two departing women. Her face seemed to reflect more than mere interest. She seemed to smile with pride. Even through the blur of his dead eyes, there was no mistaking it.

It was then that he knew . . .

He recalled the strange song of the village troubadour, who had sung of sorrow and shame descending on the planter's family.

The words of that song are true, thought Carrefour, *but the blame for those two brothers' pain lies with the woman who bore them. It was she . . .*

He sensed strongly that the fault for their sorrow lay only partly with the planter's rum-soaked brother, whose misplaced passions had threatened to shatter their familial bonds. The greater blame belonged to their own mother, a white woman well-schooled in Northern medicine, but who also dabbled adroitly in island *voodoo*.

The planter's wife who walks as a ghost . . . walks because of her . . .

Ceremonial drums pounded vibrantly as Carrefour held the planter's wife in his hand, closing his dry brown fingers around the soft, cool smooth silk of her gown. She was so small that only the tips of her feet and the top of her head protruded from the grasp of his surrounding fingers.

The *sabreur* smiled, pleased by Carrefour's interest. He reached up and tugged the tiny white doll from Carrefour's hand. He waved and gestured at it, holding the symbol aloft. Slowly Carrefour extended his arm and took the little effigy back from him. Once more the *sabreur* removed it from his grasp.

The drummers quickened their pace.

Carrefour turned and began to walk away. He had been assigned his mission.

Burdened with great purpose, he moved toward the faraway lights of Fort Holland.

There was a strong hint of ocean salt in the warm night breeze, and it slowed Carrefour's pace, causing him to step awkwardly on the unpaved trails, with his footfalls dragging as if walking under seawater. At this delayed pace, he reached the planter's home when the moon was more than halfway through its nightly arc. Bullfrogs croaked from the high grass of the surrounding marshes.

The unguarded iron gate of Fort Holland swung open silently at his touch.

Carrefour shuffled into the central courtyard, making better progress now that this flat stone surface was under his feet. Other than the scrape of his soles on the smooth stone, the only sound in here was the constant trickle of water from the fort's fountain, over which an immense wooden figurehead loomed.

Carrefour paused briefly to stare up at the huge carving, his dull and unblinking eyes struggling to take in the sight.

He had heard tales of it, but until this moment he had never seen it. Rescued from the wreckage of the slave ship *Estrella*, the figurehead was a giant effigy of Sebastian, the Christian saint from whom this island took its name. It depicted the saint during his martyrdom, with a dozen of his tormentors' arrows protruding from chest and arms. In real life, Sebastian had somehow survived this horror. So too had much of the *Estrella*'s terrified, dusky-hued cargo endured the misadventure of their shipwreck. They had lived to walk the sands of this island, if only to toil in the cane fields under the unrelenting lash of their white masters.

Carrefour continued onward past the splashing fountain, shuffling up onto the covered porch at the far side of the courtyard. He knew this was where he would find the Holland family's sleeping rooms. He could smell her now, the planter's wife, the fair white zombie wrapped in her cool silken robes. His nostrils flared, picking up the scents of the oils and perfumes with which the healer-woman had washed her, and beneath these the reek of those stinging Northern medicines which so vainly attempted to mask the woman's undeniable condition.

For she is dead, he thought. *As dead as I . . .*

He heard something stir behind billowing curtains. Someone must have heard him.

Is it . . .?

A high-pitched scream tore through the night breeze.

It was the cry of the healer-woman, roused by Carrefour's approach. She screamed again, and soon there were more sounds, doors and windows opening, frantic footsteps. A large man ran up behind him, the boards of the porch creaking under his mass.

"Stop!" he barked. His voice was deep and masculine. "Why have you come?"

Carrefour turned and found himself face to face with the planter himself, the lord of Fort Holland. He was a powerfully built and imposing white man who was wrapped in an ornate golden night-robe.

"Why have you come?" the planter asked again, his tone angry and forceful.

The sound stirred Carrefour's rage.

Something deep within him boiled to the surface, faint memories of his own life, his life before his resurrection, when he and his brother competed for the hand of the same woman. The white man's fearsome tone echoed the outrage and betrayal in Carrefour's brother's voice on that night when he had surprised them together . . .

And yet there was another, even deeper memory awakening beneath that one, faint and ghostly grey impressions of lying on the bare wooden hull of a creaking ship as it pitched upon heaving waves, men and women wallowing for days and nights in their own filth, hearing the chanting and screaming of the entire tightly packed living brown cargo, and the vicious crack of a cat o' nine tails . . .

His lips curled back in a savage snarl.

He reached out, his long brown arms grasping eagerly for planter's neck. He could crack the man's windpipe as easily as he would crush a stalk of cane. He stepped forward, making a crude lunge for his victim.

"*Carrefour!*"

The unexpected sound of his own name caused him to stop instantly, his fingers mere inches from the planter's bare white neck.

"*Carrefour!*" came the call again.

It was the voice of the Great White Mother. She turned away from him and whispered something to one of the household servants. Carrefour could not make out all the words, but he heard her say, "Salt . . . quickly . . . brick of salt . . . only . . . return them to their graves."

He saw her now, roused from her sleep, wrapped in a long woollen shawl and with her grey hair hanging loosely. She stood in a doorway which opened onto the porch. The expression on her face was difficult to discern in the deep shadows here, but her commanding tone was unmistakable as she addressed him.

"*You must go,*" she insisted.

The Great White Mother was not to be denied. Her Northern medicine was strong. He had known hundreds of fellow islanders who had finally overcome maladies such as cholera, dysentery, and malaria only by means of her cures. But her *voodoo* was just as powerful. She had become a *mambo*, the female counterpart of their own *houngan* priest, equally skilled in the ways of island magic. It was she who had solved the dilemma of her two quarrelling sons, the rum-soaked brother and the planter, by destroying the object of their tension. It was *she* who made the planter's wife walk as a zombie.

A female servant scurried to the Great White Mother's side, bearing a brick of salt from the kitchen. The Mother held up her hand, gesturing for her servant to step back. "No need for that now, Marianne," she whispered. "He will go peacefully."

Carrefour turned and shuffled off through the courtyard, past the trickling fountain, past the watchful gaze of the giant martyred saint, past the great iron gates and, finally, onto the sandy trail beyond. Warm ocean breezes embraced him as he stepped outside the walls of Fort Holland.

He headed toward the *hounfour*.

The sound of the ceremonial drums began again softly, coming from that direction.

The *tamboulas* hammered with renewed purpose, their rhythm quickening. Flickering torchlight danced over the *sabreur*, casting bizarre distortions of his shadow on the cane-husk walls. He prepared the small effigy of the planter's wife by binding its waist with one end of a long, slender thread. As the faithful chanted, he raised the white doll and asked the spirits of the field to bless the long steel *ouanga* needle he had selected.

Carrefour watched from the edge of the circle as the doll was placed at one side and the *sabreur* crouched in position at the other. Once again the beating of the drums hastened. In time with this faster rhythm, the *sabreur* began motioning with his arms, beckoning the effigy of the planter's wife to move toward him.

As one of the worshippers gently pulled the almost invisible thread, it did.

Carrefour saw her near the beach, on the sandy trail beneath which the waves broke most loudly against the horns of jagged black rock, where they sprayed the air the widest and highest with fine mists of salty water. Even in the darkness, even through the blur of his dead eyes, he knew it was her.

The wife of the planter . . .

The woman walked the irregular trail at an unvarying pace, with her golden hair hanging limp on her shoulders and the white fabric of her gown dragging along the ground behind her.

She heeds the call of the sabreur, *but how will his needle take her?*

As if in answer, a second figure appeared on the trail, moving at an awkward pace but clearly driven by an intense passion. It was the planter's brother.

The rum-soaked man . . .

He blundered along the sand much faster than the woman, quickly overtaking her.

Carrefour noticed that there was something in the man's hand, a long and slender cylindrical object which resembled a wand or a small whip. It was only as the two white figures connected at the crest of the trail, in the brief moment before they vanished behind a shield of jagged black rocks, that Carrefour recognised the instrument which the man clutched so purposefully.

An arrow from Sebastian's chest . . .

So this was the dark magic the *sabreur* had wrought. His holy *ouanga* needle, when pressed into the doll's chest, would bring about an event that ended the dead woman's empty, ceaseless walking. Carrefour had hoped for a bolt of lightning or a column of fire, even one which would set alight the dry, rain-starved cane fields and bring ruin to the region, but not an arrow pulled from the wooden figurehead over Fort Holland's fountain.

Saint Sebastian survived his martyrdom. So too will the planter's wife rise again.

Unless . . .

He shuffled as quickly as he could toward those jagged black rocks, his immense brown feet scraping the sand like shovels. As the salty air stung his nostrils, he realised at last why he had always felt at peace near the shore, why he had always been able to hear the echoes of his ancestors who had perished in the ocean.

The salt . . .

He understood now, at last making sense of those words he had overheard the Great White Mother say to her servant, wise counsel about using a brick of salt as *voodoo* magic, to subdue a zombie.

The salt will end the suffering . . .

He was too late.

As he reached the crest of the trail, he looked down on a chamber of rock and saw the rum-soaked man standing over the woman, who lay motionless in a soft bed of sand. Saint Sebastian's arrow protruded from her heart.

Weeping softly, the man withdrew the arrow and cast it aside.

Does he truly think she is finished? Can the man believe that this is truly her end?

Carrefour descended the trail and advanced toward them.

Even above the pounding of the surf, the white man somehow heard his approach and turned to face him. Seized by panic, the man began shouting and gesturing for Carrefour to get away, but Carrefour reached out with both of his hands, extending them toward him.

The man turned back and gathered up the woman in his arms. She hung limply in his grasp, but Carrefour could already see her leg beginning to kick as her inevitable re-animation began. It would not be long.

Unless . . .

"Get away from us!" the man shouted. "Away, I say!" With the woman sprawled across his arms, he began to back up into the surf. The waves broke around his ankles, then around his knees, and then around his waist. The woman's head, dangling into the seawater, was soon submerged.

Carrefour continued his advance. It was this event for which he hoped.

The salt . . . she will taste the salt . . .

It was the village fisherman who found them.

Long before dawn, when the tide was at its highest, the dark-skinned men walked barefoot in the warm coastal waters, guided in their quest by the fluttering flames of small torches. They carried spears and tridents, quickly thrusting these sharp-edged tools at the darting fins of their elusive aquatic quarry. Less than an hour had passed and already their catch had exceeded that of the past three days, until one of the younger men spied something floundering in the water, something which was not a fish.

As the sombre column moved up the trail from the beach, two fishermen bore torches in advance of the others. A group of four of the men carried the lifeless body of the planter's rum-soaked brother. Carrefour alone transported the corpse of the planter's wife, draped over his extended arms, for none of the villagers had dared to touch her.

She no longer moved.

At last, thought Carrefour, *she has found peace.*

The sky was still dark when the grim procession reached Fort Holland. The great iron gate opened for them at the hands of servants whose heads hung in woe, though Carrefour sensed their relief in the hushed whispers they exchanged as he passed. The planter stood sadly on the porch above them, with his arms around the healer-woman. Though the healer's wrenching sobs were genuine, he sensed that the planter's grief was as false as that of his servants.

The healer then wiped away her own tears with a small chequered handkerchief and began to watch the fishermen closely, with fascination, almost as if she intended later to paint a portrait of the scene. Her stare faltered only from time to time when she daubed the corners of her eyes with the moist cloth.

The healer, he thought, *she is strong. She will go North and tell this story, so that others will come to believe* . . .

The group of fishermen laid the planter's brother gently onto the cool flat stones of the courtyard. Carrefour did the same with the limp form of the planter's wife, her robes spilling out beside her. The villagers then turned and, after respectfully placing one of their torches upright near the two limp bodies, they made their way back out through the gate.

Carrefour shuffled slowly over to the courtyard's fountain, whose water trickled like bitter tears. From the waist of his rough sackcloth trousers, he drew the single arrow which the rum-soaked man had taken from here. Carrefour placed its tip back into the small hole in the centre of the big wooden saint's chest. He pushed forcefully. The arrow sank deeply into the aperture, protruding upright.

It would stay.

As Carrefour passed through the gate, lightning flickered in the distance. It was followed by a low, faraway roll of thunder.

The rain comes, he thought.

The loa *are pleased* . . .

The cane crop will be saved.

From the distance he heard the call of the ocean, the foamy waves breaking rhythmically on the shore.

I shall join them now . . .

*   *   *

The beach glistened like fine jewels as moonlight reflected off the wave-washed sand. Salty spray burst from the rocky outcroppings, lingering ghost-like in the air after each mighty crash of the surf against the beach.

Carrefour shuffled purposefully into the wet sand. His huge brown feet sank down into the soft smooth grains, each step leaving massive divots in the beach which filled up quickly with warm saltwater and were erased by the next pass of the waves. The ocean crashed around his knees and then, as it drew itself back from the shore, began to pull him along with it, beckoning him toward its depths.

He continued to walk.

The water wrapped itself around his waist like the arms of his long-ago lover, tugging him forward, deeper. Ocean salt teased his nostrils, re-awakening long dormant memories of his life before, returning him to the long-ago time when he was alive, when he was human, when he had foolishly believed that his own death, however it might come, would be final and would bring an end to his time on Earth.

And now, he thought, *at last it shall be . . .*

Men in far lands will hear of what happened here, of this island and its mysteries. They will speak of the white healer from the North, of how she travelled to join us and learn of our ways.

The warm seawater reached Carrefour's chin, wave caps surrounding and embracing his neck. He continued to walk forward, his mouth filling with its intensely salty sting, the salt seeming to explode like gunpowder, sending images flashing through his mind in time with the flashes of lightning from the great tropical storm brewing overhead.

Men will tell her story many times, he thought. *They will whisper it by firelight, and they will write it in their books. They will draw and paint its strange scenes as they grasp hopelessly to understand them. They will retell tales of the white healer in their poems and their songs . . . their troubadours will sing of how she walked these shores accompanied by one of our own living dead . . .*

Yes, so shall they sing . . . but none shall sing for me . . .

The water covered Carrefour's unblinking eyes, salt burning them until they could see no more. The ocean closed over his head and roughly plunged him down even deeper, forcing him undersea by the roots of his woolly scalp.

In the distance he heard the shouts and cries of his ancestors, the wails of his long-ago mothers and long-ago fathers when the iron shackles of the *Brillante* dragged them under the sea, joined by the howls of terror-stuck slaves aboard the *Estrella* as its wooden hull shattered against the knife-like ridges of a hidden reef.

Their wailing slowly eased into softer calls, faraway echoes of contentment and peace, of tribal drums around crackling fires, of the hooves of zebra and wildebeest thundering in the distance across hard-packed yellow earth, of the laughter of small brown children watching, of happy group-chanting as the orange sun descended slowly on the warmth of the African plains, and of the gentle whispers of love from the lips of his brother's wife . . .

For the first time in as long as he could effectively remember, something resembling a smile curled at the edges of Carrefour's dead black lips.

Until, finally, it all went dark.

ALISON LITTLEWOOD

About the Dark

ALISON LITTLEWOOD LIVES WITH her partner Fergus in West
Yorkshire, where she dreams dreams, writes fiction and hoards
a growing collection of books with the word "dark" in the
title.

Her short fiction has appeared in such magazines as *Black
Static*, *Shadows and Tall Trees*, *Crimewave*, *Not One of Us* and
the British Fantasy Society's *Dark Horizons*. Anthology appearances include *Where Are We Going?*, *Read by Dawn Volume 3*,
Midnight Lullabies, *Full Fathom Forty*, *Best Horror of the Year
4* and the charity anthology *Never Again*.

New stories are due to appear in the anthologies *Magic*,
Resurrection Engines, *Alt.Zombie*, *Terror Tales of the Cotswolds*
and *The Screaming Book of Horror*. Another story set in caves,
this time the flooded cenotes of Mexico, is available as a chapbook from Spectral Press.

The author's first novel, *A Cold Season*, was published in
January 2012 by Jo Fletcher Books and was selected for the
Richard and Judy Book Club in the UK. *Path of Needles*, a
twisted fairy tale meets crime story, is forthcoming from the
same imprint early in 2013.

"'About the Dark' is really a meditation on the source of evil,"
Littlewood explains. "We associate bad things with dark places:
they happen in secret, away from view and the relief of daylight.
And the dark never seems to be quite empty – at least, not when
you start to stare into it.

"This story takes things a step further. What if evil didn't just happen *in* the dark – what if the evil *was* the dark? And what happens when that darkness finds an answering echo inside ourselves?"

D ARK CAVE DIDN'T sound the most promising place to hang out, but it was the driest place Adam could think of away from the town centre. Adam didn't want to be in the town centre, mainly because his latest school had an "attendance optimiser", otherwise known as a truant officer. The truant officer knew what Adam looked like, partly because of the number of times he'd hauled him back to classes, and partly because of the way Adam had tried to deck him the last time he'd tried.

He'd nearly been expelled for that one, and it was only because they decided to blame his mother that expulsion had been commuted to a three day suspension; a punishment that seemed to more than fit the crime, although not in the way they'd intended. Adam grinned at the thought, then grimaced. Blaming his mother was what everyone did. No one seemed to expect anything from his dad, least of all Adam himself.

He turned now to see Sasha flick wet hair out of her face, rubbing at her black-rimmed eyes. Adam decided not to tell her she'd smudged her make-up. No doubt she'd find out later, on her own. He exchanged looks with Fuzz, so named for his shaved head rather than any liking for the police. Fuzz nodded back. He didn't tell Sash about the smudge on her cheek, either.

There was a wall of rain behind Sash, the muted grey-green of trees beyond that. She already had a cigarette clamped between her lips and she flicked her lighter, emitting a brief flame that fizzled before it could begin.

"Get under, shit-fer," Adam said. *Shit-fer brains:* his favourite mode of address. Adam stood just beneath the cave mouth, not quite far enough that the dangling ferns couldn't drip down the back of his neck. Fuzz edged onto the rock behind him, feet slipping, sending loose pebbles down to clip Adam's feet. Adam stared at them.

"Soz," said Fuzz.

Adam didn't say anything. Sometimes he didn't have to, and that was best. That was when he knew it had worked; the face he put on, the tough words, the fists. No one messed with him anymore. Now he skived off classes because it made him look hard. That wasn't why he'd done it at his last school.

Sash started giggling, trying to get the cig to light. She couldn't. Adam rolled his eyes, snatched it away, felt damp paper under his fingers and flicked it, one-handed, out into the rain. He ignored Sash's squeal of protest. Instead he turned and looked into the cave mouth, the way its misshapen walls faded into the dark.

"You going in?" He looked at Fuzz. He didn't look at Fuzz because he wanted Fuzz to lead the way: he didn't want Fuzz to lead anything. That was Adam's job. He said it as a challenge.

"Course."

Adam didn't ask Sash. He knew she'd follow. He knew that because of the way he'd told her, once, to take off her top; the way, after a moment's hesitation, she had.

Sash had full tits, for a skinny lass. Adam remembered them now, thought of how they would feel under his hands in the rain, the way her top would stick to them. He felt a flush of warmth beneath the cool air that rose from the cave. There was a smell, too; dank stone, mingling with the scent of rain. He wrinkled his nose. "Come on," he said, and stepped forward. He flicked on his own lighter as he went.

It was more difficult than Adam had expected. The lighter emitted a circular glow, highlighting each finger in glowing blood red, but not illuminating much else. It was hot and he kept switching hands, pulling a face he knew no one could see. He felt the irregular rock through his shoes. He heard the others following, their footsteps seeming more sure than his own. That wouldn't do. He couldn't show weakness; something he'd learned the hard way. Weakness painted a target on your back.

Now he was the one who punched and spat and made boasts and smoked, the one who led. He had assumed his new role when he started his new school. It had been like slipping on a new skin, but sometimes he could still feel it moving over his old one, loose and ill-fitting.

He switched hands again, jumped as Sash behind him flicked her own lighter. It lit the wall at Adam's side and he saw old lettering there, as though this place had been better used, once; the remnants of old names, old lives. Now they were little more than fragments; he couldn't make out the words. He wondered who had been here, whether they smoked or drank or fucked in the dark. He grinned as he stepped forward and, not watching his feet, slipped. He almost went down.

There came a light giggle behind him.

Adam straightened his back, started to turn. Such things couldn't be allowed to go on or they only got bigger. He knew this in ways the others didn't. As he turned, though, Sash swore and Adam heard her lighter drop, the sharp sound of plastic shattering. A moment later there came an acrid smell.

"Fucker burned me," she said. She sounded upset.

Adam knew Sash couldn't afford another lighter, couldn't afford much of anything. He opened his mouth to tell her she could use his whenever she wanted, then closed it again. "Stop pissing about," he said.

The ground beneath his feet started to slope downward. Adam lowered the light, trying to make out the way, but could see nothing. He started down anyway; realised, after a few strides, that he couldn't hear the others. He turned and saw two dark shapes against the glow from the entrance, their faces outlined by the light of his flame. "What's up?" he said.

"I'm not going down there," said Sash. She sounded close to panic. "I don't like this, Ad. It's opening out; how we gonna find our way? We could get lost."

Fuzz didn't say anything. He didn't follow Adam, either.

"There are stories," Sash said, "about Dark Cave."

Adam snorted. "Stories are for kids." He took another few steps as if to demonstrate, but when he glanced around he saw that Sash was right. The cave had broadened out; he could no longer see the walls. He looked back at Sash and Fuzz. They hadn't moved. They were still dark shapes, but their faces had gone. For a while he didn't say anything, and neither did they. It struck him that they might not speak, that it might not even be Sash and Fuzz standing there. His mates had turned tail and fled into the sunlight, leaving only these shadows behind.

Then Sash did speak, and Adam took a breath. "I don't want to," she said. "Why don't we go and have a cig, instead? I could try and find my lighter."

"Just a bit further," Adam said. "Then we'll sit down and you can tell us all about Dark Cave." He paused, deepened his voice. "Tell us ze ghost stories, mwa ha ha . . ."

Sash didn't laugh, but she did get moving. Adam turned and went on. Their footsteps echoed around him, a confusion of sound, but he knew that Fuzz would be following too. Sometimes Adam thought that kid was sweet on Sasha. Then he remembered the way Fuzz had been when Sash took off her top: the way he'd kept his eyes on Adam all the time, not saying a word. Fuzz had never even looked at Sash, at all.

"Here," Adam said, bending low and scanning the floor. A low outcrop of rocks glowed almost yellow in the flame; he sat down on the nearest. The others sat too. Fuzz made a "tch" sound and pulled something from his pocket. Another light sprung to life in the boy's hands, and Adam cursed himself for not thinking of it sooner. It was Fuzz's mobile phone. After a few seconds the light winked out and Fuzz pressed a button to light it up again. Adam wasn't sure he liked it. It made the dark draw back a little, but the bluish glow made everything cold.

Fuzz crossed one boot over the other. "Nice ere, innit," he said.

Adam cleared his throat. "So, Sash," he said. "Tell us about the ghosts."

She turned her head. Her face looked pale. "Aren't no ghosts in Dark Cave."

"But you said . . ."

"I didn't say there were ghosts. I said there were stories." She wrapped her arms around her skinny body.

"Same difference."

Sash glanced over her shoulder, into the dark. Adam looked too, but there was nothing there. There was nothing around them at all; it was like they were floating. He shivered. *It's not me*, he thought, *it's them*, and he didn't know why: only that the words were in his mind, playing over like an echo.

It's not me. It's them.

"So what are the stories, Sash?" Fuzz's voice was gentle.

"They're about old stuff. My Nan told me. About when people used to come here, and what they used to do."

Adam wanted to snort, but he did not.

"What stories, Sash?" Fuzz prompted.

"They're about what's in here." Sash glanced around again.

"So tell us."

But Sash didn't. She got to her feet, so abruptly she knocked Fuzz's phone out of his hands. There was a splay of light and a gritting sound, and then the dark ate it.

"*Sash.*"

She didn't answer.

Fuzz got up, feeling about for his phone.

"Wait," said Adam. It came out louder than he'd intended and he expected to hear his own voice coming back from the walls – *wait – wait – wait* – but there was nothing. He didn't know which was worse, hearing an echo or not hearing it. "I'll make a bit of light."

He stood, reached for his bag, rummaged through the contents. He pulled out some exercise books, flicked to the back of one, steadied it with the fist holding his lighter and ripped out the blank pages. He crumpled them, placed them where he'd been sitting. He could feel the dark at his back, and he didn't like it. He'd felt better when he was inside the circle. He bent and put the flame to the paper. It flared, and he saw what lay around them.

Their shadows rose and danced on the walls. The cavern was roughly circular. There were no other tunnels that he could see. There was more writing on the walls, though: names, dates. Adam glanced at the fire and saw the last ball of paper catch. It flared but the blackness flooded back anyway, as though the dark had grown, was reclaiming its territory. Then the fire went out.

"I'm getting out of here," said Sash. She took a couple of steps into the dark then stopped. Adam almost – not quite – reached out to pull her back.

"Wait," said Fuzz. His voice was oddly high, and it struck Adam that fear was catching, that it had leapt from one of them to the next just as the flame had spread from paper to paper. Fuzz pressed a switch and the cold blue light was back again: he had found his phone. He went after Sash and became a black shape.

Adam's own lighter flickered and went out.

He didn't curse, didn't say anything at all. He was in the dark and he could feel its cold fingers on his skin, touching his clothes, his face, his eyes. He didn't want to move; all he wanted was for it to stop. His hands shook around the lighter. Then the flame sprang up and the shadows shrank from him.

He could no longer see Sash and Fuzz. Adam kept his eyes on the flame he held, feeling the darkness massing at his back as he started after them.

"The stories are about the dark," said Sash. She held a cigarette to her lips and it shook in her hands. She was sitting on the low, twisted branch of a tree. Adam looked away, down at the woodland floor. It was covered in fallen leaves; another year dying.

"My Nan says they used to think the dark lived in the cave. So they'd send people in, you know – to test them. To see if they could handle it. Sometimes they came out and sometimes they didn't. The ones who didn't, who got fed to the dark, they had their names written on the walls, see? And then the dark would go away for another year, like they were sacrifices or something. It kept it away, right?" She paused. "I thought it was stupid. But—"

Fuzz touched Sasha's arm. "What do you mean, sometimes the dark was there? It's Dark Cave. Of course, the dark was there. It's there all the time."

"Not *this* dark," Sash said, taking another draw.

Fuzz waited. So did Adam.

"There was this special darkness, see. It was there no matter what. You could walk into that dark with the brightest torch, my Nan said, and it'd still be dark. All that'll happen is, your light'll be quenched. That's how she put it: quenched. Like thirst."

Adam scowled, shuffling his foot through withered leaves. The earth beneath it was a deep, rich black. He stopped.

"You couldn't put it out, that dark. People just went into it and there was nothing to light their way. They went in and either they came back or they didn't. No one knows what happened to the ones who didn't."

Adam thought again of the names he'd glimpsed on the walls. He let out an exasperated sound. There were so many: too many. If that many people had disappeared around here, someone would know. They'd have stopped it. More likely the cave had been the haunt of people like him. They'd written their own names there, and no one had come to wipe them away. Why would they? The cave was nothing special. It went so far and no further; like everything else in life, a disappointment. He realised the others were looking at him and scowled.

"I felt it," said Fuzz.

"Oh, for Christ's sake. You felt her panicking. And you turned chickenshit." Adam turned away. "It's about time you grew up, Fuzz." And then he thought: *It's not them. It's me. Only, I couldn't feel it because they were there.* He didn't know why he thought it. It didn't even seem quite right, not really. He only knew that the taste of the place had stayed with him, like an echo but with a feeling instead of sound.

Sash pushed herself up. "I've had enough of this. I'm off. You coming, Fuzz?"

It happened quickly. Fuzz nodded and the two of them headed away, threading between the trees. Adam opened his mouth to call after them, some insult, or a question maybe: like, where they were going. Like, what they thought they were doing, just the two of them. Then he closed it again. It didn't do to care, didn't do to let people fuck you over. If they wanted to be alone, let them. He wasn't going to make them think he gave a shit. Besides, he had better things to do. The other two could wait.

Daylight was fading when Adam found himself standing outside the cave once more, but he knew it didn't matter; it would be dark inside anyway. It was different, being in the woods on his own. He didn't know if he missed the others. He liked the clean air, the way the trees waved at him and the cave mouth opened as though to swallow him. He wasn't sure he minded the idea of disappearing into it. He thought of the way his mother had been that morning. She'd been passed out on the sofa, an empty bottle at her side. This time it was gin, not wine. Ordinarily Adam would have been upset, but it gave him the chance to take a couple of tenners from her purse.

Adam had been shopping. Now, he pulled the first item from his bag: a large torch. The weight of it was comforting and he smacked it into his palm a few times. He opened the slot, inserted the batteries he'd bought. Now it was even heavier. He flicked it on and off a few times, watched the beam disappear into the dregs of daylight. He looked towards the cave. There was nothing to wait for. He turned his back on the trees and started walking.

This time, it was easier. The torch highlighted each irregularity in the ground, filling each dip with ink-black wells. They looked almost like footprints and Adam grimaced as he placed his feet into them. When he shone the light on the walls, he saw that there *was* writing on them. He made out occasional letters; more names, maybe. Then he found an almost complete date: 1971, years ago. The paint was cracked, crumbling away. Adam wondered what the date had meant, why it was important enough for someone to write it here. Someone's birthday perhaps, or the day a couple met: sealed with a loving kiss. Sash and Fuzz, sitting in a tree, K-I-S-S-I-N-G. Adam scowled.

He stood there, listening to the sound of water dripping onto rock. There was no other noise: no traffic, no voices, no teacher droning a list of facts he was supposed to remember. This time, when he went on, Adam smiled. He reached the chamber and shone his torch around it. The space was indeed roughly circular, and about twice his height. There was writing here too, and in places it was fresher. There were more names and more dates, just like Sash had said. Adam frowned. Why only names? Dates that had once meant something to somebody, and now meant nothing that he could tell?

There was darkness in the centre of the cave. Adam looked into it. He couldn't make out the wall beyond that part. It must be too far off for his torch to reach, or perhaps there was another tunnel after all. He started to walk round the outside of the cave, tracing the wall with his fingertips. Soon he stood at the opposite side. There was no other tunnel; the wall was solid. Adam looked down at the floor and saw deep wrinkles in it, grooves leading towards the centre of the cave. They went into the dark and were lost to view. Adam shone the light along one of them. He still couldn't see where it led. He shone it up at the ceiling. Bright lines flashed down, water dripping in the torchlight. He frowned, tried to watch them all the way to the floor. He could not.

Adam didn't like the dark. He found his heart was thudding, a solid, heavy sound that reminded him he was alive, he was flesh and skin and bone, and could be taken apart quite easily. Could be sliced and bitten and ended.

He realised he couldn't see the way out now. There should be a faint glow coming from the entrance, but it wasn't there. Adam shone the torch straight ahead, into the dark. The beam was swallowed up. He heard his own breath, too loud. It sounded like some animal: a bear perhaps, or a wolf. He blinked. It made no difference to what he could see and what he couldn't.

He shuffled quickly on around the cave wall, and realised he could see the tunnel after all. It was as though something had been blocking his sight. As he went on a few more steps, the whole, roughly circular shape of it came into view.

Adam closed his eyes. He was letting Sasha's stories get to him. Of course, he hadn't been able to see the tunnel: the torchlight had spoiled his night vision. If he'd just turned it off, let his eyes adjust, he would have seen it all the time.

Now he stood by the way out and turned back towards the centre of the cave. The darkness was there. There was something wrong with it. Adam frowned. There was one way to prove this was stupid, that Sasha was wrong, and that was to go in. He would go into the dark and banish the thought of the way she'd looked at him when she walked away with Fuzz.

Sash with her smooth, pale tits. Her laugh. Her grin.

Adam still didn't move. He didn't like the dark. It looked too solid somehow, especially when he looked at it dead on. Like a roughly circular patch of – *something*. And there was something else; a feeling of watchfulness, of waiting. Of presence.

Adam shook his head. It was like standing in an old house and telling yourself not to think of ghosts. The moment you did, every shadow was brought to life, every room given breath. It wasn't that anything was there, not really. "Nothing outside your mind," he said out loud, and wished he hadn't. He let out another sound; a hiss of irritation, at himself and this whole stupid place, the way the three of them had parted. It was this place's fault. He had done everything right, put on the skin he'd needed, the bravado and the toughness that got him through. It was the cave that had fucked everything up.

"I'll show you," he said, and this time it seemed all right to say it out loud.

Adam shone the torchlight down at the floor. It found one of those deep grooves, and he placed his feet on either side of it. He took one step forward, and another. It was easy once he'd started. One after the next. The light moved forward and the dark retreated. When Adam looked into it, though, it seemed to swirl in front of his eyes. Coalescing. Massing. He took another step and the light went out.

Adam caught his breath, started back the way he'd come. He couldn't stop himself. He didn't think about where he was putting his feet, slipped into that groove in the floor, caught himself from falling. He had to get away; had to put some space between him and the dark before he could turn his back on it. When he'd gone far enough he turned and ran, not stopping to take out his lighter. Adam didn't stop running until he was out of the cave mouth and into the trees, turning again so that the cave was no longer behind him. He leaned against a tree trunk, panting, hands on his knees. He let his breath come quick and fast. Then he started to laugh.

The torch was still in his hand and he shook it. The batteries rattled in their compartment. Duff batteries: of course they were. That was all there was to it, just his sodding luck. He laughed again. He turned the torch over in his hands, flicked the switch. His eyes shut involuntarily as bright light flooded his face.

"Hey: Fuzz, Sash." They stood by the tree, a sorry thing that had been shorn of its lower branches. The tree stood in the centre of the school yard and its branches had been cut off to stop kids from swinging on them.

Sash scraped her foot across the concrete, staring at it fixedly. It was Fuzz who said, "All right?"

"I'm going back to the cave." Adam said the words casually then wished he hadn't. He should have made it a boast, one they'd have to rise to. Now Sash looked away, staring at the school as though she longed to be inside.

"Tonight. I've got a torch. You coming? It'll be a laugh." Adam stuck his hands in his pockets, straightened his back.

After a moment, Fuzz shook his head. "Sash is coming to ours," he said. He made a movement, a jerk of his arm as though he'd been going to reach for her.

"You're scared," Adam tried. "Chickenshit."

"All right," said Fuzz. He wiped his sleeve across his mouth. "We're chickenshit. Come on, Sash. We need to get to French."

She nodded. Then she met Adam's eye. "I'm not going back," she said.

Adam looked at her for a moment. He remembered the way she'd taken off her top. The way he'd thought it meant something: the way he'd looked at her and Fuzz hadn't. Now he realised that maybe it did.

But Fuzz was already moving. He took Sash's arm, kept hold of it as he led her away. As he *led*. *Fuzz*.

Adam scowled after them. If they chose not to be a part of this, fair enough. It was something special he had found, that he had led them to. If they turned their back on it . . . he spat. Their loss.

It's not them. It's me.

He turned and started walking towards the road. If the others weren't coming, there was no need for him to wait. No need to wait, at all.

The mouth of the cave looked smaller than Adam remembered. It didn't look scary, or forbidding, or welcoming. It didn't look like anything special. It just looked like what it was, an unexciting cave in an unexciting wood, clinging to the edge of an unexciting town. Adam thought of the first time they'd come here, the three of them laughing, hurrying into the cave so that Sash could light her cigarette. No, not laughing.

He shook his head. The others had no part in this. The dark was for him, and him alone. He was supposed to go inside. He knew the cave had drawn him back: he just didn't know why.

He got the torch from his bag and it lit when he flicked the switch. He started walking.

The next time Adam looked about, he was in the chamber. He blinked. He didn't remember the tunnel, didn't remember if the footing had been damp or dry, whether he had slipped. It was nothing; just a blank. Like the space he saw in front of him.

The dark was there. Adam looked into it, and it seemed to him that the dark looked back. Adam listened. He felt he should be able to hear something, but there was only a faint silvering on the edge of hearing; something that could have been the blood in his veins or the wind outside or the sound the dark made.

Adam put down the torch and his bag, rummaged through what was inside. More exercise books, one with the blank pages missing. He couldn't remember which went with which subject, which classroom, which teacher. It didn't matter. This time he tore all the pages out, crumpled some so that they would catch. He got his cigarette lighter and set it to the paper, used another book to bat the flame towards the middle of the cave.

It fluttered to the ground and went out. It hadn't gone far enough. Adam knew this because he could still see a faint glow where the paper smouldered.

This time he went closer before he flung the fire into the dark. Again, it went out. This time the change was so sudden Adam blinked. One moment the paper was there; the next it was not. It had fallen further in this time. There was nothing left to see, not a single smouldering page. The dark had taken it.

What was it Sash had said? *They'd send people in. Sometimes they came out, and sometimes they didn't.*

Adam stood there. He thought about his mother, waiting back home. No, not waiting. Drinking. His mother's mouth to the bottle as though she was sucking in life. His father at the television, taking in its babble with greedy eyes.

Sometimes they didn't.

Adam's heart beat faster. It was a small, captured thing between his ribs. He wondered what would happen to it if he went into the dark; whether it would end up somewhere new, or if it would burst. He took a step forward, hadn't known he was going to. And he realised he could see something in the dark, after all: something that was only for him. It was waiting. Adam didn't close his eyes. As he walked into the dark, he knew it wouldn't make the slightest bit of difference.

* * *

Adam stepped towards the edge of the cavern. The torch had gone out, but he could see everything. It was all so bright, now. He swept up the torch and his bag then let them fall again. He didn't need them any longer. He smiled. The dark had filled him. There were no longer any questions, any worries. He was full, entirely full; no room left for different skins, different faces. That was behind him now. The dark had swallowed him, making him whole. Making Adam truly himself.

He looked around and saw the names written on the walls. He could see them clearly, even the ones where no ink remained. Adam smiled: almost laughed. The words he had heard on his first visit echoed through him. He had been right after all: *it's not me. It's them.*

He had expected to find his name written here, but it was not. These were not the names of the chosen, the initiated, the others like him. These were the names of the reluctant, of all those who had looked into the dark and turned away, denied its name. They were the ones who disappeared: the unwilling. The ones who had to be forced, to be made to see. Like Sasha and Fuzz. So that they were made a part of it; part of the dark. The ones who needed to be led.

Adam leaned into the wall, running his hands over its roughness. He could sense that he was close. He searched until he found the right place. There was a sharp jut of rock and he cut his palm against it, wiped the blood onto his fingers. He glanced towards the centre of the cave. He knew it was different now; the dark wasn't there anymore, not really. Adam wasn't worried. He carried it inside him, and when he needed it, it would be there. He turned back to the wall, could see every dip and wrinkle in the rock. He stared at it, eyes wide and bulging. And he smiled as he smeared the blood across it; the pact-blood that acknowledged what he was going to do. Acknowledged it and let it in as he wrote their names.

DANIEL MILLS

The Photographer's Tale

DANIEL MILLS LIVES IN Vermont, New England. He is the author of the novel *Revenants*: *A Dream of New England* from Chômu Press, and his short fiction has appeared or is forthcoming in a variety of venues, including *Historical Lovecraft*, *Delicate Toxins*, *Supernatural Tales 20*, *Aklonomicon*, *Dadaoism*, *A Season in Carcosa* and *The Grimscribe's Puppets*.

"Spirit photography has existed for nearly as long as the photographic medium itself," explains Mills. "As early as 1869, engraver and amateur photographer William H. Mumler was tried on charges of fraud in relation to his purported images of the dead.

"Likewise the haunted photograph is a well-established horror trope, one that has far outlasted the heyday of spirit photography. In such stories, the haunting is typically presented to the reader as a phenomenon of the development process – i.e. a photograph of an unremarkable scene is developed to reveal the otherwise invisible presence of a ghost. Horror ensues.

"'The Photographer's Tale' attempts a variation on the now-familiar model. Here the camera lens itself – rather than the process of development – serves as the agent of unearthly revelation. In the viewfinder, the protagonist Lowell obtains a glimpse of the Other – of the future, perhaps, the soul in all of its grotesque splendour.

"This other reality defies all attempts at illumination, all of Lowell's efforts to capture or contain it via film. As he himself describes it: 'There are places – interiors, I mean – corners so dark they cannot be lighted.' His flash powder burns but cannot chase away the darkness.

"By the time his tale concludes, he is left alone, with nothing save his guilt, his unconfessed sins, and the endless New England winter."

I HEARD THIS STORY from a passing acquaintance, a fellow photographer whom we shall call Lowell. I met Lowell in June of last year at a mountaintop resort in northern Vermont. I had travelled there for my health and was surprised to meet another who shared my profession.

The two of us struck up a conversation one evening after supper as we took cigars on the veranda – two old men alone with the wild hills before us. The darkness covered us completely and Lowell's haggard features were visible only by the pale orange tip of his cigar.

Photographic technique was the object of our discussion. As I recall, we argued back and forth for some time regarding the utility of the new flash lamp.

"I'm not denying that it might be useful," Lowell conceded. "But only up to a point. There are places – interiors, I mean – corners so dark they cannot be lighted."

I shook my head. "I'm afraid I don't follow you."

He exhaled heavily, releasing a cloud of smoke. His mood was unreadable. Turning from me, he looked out toward the distant mountains, black beneath the hidden moon. A long minute elapsed, a silence spun from the murmur of crickets, the occasional scrap of bird song.

He sighed. "Perhaps I had better explain."

The morning of 1 December, 1892 dawned cold and grey, promising an early snowfall. After breakfasting in his apartment, Lowell descended the back stair to his studio, where he was surprised to find that a shipping crate had been left for him with the first post. There was no return address, but he recognised the handwriting on the label and knew it to be from Patrick.

Lowell had first encountered the boy on the streets of Providence some twelve years before. Patrick was no more than eight or nine at the time, one among hundreds of beggar children who had resorted to thievery and worse in order to survive. One night in October, Lowell returned to his studio to find the boy curled up in the doorway: soaked and shivering, delirious with fever. Lowell brought him inside and allowed him to spend the night.

Days went by – Patrick's health improved – but Lowell did not turn him out. The boy served as his apprentice for the next seven years, assisting in the darkroom in exchange for room and board. Their relationship was a close one, and in time, the unmarried Lowell came to regard the lad as his own son, only for Patrick to leave him – as sons will do – at the age of sixteen.

Whatever its cause, their final parting, when it came, was not amicable. Lowell blamed himself for it. He sought shelter in alcoholism and later in the Church. Five years passed. His letters to Patrick went unanswered but from time to time he received word of his former apprentice from colleagues in New York.

In 1892, Patrick was just twenty-one years old but already esteemed an expert in the field of portrait photography. He was said to possess an eye for hidden beauty and feeling that allowed him to reveal, with considerable skill, "the very soul" of his subject. Lowell admitted to a twinge of jealousy in this. Certainly, his own work had never inspired such hyperbole.

He knelt before the shipping crate and lifted the lid, peeling back layers of straw and brown paper to reveal a view camera. It was a newer model, equipped with a built-in viewfinder and little used by its appearance. A length of ribbon had been fastened around the front standard, the ends tied up in an elaborate bow.

Lowell plucked the camera out of the crate and tested the action of the shutter. *Click*. Hearing the sound, he exhaled, his anxiety evaporating like shadows at sundown. He hurried to the doorway and took down his hat and coat. His first client was not due for another hour, giving him plenty of time to walk to the post office and send off a telegram of thanks to New York.

Outside, the weather was dismal, but the avenue bustled with the usual crowds of carriages and pedestrians. Clerks and scriveners scurried past Lowell en route to their respective offices while paperboys shouted the day's headlines from every corner, their voices ringing shrilly above the rattle of wheels on cobble.

A pair of young women proceeded down the pavement in his direction – sisters, evidently, their good humour unaffected by the wind and imminent snow. The two walked arm-in-arm, laughing, even as their guardian gasped and panted behind them, burdened by a picnic basket and a pair of canvas shopping bags.

One of the sisters smiled at Lowell. The other tittered and tightened her grip on her sister's elbow. Their treatment of their guardian showed them to be callous, even cruel, but Lowell grinned back at them all the same. He could hardly do otherwise: they were simply too young, too beautiful, too alive.

He crossed the street to the next block and passed Saint Andrew's church, where he had begun attending mass. Every Sunday morning, he knelt before the altar and prayed, rocked by yearning though he dared not take the Host. That morning, walking past, he let his fingers trail along the rough stones and sighed as the great bell struck the half-hour.

At the post office, he composed a brief message to be wired to Patrick's studio in New York. *Rec'd camera*, the wire read. *Deepest thanks. Please write.*

He asked the clerk to contact him in the event of any delays and then hurried home to keep his first appointment, smiling first at the sisters, whom he passed once more, and then at the paperboy, unable to contain his elation, even in that late season, even as the first flakes of snow drifted down and settled in his hair.

Mrs Lavinia Perkins was Lowell's most reliable client, a middle-aged teetotaller of extraordinary vanity and peculiar habit – to wit, her insistence on having a new photograph of herself taken on the first of every month. She used these to chart the course and extent of her ageing, scouring each monochrome image for signs of greying hair. This was, of course, an impossible task, but perhaps this was why she preferred the photographer's lens to that more ordinary (and less expensive) instrument: the mirror.

On that morning she breezed into the room with the haughty assurance of a beloved monarch. She did not even wish Lowell good morning but instead assumed her usual pose against her favourite backdrop: a canvas sheet painted with a classical motif, three ruined columns like a row of broken teeth.

Lowell had already positioned Patrick's camera on the tripod and focused the lens. The plate was loaded, the flash box readied, and he wasted no time in going beneath the hood.

"Are you ready?" he asked.

Her pose spoke for itself. She stood perfectly erect, one arm draped over the Brady stand, and turned her face from the camera so that she appeared in profile.

He lifted the flash box with one hand and sighted the widow through the viewfinder. He steadied his fingers over the triggers for flash and shutter and began to count down, whispering the numbers to himself in the blackness of the hood.

Three. Two. One.

The widow changed.

Her brown curls turned wiry and grey even as her cheekbones sloped inward and stretched the mottled skin to breaking. From beneath her sallow flesh there emerged the outline of a skull, which threatened to burst from the tattered sinews of her once-beautiful face. Even her teeth, usually white, had become brown and stained by the corruptions of the grave.

Lowell wanted to close his eyes but in the manner of a nightmare found that he could not – not even when the tail of a worm thrust out from behind her ear, puncturing the skin so that a shower of corpse dust drifted to the ground.

"Well?" the widow inquired. Her voice, at least, was unaltered, but the coolness of her tone did nothing to dispel the image in the viewfinder. "Is something wrong?"

"Ah – um?"

Sweat poured from Lowell's brow.

"What is the delay?"

The widow turned to face him. Her eyes were gone: the sockets empty, rimmed with pitted bone. A mass of white worms writhed within the hollow of her skull.

He released the trigger on the flash box. The magnesium ignited and a wave of cleansing light flooded the room. Somehow he possessed the presence of mind to open and close the shutter, capturing the widow in a blast of white lightning.

He wrenched his head from the hood and dashed to the side cabinet. There he found the brandy bottle, untouched in the days since his conversion. His heart galloped, fuelling his panic, and his lungs heaved in his chest – faster and faster, refusing to slow.

He poured himself a glass. He gulped it down.

"Whatever is the matter?" Mrs Perkins asked. "You're acting most peculiarly."

The room shimmered, retreating from Lowell as the alcohol took hold. He clenched his eyes shut. He shook his head but could not speak.

"Open your eyes," she snapped. "Look at me!"

It required all of his courage for Lowell to lift his head and address the widow. Her appearance had returned – mercifully – to normal. She peered at him through the lenses of her silver lorgnette, her magnified eyes more hawk-like than ever.

"I'm – quite well," Lowell gasped. "It's the – weather. My gout—"

She nodded thoughtfully. "I'm glad it's nothing serious," she said. "Did you get the picture?"

He shivered. He poured another glass and drained it in a swallow. Tears leapt to his eyes as the familiar ache spread through his chest. Mrs Perkins sniffed in disapproval, but at that moment, he scarcely cared. Even the thought of that photograph chilled him to the marrow.

"Well?" she demanded. "Shall we take another?"

"No," he said quickly. "There's – no need."

"Good." She cast a scornful glance at the glass in his hand. "I shall come by later this week to collect it. Good day."

She proceeded to the door and let herself out.

The catch slammed behind her.

Lowell gulped down another drink. The alcohol steadied his hands somewhat but could not drive out the images that crowded about him. When he shut his eyes, he saw the widow as she had appeared through the viewfinder: gaping eye-sockets, the skull that surfaced from beneath her thinning skin. Other images too. Blue eyes, bruises. A palm-print on white skin.

He poured a fourth glass and contemplated the liquid for a full minute before returning it to the bottle. Already he regretted this return to his old habits. Guilt rose like a tumour in his throat, an ever-familiar gorge he could not spit out or swallow.

He mopped the sweat from his brow. Turning his attention to more material concerns, he replaced the bottle in the side cabinet and went into the darkroom to ready the developer.

In the years since his conversion, Lowell had come to see the development process as a kind of miracle. While he was familiar with the various chemical principles at work, he could not but marvel at the thing itself, which he understood as a singular indicator of God's grace. To watch a human face form on albumen paper, to see it slowly assume shape, its fine lines betraying either hope, or grief, or pain—

In those moments, Lowell admitted, his very soul ached, and he imagined the birth of the planet from the void, the first word of light like the flash of torched magnesium.

But that morning he found no joy in developing the plate. His hands shook with fright, and his fingers kneaded the flesh of his palms, his nails drawing blood as the positive image formed on the albumen.

His fears proved baseless. The widow Perkins appeared looking much as she always did. While her pose was slightly different – for here she looked directly into the camera, confusion playing on her features – the photograph closely resembled the three dozen he had already taken of the widow. In no way did it hint at the horror he had witnessed through the viewfinder.

He made a second print of the photograph and left the darkroom, feeling neither terror nor relief – only a persistent unease. He settled himself down in a chair beside the window and allowed his gaze to stray into the street.

Snow continued to fall. Nearly an inch had accumulated in the last hour, covering over muck and dirtied straw. The clustered roofs and gambrels of the block opposite bore a fine dusting, as iridescent and fine as a poplar's cotton. Even the soot-black stacks of the distant metal-works appeared white and pure, standing like twin ghosts against the horizon, holding back the early dark. Soon the city would be covered, first by snow and then by night – all beauty and squalor erased by the whispered sough of white on black.

* * *

His sleep proved shallow and troubled, haunted by visions of blazing cities and crumbling churches, the worm-filled skull of the widow Perkins. To his relief, he was roused by the sound of the bell. He wiped the sleep from his eyes and went to answer.

He opened the door to reveal a clerk from the post office. The young man was clearly possessed of a nervous disposition. His eyes darted furtively from side to side, settling on Lowell seemingly by accident.

"Your wire, sir—"

"Yes?"

"It came back, sir."

"Came back?"

"Could not be delivered, sir."

"Has he moved?" wondered Lowell, half to himself.

"I don't know, sir," said the clerk, miserably.

"Then find out!" snapped Lowell. "Wire New York and see what you can learn from them. Then try sending the message through again. It's – important."

"Yes, sir. Of course, sir."

"Good."

The clerk looked down at his feet. His natural nervousness grew more apparent with every second he lingered on the stoop.

Lowell sighed, regretting his outburst. "Go on then," he said, as gently as he could manage. "I'll try and drop by later. That should save you the trip."

"Yes, sir. Thank you, sir."

The clerk donned his hat and shuffled from the stoop. Lowell watched him disappear down the alleyway and then looked up, finding the sky in a crack between two buildings. The blizzard had intensified since morning, leaving the heavens snow-filled and sunless, iron-grey but for a varicose network of dark veins and fractures.

He turned from the doorway. A quick consultation of his watch showed the time to be a quarter to three. He pushed shut the door and returned to the studio to ready it for his next appointment. Less than an hour remained before Arthur Whateley and his young wife, married in November, were due to arrive.

He unrolled the pastoral background on which they had already agreed, arranged two chairs before it, and fell to the task of readying the camera – Patrick's camera. While the results of the development process had not put his earlier terror to flight, they had at least given him courage, and he resolved to confront his fears. To this end, he positioned Patrick's camera at the appropriate distance from the canvas and drew a breath before lifting the flaps over his head.

He peered through the viewfinder at the wall of his studio. His palms were slick – his breathing rapid – but no dread apparition materialised to confront him. Instead he saw only the painted trees of the familiar country scene. Their leaves wavered, delicate and still, as though waiting for the first breath of wind, a summer storm sure to come.

Arthur Whateley was one of those rare men upon whom Fortune has never ceased to smile. Wealthy, well groomed, and recently wed, his generosity was matched only by the honeyed warmth of his voice and by the kindness of his demeanour. He was handsome, notably so, but his dusky good looks were more than equalled by the beauty of his wife Gertrude, a noted heiress. She was, like him, dark of hair and eye, but blessed with a delicate complexion, with cheeks that flushed to a subtle rose-colour and would not tolerate the sun.

Whateley himself was in all respects a consummate gentleman. Lowell had met him for the first time two weeks before when the young tycoon first came to the studio to make arrangements for his formal wedding portrait. Lowell had found him as charming and personable as any man he had ever met, well versed in an array of subjects ranging from architecture to the theatre and indeed most topics one could name.

He was also exceedingly punctual. At half-past three, the bell sounded, and Lowell hurried to the door to admit the happy couple. Arthur grinned broadly and offered his hand. Mrs Whateley blushed to meet Lowell's gaze and wished him a soft "how do." She wore an unusual amount of face powder and the skin surrounding her eyes was strikingly pale.

"Please come in," said Lowell. "Everything's ready."

"Excellent!" Arthur exclaimed. "But I'm afraid we cannot stay long. My wife and I are expected at the Grand in half-an-hour's time."

"I understand perfectly," said Lowell. "This will not take a minute."

"Have you been?"

"To – to the Grand?"

"No? Then you must join us there sometime."

"Why – of course," said Lowell, taken off guard. "I would be honoured."

"It's settled, then. Shall we take the picture?"

"By all means." Lowell gestured in the direction of the prepared background. "I believe we agreed on a seated portrait?"

"Indeed we did," said Arthur.

He steered his wife across the room and helped her settle into a chair before taking the seat beside her, one hand thrust into his jacket, the other resting lightly on her knee.

"Ready when you are," said Arthur.

Lowell approached the tripod. "And you, Mrs Whateley?"

Her husband answered. "Oh, you needn't worry about Gertie," he said cheerfully. "Isn't that right, darling?"

Mrs Whateley nodded but said nothing.

"Shall we proceed?" asked Arthur.

"Of course," said Lowell, nodding. He had already prepared the collodion mixture and adjusted the lens. All that remained was to open the shutter. Taking up the flash box, he slipped his head under the cover and placed his eye against the viewfinder.

The powder had vanished from Mrs Whateley's brow. In its place he noted the swelling of an under-skin bruise. As Lowell watched, the colours continued to deepen and spread, leaching through flesh and tissue to collect in a series of purple bruises down her neck, forming the imprint of a man's hand around her throat.

Lowell's stomach clenched. The air left his lungs, and he gasped for breath that would not come. She looked up at him then – perhaps only to wonder what was taking so long – and in her eyes he saw a silent suffering, such as he had once glimpsed in the eyes of another, and all at once, he understood everything.

Whateley had come to him seeking concealment. Like many clients, he wanted an image of false happiness, another mask for the violence and cruelty they both strove to hide – he with his airs and false benevolence and she with her daubs and powders. Mrs Whateley gazed back at Lowell through the viewfinder, her eyes bloodied and sightless.

He swallowed.

"I'm sorry," he said. He withdrew from the hood and stepped away from the camera. "But I'm afraid I cannot take the picture. You will have to go elsewhere."

"You're *sorry*?" erupted Whateley. "What in God's name are you talking about? Is there some kind of – problem – with the camera?"

Lowell shook his head.

"What, then?"

"I cannot take the picture," he repeated. "I'm sorry."

"You owe me an explanation."

Lowell looked from the camera to the seated couple. He exhaled. "Yes," he conceded. "Perhaps you're right."

"Well?"

He pointed to the area above his own right eye and nodded toward Mrs Whateley. "It's her make-up. It's playing havoc with this light. Could we try one without?"

Whateley's face turned crimson. He sprang up from the chair and grabbed hold of his wife's arm. Without a word, he dragged her to her feet and spirited her toward the doorway.

In the entryway, he retrieved his cane and spun on his heel to address Lowell.

"You have wasted my afternoon, sir," he declared coldly. "And you will not see me again. Nor will you see my friends again, either. I will certainly warn them to stay far away from an *amateur* such as yourself."

He stepped through the doorway, pulling his wife after him. She tripped on the stoop and looked back at Lowell, her expression at once pleading and resigned, as though craving a deliverance she no longer expected. Her despair bit deep, instilling in Lowell a terrible, inescapable guilt.

He ran after them into the alleyway. Dusk was descending. A heavy snow filled the air. "You swine!" he shouted after Whateley. "I will tell the world what you are!"

Whateley halted and turned around. He released his grip on his wife's arm and advanced on Lowell with a menacing sneer, brandishing his cane like a common thug, the weighted end tapping against his open palm.

"Run!" Lowell shouted to Mrs Whateley. "He will kill you – don't you see that?"

She did not move. She merely looked on without expression, watching as her husband approached her would-be rescuer. Two yards away, Whateley lifted the cane high above his head and brought it down across his chest, a pendulum descending.

Lowell dodged to his right and managed to escape the blow. The cane impacted the frozen ground with a hollow report. Whateley cursed. Lowell saw his opening and took the offensive, dashing toward Whateley with fists raised.

The other man was ready for him.

Whateley stepped to one side and caught Lowell with an outstretched boot, scooping his legs out from under him. The photographer dropped to the ground, his weight landing on his elbow. His arm went numb.

Lowell attempted to regain his feet, but Whateley was too quick for him. The younger man kicked the photographer in the side and stomped down on his exposed gut. Lowell screamed. He rolled over and attempted to crawl away, dragging himself through the snow with his good arm.

Whateley followed him. Wielding the cane like a riding crop, he delivered a series of rapid blows across Lowell's back, dropping the photographer onto his stomach. Lowell tried to speak – to apologise, to plead for mercy – but found he had not the breath for it.

From the corner of his eye, he saw Whateley raise the cane and take aim at his left temple. The blow connected with a startling crack. The world flashed white before him and the vision in his left eye flickered and dimmed. A warm trickle poured from the torn scalp, staining his shirt and collar. He collapsed onto his stomach and closed his eyes.

Snow settled above his brow and melted. Cold fluid streamed down his forehead and into his damaged eye. Patrick's face returned to him in that moment, surfacing from the crimson cloud that obscured his vision.

"Forgive me," he murmured. "Please."

"Scum."

Whateley wiped his stick on Lowell's shirt and spit on him as he would a beggar or criminal. Then he turned away. His footsteps retreated, muffled by fresh snow.

"Come," Lowell heard him say. "We're due at the Grand."

He opened his eyes.

Night had fallen. Hours might have passed or mere minutes – he could not be sure – but the agony he experienced on waking was indescribable. His chest ached. His temples pounded, and he had lost the sight in his left eye. Nauseous, he rotated his head and threw up into the fresh snow. His vomit was yellow and dark, the colour of old bruises.

He crawled to the nearest wall and propped himself against it. Slowly he counted down from five, whispering the words to himself as he did before a picture. When he reached the end, he vaulted himself into a standing position. He wobbled dangerously, nearly fell, but caught himself against the wall. He cast his gaze back in the direction of his studio. The door was open, but he could not bring himself to return there, not now.

Breathing heavily, he hauled himself hand over hand down the alleyway and emerged into the gas-lit sheen of the street. Only this morning he had walked this same block, but tonight, everything had changed. Providence itself now swam in the lens of Patrick's camera. Even the newest buildings bore the signs of decay, marked by smoke stains and fallen roofs, brown curls of dying ivy on every wall.

It was late – too late – but the city hummed with activity. An endless stream of carriages clattered over the cobbles. Lowell stumbled into the path of a police officer, but the man simply ignored him, turning up his collar to hurry past.

No one else seemed to notice him. He passed among the midnight crowds – anonymous, unseen – cursed by solitude as in the year that Patrick left him. A dogcart flew past, missing him by less than a yard. Reeling, he took two steps backward, lost his footing, and tumbled into the gutter.

He lay there for a time, quite collapsed, while men and women passed him by. At one point he spotted the two sisters from the morning and observed that their faces had grown heavy with the accumulation of years, all vestiges of their former beauty spoiled.

On a chain between them, they carried a purse that bulged with miserly excess.

Behind them, shackled to the purse by a pair of manacles, walked a young woman of waxy countenance who wore nothing but a cotton shift. Lowell could see that she alone understood his plight, but she only lifted her shackled wrists, as though to indicate her own helplessness, and then shuffled past, dragged on like a dog by the women she served.

No one would help him – that much was clear – and he called on reserves of strength he did not know he possessed in order to regain his feet. Once he had steadied himself, he began to walk, continuing down the pavement toward Saint Andrew's. He thought he must be dying. He shivered in his shirtsleeves, occasionally spitting blood into the slush at his feet.

On the corner, he passed the paperboy. The lad grinned wickedly through his front teeth and shoved the evening circular into his face.

"No," Lowell gasped. "I don't need it."

"Yessir," the boy drawled. "But ye do *want* it, don't ye?"

Lowell tore the paper from the boy's grasp and threw it into the street. He pressed past him to the church of Saint Andrew's, where he mounted the stone stairs. He took them slowly, his legs weakening with each step. At last he reached the high doors. He rattled the handles but to no effect. Locked fast: even the Church had closed its doors to him.

In despair he cast his gaze heavenward, seeking out that point in space where the cross-topped spire disappeared into endless snowfall. Then he saw it: the cross had become a crucifix. A living figure writhed in agony on that bronze tree, naked and abandoned with only the dark for comfort. Lowell recognised him at once, even at that great distance.

He fell to his knees, trembling as before the altar. He heard a cry – a boy's voice, he fancied, though he could not make out the words. The world was falling from him, a garment shed. His head tipped back and he tumbled into nothingness.

He woke up swathed in snow. His clothes had frozen in conformance to the shape of his body, and the blood had thickened in his beard. He wiped the snowmelt from his face, relieved to find he could see through his left eye, and levered himself into a crouch. The pain was excruciating, but perhaps not as intolerable as before.

He was in the alleyway behind his studio. His nightmare, then, had been a nightmare in truth, a vision brought on by the blow to his skull. It made no difference. He was a man haunted, damned beyond atonement. He understood this now. Though years might pass, nothing could erase from his mind the image of that crucified figure.

He struggled to his feet and limped back into the studio. A fire smouldered in the grate and the room was still warm. From this he concluded that his unconsciousness could not have lasted more than an hour. He went to the side cabinet and extracted the brandy bottle. He took three quick slugs before replacing it.

He crossed the room to the corner where the shipping crate lay discarded, left behind in his excitement over Patrick's camera. He turned it upside down. A brown envelope slipped free and drifted to the floor. No name was indicated, but he knew it was meant for him.

Inside was a photograph. Lowell recognised it as one that he himself had taken many years before. In the picture, a young child regarded the camera without smiling. Patrick. The child's features were fair, his nose turned slightly to the right where it had once been broken. His eyes were blue: wide with terror, blank with suffering.

Lowell blinked. His vision blurred. The room swam before him and the blood rushed to his ears. He thrust the photograph into the fire. He watched it light – the child's face blackening, falling through – and then lunged for Patrick's camera.

He toppled the tripod, dashing the instrument onto the floor. Dropping to his knees, he ripped free the hood and shattered the slide loader, punching through the mahogany frame, his knuckles splitting where they connected with brass. He plucked out the lens from the viewfinder and carried it into the darkroom, the glass slipping between his injured fingers. In the darkroom, he held up the lens to the mirror and glimpsed himself in its depths.

What did he hope to see there? Lowell could not say. Some hidden truth, perhaps – some veiled hope of which he was only half-aware. But his appearance had not altered. In the lens, he saw only the same broken man as in the mirror, a bloodied beast stalked by the same demons, the same ghosts. With a roar of agony, more animal than human, he hurled the lens against the far wall and heard it shatter.

He returned to the studio and shot the deadbolt, the better to escape down the neck of a brandy bottle. And so the night passed. He drank – he did not pray – and the darkness drew near as with the rustle of fabric, a starless hood that stretched to cover the city, to gather all creation in its sweep. At dawn, the wind turned southerly. The snow became a bitter rain that drummed like pebbles on the walls of the studio.

He was awakened by the doorbell. It was midday, the sun's glare doubled by slush and snowmelt. He went to the door and cracked it open, withdrawing the chain when he recognised the clerk from the post office.

"Yes?" he croaked. "What do you want?"

The clerk started, shocked by the change in Lowell's appearance.

"You didn't stop by, sir. Yesterday, sir. Before we locked up."

"No," he said. "I was – delayed."

"I have this for you," said the clerk. "I'm sorry, sir."

The tersely-worded missive contained the news of Patrick's death.

On 29 November, the young man had sold off his apartment and settled his debts before returning to the studio. After he failed to emerge, his friends had summoned the officers, who found him in the darkroom, a suicide.

It was later reported that Patrick had boxed up all of his possessions prior to his death: his books, his papers, his prints. Only his camera was found to be missing.

Lowell's story ended there. For a time neither of us spoke. Crickets sang in the nearby underbrush. The moon emerged from a bank of clouds, recasting the landscape from shades of silver. Lowell stubbed out his cigar and disappeared inside.

Five years have passed since our brief meeting, and yet I find his story has not left me. Lowell spoke eloquently of light and darkness – and of the dark that cannot be illumined – and within his tale itself there is another kind of darkness, a history hidden from the light of narrative: shadowed, secret, and thus ineradicable.

I woke the next morning to find that he had gone. He had departed the resort at first light and returned to Providence. I do not know what has become of him. Sometimes I like to think that he has found some measure of peace, whatever the nature of his past sins. In any event, I doubt that I shall see him again.

MARK SAMUELS

The Tower

MARK SAMUELS LIVES ALONE in a garret in London, England. He is the author of four acclaimed short story collections: *The White Hands and Other Weird Tales* (Tartarus Press, 2003), *Black Altars* (Rainfall Books, 2003), *Glyphotech & Other Macabre Processes* (PS Publishing, 2008) and *The Man Who Collected Machen* (Ex Occidente, 2010; reprinted by Chômu Press, 2011), as well as the short novel *The Face of Twilight* (PS Publishing, 2006).

"The Tower" is the seventh of his tales to appear in *The Mammoth Book of Best New Horror*. New fiction from his pen is forthcoming in issues of the journal *Sacrum Regnum*, published by Hieroglyph Press.

About the following story, Samuels reveals: "Actually, this is more of an autobiographical piece than a work of fiction. In psychological and spiritual terms, every word of it is the truth."

M Y CUSTOM, FOR many weeks, just after awaking at dawn, was to walk the streets in the region around King's Cross. They are a bewildering mixture of decay and modern renovation. A number of the buildings seem in danger of being pulled down, because they do not appear to fit the image of the brand new and commercially successful ideal the redevelopers have in mind.

I think of the "Lighthouse" (which has no light) atop a dilapidated building on the corner of the Gray's Inn Road, just opposite the station.

I think of the old Eastern Goods Yard just north of the station, its sidings abandoned, the vast wooden structure now scarcely covered by the paint that has turned grey and peeled off, its bulk surrounded by a field of weeds that have broken through the pavement. It, along with Granary Square, will soon be remade, and turned into something as grotesque in appearance as an elderly woman who has become the casualty of too much plastic surgery.

I think also of the wharves, where cargoes were offloaded from narrowboats on Regent's Canal, the buildings now lost to chic design companies who produce nothing of lasting value.

It is still possible to wander in this area and discover corpse structures: closed-down and boarded-up pubs left abandoned, the silent remains of a record shop that sold vinyl, an empty sex shop with dust-obscured windows, fast food restaurants where now only hordes of vermin feed. I remember passing by all of these places when they were still active. Now they are gutted, with only decaying outward shells as reminders of their having been there at all. In a few more years even these remnants will have vanished completely – "regenerated" into yet another useless tentacle of corporate nonsense.

As I wandered in the early morning sunlight, golden and dazzling, it seemed to me that the remains of the past were more beautiful than what was to come. The future offered no prospect but a soulless death, all the more terrifying for its not being acknowledged. The solidity of the past, the idea of permanence, was over, and it had been replaced by a new ethos of disposability and change for its own sake, under the guise of so called "progress". But progress towards what destination?

For no destination seemed to be in mind, only "progress" for its own sake, only an end that could not be reached, only the doing away with all that shows any sign of having reached old age. The human race now lives solely in order to try and prolong its own youth indefinitely. And that was progress?

Those ruined and decayed remains of buildings that have been abandoned due to their commercial worthlessness have more mystery about them than any number of new glass and steel developments. They are testaments to the truth that the city is not solely the business centre its rulers would have us take pride in, but that it is an organic entity with an occult life and history of its own. For there are still ghosts in those shells, and, just as long as memory lingers and imagination is not stamped out by the profit motive, the ghosts will live on.

And so, when morning was over, once the sun had risen higher in the sky, once the traffic had begun to swarm, and the commuters had streamed out of St Pancras, King's Cross and Euston, to tramp the streets and take possession of the buildings like an army of occupation, once commercial activities reigned, I retreated to my garret in a squalid, horrible edifice further north, and I pursued my campaign of resistance in occupied territory: my enemies being the fearful foes who would reduce all spirit, wonder and beauty to mere semantics, madness and insignificance. I continued, against all obstacles, to resist the vengeful by refusing to recognise their dominion.

After a while I ceased to visit the region around King's Cross, having reached the point where I could no longer bear its transformation, and I made the district wherein I dwelt the limit of my universe. With this act of psychogeographical withdrawal, and perhaps as a consequence of it, the Tower appeared for the first time.

On that morning the entire city was shrouded with a deep mist, rendering existence within its confines ghostly. All other edifices became nebulous, but this one structure seemed to draw its own clarity from the degree to which others were obscured. It stood out in stark relief against the grey murky atmosphere that had descended like a pall. Naturally, I thought myself to be, at first, the victim of my own imagination. I was acutely aware of the degree to which I had become isolated from other people, and aware of the pitfalls that follow an intense degree of self-absorption. I had suffered periods of paranoia, of depression and of loneliness, but I regarded myself as nevertheless psychologically intact, since my capacity to make critical judgements with regards to my own state of mind remained clear.

I had, of course, seen the same view innumerable times before, and it was quite familiar to me. But this time, from the profusion of the mist, there appeared this fantastic new structure, as if risen up from inconceivable depths; with one lone Tower breaking the waves and the tolling of immense bells heralding the return of an Atlantean cathedral wreathed in sea-fog.

In design the Tower was fantastically lofty, a dizzying physical projection capable of being conceived only in the mind of an individual given over wholly to dream. It radiated an aura of antiquity, and the surface of its brickwork was thick with the grey dust of untold centuries. The titanic spire that formed its pinnacle was bewildering to the imagination, for its height surpassed any of the skyscrapers of the "triumphant" modern era. It was as if the Tower was the spectre of a structure that had been destroyed, but which had forced its way back into existence, or back into human consciousness, which – nevertheless – amounts to the same thing.

The appearance, overnight, of a structural invader amidst the architectural vista to which one has become accustomed, seen from one's own window, provokes terror.

Doubtless some puerile Freudian analyst would have had the temerity to designate the appearance of the Tower as evidence of a phallic symbol erupting into my consciousness from the depths of repression, but, in opposition to such a notion, one that cannot be disproved since its basis is ideological, I can do little more save express my scorn and contempt. The anthropodeist perspective is so ingrained into modern man that to the absolutely convinced any attempt at denial contains the seeds of its own defeat. Unable to acquiesce, I felt to protest the thesis was to confirm it.

By the time I had rapidly dressed and was ready to venture out into the mist, it had lifted and when next I looked out of the window, the Tower had vanished utterly.

I cursed myself for a fool and a victim of my own imaginings, for I have always been a dreamer, and such a one is often prone to delusion.

I could not help but conclude that the Tower could be seen only when the mist was present, and was not merely the by-product of my own mind having become disordered. This I realised over the course of many weeks observation, seeking in vain for the elusive structure. It was not a phantom edifice conjured by a mental fugue. Its first appearance occurred moments after I had awoken for the day, had lit a cigarette and sat absent-mindedly in my easy chair looking out the window, with a completely clear frame of reference. Since my rooms (which I had occupied for just over a month) are on the third floor a quarter of the way up the steep rise of this district's hill, the view is extensive and I can see over huddled rooftops all the way to the summit.

If only it were not the case that the noise of tolling bells in the Tower had been so ghostly, more like the shadow of a sound than a sound itself, then I could have hoped others might notice, but it could be heard only late at night, at those moments when the world is at its quietest, when conversations die, when broadcasts and recordings are turned off, when dreams replace thoughts. And then there was the anti-light therein, not darkness, but of a negative intensity that, though glimpsed only through the Tower's narrow, gaunt apertures, formed streaming shafts of an unknown colour, and penetrated the gloom of the mist that lay without like mystical searchlights.

Though I tried not to allow this vision to dominate my day-to-day life, I could not resist its allure. Only when a mist descended was the Tower visible. I became a devotee of its capricious nature and longed, like a spurned lover, to further what opportunities were available for me to glimpse again the half-ruined edifice from which strange, distant chants seemed eventually to mingle with the tolling bells and whose warped architecture told a tale of madness beyond the apprehension of those who went about their commonplace lives.

I alone knew that some ultimate mystery was to be found within, and only inside the immense confines of the apparition would I discover the symbol for which the Tower stood. I was prepared always for the advent of mist, whether in the early morning or during the midnight hours, and went abroad in pursuit of the titanic structure, wandering the streets in a desperate attempt to get closer and closer. Yet, despite my best endeavours, I found it impossible to draw near, for the Tower seemed to maintain a fixed distance, one unrelated to my own conceptions of proximity.

It was, of course, not a physical, but rather a *spiritual*, phenomenon. The matter of my approach depended less on my physical route and the speed with which I acted, than upon my own state of mind. The Tower was not a structure visible to all, for it appeared only to those who had been initiated into its mysteries. I dared not speak of it to anyone else, lest the spell be broken by my own faithlessness, and the mystery be snatched away from me.

I wondered then whether the fog, too, existed in my own mind, and formed as much a part of the initiatory sequence as any other component of the process of transformation.

True, I had been drinking a great deal. True also, that the small capital upon which I had been drawing in order to keep me from ruin, was close to exhaustion. My attempts to connect with the so-called "real world" had been unsuccessful. My rent was several weeks in arrears. What food I could afford to purchase was of the cheapest and least nutritious kind: instant noodles, bread on the last day of its expiry date, vegetables close to mouldering, and the contents of tins with peeling labels that, for the most part, lay dusty on shelves; the type viewed only as insurance by the majority of people against some long period of unexpected war or other disaster.

What few job interviews I obtained were useless, for when I was questioned upon business aptitude and commercial considerations, my answers were of a kind that revealed at once the gulf between an autocratic dreamer and a man of this world, sharing in its values. I did not tell anyone directly of the Tower, but dropped hints that I hoped might prove to be the equivalent of a password, or a secret sign, admitting me into that otherworldly realm where I hoped to find at least one other individual who knew of its cryptic existence and who was prepared to acknowledge its awful, and infinitely essential, character.

But always I encountered only those with television eyes whose own imaginative vision had dimmed, those whose values were formed by the irresistible tsunami of gossip and infotainment. Those whose gazes were fixed on bright plasma and LED screens, those addicted to shows where the value of a person was determined by his ability to entertain, to financially enrich or to sexually arouse, an agenda driven in turn by those who were drained of their own thought-processes by the media's mental vampires. Pity those who, through the process of electronic devolution, had allowed themselves to be turned into a pack of obedient dogs, eagerly lapping up the anti-individualistic, collectivist poison provided by their supremely powerful masters, lapping up the noxious gruel, the sewage diet of self-destruction, and being told that this wave of conformist propaganda is freedom. Pity those who thought they had the solution, and who paid lip-service to an alternate system of totalitarianism, which they called freedom, but in which the mass of men were only components; oppressed economic units rather than individuals.

For a time I wallowed in the icy consolations of pessimism, that anti-gospel which provides solace in the creed that the universe is so ordered as to be inimical to humanity itself. Relieved from the onus of developing a measure of stoic acceptance of life's vicissitudes, I found respite in a grand conspiracy theory in which the cosmos was intrinsically malignant to men. Intrinsically, but not *consciously*, malignant, you will note; rather like a natural poison-zone, in which sentience was an aberration of such jarring uniqueness that it could be nothing other than doomed to final destruction when confronted with the revelation of an ultimate, dead, and bleak reality.

And yet this scheme, like all the others, I found unsatisfying. It answered all questions, allayed all doubts, *provided* one acquiesced in its inhuman principles, and so I concluded it was a hoax. For if the advocates of pessimism were correct, they would surely have destroyed themselves, negating all that their continued existence represented. Instead, they lingered on within life, filling time in the fruitless quest to persuade others, the bulk of mankind, that all men are nothing more than mindless puppets, and, thereby, themselves playing at being the *puppet-master*.

Their excuses were hollow – especially when they retorted that their deaths would cause unwarranted distress to those they left behind – or why should they care at all for the temporary and negligible reactions of others whom, their logic dictated, were as doomed and ensnared by human illusions as were they? Suicide, instead of causing pain (though doubtless they would) should have been viewed, by the true pessimist, as being an *authentic act*, an *example to follow*, not as an occasion for mourning.

A pessimist is a liar, unless he destroys himself, and no less of a hypocrite than a priest who defiles the holy.

For, in truth, is not all human philosophy simply the piling up of one word after another in a self-absorbed train of thought and justification? To pull the strings of mental association, to prompt the idea, to suggest the conclusion, to lead, to guide, to steal back into the shadows and work one's "magic" from afar?

What then, of *experience* as opposed to *reason*? Can the experience of any one man be of significance to all others? And if experience be incommunicable, what then of a *better example* one man might set? Alas, even had I endeavoured to turn myself into a saint, such a course was beyond my powers. Fallen too far into the morass of materialism, my soul had begun to rot, my imagination had dried up, and I had reached the stage of dreading any contact with my fellow human beings.

I emphasise it now; I had little-to-nothing in common with other people. Their values I did not comprehend, their ideals were to me a living horror. Call it ostentatious but I even sought to provide tangible proof of my withdrawal from the world. I posted a sign in the entrance to the building wherein I dwelt; a sign that indicated I had no wish to be disturbed by anyone, for any purpose whatsoever.

As these convictions took hold of me and, as I denied, nay even *repudiated*, the hold that the current society of men possesses over its ranks, as I retreated into a hermitage of the imagination, disentangling my own concerns from those paramount to the age in which I happened to be born, an age with no claim to be more enlightened, significant or progressive than any other, I tried to make a stand for the spirit. Tyranny, in this land, I was told, was dead. But I contend that the replacement of one form of tyranny with another is still tyranny. The secret police now operate not via the use of brute force in dark underground cells; they operate instead by a process of open brainwashing that is impossible to avoid altogether. The torture cells are not secret; they are everywhere, and so ubiquitous that they are no longer seen for what they are.

One may abandon television; one may abandon all forms of broadcast media, even the Internet, but the advertising hoardings in every street, on vehicles, inside transport centres, are still there. And they contain the same messages.

Only the very rich can avoid their clutches utterly. Those who have obtained sufficient wealth may choose their own surroundings, free from the propaganda of a decayed futurity. And yet, and yet, in order to obtain such a position of freedom it is first necessary to have served the ideals of the tyranny slavishly, thereby validating it.

Still, even if one is not rich, there is freedom in the imagination. I recall, in particular, a certain night on the dreary stretch of the busy Archway Road. The rain was falling quite heavily, and beneath the stellar street-lamps the droplets beat down like a majestic mystery upon the sodden and wet pavements, creating a world of splendour and of intense fascination. Reality was transformed; a deeper glimpse into the realm of possibilities was made apparent, one that suggested much more than a single moment, but which revealed itself as a shard from a greater eternity.

When I realised this, I began to see the vision of the Tower outside of those times when the mist seemed to bring it into existence, for it appeared my imagination had sufficient power to carry me more frequently into that other realm of spirit. And with each mental voyage, the next became less arduous.

Eventually, the Tower appeared omnipresent. I saw it, whenever I looked for it, at all hours of the day and night. Believing its appearance as a constant to be an indication of the mysterious structure that was now gaining a firmer foothold in reality – or what I took to be reality, or even some new reality imposed by my imagination – I naturally attempted to gain entrance to its immediate grounds, and perhaps even to its interior confines.

But when I tramped the maze of streets that I thought would draw me closer to the Tower, I found that, despite the ease with which I conjured it into being, still I got no nearer to my destination, and it remained as distant as when I first glimpsed it. Several times I made the attempt, but each one ended in exhaustion, and with a resultant bodily collapse dozens of miles from my home. Naturally, when asked about the object of my quest I dared not tell the truth lest I was regarded as being of completely unsound mind, and thereby unable to care for myself; a prospective candidate for the close attention and palliative care of the state (that is, of a society whose, albeit unconscious, aim is to crush any form of deviation from its own standards).

What was contained inside the Tower? Was it not the case that it was less important in and of itself than the secret within? Increasingly, I thought so.

Physical distance was not the barrier to the attainment of close proximity; rather was it a question of spiritual distance.

I felt myself to be subject to a form of discipline, a form almost totally alien to that of the world in which I felt myself stranded, and something beyond even the increased power of my imagination. And this discipline was being imposed from without; from a force that was entirely transcendent of the self-absorbed and self-consuming world in which I dwelt. Without the discipline one could not advance. Moreover one did not seek the discipline, rather was one called to it by its source. But I knew nothing of the nature of that source or of its meaning (if it was possessed of either).

The discipline required was precisely that form of introspection into which I had fallen, or to which I had succumbed. It was an ordered withdrawal from all the demands of the everyday. Not, I must add, *as an escape*. The process, I suppose, was most closely akin to meditation; an immersion into the essence of one's very consciousness, and the Tower stood as a signpost, one not representing some external object but the nucleus of my own mind, and not the nebulous dreams that surrounded it.

One may escape from the prisons of experience, ideology or philosophy, but it is impossible to escape from the reality of one's innermost self. Understanding this, I had freed myself from nostalgia, and having done so, what remained was to free myself from the prospect of the future.

Although the discipline was imposed from outside, I knew that my withdrawal was not ordered by any force other than my own self, in its own intrinsic desire to find its true purpose – the absorption into a greater meaning, one that I might finally attain by entry into the Tower.

When one has given up all the petty jealousies of ambition, all the siren-calls of satiety, when one instead recognises that the loss of all one holds dear in this materialistic paradigm is not an escape but a liberation, a moving on, a step into the next stage of being, that this is the only form of authentic revelation that there is, then one approaches true freedom.

Within the Tower was the mystery of untold ages, and without there was only certainty. For every man there exists an individual Tower, but all the Towers are One.

And I know now, gazing upon the reflection that stares back at me from the mirror in the apartment wherein I dwell, that to see the Tower is to pass from this world to the next. My body is that of a white-haired ancient, one whose flesh is honeycombed with innumerable lipomas, one whose skeletal structure has become strangely distorted, one whose face is a maze of criss-crossed lines harbouring rheumy, cataract-clouded blue eyes, one whose yellow skin, dry as parchment, is stretched tightly over a death's-head skull.

Time becomes fluid and non-linear as the liberty of disintegration takes hold. Time torments those who immerse themselves in its infinite progressions and regressions. Time, *experienced in its entirety*, is incomprehensible.

And indeed, since my discovery of the Tower, decades have passed in days and seconds have become aeons.

Across the whitewashed walls inside this overground tomb, there are scrawled indecipherable words and equations, each either haunted with antiquity or else pregnant with futurity.

Their meaning is lost, but their significance is not.

PETER ATKINS

Dancing Like We're Dumb

PETER ATKINS WAS BORN in Liverpool, England, and now lives in Los Angeles, California. He is the author of the novels *Morningstar*, *Big Thunder* and *Moontown*, and the screenplays *Hellbound: Hellraiser II*, *Hellraiser III: Hell on Earth*, *Hellraiser IV: Bloodline*, *Wishmaster* and *Prisoners of the Sun*.

His short fiction has appeared in such anthologies as *The Museum of Horrors*, *Dark Delicacies II*, *Hellbound Hearts* and the first two volumes of the "mosaic novel" series *Zombie Apocalypse!*. Magazines to which he has contributed include *Weird Tales*, *The Magazine of Fantasy & Science Fiction*, *Cemetery Dance* and *PostScripts*.

"Dancing Like We're Dumb" first appeared in the author's short story collection *Rumours of the Marvellous*, and is the third story to feature his lesbian detective character Kitty Donnelly as first-person narrator.

"The real Kitty Donnelly," Atkins says, "was my paternal grandmother, and I'm horribly aware of just how much that good Irish Catholic, born while Victoria was still on the throne, would want to wash her fictional namesake's filthy mouth out with soap.

"I like to believe, though, that she might quietly approve of young Kitty's take-no-prisoners attitude . . ."

Punk in the back seat didn't look so tough, but the jittery eagerness with which he pressed the barrel of his Ruger against the back of my headrest talked me out of giving him the kind of shit I'd normally enjoy throwing his way.

I was in the front passenger seat – annoying to begin with because it was my fucking car – and Jumpy McHandgun back there was the monkey to Cody Garrity's organ-grinder. Cody was driving. Not driving well, it has to be said, but certainly letting the State know what it could do with its posted speed limits.

I'd had the pleasure of their acquaintance a mere four minutes or so, and I knew Cody's name only because he was the kind of tool that liked to introduce himself when he was car-jacking you.

"Hi, I'm Cody Garrity," he'd said. "Slide over." His Smith & Wesson .38 had been on display for me, but held flat against his stomach to avoid alarming anyone else in the Albertson's parking lot.

I got to give them props for the smoothness of their work. Cody'd ambled schlub-like between the spots like some harmless stoner who'd forgotten where he'd parked, while his neck-tattooed catamite kept himself completely out of sight until Cody'd already got the drop on me.

I'd only been driving Ilsa, She-wolf of the SS, for a month or so and, while she may have been merely an entry-level Mercedes, she was still a Mercedes, so I should have been paying more fucking attention. It's true that it was four o'clock in the afternoon of another perfect LA day and that seven years of driving third-hand Detroit may well have dulled my douchebags-who-want-your-stuff antenna, but I'm not going to make excuses. I'd been sitting there checking my mental shopping list with the driver door wide open like some middle-class moron who thinks crime only happens to other people, so I've got no one to blame but Mrs Donnelly's youngest.

Cody, jumping lights and ignoring stop signs, was tearing down Griffith Park Boulevard now, pushing Ilsa like he had her on a Nascar track instead of a residential street, and her engine was purring pleasurably in response to his aggression. Little Kraut slut.

"What you got on your pre-sets?" Cody asked, but was already stabbing at the radio's buttons. The speakers burst into life and the godlike genius known to an undeserving world as Ke$ha told us she had Jesus on her necklace.

Cody gave me a superior look. "Top forty," he said, like I needed my channels explaining to me. His tone was derisive, and the epsilon in back snorted in agreement. Their disdain didn't surprise me. What did surprise me – confused me, in fact – was that I was still in the damn car. I don't know if Cody and his chimp had ever read *Carjacking for Dummies* but, if they had, I'm pretty sure they'd have learned that the place to say goodbye to their new vehicle's previous owner was back at the point of purchase.

It's never a good idea to point out examples of their own stupidity to boys who like to play with guns but I needed to let them know that, now that they had the car and all, it was time that they thought about ditching the unwanted baggage. I turned to look at Cody – always smarter to talk to the less-amped one – and pointed ahead to the next intersection.

"You could drop me at the corner of Hyperion," I said, calm as a tween on Ritalin. "I can pick up a slice at Hard Times and—"

"Hey, lesbo-at-frontseat-dot-com," his partner interrupted. "Shut the fuck up."

Well, that was alarming. Not a single Melissa CD or Ellen bio in sight and me in my usual show-the-boys-what-they're-missing drag, but still Antsy Von Rugerstein – who I'm guessing wasn't the brightest bitch in his pack – had me down as a friend of Radclyffe Hall. Which meant he had to have come armed with prior knowledge. Which meant he and his alpha hadn't been targeting Ilsa at all. They'd been targeting *me*.

Huh. And the day'd started off so quiet.

Started off nice, in fact. Coffee at my place with a pretty girl.

Anna was almost eighteen, exclusively and unfortunately hetero, and was part of a girl power trio called The Butchered Barbies. Anna had two jobs in the band – to play bass and to look hot – and was good at one of them. The Barbies – who were almost big in what remained of the Silverlake scene – were all buzzsaw guitar and Jenny Rotten snarls, like the last thirty years had never happened. I'd tried to point out to Anna on more than one occasion that their whole schtick was as charmingly anti-quarian as crinolines and afternoon tea but she wasn't having it. Fucking kids. No telling them.

Anyway, Anna had come calling this morning because she'd misplaced a piece of vinyl that meant a lot to her, and was flirting with the idea that it had been stolen and wanted me to flirt with the idea of making it my next case.

Next case. Jesus Christ. Truth is I feel weird even talking about *cases*. I mean, with my impressive juvenile resumé of drug-running and related criminal activities, it wasn't like the State was going to fucking *license* me any time soon. And, besides, most of the people who came to me with their little problems weren't the sort of people who were likely to want the authorities anywhere within sniffing distance of their own shit. Nevertheless, for the last eighteen months or so, the Donnelly larder had been stocked pretty exclusively by the proceeds of a series of adventures in private investigation, so turns out – licensed or not – I'd sashayed my way into becoming Nancy Drew for the meh generation.

"It was that guy," Anna said. "I'm pretty sure. Have you got any more coffee?" She looked around my kitchenette with a hopeful expression, like the coffee could perhaps be somewhere other than the auto-drip's empty pitcher and waggled her mug on the counter-top like she might tempt it out of hiding.

"I'll make some," I said, getting up. "What guy?"

"The *guy*," she said, giving me a look like what the fuck was wrong with me not keeping up with her tweets.

"Remind me," I said, walking to the machine and swapping out the used filter.

"Took a stranger home after a gig," she said. "Fucked him. Gone when I woke up. No name, no number. One of my 45s was missing."

Come on. Of course that's not what she said. What she *said* took the entire brew-cycle, but I've done you the courtesy of editing out the how-she-felt and the what-she-wore and the how-he-seemed-nice and the Emma's-cool-but-she-can-be-*so*-jealous and all the rest of her Proustian-level-of-detail shit. Trust me, you owe me big.

I'd press her later for more clues to the identity of the gentle and sensitive young poet with whom she'd shared those brief idyllic moments, but first I wanted to know if what might have been stolen was something actually worth stealing. I asked her the name of the missing single.

"You probably haven't heard of it, Kitty," she said gently – you know, me being twenty-five and such a fucking square and all. "It's called 'The Devil Rides Shotgun', by Guest Eagleton."

Bless her. Everything's new to seventeen-year-olds, even history. The record in question was certainly a rarity, but the story behind it was hardly obscure. They even made a bad TV movie about it in the early eighties, something I resisted telling Anna for fear it would break her hip little heart. Rockabilly legend Eagleton – not a legend at the time, of course, just another redneck punk lucky enough to be making a third single because his second had crossed over from the regional charts to the lower reaches of the Billboard Hot 100 – recorded 'The Devil Rides Shotgun' in 1957. By all accounts, the recording itself went fine – single hanging mike, three-piece band, two takes and off to the cathouse, those were the days – but between the day of the recording and the release of the single Guest finally got around to reading his contract.

Discovering that the label's owner – a scurrilous one, imagine that – had put himself up as co-writer of the song, young Guest, still fresh from the Kentucky hills and not one to wait for lawyers when there's a sawn-off handy, broke into the record plant to personally stop the pressing of the 45.

Here's the part of the story where fact shades into legend. It's a fact Guest was shot by the first cop on the scene. It's a fact that he fell from the gantry into the production line below. I don't know for a fact he was dead before his face landed in the hot wax vat, but I sure hope so. It's a fact that twenty-seven copies of the 45 were pressed before they could shut the line down. And the legend, of course, is that each of those twenty-seven copies contains microscopic remnants of their late creator because the flesh that was stripped from his skull by the molten vinyl was swirled away with it and stamped into the records themselves. You can believe it if you like. Snopes gives it a cautious "hasn't actually been disproved" kind of rating.

Anyway, the final fact is that – whether the story of their extra
ingredient was true or not – those copies of the single, though
never officially released, have become Grail-like to serious vinyl
junkies over the years. Springsteen paid nearly twenty grand for
his copy back in his glory days, the nerd from Coldplay almost
twice as much at a Sotheby's auction three years ago. Anna got
hers as a gift. Like I said, pretty girl.

It wasn't even lunchtime before I was cooling my heels in the
lobby of a mid-level talent agency on Beverly waiting to see the
douche who'd picked Anna up and ask him nicely for the return
of her property.

Here's the thing about detecting that my more invested-in-the-
myth colleagues don't want you to know: like every other job,
it's really easy except for those rare but annoying times when it's
not. This thing of Anna's took me one phone call to a barman I
knew at the club where the Barbies had played, another to a
customer he knew who'd spent time talking to the aforemen-
tioned douche, and a quick Internet search of employment
records.

I'd given my name to the pretty young man at the reception
desk and told him I needed to see Andy Velasco on a personal
matter of some urgency. He'd told me he'd do what he could,
but that Mr Velasco was very busy, and I'd bit my tongue and
sat down to wait. But by the time I'd read *Variety* from cover to
cover I figured I'd waited long enough and, in the next brief gap
in the endless phone calls the receptionist was fielding, walked
back over to his desk and said, "Where's his office?"

The receptionist pulled a face. "I'm going to need you to sit
down and be patient."

"When?" I asked him.

"Excuse me?"

"When are you going to need me to do that?"

He hesitated, because – how the hell would *he* know – maybe
I actually was that stupid.

"Now," he said, with that weary politeness that's supposed to
let you know you're dealing with a trained professional.

"Now?" I said. "So what's with all the 'I'm going to' crap?
Present tense. Future tense. They're different for a reason." Poor

bastard. Wasn't like he was the only idiot to talk that way but, you know, millionth customer gets the confetti and the coupon-book. Luck of the draw.

"I need you to sit down," he said. "*Now.*" Giving it his best firm and authoritative, just like the manual must've told him. Adorable.

"Well, *I* need Scarlett Johansson and a fistful of Rohypnol," I said. "So that's two of us that are shit out of luck."

"I have no problem with calling the police," he said.

"Me neither," I said. "But I can guarantee you your Mr Velasco would." He came up short on the snappy comeback front so I pressed on. "Tell him I've got a pitch for him. Re-imagining of an old classic. *Statutory Rape and the Single Rockchick*. Pretty sure he'll want to hear it."

Five minutes later, I was driving the single back to Anna's place in Echo Park.

And five hours later, after a breakneck jaunt up and around the curves of Mulholland, I was about to be ushered in to a mansion on a hill by my new friend, Cody Garrity.

His little helper had clambered into Ilsa's driver seat when Cody and I'd got out and, as he slipped her back into drive and started out of the courtyard roundabout, he dropped the window, grinned at me, and pantomimed a shot to my head. Charm. It's just something you're born with.

I returned the smile and nodded. "Catch you later," I said.

He didn't much care for the way I'd said it, I guess, because he slammed back into park like he was ready to get out and teach the bitch some manners.

"Scott . . ." Cody said. Not much spin on it, but apparently enough to get the little tyke back in his cage. He drove off, and I watched him exit through the big wrought-iron gates. Neck tattoo, five-foot-six, name of Scott. Should be enough. And it's always nice to have something to look forward to.

"Long walk back," I said to Cody. "But at least it's downhill."

"I got a ride," he said, cocking his head in the direction of a late model Cadillac parked outside a separate Carriage House. "And you're not going to need one."

"Ominous," I said. "I'm all a-tremble."

"Comedienne," he said – yeah, four syllables, gender-specific and everything, who knew? – and waved me toward the front door of the main house with his gun.

Quite a place. And it sure as hell didn't belong to Cody. Nor did it belong to a pissant junior agent like Andy Velasco – to whom I should perhaps have paid more attention when he told me that he was just a middleman and that his client was not going to be happy – because this place was money. Real money.

The three rooms and a hallway we walked through to get where we were going were high-end SoCal class. Impressive and imposing, but nothing you haven't seen in the glossies. The room we ended up in, though, was something quite different. Black marble and red lacquer and display cases full of books, artefacts, and impedimenta of a very specific nature.

Shit.

Magic. I *hate* magic.

LA's just full of Satanists. Always has been. I don't know if it's some kind of yin–yang natural balance thing – all that sun, surf, and simplicity needing to be contrasted by some really dark shit – but it certainly seems that way. Into every Brian Wilson's life, a little Charlie Manson must fall.

Most of the Golden State's followers of the left-hand path are of course idiot dilettantes chasing tail and money, but every now and then something real fucking ugly breaks surface. Something that knows what it's doing.

It was hard to think of the seventy-year-old guy who'd been waiting for us in the room as someone who knew what he was doing, though, at least when it came to raising demons and the like. Getting into pickles with pretty sitcom moms, sure, or raising exasperated eyebrows at the antics of adorable juvenile leads maybe. I recognised him immediately, and you would've too. I doubt you could watch four hours of TV Land without seeing him at least twice. Never had his own show, but from the late sixties through the mid-eighties he was very solidly employed. You'd have as hard a time as I did remembering the name – Frankie Metcalfe, I eventually recalled – but you'd know the face in a heartbeat. Still worked now and then; he did one of those standard Emmy-baiting loveable-old-curmudgeon-with-Cancer bits on *Grey's Anatomy* couple of seasons back.

"Really?" I said. "*There Goes the Neighborhood* residuals can get you a place like this?"

"Hardly," he said. "Bequest from an acolyte. So you're the interfering little cunt who decided she'd piss on my parade?"

Whoa. Quite a mouth. And from *this* guy? It was like hearing Howie Cunningham tell you to go fuck your mother.

"Why didn't you just make Anna an offer?" I said. "You probably could have got the damn single for less than a month's worth of property tax."

"Not an option," he said. "The ritual has its rules."

Christ almighty. Always with the rules and rituals, these dickheads. Flying the flag for transgression and the dark arts, but as prissy about it as a chapter of the fucking DAR.

"Esoteric as all get out, I'm sure," I said. "Can I give you a piece of friendly advice? Payback for all those hours of televisual pleasure? If you have a gun handy, you might want to get it now."

"Because?"

"Because sometime in the next five or ten minutes I'm going to relieve Cody of his and blow the top of his fucking head off, and I'd hate for you to be caught at a disadvantage."

Cody bristled at that – big fucking deal, I've been bristled at before – but Frankie laughed. I think he was starting to like me.

I wondered why he'd sent his boys to grab *me* instead of just having them snatch the single again, and asked him.

"Your friend was apparently so moved by its safe return that she's keeping it about her person," Frankie said. "Which wouldn't be a problem, but her group is currently travelling." He looked to Cody for details.

"They got a gig in Bakersfield tonight," Cody said.

"Bakersfield?" I said. "Seriously, the Barbies? Buck Owens must be turning over in his grave."

Frankie ignored the sidebar. "So, no *memento mori* of the unfortunate Mister Eagleton," he said. "Still, not to worry. We've got you instead."

"I'm a girl of many talents," I said. "But singing isn't one of them."

"Then how lucky we are that all you'll be required to do is die. Let's move the party down below, shall we?"

We were on the ground floor, in case I haven't made that clear. "Down below," I said. "That's quite unusual for Los Angeles." Look at me, being all up on my building codes and shit.

"What's unusual?" Frankie asked.

"Having a basement."

"Oh, I don't have a basement," he said.

He was right. He didn't have a basement. What he had was a cavern. I'd have made the requisite Bruce Wayne jokes, except the sight of it didn't really inspire humour.

It was huge, for starters, like the hill beneath his house and those of his neighbours lower down on the slope was absolutely hollow. And the hollowness was new. I don't mean man-made new – there'd been no excavation here, at least not by natural means – but alarmingly, preternaturally new, like the hill was eating itself hollow in preparation for something. The hill was being rewritten, I thought, though I'd have preferred not to.

The cavern walls weren't of rock, but of whatever primordial clay once hardened into rock. They were pale brown, and wet. Oozing wet, like the whole thing was sweating feverishly. The floor was the same, sucking at our feet with every step. That I could handle. It was the breathing that freaked me the fuck out.

It was slow and laboured and, apart from being a hundred times as loud and coming from everywhere at once, sounded like the melancholy and heartbreaking sound of someone on their deathbed. But this wasn't the sound of something dying. It was the sound of something being born. And it bothered me. A lot.

But not as much as it bothered Cody.

We'd descended by rope ladder from a trapdoor in Frankie's souvenir shop – the descent being, too bad for me, textbook smart; guy with gun first, unarmed chick second, creepy old guy third – and ever since we'd got here, Cody'd evidenced increasing signs of having got himself into something that wasn't what he thought he'd signed up for.

Yeah, well too damn bad, Gangsta.

Once his awestruck and unhappy glances at his surroundings started to occupy more of each of his last minutes on earth than his glances at me did, I figured it was time to put him out of his misery.

I couldn't even feel smug about it, guy was so out of his comfort zone. A slight hesitation, as if I was mesmerised by one of the clay-like excrescences that bloomed from the dripping walls like attempts at imitating local flora, a misdirecting glance back behind him, and then a well-placed heel and elbow, and he was on his knees, gasping for breath, and his gun was in my unforgiving hand.

"Say goodnight, Cody," I said, and put one through the centre of his forehead.

I was swinging back towards where I'd last seen Frankie when I heard the click of his safety and felt his barrel at the back of my neck. Cargo pants don't look that great on guys his age, but they do have a lot of pocket space.

"Leave it with him," Frankie said, and I dropped the .38 on Cody's dead chest.

"Watch," Frankie said, trying for dispassionate but failing to completely mask the fascination and excitement.

So I watched. Partly because information is power, and partly because Mom always told me it's a bad idea to piss off a crazy old fucker with a gun.

The blood jetting out of Cody's shattered skull was being sucked into the liquid sheen of the clay like mother's milk into the mouth of a greedy newborn. And it was a two-way street. Cody's flesh was invaded by the faecal brown of the mud he'd died on until, inside of a minute, he looked like something somebody'd moulded from the wet and alien earth itself.

So much for any lingering hope that this could all be explained away by sedimentary settlement.

"It accepts the offering," Frankie said, more out there by the fucking minute. "But don't entertain any hope that this can replace your own sacrifice. There was no gravitas here. No ceremony. The unfortunate news for you is that your death needs to be both slow and somewhat spectacular."

Fuck me. With the exception of his charming opening gambit with the C-word back in his trophy room, everything this guy said sounded like he'd lifted it from his back catalogue of crappy scripts. Case in point, his subsequent lurid description of what I had to look forward to before the day was much older.

"I'm going to blah blah blah. Blah blah blah, Kitty, blah blah blah." On and fucking on. Use your imagination. I assure you it's at least as good as his.

"That how you get it up?" I said, when he was finally done. "Telling girls what you're going to do to them?"

"No, Ms Donnelly," he said. "I get it up watching people's eyes turn glassy with dread as they feel all hope of escape disappear." TV's Frankie Metcalfe, Ladies and Gentlemen. A real fucking sweetheart. "Now, let's move on to the central chamber."

We moved ahead through a curving anterior walkway. Only then, within its lower ceiling and narrower walls, did I pause to wonder where the hell the light was coming from. But it was a meaningless question. I could see perfectly well. And I had no idea how or why.

Another of those misshapen flowers was growing from the weeping wall to our left. This one was vanguard minded, attempting an impression of colour, its stalk and leaves blood red, its petals an eerie and bilious yellow. Frankie's left hand plucked it from the wall with a flourish.

"Here," he said, shaking some of its slime from his fingers and flinging it at me. "Pretend it's Prom Night."

"Thanks," I said, catching it and pretending to sniff it before holding it to my wrist like a corsage. "Every time I smell it, I'll think of you."

He gave me a look that told me he was smart enough to know I'd stolen the line, but not sharp enough to remember from whom – let me save you the Google; it was my fellow Irish deviant, Oscar Wilde – and then, all done with our little time-out flirtation, waved me ahead impatiently, waggling the gun like a signalling device.

"Got it," he said. "You're un-fucking-flappable. Now get moving, or I'll drag you there by the short-and-curlies."

Sad old bastard. Like anybody has pubic hair anymore. I dropped the nasty little flower – wet and rubbery and pulsing unpleasantly like it hadn't yet decided its final shape – and moved ahead of him, conceding reluctantly to myself as I walked on that things were not looking good for our plucky girl detective. Fact, I could feel *The Adventure of the Hollow Hill* lobbying to give itself a real fucking downer of an ending as I stepped out from the walkway into what he'd called the central chamber. There was a bubbling quicksand-like pool at its heart, surrounded by several ill-defined shapes that put me in mind of the grotesque statue that Cody's body had become. More formal offerings, I thought. The place was a compost heap, a mulch pit, and Frankie's ode to its insane splendour confirmed as much.

"You've doubtless seen all that pentagram and puff of smoke nonsense in the movies," he said. "But the truth is it takes time and effort to actually effect a materialisation. The ground must be prepared. I've been seeding it for years, Kitty. Seeding it with frozen pain, with artefacts that contain the captured essence of human suffering. I've brought such treasures here. The skulls of slaughtered children, a letter to the media that one of our most celebrated serial killers wrote in the blood of a victim, a copy of the *De Vermis Mysteriis* bound in human skin. 'The Devil Rides Shotgun' would have been a beautiful addition, but alas . . ."

He let his voice trail off theatrically. Prime fucking ham.

I'd have asked him the obvious question – *why the hell are you doing this?* – but I knew there was no point. He wouldn't have an answer because he wasn't really here anymore. He was as hollow as his hill, and just as much in the process of transformation. Whatever the human motivations that had kicked him off – curiosity, excitement, thrill of the forbidden, whatever – he was now merely a vessel of the Other's desire to manifest itself. He had nothing to do with it. He was long gone. Whatever was blossoming in his cavern had eaten Frankie Metcalfe from the inside too.

So why leave the crust?

He was staring at the bubbling pool at the heart of it all and, for a second or two, hardly paying attention to me. I'd think later that perhaps either outcome was equally acceptable to what was left of the man he used to be, but I wouldn't think about it much because it allowed for too much human ambiguity in the monster he'd become. I sure as shit didn't think about it in the moment. I was younger and faster, and all his meditative pause in the proceedings meant to me was this: forget the gun, close the gap, get one hand on his skull and the other on his chin, and snap his wretched ancient neck like a fucking twig.

I'd have run anyway, but the terrifying re-ossification of the whole cavern lent my legs a whole new level of motivation. Killing Frankie had been like flipping a power-down switch on whatever he'd been ushering in to our world. It made sense, I suppose. Any other death down here – like, you know, *mine* – would have been just more mulch on the shit-pile of its becoming, but the death of its possessed summoner threw everything into reverse. Whatever had been coming was now retreating, and the hill was reclaiming its solidity. Reclaiming it, thank fuck, not quite as fast as I reclaimed the rope ladder and clambered my way back up into the house.

By the time I let myself out of the front door and headed for the Cadillac, the sun was just starting to set. California perfect. Orange and blue and purple and beautiful.

But I wasn't really thinking about that. I was thinking about this:

Neck tattoo, five-foot-six, name of Scott.

Catch you later.

SIMON STRANTZAS

An Indelible Stain Upon the Sky

SIMON STRANTZAS IS THE critically acclaimed author of *Nightingale Songs, Cold to the Touch* and *Beneath the Surface* – three collections of the strange and supernatural currently available from Dark Regions Press.

His award-nominated fiction has appeared previously in the *Mammoth Book of Best New Horror* series, *Zombie Apocalypse! Fightback, PostScripts* and *Cemetery Dance*.

At the moment he is hard at work on his fourth collection, while also editing an anthology about thin places by some of the genre's best new talent. He still lives in Toronto, Canada, with his ever-patient wife and an unyielding hunger for the flesh of the living.

"My wife and I once took a weekend trip on the advice of a friend," Strantzas recalls, "and it turned out to be the most horrendous experience either of us had ever had. So horrendous, in fact, that it did not take long for aspects of the trip to end up incorporated into my fiction, along with my long-standing fear of punishment dolls and my obsession with regret.

"But it wasn't until I incorporated the oil spill from one of my failed novellas that the piece really clicked, and the echoes of past and present began to clearly assert themselves.

"It's a story of loss and despair – the perfect combination for an easy summer holiday on the beach."

I WALK THE SHORELINE as I did ten years ago but everything has changed. The intervening decade has not been long enough for wounds to heal; everywhere I look I see the scars of what's been done. It all looks dead, covered in a thin viscous layer of regret.

The name is infamous even now. The oil tanker *Madison*, one thousand feet long and one-sixth that wide, ran ashore on the reef not twelve miles from where I stand, and the sharp coral sliced through its two hulls as though they were made of paper. From that long gash flowed the darkest, most vile blood into McCarthy Sound, and it spread faster than any estimate could predict. It raced towards the shore, hungry for life to feed on, and it took all birds and fishes and animals in its way until their deaths numbered into the thousands. Everything it touched withered and died, and then it took the life of Port McCarthy, the once peaceful town that could do nothing but watch itself succumb.

Suzanne and I had been there only a few months earlier, when everything seemed as though it would remain beautiful forever. It was still early June, when the days stretch their longest and we had nothing but warm weather to look forward to. We had by then only been together a short while, yet like the summer I could only see happiness laid before us, mapped out across the white sands of the beach. It's strange now to remember; the accident was so close, and in hindsight I can see the ripples it sent backwards through time, yet I was too ignorant to recognise them for what they were. Portents of change, and what they promised has haunted me every day since.

We had driven half a day to reach the small town, sent on the recommendation of a close friend. Suzanne wore a straw hat, and through its wide woven brim a checkerboard of light dappled her soft face and filled her eyes with something akin to a sparkle every time she looked at me. Her laugh made me in turn laugh, and I still recall the sight of her newly shaven legs rubbing against one another and the feeling of absolute happiness it brought me. Were I somehow able to have frozen that moment, I would gladly have spent my remaining life there, wrapped in that beatific feeling of joy. That is the worst of the hauntings: the reminders of what I shall never again have.

The Port McCarthy that lies before me now is overcast, and I must work to remember that this is due to the shorter late autumn days and not that the oil has stained the sky.

I check myself into the Windhaven Inn, the same place where Suzanne and I stayed those many years ago. I must admit I'm surprised it's still there and doing business, but one step inside shows me that it has hung on only by the thinnest of threads. The smiling woman who greeted us a decade ago is nowhere to be seen. Instead, in her place, a girl no more than sixteen, her faded black clothes stretched over her thick body, coils of seeping tattoos wrapped around her arms. I notice her pierced tongue as she speaks to me, and the words leave me feeling cold and wet.

"I've a reservation," I tell her. "For the weekend."

"Sign here," she says, and I see her chipped nails are painted a matching dull black as she points to an empty space in the smudged guest book. I take the pen and try to sign my name, but after more than two attempts the ink still refuses to run. She takes the pen from me wordlessly and dabs it on her studded tongue. When she hands it back it works, but the ink it dispenses is clotted and old.

I follow her upstairs, carrying my small leather bag over my shoulder. I make the mistake of touching the banister and my hand comes away feeling sticky. I try to discreetly rub it clean on the leg of my trousers, but instead stain them as well. When I ask after the woman I'd seen there years before, the young girl explains that she is that woman's daughter, and hints that the *Madison* spill changed her mother in inexplicable ways, ways impossible to come back from. My smile is weak as I look away though I don't know if it's because of the girl's mother or the mother's child. The young girl gives me a half-hearted tour of the inn, her well-practised voice unable to disguise her boredom. She takes me down a corridor and along its length I see three other bedrooms. Only one door is ajar however, and I try to glance in while we pass but the gap is too narrow and the girl has guided me too quickly to catch more than a fleeting glimpse of something dark and wet seeping across the floor.

"This is your room," she says, and hands me a key large enough for only a child's hand. "The lock sticks sometimes and you need to pull it shut to move the bolt." I smile and nod but she doesn't return the courtesy. Instead, she tells me breakfast will be served downstairs at seven, and warns me not to be late.

I close the door and, after struggling with the lock, inspect the small room. It's the same one in which Suzanne and I spent those past days together and for a moment my memories are superimposed over what is truly there. Instead of the stained wallpaper under an overcast day, I see sunlight and warmth; instead of a sagging bed and carpet that looks matted by a million little feet, I see Suzanne laughing as she jumps on the bed, the springs bouncing suggestively. I smile, and the act of smiling causes the mirage to dissipate, revealing the truth of the room, and the first thing I see is a crack that runs down the wall, starting a foot from the ceiling. At its base there is a dark wet mould that has grown into the carpet. I breathe out slowly and look in the mirror on top of the dresser. It too is covered in some greasy film, obscuring my features or twisting them into someone who looks far too old. I hear a noise and look towards the window but I see nothing there. Nothing at all.

I walk over a small bridge into the town of Port McCarthy. To my right, between the rooftops of the tiny stores, the dark grey clouds roll towards me, while beneath them dark waters churn. No one walks the streets but me, and it's clear why as soon as I reach the grimy storefronts. They are closed; boarded for the coming winter. I wonder if it's my timing that's the issue. Had I arrived earlier, in June as before, would the town be bustling with the tourists that I remember Suzanne and I walking past, hand in hand, as we investigated the narrow streets? The two of us spent hours there, wandering through the tiny shops filled with trinkets and home-made crafts, each one comprising a tiny piece of a town that neither of us wanted to leave or ever forget. How different, I think, to now, when all I want is to somehow rid myself of the memories. I look just off the main street and the spectre of Suzanne is there waiting for me, wanting to evoke a memory I'd long ago suppressed.

Suzanne, standing in the sun, an ice-cream cone in one hand fresh from a cart by the edge of the water, pointing at a small sign affixed to a faux-antique lamppost.

"Look," she said, "A new store's just opened. Do you want to see inside?"

"I'm pretty tired," I laughed. "And we've been on our feet for hours. Can't we just rest for a bit?"

She handed me her cone.

"You sit on that bench. I'll only be a minute."

And she was off.

I laughed and waited, and as her treat melted I ate it with selfish glee. Yet, after twenty minutes she had not yet returned and I decided I'd had enough of sitting. I followed the direction she had taken until I came to an old house at the end of the small street. It looked much like any of the houses beside it, yet it had a hand-painted sign with the word ALICE'S written on it in children's paint. The screen door was slightly ajar and I pulled it open to step into the dim room beyond.

It took a few moments to get my bearings, my eyes unable to cope with the change in light. A shadow moved before me and I tried unsuccessfully to blink away the spots that blinded me. In the faux darkness, small black blobs squirmed across my vision, making the world appear murky. As my sight cleared, the first thing I saw was Suzanne, inspecting a polyester dress that hung shapelessly from its hanger. Around me were the beginnings of a consignment shop, filled with crafts of all different kinds, each vying for the attention of tourists. But beyond the items displayed for sale it was clear that no other work had been done to transform the house into a proper store.

"This place fascinates me," she said. "I could spend hours in here."

From room to room we travelled while Suzanne inspected the clothes slowly, her fingers lingering on sizes that would forever be too large for her, and in every corner I saw the same traces of the store's previous function. A single standing lamp in each room were the only sources of illumination, and those oversized ugly dresses were displayed from small hooks screwed into the rafters and walls. I shook my head. It was a terrible place, that converted former house. I thought I heard it scream for release, then realised it was not the house, but Suzanne, and I was immediately certain I had underestimated just how bad things would become.

In my memory, the events play out in slow motion, as though trapped in amber, or perhaps oily tar. I know these things occurred many years ago – so many they may not have happened at all. All I have left of those times are ghosts; dark shadowy ghosts that hover and remind me of what I've lost, of what I've given away without thinking. They are blemishes on my life, like the stains on the Port McCarthy beach that are still working their way into the ground a decade later, killing the seeds of any life they find.

"Look at this. Who *makes* these things?"

Suzanne whispered to me in that converted house, and though it must have been loud enough for anyone to hear, I was far too unnerved by spinning uncontrollable fear to check. There before us stood a doll the size of a small child, dressed in a small child's clothes. It faced the wall as though it were being punished, its arms raised to cover its missing eyes. I shivered, and then saw a second doll. Then, another. They stood throughout the house in the same manner, faces turned to the wall, their little bodies impossibly real. Except their faces. I knew immediately that if I were to check the dolls' faces they would be blank, lifeless, and part of me wished that would not be the case.

"They're *so* creepy," Suzanne said. "They look so real."

"I don't know who would buy one," I said, looking away because I could no longer bear the sight. An older man across the room smiled at me from behind a counter, his teeth too large.

"The sign says they're called 'hide and seek dolls'," Suzanne said. "Where do they get their clothes?"

"Maybe from their dead children," I said, mesmerised by the man's widening smile – so wide I doubted reality for a moment. Then my own words registered, and the sickness they filled me with snapped me back to attention. "I mean, they were probably donated. Some kid outgrew them." I smiled at Suzanne in hopes she had forgotten what I had said. Instead, she grimaced.

I carry that image of her in my head still, and sometimes it amazes me it's there at all when so many other things I wish I could recall have been forgotten. Memories are strange and elusive, yet they can return at a moment's notice and from out of nowhere, appearing so vividly it feels as though time has not passed. But time *has* passed, and those memories that return most often have crashed just off the shore of my life, and the dark sweep of destruction continues to move towards me over the churning water's surface.

I can't be sure if it's going to rain, but the air feels wet and chilled and I decide I don't want to take the chance. By the time I return to the Windhaven Inn, I know I was right, as the rain has started, but even so it is not a hard cleansing rain. Rather, it's a drizzle, barely more than a mist, and all it succeeds in doing is making my shoes damp enough that each step feels as though I am wading through water.

Outside the Inn's front door is a small garden in which an old cat squats. Its fur is grimy and matted as though it has spent an inordinate amount of time underground, and there is a glazed look in its dull ancient eyes. It chews grass slowly, and doesn't seem to know I'm there, or if it does it cannot be bothered to acknowledge me. Perhaps one of us is a ghost, though neither of us is sure which.

"It has six toes, you know. Born like that. Six on every foot. You know what they say about *that*, don't you?"

It is the young tattooed woman. She stands at the door smoking a cigarette, looking at me as though I have disturbed her with my thoughts. I smile weakly.

"No. What does it mean?"

She shakes her head, disappointed, and looks up at the sky. I look too, but the rain is a cloud hovering too close to the ground.

"Your key is at the front desk."

I nod. She signals me with some hand sign that belies her youth, then retreats inside. I try and push the cat out of the way with my foot, but it doesn't move, not at first. My foot sinks into sickly soft fur that feels no different from a dish of rotted meat. The cat makes a low gurgling noise, and finally gets to its feet and staggers a few steps before falling on its side, out of breath.

My room is dark when I return to it, the overcast day filling the emptiness with the kind of shadows that do not dissipate when I turn on the lamps. I take my shoes and socks off to dry them, then sit on the edge of the bed. I scratch at the underside of my beard, less from discomfort and more for something to do with my hands, and look out the window at the solid wall of mist that hovers there. Part of me wants to draw the drapes, but I can't. The swirling reminds me of a flood that will wash over everything and make it new. I just wish I knew what colour the water would be.

Suzanne and I made love that first night at the Inn, when the summer was warm and the scent of the beach was in the air. I remember it clearly, remember how soft and slow it was, remember us pausing to share a cigarette afterward, the smoke curling around the curve of her small breasts. And then I again see her grimacing face before me, only now she's joined me on the edge of the bed, and with a sense of ten-year-old *déjà vu* I ask what's wrong. She hangs her head so I can't see her face behind her hair, and covers her eyes. "A ghost must have just walked past me." She laughs and I laugh with her though I'm not sure why. The vision begins to recede again until all that is left is the memory of a sky turned dark orange, and Suzanne's hand fidgeting awkwardly as it lights on her abdomen. But there is something else, a flicker on the edge of my vision. I turn to the source and see in the darkness that the crack in the wall is longer, and the stain spreading from it is creeping across the carpet towards me. There's something intriguing about it, but before I can determine just what that is I realise the stain is in fact something more.

In my head, words still echo like ripples in time spreading out from the past. I try to push them aside, try to drown them with alcohol or noise, but I can still hear them as they leave an indelible mark on my soul.

"What are we going to do?" I remember Suzanne asking me, her eyes wide while I only wanted to close my own to dull the throbbing.

"What *can* we do?"

There were no answers. What had seemed so clear only a few hours before we spoke had become suddenly so muddy, as though the oil that had flooded McCarthy Sound had contaminated my mind. I rubbed my temples as she spoke, and the fear she filled me with was thick and suffocating. She cried and hugged herself because I could do neither for her. I was afraid. I was young and afraid and selfish, and I could not understand why such a thing was happening.

"Why is this happening?" she echoed.

My apartment seemed filled by her presence, and as she sat at my kitchen table quietly sobbing I tried to think. Behind me, the television news was stuck in a loop, repeating the story of the tanker *Madison* and the wave of inevitable death that advanced upon the idyllic town of Port McCarthy. The words repeated in my mind until it seemed as though the voices were talking about me – talking *to* me. The accident was dire; everything had to be cleaned – I heard the words over and over until it seemed the only logical course, and yet Suzanne did not agree, not at first. I managed to convince her, though. I wore her down until she believed it was for the best. That ghost, too, continues to haunt me. It yelps at me, demanding my attention, and as I'm drawn from my reverie I realise it's the sound of a dog in the next room. At least, I believe it's a dog. I can't be sure. It is unlike any sound I've ever heard, and it cuts into my nerves.

Yet I can't help but feel dissociated from that part of myself, far away from the place I truly am, for when I see the shape of the shadow standing before me, I barely register its impossibility. The illusion is darker than anything I've ever seen, and beneath its form is a stain that has crept across the carpet towards me, a stain of what was spilled here so long ago. And yet, that darkness looks familiar to me, as though I should recognise its shape but cannot. It's a puzzle that my brain doesn't comprehend. Not until the shadow moves. It's then that the image shifts into focus, and I realise to my horror what I am witnessing.

I don't know where he comes from or what he's made of, but before the wall stands a child formed from the black oil that is spread like a thin blanket over every surface of Port McCarthy. The boy-shaped shadow ripples, standing with his back to me as he shields his eyes from the deep fissure he was born from. He hides his face as though playing a game, a game meant to tell me something, but I'm not sure what that might be. Whatever knowledge he is trying to impart has been washed away by the flood of regret that pours from my heart like oil from a ruptured ship. I stand, intent on going nearer to him, wanting to inspect the vision to be sure my eyes are not deceiving me, but I travel no more than a step before I find myself hesitating, unsure I truly want to know the truth. In my terror I am unable to confront him and the wave of my regret threatens to overwhelm me. The only way I might breathe again is to turn my back, to hide from the childlike shadow as it hides from me, and wait until the world seems familiar again. But instead all I can see is the dresser mirror, and the reflection of a shivering child smeared and fractured within it.

The accident's effects were not clear to me at first. I thought naïvely that the world would revert to what it once had been. Suzanne returned to work, I to my writing, and though we still bore the knowledge of what had happened I thought for a while that it meant nothing, that ultimately our love – that love shared between us in the sun of Port McCarthy, that had taken seed and grown further there – would be enough to heal us. I could not allow myself to believe that the accident would rob us of that idyllic life and erase everything that had preceded it. Yet, over time, my confidence faltered. The first sign things had altered irrevocably I did not immediately notice. Each return of Suzanne home from work was progressively later, until eventually I realised it had been months since I'd seen her in daylight. The darkness, it wore on her. Deep circles appeared beneath her swollen eyes, her blonde hair dried and lost its lustre. She no longer smiled, and try as I might to retain what we once had I could feel it slipping through my fingers like the fine grains of sand along the Port McCarthy beach. The life Suzanne and I once shared had withered after the accident, and though a portion of me understood that I still refused to believe the part I had played. Port McCarthy, where all our happiness once lay, had become ruined by the black oil that lapped its shores. It had become a barren place to which neither of us could return; we no longer belonged there. The accident had banished us forever. I know this because ten years later I *have* returned, and as I stand in nearly the same spot, in the same room, as I did then when I told Suzanne I loved her, I cannot face what we made reflected in the mirror before me. Instead, I weep over all that has been taken from me and all that has been lost, never to return.

The knock at the door startles me. The world that had been so quiet before returns and I find myself caught in a limbo state between what is real and what cannot be. As though I am awakening from a dream, the sensation is enough to disorient me, and looking around everything appears to be wrong. Understanding of what has happened is frustratingly out of reach. The knock returns, a voice calling to me from the door, and shaking off my delirium I stumble towards it, keenly aware of the presence that stands behind me, not looking my way. I don't dare turn to see if it has vanished.

"Are you okay in there?" the young woman from the desk asks through the door. Her concerned words belie her distaste for me. I hear her fumbling with the lock, trying to open it. I place my foot surreptitiously against the base of the door.

"I'm fine. Fine."

"Can you open the door?" she asks. I jiggle the handle ineffectually from my side, feigning effort.

"It seems to be stuck."

"That's okay. I've just come to tell you—" she lowers her voice and I'm not sure at first I've heard her properly. "There've been some complaints. The walls here are a bit thin; things pass through them."

"Things? What things?" I say, growing cold. Is it possible I feel the fissure behind me growing wider? Feel it like a crack in my own being?

"Like I don't know what. Like whatever you're doing in here. Can you keep it down?"

I am not sure what she means but I agree. What else can I do? I'm afraid she's going to push into the room and see the wall and what has emerged from it. Or, perhaps, I'm more afraid she won't. I close my eyelids and listen to her walk away then hear nothing more – nothing but the slow leaking tap, or perhaps it's the rain outside. Or is it a small figure made of oil, its back turned to me as mine is to it, no longer able to keep its shape and exist in this world, that drips darkness onto the carpet? I open my eyelids finally and turn around to see which it is.

The town of Port McCarthy died slowly, choked by the darkness that rolled towards it without warning on waves as black as night. While the rest of the world saw this from a distance, Suzanne and I suffered the full brunt of the accident there, we suffered the crashing waves of darkness that would not stop, would not end, until it spread through our lives as surely as it had through Port McCarthy. Even now I feel it, and even now I wish I had known some way to halt its progress before it was too late. But that's the way with accidents; they come when we are not prepared, and in their wake they leave devastation and death. As soon as that black oil was spilled in Port McCarthy, there was no hope for me, for Suzanne, for us. It doesn't surprise me in hindsight that there is no sun in Port McCarthy, instead only dark clouds. The sun forsook us then. While we laughed and smiled and embraced in ignorance the seeds of our destruction had already been planted.

It doesn't take me long to pack my bag, my distaste for the town all but palpable. The dog in the next room has not made a noise in some time, and I pray it doesn't start because I worry what I will do if it does. Not once do I look at the crack in the wall, at the stain that has spread from it across the carpet. I want to, but if I succumb I fear I will be drawn too far into the darkness to ever extricate myself.

I rush down the stairs, nearly slipping on something that coats them. The tattooed girl at the front desk clicks her studded tongue against her teeth as I sign out and hand her the key.

"You aren't staying?"

"There's nothing here to see anymore," I mutter, my head down, and scurry from the Windhaven Inn while trying to dispel the image of that dark child from my memory. If the girl says anything more to me, it does not register.

I stop on the porch of the Windhaven Inn, my hastily packed bag in my hand, and look up at the dark clouds that are like an indelible stain upon the sky. And I wonder, for a moment, if it's not my soul that has been so marked.

Then, at the foot of the steps, I see the large six-toed cat once again. It still stares blankly ahead as though it is waiting for something but has forgotten what. It sits, blocking my passage, but I don't dare touch it – I cannot bring myself to relive the experience of feeling its matted fur slide across its body. As I watch I see that what it chews is not grass, not any longer. I put my bag down and take a hesitant step towards the creature, not heeding the low growl it gives as warning. Instead, I crane my head further until what I see between its teeth is the head of a flower from which a long stem trails back to the ground; a flower that has impossibly sprouted through a dark oily film and beneath an even darker sky.

A flower. A life for a life. A promise of re-growth.

I reach towards the old cat but it only growls and bites.

JOAN AIKEN

Hair

JOAN DELANO AIKEN MBE (1924–2004) was born in Rye, East Sussex, the daughter of Pulitzer Prize-winning American poet and ghost story author Conrad Aiken. She began writing at an early age, and in her early twenties she had some of her stories broadcast by the BBC.

In the 1950s she joined the editorial staff of *Argosy* magazine which, along with a number of other popular periodicals at the time, published her short fiction. During this period she also produced her first two collections of children's stories and began work on her classic novel *The Wolves of Willoughby Chase* (1962), which was set in an alternate history of Britain.

By now a full-time writer, she produced two or three books a year for the rest of her life. Her more than 100 titles included *Midnight is a Place*, *Black Hearts in Battersea*, *The Cuckoo Tree*, *Dark Interval*, *The Crystal Crow*, *Voices in an Empty House*, *The Kingdom Under the Sea*, *The Cockatrice Boys*, *The Scream*, *Midwinter Nightingale* and *The Witch of Clatteringshaws*, along with a series of historical novels based around Jane Austen's characters.

Aiken was also a life-long fan of ghost stories, particularly the works of M. R. James and Fitz James O'Brien, and her own contributions to the genre include the novels *The Shadow Guests* and *The Haunting of Lamb House*, along with the collections *The Windscreen Weepers*, *A Whisper in the Night* and *A Creepy Company*.

More recently, Small Beer Press published *The Monkey's Wedding and Other Stories*, a posthumous collection that included seven previously unpublished stories, including the macabre tale that follows.

A Guest of Honour at the 1997 World Fantasy Convention in London, Joan Aiken won the Guardian Award and the Edgar Allan Poe Award, and in 1999 was presented with an MBE for her services to children's literature.

T OM ORFORD STOOD leaning over the rail and watching the flat hazy shores of the Red Sea slide past. A month ago he had been watching them slide in the other direction. Sarah had been with him then, leaning and looking after the ship's wake, laughing and whispering ridiculous jokes into his ear.

They had been overflowingly happy, playing endless deck games with the other passengers, going to the ship's dances in Sarah's mad, rakish conception of fancy dress, even helping to organise the appalling concerts of amateur talent, out of their gratitude to the world.

"You'll tire yourself out!" somebody said to Sarah, as she plunged from deck-tennis to swimming in the ship's pool, from swimming to dancing, from dancing to ping pong. "As if I could," she said to Tom. "I've done so little all my life, I have twenty-one years of accumulated energy to work off."

But just the same, that was what she had done. She had died, vanished, gone out, as completely as a forgotten day, or a drift of the scent of musk. Gone, lost to the world. Matter can neither be created nor destroyed, he thought. Not matter, no. The network of bones and tendons, the dandelion clock of fair hair, the brilliantly blue eyes that had once belonged to Sarah, and had so riotously obeyed her will for a small portion of her life – a forty-second part of it, perhaps – was now quietly returning to earth in a Christian cemetery in Ceylon. But her spirit, the fiery intention which had co-ordinated that machine of flesh and bone and driven it through her life – the spirit, he knew, existed neither in air nor earth. It had gone out, like a candle.

He did not leave the ship at Port Said. It was there that he had met Sarah. She had been staying with friends, the Acres. Orford had gone on a trip up the Nile with her. Then they had started for China. This was after they had been married, which happened almost immediately. And now he was coming back with an address, and a bundle of hair to give to her mother. For she had once laughingly asked him to go and visit her mother, if she were to die first.

"Not that she'd enjoy your visit," said Sarah dryly. "But she'd be highly offended if she didn't get a lock of hair, and she might as well have the lot, now I've cut it off. And you could hardly send it to her in a registered envelope."

He had laughed, because then death seemed a faraway and irrelevant threat, a speck on the distant horizon.

"Why are we talking about it, anyway?" he said.

"Death always leaps to mind when I think of Mother," she answered, her eyes dancing. "Due to her I've lived in an atmosphere of continuous death for twenty-one years."

She had told him her brief story. When she reached twenty-one, and came into an uncle's legacy, she had packed her brush and comb and two books and a toothbrush ("All my other possessions, if they could be called mine, were too ugly to take"), and, pausing only at a hairdresser's to have her bun cut off (he had seen a photograph of her at nineteen, a quiet, dull-looking girl, weighed down by her mass of hair) she had set off for Egypt to visit her only friend, Mrs Acres. She wrote to her mother from Cairo. She had had one letter in return.

"My dear Sarah, as you are now of age I cannot claim to have any further control over you, for you are, I trust, perfectly healthy in mind and body. I have confidence in the upbringing you received, which furnished you with principles to guide you through life's vicissitudes. I know that in the end you will come back to me."

"She seems to have taken your departure quite lightly," Orford said, reading it over her shoulder.

"Oh, she never shows when she's angry," Sarah said. She studied the letter again. "Little does she know," was her final comment, as she put it away. "Hey, I don't want to think about her. Quick, let's go out and see something – a pyramid or a cataract or a sphinx. Do you realise that I've seen absolutely nothing – nothing – nothing all my life? Now I've got to make up for lost time. I want to see Rome and Normandy and Illyria and London – I've never been there, except Heathrow – and Norwegian fjords and the Taj Mahal."

Tomorrow, Orford thought, he would have to put on winter clothes. He remembered how the weather had become hotter and hotter on the voyage out. Winter to summer, summer to winter again.

London, when he reached it, was cold and foggy. He shrank into himself, sitting in the taxi which squeaked and rattled its way from station to station, like a moving tomb. At Charing Cross he ran into an acquaintance who exclaimed, "Why, Tom old man, I didn't expect to see you for another month. Thought you were on your honeymoon or something?"

Orford slid away into the crowd.

"And can you tell me where Marl End is?" he was presently asking, at a tiny ill-lit station which felt as if it were in the middle of the steppes.

"Yes, sir," said the man, after some thought. "You'd best phone for a taxi. It's a fair way. Right through the village and on over the sheepdowns."

An aged Ford, lurching through the early winter dusk, which was partly mist, brought him to a large redbrick house, set baldly in the middle of a field.

"Come back and call for me at seven," he said, resolving to take no chances with the house, and the driver nodded, shifting his gears, and drove away into the fog as Orford knocked at the door.

The first thing that struck him was her expression of relentless, dogged intention. Such, he thought, might be the look on the face of a coral mite, setting out to build up an atoll from the depths of the Pacific.

He could not imagine her ever desisting from any task she had set her hand to.

Her grief seemed to be not for herself but for Sarah.

"Poor girl. Poor girl. She would have wanted to come home again before she died. Tired herself out, you say? It was to be expected. Ah well."

Ah well, her tone said, it isn't my fault. I did what I could. I could have prophesied what would happen; in fact I did; but she was out of my control, it was her fault, not mine.

"Come close to the fire," she said. "You must be cold after that long journey."

Her tone implied he had come that very night from Sarah's cold un-Christian deathbed, battling through frozen seas, over Himalayas, across a dead world.

"No, I'm fine," he said. "I'll stay where I am. This is a very warm room." The stifling, hothouse air pressed on his face, solid as sand. He wiped his forehead.

"My family, unfortunately are all extremely delicate," she said, eyeing him. "Poor things, they need a warm house. Sarah – my husband – my sister – I daresay Sarah told you about them?"

"I've never seen my father," he remembered Sarah saying. "I don't know what happened to him – whether he's alive or dead. Mother always talks about him as if he were just outside in the garden."

But there had been no mention of an aunt. He shook his head.

"Very delicate," she said. She smoothed back her white hair, which curved over her head like a cap, into its neat bun at the back. "Deficient in thyroid – thyroxin, do they call it? She needs constant care."

Her smile was like a swift light passing across a darkened room.

"My sister disliked poor Sarah – for some queer reason of her own – so all the care of her fell on me. Forty years."

"Terrible for you," he answered mechanically.

The smile passed over her face again.

"Oh, but it is really quite a happy life for her, you know. She draws, and plays with clay, and of course she is very fond of flowers and bright colours. And nowadays she very seldom loses her temper, though at one time I had a great deal of trouble with her."

I manage all, her eyes said, I am the strong one, I keep the house warm, the floors polished, the garden dug, I have cared for the invalid and reared my child, the weight of the house has rested on these shoulders and in these hands.

He looked at her hands as they lay in her black silk lap, fat and white with dimpled knuckles.

"Would you care to see over the house?" she said.

He would not, but could think of no polite way to decline. The stairs were dark and hot, with a great shaft of light creeping round the corner at the top.

"Is anybody there?" a quavering voice called through a half-closed door. It was gentle, frail, and unspeakably old.

"Go to sleep, Miss Whiteoak, go to sleep," she called back. "You should have swallowed your dose long ago."

"My companion," she said to Orford, "is very ill."

He had not heard of any companion from Sarah.

"This is my husband's study," she told him, following him into a large, hot room.

Papers were stacked in orderly piles on the desk. The bottle of ink was half full. A half-written letter lay on the blotter. But who occupied this room? "Mother always talks as if he were just outside."

On the wall hung several exquisite Japanese prints. Orford exclaimed in pleasure.

"My husband is fond of those prints," she said, following his glance. "I can't see anything in them myself. Why don't they make objects the right size, instead of either too big or too small? I like something I can recognise, I tell him."

Men are childish, her eyes said, and it is the part of women to see that they do nothing foolish, to look after them.

They moved along the corridor.

"This was Sarah's room," she said.

Stifling, stifling, the bed, chair, table, chest all covered in white sheets. Like an airless graveyard waiting for her, he thought.

"I can't get to sleep," Miss Whiteoak called through her door. "Can't I come downstairs?"

"No, no, I shall tell you when you may come down," the old lady called back. "You are not nearly well enough yet!"

Orford heard a sigh.

"Miss Whiteoak is wonderfully devoted," she said, as they slowly descended the stairs. "I have nursed her through so many illnesses. She would do anything for me. Only, of course, there isn't anything that she can do now, poor thing."

At the foot of the stairs an old, old woman in a white apron was lifting a decanter from a sideboard.

"That's right, Drewett," she said. "This gentleman will be staying to supper. You had better make some broth. I hope you are able to stay the night?" she said to Orford.

But when he explained that he could not even stay to supper she took the news calmly.

"Never mind about the broth, then, Drewett. Just bring in the sherry."

The old woman hobbled away, and they returned to the drawing room. He gave her the tissue-paper full of Sarah's hair.

She received the bundle absently, then examined it with a sharp look. "Was this cut before or after she died?"

"Oh – before – before I married her." He wondered what she was thinking. She gave a long, strange sigh, and presently remarked, "That accounts for everything."

Watching the clutch of her fat, tight little hands on the hair, he began to be aware of a very uneasy feeling, as if he had surrendered something that only now, when it was too late, he realised had been of desperate importance to Sarah. He remembered, oddly, a tale from childhood: "Where is my heart, dear wife? Here it is, dear husband: I am keeping it wrapped up in my hair."

But Sarah had said, "She might as well have the lot, now I've cut it off."

He almost put out his hand to take it back; wondered if, without her noticing, he could slip the packet back into his pocket.

Drewett brought in the sherry in the graceful decanter with a long, fine glass spout at one side. He commented on it.

"My husband bought it in Spain," she said. "Twenty years ago. I have always taken great care of it."

The look on her face gave him again that chilly feeling of uneasiness. "Another glass?" she asked him.

"No, I really have to go." He looked at his watch, and said with relief, "My taxi will be coming back for me in five minutes."

There came a sudden curious mumbling sound from a dim corner of the room. It made him start so violently that he spilt some of his sherry. He had supposed the place empty, apart from themselves.

"Ah, feeling better, dear?" the old lady said.

She walked slowly over to the corner and held out a hand, saying, "Come and see poor Sarah's husband. Just think – she had a husband – isn't that a queer thing?"

Orford gazed aghast at the stumbling slobbering creature that came reluctantly forward, tugging away from the insistent white hand. His repulsion was the greater because in its vacant, puffy-eyed stare he could detect a shadowy resemblance to Sarah.

"She's just like a child, of course," said the old lady indul-gently. "Quite dependent on me, but wonderfully affectionate, in her way." She gave the cretin a fond glance. "Here, Louisa, here's something pretty for you! Look, dear – lovely hair."

Dumbly, Orford wondered what other helpless, infirm pieces of humanity might be found in this house, all dependent on the silver-haired old lady who brooded over them, sucking them dry like a gentle spider. What might he trip over in the darkness of the hall? Who else had escaped?

The conscious part of his mind was fixed in horror as he watched Louisa rapaciously knotting and tearing and plucking at the silver-gold mass of hair.

"I think I hear your taxi," the old lady said. "Say good-night, Louisa!"

Louisa said good-night in her fashion, the door shut behind him – and he was in the car, in the train, in a cold hotel bedroom, with nothing but the letter her mother had written her to remind him that Sarah had ever existed.

STEVE RASNIC TEM

Miri

STEVE RASNIC TEM'S LATEST novel is *Deadfall Hotel* from Solaris Books, while New Pulp Press has recently published a collection of the best of his *noir* and crime fiction, *Ugly Behavior*. Forthcoming is *Celestial Inventories*, a major collection of his more recent strange fiction from ChiZine.

"'Miri' came out of a meditation on vampirism," explains the author, "and those extremely needy people who leave you drained even in the most casual of relationships. Good sense tells you to stay away, and yet your humanity will not let you simply ignore the sadness of their situation – balancing the two impulses is never easy.

"Along the way the difficulty of acting honourably in such a relationship entered into the equation, and the shame we sometimes feel that our younger selves failed to meet our current standards."

THEY SPREAD THE blanket over the cool grass and took their places. The puppet stage was broad and brightly lit, with a colourful and elaborate jungle set. Rick framed his children inside the LCD screen on the back of his camera as they settled in front of him: Jay Jay who was too old for this sort of thing but would enjoy it anyway, and seven-year-old Molly, worrisomely thin, completely entranced, her large eyes riveted on the stage as oversized heads with garishly painted faces danced, their mouths magnified into exaggerated smiles, frowns, and fiercely insistent madness.

The colours began to fade from the faces – the painted ones, and his children's – he took his eyes away from the camera and blinked. The world had become a dramatic arrangement of blacks and whites. Molly raised her stark face and stared at him, her eyes a smoulder of shadow. *Where is she?* he thought, and looked around. He thought he caught a glimpse – there by a tree, a pale sliver of arm, a fall of black hair, lips a smear of charcoal. He could feel the breath go out of him. *Not here.* But he couldn't be sure. He closed his eyes, tried to stop the rising tide of apprehension, opened them, and found that all the colours had been restored to the world with sickening suddenness.

He quickly took a dozen or so more shots, his finger dancing on the shutter button. Elaine patted his hand and took the camera away. "Enough already," she whispered into his ear. He tried not to be annoyed, to no avail. She had no idea what she was talking about. It didn't matter how many pictures he took – it would never be enough.

Between the kids lay the pizza box with their ragged leftovers. Jay Jay would finish it if they let him. Molly would sneak a guilty glance but would not touch it. Rick had no idea what to do to help her; next week he would make more calls.

"You're a wonderful dad, and a really good person," Elaine whispered, and kissed that place above his ear where his hairline had dramatically begun to recede. Especially in this early evening light she was lovely – she still managed to put a hitch into his breath.

He smiled and mouthed *thanks*, even though such naked compliments embarrassed him. He'd finally learned it was bad form, and unattractive, to argue with them. So even though he was thinking he just had a few simple ideas, like always giving your kids something to look forward to, he said nothing. In any case it would be hypocritical. Because he also would not be confessing that he wasn't the good person she thought he was. Or telling her how often he wished he'd didn't have kids – it had never been his dream, and sometimes spending an entire day with them and their constant need left him drained, stupid, and angry. He was ashamed of himself – perhaps that was why he sometimes made himself so patient.

An unreal ceiling of stars hung low over the lake, the park, the puppet stage, and all these families sitting out on their assorted colourful blankets. Elaine pulled closer to him, mistakenly saying "I love that you still love the stars."

But he didn't. These stars were a lie. This close to the centre of the city you couldn't see the stars because of the electric lights. And the dark between them had a slightly streaked appearance, as if the brush strokes were showing. Somehow this sky had been faked – he just didn't know how. But he knew by whom.

Was he lying when he allowed Elaine to mistake his silence or his distraction, for something sweet and good? If so he was a consistent and successful liar.

His gaze drifted. Off to his left an elderly couple standing on their blanket looked a bit too textured, too still. At the moment he decided they were cut-outs the vague suggestion of a slim female form moved slowly in behind them, looking much the cut-out herself, a black silhouette with a painted white face, a dancing paper doll. She turned her head toward him, graceful as a ballerina, presenting one dark eye painted against a background of china white, framed expressionistically by black strokes of hair, black crescent cheekbones, before she turned sideways and vanished.

"I'll be right back," he whispered to Elaine. "Bathroom." He climbed absently to his feet, feeling as if his world were being snatched out from under him. *If I could just get my hands on that greedy, hungry bitch.*

The kids didn't even notice him leave, their eyes full of the fakery on stage. He quickly averted his glance – the colour in their faces, the patterns in their shirts, were beginning to fade.

He moved through the maze of blankets quickly, vaguely registering the perfectly outfitted manikin couples with rudimentary features, their arms and legs bent in broken approximations of humanity. Near the outer edge of the crowd he bumped into a stiff tree-coat of a figure with a grey beard glued to the lower part of its oval head. He pardoned himself as it crashed to the ground, scattering paper plates and plastic foods onto the silent shapes of a seated family.

He passed into the well-mannered trees, which grew in geometric patches around the park. He could see her fluttering rapidly ahead of him, alternating shadow side and sunny side like a leaf twirling in the breeze off the water. She peeked back over her shoulder, her cheek making a dark-edged blade. She laughed as sharply, with no happiness in it. Something was whipping his knees – he looked down and the flesh below his shorts had torn on underbrush that hadn't been here before, that had been allowed to grow and threaten. He started to run and the trees greyed and spread themselves into the patchy walls of an ill-kept hallway – inside the residential hotel he'd lived in his last few years of college. Dim sepia lighting made everything feel under pressure, as if the hall were a tube travelling through deep water.

Wearily he found his door and stepped into a room stinking of his own sweat. He slumped into a collapsed chair leaking stuffing. He thought to watch some television, but couldn't bring himself to get up and turn the set on. Gravity pushed him deeper into the cushion, adhering his hands to the chair's palm-stained arms.

The knock on the door was soft, more like a rubbing. "Ricky? Are you home?"

He twisted his head slightly, unable to lift it away from the thickly-padded back. He watched as the doorknob rattled in its collar. He willed the latch to hold.

"Ricky, it's Miri," she said unnecessarily. "We don't have to do anything, I swear. We could just talk, okay?" Her voice was like a needy child's asking for help. How did she do that? "Ricky, I just need to be with somebody tonight. Please."

She knew he was there, but he didn't know how. He'd watched his building and the street outside long before he came in – she'd been nowhere in sight.

"Are you too tired, Ricky? Is that it? Is that why you can't come to the door?"

Of course he was tired. That had been the idea, hadn't it? Everything was so incessant about her – you couldn't listen without being sucked in. She wanted him too tired to walk away from her. He closed his eyes, could feel her rubbing against the door.

He woke up in his living room, the TV muted, the picture flickering in a jumpy, agitated way. It looked like one of those old black and white Val Lewton films, *Cat People* perhaps, the last thing he'd want to watch in his state of mind. He was desperate to go to bed, but he couldn't move his arms or legs. He stared at his right arm and insisted, but he might have been gazing at a stick for all the good it did. He blinked his grainy eyes because at least he could still move them. After a few moments he was able to jerk his head forward – and his body followed up and out of the chair. He almost fell over but righted himself, staggering drunkenly down to their bedroom.

He couldn't see Elaine in the greasy darkness, but she whispered from the bed. "I know it's the job, wearing you out, but the kids were asking about you. They were disappointed you didn't come say goodnight – they wanted to talk more about the puppet show. Go and check on them – at least tomorrow you can tell them you did that."

He felt like lashing out, or weeping in frustration. Instead he turned and stumbled back out into the hall. He could have lied to her, but he went down to Jay Jay's room.

The boy in the bed slept like a drunk with one foot on the floor. He looked like every boy, but he didn't look anything like his son. What his son actually looked like, Rick had no idea.

Molly had kicked all the covers off, and lay there like a sweaty, sick animal, her hair matted and stiff, her mouth open exposing a few teeth. She seemed too thin to be a child – he watched as her ribs made deep grooves in the thin membrane of her flesh with each ragged breath. How was he expected to save such a creature? He walked over and picked her sheet off the floor, tucked her in and, when she curled into a sigh, kissed her goodnight.

When he climbed into bed Elaine was asleep. He avoided looking at her, not wanting to see whatever it was he might see. He must have looked at his wife's face tens of thousands of times over the years of their marriage. If you added it all up – months certainly – of distracted or irritated or loving or passion-addled gazes. And yet there were times, such as after the 3 a.m. half-asleep trudge to the bathroom, when he imagined that if he were to return to their bedroom and find Elaine dead, it wouldn't be long before he'd forget her lovely face entirely.

He sometimes loved his family like someone grieving, afraid he would forget what they'd looked like. An obsession with picture-taking helped keep the fear at bay, but only temporarily. As a graphic designer he worked with images every day. He knew what he was talking about. It didn't matter how many snapshots he kept – we don't remember people because of a single recognisable image. In his way, he'd conducted his own private study. We remember people because of a daily changing gestalt – because of their ability to constantly look different than themselves. The changing set of the mouth, the tone of the skin, the engagement of the eyes. The weight lost and the weight gained. The changing tides of joy and stress and fatigue. That's what keeps people alive in our imaginations. Interrupt that flow, and a light leaves them. That's what Miri had done, was doing, to him. She was draining the light that illumined his day. Sometime during the night he turned over and made the error of opening his eyes, and saw her face where Elaine's used to be.

"Rick, you're gonna have to redo these." Matthew stood over him, a sheaf of papers in hand, looking embarrassed. They'd started in college together, back when Rick had been the better artist. Now Matthew was the supervisor, and neither of them had ever been comfortable with it.

"Just tell me what I did wrong this time – I'll fix it."

"It's this new character, the goth girl. The client will never approve this – it's the wrong demographic for a mainstream theatre chain."

"I didn't—" But seeing the art, he realised he had. The female in each of the movie date scenes was dark-haired and hollow-eyed, depressed-looking. And starved.

"She looks like that woman you dated in college."

"We didn't date," Rick snapped.

"Okay, went out with."

"We never even went out. I'm not sure what you'd call what we did together."

"I just remember what a disaster she was for you, this freaky goth chick—"

"Matt, I don't think they even had goths back then. She was just this poor depressed, suicidal young woman."

He smirked. "That was always your type, if I recall. Broody, skinny chicks."

Now his old friend had him confused with someone else. There had never been enough women for Rick to have had a type. "Her *name* was Miriam, but she always went by Miri. And do you actually still use that word 'chick'? Do you understand how disrespectful that is?"

"Just when I'm talking about the old days. No offence."

"None taken. I'll have the new designs for you end of the week."

Rick spread the drawings out over his desk and adjusted his lamp for a better look. He never seemed to have enough light anymore. There was an Elvira-like quality to the figures, or like that woman in the old Charles Addams panel cartoons, but Miri had had small, flattened breasts. It embarrassed him that he should remember such a thing.

In college all he ever wanted to do was paint. But it had really been an obsession with colour – brushing it, smearing it, finding its light and shape and what was revealed when two colours came against each other on the canvas. He'd come home after class and paint late into the night, sometimes eating with his brush in the other hand. Each day was pretty much the same, except Saturday when he could paint all day. Then Sunday he'd sleep all day before restarting the cycle on Monday.

Women were not a part of that life. Not that he wasn't interested. If he wanted anything more than to be a good painter it was to have the companionship and devotion of a woman. He simply didn't know how to make that happen – he didn't even know how to imagine it. To ask a woman for a date was out of the question because that meant being judged and compared and having to worry if he would ever be good enough and unable to imagine being good enough. He'd had enough of that insanity growing up.

At least he was sensitive enough to recognise the dangers of wanting something so badly and believing it forever unobtainable. He wasn't about to let it make him resentful – he wasn't going to be one of those lonely guys who hated women. The problem was his, after all.

He was aware a female had moved into the residential hotel, because of conversations overheard and certain scents and things found in the shared bathroom or the trash. Then came the night he was at the window, painting, and just happened to glance down at the sidewalk as she was glancing up.

Her face was like that Ezra Pound poem: a petal on a wet black bough. Now detached from its nourishment, now destined for decay.

A few minutes later there was a faint, strengthless knocking on his door. At first he ignored it out of habit. Although it didn't get louder it remained insistent, so eventually he wiped the paint off his hands and went to answer.

Her slight figure was made more so by a subtle forward slump. She gazed up at him with large eyes. "I'm your neighbour," she said, "could I come inside for a few minutes?"

He was reluctant – in fact he glanced too obviously at his unfinished painting – but it never occurred to him to say no. She glided in, the scarf hanging from her neck imbued with a perfume he'd smelled before in the hall. Her dress was slip-like, and purple, and might have been silk, and was most definitely feminine. Ribbons of her dull black hair appeared in the cracks among multiple scarves covering her head. She sat down on a chair right by his easel, as if she expected him to paint her.

"You're an artist," she said.

"Well, I want to be. I don't think I'm good enough yet, but maybe I will be."

"I'll let you paint me sometime." He stumbled for a reply and couldn't find one. "I have no talents. For anything. But it makes me feel better to be around men who do."

She didn't say anything more for a while, and he just stood there, not knowing what to do. But he kept thinking about options, and finally said, "Can I get you something to eat?"

There was a slight shift in her expression, a strained quality in the skin around the mouth and nose. "I don't eat in front of other people," she finally said. "I can't – it doesn't matter how hungry I am. And I'm always hungry."

"I'm sorry – I was just trying to be a good host."

She looked at him with what he thought might be amusement, but the expression seemed uncomfortable on her lips. "I imagine you apologise a lot, don't you?"

His face warmed. "Yes. I guess I really do."

"I'd like to watch you paint, if that's okay."

"Well, I guess. It'll probably be a little boring. Sometimes I do a section, and then I just stare at the canvas for a while, feeling my way through the whole, making adjustments, or just being scared I'll mess it up."

"I'd like to watch. I'm not easily bored."

And so she sat a couple of hours as if frozen in place, watching him. He might have thought she was sleeping if not for the uncomfortably infrequent blinking. Now and then he would glance at her, and although she was looking at him, he wasn't sure somehow that she was seeing him. And his dual focus on her and on his painting was rapidly fatiguing him. He appreciated her silence, however – he might not have been able to work at all if she'd said anything. It occurred to him she smelled differently. Under the perfume was a kind of staleness – or gaminess for lack of a better word. Like a fur brought out of storage and warming up quickly. Finally it was he who spoke.

"You're great company." It was the first time he'd ever said such a thing. "But I'm feeling so tired, I don't know why, but I think I might just fall over. I'm sorry – I usually can work a lot longer."

"You should lie down." She stood and led him to the bed in the other room of the small apartment. So quickly there hardly seemed a transition. Despite her slightness she forced him down into a reclining position. And without a word lay down beside him, close against him like a child. But even if she had said something, even if she had asked, he would not have said no. And of course he didn't stop her when she first removed his clothes, then threw off her own. It was all such a stupid cliché, he would think later, and again and again, for the six months or so their relationship lasted, and for years afterward. All the bad jokes about how men could not really be seduced, because they were always ready to have sex with anyone, with anything – it was just part of their nature. They couldn't help themselves. It embarrassed him, he felt ashamed. He'd never thought it was true, and now look at how he was behaving.

For there was this other sad truth. Men who never expected to be loved, who'd never even felt much like men, had a hard time saying no when the opportunity arrived, because when would it ever come again?

At least he had never been able to fool himself into believing that she actually enjoyed what they were doing. Most of the time she lay there with her eyes closed, as if pretending to be asleep or in some drug-induced semi-consciousness. He was never quite sure if he was hurting her, the way her body rose off the bed as if slapped or stabbed, her back arching, breath coming out in explosions from her as-if wounded lungs, eyes occasionally snapping open to stare from the bottom of some vast and empty place. Certainly there couldn't be any passion in her for it, as dry as she was, her pubic hair like a bit of thrown-out carpet, so that at some point every time they did it he lost his ability to maintain the illusion, so much it was like fucking a pile of garbage, artfully arranged layers of gristle and skin, tried to escape, but like that moment in the horror movies when the skeleton reaches up and embraces you, she always pulled her bony arms around him, squeezing so hard he could feel her flailing heart right through the fragile web of her ribcage, as they continued to rock and bump the tender hangings of their flesh until bruised and bloody.

"Daddy! I *said* I saw a monkey at the zoo today!" Across from him at the dinner table, Molly looked furious.

"I know, honey," he said. "I heard you."

"No you didn't! You weren't paying attention!"

He looked at Elaine, maybe for support, or maybe just for confirmation that he had screwed up. She offered neither, was carefully studying the food on her plate. "Honey, I'm sorry. Sometimes I don't sleep too well, and the next day I have a hard time focusing, so by the time I get home from work I'm really very tired. But I'm going to listen really closely to you, okay? Please tell me all about it."

Apparently she was willing, because she began again, telling a long story about monkeys, and thrown food, and how Brian got on the bus and started throwing pieces of his lunch like *he* was the monkey, and what the bus driver said, and what their teacher said, and how lunch was pretty sick-looking, so she couldn't eat anything again anyway, except for a little bit of a juice box, and some crackers. And the entire time she was telling this story a tiny pulse by her left eye kept beating, like the recording light on a video camera, but he still kept his eyes on her, and he made himself hear every tedious word, and he let the pictures of what she was telling him make a movie in his brain, so that he felt right there.

Even though at the corners of his eyes his view of the dining room, and his daughter speaking at the centre of it, was breaking down into discordancy, into a swarm of tiny black and white pixels, and even though Miri's face was at one edge of the dining room window, peering in, before her silhouette coiled and fell away.

So that by the end of his daughter's little story he had closed his eyes by necessity, and spoke to her as if in prayer. "That's a really nice story, sweetheart, thanks so much for telling it. But you know you really must eat. Why, tonight you've hardly touched anything on your plate. That little piece of meat hung up in the edge of your mouth – I can't tell if it's even food. But you have to keep your strength up, you're really going to need every bit of strength you can find."

The rest of the evening was awkward, with Elaine pleading with him to see a doctor. "You're not here with me anymore," she was saying, or was that Miri, and that was the problem, wasn't it? He no longer knew when or with whom he was. It was all he could do to keep his eyes in the same day and place for more than a few minutes at a time.

By the end Rick had known Miriam for six months or so. He'd told Matt about her, but then had been reluctant to share more than a very few of the actual details. He just wanted someone to know, in case – but he didn't understand in case of what. Matt ran into them once, when Rick had tried to drive her to a restaurant. He'd been so stupid about it – he should have been driving her to a hospital instead. She'd lost enough fat in her face by then that when she reacted to anything he couldn't quite tell what the emotion was – everything looked like a grimace on her. When she walked she was constantly clicking her teeth together and there was a disturbing wobble in her gait. He knew she must eat – how could she not? But it could not be much, and she had to be doing it in secret because he'd never actually seen her put anything into her mouth except a little bit of water.

When she breathed sometimes it was as if she were attempting to devour the space around her – her entire frame shook with the effort. When he first experienced this he tried to touch her, pull her in to comfort a distress he simply could not understand. But soon he learned to keep his distance, after getting close enough he felt he might dissolve from the force of what was happening to her.

He hadn't told her they were going to a restaurant. He said he just wanted to get out of that building where they spent virtually all of their time. Finally she stumbled into his car and caved into the passenger seat. He drove slowly, telling her it was time they both tried new things.

"What, you're breaking up with me?" A thin crimson line of inflammation separated her eyes from their tightly wrinkled sockets.

"No, that's not what I meant at all. I mean try new things together, as a couple. Go places, do things."

"You have the only new thing I need, lover." Her leer ended with a crusted tongue swiped over cracked lips.

"It doesn't feel healthy staying in the way we do. Maybe it's okay for you, but it doesn't work for me."

He pulled up in front of a little Italian place. It wasn't very popular – the flavours were a bit coarse – but the food was always filling.

"No," she said, and closed her eyes. She was wearing so much eye make-up that it looked as if her eyelids had caved in.

"All I'm asking is that you give it a try. If you don't like it, okay. No problem. We'll just go home."

She slapped his face then, and it felt as if she'd hit him with a piece of wood. She continued hitting him with those hands of so little padding, spitting the word "lover!" at him, as if it were some kind of curse.

He had no idea what to do. He'd never been struck by a woman before. He couldn't remember the last time he'd been in a physical fight with anyone. And now she was screaming, the angular gape of her mouth like an attacking bird's.

"Hey! Hey!" The car door was open, and someone was pulling her away from him. Miri was beside herself, struggling, kicking. Rick was leaning back as far as possible to avoid her sharp-pointed shoes. Over her shoulder he saw Matt's face, grimly determined, as he jerked her out of the car.

She spat at both of them, walking back toward her apartment with one shoe missing, her clothes twisted around on her coat-hanger frame.

"I should go get her, try to coax her back into the car," Rick said, out of breath.

"Glad you finally introduced us." Matt was bent over, wheezing.

Of course she had apologised in her own way, showing up at Rick's door the next night, naked, crying and incoherent. He got her inside before anyone else could see. And then she would not leave for weeks, sleeping in his bed, watching him eat or stand before his easel unable to paint. Most of the time he slept on the floor, but sometimes he had to have something softer, and lay on the bed trying to ignore her mouth and hands all over him, in that fluttering way of hers, until she stopped and lay cold against him.

"I'm glad you were able to join us today." Matt stood at Rick's office door, looking unhappy. "Were you really sick, or did you get Elaine to call in and lie for you every day?"

Rick was unable to do anything but stare as Matt's words rushed by him. He'd been in the office for only five minutes or so and already he was feeling disoriented. Papers were stacked all over his desk, and message notes were attached around his monitor, even to his lamp base. He never left things like this.

Finally, he looked up at his old friend. "I have no idea what you're talking about."

"You haven't been here in four days! I can't keep coming up with excuses for you with the partners."

"Four days?"

Matt stared at him. It made him uncomfortable, so he started sifting through the piles of papers. But these were piles of print on paper, black on white, black and white. Before he could turn away he was seeing the shadows of her eyes, the angles of her mouth in the smile that wasn't a smile. "Maybe you *are* sick," Matt said behind him.

"You said Elaine called in every day?"

"Right after the office opened, once before I even got in."

"Elaine never lies. That's one of the best things about her. I don't think she even knows how," Rick said absently, looking around the office, finding more phone messages. Some appeared to be in his own handwriting.

"Well, I know. Of course. Look, I didn't mean—"

"Are you sure it wasn't someone who just *pretended* to be Elaine?"

But then someone was softly knocking, or rubbing, on the door outside. And Rick couldn't bring himself to speak anymore.

"Ricky?" she had said. "Are you home?"

But he couldn't get out of his so well-cushioned chair. The doorknob rattled in its collar. He willed the latch to hold.

"Ricky, we don't have to do anything," she said in her child's voice, muffled by the door.

"Ricky, I just need – are you too tired, Ricky? I just need—"

After a few weeks she had stopped. Later he heard she'd killed herself, but he never saw a word about it in the papers. One afternoon a truck came and took away all the stuff in her apartment. A white-haired man came by, knocking on each door. But Rick hadn't answered when the old man knocked on his. Later one of the other tenants would tell Rick the white-haired man had claimed to be her uncle.

The next week was when the colour-blindness had come over him like some sort of virus, intermittently, then all at once. One of the doctors he saw said it appeared to be a hysterical reaction of some sort. Whatever the source, or the reason, he stopped painting, and she mostly left him alone for a long time after that, reappearing now and then to monochrome the world for a while, or to take a day or two, or to eat one of his new memories and leave one of the tired old ones in its place.

And now it had looked as if he was going to be happy, or at least the possibility was there, and she couldn't just leave that be.

The bedroom was completely black, except for a few bright white reflections of window pane. And the side of Elaine's face, as she slept on her back. Lovely and glowing and ghostly.

The children were out there asleep in their own beds, or should be. At least he hadn't heard them in hours. He prayed they were. Sleeping.

But it was all so black, and white, and something was rubbing at the door.

GEETA ROOPNARINE

Corbeaux Bay

GEETA ROOPNARINE WAS BORN in Trinidad and Tobago and now
lives in Greece. She is also a visual artist and is currently working
on her first novel, which does not deal with corbeaux but has
one sitting on a fence.

"There is an *otherness* about this bird which induces in me a
feeling of disquiet, and a kind of admiration too," says the
author.

"Corbeaux in Trinidad act as if they were almost civilised: at
the seaside, they come within a foot or so of where you might be
gutting a fish and wait patiently for the entrails. Yet if you see
them sitting on the top of a coconut tree, there is a peculiar stillness about them – as though they are waiting for a sign, waiting
to act in an unforeseen manner, as if they have a collective
intelligence.

"And it is really spooky coming upon them on a deserted
beach . . ."

IT IS THEIR summer holidays. He has gone for a run along the
beach, early in the morning, every day except today. Last night
he slept uneasily, disturbed by the peculiar sound of a night bird.

Sunday, and the beach is already swarming with people gaily
mapping their domains with rectangular pieces of scraggy
matting. The fishermen have returned from their trawling and

Christine is at work in the lean-to. She slits, disembowels, and segments strange sea creatures that she has picked up from the nets; they may not be marketable but they do make nourishing soups. She looks like a Pied Piper but with a flock of black scrawny corbeaux, turkey vultures, some as tall as their youngest son. She throws the inner parts of the head, the gills, and the shining entrails to them without looking and they eagerly scoop up the offal, their curved beaks slicing, spilling the juices of the soft material. They are fast eaters, intent on their portions and defensive of their territory, fiercely pecking.

He is uneasy that she feeds the birds while the children watch from the balcony, but she laughs and says it is because he is from the city and does not understand the ways of nature, that when she was a girl her mother did the same and she sees no reason to change.

As he hurries along the pathway to the garden, one of the corbeaux, intent on feasting, on staining the cement red, is unaware of his approach. He aims a kick at it. The bird staggers a few feet away with a weird side-stepping gait and gazes at him. The flock also pause for a moment, their heads cocked to one side, and look up. Christine continues to pull, to stretch, to empty.

When he is almost at the gate, she notices him in his sneakers and tells him to take his mobile phone.

"What?" he says. "And have you calling every five minutes to tell me which child is using dirty words, or which one is making his kaka." He goes back inside and puts away his phone and his watch.

Then he bares his arm at her. "I am on holiday."

He goes for his run but soon returns. The sun is high in the sky and the people on the beach upset him, playing handball and shrieking as if the beach belongs to them. Tomorrow, he promises himself, he will leave early in the morning, and explore beyond the coconut trees on to the shoreline bordered by the jungle.

The birds have gone and he is pleased that he doesn't have to look at their bare wrinkled necks, their curved beaks, their staring eyes.

Next day he leaves at 6 a.m., before the sun is up. He takes a small bottle of water, strapped to his waist. He picks up his mobile phone, remembers his conversation with his wife the day before, and puts back it down.

The beach is white, pristine. There is not a soul in either direction. The sea is grey, untouched yet by the morning sun. It looks fresh, newly formed.

He pulls off his socks, balls them up, places them in his sneakers and runs in the fine sand, his feet caressed by the soft swell of the water. He leaves no trail, and in front, the beach stretches out clean, unmarked.

He goes further and further until he leaves the swelter of houses, humped together like ticks. After an hour he reaches the end of the long beach and the sand gives way to a rocky outcrop. Here, the coconut palms surrender to the tangled growth of the tropics. He dries his feet, puts on his socks and sneakers, and climbs the rocky incline. Another, shorter beach stretches out in front of him. In the distance, beyond a protrusion of blood-red rocks, a second bay shimmers.

The small village has vanished behind the curve of the sea. He drinks the rest of his water and decides to go as far as the red rocks, maybe take a small sample for the boys. In the sky, a bird circles lazily.

He jogs slowly, taking care. The sand is littered with debris: broken plastic, bottle tops, a single rubber flip-flop. He looks at the orientation of the shore, at an angle to the long beach, and it appears that the sea rages through here at intervals. As he goes on, it becomes rocky. He wonders whether he should turn back. The sun is already high and Christine would be looking towards the beach. Then he reasons it is a pity to come so far and not see what is on the other side.

The liver-coloured rocks are jagged with thin spikes and he is amazed at the different shades of red, rust and brown that swirl through the small peaks. He is dizzy from the long run, not having had breakfast, and the hot sun, but he is determined to climb to the top, to master this wilderness.

The top does not disappoint. It is wild and rugged. In the forest, the trees seem alive, listening. Here, too, he sees that the ocean comes in with a vengeance. Large logs are piled up at the edge of the narrow strip of beach as if protecting it from the forest or something unknown.

The tip of the rocky outcrop is covered with huge globs of white with black feathers sticking out here and there. He looks up. More birds are circling but they are too far away for him to identify. Probably those damn corbeaux looking for another gullible housewife to feed them.

He peers down. On a ledge cut into the rock, he sees nests with broken shells, but one has two eggs. They are large, speckled with grey. An image of Christine's face, frowning, passes across his mind as she sees him with the egg, when her monopoly on nature is broken, and the boys touch the egg with their small, sensitive fingers.

As he balances himself and stretches precariously to get at the egg, his attention is caught by some markings on the beach below like symbols in a strange language.

He falls and as he moves through the air, slowly, he sees a multitude of black figures huddling under a projecting ledge. He hits one of the tall spikes in the rocks below and feels something ram into his stomach. Then, the spike breaking, he falls again.

He is lying on the beach. He takes a deep breath. There is no pain yet. He sees himself take a hold of the spike with both hands and pull hard. He flings it away and at first there are no fluids, no blood, no acids.

He rolls onto his stomach, closes his eyes and gives in to the pain, his face pressed against the sand. When he opens his eyes, the markings, the symbols, are no more than hundreds of V-shaped footprints of birds.

A stain spreads across his T-shirt and he pulls it off, tears it and makes a bandage of sorts. He reaches towards his pocket and then his hand falls away; he pictures the mobile on the table where he left it.

A movement above catches his eye. On the hidden ledge, something is causing the birds to stir. They raise their heads and seem to sniff at the air. Then they are quiet, watchful, their heads cocked to one side as if listening to some signal.

They take to the air, fly high. He exhales slowly. He turns his head towards the forest. It looks dark, impenetrable. The only way is back over the cliffs. He tries to move forward, but the pain leaves him weak.

He hears a movement and moves his head slowly. A corbeau is on the beach, side-walking like a bashful virgin, its beak contained, quiet.

Another movement, and more feet making V-shaped symbols on the sand.

His mouth is dry; the hot rays seem to pour down his throat.

He wishes he could talk to his sons, listen to their little squabbles falling around his ears like soft rain.

Then, a stirring of wings blots out the sun.

MICHAEL MARSHALL SMITH

Sad, Dark Thing

MICHAEL MARSHALL SMITH IS a novelist and screenwriter. Under this name he has published the modern SF novels *Only Forward*, *Spares* and *One of Us*, and is the only person to have won the British Fantasy Award for Best Short Story four times – along with the August Delerth, International Horror Guild and Philip K. Dick awards.

Writing as "Michael Marshall" he has published six international best-selling novels of suspense, including *The Straw Men* and *The Intruders*, currently in development with the BBC. His most recent novel is *Killer Move*, while *The Forgotten* is forthcoming.

He currently lives in Santa Cruz, California, with his wife and son.

"This story was born out of two things," explains the author. "The atmosphere of the forests of the Santa Cruz mountains – a place where I'd just vacationed – and a title, given by a friend. The two collided in my head and produced the story almost without any intervention on my part.

"The strange thing is that I'm now living about fifteen minutes' drive from the kind of place where the story is set. I hope the protagonist's story will not become my own, however – hope so very much indeed."

Aimless. a short, simple word. It means "without aim", where "aim" derives from the idea of calculation with a view to action. Without purpose or direction, therefore, without a considered goal or future that you can see. People mainly use the word in a blunt, softened fashion. They walk "aimlessly" down a street, not sure whether to have a coffee or if they should check out the new magazines in the bookstore or maybe sit on that bench and watch the world go by. It's not a big deal, this aimlessness. It's a temporary state and often comes with a side order of ease. An hour without something hanging over you, with no great need to do or achieve anything in particular? In this world of busy lives and do-this and do-that, it sounds pretty good.

But being wholly without purpose? With no direction home? That is not such a good deal. Being truly aimless is like being dead. It may even be the same thing, or worse. It is the aimless who find the wrong roads, and go down them, simply because they have nowhere else to go.

Miller usually found himself driving on Saturday afternoons. He could make the morning go away by staying in bed an extra half-hour, tidying away stray emails, spending time on the deck, looking out over the forest with a magazine or the iPad and a succession of coffees. He made the coffees in a machine that sat on the kitchen counter and cost nearly eight hundred dollars. It made a very good cup of coffee. It should. It had cost nearly eight hundred dollars.

By noon a combination of caffeine and other factors would mean that he wasn't very hungry. He would go back indoors nonetheless, and put together a plate from the fridge. The ingredients would be things he'd gathered from delis up in San Francisco during the week, or else from the New Leaf markets in Santa Cruz or Felton as he returned home on Friday afternoon. The idea was that this would constitute a treat, and remind him of the good things in life. That was the idea. He would also pour some juice into one of the only two glasses in the cabinet that got any use. The other was his scotch glass, the one with the faded white logo on it, but that only came out in the evenings. He was very firm about that.

He would bring the plate and glass back out and eat at the table which stood further along the deck from the chair in which he'd spent most of the morning. By then the sun would have moved around, and the table got shade, which he preferred when he was eating. The change in position was also supposed to make it feel like he was doing something different to what he'd done all morning, though it did not, especially. He was still a man sitting in silence on a raised deck, within view of many trees, eating expensive foods that tasted like cardboard.

Afterward he took the plate indoors and washed it in the sink. He had a dishwasher, naturally. Dishwashers are there to save time. He washed the plate and silverware by hand, watching the water swirl away and then drying everything and putting it to one side. He was down a wife, and a child, now living three hundred miles away. He was short on women and children, therefore, but in their place, from the hollows they had left behind, he had time. Time crawled in an endless parade of minutes from between those cracks, arriving like an army of little black ants, crawling up over his skin, up his face, and into his mouth, ears and eyes.

So why not wash the plate. And the knife, and the fork, and the glass. Hold back the ants, for a few minutes, at least.

He never left the house with a goal. On those afternoons he was, truly, aimless. From where the house stood, high in the Santa Cruz mountains, he could have reached a number of diverting places within an hour or two. San Jose. Saratoga. Los Gatos. Santa Cruz itself, then south to Monterey, Carmel and Big Sur. Even way down to Los Angeles, if he felt like making a weekend of it.

And then what?

Instead he simply drove.

There are only so many major routes you can take through the area's mountains and redwood forests. Highways 17 and 9, or the road out over to Bonny Doon, Route 1 north or south. Of these, only 17 is of any real size. In between the main thoroughfares, however, there are other options. Roads that don't do much except connect one minor two-lane highway to another. Roads that used to count for something before modern alternatives came along to supplant or supersede or negate them.

Side roads, old roads, forgotten roads.

Usually there wasn't much to see down these last roads. Stretches of forest, maybe a stream, eventually a house, well back from the road. Rural, mountainous backwoods where the tree and poison oak reigned supreme. Chains across tracks which led down or up into the woods, some gentle inclines, others pretty steep, meandering off toward some house which stood even further from the through-lines, back in a twenty- or fifty-acre lot. Every now and then you'd pass one of the area's very few tourist traps, like the "Mystery Spot", an old-fashioned affair which claimed to honour a site of "Unfathomable Weirdness" but in fact paid cheerful homage to geometry, and to man's willingness to be deceived.

He'd seen all of these long ago. The local attractions with his wife and child, the shadowed roads and tracks on his own solitary excursions over the last few months. At least, you might have thought he would have seen them all. Every Saturday he drove, however, and every time he found a road he had never seen before.

Today the road was off Branciforte Drive, the long, old highway which heads off through largely uncolonised regions of the mountains and forests to the south-east of Scott's Valley. As he drove north along it, mind elsewhere and nowhere, he noticed a turning. A glance in the rear-view mirror showed no one behind and so he slowed to peer along the turn.

A two-lane road, overhung with tall trees, including some redwoods. It gave no indication of leading anywhere at all.

Fine by him.

He made the turn and drove on. The trees were tall and thick, cutting off much of the light from above. The road passed smoothly up and down, riding the natural contours, curving abruptly once in a while to avoid the trunk of an especially big tree or to skirt a small canyon carved out over millennia by some small and bloody-minded stream. There were no houses or other signs of habitation. Could be public land, he was beginning to think, though he didn't recall there being any around here and hadn't seen any indication of a park boundary, and then he saw a sign by the road up ahead.

STOP

That's all it said. Despite himself, he found he was doing just that, pulling over toward it. When the car was stationary, he looked at the sign curiously. It had been hand-lettered, some time ago, in black marker on a panel cut from a cardboard box and nailed to a tree.

He looked back the way he'd come, and then up the road once more. He saw no traffic in either direction, and also no indication of why the sign would be here. Sure, the road curved again about forty yards ahead, but no more markedly than it had ten or fifteen times since he'd left Branciforte Drive. There had been no warning signs on those bends. If you simply wanted people to observe the speed limit then you'd be more likely to advise them to 'Slow', and anyway it didn't look at all like an official sign.

Then he realised that, further on, there was in fact a turning off the road.

He took his foot off the brake and let the car roll forward down the slope, crunching over twigs and gravel. A driveway, it looked like, though a long one, bending off into the trees. Single lane, roughly made up. Maybe five yards down it was another sign, evidently the work of the same craftsman as the previous.

TOURISTS WELCOME

He grunted, in something like a laugh. If you had yourself some kind of attraction, of course tourists were welcome. What would be the point otherwise? It was a strange way of putting it.

An odd way of advertising it, too. No indication of what was in store or why a busy family should turn off what was already a pretty minor road and head off into the woods. No lure except those two words.

They were working on him, though, he had to admit. He eased his foot gently back on the gas and carefully directed the car along the track, between the trees.

*   *   *

After about a quarter of a mile he saw a building ahead. A couple of them, in fact, arranged in a loose compound. One a ramshackle two-storey farmhouse, the other a disused barn. There was also something that was or had been a garage, with a broken-down truck/tractor parked diagonally in front of it. It was parked insofar as it was not moving, at least, not in the sense that whoever had last driven the thing had made any effort, when abandoning it, to align its form with anything. The surfaces of the vehicle were dusty and rusted and liberally covered in old leaves and specks of bark. A wooden crate, about four feet square, stood rotting in the back. The near front tyre was flat.

The track ended in a widened parking area, big enough for four or five cars. It was empty. There was no sign of life at all, in fact, but something – he wasn't sure what – said this habitation was a going concern, rather than a collection of ruins that someone had walked away from at some point in the last few years.

Nailed to a tree in front of the main house, was another cardboard sign.

WELCOME

He parked, turned off the engine, and got out. It was very quiet. It usually is in those mountains, when you're away from the road. Sometimes you'll hear the faint roar of an airplane, way up above, but apart from that it's just the occasional tweet of some winged creature or an indistinct rustle as something small and furry or scaly makes its way through the bushes.

He stood for a few minutes, flapping his hand to discourage a noisy fly which appeared from nowhere, bothered his face, and then zipped chaotically off.

Eventually he called out. "Hello?"

You'd think that – on what was evidently a very slow day for this attraction, whatever it was – the sound of an arriving vehicle would have someone bustling into sight, eager to make a few bucks, to pitch their wares. He stood a few minutes more, however, without seeing or hearing any sign of life. It figured. Aimless people find aimless things, and it didn't seem like much was going to happen here. You find what you're looking for, and he hadn't been looking for anything at all.

He turned back toward the car, aware that he wasn't even feeling disappointment. He hadn't expected much, and that's exactly what he'd got.

As he held up his hand to press the button to unlock the doors, however, he heard a creaking sound.

He turned back to see there was now a man on the tilting porch that ran along half of the front of the wooden house. He was dressed in canvas jeans and a vest that had probably once been white. The man had probably once been clean, too, though he looked now like he'd spent most of the morning trying to fix the underside of a car. Perhaps he had.

"What you want?"

His voice was flat and unwelcoming. He looked to be in his mid–late fifties. Hair once black was now half grey, and also none too clean. He did not look like he'd been either expecting or desirous of company.

"What have you got?"

The man on the porch leant on the rail and kept looking at him, but said nothing.

"It says 'Tourists Welcome'," Miller said, when it became clear the local had nothing to offer. "I'm not feeling especially welcome, to be honest."

The man on the porch looked weary. "Christ. The boy was supposed to take down those damned signs. They still up?"

"Yes."

"Even the one out on the road, says 'Stop'?"

"Yes," Miller said. "Otherwise I wouldn't have stopped."

The other man swore and shook his head. "Told the boy weeks ago. Told him I don't know how many times."

Miller frowned. "You don't notice, when you drive in and out? That the signs are still there?"

"Haven't been to town in a while."

"Well, look. I turned down your road because it looked like there was something to see."

"Nope. Doesn't say anything like that."

"It's implied, though, wouldn't you say?"

The man lifted his chin a little. "You a lawyer?"

"No. I'm a businessman. With time on my hands. Is there something to see here, or not?"

After a moment the man on the porch straightened, and came walking down the steps.

"One dollar," he said. "As you're here."

"For what? The parking?"

The man stared at him as if he was crazy. "No. To see."

"One dollar?" It seemed inconceivable that in this day and age there would be anything under the sun for a dollar, especially if it was trying to present as something worth experiencing. "Really?"

"That's cheap," the man said, misunderstanding.

"It is what it is," Miller said, getting his wallet out and pulling a dollar bill from it.

The other man laughed, a short, sour sound. "You got that right."

After he'd taken the dollar and stuffed it into one of the pockets of his jeans, the man walked away. Miller took this to mean that he should follow, and so he did. It looked for a moment as if they were headed toward the house, but then the path – such as it was – took an abrupt right onto a course that led them between the house and the tilting barn. The house was large and gabled, and must once have been quite something. Lord knows what it was doing out here, lost by itself in a patch of forest that had never been near a major road or town or anyplace else that people with money might wish to be. Its glory days were long behind it, anyway. Looking up at it, you'd give it about another five years standing, unless someone got onto rebuilding or at least shoring it right away.

The man led the way through slender trunks into an area around the back of the barn. Though the land in front of the house and around the side had barely been what you'd think of as tamed, here the forest abruptly came into its own. Trees of significant size shot up all around, looking – as redwoods do – like they'd been there since the dawn of time. A sharp, rocky incline led down toward a stream about thirty yards away. The stream was perhaps eight feet across, with steep sides. A rickety bridge of old, grey wood lay across it. The man led him to the near side of this, and then stopped.

"What?"

"This is it."

Miller looked again at the bridge. "A dollar, to look at a bridge some guy threw up fifty years ago?" Suddenly it wasn't seeming so dumb a pricing system after all.

The man handed him a small, tarnished key, and raised his other arm to point. Between the trees on the other side of the creek was a small hut.

"It's in there."

"What is?"

The man shrugged. "A sad, dark thing."

The water which trickled below the bridge smelt fresh and clean. Miller got a better look at the hut, shed, whatever, when he reached the other side. It was about half the size of a log cabin, but made of grey, battered planks instead of logs. The patterns of lichen over the sides and the moss-covered roof said it had been here, and in this form, for a good long time – far longer than the house, most likely. Could be an original settler's cabin, the home of whichever long-ago pioneer had first arrived here, driven west by hope or desperation. It looked about contemporary with the rickety bridge, certainly.

There was a small padlock on the door.

He looked back.

The other man was still standing at the far end of the bridge, looking up at the canopy of leaves above. It wasn't clear what he'd be looking at, but it didn't seem like he was waiting for the right moment to rush over, bang the other guy on the head, and steal his wallet. If he'd wanted to do that he could have done it back up at the house. There was no sign of anyone else around – this boy he'd mentioned, for example – and he looked like he was waiting patiently for the conclusion of whatever needed to happen for him to have earned his dollar.

Miller turned back and fitted the key in the lock. It was stiff, but it turned. He opened the door. Inside was total dark. He hesitated, looked back across the bridge, but the man had gone.

He opened the door further, and stepped inside.

The interior of the cabin was cooler than it had been outside, but also stuffy. There was a faint smell. Not a bad smell, particularly. It was like old, damp leaves. It was like the back of a closet where you store things you do not need. It was like a corner of the attic of a house not much loved, in the night, after rain.

The only light was that which managed to get past him from the door behind. The cabin had no windows, or if it had, they had been covered over. The door he'd entered by was right at one end of the building, which meant the rest of the interior led ahead. It could only have been ten, twelve feet. It seemed longer, because it was so dark. The man stood there, not sure what happened next.

The door slowly swung closed behind him, not all the way, but leaving a gap of a couple of inches. No one came and shut it on him or turned the lock or started hollering about he'd have to pay a thousand bucks to get back out again. The man waited.

In a while, there was a quiet sound.

It was a rustling. Not quite a shuffling. A sense of something moving a little at the far end, turning away from the wall, perhaps. Just after the sound, there was a low waft of a new odour, as if the movement had caused something to change its relationship to the environment, as if a body long held curled or crouched in a particular shape or position had realigned enough for hidden sweat to be released into the unmoving air.

Miller froze.

In all his life, he'd never felt the hairs on the back of his neck rise. You read about it, hear about it. You knew they were supposed to do it, but he'd never felt it, not his own hairs, on his own neck. They did it then, though, and the peculiar thing was that he was not afraid, or not only that.

He was in there with something, that was for certain. It was not a known thing, either. It was . . . he didn't know. He wasn't sure. He just knew that there was *something* over there in the darkness. Something about the size of a man, he thought, maybe a little smaller.

He wasn't sure it was male, though. Something said to him it was female. He couldn't imagine where this impression might be coming from, as he couldn't see it and he couldn't hear anything, either – after the initial movement, it had been still. There was just something in the air that told him things about it, that said underneath the shadows it wrapped around itself like a pair of dark angel's wings, it knew despair, bitter madness and melancholy better even than he did. He knew that beneath those shadows it was naked, and not male.

He knew also that it was this, and not fear, that was making his breathing come ragged and forced.

He stayed in there with it for half-an-hour, doing nothing, just listening, staring into the darkness but not seeing anything. That's how long it seemed like it had been, anyway, when he eventually emerged back into the forest. It was hard to tell.

He closed the cabin door behind him but he did not lock it, because he saw that the man was back, standing once more at the far end of the bridge. Miller clasped the key firmly in his fist and walked over toward him.

"How much," he said.

"For what? You already paid."

"No," Miller said. "I want to buy it."

It was eight by the time Miller got back to his house. He didn't know how that could be unless he'd spent longer in the cabin than he realised. It didn't matter a whole lot, and in fact there were good things about it. The light had begun to fade. In twenty minutes it would be gone entirely. He spent those minutes sitting in the front seat of the car, waiting for darkness, his mind as close to a comfortable blank as it had been in a long time.

When it was finally dark he got out the car and went over to the house. He dealt with the security system, opened the front door and left it hanging open.

He walked back to the vehicle and went around to the trunk. He rested his hand on the metal there for a moment, and it felt cold. He unlocked the back and turned away, not fast but naturally, and walked toward the set of wooden steps which led to the smaller of the two raised decks. He walked up them and stood there for a few minutes, looking out into the dark stand of trees, and then turned and headed back down the steps toward the car.

The trunk was empty now, and so he shut it, and walked slowly toward the open door of his house, and went inside, and shut and locked that door behind him too.

It was night, and it was dark, and they were both inside and that felt right.

*   *   *

He poured a small scotch in a large glass. He took it out through the sliding glass doors to the chair on the main deck where he'd spent the morning, and sat there cradling the drink, taking a sip once in a while. He found himself remembering, as he often did at this time, the first time he'd met his wife. He'd been living down on East Cliff then, in a house which was much smaller than this one but only a couple of minutes' walk from the beach. Late one Saturday afternoon, bored and restless, he'd taken a walk to the Crow's Nest, the big restaurant that was the only place to eat or drink along that stretch. He'd bought a similar scotch at the upstairs bar and taken it out onto the balcony to watch the sun go down over the harbour. After a while he noticed that, amongst the family groups of sunburned tourists and knots of tattooed locals there was a woman sitting at a table by herself. She had a tall glass of beer and seemed to be doing the same thing he was, and he wondered why. Not why she was doing that, but why he was – why they both were. He did not know then, and he did not know now, why people sit and look out into the distance by themselves, or what they hope to see.

After a couple more drinks he went over and introduced himself. Her name was Catherine and she worked at the university. They got married eighteen months later and though by then – his business having taken off in the meantime – he could have afforded anywhere in town, they hired out the Crow's Nest and had the wedding party there. A year after that their daughter was born and they called her Matilde, after Catherine's mother, who was French. Business was still good and they moved out of his place on East Cliff and into the big house he had built in the mountains and for seven years all was good, and then, for some reason, it was no longer good any more. He didn't think it had been his fault, though it could have been. He didn't think it was her fault either, though that too was possible. It had simply stopped working. They'd been two people, and then one, but then two again, facing different ways. There had been a view to share together, then there was not, and if you look with only one eye then there is no depth of field. There had been no infidelity. In some ways that might have been easier. It would have been something to react to, to blame, to hide behind. Far worse, in fact, to sit on opposite sides of the breakfast table and wonder who the other person was, and why they were there, and when they would go.

Six months later, she did. Matilde went with her, of course. He didn't think there was much more that could be said or understood on the subject. When first he'd sat out on this deck alone, trying to work it all through in his head, the recounting could take hours. As time went on, the story seemed to get shorter and shorter. As they said around these parts, it is what it is.

Or it was what it was.

Time passed and then it was late. The scotch was long gone but he didn't feel the desire for any more. He took the glass indoors and washed it at the sink, putting it on the draining board next to the plate and the knife and the fork from lunch. No lights were on. He hadn't bothered to flick any switches when he came in, and – having sat for so long out on the deck – his eyes were accustomed, and he felt no need to turn any on now.

He dried his hands on a cloth and walked around the house, aimlessly at first. He had done this many times in the last few months, hearing echoes. When he got to the area which had been Catherine's study, he stopped. There was nothing left in the space now bar the empty desk and the empty bookshelves. He could tell that the chair had been moved, however. He didn't recall precisely how it had been, or when he'd last listlessly walked this way, but he knew that it had been moved, somehow.

He went back to walking, and eventually fetched up outside the room that had been Matilde's. The door was slightly ajar. The space beyond was dark.

He could feel a warmth coming out of it, though, and heard a sound in there, something quiet, and he turned and walked slowly away.

He took a shower in the dark. Afterward he padded back to the kitchen in his bare feet and a gown and picked his scotch glass up from the draining board. Even after many, many trips through the dishwasher you could see the ghost of the restaurant logo that had once been stamped on it, the remains of a mast and a crow's nest. Catherine had slipped it into her purse one long-ago night, without him knowing about it, and then given the glass to him as an anniversary present. How did a person who would do that change into the person now living half the state away? He didn't know, any more than he knew why he had so little to say on the phone to his daughter, or why people sat and looked at views, or why they drove to nowhere on Saturday afternoons. Our heads turn and point at things. Light comes into our eyes. Words come out of our mouths.

And then? And so? Carefully, he brought the edge of the glass down upon the edge of the counter. It broke pretty much as he'd hoped it would, the base remaining in one piece, the sides shattering into several jagged points.

He padded back through into the bedroom, put the broken glass on the nightstand, took off the robe, and lay back on the bed. That's how they'd always done it, when they'd wanted to signal that tonight didn't have to just be about going to sleep. Under the covers with a book, then probably not tonight, Josephine.

Naked and on top, on the other hand . . .

A shorthand. A shared language. There is little sadder, however, than a tongue for which only one speaker remains. He closed his eyes, and after a while, for the first time since he'd stood stunned in the driveway and watched his family leave, he cried.

Afterward he lay and waited.

She came in the night.

Three days later, in the late afternoon, a battered truck pulled down into the driveway and parked alongside the car that was there. It was the first time the truck had been on the road in nearly two years, and the driver left the engine running when he got out because he wasn't all that sure it would start up again. The patched front tyre was holding up, though, for now.

He went around the back and opened up the wooden crate, propping the flap with a stick. Then he walked over to the big front door and rang on the bell. Waited a while, and did it again. No answer. Of course.

He rubbed his face in his hands, wearily, took a step back. The door looked solid. No way a kick would get it open. He looked around and saw the steps up to the side deck.

When he got around to the back of the house he picked up the chair that sat by itself, hefted it to judge the weight, and threw it through the big glass door. When he'd satisfied himself that the hole in the smashed glass was big enough, he walked back along the deck and around the front and then up the driveway to stand on the road for a while, out of view of the house.

He smoked a cigarette, and then another to be sure, and when he came back down the driveway he was relived to see that the flap on the crate on the back of his truck was now closed.

He climbed into the cab and sat a moment, looking at the big house. Then he put the truck into reverse, got back up to the highway, and drove slowly home.

When he made the turn into his own drive later, he saw the STOP sign was still there. Didn't matter how many times he told the boy, the sign was still there.

He drove along the track to the house, parked the truck. He opened the crate without looking at it, and went inside.

Later, sitting on his porch in the darkness, he listened to the sound of the wind moving through the tops of the trees all around. He drank a warm beer, and then another. He looked at the grime on his hands. He wondered what it was that made some people catch sight of the sign, what it was in their eyes, what it was in the way they looked, that made them see. He wondered how the man in the big house had done it, and hoped he had not suffered much. He wondered why he had never attempted the same thing. He wondered why it was only on nights like these that he was able to remember that his boy had been dead twenty years.

Finally he went indoors and lay in bed staring at the ceiling. He did this every night, even though there was never anything there to see: nothing unless it is that sad, dark thing that eventually takes us in its arms and makes us sleep.

ROBERT SILVERBERG

Smithers and the Ghosts of the Thar

ROBERT SILVERBERG IS A multiple winner of both the Hugo and Nebula Awards, and he was named a Grand Master by the Science Fiction and Fantasy Writers of America in 2004.

He began submitting stories to science fiction magazines in his early teens, and his first published novel, a children's book entitled *Revolt on Alpha C*, appeared in 1955. He won his first Hugo Award the following year.

Always a prolific writer – for the first four years of his career he reputedly wrote a million words a year – his numerous books include such novels as *To Open the Sky*, *To Live Again*, *Dying Inside*, *Nightwings* and *Lord Valentine's Castle*. The latter became the basis for his popular "Majipoor" series, set on the eponymous alien planet. His most recent book is the seventh volume in his *Collected Short Stories* from Subterranean Press.

"I am not, of course, noted for writing ghost stories," Silverberg admits, "but I have had a life-long interest in them, going back to my discovery of the classic Wise & Fraser *Great Tales of Terror and the Supernatural* when I was ten.

"My unsurprising favourites have been, all these years, Machen, Blackwood, and M. R. James, whom I have read and re-read many times.

"Another favourite of mine since childhood has been Kipling; and so, when Nick Gevers and Jack Dann invited me to contribute to an anthology of modern ghost stories paying homage to the British masters, I fell immediately on the idea of doing a Kiplingesque ghost story for them."

WHAT HAPPENED TO Smithers out there in the Great Indian Desert may seem a trifle hard to believe, but much that happens in Her Imperial Majesty's subcontinent is a trifle hard to believe, and yet one disbelieves it at one's peril. Unfortunately, there is nobody to tell the tale but me, for it all happened many years ago, and Yule has retired from the Service and is living, so I hear, in Palermo, hard at work on his translation of Marco Polo, and Brewster, the only witness to the tragic events in the desert, is too far gone in senility now to be of any use to anyone, and Smithers – ah, poor Smithers—

But let me begin. We start in Calcutta and the year is 1858, with the memory of the dread and terrible Mutiny still overhanging our dreams, distant though those bloody events were from our administrative capital here. That great engineer and brilliant scholar Henry Yule – Lieutenant-Colonel Yule, as he was then, later to be Sir Henry – having lately returned from Allahabad, where he was in charge of strengthening and augmenting our defences against the rebels, has now been made Secretary of the Public Works Department, with particular responsibility for designing what one day will be the vast railroad system that will link every part of India. I hold the title of Deputy Consulting Engineer for Railways. Our young friend Brewster is my right-hand man, a splendid draughtsman and planner. And as my story opens Brewster has come to us, looking oddly flushed, with the news that Smithers, our intense, romantic, excitable Smithers, whom we have sent off on a surveying mission to Jodhpur and Bikaner and other sites in the remote West, has returned and is on his way to us at this very moment with an extraordinary tale to tell.

"Is he now?" Yule said, without much sign of animation. Yule is a Scot, stern and outwardly dour and somewhat fierce-looking, though I am in a position to know that behind that grim bearded visage lies a lively mind keenly alert to the romance of exploration. "Did he find a railroad already in place out there, I wonder? Some little project of an enterprising Rajput prince?"

"Here he comes now," said Brewster. "You will hear it all from the man himself." And an instant later Smithers was among us.

Smithers was fair-haired and very pink-skinned, with gleaming blue eyes that blazed out from his face like sapphires. Though he was somewhat below middle height, he was deep-chested and wide-shouldered, and so forceful was his physical presence that he could and did easily dominate a room of much taller men. Certainly he dominated his friend Brewster, who had known him since childhood. They had been to university together and they had entered the service of the East India Company together, taking appointment with the Bengal Engineers and making themselves useful in the Public Works Department, specialising in the building of bridges and canals. I could best describe the lanky, dark-complected Brewster as timid and cautious, one who was designed by Nature as a follower of stronger men, and Smithers, who in his heart of hearts looked upon himself as part of a grand English tradition of adventurous exploration that went back through Burton and Rawlinson and Layard to Walter Raleigh and Francis Drake, was the man to whom he had attached himself.

"Well, Smithers?" Yule asked. "What news from Bikaner?"

"Not from Bikaner, sir," said Smithers, "but from the desert beyond. The Thar, sir! The Thar!" His blazing blue eyes were wilder than ever and his face was rough and reddened from his weeks in the sun.

Yule looked startled. "You went into the Thar?" A reconnaissance of the vast bleak desert that lies beyond the cities of Rajputana had not been part of Smithers' immediate task.

"Only a short way, sir. But what I learned – what I have heard—!"

Yule, who can be impatient and irritable, made a swift circular beckoning gesture, as though to say, "Aye, out with it, man!" But Smithers needed no encouragement. Already a story was tumbling from him: how in the desert city of Bikaner he had fallen in with an itinerant Portuguese merchant newly returned from a venture into the Great Indian Desert – the Thar, as the natives call it, that immense waterless void a hundred and fifty miles in breadth that stretches north-eastward for some four hundred miles from the swampy Rann of Cutch. Breathlessly Smithers retold the tale the Portuguese had told him: an unknown valley far out in the Thar, the sound of strange voices floating on the air, sometimes calling alluringly, sometimes wailing or sobbing, voices that could only be the voices of spirits or demons, for there was no one to be seen for miles around; the eerie music of invisible musicians, gongs and drums and bells, echoing against the sands; and above all a distinct sensation as of *summoning*, the awareness of some powerful force pulling one onward, deeper into that valley.

The Portuguese had resisted that force, said Smithers, for he was a hard-nosed trader and was able to keep his mind on business; but from villagers at an oasis town the man had picked up fragmentary anecdotes of an entire ancient city hidden away in that valley, a lost civilisation, a land of ghosts, in fact, from which that potent summons came, and into whose mysterious realm many a traveller had vanished, never to return.

I saw what I took to be the unmistakable glint of scepticism in Yule's eyes. He has never been a man to suffer foolishness gladly; and from the knotting of his bristling brows I interpreted his response to Smithers' wild fable as annoyance. But I was wrong.

"Singing spirits, eh?" Yule said. "Gongs and drums and bells? Let me read you something, and see if it sounds familiar."

He drew from his desk a sheaf of manuscript pages that were, we already knew, his translation of *The Book of Ser Marco Polo* – the earliest draft of it, rather, for Yule was destined to spend two decades on this magnum opus before giving the world the first edition in 1870, nor did he stop revising and expanding it even then. But even here in 1858 he had done a substantial amount of the work.

"Marco is in the Gobi," said Yule, "in the vicinity of the desert town of Lop, and he writes, 'The length of this desert is so great that 'tis said it would take a year and more to ride from one end of it to the other. Beasts there are none, for there is nought for them to eat. But there is a marvellous thing related of this desert, which is that when travellers are on the move by night, and one of them chances to lag behind or to fall asleep or the like, when he tries to gain his company again he will hear spirits talking, and will suppose them to be his comrades. Sometimes the spirits will call him by name; and thus shall a traveller oft-times be led astray so that he never finds his party. And in this way many have perished.'"

"It is much like what the Portuguese told me," said Smithers.

Yule nodded. "I will go on. 'Sometimes the stray travellers will hear as it were the tramp and hum of a great cavalcade of people away from the real line of road, and taking this to be their own company they will follow the sound; and when day breaks they find that a cheat has been put upon them and that they are in an ill plight. Even in the daytime one hears those spirits talk-ing. And sometimes you shall hear the sound of a variety of musical instruments, and still more commonly the sound of drums.'"

Smithers said, and his face grew even redder, "How I long to hear those drums!"

"Of course you do," said Yule, and brought out the whisky and soda, and passed around the cigars, and I knew that look in Yule's formidable glittering eyes had not been one of scepticism at all, but of complete and utter captivation.

He went on to tell us that such tales as Marco Polo's were common in medieval travel literature, and, rummaging among his papers, he read us a citation from Pliny of phantoms that appear and vanish in the deserts of Africa, and one from a Chinese named Hiuen Tsang six centuries before Marco that spoke of troops with waving banners marching in the Gobi, vanishing and reappearing and vanishing again, and many another tale of goblins and ghouls and ghostly dancers and musi-cians in the parched places of the world. "Of course," said Yule, "it is possible to explain some of this music and song merely as the noises made by shifting sands affected by desert winds and extreme heat, and the banners and armies as illusions that the minds of men travelling under such stressful conditions are likely to generate." He stared for a moment into his glass; he took a reflective puff of his cigar. "And then, of course, there is always the possibility that these tales have a rational origin – that somewhere in one of these deserts there does indeed lurk a hidden land that would seem wondrously strange to us, if only we could find it. The great age of discovery, gentlemen, is not yet over."

"I request leave, sir, to look into the Thar beyond Bikaner and see what might be found there," Smithers said.

It was a daring request. Smithers was our best surveyor, and the entire subcontinent needed measuring for the system of railways that we intended to create in its immense expanse, and nobody was planning to run track through the desert beyond Bikaner, for there was nothing there. Plenty of urgent work awaited Smithers between Delhi and Jodhpur, between Calcutta and Bombay, and elsewhere.

But Yule rose with that glitter of excitement in his eyes again and began pulling maps from a portfolio under his desk and spreading them out, the big thirty-two-miles-to-the-inch map and a smaller one of the Frontier, pointing to this place and that one in the Thar and asking if one of them might have been the one of which that Portuguese had spoken, and we knew that Smithers' request had been granted.

What I did not expect was that Brewster would be allowed to accompany him. Plainly it was a dangerous expedition and Smithers ought not to have been permitted to undertake it alone, but I would have thought that a subaltern or two and half a dozen native trackers would be the appropriate complement. Indeed Brewster was a strong and healthy young man who would readily be able to handle the rigours of the Thar, but an abundance of work awaited him right here in Calcutta and it struck me as remarkably extravagant for Yule to be willing to risk not one but two of our best engineers on such a fantastic endeavour at this critical time in the development of the nascent Indian railway system.

But I had failed to reckon with two traits of Yule's character. One was his insatiable scholarly curiosity, which had drawn him to the close study not only of Marco Polo's huge book but of the texts of many another early traveller whose names meant nothing to me: Ibn Batuta, for example, and Friar Jordanus, and Odoric of Pordenone. We were living at a time when the remaining unknown places of the world were opening before us, and the discovery – or rediscovery – of strange and marvellous regions of Asia held great fascination for him. Though he himself could not leave his high responsibilities in Calcutta, Smithers would serve as his surrogate in the far-off Thar.

Then, too, I had overlooked Yule's profound complexity of spirit. As I have already noted, he is not at all the grim, stolid, monolithic administrator that he appears to a casual observer to be. I have spoken of his irritability and impatience; I should mention also his bursts of temper, followed by spells of black depression and almost absolute silence, and also the – well, *eccentricity* that has led him, a man who happens to be colour-blind, to dress in the most outlandish garb and think it utterly normal. (I have in mind his brilliant claret-coloured trousers, which he always insisted were silver-grey.) He is complicated; he is very much his own man. So if he had taken it into his mind to send our highly valued Smithers off to look for lost cities in the Thar, nothing would stop him.

And when he asked Smithers what sort of complement he thought he would need, Smithers replied, "Why, Brewster and I can probably deal with everything all by ourselves, sir. We don't want a great silly crowd of bearers and trackers, you know, to distract us as we try to cope with those musical spectres in the desert."

Quickly I looked at Brewster and saw that he was as amazed as I was to find himself requisitioned for the expedition. But he made a quick recovery and managed a grin of boyish eagerness, as if he could think of nothing more jolly than to go trekking off into a pathless haunted desert with his hero Smithers. And Yule showed no reaction at all to Smithers' request: once again he demonstrated his approval simply through silence.

Of course, getting to the Thar would be no easy matter. It lies at the opposite side of the subcontinent from Calcutta, far off in the north-west, beyond Lucknow, beyond Agra, beyond Delhi. And, as I have said, all of this was taking place at a time before we had built the Indian railway system. Smithers had just made the round trip from Calcutta to Bikaner and back, fifteen hundred miles or more, by an arduous journey down the Grand Trunk Road, India's backbone before the railways existed. I have no idea how he travelled – by horse, by camel, by bullock-cart, by affiliating himself with merchant caravans, by any such means he could. And now he – and Brewster – would have to do it all over again. The journey would take months.

I should mention that Smithers had been engaged for the past year and a half to the Adjutant's daughter, Helena, a young woman as notable for her beauty as for her sweetness of temperament, and the wedding was due to take place in just another dozen weeks or so. I wondered how Smithers would be able to prevail on her for a postponement; but prevail he did, either through his own force of personality or the innately accommodating nature that is so typical of women, and the wedding was postponed. We held a grand farewell party for Smithers and Brewster at Fort William, where nothing was asked and nothing was volunteered about the reason for their departure, and in the small hours of the night we stood by the bank of the river with brandy-glasses in hand, singing the grand old songs of our native country so far away, and then in the morning they set out to find whatever it was that they were destined to find in the Great Indian Desert.

The weeks passed, and turned into months.

Helena, the Adjutant's lovely daughter, came to us now and again to ask whether there had been any word from her wandering fiancé. Of course I could see that she was yearning to get him back from the Thar and take him off to England for a lifetime of pink-faced fair-haired children, tea, cool fresh air, and clean linens. "I love him so," she would say.

The poor girl! The poor girl!

I knew that Smithers was India through and through, and that if she ever did get him back from the Thar there would be another quest after that, and another, and another.

I knew too that there had been an engagement before she had met Smithers, a Major invalided home from Lahore after some sort of dreary scandal involving drinking and gambling, about which I had wanted to hear no details. She was twenty-six, already. The time for making those pink-faced babies was running short.

The months went by, and Smithers and Brewster did not return from the Thar. Yule began to grow furious. His health was not good – the air of India had never been right for him, and Bengal can be a monotonous and depressing place, oppressively dank and humid much of the year – and he could see retirement from the Service not very far in his future; but he desperately wanted to know about that valley in the Thar before he left. And, for all that desperate curiosity of his, work was work and there was a railroad line to build and Smithers and Brewster were needed here, not drifting around in some sandy wasteland far away.

Yule's health gave way quite seriously in the spring of 1859 and he took himself home to Scotland for a rest. His older brother George, who had not been out of India for thirty years, went with him. They were gone three months. Since the voyage out and the voyage back took a month each, that left them only a month at home, but he returned greatly invigorated, only to be much distressed and angered by the news that Smithers and Brewster were still unaccounted for.

From time to time the Adjutant's daughter came to inquire about her fiancé. Of course I had no news for her.

"I love him so!" she cried.

The poor girl.

Then one day there was a stir in town, as there often is when a caravan from some distant place arrives, and shortly thereafter Brewster presented himself at my office at the Public Works Department. Not Brewster and Smithers: just Brewster.

I scarcely recognised him. He was decked out not in his usual khakis but in some bizarre native garb, very colourful and strange, flowing robes of rose, magenta, turquoise blue, but that was not the least of the change. The Brewster I had seen off, the year before, had been dark-haired and youthful, perhaps thirty-two years old at most. The man I saw before me now looked forty-five or even fifty. There were prominent streaks of grey in his thick black hair, and the underlying bony structure of his cheeks and chin seemed to have shifted about to some degree, and there was a network of fine lines radiating outward from the corners of his eyes that no man of thirty-two should have had. His posture had changed, too: I remembered him as upright and straight-backed, but he had begun to stoop a little, as tall men sometimes do with the years, and his shoulders seemed rounded and hunched in a way I did not recall. My first thought, which in retrospect shows an amazing lack of insight, was merely that the journey must have been a very taxing one.

"Welcome, old friend," I said. And then I said, carefully, "And Smithers—?"

Brewster gave me a weary stare. "He is still there."

"Ah," I said. And again: "Ah."

Brewster's reply could have meant anything: that Smithers had found something so fascinating that he needed more time for research, that he had fallen under the sway of some native cult and was wandering naked and ash-smeared along the ghats of Benares, or that he had perished on the journey and lay buried somewhere in the desert. But I asked no questions.

"Let me send for Yule," I said. "He will want to hear your story."

There had been a change in Yule's appearance, too, since Brewster's departure. He too had grown bowed and stooped and grey, but in his case that was no surprise, for he was nearly forty and his health had never been strong. But it was impossible not to notice Yule's reaction at the great alteration Brewster had undergone. Indeed, Brewster now looked older than Yule himself.

"Well," said Yule, and waited.

And Brewster began to tell his tale.

They had set forth in the grandest of moods, Brewster said. Smithers was almost always exuberant and enthusiastic, and it had ever been Brewster's way, although he was of a different basic temperament, readily to fall in with his friend's customarily jubilant frame of mind. It had been their plan to go with the Spring Caravan heading for Aurangabad, but in India everything happens either after time or before time, and in this case the caravan departed before time, so they were on their own. Smithers found horses for them and off they went, westward along the Grand Trunk Road, that great long river-like highway, going back to the sixteenth century and probably to some prehistoric precursor, that carries all traffic through the heart of India.

It is a comfortable road. I have travelled it myself. It is perfectly straight and capably constructed. Trees planted on both sides of it give welcome shade the whole way. The wide, well-made middle road is for the quick traffic, the sahibs on their horses, and the like. It was on that road that the British armies moved swiftly out of Bengal to conquer the north Indian plain. To the left and right are the rougher roadbeds where the heavy carts with creaking wooden wheels go groaning along, the ones that bear the cotton and grain, the timber, the hides, the produce. And then there is the foot traffic, the hordes and hordes of moneylenders and holy men and native surgeons and pilgrims and peddlers, swarms of them in their thousands going about the daily business of India.

As travelling sahibs, of course, Smithers and Brewster encountered no problems. There are *caravanserais* at regular intervals to provide food and lodging, and police stations set close together so that order is maintained. When their horses gave out they rented others, and later they hired passage for themselves in bullock-carts until they could find horses once again, and after that they rode on camels for a time. From Durgapur to Benares they went, from Kanpur and Aligarh to Delhi, and there, although the Grand Trunk Road continues on north-westward to Lahore and Peshawar to its terminus, they turned to secondary roads that brought them down via Bikaner to the edge of the desert.

The Thar, then! The vast unwelcoming Thar!

Brewster described it for us: the deep, loose, fine-grained sands, the hillocks that the winds have shaped, running from south-west to north-east, the dunes that rise two hundred feet or more above the dusty plain, the ugly gravel plains. As one might expect, there are no real rivers there, unless you count the Indus, which flows mostly to the west of it, and the Luri, which runs through its southern reaches. The Ghaggar comes down into it from the north but loses itself in the desert sands. There are some salt lakes and a few widely spaced freshwater springs. The vegetation, such as it is, is mostly thorny scrub, and some acacia and tamarisk trees.

Why anyone would plant a city in such a desolate place as the Thar is beyond my comprehension, but men will found cities

anywhere, it seems. Most likely they chose sites along the eastern
fringe of the desert, which is relatively habitable, because that
great forbidding waste just beyond would protect them against
invasion from the north-west. So along that fringe one finds the
princely states of Rajasthan, and such royal capitals as Jodhpur,
Jaipur, and Bikaner; and it was the walled city of Bikaner,
famous for its carpets and blankets, that became expedition
headquarters for Smithers and Brewster.

Brewster, who was something of a linguist, went among the
people to ask about haunted valleys and invisible drum-players
and the like. He did not quite use those terms, but his persistent
questioning did get some useful answers, after a while. One old
fakir thought that the place they sought might lie between
Pakpattan and Mubarakpur. Smithers and Brewster bought
some camels and laid in provisions and headed out to see. They
did not find any lost civilisations between Pakpattan and
Mubarakpur. But Smithers was confident that they would find
something somewhere, and they went north and then west and
then curved south again, tacking to and fro across a pathless
sea of sand, making an intricate zigzagging tour through territory so forlorn, Brewster told us, that you felt like weeping
when you saw it. And after a week or two, he said, as they
plodded on between nowhere and nowhere and were close to
thinking themselves altogether and eternally lost, the sound of
strange singing came to them on the red-hot wind from the
west.

"Do you hear it?" Smithers asked.

"I hear it, yes," said Brewster.

He told us that it was like no singing he had ever heard: delicate, eerie, a high-pitched chant that might have been made up of
individual words, but words so slurred and blurred that they
carried no meaning at all. Then, too, apart from the chanting
they heard spoken words, a low incomprehensible whispering in
the air, the urgent chattering conversation of invisible beings,
and the tinkling of what might have been camel-bells in the
distance, and the occasional tapping of drumbeats.

"There are our ghosts," Smithers said.

It was a word he liked to use, said Brewster. Like most of us
Brewster had read a few ghost stories, and to him the word

"ghosts" summoned up the creaking floorboards of a haunted house, shrouded white figures gliding silently through darkness, fluttering robes moving of their own bodiless accord, strangely transparent coaches travelling swiftly down a midnight road, and other such images quite remote from the chanting and drumming of desert folk in gaudy garb, with jingling anklets and necklaces, under a hot fierce sun. But the sounds of the Thar came from some invisible source, and to Smithers they were sounds made by ghosts.

Everything was as the Portuguese merchant had said it would be, even unto the mysterious *summoning* force that emanated from some location to the west. The Portuguese had fought against that pull and had won his struggle, but Smithers and Brewster had no wish to do the same, and they rode onward, wrapping their faces against the burning wind and the scouring gusts of airborne sand. The sounds grew more distinct. It seemed to them both that the voices they heard were those of revellers, laughing and singing in the marketplace of a populous city; but there could be no cities here, in this abysmal trackless wilderness of sand and thin tufts of grass and empty sky. There was nothing here whatsoever.

And then they entered a narrow canyon that showed a shadowy slit at its farther end. They went toward it – there was scarcely any choice, now, so strong was the pull – and passed through it, and, suddenly, without any sense of transition, they were out of the desert and in some new and altogether unexpected realm. It was more than an oasis; it was like an entire faery kingdom. Before them stretched groves of palms and lemon trees along gently flowing canals, and beyond those gardens were rows of angular, many-windowed buildings rising rank upon rank above a swiftly flowing river that descended out of low, softly rounded green hills in the west. Brewster and Smithers stared at each other in amazement and wonder. When they looked back they no longer could see the desert, for a thick grey film, a kind of solid vapour, stretched like an impenetrable band across the mouth of the canyon.

"A moment later," said Brewster, "we found ourselves surrounded by the inhabitants of this place. They rose up out of nowhere, like phantoms indeed, a great colourful horde of them, and danced a welcome about us in circles, singing and waving their arms aloft and crying out in what we could only interpret as tones of gladness."

The people of the hidden valley, Brewster told us, were a tall, handsome folk, plainly of the Caucasian race, dark-eyed but light-skinned, with sharp cheekbones and long narrow noses. They seemed rather like Persians in appearance, he thought. They dressed in loose robes of the most vibrant colours, greens, reds, brilliant yellows, the men wearing red or gold pointed skullcaps or beautiful soft-hued turbans striped with bright bands of lemon, pink, yellow or white, and the women in voluminous mantles, filmy clouds of crepe, shawls shot through with gold brocade, and the like. Below their cascading robes both sexes wore white trousers of a ballooning sort, and an abundance of silver anklets. Their feet were bare. Of course throughout India one sees all manner of flamboyant exotic garb, varying somewhat from region to region but all of it colourful and almost magical in its beauty, and the way these people looked was not fundamentally different from the look of the dwellers in this district of Hindustan or that one, and yet there *was* a difference, a certain quaint touch of antique glamour, an element of the fantastic, that left the two travellers thinking that they had drifted not into some unknown valley but into the thousand-year-old pages of the *Thousand Nights and a Night*.

At no time did they feel as though they were in danger. Perhaps these people might be ghosts of some sort, but goblins, ghouls, demons, no. They were too amiable for that. The welcoming party, never ceasing its prancing and chanting, conducted them into the town, the buildings of which were of wattled mud plastered in white and over-painted with elaborate patterns of the same brilliant hues as the clothing. From there on it was all rather like entering into an unusually vivid dream. They were shown to a kind of *caravanserai* where they were able to rest and bathe. Their camels, which were the object of great curiosity, were taken away to be given provender and water, and they themselves were supplied with clothing of the native sort to replace the tattered garments in which they had crossed the desert.

"They fed us generously," said Brewster, "with an array of curried meats, and some fruits and vegetables, and a drink much like yoghurt, made of the fermented milk of I know not what creature."

The flavour of the food was unfamiliar, rich with spices, particularly black pepper, but wholly lacking in the fiery red capsicums that we associate with the cuisine of the land. Of course the capsicum is not native to India – the Portuguese, I think, brought it here from the New World centuries ago – and perhaps it was impossible to obtain them here in the Thar; but their absence from the food was something that Brewster found especially notable.

He and Smithers were the centre of all attention, day after day, as if they were the first to make their way into the valley from the outside world in many years, as most probably they were. Village notables came to them daily, men with flowing white beards and glorious turbans, one of them of particularly majestic bearing who was surely the rajah of the city, and pelted them with an endless flow of questions, none of which, of course, either man could understand. English was unknown here, and when Brewster and Smithers tried Hindustani or Rajasthani or such smatterings of Urdu and Sindhi that they knew, no connection was made. Gradually it dawned on Brewster, who was, as I have said, quite a good linguist, that they were speaking a primitive form of Hindi, something like the Marwari dialect that they speak in and around Bikaner, but as different from it as the English of Chaucer is from that of Queen Victoria's times. He did indeed manage to pick out a few words correctly, and achieved some few moments of successful communication with the valley folk, each time touching off a great gleeful volley of the local kind of applause, which involved stamping of the feet and jingling of the anklets.

In the succeeding weeks Smithers and Brewster became, to some degree, part of the life of the village. They were allowed to wander upriver by themselves, and found garden plots there where spices and vegetables were growing. They saw the workshops where cloth was laboriously woven and cut by women sitting cross-legged. They saw the dyers' tanks, great stone-walled pools of scarlet and mauve and azure and crimson. They saw the fields where livestock grazed.

It was a closed community, utterly self-sufficient, sealed away from the forbidding desert that surrounded it and completely able to meet all its own needs, while outside the valley the world of kings and emperors and railroads and steam engines and guns and newspapers ticked on and on, mattering less than nothing to these oblivious people – these ghosts, as Smithers persisted in calling them.

And yet there was leakage: those sounds of gongs and drums and singing, drifting through that foggy barrier and into the wasteland beyond, and occasionally summoning some outsider to the valley. That was odd. Brewster had no explanation for it. I suppose no one ever shall.

Before long the irrepressible Smithers' innate exuberance came to the fore. He was full of ideas for transforming the lives of these people. He wanted to teach them how to build aqueducts, steam engines, pumps, looms. He urged Brewster, who even now could manage only a few broken sentences in their language, to describe these things to the rajah and his court. Brewster was not convinced that these folk needed aqueducts or pumps or any of the other things Smithers yearned to bestow on them, but he did his best, which was not nearly good enough. Smithers, impatient, began to try to learn their language himself. One of the women of the village – a girl, rather, a striking keen-eyed girl of about twenty, half a head taller than Smithers – seemed to have volunteered to be his tutor. Brewster often saw them together, pantomiming words, acting out little charades, laughing, gesturing. He might perhaps be learning something, Brewster thought.

But Brewster knew that they could not stay there long enough to build aqueducts. Fascinating though the place was, the time had come, he thought, to begin the journey back into the modern world. And so he said, one morning, to Smithers.

At that point in his narrative Brewster fell silent. He seemed entirely played out. "So you would call it truly a lost civilisation?" Yule asked, when Brewster had said nothing for what might have been several minutes. "Cut off in the desert for hundreds of years or even more from all contact with the rest of India?"

"I would call it that, yes," said Brewster.

"And when the time came for you to leave, Smithers chose to remain?"

"Yes," said Brewster, showing some signs of uneasiness at the question. "That is exactly what happened."

He did not offer details, but merely said that after some weeks he felt that it was incumbent upon them to return to Calcutta and make their report, and, when Smithers insisted on remaining to conduct further studies, of the type that so many venturesome men of our nation have carried out in Africa and Asia and the Americas, Brewster, finding it impossible to shake his resolve, at last reluctantly resolved to leave without him. The valley people seemed distressed at the thought of his departure, and indeed made it so difficult for him to locate the camels that he thought they might intend to restrain him from going; but eventually he found them, and – this part was very difficult too – went back out of the canyon, blundering around in one direction and another in that thick band of vapour before finding the one and only exit into the desert. Getting back to Bikaner from there was another great challenge, and only by some lucky guesswork was he able to retrace his earlier path. And after a lengthy and evidently toilsome journey back across the subcontinent, a journey that he did not choose to describe, but which I thought must have been so exhausting that it had put that strange appearance of premature age upon him, here he was among us once more in Yule's office.

Yule said, when he was done, "And would you be able to find that place again, if you had to? If I were to ask you to go back there now to get Smithers?"

Brewster seemed stunned by the request.

He winced and blinked, like one stepping out of a dark room into Calcutta sunlight. I could see signs of a struggle going on within him. Yule's question had caught him completely by surprise; and plainly he was searching for the strength to refuse any repetition of the ordeal he had just been through. But the indomitable Yule was waiting grimly for a reply, and finally, in a barely audible voice, Brewster said, "Yes, I think that I could. I think so, sir. But is it necessary that I do?"

"It is," said Yule. "We can hardly do without him. It was wrong of you to come away with him still there. You must go back and fetch him."

Brewster considered that. He bowed his head. I think I may have heard a sob. He looked ragged and pale and tired. He was silent a great while, and it seemed to me that he was thinking about something that he did not care to discuss with us.

Yule, waiting once again for a reply, appeared terribly tired himself, as though he wanted nothing more than a year's rest in some gentler clime. But the great strength of the man was still evident, bearing down on poor Brewster with full force.

After a long, an interminable silence, whatever resistance Brewster had managed to muster seemed to snap. I saw him quiver as it happened. He said quietly, huskily, "Yes, I suppose I must." And planning for the return trip began forthwith.

I was with Brewster the next day when Helena came to inquire about her errant fiancé. Brewster told her that Smithers was making great discoveries, that his discovery of this lost land would assure him eternal fame in the annals of exploration. He has remained behind for a while to complete his notes and sketches, Brewster said. I noticed that he did not meet the Adjutant's daughter's eager gaze as he spoke; in truth, he looked past her shoulder as though she were a creature too bright to behold.

This time there was no grand farewell party. Brewster simply slipped away alone to the Grand Trunk Road. He had insisted that no one should accompany him, and he did so with such unBrewsterlike firmness that even Yule was taken aback, and yielded, though to me it seemed like madness to let the man make that trip by himself.

And so Brewster departed once more for that valley in the Thar. Soon Yule left us again also – he had another breakdown of his health, and went on recreational leave to Java – and, since we were now in the full throes of planning the Indian railway system and our staff was already undermanned, my own responsibilities multiplied manifold. In 1857 we had had only 200 miles of track in operation in all of India. Our task was to increase that a hundredfold, not only for greater ease in our own military operations, but also to provide India with a modern system of mass transportation that would further the economic development of that huge and still largely primitive land. As the months went along and my work engulfed me, I confess that I forgot all about Brewster and Smithers.

Yule returned from Java, looking much older. Before long he would resign from the Service to return to England, and then, as his wife's health weakened also, on to the more benevolent clime of Italy, where he would complete and publish his famous translations of Marco Polo and other medieval travellers in Asia. In his remaining time in Calcutta he said nothing about Brewster and Smithers either; I think they had fallen completely out of his mind, which had no room for the irresponsible Smitherses and feckless Brewsters of the world.

One day in 1861 or early 1862 I was hard at work, preparing a report for the Governor-General on the progress of the Bombay–Calcutta line, when an old man in faded robes was shown into my office. He was thin and very tall, with rounded shoulders and a bent, bowed posture, and his long, narrow face was deeply lined, so that his eyes looked out at me from a bewildering webwork of crevices. He was trembling as though palsied, though more likely it was just the tremor of age. Under his arm he carried a rectangular box of some considerable size, fastened with an ornate clasp of native design. Because his skin was so dark and he was wearing those loose robes I mistook him for a native himself at first, but then I began to think he might be a deeply tanned Englishman, and when he spoke his accent left no doubt of that.

"You don't recognise me, do you?" he asked.

I stared. "I'm sorry. I don't think I do." I was annoyed by the interruption. "Are you sure that the business you have is with the Public Works Department?"

"I am, in fact, an employee of the Public Works Department. Or was, at least."

His face was still unrecognisable to me. But the voice—

"Brewster?"

"Brewster, yes. Back at last."

"But this is impossible! You're – what, thirty-five years old? You look to be—"

"Sixty? Seventy?"

"I would have to say so, yes."

He studied me implacably.

"I am Brewster," he said. "I will be thirty-seven come January."

"This is impossible," I said, though aware of the foolishness of my words as soon as I spoke them. "For a man to have aged so quickly—"

"Impossible, yes, that's the word. But I am Brewster."

He set that box down on my desk, heedless of the clutter of blueprints and maps on which he was placing it. And he said, "You may recall that Lieutenant-Colonel Yule ordered me to return to a certain valley in the Thar and bring Major Smithers out of it. I have done so. It was not an easy journey, but I have accomplished it, and I have returned. And I have brought Smithers with me."

I peered expectantly at him, thinking that he would wave his age-withered arm and Smithers would come striding in from the hall. But no: instead he worked at the clasp of that big wooden box with those trembling fingers of his for what seemed like half an hour, and opened it at last, and lifted the lid and gestured to me to peer in.

Inside lay a bleached skull, sitting atop a jumble of other bones, looking like relics exhumed from some tumulus of antiquity. They were resting on a bed of sand.

"This is Smithers," he said.

For a moment I could find nothing whatsoever to say. Then I blurted, "How did he die?"

"He died of extreme age," Brewster said.

And he told me how, after expending many weeks and months crossing India and bashing around in the Thar, he had finally heard the ghostly singers and the distant drums and gongs again, and they had led him to the hidden valley. There he found Smithers, fluent now in the local lingo and busy with all manner of public-works projects in a full-scale attempt to bring the inhabitants of the valley into the nineteenth century overnight.

He was married, Brewster said, to that lovely long-legged native princess who had been teaching him the language.

"Married?" I repeated foolishly, thinking of mournful Helena, the Adjutant's beautiful daughter, faithful to him yet, still waiting hopefully for his return.

"I suppose it was a marriage," said Brewster. "They were man and wife, at any rate, whatever words had been said over them. And seemed very happy together. I spoke to him about returning to his assignment here. As you might suspect, he wasn't eager to do so. I spoke more firmly to him about it." I tried to imagine the diffident Brewster speaking firmly to his strong-willed friend about anything. I couldn't. "I appealed to his sense of duty. I appealed to him as an Englishman. I spoke of the Queen."

"And did he yield?"

"After a while, yes," Brewster said, in a strange tone of voice that made me wonder whether Brewster might have made him yield at gunpoint. I could not bring myself to ask. "But he insisted that we bring his – wife – out of the valley with us. And so we did. And here they are."

He indicated the box, the skull, the bones beneath, the bed of sand.

"Hardly had we passed through the barrier but they began to shrivel and age," he said. "The woman died first. She became a hideous crone in a matter of hours. Then Smithers went."

"But how – how?"

Brewster shrugged. "Time moves at a different rate within the valley. I can't explain it. I don't understand it. The people in there may be living six or eight hundred years ago, or even more. Time is suspended. But when one emerges – well, do you see me? How I look? The suspended years descend on one like an avalanche, once one leaves. I spent a few weeks in that village the first time. I came back here looking ten or twenty years older. This time I was there for some months. Look at me. Smithers had been under the valley's spell for, what, two or three years?"

"And the woman for her entire life."

"Yes. When they came out, he must have been a hundred years old, by the way we reckon time. And she, perhaps a thousand."

How could I believe him? I am an engineer, a builder of railroads and bridges. I give no credence to tales of ghosts and ghouls and invisible spectres whose voices are heard on the desert air, nor do I believe that time runs at different rates in different parts of our world. And yet – yet – the skull, the bones, the withered, trembling old man of not quite thirty-seven who stood before me speaking with Brewster's voice—

I understood now that Brewster had been aware of what going back into that terrible valley to fetch Smithers would do to him. It would rob him of most or all of the remaining years of his life. He had known, but Yule had ordered him to go, and, yes, he had gone. The poor man. The poor doomed man.

To cover my confusion I reached into the box. "And what is this?" I asked, picking up a pinch of something fine and white that I took for desert sand, lying beneath the little heap of bones like a cushion. "A souvenir of the Thar?"

"In a manner of speaking. That's all that remains of her. She crumbled to dust right in front of me. Shrivelled and died and went absolutely to dust, all in a moment."

Shuddering, I brushed it free of my fingers, back into the box. I was silent for a while.

The room was spinning about me. I had spent all my days in a world in which three and three make six, six and six make twelve, but I was no longer sure that I lived in such a world any longer.

Then I said, "Take what's left of Smithers to the chaplain, and see what he wants to do about a burial."

He nodded, the good obedient Brewster of old. "And what shall I do with this?" he asked, pointing to the sandy deposit in the box.

"Scatter it in the road," I said. "Or spill it into the river, whatever you wish. She was Smithers' undoing. We owe her no courtesies."

And then I thought of Helena, sweet, patient Helena. She had never understood the first thing about him, had she? And yet she had loved him. Poor, sweet Helena.

She must be protected now, I thought. The world is very strange, and too harsh, sometimes, and we must protect women like Helena from its mysteries. At least, from such mysteries as this one – not the mystery of that hidden valley, I mean, though that is mysterious enough, but the mysteries of the heart.

I drew a deep breath. "And – with regard to the Adjutant's daughter, Brewster—"

"Yes?"

"She will want to know how he died, I suppose. Tell her he died bravely, while in the midst of his greatest adventure in Her Majesty's Service. But you ought not, I think, to tell her very much more than that. Do you understand me? He died bravely. That should suffice, Brewster. That should suffice."

REGGIE OLIVER

Quieta Non Movere

REGGIE OLIVER HAS BEEN a professional playwright, actor, and theatre director since 1975. Besides plays, his publications include the authorised biography of writer Stella Gibbons, *Out of the Woodshed*, published by Bloomsbury in 1998, and five collections of stories of supernatural terror, of which the latest, *Mrs Midnight*, is now in paperback, having sold out its hardback edition from Tartarus.

His novel, *The Dracula Papers I: The Scholar's Tale*, is the first of a projected four, and he is now working on the second volume, *The Monk's Tale*. Meanwhile, an omnibus edition of his short stories entitled *Dramas from the Depths* is being published by Centipede Press, as part of that imprint's "Masters of the Weird Tale" series.

The author's stories have appeared in more than thirty anthologies, including several previous volumes of *The Mammoth Book of Best New Horror*.

"There is no point in denying it: this story is a deliberate pastiche of M. R. James' style and manner, and set in his period," Oliver confesses, "though perhaps with a few flourishes that are my own.

"It was originally written as an inset story inside a tale called 'The Giacometti Crucifixion', and appears as such in my latest collection, *Mrs Midnight*.

"There, it is purported to have been written by 'The Rev. A. C. Lincoln', an Oxford contemporary and rival of James'.

However, the story was thought capable of standing on its own and appears as such in *The Eighth Black Book of Horror*.

"It is one of a number of stories I have written located in the fictional English cathedral city of Morchester. Readers who know the lovely old city of Salisbury will have some idea of my inspiration for Morchester."

O NE OF MY first clerical positions was that of a curate to a parish just outside the cathedral city of Morchester. Being of a naturally studious inclination, I devoted my spare time to researching the history of the district and, in particular, the cathedral. I even proposed to write a short monograph on some of the more curious funerary monuments to be found in that building. One in particular attracted my attention because of its strange inscription and carving. My enquiries about this particular monument elicited a story of some very shocking events connected with that tomb which happened some ten years prior to my arrival in Morchester. Despite the passing of a decade, the events were still very clear in the minds of those who witnessed them and who were willing to speak to me. Their accounts are the foundations of the story I am about to tell.

Let me therefore remove you a while to the ancient city of Morchester in the County of Morsetshire in the year 1863. Though the railway had arrived some fifteen years previously, it could be said that in all other respects time had stood still in the city for many decades. It had been and remained a prosperous market town; it boasted a fine cathedral, mostly in the Early English and Decorated styles. Rooks cawed among its towers and in the immemorial elms that punctuated the sward of its fine old close.

One cloudless afternoon in the July of that year the great bell of the cathedral began to sound its bass note, summoning the city to the funeral of one of its servants. The Dean was dead. That ancient knell, that call to remembrance and reminder of mortality, would no doubt have seemed to Morchester's inhabitants no more than a slight eddy in the changeless flow of life and death which washed about its walls. Who could have foreseen that it tolled the commencement of a series of horribly inexplicable events?

In all conscience, the passing of The Very Rev. William Ainsley, Dean of Morchester was greeted with little sadness, and was the occasion, in some quarters, of no small relief. Dean Ainsley had for many years been infirm and fulfilled his decanal duties with a listlessness only just short of rank incompetence. When, on the day of his funeral, the Very Rev. Stephen Coombe, acceded to the position and sat in his stall in the choir, there was much talk of new brooms sweeping clean. Even those who did not find such a metaphor entirely reassuring were compelled to admit that anything was preferable to the disarray of the previous regime.

Dean Coombe was a tall lean man in his forties, heavily whiskered as was the fashion in those days, and of High Church leanings. He was in possession of a wife and a daughter, almost as angular as he was. He was an upright man, but stiff and overbearing; he inspired respect perhaps, but no great affection. Being active and zealous in all his dealings, he very soon began to turn his attention to the fabric of Morchester Cathedral which was indeed in a woeful state of disrepair.

The tenure of Dean Ainsley had been marked by neglect towards the great building he was appointed to maintain, so it was perhaps only just that this legacy of dereliction should be mitigated by his posthumous one. The late Dean had left his entire and considerable fortune to the cathedral, with the provision that a chapel, dedicated to the Virgin Mary, in the north transept should be made as a permanent memorial to him. As the legacy more than amply provided for this, it was resolved, by the dean and chapter, to accept it. There had been murmurings from some of the more low church canons that the building of a Lady Chapel might give rise to accusations of popery, but these were properly dismissed as old fashioned. The Dean was a forceful man and was used to carrying all before him.

An architect was engaged and there needed only a decision to be made over the location of the chapel. The obvious place was an area closest to the crossing and facing east. This would entail the partial destruction of the eastern wall of the north transept, an exercise which would require the relocation of a number of funereal plaques and stones, the most significant of which was a sixteenth century memorial to a Canon of Morchester Cathedral, one Jeremiah Staveley. It was quite an elaborate affair in polished black basalt about seven foot in height overall, set into the wall some three feet above the ground. It consisted in a slab topped with scrollwork, crudely classical in feel with a niche in which was set a painted alabaster image of the Canon, standing upright in his clerical robes with his arms crossed over his chest. The figure was tall and narrow, the bearded face gaunt: a somewhat disconcerting image which looked as if it portrayed the corpse rather than the living being. Beneath this on the polished slab an inscription had been incised, the lettering picked out in white. It read:

JEREMIAH STAVELEY

Canonus Morcastriensis, obiit anno 1595 aetat 52

It was followed by these verses in bold capital letters:

BEHINDE THESE SACRED STONES IN DEATH STAND I
FOR THAT IN LIFE MOST BASELY DID I LIE
IN WORD AND SINNE FORSAKING GOD HIS LAWE,
I DANCED MY SOULE IN SATANN'S VERIE MAWE.
WHEREFORE IN PENANCE I THIS VIGILL KEEPE
ENTOMBÉD UPRIGHT THUS WHERE I SHOULDE SLEEPE.
WHEN DEAD RISE UP I'LL READYE BE IN PLACE
TO MEET MY JUDGE AND MAKER FACE TO FACE.
STRANGER, REST NOT MY CORSE UNTIL THAT DAYE
LEST I TORMENT THEE WITH MY SORE DISMAYE.

The implication of these lines, that the body of Canon Staveley was actually entombed behind the slab, was borne out by the cathedral records and one of the old vergers whose family had been connected with the cathedral since time immemorial. Dean Coombe was disposed to be rather benevolent towards this worthy whose name was Wilby. The man was a repository of cathedral history and lore and the Dean was content to listen politely to Wilby's ramblings, but he did not expect his condescension to be rewarded by opposition to his plans.

"Mr Dean," said Wilby one afternoon, as they stood before the memorial in the north transept. "You don't want to go a moving of that there stone, begging your pardon, sir."

"My dear man, why ever not?"

"Don't it say so plain as brass on that there 'scription? 'Tis ill luck to move the bones of the wicked. So said my granfer, and his before him."

"And who says this Canon Staveley was a wicked man?"

"Why 'tis well known. There are tales that have passed down about Jeremiah Staveley, which I might blush to tell you, Mr Dean. The poor women of this city were not safe in their beds from him, they say. A harsh man too, to those below him. But he was a fair man of music and when I were a lad in the choir they still sang his setting to the Psalm one hundred and thirty seven. 'By the waters of Babylon . . .', all nine verses too. With the dashing of children agin the stones and all. Some said he would have fain dinged his choir lads agin the stones, too, when they were singing awry. Certain it was, he spared not the rod among them. And there were tales of meeting at night in the church with a man all in black and a gold treasure that he found under the earth in a field that the black man took him to. But it weren't no good for him, for soon as he was by way of enjoying his gold, the plague fell on him and he wasted to a wraith of skin and bone, and him as tall and narrow as may be already. And when at last he came to be in extreme, as you say, and within a hand's breadth of mortality, he summons the Dean, as it might be you, sir, a man with whom he had had some mighty quarrel, and begs him for forgiveness and to be shriven of his many sins. And all his treasure they say he left to the dean and chapter but saying he must be buried upright, to keep him awake, he says. Because in the last days he suffered terribly from dreams and was as mortally afeared of sleep as he was of death. So he begged to be buried upright that he might not sleep till the Last Judgement, even as a dead man. And when the Dean of that time, Dean Cantwell, as I think it was, came out from seeing Canon Staveley in his deathbed, they say the Dean's face was as white as a linen altar cloth and he spoke not a word to a mortal soul for seven days. This I had from my granfer who had it from his, and it came down in the family with a warning, as my old father used to say. 'Don't you touch the Staveley stone, nor go nigh it at night, nor suffer his bones to be moved.' And that's what I say to you, begging your pardon, Mr Dean."

"Well, well, Wilby," said Dean Coombe who was rather more shaken by this recitation than he cared to admit, "that is indeed a most fascinating legend. Most interesting. I must write some of it down."

"It weren't no legend, Mr Dean," said old Wilby. "I had it from my granfer, and he—"

"Quite so, quite so, my dear man," said the Dean hurriedly. "Nevertheless, move this old monument we must. But make no mistake, we shall re-site it well, for it is certainly a curiosity, and if there are any human remains behind it we shall lay them to rest with all due respect. Goodness me! What was that noise?"

Both Wilby and Dean Coombe heard it, a sound like a long inhalation of breath, ragged and rattling, somewhat as if the breather – if such there was – was experiencing difficulty in drawing in air. It was magnified and distorted by the cathedral's echo which was particularly reverberant in that part of the building. Dean Coombe was not a fanciful man but he had been at his father's deathbed and he knew the sound of a man's breathing as he nears the end. This sound was uncomfortably like it.

"Dear me," said the Dean. "I really must have that organ seen to."

Wilby gave the Dean a quizzical stare, then, bidding him a hurried "Good day, Mr Dean", he began to shuffle off in the direction of the west door with surprising swiftness. Dean Coombe remained behind standing before the monument. A passer-by was surprised to hear him mutter.

"Hah! You won't affright me that easy, Master Staveley. We shall see!"

The following day the workmen moved in and began the demolition of the eastern wall of the north transept. Dean Coombe had given explicit instructions that the memorial slabs were to be most carefully removed, and, towards evening, he was on hand when the dismantling of the Staveley Memorial began. Palmer, the head mason, had set up scaffolding and constructed a wooden cradle in which to take the stone.

Dean Coombe suggested that the painted alabaster effigy in the niche be removed first, but this proved unexpectedly troublesome. The statue had been very securely cemented to its base, and one of the workmen cut himself on one of the folds of the statue's long gown. The workmanship was unusually precise and unworn by time.

When the effigy was finally removed, Dean Coombe was intrigued to find that it had been carved all round and that the back of the figure, which had been unseen by any living soul since it had been placed in the niche over two hundred and fifty years ago, had been carved with as much care as the visible front. He noted with particular interest the minuteness with which the sculptor had represented every snaking strand of the subject's unusually long black hair. He had also taken care to represent a gold seal ring on the third finger of the left hand, even incising the seal with a strange geometrical figure.

The face too repaid closer inspection. As Dean Coombe remarked to a colleague the following day, in a rather striking phrase, it would seem to have been "done from the death rather than from life". The skin had been painted white, with a slight yellow tinge, the cheeks were sunken and gaunt and – a rather troubling detail – the mouth gaped slightly, revealing a tiny set of jagged greenish teeth. Then there were the eyes.

Dean Coombe did not care to dwell long on the eyes. There was, as he later remarked, something "not quite dead" about them. Under the heavy lids an area of creamy white showed punctuated by the pinpoint of a pupil in a cloudy, greyish iris. The impression given was of a last wild stare at life. The painter of the statue had somehow managed to convey the terror of the sinner at the very point of death.

Despite a certain distaste (as he chose to call it) Dean Coombe was impressed by the remarkably fine workmanship of the image. In the few moments of leisure that he allowed himself he was something of an antiquarian which was why one of his many projects for the cathedral was the setting up of a museum in the chapter house where some of the old plate and vestments of the cathedral could be displayed for the benefit of both the public and the cathedral which would take its sixpences.

"This is such fine work," said the Dean, in reality thinking aloud, but ostensibly addressing Palmer the mason. "I wonder if the craftsmanship could be Spanish, though they tended to carve in wood rather than alabaster. Certainly whoever did the painting, not necessarily the sculptor, for the painting of sculpture was a specialised art in those days, you know, looks to have been trained in the peninsular. Most unusual. I must get up something to one of the learned journals on the subject. Now then, Palmer, I want you to set this aside. Take great care of it. I shall have a plaster copy made. The replica we will put back in the niche and we can display the original in my chapter house museum, in a glass case where it may be appreciated from all angles – Good gracious, what was that?"

There had been a cry of pain accompanied by – had it been an oath? Palmer and the Dean looked around much startled as they had been absorbed in the contemplation of the effigy. However they soon discovered the cause: it was one of the workmen who had accidentally dropped a lump hammer on his foot. He was much rebuked both by Palmer for carelessness and by Dean Coombe for making an unseemly noise in a sacred building. The man protested that some mysterious force had knocked the hammer from his hand, but he was not listened to, for by this time the light was dimming and it was decided to abandon work for the day.

And so Dean Coombe began to make his way home to the Deanery across the darkling close on that cool March evening. Picture him if you will as he takes this journey, a man you might say not much given to strange fears and frets. Here is a man who walks in life both inwardly and outwardly straight ahead, looking neither to left nor right, untroubled by fancy. This is what you would have said had you seen him stride out from the west door to face a sun which was falling behind the ancient elms in an untidy wrack of clouds. Now he turns a little to his left, and sets forth diagonally across the grass to where the Deanery is situated at the south-west corner of the great close which surrounds the edifice of St Anselm's, Morchester.

Barely has he begun on this journey when a whole crowd of rooks, a "building" of them, if I may use the correct ornithological term, rises as one from the elms and begins to wheel about above the trees uttering their distinctive "kaa, kaa" sound. Dean Coombe must have witnessed this behaviour countless times, and yet he starts and stops for a moment to consider those birds. Their flappings across the ensanguined sky of evening appear to him more than usually agitated and chaotic, and their strange, forlorn cries, more desolate even than normal. But these thoughts occupy him for no longer than a few seconds, and then he is on his way once more.

He quickens his pace, now more resolved than ever to reach his destination. Yet once or twice we see him glance quickly behind him, so quickly that one wonders if he truly wants to see if anything follows. By the time he reaches the gate of the Deanery passers-by are amazed to see that this very sober divine is almost running. The housemaid is equally astonished to open the door to a breathless man.

We will pass over the Dean's next few hours. Let us say only that the Deanery, though spacious, is a chilly, damp old house, rather too near the river for comfort. Its physical atmosphere, moreover, is matched by that which exists among its inhabitants. Relations between the Dean and his wife have become distant over the years, and his daughter is a silent creature who longs to escape the Deanery but possesses neither the youth, nor the looks, nor the accomplishments to do so.

After dinner the Dean spends some time in his study before retiring to bed writing letters and making notes for the forthcoming chapter meeting. His wife passes by his study door twice bearing an oil lamp. She has taken to these nocturnal perambulations lately because she cannot sleep. On the second occasion, it being close on midnight, she looks in to remind her husband of the fact and finds him not writing, but staring dully at the dying embers of his fire. When he becomes aware of her presence he starts violently and stares at her as if she were a stranger. Coolly Mrs Coombe reminds him of the hour, a remark which he dismisses with a perfunctory: "Thank you, my dear." Soon afterwards she hears his heavy tread on the stairs as he goes to his bedroom.

Unlike his wife Dean Coombe is accustomed to sleeping soundly, and it is one of the reasons why he sleeps apart from his wife. She would plague him far into the night with troublesome questions and admonitions if they still shared a bed. She has acquired a habit of discontent of late and he lacks the imagination to supply the remedy.

His own bedroom is small, for Mrs Coombe occupies the official matrimonial chamber, but it has a fine view over the close, and from the bed, if the curtains are open, you may just see the western front of St Anselm's. Dean Coombe does not close the curtains because he likes to imagine himself the guardian of this great edifice, keeping watch over it by day and night.

Once his night-shirt is on the Dean feels suddenly exhausted, but still he kneels dutifully by the bed to say his prayers. But when he has climbed into bed he falls almost immediately into a heavy sleep from which two hours later he is awakened with almost equal suddenness.

The moon is up and shines across his bedchamber with a clear cold light. Coombe thinks he has been awakened by a noise, but all is silence. Then he hears a sound. It is like wings fluttering in a confined space, a bird trapped in a box perhaps, but he cannot tell whether it comes from within the room or just outside the window. He chooses to believe the latter and sits up in bed to see out. There is not a cloud in the sky and the pitiless stars are out. The west front of the cathedral, whose details he can barely make out, looks to him like a hunched old man in rags, the dark rents in his clothing formed by the windows and niches of its elaborate façade. He is invaded by a feeling of infinite solitude, and in the silence that follows his ears become increasingly alert to any noise, but none comes. The stillness now seems to him unnatural.

As he continues to stare at the view beyond the window, screwing and unscrewing his eyes to get a better sight of it, he begins to be troubled by what he is looking at. For some moments he tries to find a rational explanation. At length his eyes become concentrated upon a dark bump or lump at the bottom of the window and beyond the glass. It looks to him as if he is staring at the top of a man's head, the greater part of which is below the window. He even thinks he can make out a few wayward strands of hair upon it.

"Nonsense!" he says to himself several times. "Ridiculous! Impossible!" But the fancy does not leave him. Then the head begins to move and lift itself up, as if to look at him.

With a great cry Coombe leaps out of bed and dashes to the window in time to see a rook, which had been perched on the sill, flap away towards its building among the elms. It was only a rook! But then, rooks are not in the habit of perching on windowsills at dead of night.

Nothing more happened to the Dean that night, but he did not sleep. At breakfast the following morning his wife noted how pale and drawn he looked, but she offered no solicitude. That would have been to break the barrier that had arisen between them, and she could not do that. She felt safer behind it. The Dean would have been glad of some comfort, but he, like her, had passed the point of being able to ask for it.

That afternoon in the cathedral Dean Coombe was present when Palmer and his men began to ease away the memorial slab to Jeremiah Staveley. All had been prepared for the possibility of human remains being found in a recess behind the stone, but no one had anticipated the smell. As the slab, supported by ropes, came slowly away to be laid on a specially constructed wooden cradle, an overpowering odour pervaded not only the north transept but the whole cathedral. The organist stopped playing and several of the workmen took their hands off the stone slab to put handkerchiefs up to their noses. For a moment the memorial stone swung free on its ropes and threatened to crash into the wall and break into fragments, but just in time Palmer called his men to order and the object was laid to rest in its cradle on the scaffolding.

For almost half a minute after this had happened, nothing could be heard in that great cathedral but the sound of coughing and retching. One of the apprentice boys was violently ill into the font. Those who recalled the incident to me describe the odour as being one of mould, more vegetable than animal, "like," as one told me, "a heap of decaying cucumbers in a damp cellar." Others offered different similes, but all agreed that the scent stayed with them, on their clothes and in their nostrils for several days. Another told me that from that day forward he could never so much as look at a ripe cheese without feeling ill.

It was a while therefore before those present could bear to look at what the removal of the slab had revealed. When they did they found themselves looking at a figure that strikingly resembled the painted alabaster effigy which had been removed the previous day.

It was the body of a man in a black clerical gown with his arms crossed over his chest. The skin was still present, but dark yellow, leathery and stretched tightly over the bones. The eyes had fallen into the skull, the nose was somewhat flattened, but otherwise the face was in a remarkable state of preservation. As with the alabaster effigy, the mouth gaped slightly to reveal a set of jagged and discoloured teeth. The hair and beard were an intense and almost lustrous black. Even the nails were still present on the digits of the skeletal hands and feet. A seal ring on the third finger of the left hand was of bright, untarnished gold incised with an unusually elaborate geometrical figure.

In silence the company wondered at this strange vision, and it occurred to several of them that it was astonishing that the corpse still remained upright. Then, as they looked the body began to collapse and disintegrate before their eyes. The first thing to go was the lower jaw, which fell off the face and shattered into a thousand dusty fragments on the cathedral floor. Then, almost like a living thing, the corpse buckled at the knees, lurched slightly forward and plunged to the ground from its recess. A dreary sound, half way between a rattle and a sigh, accompanied this final dissolution.

It was a shocking moment, but the Dean was the first to recover from it. He commanded that the remains should be gathered up and placed in the long deal box which had been provided for the purpose.

While this was being done the Dean suddenly uttered a sharp: "No you don't, young man!" and sprang upon one of the apprentices who had been putting Canon Staveley's bones into the box. Dean Coombe thrust his hand into one of the boy's pockets and brought out a bright, golden object. It was Staveley's seal ring.

When I interviewed that boy ten years later, he was by then a most respectable young man, and the owner of a thriving building business in Morchester. He told me honestly that he had intended to steal the ring and sell it to buy medicine for his sick mother. Nevertheless, he said, he came to be very glad that he had been caught out in the theft. He also told me that Dean

Coombe had not returned the ring to the deal box but had placed it in his waistcoat pocket, muttering something about "the cathedral museum". I can testify that there is no sixteenth century seal ring among the antiquities on display in the Morchester Cathedral Museum.

When he left the cathedral later that day Dean Coombe seemed in more than usually good spirits. So we will leave him for a moment and return to the young apprentice whom I have mentioned. His name was Unsworth and he told me that Palmer, the head mason, a strict but fair man, had spoken to him sharply about the attempted theft, but knowing his situation with a sick mother and no father, said he would not dismiss him. Nevertheless, as a punishment, he made the boy stay on in the cathedral to sweep and tidy up after the other workmen had gone. Never, Unsworth told me, had he performed a task with greater reluctance.

If there had not been a verger or somebody about – Unsworth heard footsteps occasionally and some fragments of dry, muttered conversation – the boy might have fled the scene and braved the consequences. As it was, he did his work conscientiously in spite of the smell which was still all-pervasive.

One of his last tasks was to nail down the lid of the deal box which held the remains of Canon Staveley. Before the body was hidden forever from public gaze Unsworth felt a compulsion to take a last look at the corpse. Much of it had turned to dust but parts of the skull and the long thin limbs were intact with shreds of parchment skin still clinging to the bone. Curiously, the black gown in which Staveley was clothed had suffered even more than the body from exposure to the air. It was now in rags and tatters, no longer recognisable as a cassock.

Unsworth covered the deal box with the lid and banged in the nails with a hammer to secure it. With each blow of the hammer Unsworth fancied he heard a cry, distant, perhaps coming from a dog or a cat outside the cathedral. He finished his work with reckless speed.

As he left the cathedral, Unsworth told me, some sort of choir practice was in progress. He remembers the groan of the organ and a piercingly high treble voice singing in a style that was unfamiliar to him. Nevertheless he remembered the words because he knew that they came from the end of the 137th Psalm:

"Happy shall he be that taketh thy children and dasheth them against the stones."

As he stepped outside the cathedral Unsworth saw that the sun was low in the horizon sinking through a yellow sky dappled with purple cloudlets. He breathed the untainted evening air with relief. There were not many people about in the close and the noise of the day was hushed. The rooks had settled into their nests in the elms. It was a still evening with very little wind, perhaps even a trifle oppressive.

Unsworth had come out of the west door of the cathedral, the only one open at that time of day, but his home lay to the east of it. His quickest route home took him around the northern side of the cathedral with the setting sun behind him. Unsworth remembers feeling a vague sense of apprehension as he set off.

Along the northern side of the close were a few private dwellings and a long low stretch of almshouses occupied by the poor pensioners of the diocese. Unsworth could see a few of their windows dimly glowing. In front of these almshouses were little gardens bordered by a low stone wall with gates in them for each dwelling. Most of these gates were wooden and painted white which showed up against the grey stone houses and the deepening violet of the northern sky. As he rounded the north transept of the cathedral Unsworth had to pass quite near to these gates and it was then that he saw a human figure silhouetted against one of them.

He took the figure to be that of a man because he could see the legs which were unnaturally long and thin, almost stick-like in appearance. The arms were similarly emaciated and the head narrow and oblong. He could not see any clothes on the creature except for a few black rags, which fluttered faintly in the mild evening breeze.

He did not care to look too closely, but he took it to be some drunken vagrant, not simply because of the rags but because of the way it moved. It was swaying uneasily from side to side and waving its arms about. Unsworth told me that he was reminded of some long-legged insect, perhaps a spider, that has become stuck in a pool of jam and is making frantic efforts to escape from its entrapment. The thinness of those writhing legs and arms appalled him.

Unsworth started to run, but was brought up short by the sound of a cry. It was perfectly expressive, but so high above a human pitch that it resembled a dog whistle. It pierced his brain and stopped him from moving. The noise spoke to him of desolation and rage, like that of a child that has been left to scream in its cot, except that the cry was even more shrill and had no innocence to it. It was the shrieking fury of an old, old man. Unsworth found that his legs could not move. Looking behind him he saw that the stick creature had begun to stagger stiffly towards him, still uncertain on its feet, but with growing confidence.

A succession of little screams accompanied these staggering steps which seemed to indicate that movement was causing it pain, but that it was determined to stir. With its long attenuated legs it began to make strides towards him. It was coming on, but still Unsworth told me, he could not stir, "like in those dreams, sir," he said, "when you want to fly but cannot."

Suddenly the great bell of the cathedral boomed out the hour of seven and Unsworth was released from his paralysis. He ran and ran until he reached the gatehouse at the eastern end of the close where he stopped for breath and looked back. The creature was no longer coming towards him. He could see its starved outline clearly against the last of the setting sun. It had turned south-west and with long, slightly staggering strides was making its way, as Unsworth thought, towards the Deanery.

Let us now go there ourselves before whatever it was that Unsworth saw arrives.

Dean Coombe sups, as usual, with his wife and daughter. Conversation, even by Deanery standards, is not lively during this meal. It is plain to Mrs Coombe and her daughter Leonora that their master is preoccupied and anxious to escape from them to his study. Perhaps he has a sermon to write, thinks Mrs Coombe idly, half remembering a time when she interested herself passionately in his doings. Even the fact that her husband seems quite indifferent to her company no longer troubles her.

The Dean has barely taken his last mouthful when, with a muttered apology, he wipes his mouth with his napkin and excuses himself from the table. A few minutes later we find him in his study. A fire is glowing in the grate and an oil lamp illumines the desk on which it has been placed. Outside the uncurtained window dusk is falling rapidly over the cathedral close.

The Dean begins to take several volumes down from his shelves. One of those he needs is on the very topmost shelf, and to obtain it he makes use of a set of library steps. He plucks the book from its eyrie and, for some moments, he leafs through it rapidly on the top of the steps until we hear a little sigh of satisfaction. He descends the steps with his book which he places beneath the lamp on his desk. The work is Barrett's *Magus* and the page at which it is open has many sigils and diagrams printed on it. The Dean now takes the gold seal ring from his waistcoat pocket and begins to compare the design incised upon it with those in the book.

There is a rap at the door. The Dean looks up sharply and plunges the golden ring back into his pocket.

"Yes!" he says in a voice, half-irritable, half-fearful.

The door opens. It is his wife. She says: "Stephen, did you hear that dreadful noise just now?"

"What noise, my dear?"

"A sort of shrieking sound. From the close. Do you think it is those boys from the workhouse making a nuisance of themselves again? Hadn't you better see what is going on?"

"My dear, I heard nothing. Are you sure it wasn't a bird of some kind?"

"No, of course, it wasn't a bird. It was nothing like a bird. I would have said if it was a bird. Are you sure you heard nothing?"

"Quite sure, my dear," says Dean Coombe in his mildest voice, though inwardly he seethes with impatience. The truth is, he *has* heard something, but he does not want to prolong the conversation with his wife. Mrs Coombe expresses her incredulity with a pronounced sniff and leaves the room, shutting the door in a marked manner.

As soon as she is gone the Dean has taken the ring from his pocket once again and begins to pore over the designs in the book. So intent is he on his studies that at first he really does not hear the odd crackling noise that begins to manifest itself outside his window. It is a sound like the snapping of dry twigs. Slowly however, he becomes vaguely aware of some mild irritant assaulting the outer reaches of his consciousness, but he applies himself all the more ferociously to his research. Then something taps on his window.

Startled he looks up. What was it? The beak of a bird? There it is again! No, it is not a bird. Some sort of twig-like object or objects were rattling against the pane. Perhaps his wife had been right and it was those wretched workhouse boys up to their pranks. Dean Coombe goes to the window and opens it.

It was at this moment that a Mrs Meggs happened to be passing the Deanery. She was the wife of a local corn merchant and a woman of irreproachable respectability. I had the good fortune to interview her at some length about what she saw that evening, and, after some initial reluctance, she proved to be a most conscientious witness.

Despite the gathering dusk, she told me, there was still light enough to see by. What she saw first was something crouching in the flowerbed below the window of the Dean's study. It appeared to be a man in rags, "though 'twas all skin and bone, and more like a scarecrow than a living being," she told me. The man's hands were raised above his head, and with his immensely long and narrow fingers he appeared to be rattling on the Dean's window. Then Mrs Meggs saw the Dean open the window and look out, "very cross in the face," as she put it. Immediately the figure that had been crouched below the windowsill reared up and appeared to embrace the Dean with its long thin arms. It might have looked like a gesture of affection except that for a moment Mrs Meggs saw the expression on Dean Coombe's face which, she said, was one of "mortal terror".

"Next moment," Mrs Meggs told me, "the thin fellow in rags had launched himself through the window after the Dean and I heard a crash inside. Then I heard some shouting and some words, not distinct, but I do remember hearing the Dean cry out, 'God curse you, take your ring back, you fiend!' And I remember thinking such were not the words that should be uttered by a Man of God, as you might say. Then comes another crashing, and a cry such as I never hope to hear again as long as I live. It was agony and terror all in one. Well, by this time I was got to the door of the Deanery and banging on it with my umbrella for dear life. The maid lets me in, all of a flutter, and when we come to the Dean's study, Mrs Dean and Miss Leonora, the Dean's daughter, were there already, and Miss Leonora screaming fit to wake the dead. And who could blame her, poor mite? For I saw the Dean and he was all stretched back in his chair, his head twisted, and his mouth open and black blood coming out of it. There was no expression in the eyes, for he had no eyes, but only black and scorched holes as if two burning twigs had been thrust into their sockets."

Only one thing remains to tell. At the Dean's funeral in the cathedral some weeks later it was noticed that, though the widow was present, Dean Coombe's daughter, Leonora was not. However, as the congregation were leaving the cathedral after the service, they heard a cry in the air above them. Looking up they saw a tiny figure on the south tower of the west front. It appeared to be that of a woman waving her arms in the air. Some of the more sharp-sighted among the crowd recognised the figure as that of Miss Leonora Coombe.

In horrified impotence they watched as Leonora mounted the battlements of the tower and hurled herself off it onto the flag-stone path at the base of the cathedral. Her skirts billowed out during the fall but did nothing to break it, and, as she descended, all the rooks in the elms of the close seemed to rise as one and set up their hoarse cries of "kaa, kaa, kaa".

When Leonora hit the ground her head was shattered, and the only mercy of it was that she had died instantly.

Later, in recalling this final episode of the tragedy, several witnesses quoted to me, as if compelled by some inner voice, those final words of the 137th psalm:

"Happy shall he be that taketh thy children and dasheth them against the stones."

JOE R. LANSDALE

The Crawling Sky

JOE R. LANSDALE IS the author of over thirty novels, the latest of which is *Edge of Dark Water*. He has written numerous short stories and articles, screenplays, teleplays for animated TV shows, and comic scripts.

Lansdale is a recipient of the Edgar Award, the British Fantasy Award, nine Bram Stoker Awards, and a Grandmaster Award and Lifetime Achievement Award from The Horror Writers Association, amongst many others.

His novella "Bubba Ho-Tep" was filmed by Don Coscarelli in 2002 and is considered an independent film classic. He is currently writing a new novel and producing and co-producing films.

As the author explains: "'The Crawling Sky' is one of the stories I've written about the Reverend, a reluctant servant of God.

"He is inspired by Robert E. Howard's weird westerns – maybe there's a bit of Solomon Kane, certainly there's some Jonah Hex and Sergio Leone, working in the background, and then for this tale there's also Lovecraft, and every creepy-crawly comic I ever read.

"Add to that an odd sky formation I watched for a while, you have this story."

I. Wood Tick

WOOD TICK WASN'T so much as town as it was a wide rip in the forest. The Reverend Jebediah Mercer rode in on ebony horse on a coolish autumn day beneath an overcast sky of humped up, slow-blowing, gun-metal-grey clouds; they seemed to crawl. It was his experience nothing good ever took place under a crawling sky. It was an omen, and he didn't like omens, because, so far in his experience, none of them were good.

Before him, he saw a sad excuse for a town: a narrow clay road and a few buildings, not so much built up as tossed up, six altogether, three of them leaning south from northern winds that had pushed them. One of them had had a fireplace of stone, but it had toppled, and no one had bothered to rebuild it. The stones lay scattered about like discarded cartridges. Grass, yellowed by time, had grown up through the stones, and even a small tree had sprouted between them. Where the fall of the fireplace had left a gap was a stretch of fabric, probably a slice of tent; it had been nailed up tight and it had turned dark from years of weather.

In the middle of the town there was a wagon with wooden bars set into it and a flat heavy roof. No horses. Its axle rested on the ground giving the wagon a tilt. Inside, leaning, the Reverend could see a man clutching at the bars, cursing at a half-dozen young boys who looked likely to grow up to be ugly men, who were throwing rocks at him. An old man was sitting on the precarious porch of one of the leaning buildings, whittling on a stick. A few other folks moved about, crossing the street with the enthusiasm of the ill, giving no mind to the boys or the man in the barred wagon.

Reverend Mercer got off his horse and walked it to a hitching post in front of the sagging porch and looked at the man who was whittling. The man had a goitre on the side of his neck and he had tied it off in a dirty sack that fastened under his jaw and to the top of his head and was fastened under his hat. The hat was wide and dropped shadow on his face. The face needed concealment. He had the kind of features that made you wince; one thing God could do was he could sure make ugly.

"Sir, may I ask you something?" the Reverend said to the whittling man.

"I reckon."

"Why is that man in that cage?"

"That there is Wood Tick's jail. All we got. We been meaning to build one, but we don't have that much need for it. Folks do anything really wrong, we hang 'em."

"What did he do?"

"He's just half-witted."

"That's a crime?"

"If we want it to be. He's always talkin' this and that, and it gets old. He used to be all right, but he ain't now. We don't know what ails him. He's got stories about haints and his wife done run off and he claims a haint got her."

"Haints?"

"That's right."

Reverend Mercer turned his head toward the cage and the boys tossing rocks. They were flinging them in good and hard, and pretty accurate.

"Having rocks thrown at him can not be productive," the Reverend said.

"Well, if God didn't want him half-witted and the target of rocks, he'd have made him smarter and less directed to bullshit."

"I am a man of God and I have to agree with you. God's plan doesn't seem to have a lot of sympathy in it. But humanity can do better. We could at least save this poor man from children throwing rocks."

"Sheriff doesn't think so."

"And who is the sheriff."

"That would be me. You ain't gonna give me trouble are you?"

"I just think a man should not be put behind bars and have rocks thrown at him for being half-witted."

"Yeah, well, you can take him with you, long as you don't bring him back. Take him with you and I'll let him out."

The Reverend nodded. "I can do that. But, I need something to eat first. Any place for that?"

"You can go over to Miss Mary's, which is a house about a mile down from the town, and you can hire her to fix you somethin'. But you better have a strong stomach."

"Not much of a recommendation."

"No, it's not. I reckon I could fry you up some meat for a bit of coin, you ready to let go of it."

"I have money."

"Good. I don't. I got some horse meat I can fix. It's just on this side of being good enough to eat. Another hour, you might get poisoned by it."

"Appetising as that sounds, perhaps I should see Miss Mary."

"She fixes soups from roots and wild plants and such. No matter what she fixes, it all tastes the same and it gives you the squirts. She ain't much to look at neither, but she sells out herself, you want to buy some of that."

"No. I am good. I will take the horse meat, long as I can watch you fry it."

"All right. I'm just about through whittling."

"Are you making something?"

"No. Just whittlin'."

"So, what is there to get through with?"

"Why my pleasure, of course. I enjoy my whittlin'."

The old man, who gave the Reverend his name as if he had given up a dark secret, was called Jud. Up close, Jud was even nastier looking than from the distance of the hitching post and the porch. He had pores wide enough and deep enough in his skin to keep pooled water and his nose had been broken so many times it moved from side to side when he talked. He was missing a lot of teeth, and what he had were brown from tobacco and rot. His hands were dirty and his fingers were dirtier yet, and the Reverend couldn't help but wonder what those fingers had poked into.

Inside, the place leaned and there were missing floor boards. A wooden stove was at the far end of the room, and a stove pipe wound out of it and went up through a gap in the roof that would let in rain, and had, because the stove was partially rusted. It rested heavy on the worn flooring. The floor sagged and it seemed to the Reverend that if it experienced one more rotted fibre, one more termite bite, the stove would crash through. Hanging on hooks on the wall there were slabs of horse meat covered in flies. Some of the meat looked a little green and there was a slick of mould over a lot of it.

"That the meat you're talkin' about?"

"Yep," Jud said, scratching at his filthy goitre sack.

"It looks pretty green."

"I said it was turnin'. Want it or not?"

"Might I cook it myself?"

"Still have to pay me."

"How much?"

"Two bits."

"Two bits, for rancid meat I cook myself."

"It's still two bits if I cook it."

"You drive quite the bargain, Jud."

"I pride myself on my dealin'."

"Best you do not pride yourself on hygiene."

"What's that? That some kind of remark?"

Reverend Mercer pushed back his long black coat and showed the butts of his twin revolvers. "Sometimes a man can learn to like things he does not on most days care to endure."

Jud checked out the revolvers. "You got a point there, Reverend. I was thinkin' you was just a blabber mouth for God, but you tote them pistols like a man whose seen the elephant."

"Seen the elephant I have. And all his children."

The Reverend brushed the flies away from the horse meat and found a bit of it that looked better than rest, used his pocket knife to cut it loose. He picked insects out of a greasy pan and put the meat in it. He put some wood in the stove and lit it and got a fire going. In short time the meat was frying. He decided to cook it long and cook it through, burn it a bit. That way, maybe he wouldn't die of stomach poisoning.

"You have anything else that might sweeten this deal?" the Reverend asked.

"It's the horse meat or nothin'."

"And in what commerce will you deal when it turns rancid, or runs out?"

"I've got a couple more old horses, and one old mule. Somebody will have to go."

"Have you considered a garden?"

"My hand wasn't meant to fit a hoe. It gets desperate, I'll shoot a squirrel or a possum or a coon or some such. Dog ain't bad you cook 'em good."

"How many people reside in this town?"

"About forty, forty-one if you count Norville out there in the box. But, way things look, considerin' our deal, he'll be leavin'. Sides, he don't live here direct anyway."

"That number count in the kids?"

"Yeah, they all belong to Mary. They're thirteen and on down to six years. Drops them like turds and don't know for sure who's the daddy, though there's one of them out there that looks a mite like me."

"Bless his heart," the Reverend said.

"Yeah, reckon that's the truth. Couple of 'em have died over the years. One got kicked in the head by a horse and the other one got caught up in the river and drowned. Stupid little bastard should have learned to swim. There was an older girl, but she took up with Norville out there, and now she's run off from him."

When the meat was as black as a pit and smoking like a rich man's cigar, Reverend Mercer discovered there were no plates, and he ate it from the frying pan, using his knife as a utensil. It was a rugged piece of meat to wrestle and it tasted like the ass end of a skunk. He ate just enough to knock the corners off his hunger, then gave it up.

Jud asked if he were through with it, and when the Reverend said he was, he came over picked up the leavings with his hands and tore at it like a wolf.

"Hell, this is all right," Jud said. "I need you on as a cook."

"Not likely. How do people make a living around here?"

"Lumber. Cut it and mule it out. That's a thing about East Texas, plenty of lumber."

"Some day there will be a lot less, that is my reasoning."

"It all grows back."

"People grow back faster, and we could do with a lot less of them."

"On that matter, Reverend, I agree with you."

When the Reverend went outside with Jud to let Norville loose, the kids were still throwing rocks. The Reverend picked up a rock and winged it through the air and caught one of the kids on the side of the head hard enough to knock him down.

"Damn," Jud said. "That there was a kid."

"Now he's a kid with a knot on his head."

"You're a different kind of Reverend."

The kid got up and ran, holding his hand to his head squealing.

"Keep going you horrible little bastard," Reverend Mercer said. When the kid was gone, the Reverend said, "Actually, I was aiming to hit him in the back, but that worked out quite well."

They walked over to the cage. There was a metal lock and a big padlock on the thick wooden bars. Reverend Mercer had wondered why the man didn't just kick them out, but then he saw the reason. He was chained to the floor of the wagon. The chain fit into a big metal loop there, and then went to his ankle where a bracelet of iron held him fast. Norville had a lot of lumps on his head and his bottom lip was swollen up and he was bleeding all over.

"This is no way to treat a man," Reverend Mercer said.

"He could have been a few rocks shy of a dozen knots, you hadn't stopped to cook and eat a steak."

"True enough," the Reverend said.

II. Norville's Story: The House in the Pines

The sheriff unlocked the cage and went inside and unlocked the clamp around Norville's ankle. Norville, barefoot, came out of the cage and walked around and looked at the sky, stretching his back as he did. Jud sauntered over to the long porch and reached under it and pulled out some old boots. He gave them to Norville.

Norville pulled them on, then came around the side of the cage and studied the Reverend.

"Thank you for lettin' me out," Norville said. "I ain't crazy, you know. I seen what I seen and they don't want to hear it none."

"Cause you're crazy," Jud said.

"What did you see?" the Reverend asked.

"He starts talkin' that business again, I'll throw him back in the box," Jud said. "Our deal was he goes with you, and I figure you've worn out your welcome."

"What I've worn out is my stomach," Reverend Mercer said. "That meat is backing up on me."

"Take care of your stomach problems somewhere else, and take that crazy sonofabitch with you."

"Does he have a horse?"

"The back of yours," Jud said. "Best get him on it, and you two get out."

"Norville," the Reverend said, "come with me."

"I don't mind comin'," Norville said, walking briskly after the Reverend.

Reverend Mercer unhitched his horse and climbed into the saddle. He extended a hand for Norville, helped him slip up on the rear of the horse. Norville put his arms around Reverend Mercer's waist. The Reverend said, "Keep the hands high or they'll find you face down outside of town in the pine straw."

"You stay gone, you hear?" Jud said, walking up on the porch.

"This place does not hold much charm for me, Sheriff Jud," Reverend Mercer said. "But, just in case you should over value your position, you do not concern me in the least. It is this town that concerns me. It stinks and it is worthless and should be burned to the ground."

"You go on now," Jud said.

"That I will, but at my own speed."

The Reverend rode off then, glancing back, least Jud decide to back shoot. But it was a needless concern. He saw Jud go inside the shack, perhaps to fry up some more rancid horse meat.

They rode about three miles out of town, and Reverend Mercer stopped by a stream. They got down off the horse and let it drink. While the horse quenched its thirst, the Reverend removed the animal's saddle, then he pulled the horse away from the water lest it bloat. He took some grooming items out of a saddlebag and went to work, giving the horse a good brushing and rub down.

Norville plucked a blade of grass and put it in his mouth and worked it around, found a tree to sit under, said, "I ain't no bowl of nuts. I seen what I seen. Why did you help me anyway? For all you know I am a nut."

"I am on a mission from God. I do not like it, but it is my mission. I'm a hunter of the dark and a giver of the light. I'm the hammer and the anvil. The bone and the sinew. The sword and the gun. God's man who sets things right. Or at least right as God sees them. Me and him, we do not always agree. And let me tell you, he is not the God of Jesus, he is the God of David, and the angry city killers and man killers and animal killers of the Old Testament. He is constantly jealous and angry and if there is any plan to all this, I have yet to see it."

"Actually, I was just wantin' to know if you thought I was nuts."

"It is my lot in life to destroy evil. There is more evil than there is me, I might add."

"So . . . You think I'm a nut, or what?"

"Tell me your story."

"If you think I'm a nut are you just gonna leave me?"

"No. I will shoot you first and leave your body . . . Just joking. I do not joke much, so I'm poor at it."

The Reverend tied up the horse and they went over and sat together under the tree and drank water from the Reverend's canteen. Norville told his story.

"My daddy, after killin' my mother over turnip soup, back in the Carolinas, hitched up the wagon and put me in my sister in it and come to Texas."

"He killed your mother over soup?"

"Deader than a rock. Hit her upside the head with a snatch of turnips."

"A snatch of turnips? What in the world is a snatch of turnips?"

"Bunch of them. They was on the table where she'd cut up some for soup, still had the greens one 'em. He grabbed the greens, and swung them turnips. Must have been seven or eight big ole knotty ones. Hit her upside the head and knocked her brain loose I reckon. She died that night, right there on the floor. Wouldn't let us help her any. He said God didn't want her to die from getting' hit with turnips, he'd spare her."

"Frankly, God is not all that merciful . . . You seen this? Your father hitting your mother with the turnips?"

"Yep. I was six or so. My sister four. Daddy didn't like turnips in any kind of way, let alone a soup. So he took us to Texas after he burned down the cabin with mama in it, and I been in Texas ever since, but mostly over toward the middle of the state. About a year ago he died and my sister got a bad cough and couldn't get over it. Coughed herself to death. So I lit out on my own."

"I would think that is appropriate at your age, being on your own. How old are you. Thirty?"

"Twenty-six. I'm just tired. So I was riding through the country here, living off the land, squirrels and such, and I come to this shack in the woods and there weren't no one livin' there. I mean I found it by accident, cause it wasn't on a real trail. It was just down in the woods and it had a good roof on it, and there was a well. I yelled to see anyone was home, and they wasn't, and the door pushed open. I could see hadn't nobody been there in a long time. They had just gone off and left it. It was a nice house, and had real glass in the windows, and whoever had made it had done good on it, cause it was put together good and sound. They had trimmed away trees and had a yard of sorts.

"I started livin' there, and it wasn't bad. It had that well, but when I come up on it for a look, I seen that it had been filled in with rocks and such, and there wasn't no gettin' at the water. But there was a creek no more than a hundred feet from the place, and it was spring fed and I was right at the source. There was plenty of game, and I had a garden patch where I grew turnips and the like."

"I would have thought you would have had your fill of turnips in all shapes and forms."

"I liked that soup my mama made. I still remember it. Daddy didn't have no cause to do that over some soup."

"Now we are commanding the same line of thought."

"Anyway, the place was just perfect. I started to clean out the well. Spendin' a bit of time each day pullin' rocks out of it. In the meantime, I just used the spring down behind the house, but the well was closer, and it had a good stone curbin' around it, and I thought it would be nice if it was freed up for water. I wouldn't have to tote so far.

"Meanwhile, I discovered the town of Wood Tick. It isn't much, as you seen, but there was one thing nice about it, and every man in that town knew it and wanted that nice thing. Sissy. She was one of Mary's daughters. The only one she knew who her father was. A drummer who passed through and sold her six yards of wool and about five minutes in a back room.

"Thing is, there wasn't no real competition in Wood Tick for Sissy. That town has the ugliest men you ever seen, and about half of them have goitres and such. She was fifteen and I was just five years older, and I took to courtin' her."

"She was nothing but a child."

"Not in these parts. Ain't no unusual thing for men to marry younger girls, and Sissy was mature."

"In the chest or in the head?"

"Both. So we got married, or rather, we just decided we was married, and we moved out to that cabin."

"And you still had no idea who built it, who it belonged to?"

"Sissy knew, and she told me all about it. She said there had been an old woman who lived there, and that she wasn't the one who built the house in the first place, but she died there, and then a family ended up with the land, squatted on it, but after a month, they disappeared, all except for the younger daughter who they found walkin' the road, talkin' to herself. She kept sayin' 'It sucked and it crawled' or some such. She stayed with Mary in town who did some doctorin', but wasn't nothing could be done for her. She died. They said she looked like she aged fifty years in a few days when they put her down.

"Folks went out to the house but there wasn't nothin' to be found, and the well was all rocked in. Then another family moved in, and they'd come into town from time to time, and then they didn't anymore. They just disappeared. In time, one of the townspeople moved in, a fellow who weaved ropes and sold hides and such, and then he too was gone. No sign as to where. Then there was this man come through town, a preacher like you, and he ended up out there, and he said the house was evil, and he stayed on for a long time, but finally he'd had enough and came into town and said the place ought to be set afire and the ground ploughed up and salted so nothing would grow there and no one would want to be there."

"So he survived?"

"He did until he hung himself in a barn. He left a note said: 'I seen too much'."

"Concise," the Reverend said.

"And then I come there and brought Sissy with me."

"After all that, you came there and brought a woman as well. Could it be, sir, that you are not too bright?"

"I didn't believe all them stories then."

"But you do now?"

"I do. And I want to go back and set some thing straight on account of Sissy. That's what I was tryin' to tell them in town, that somethin' had happened to her, but when I told them what, wouldn't nobody listen. They just figured I was two nuts shy a squirrel's lunch and throwed me in that damned old cage. I'd still have been there wasn't for you. Now, you done good by me, and I appreciate it, and I'd like you to ride me over close to the house, you don't have to come up on it, but I got some business I want to take care of."

"Actually, the business you refer to is exactly my business."

"Haints and such?"

"I suppose you could put it that way. But please, tell me about Sissy. About what happened."

Norville nodded and swigged some water from the canteen and screwed the cap on. He took a deep breath and leaned loosely against the tree.

"Me and Sissy, we was doin' all right at first, makin' a life for ourselves. I took to cleanin' out that old well. I had to climb down in it and haul the rocks up by bucket, and some of them was so big I had to wrap a rope around them and hook my mule up and haul them out. I got down real deep, and still didn't reach water. I come to where it was just nothin' but mud, and I stuck a stick down in the mud, and it was deep, and there really wasn't anymore I could do, so I gave it up and kept carrying water from the spring. I took to fixin' up some rotten spots on the house, nailin' new shingles on the roof. Sissy planted flowers and it all looked nice. Then, of a sudden, it got so she couldn't sleep nights. She kept sayin' she was sure there was somethin' outside, and that she'd seen a face at the window, but when I got my gun and went out, wasn't nothin' there but the yard and that pile of rocks I'd pulled out of the well. But the second time I went out there, I had the feelin' someone was watching, maybe from the woods, and my skin started to crawl. I ain't never felt that uncomfortable. I started back to the house, and then I got this idea that I was bein' followed. I stopped and started to look back, but I couldn't bring myself to do it. Just couldn't. I felt if I looked back I'd see somethin' I didn't want to see. I'm ashamed to say I broke and ran and I closed the door quickly and locked it, and outside the door I could hear somethin' breathin'.

"From then on, by the time it was dark, we was inside. I boarded up all the windows from the inside. In the day, it seemed silly, but when night come around, it got so we both felt as if something was moving around and around the house, and I even fancied once that it was on the roof, and at the chimney. I built a fire in the chimney quick like, and kept one going at night, even when it was hot, and finally, I rocked it up and we cooked outside durin' the day and had cold suppers at night. Got so we dreaded the night. We were frightened out of our gourds. We took to sleepin' a few hours in the day, and I did what I could to tend the garden and hunt for food, but I didn't like being too far from the house or Sissy.

"Now, the thing to do would have been to just pack up and leave. We talked about it. But the house and that land was what we had, even if it was just by squatter's rights, and we thought maybe we were being silly, except we got so it wasn't just a feelin' we had, or sounds, we could smell it. It smelled like old meat and stagnant water, all at once. It floated around the house at night, through them boarded windows and under the front door. It was like it was gettin' stronger and bolder.

"One mornin' we came out and all the flowers Sissy had planted had been jerked out of the ground, and there was a dead coon on the doorstep, its head yanked off."

"Yanked off?"

"You could tell from the way there was strings of meat comin' out of the neck. It had been twisted and pulled plumb off, like a wrung chicken neck, and from the looks of it, it appeared someone, or something, had sucked on its neck. Curious, I cut that coon open. Hardly had a drop of blood in it. Ain't that somethin'?"

"That's something all right."

"Our mule disappeared next. No sign of it. We thought it over and decided we needed to get out, but we didn't know where to go and we didn't have any real money. Then one mornin' I come out, and on the stones I'd set in front of the house for steps, there was a muddy print on them. It was a big print and it didn't have no kind of shape I could recognise, no kind of animal, but it had toes and a heel. Mud trailed off into the weeds. I got my pistol and went out there, but didn't find nothin'. No more prints. Nothin'.

"That night I heard a board crack at the bedroom window, and I got up with a gun in my hand. I seen that one of the boards I'd nailed over the window outside had been pulled loose, and a face was pressed up against the glass. It was dark, but I could see enough cause of the moonlight, and it wasn't like a man's face. It was the eyes and mouth that made it so different, like it had come out of a human mould of some sort, but the mould had been twisted or dropped or both, and what was made from it was this . . . This thing. The face was as pale as a whore's butt, and twisted up, and its eyes were blood red and shone at the window as clear as if the thing was standin' in front of me. I shot at it, shatterin' an expensive pane of glass, and then it was gone in the wink of that pistol's flare.

"I decided it had to end, and I told Sissy to stick, and I gave her the pistol, and I took the fire wood axe and went outside and she bolted the door behind me. I went on around to the side of the house, and I thought I caught sight of it, a nude body, maybe, but with strange feet. Wasn't nothin' more than a glimpse of it as it went around the edge of the house and I ran after it. I must have run around that damn house three times. It acted like it was a kid playin' a game with me. Then I saw somethin' white that at first I couldn't imagine was it, because it seemed like a sheet being pulled through the bedroom window I'd shot out.

"You mean it was wraith like . . . A haint, as you said before?"

Norville nodded. "I ran to the door, but it was bolted of course, way I told Sissy to do. I ran back to the window and started using the axe to chop out the rest of the boards, knocked the panes and the frame out, and I crawled through, pieces of glass stickin' and cuttin' me.

"Sissy wasn't there. But the pistol was on the floor. I dropped the axe and snatched it up, and then I heard her scream real loud and rushed out into the main room, and there I seen it. It was chewin' . . . You got to believe me, preacher. It had spread its mouth wide, like a snake, and it had more teeth in its face than a dozen folk, and teeth more like an animal, and it was bitin' her head off. It jerked its jaws from side to side, and blood went everywhere. I shot at it. I shot at it five times and I hit it five times.

"It didn't so much as make the thing move. I might as well have been rubbin' its belly. It lifted its eyes and looked at me, and . . . As God is my witness, it spat out what was left of poor Sissy's head, and slapped its mouth over her blood pumpin' neck, and went to suckin' on it like a kid with a sucker.

"I ain't ashamed to admit it, my knees went weak. I dropped the pistol and ran and got the axe. When I turned, it was on me. I swung that axe, and hit it. The blade went in, went in deep . . . and there wasn't no blood, didn't spurt a drop. Thing grabbed me up and flung me at the window, and damned if I didn't go straight through it and land out on my back, on top of some of them rocks I'd pulled out of the well. It flowed through that window like it was water, and it come at me. I rolled over and grabbed one of the rocks and flung it and hit that thing square in its bony chest. What five shots from a pistol and a hack from an axe couldn't do, the rock did.

"Monster yelled like the fire of hell had been shoved down its throat, and it ran straight away for the well faster than I've ever seen anything move, its body twistin' in all directions, like it was going to come apart, or like the bones was shiftin' inside of it. It ran and dove into the well and I heard it hit the mud below.

"I climbed back through the window, rushed into the main room, tryin' not to look at poor Sissy's body, and I got the double barrel off the mantle and lit a lantern and went back outside through the front door with the lantern in one hand, the shotgun in the other.

"First I held the lantern over the well, got me a look, but didn't see nothin' but darkness. I bent over the curbin' and lowered the lantern in some, fearin' that thing might grab me. The sides of the well were covered with a kind of slime, and I could see the mud down below, and if the thing had gone into it, there wasn't no sign now except a bit of a ripple.

"I hid out in the woods. I went back the next mornin' and got Sissy's body and buried it out back of the place, and then before it was dark, I boarded up all the windows good and locked the door and I got the shotgun and sat with it all night in the middle of the big room. I knew it wouldn't do me no good, but that was all I had. Me and that shotgun.

"But didn't nothin' bother me, though I could hear it and smell it movin' around outside the house. Come morning, I was brave enough to go out, and Sissy's body had been pulled from the grave and gnawed on. I reckon animals could have done it in the night, but I didn't think so. I buried her again, this time deep, and mounded up dirt and packed it down. I cut some sticks and tied a cross together and stuck that up, then I walked into town and told my story. They didn't even think I was a murderer. They didn't question if I might have killed Sissy, which is what I thought they might do. They locked me up for bein' a crazy, and wasn't no one cared enough to come and see if her body was at the cabin or not. They wasn't interested. I done taken Sissy off and wasn't no man wanted her back now that she had been with me, which considerin' the kind of women they was usually with didn't make no sense, but then there ain't much about Wood Tick that does make sense.

"And then you come along, and you know the rest from there."

III. The Thing Down There

The sun was starting to slant to the West, but there was still plenty of daylight left when they arrived on horseback. The house was built of large logs and it looked solid. The chimney appeared sound. The shingles well cut and nailed down tight. It was indeed a good cabin and the Reverend understood the attraction it held for those who passed by.

Norville slipped off the back of the horse and hurried around behind the cabin. After the Reverend tied up his horse, he too went out back. Norville stood over an empty grave, the cross turned over and broken. Norville and the Reverend stood there for a long moment.

Norville fell to his knees. "Oh, Jesus. I should have taken her off somewhere else. He's done come and got her."

"It is done now," Reverend Mercer said. "Stand up, man. None of this does any good. Let's look around."

Norville stood up, but he looked ready to collapse.

"Buck up, man," Reverend Mercer said. "We have work to do."

No sight or parcel of the body was found. The Reverend went to the well and bent over and looked down. It was deep. He took out a match and struck it on the curbing and dropped it down the shaft, watched the little light fall. The match hissed out in the mud below.

"Do you believe me," Norville said, standing back from the well a few paces.

"I do."

"What can I do?"

"Whatever you do, you will not do alone. I will be here with you."

"Kind of you, Reverend, but what can you do?"

"At the moment, I'm uncertain. Let's look inside the house."

The cabin, though not huge, had two rooms. A small bedroom and a large main room with a kitchen table and a rocked-in fireplace and some benches and a few chairs. There was blood on the floor and on a rug there, and on the walls and even on the ceiling. The Reverend paused at the rocked-up fireplace. He bent down and looked at the rocks. Did you notice a lot of these rocks have a drawing in them?"

"What now?"

"Look here." Reverend Mercer touched his finger to one of the stones. There was a strange drawing on it, a stick figure with small symbols written around it in a circle. "It's on a lot of the rocks, and my guess is, if you were to pull the ones without visible symbols free, you could turn them over and the marks would be on the other side. They came from inside the well, correct?"

"Nearly all of them. It's a very deep well."

"As I have seen. Did you not notice the marks?"

"Guess I was so anxious to get those rocks out of there I didn't."

"It is only visible if you're looking for it."

"And you were?"

"I was looking for anything. This is my business. When you said you hit this thing with a rock and it fled after shooting it and hitting it with an axe had no effect, I started to wonder. I believe these are symbols of protection."

The Reverend began walking about the house. He looked under the bed and at the walls and checked nooks and crannies. He bounced himself on the floor to test the boards. He stood looking down at the blood stained rug for a while. He picked up the edge of the rug and saw there were a series of short boards that didn't extend completely across the floor.

Sliding the rug aside, the Reverend used his knife and stuck it under the edge of one of the boards and pried it up. There was a space beneath and a metal box was in the space. The Reverend removed a few more boards so he could get a good look at the box. It had a padlock on it.

"Find the axe," the Reverend said.

Norville went outside and got the axe and brought it back. It was a single edge, and the Reverend turned the flat side down and swung and knocked the lock off with one sure blow. He opened the box. Inside was a book.

"Why would someone put a book under lock and key?" Norville said.

The Reverend went to the table and sat on the long bench next to it. Norville sat on the other side. The Reverend opened the book and studied it. He looked up after a moment, said,

"Whoever built this house originally, their intentions for us were not good."

"Us?" Norville said. "How would they, whoever that is, know we would be here?"

"Not you and I. Us as in the human race, Norville. They, meaning the ones who possess this book, called *The Book of Doches*. The ones who find it or buy it or kill to possess it, always believe they will make some pact with the dark ones, the ones darker than our god, much darker, and they believe that if they allow these dark ones to break through they will be either its master or its trusted servant. The latter is sometimes possible, but the former, never. And in the end, a trusted servant is easily replaced."

"What are you talkin' about?" Norville said.

"There are monsters on the other side of the veil, Norville. A place you and I can't see. These things want out. Books like this contain spells to free them, and sometimes the people who possess the book want to set them free for rewards. Someone has already set one of them free."

"The sucking thing?"

"Correct," the Reverend said, shaking the book. "Look at the pages. See. The words and images on the pages are hand-printed? The pages, feel them."

Norville used his thumb and finger to feel.

"It's cloth."

"Flesh. Human flesh is what the book says."

Norville jerked his hand back. "You can read this hen scratch?"

"Yes. I read a translation of it long ago, taught myself to understand the original symbols."

"You have the same book?"

"Had. One of them got away from me, the one adapted into English. The other I destroyed."

"How did it get away from you?"

"That's not important to us today. Whoever built this house may have brought this copy here. But their plans didn't work out. They released something, one of the minor horrors, and that minor horror either chased them off, or did to them what they did to your poor Sissy. This thing they called up. The place where it is from is wet, and therefore it takes to the well. And it is hungry. Always hungry. A minor being, but a nasty one."

"But if this beast is on the other side, as you call it, why would anyone bring it here?"

"Never underestimate the curiosity and stupidity and greed of man, Norville."

"If the book set this thing free, then burn the book."

"Not a bad idea, but I doubt that would get rid of anything. In fact, I might do better to study the book. My guess is whoever first brought the book, loosed the creature. They then decided they had made a mistake, made the marks of power on the stones and sealed the thing in the well where it preferred to reside – it liked the dampness, you see. And then, someone, like you, took the rocks from the well and the thing was let loose. One of the other survivors, the preacher for example, may have figured out enough to seal the thing back in the well. And then you let it out again."

"Then we can seal it back up," Norville said.

The Reverend shook his head. "Then someone else will open the well."

"We can destroy the well curbing, put the rocks in, build a mound of dirt over all of it."

"Still not enough. That leaves the possibility of it being opened up in the future, if only by accident. No. This thing, it has to be destroyed. Listen here. It's light yet. Take my horse and walk it and take off its saddle, and then bring it inside where it will be safer."

"The house?"

"Since when are you so particular? I do not want to leave the horse for that thing to kill. If it must have the horse or us, then it will have to come and get the lot of us."

"All right then."

"Bring in my saddle and all that goes with it. And those rocks from the well. Only the rocks from the well. Start bringing them in by the pile."

"Aren't there enough here in the fireplace?"

"They are in use. One may cause this thing to flee, but that doesn't mean one will destroy it. I have other plans. Do it,

Norville. Already the sun dips deep and the dark is our first enemy."

When the horse was inside and the stones were stacked in the middle of the floor, the Reverend looked up from the book, said, "Place the stones in a circle around us. A large circle. Make a line of them across the back of this room and put the horse against the wall behind them. Give him plenty of room to get excited. Hobble him and put on his bridle and tie him to that nail in the wall, the big one."

"And what exactly will you be doin'?"

"Reading," the Reverend said. "You will have to trust me. I'm all that is between you and this thing."

Norville went about placing the stones.

It was just short of dark when the stones were placed in a circle around the table and a line of them had been made behind that from wall to wall, containing the tied up horse.

Reverend Mercer looked up from the book. "You are finished?"

Norville said, "Almost. I'll board up the bedroom window. Not that it matters. He can slip between some small spaces. But it will slow it down."

"Leave it as is, and leave the door to the bedroom partially cracked."

"You're sure?"

"Quite."

The Reverend placed one of the rocks on the table, removed the bullets from his belt and took his knife and did his best to copy the symbols in small shapes on the tips of his ammunition. The symbols were simple, a stick man with a few twists and twirls around it. It took him an hour to copy it onto twelve rounds of ammunition.

Finished, he loaded six rounds in each of his revolvers.

"Shall I light the lamp?" Norville asked.

"No. You have an axe and a shotgun lying about. We may have need for both. Recover them, and then come inside the ring of stones."

IV. The Arrival

While they waited, sitting cross-legged on the floor inside the circle of stones, the Reverend carved the symbols on the rocks onto the blade of the axe. He thought about the shotgun shells, but it wouldn't do any good to have the symbols on the shells and not on the load, and since the shotgun shot pellets, that was an impossible task.

Lying the axe between them, the Reverend handed the shotgun to Norville. "The shotgun will be nothing more than a shotgun," he said. "And it may not kill the thing, but it will be a distraction. You get the chance, shoot the thing with it, otherwise, sit and do not, under any circumstances, step outside this circle. The axe I have written symbols on and it may be of use."

"Are you sure this circle will keep him out?"

"Not entirely."

Norville swallowed.

They sat and they listened and the hours crept by. The Reverend produced a flask from his saddlebags. "I keep this primarily for medicinal purposes, but the night seems a little chill, so let us both have one short nip, and one short nip only."

The Reverend and Norville took a drink and the flask was replaced. And no sooner was it replaced, than a smell seeped into the house. A smell like a charnel house and a butcher shop and an outhouse all balled into one.

"It's near," Norville said. "That's its smell."

The Reverend put a finger to his lips to signal quiet.

There were a few noises on the outside of the house, but they could have been most anything. Finally there came a sound in the bedroom like wet laundry plopping to the floor.

Norville looked at the Reverend.

Reverend Mercer nodded to let him know he too had heard it, and then he carefully pulled and cocked his revolvers.

The room was dark, but the Reverend had adjusted his eyesight and could make out shapes. He saw that the bedroom door, already partially cracked open, was slowly moving. And then a hand, white and puffy like the leaves of an orchid, appeared around the edge of the door, and fingers, long and stalk like, extended and flexed, and the door moved and a flow of muddy water slid into the room along the floor.

The Reverend felt Norville move beside him, as if to rise, and he reached out and touched his shoulder to steady him.

The door opened more, and then the thing slipped inside the main room. It moved strangely, as if made of soft candle wax. It was dead white of flesh, but much of the skin was filthy with mud. It was neither male nor female. No genitals; down there it was as smooth as a well-washed river rock. It was tall, with knees that swung slightly to the sides when it walked, and there was an odd vibration about it, as if it were about to burst apart in all directions. The head was small. Its face was mostly a long gash of a mouth. It had thin slits for eyes and a hole for a nose. At the ends of its willowy legs were large flat feet that splayed out in shapes like claw-tipped four-leaf clovers.

Twisting and winding, long stepping, and sliding, it made its way forward until it was close to the Reverend and Norville. It leaned forward and sniffed. The hole that was its nose opened wider as it did, flexed.

It smells us, thought the Reverend. Only fair, because we certainly smell it.

And then it opened its dripping mouth and came at them in a rush.

As it neared the stones, it was knocked back by an invisible wall, and then there came something quite visible where it had impacted, a ripple of blue fulmination. The thing went sliding along the floor on its belly in its own mud and goo.

"The rocks hold," the Reverend said, and it came again. Norville lifted the shotgun and fired. The pellets went through the thing and came rattling out against the wall on the other side. The hole made in its chest did not bleed, and it filled in rapidly, as if never struck.

Reverend Mercer stood up and aimed one of his pistols, and hit the thing square in the chest, and this time the wound made a sucking sound and when the load came out on the other side, goo and something dark went with it. But it didn't stop the creature. It hit the invisible wall again, bellowed and fell back. It dragged its way around the circle toward the horse, tied behind the line of stones. The terrified horse reared and snapped its reins as if they were non-existent. The horse went thundering across the line, and then across the circle of stones, causing them to go spinning left and right, and along came the thing, entering the circle through the gap.

The Reverend fired again. The thing jerked back and squealed like a pig. Then it sprang forward again, grabbed the Reverend by the throat and sent him flying across the room, slamming into the side of the frightened horse.

Norville swung the shotgun around and fired right into the thing's mouth, but it was like the thing was swallowing gnats. It grabbed the gun barrel, used it to sling the clutching Norville sliding across the floor, collecting splinters until he came up against the bedroom door, slamming it shut.

It started forward, but it couldn't step out of the circle. Not that way. It wheeled to find the exit the horse had made, and as it did, Reverend Mercer, now on his feet, fired twice and hit the thing in the back, causing it to stagger through the opening and fall against the line of rocks that had been there to protect the horse. Its head hit the rocks and the creature cried out, leaping to its feet with a move that seemed boneless and without use of muscle. Its forehead bore a sizzling mark the size of the rock.

"Get back inside the circle," the Reverend said. "Close it off."

Norville waited for no further instruction. He bolted and leaped into the circle and began to clutch at the displaced stones. The Reverend put his right leg forward and threw back his coat by bending his left hand behind him; he pointed the revolver and took careful aim, fired twice.

Both shots hit. One in the head, one in the throat. They had their effect. The horror splattered to the floor with the wet laundry sound. But no sooner had it struck the ground, then it began to wriggle along the floor like a grub worm in a frying pan; it came fast and furious and grabbed the Reverend's boot, and came to spring upright in front of the Reverend with that strange manner it had of moving.

Reverend Mercer cracked it across the head with his pistol, and it grabbed at him. The Reverend avoided the grab and struck out with his fist, a jab that merely annoyed the thing. It spread its jaws and filled the air with stink. The Reverend drew his remaining pistol and fired straight into the hole the thing used for a nose, causing it to go toppling backward along the floor gnashing its teeth into the lumber.

Reverend Mercer ran and leaped into the circle.

When he turned to look, the monster was sliding up the wall like some kind of slug. It left a sticky trail along the logs as it reached the ceiling and crawled along that with the dexterity of an insect.

The horse had finally come to a corner and stuck its head in it to hide. The thing came down on its back, and its mouth spread over the horse's head, and the horse stood up on its hind legs and its front legs hit the wall, and it fell over backward, landing on the creature. It didn't bother the thing in the least. It grabbed and twisted the horse over on its side as if it were nothing more than a feather pillow. There was a crunch as the monster's teeth snapped bones in the horse's head. The horse quit moving, and the thing began to suck, rivulets of blood spilling out from the corners of its distended mouth.

The Reverend jammed his pistol back into its holster, bent and grabbed the axe from the floor and leaped out of the circle. The thing caught sight of the Reverend as he came, rolled off the horse and leaped up on the wall and ran along it. As the Reverend turned to follow its progress, it leaped at him.

Reverend Mercer took a swing. The axe hit the fiend and split halfway through its neck, knocking it back against the wall, then to the floor. Its narrow eyes widened and showed red, and then it came to its feet in its unique way, though more slowly than before, and darted for the bedroom door.

As it reached and fumbled with the latch, the Reverend hit the thing in the back of the head with the axe, and it went to its knees, clawed at the lumber of the door, causing it to squeak and squeal and come apart, making a narrow slit. It was enough. The thing eased through it like a snake. The Reverend jerked the door open to see it going through the gap in the window. He dropped the axe and jerked the pistol and fired and struck the thing twice before it went out through the breach and was gone from sight.

Reverend Mercer rushed to the window and looked out. The thing was staggering, falling, rising to its feet, staggering toward the well. The Reverend stuck the pistol out the window, resting it on the frame, and fired again. It was a good shot in the back of the neck, and the brute went down.

Holstering the revolver, rushing to grab the axe, the Reverend climbed through the window. The monster had made it to the well by then, crawling along on its belly, and just as it touched the curbing, the Reverend caught up with it, brought the spell marked axe down on its already shredded head as many times as he had the strength to swing it.

As he swung, the sun began to colour the sky. He was breathing so hard he sounded like a blue norther blowing in. The sun rose higher and still he swung, then he fell to the ground, his chest heaving.

When he looked about, he saw the thing was no longer moving. Norville was standing nearby, holding one of the marked rocks.

"You was doin' so good, I didn't want to interrupt you," Norville said.

The Reverend nodded, breathed for a long hard time, said, "Saddlebags. If this is not medicinal. I do not know what is."

A few moments later, Norville returned with the flask. The Reverend drank first, long and deep, and then he gave it to Norville.

When his wind was back, and the sun was up, the Reverend chopped the rest of the monster up. It had already gone flat and gushed clutter from its insides that were part horse bones, gouts of blood, and unidentifiable items that made the stomach turn; its teeth were spread around the well curbing, like someone had dropped a box of daggers.

They burned what would burn of the beast with dried limbs and dead leaves, buried the teeth and the remainder of the beast in a deep grave, the bottom and top and sides of it lined with the marked rocks.

When they were done chopping and cremating and burying the creature, it was late afternoon. They finished off the flask, and that night they slept in the house, undisturbed, and in the morning, they set fire to the cabin using *The Book of Doches* as a starter. As it burned, the Reverend looked up. The sky had begun to change, finally. The clouds no longer crawled.

They walked out, the Reverend with the saddlebags over his shoulder, Norville with a pillowcase filled with food tins from the cabin. Behind them, the smoke from the fire rose up black and sooty and by night-time it had burned down to glowing cinders, and by the next day there was nothing more than clumps of ash.

CONRAD WILLIAMS

Wait

CONRAD WILLIAMS IS A three-time recipient of the British Fantasy
Award. He is the author of the novels *Head Injuries*, *London
Revenant*, *The Unblemished*, *One*, *Blonde On a Stick*, *Decay
Inevitable* and *Loss of Separation*.

Some of his short fiction has been collected in *Use Once Then
Destroy* and *Born with Teeth*. He is also the editor of *Gutshot*,
an anthology of "weird west" stories from PS Publishing.

The author is currently working on a novel that will act as a
prequel for a major videogame from Sony, and a novel of supernatural terror set in France.

"'Wait' came about directly after a visit to Poole's Cavern in
Buxton, Derbyshire," Williams reveals. "At the end of the system
is a boulder choke. A radar scan in 1999 established that a
greater network of chambers lie beyond it.

"It was quite awe-inspiring to think that we were feet away
from a place that has not been seen by human eyes since the
glaciers carved it out two million years ago.

"And then I began to think about means of access, and how
every entrance can also be an exit . . ."

THE SNOW HAD never really gone away. It swirled in his head,
in memories of Julie's cheap little ornament. And here was
the same whitened motorway turn-off. Here the same

crystallised countryside swelling against the verge. He had to stop the car at the accident site, although he had persuaded himself over the three-hour duration of his drive up here that he would not.

He parked in a lay-by and walked back. The telegraph post was no longer there. The car had almost torn it out of the ground, and might have done so had it not destroyed the passenger side of the car first.

Julie had not stood a chance.

The doctors he spoke to reassured him that she was unlikely to have felt anything, the impact was so swift, so massive. There was nothing to suggest an accident had taken place here.

Don had received a face full of broken glass, but he was otherwise unmarked. He could walk. He could get in and out of bed. He could turn his head. Everything that Julie could not. Even the cuts on his face had healed without leaving obvious scars. The scar he needed to heal was inside him. That was partly the reason for this trip. To confront the moment of his wife's death, and to carry on to the place they had meant to be journeying. To find a way forward.

They had been a scant ten minutes away from Sheckford, that awful day. Now Don went back to the car and switched on the engine. He pulled out into the road. A blade of sunshine sliced through clouds and turned the snow golden. Apart from the streak of red far off in the distance, on one of the hills surrounding the town.

A lorry thundered by him, dragging up a great fan of slush that covered his windscreen, blinding him for a moment. His heart racing, he cleared the filth from the glass, his head full of collisions and the feel of all those icy pebbles of windscreen assaulting his face. The shock of cold air as his car was bisected. No scream. No sounds at all.

Now the red was gone from the hill. Or maybe it was a different hill, a different angle, an illusion formed by the sun and the strange refracted light coming off the crystals of snow and ice.

Maybe it was in his own eyes.

The doctor had explained to him that all that exploded glass had to go somewhere. There would have been some splinters he wouldn't even feel. The force of the impact would have sent them into his flesh so fast, so smoothly, that there would have been no blood. There was the likelihood that he would carry minute slivers of glass around in his flesh for the rest of his life. Some survivors of bomb blasts, he was told, had suffered hundreds of tiny splinters of glass passing right through their bodies.

He was a year further away from her. He was a year closer to her.

Don would not let himself get distracted again. He completed his journey concentrating fully on his driving, checking his speed, his rear-view mirrors and keeping his hands at ten to two on the steering wheel. He let out a long, low sigh when he arrived at the hotel car park and turned the engine off. He listened to it ticking like some horrible countdown. Keep busy. Keep moving.

He got out of the car and strode past a woman holding a leash, calling into a clump of bushes for a dog that would not come. From the sounds of her, she'd been calling for some time. A red glove came up and rubbed at her face, perhaps in an attempt to coax the worry from it.

He checked into the hotel and tossed his suitcase on to the bed. The exact room they would have taken a year previously.

Why are you doing this to yourself?

He turned but of course there was nobody else in the room. He stared at the reflection of himself in the full-length mirror fitted into the panels of the wardrobe doors. The mirror was not the best quality. Red paint edged it, indicating that at some previous time it had been part of some other furniture. The tain was scarred and there was foxing in the corners. A look of shabby chic, he supposed the hotel was going for, but it appeared out of place when compared to the rest of the room, which was formal, Edwardian, verging on the cold.

"God, you'd have hated this, Ju," he whispered.

He sat on the edge of the bed and stared at his fingers. Julie liked his fingers. She had described them as surgeon's fingers, as early as their first date. He could do nothing for her, though, with these delicate fingers. He could not stave off death. He couldn't find the life in her and coax it back, make it bloom, make it overpower the hurt that took her away. He felt bad that he had escaped with little more than bruises and shock (poor thing) while she had the life slammed from her in less than a millisecond. He wishes she were merely lost, like that dog in the bushes.

He unpacked, desultory, quietly panicked by his decision to come here. He didn't know what to do. He had been filled with plans when he took that journey up with his wife. They were celebrating their third anniversary. Glass, ha ha. But also he'd meant this trip to be a way for them both to shed the tension that had been building up in London. Julie's homeopathic shop in Camden had been hit hard by the recession. She relied on the Christmas shopping period to tide her over the following half-year, but trade had been anything but brisk. She had had to let one of her assistants go and, although she enjoyed a steady supply of small orders via the website, and as a practising herbalist was able to lean on the money she made from her patients, it was not enough to help them scramble out of the red. Another twelve months like this would have buried the business. Instead, they buried Julie, and all the worry over the business meant less than nothing. It was sold. It was over.

As for Don, he was teaching guitar to a class of young boys and girls at the local primary school. They had more often than not been bought the instrument for Christmas, or their birthdays, but little thought had gone into it. The parents tended to buy expensive items, without pause to consider if the guitar would be too big or small, the neck too wide for the child to be able to shape a decent barre chord. In the main his pupils had no natural aptitude. No promise. One boy had picked up the guitar like a double bass. Another had held the guitar in the correct manner but, astonishingly, had used his strumming hand to fret chords and vice versa. It was enough to make him want to restring his Gibson via their scrawny little throats.

It had been such a long time since he had relaxed, or even tried to. He stared out of the window at the square and the people milling around it. The opera house and the park were possible places to visit, but he didn't feel like being among other people. He shaved because it ate up some time. As he did so, he thought about guitars and people. He wanted to write a song about Julie, but he didn't know how to begin. All the great songs written by guitarists for important people in their lives. John for Julia; Eric for Conor; Joni for Kelly; George for Patti. Mothers and fathers, sons and daughters. Lovers. There ought to be something in him for Julie, but every time he thought of music, he felt guilty. How could he even begin to consider the positioning of notes on the stave when she would never again be able to do the things she loved?

He felt a twinge in his cheek and ran his finger over the skin there. He hadn't nicked himself shaving but there was a lump in his cheek. *Great*, he thought, *I survive a major road traffic accident only to fall foul of cancer*. He checked in the mirror. Maybe the blade had taken the top off a pimple he hadn't noticed. The edges of the lump were raised. It felt tender. He tried squeezing it, convinced now that it was filled with pus and he would have to clean it or run the risk of it becoming a boil, or worse. He stopped immediately. The slightest pressure told him that there was something solid beneath the skin.

He called down to reception and asked for ointment, plasters and painkillers. He poured vodka from the miniature in his mini-bar and drank it in one swallow. When the packets and pills came, brought by a young man whose expression clearly spoke of his disdain for anybody who asks for such things from room service, Don tenderly applied to his cheek some of the ointment – which contained a substance he recognised from Julie's work in homeopathy, something that was good at drawing out foreign bodies – and placed one of the plasters over it. He stomached the pills with more vodka. He changed into a shirt and trousers, went down to the bar and had a cocktail, read the newspaper and, when the bar started to become busy, retired to his room, more than a little drunk, where he slept fitfully.

At one point during the night, he was sucked deep enough into sleep to suffer a nightmare. He dreamed he was hiding from something that was trying to sniff him out. Something that had poor eyesight, but keen olfactory organs. Something that was intensely hungry for Don.

He had hidden in a city filled with black glass. But its surfaces made poor reflections, clinging jealously to their colour as if they would reveal terrible pictures if they were allowed to clear. There was no light anywhere. Whenever Don thought he had discovered somewhere safe, cracks would appear in the glass and he would see his pursuer's thin, long fingers, scabbed and pitted, picking through the fractures in a bid to get nearer to him, near enough to be able to swipe at Don's clothes. This happened, finally, and he felt the fingers like needles piercing the skin of his thigh. He was swept towards the crack in the glass and unceremoniously dragged through it. He was choking on splinters. And if he looked through the thin aperture, an aperture whose edges he was unravelling messily upon, he could see the shadow of its face and the writhing puncture at its centre ringed with shattered white teeth, surely too thin and weak to be able to do all *this*.

"Name's Kerner. Grant Kerner. How's your breakfast?"

Now that Kerner had drawn attention to it, Don realised he no longer wanted his food. It was swimming in grease. The bacon was undercooked, the tomato blistered black on the outside, solid and cold in the centre. And he was still mindful of the unhealthy, yawning mouth he had witnessed in his dreams. He couldn't remember the last time he had been hungry, or enjoyed a meal. He pushed the plate away and drew his coffee nearer. Caffeine and alcohol seemed to form the limit of his appetites these days.

Kerner was eating muesli loaded with extra whole hazelnuts and dried apricots. Don's jaws ached just watching him.

Kerner was obviously one of those people who liked to winkle information out of people and he perhaps saw Don as something of a challenge. He kept on at him throughout Don's second cup of coffee and while he wrapped miniature pots of jam in a serviette and stashed them in his coat pocket.

"I'm a photographer," Kerner said, although Don had not asked him his occupation. "I take pictures of crippled things. Cars, buildings. Broken architecture. People, if I can get away with it. Things that don't work the way they ought to. What do you do?"

Don thought of his job. For so long he had been going through the motions it was as if he was working from a script every day. In a way he was, following the slavish schedules set down by a government eager to have its target figures bolstered by achievable test results.

He showed the children how to play basic chords, the first few essentials: A, D and E, corrected them when they went wrong – which was often – and put on excruciating "musical" events for their parents to come and listen to. Interaction was at a minimum. He thought the children could see right through him, though they were all under ten years of age. He wondered if he resented them, since Julie's death. He wondered if maybe he was taking out the fact that he was fatherless, and had never intended to be – certainly not at this age – on them.

"I'm unemployed," Don said. He tried to think of a job so far removed from who Kerner seemed to be that he wouldn't ask him any follow-up questions about it. "I used to work in Human Resources."

That worked. Kerner's smile froze a little; he nodded, gazed outside. "That your car?" he asked brightly, apparently happy to find another conversational topic.

"The Focus? Yeah." Don closed his mouth. We used to have a Volvo. You know, safest car in the world." *Until I totalled it. And my wife.*

"I drive a Lexus."

"Nice."

"Yeah," Kerner said. "I like to drive gone midnight. Empty roads. Good up here. Some good roads. Hairpin bends and suchlike."

"It's just a metal box to get me from one place to another." Don had bought a second-hand car a week after the accident. He forced himself into the driver's seat. He would not allow it to lock him down. *Metal boxes. Wooden boxes. Snow globes.*

"Well, I must go," Kerner said, and drained his cup. "Some good light here in the mornings. Click-click and all that. Peace out, rainbow trout."

Don watched Kerner move through the dining room to the door. The other man was of a similar age to Don, he reckoned, but there was a world of difference in their physiques. Kerner's limbs were slender, he was lithe and stealthy. He panthered across the room. Don hated his own rounded posture. He was all clump and jostle. Too many hours hunched over his guitar. He resolved to do something about it – cut back on the alcohol, eradicate the fast food from his diet, try to exercise more – but even as he left the hotel lobby and walked across the square to his car, he knew this would never be the case. Some people were born to the shape they would occupy all their lives.

I'm going to take you to the school I attended. I was a model pupil. Don't laugh. I was a senior prefect. I never had a day's absence. I took eight "O" levels and scored As for all of them.

Don sat in his car wondering how he had arrived here; the journey was a blur. It angered him that he should still be able to switch off whenever he drove, considering what had happened. He got out, stalked away from his little metal box, his mobile coffin, and loitered by the school gates. So this was his old seat of learning, Sheckford Junior. So what? It might have meant something had she been with him.

There's the veranda where I used to sit with Belinda Smart, under our coats, feeding each other toffees. There's the playground where Johnny Dobson fought back against Mr Addison. There's the school field where I got ambushed on my birthday and I was egged to within an inch of my life. Now it was all just memories. Then and now. No context. His life was a flatline without detail. Bedtime stories, and not very good ones at that.

He walked along the edge of the school grounds until he reached the gym. Everything the same. Everything changed. His youth was so close sometimes, he felt he could feel it beneath his fingers. He saw himself every day in any number of mirrors, and it was Don, it was him. But a photograph from even as recent as five years ago displayed to him a massive change in how he looked. His skin greyer now, his eyebrows lighter, his eyes more sunken. But he had not seen it happen. He had been tricked.

He was a prisoner to the calendar, he realised, as we all were. He thought in little boxes that were to be ticked off and filled with things to do. Almost every day he thought back to what he had been doing ten years ago, twenty years ago, further. He lived in the past, by his diary. He was a history man, his head full of dead leaves. It was a form of reassurance, he knew. There were too many roads into the future and he didn't like not having a map for it.

Movement. He turned and gazed out over the school fields

pelting Debbie Epstein with snow, winning the high jump and just missing out on the 800 metres title, kissing Penny Greig for the first time near the pavilion

and saw a couple gesticulating wildly at each other as they raced across the grass towards the main road. She was having to run to keep up with him, her red scarf flapping at her throat like a terrible wound. She spotted Don and pointed at him. The man's head snapped up. Little hair. It was like a pink oval, a beige egg sitting on an elaborate eggcup. They arrowed towards him. The man was rolling his sleeves back as if setting himself for a scrap.

"Martin," she was calling. Don shook his head, but then realised she wasn't attempting to address him.

"Have you seen Martin?" Her voice was brittle. She was at the edge of tears.

"My boy," the man explained, and he was full of accusation. "Our boy. He was playing in our garden on Kent Lane, just down there at the foot of the fields. Keepy-uppy. In our garden."

"I was washing dishes," said the woman. "I could see him. And then I went to empty the washing machine and when I came back he was gone and the back gate was swinging open."

"Maybe he kicked his ball over the wall," Don said.

"Martin is six," the man said, as if that was explanation enough.

"He can't reach the latch," the woman said.

"I haven't seen anyone," Don said. "I just got here."

The man looked him over as if Don might somehow be concealing Martin on his person. "The police," he said at last. "We have to bring the police into this."

"Oh, God," the woman said. And then she screamed Martin's name.

Don drove back to the hotel and forced himself to face up to what was going on. His coming here was nothing to do with a pilgrimage. It wasn't a personal tribute. It was running away. All of those responsibilities back home; they'd still be there when he returned. Debts and deadlines and demands. Julie was the soft barrier that prevented him injuring himself against all that bureaucracy. She organised, she delegated, she controlled. It might have lapped around their ankles occasionally, but the water never rose around their throats, as it seemed to be doing these days.

Now Julie was gone, every day was like crashing his car. There were impacts everywhere. He missed her so desperately it was as if he could still feel the mass of her in his hands. Her smell was in every room she'd inhabited. There were shadows and shades of her in everything he owned. When the sun shone she was splintered within it; when it rained, each drop carried a fragment of her reflection.

He had tried to find that snow globe of hers, after the crash. She took it everywhere with her. It had been a gift from her childhood. A lucky token. He had wandered around in the ruins for an age until the ambulances arrived, his face dripping into the snow around the wreckage, poking with his toe amidst the mangled aluminium, the torn fabric seat covers, the shreds of her. It was gone.

This is madness, he thought now, but there was no way he could stop being dragged under. To tackle that might mean he had to force her out of his life altogether and he was not ready for it.

The stress of the afternoon was in him like hot pins. The way that poor woman had screamed for her son. It was animalistic. He could understand her need. He had wanted to howl like that, for Julie. It built up inside you. You forgot who you were.

He tried to make the room comfortable enough so that Julie might come to him in some way. He needed to be warm and clean and relaxed. He bathed and drank a glass of whisky. He put her favourite music station on the radio. He sat by the window and closed his eyes. He determined what each sound was and relegated it to the back of his mind. There was space here for her.

He felt himself slide towards sleep. But she was not there to greet him. She had not been a part of this intimate darkness since before her death. It was as if, in dying, she had ceased to exist for him during the moments when he ought to be most receptive to her. Gazing at photographs of her was like assessing a stranger. She mugged for the camera. She was never her natural self. He felt panic at the thought that, day by day, this memory of the truth was gradually leaving him. It scared him more than the nightmares that were so ready to enter that vacuum he'd created just for her.

That evening, after another challenging meal in the hotel restaurant, Don sat in the bar nursing a glass of Scotch. He'd decided on an early night and a quick escape back to London in the morning. He'd look into therapy. He'd consider a holiday away from the UK. He needed to map out his career. Find a new hobby, some new friends. Do the unthinkable. Find someone else. *Why not just dig her up and spit into what's left of her face?*

"Hello again!"

"You bastard."

"Excuse me?"

"Sorry . . . Grant, isn't it? I'm very sorry. I was talking to myself. I was thinking about someone."

Kerner was observing him with a mixture of scepticism and distaste.

"Really," Don pressed. "I'm sorry. That was aimed at me, actually."

The doubt in Kerner dissolved. Maybe he could see something in Don's own features, his posture. Defeat, quite possibly.

"Then I apologise for interrupting you."

"I'm glad you did. There's only so much abuse I can put up with."

Kerner laughed; the tension lessened. He assessed Don as if for the first time. There was a sense of him weighing up what to do next. Don could feel an invitation growing within; he was all too ready to refuse it. But he surprised himself by accepting, when Kerner asked if he would like to accompany him on a visit to Kayte's Cavern.

They walked. It was not far. There was a place to buy tickets and tat. A café. All of it closed now. A little display, showing the history of the cave and what had been found there. Roman coins and bones and bronze brooches. Over time it had been a burial ground, a shelter, and the hideaway for a robber, the eponymous Nathaniel Kayte, who used the darkness and the depth and the churning noise of the water sluicing through it to his advantage when hiding from his pursuers.

Later it was a tourist trap. People travelled great distances to see the flowstone curtains, the stalactites and stalagmites, the great chambers of pale crystal, glowing in the dark as if lit from within. After that it became a big draw for the Victorians, who were led by candlelight deep into the cavern and then, the flames blown out by their canny guides, asked for more money if they wished to be taken back to safety.

"Isn't it a bit late for this?" Don asked again. "I thought you meant we'd go in the morning."

"Caves are dark whether the sun's shining or the moon's up, no?" Kerner said. "My mate's on duty tonight. We can get in without paying. And anyway, the cavern's closed while they do some exploratory digging. I think they're going to go deep. Open up some new chamber that has never before been seen by human eyes." Kerner deepened his voice at this last sentence, turning to Don and peering at him with theatrical menace.

"What's your interest in this place?" Don asked Kerner as a black-clad figure in a peaked cap swung open the gates and directed them to the cavern's mouth. "I thought you photographed broken things."

"Not exclusively. Anyway, I'm not working. I might not even switch my camera on."

There were signs saying NO ENTRY and DANGER. Another which read CLOSED TO THE PUBLIC UNTIL JANUARY. Don felt a pang of claustrophobia when he saw the size of the entrance. He would have to bend over slightly, and then the gap narrowed and the ceiling came down further and it was as if he were being swallowed by some gigantic, scabrous throat.

When the cave was first discovered, back in the 1500s (Kerner explained), long before explosives were used to blast a more comfortable passage, you had to crawl through on your belly.

Don felt water drip on to his neck. He could feel the damp in the air. There were footlights guiding you into the cavern along a concretised strip, but then the cave floor took over and it was uneven, treacherous. There was a giddy moment when he wasn't sure if he was even the right way up.

We become so used to flatness, to stability, he almost said to Kerner. The horizon and the vertical. Take the straight lines away and we lose direction.

Kerner seemed to have no such problem. The bigger man bustled through the gap as if he were pushing himself to the front of the queue on sale day.

"Shouldn't we have a guide?" Don asked.

"No guides for us," Kerner said. "I know this place like the back of my gland. I slipped Mac back there a tenner. He's happy to warm his hands on another cup of tea. We're doing his patrol for him. We're doing a public duty."

Don didn't like that. He had never strayed too far away from the rules. Even when teaching, he stuck to the tried and tested. A gradual accumulation of knowledge. A natural progression. Chords. Barre chords. Finger-picking. Scales. Power chords and riffs were not on his syllabus. It was lazy. It was a fast-track to sloppy playing. You had to have the foundation. Deep roots. Core. He was an oak, Don decided now, enjoying the analogy. It was distracting him from the pressing in of the cave walls. He was an oak to Kerner's weak bough, flapping in the wind.

"You've been in here before then?" Don asked, to stop himself from laughing.

"Many times. I could serve as a guide myself, I reckon."

"Do you have a torch?" The entrance lights only illuminated so far. Up ahead, the blackness was deeper than anything Don had ever known. He had never thought of the dark possessing a physicality, but that's what it seemed like. There was substance in it. You'd be forgiven for thinking you had to pierce some part of it in order to get through at all.

"We don't need a torch," Kerner said.

"What are you, part owl?"

Kerner chuckled. And then light exploded around them. Don felt suddenly foolish. The space within the cavern was voluminous. The ceiling of it was sixty, seventy feet from where they were standing. Its geology seemed a living thing. It was sinuous in some places, jagged in others. He sensed Kerner watching him, his finger on a light switch hidden behind a curtain of rock.

"Timer switch," Kerner said. "Switches off automatically, after a while. This place closed down in the 1950s. Lack of interest. Nobody to fund it. It was taken over in the 1970s. Given a real spring clean. They put in the electricity then. No more of those dodgy gas lamps the Victorians used."

"The rock," Don said. He wasn't sure what he meant to follow that with. It seemed anything he might say would not do justice to his surroundings.

"Amazing, isn't it?"

"That it is."

"Limestone, in the main," Kerner said, clearly relishing his role. "You're looking at rock that was formed around three hundred and fifty million years ago, when modest little Derbyshire was part of a continental landmass close to the equator. Volcanic activity pushed the limestone up and into the fractures that were created, hot minerals poured. So you've got your galena, your flourspar, your barytes, your calcite. Veins and seams. Ore. This glittering wonderland. This cave was formed by water. Rain becomes acidic when it passes through organic matter, like soil, as I'm sure you know. It dissolved the limestone. Streams eroded it further. You can hear the water crashing through. We'll see it up ahead. All this water coming through here, it's been going on for two million years."

My God, thought Don. He thought of Julie. She would have loved this. She had been dead for one year. The water coming through here, it was difficult to imagine it would ever stop. It would still be sluicing through two million years hence. The cave wider, deeper, but essentially the same. People coming and going so quickly, like glyphs on the pages of a flicker book.

The colours were amazing. Blues and greys and greens. Orange heating up to red. Stalagmites reached up to stalactites, fangs in a closing jaw.

"How big is the cave?"

"Who knows," Kerner said. "It extends further than anybody thought. Come on, I'll show you."

They advanced through the cave, and it expanded around them. Handrails and steps had been put in. The electric lights, subtly positioned, showed off the ripples and thrusts of rock while ensuring there was no chance of becoming lost. Behind them, the lights shut off, like portions of a stage during a play. It was all very dramatic.

Don gradually relaxed. Kerner was a knowledgeable and amiable guide and Don grew to become grateful for his company. They walked through various sections, separated by natural kinks in the path they were following; all were given grandiose names: Hall of the Kings, The Chamber of Hanging Knives, Grey Lion's Lair. The names were attributed to the shapes in the rock. Some looked like crowns, or daggers, or a flowing mane. It was like hunting for faces in the fire, or the clouds.

The path ran out at a boulder choke surrounded with safety rails and more threatening red signs. Don had been so engaged by the alien surroundings, the assault of the cold and the clean, mineral flavour in his nostrils and throat, that he'd completely forgotten about the lump on his cheek. But now, as its pain re-announced itself to him, he stopped and pressed his hand to his skin.

"Okay?" Kerner asked.

"Yeah, just . . . I don't know. Spot or something."

"Oh, I noticed that too, but I didn't say anything."

Don tried to laugh it off but the sound came out all wrong. Beautiful place, unkind acoustics. "I'm turning into a teenager again," he said.

"You should maybe see a doctor. It might be an infection. You don't want it to become an abscess or anything like that. They'll have to cut a big chunk out of you. Bad scars. I have photographs of people, post-op. People who had tumours. One guy who was bitten by a flea or a tick or something. Half his face turned rotten, virtually slid off him. Imagine that."

Don tried to ignore him. He removed the sticking plaster from his skin and pushed ahead, leaving Kerner to his study of a small, visible stretch of churning water. His fingers fretted at the sore. The surrounding skin was puffed up and tender. There was a hard core beneath. It wobbled under the dome of taut skin, making him queasy. Maybe it was the air pressure that was nagging at it. Or the cold. Something was being drawn out. Maybe it was just time. The body healed itself of most things, given enough time.

"Look, see," Kerner said. He was pointing at a small hole in a cluster of rocks at the foot of the choke. "They dropped cameras through that last year and found a huge . . . I don't know how you'd describe it . . . amphitheatre of white rock. They dubbed it 'the blizzard bowl'. Crystal city. Like landing in one of those daft ornaments, you know. What are they called?"

"Snow globes," Don whispered.

"Snow globes, yeah. That's the chappy. Anyway, the idea is they're going to send a man down there. Apparently there's a guy known as Rat lives in the village. Spelunker *extraordinaire*. He can squirm his way into holes like that. No fear in him. He's going to see what's what and then they're going to open the whole thing up. I mean, it's anyone's guess. How far can you go? There might be worlds upon worlds beyond that blizzard bowl. Who knows what we might find? There are new species being discovered every day in the rainforests."

There was a moment, just as the lights were turned off, and they began the walk back to the cavern entrance, when Don thought he heard the scrabble of movement, but he chose not to mention it, because he didn't want to appear nervous, or stupid to Kerner. The slide of insecure pebbles. A rat, or a bat. It was nothing.

"Let's have a pic," Kerner said, when they were outside. He got Mac to take a photograph of them, standing in front of the cavern entrance, and then they were ushered out of the grounds and it was much colder out here and the stars were studs of glass scattered across an oily hard shoulder.

"Nightcap?" Kerner asked.

Don shook his head. "I'm wiped," he said. "Thanks for an interesting evening."

"Sad to leave ya, Eurasian beaver."

"Good night."

Again. Did it become a ritual if it happened more than once?

A hot bath. The Scotch. The music she loved, Joni Mitchell. He mustered the memory of the smells that made her who she was. Tea tree oil. Fennel. He thought back to the last time they had made love. The flush of red on her chest. The eyes closing. The quickening of her breath. *Don, Don.*

Sleep was over him and around him, closing, like a thin blanket, but it was not yet in him. His breath deepened. His eyes rolled back. He submitted himself. Sleep sank into him like something taking a bite. And just at the moment he felt himself go under, he was aware, in the dark, of a shape at the foot of his bed. It was heart-shaped, a muted grey, and it took a while to understand that it was the shape of someone's back: the arms and head lost to shadow. Slowly, it shifted. He heard the shiver of nylon moving against itself. He saw the nubs of vertebrae in a spine curve subtly against the fabric of a cardigan. And it was *her* cardigan. His heart leaped. Until:

Why are you doing this?

He flinched. Her voice was too close, as if she were whispering in his ear. And there was something wrong with it. She sounded as though she was thirsty. The voice, full of holes.

I love you but you have to let me go don't blame yourself

"Julie? Julie, what can I do? Where are you?" He stared at the figure at the end of the bed as it stretched and writhed. "Don't leave me. It was so sudden."

I have to go I want to go to the white I want to run through the snow you can set me free

The shush of her nylons . . . but she never wore tights.

"Julie?" He jerked upright in bed, blinking himself awake. The shape toppled forward, turning. Her hair fell across her face so he could see only a sliver of gleaming eye through the mouse blonde bands of it. She raised her thin limbs and showed him where she'd cut through the veins of her arms with the shattered remnants of her snow globe.

The blood hissing like water from punctured hoses, eternal.

I'd have killed myself anyway, eventually . . . don't blame yourself

In the second it took him to wrench himself free of the bedclothes, winter sunshine was streaming through the window and his alarm clock was droning and she was gone. He turned back to see his pillow, streaked with red. A pebble of glass sitting there like something the tooth fairy had forgotten to collect.

"Woah, pal. Easy. What bit you this morning?"

Don had dropped his glass of cranberry juice. He watched the spreading red stain around his breakfast plates and tried to stop his hands from shaking. Surely everyone could see that. They'd think he'd been drinking at daybreak. Or that he had something terrible to hide. Kerner watched him while he chewed his interminable muesli. His question hung in the air. Don ignored it.

He poured coffee and tried to hide in its steam. The plaster on his face felt tight and itchy, but he wasn't going to sit there with a wet hole flapping in front of all these people while they tucked into their grilled tomatoes.

After his shower that morning he'd noticed there were other points on his face beginning to flare up. Most worryingly, there was an ache building behind his left eye. Another in his chest. The windscreen had shattered into a million pieces. How many of them had disappeared inside him? How many were now worming their way out, rejected by his flesh after the slow journey of a year? In the horror of it, came the thrill. The glass might have connected him to his wife. What if, as he had read once, it was possible for slivers of glass to pass through your body? Perhaps some of them had become embedded in her. He was in her, then, after a fashion. And now that he was here, in Sheckford, some numinous frequency, made in blood, had been opened between them. It was the kind of thing she believed in. The end was never the end. We were all passengers in transit.

"There's something wrong with my camera," Kerner said. "Just found out this morning."

"I think there's a camera shop in the village. Maybe they'd have a look at it for you." Don hated the sound of his own voice. It was weak, pathetic, more so since his eventful night.

"Not this. Specialist job, I reckon. Fault somewhere. And not with my picture-taking abilities, for once. It's as if I'd forgotten to take the film out and rewound it and taken more exposures over the top."

"Have you checked that?"

Kerner gave him a look. He checked his watch. "Hmm," he said. "Says here that it's still the twenty-first century. That must mean I've got a digital camera."

The sudden, spearing conclusion that he didn't like Kerner. Don was glad his camera was knackered. He hoped it would cost him a fortune to repair it.

"Look, see," Kerner said, pushing his bowl to one side and setting the expensive camera on the table. He pressed a few buttons and the screen on the rear flashed up a picture: the one Mac had taken the previous evening.

Don came around the table and squinted at the glass oblong. "Christ," he said.

The two of them, standing in front of the cavern entrance, the blue guide lights set into the floor illuminating them from below, giving them an unhealthy, cyanotic glow. Shadows falling on the uneven rock behind them: Kerner's, Don's, and someone else's.

"See that?"

"Yeah. It can't be Mac's shadow, can it?"

"Hey?" Kerner leaned in closer. "I hadn't actually noticed that. I was talking about that . . . glow, in your chest."

Now Don saw it. In roughly the position where his heart might be, a fist-sized lump of grainy light, like the diffuse aura cast by a sodium street-lamp. He pressed his fingers to his breastbone.

"What could it be?" he asked. His voice sounded perilously close to choking. Tears ganged up. But Kerner seemed not to notice.

"Could just be some hot pixels on the sensor, maybe. Maybe a lens problem. But I have some pictures I took before and after, and they seem clean. That shadow you point out though . . . it's obvious something's not right. Bollocks. It's quality glass that. Spent a fortune on it . . ."

"I have to go," Don said.

Kerner nodded, smiled. His fingers fidgeted with the buttons on the camera body. "*Adieu*, caribou."

Go home. Leave this place. Let it sink into time, let it become a fossil in your memory.

But how could it? This was as much Julie's place as his now. They were inextricably linked by Sheckford, the things that happened to them here.

He was back in his room, standing in front of the mirror, his shirt off, staring at his chest, willing the glow to reappear. *It's you, isn't it? Julie?*

He switched on the light and his breath caught. Two shadows. But one was merely a copy of the other, bounced back by the silvered glass. He pressed his fingers against his skin and felt something hard. It was like a swelling. All of the other hotspots of pain in his skin sang out. He buttoned his shirt and returned to the bedroom. There was a sense of someone having just departed. The mattress seemed to be rising slightly, where it might have cushioned a body moments before. There was a slight shift in the temperature of the room. A microscopic change in its pressures.

I want to go to the white I want to run through the snow

The crystal snow globe had been so important to her. It had been with her for much of her life, and it had helped to end it too. She had often told him how lovely it would be to live in a snow globe, to be protected from all the evils in the outside world by that perfect glass. The silence, the beauty.

He was out of the hotel and walking hard along the street before he had any concrete notion of where he was heading.

His mind was filled with white.

Mac let him through the gate but was unsympathetic when Don told him he might have lost his car keys in the cavern. "It's not really my job to go hunting for lost property. I'm a security guard."

"I'll go," Don said.

"I don't think so. This isn't a drive-through restaurant. You don't just pop back whenever you feel like it."

A twenty-pound note changed his mind.

Don steeled himself at the entrance, but only because the pain in his chest ramped up a notch. It was like heartburn, only a hundred times worse. He thought he might retch, but nothing would come when he leaned over. Something felt sharp just beneath the skin. Something was coming.

He could hear the water ploughing over and under and through the rock as it had done for so many millions of years. It had churned through this cavern at the moment of his birth and at the moment of Julie's death. He staggered along the pathway, grateful for its enormous sound; it meant he did not have to listen to his own skin tearing open.

He reached the boulder choke and stared at the foot of it, where the tiny opening was like a pupil in a dead eye. He imagined great acres of untouched white crystal beyond it, like a field of virgin snow before the children have wakened, like Heaven.

"Julie?" he called out, but his voice was unable to best the roar. It hurt too much to try again. He felt his chest fail, and lifted his hands as if he might prevent himself from tipping out on the cold, wet path. What was there in his chest cut his hand.

Blood sped from him, slicking his fingers. It was difficult now, to find purchase on the slippery curve of the glass in him.

He saw movement at the lip of the aperture. Julie? But of course it wasn't. What could he have hoped from this? Julie was cold and dead as the piece of glass within him.

Long, white nails attached to long white fingers. The skin of something eternally damp, of something that had never known sunlight. It skittered out, all elbows and fish-thin ribs pulsing beneath translucency. A sore-looking jaw, red-rimmed, loaded with icy needles that glittered like Hoar frost, splinters of the missing packed between them. It made a sound that was almost beyond a frequency audible to him. It sounded like metal scraped across glass. It turned an eye to him that was as pale as moonstones.

Don turned to run, but his foot slid in his own filth. The chunk in his chest shifted. As he gripped it and pulled, closing his eyes to the terrible suck as the glass came free, the lights went out and it fell on him, all too keen to lend him its assistance.

SIMON KURT UNSWORTH

The Ocean Grand, North West Coast

SIMON KURT UNSWORTH WAS born in Manchester in 1972. He currently lives on a hill in the north of England with his wife and child, where he writes essentially grumpy fiction (for which pursuit he was nominated for a 2008 World Fantasy Award for Best Short Story).

His work has been published in a number of critically acclaimed anthologies, including *At Ease with the Dead*, *Shades of Darkness*, *Exotic Gothic 3*, *Gaslight Grotesque*, *Never Again* and *Lovecraft Unbound*. He has also appeared in three previous volumes of *The Mammoth Book of Best New Horror* and also *The Very Best of Best New Horror*.

His first collection of short stories, *Lost Places*, was released by Ash-Tree Press in 2010, and his second, *Quiet Houses*, followed from Dark Continents Publishing a year later. A further collection, *Strange Gateways*, is now available from PS Publishing, with another set to launch the "Spectral Press Spectral Signature Editions" imprint in 2013.

"'The Ocean Grand, North West Coast' first appeared in *Quiet Houses*, my portmanteau collection set as far as possible in real locales," explains Unsworth. "This particular story is based on the Midland Hotel in Morecambe.

"The Midland has a long and chequered history, and when I first went there ten years ago it was just before it closed amid accusations of mismanagement and ownership wrangles. Back then, it was a perfect example of faded seaside glamour; it had the most beautiful fixtures and fittings, but they were falling to pieces.

"We used to go on Saturday evenings and have an after-dinner drink, sitting in a long glass corridor that extended across the rear of the hotel and gave out on magnificent views of Morecambe Bay and, in the distance, the Barrow headlands. It was always freezing in the sun corridor because the heating was never on and half the windows were broken, but it was worth it for the sight of the ocean and the sense of being somewhere that had a foot placed firmly within a magnificent past.

"The story came about because I'd read Barry Guise and Pam Brook's excellent history of the Midland, *The Midland Hotel: Morecambe's White Hope* (Palatine Books, 2007) and it made me think about how buildings made to be full of people might feel if they were closed and empty, and about art created to be viewed being alone and going slowly, claustrophobically mad.

"Gravette and Priest and the art they created for the Ocean Grand are very, *very* loosely based on the work and philosophies of the architect Oliver Hill and the artists Eric Gill and Marion Dorn, who designed and decorated the Midland originally. But mostly they're my creations. Make of that what you will.

"The Midland, after years of closure, has been completely refitted and has re-opened, and looks spectacular. I'd urge you to visit and to have a drink in the new sun corridor or a meal in one of the restaurants.

"Me, I'm still a little nostalgic for those Saturday nights in the old sun corridor, when we had to keep our coats on because of the cold and when the wind danced in through the broken windows smelling of brine and sand."

Arrival; Initial Impressions

MANDEVILLE TWISTED ON the key, hard, and felt it grate in the lock. With a final yank, it came around and then the Ocean Grand was open for the first time in fifteen years.

The central door was large and heavy and, even unlocked, it took him several hard shoves to open it fully; it had swollen from the years of disuse, clinging and screeching as it moved and cutting tracks through the dirt on the floor. Pieces of crumpled paper shifted away in the light breeze that entered the hotel around Mandeville. Of course, he thought, it wasn't really the first time the building had been open for fifteen years, and he had to be careful not to romanticise the experience or what he found inside. Safety assessors had been inside only recently and security checks were carried out monthly, but he was the first *outsider* to gain entrance since it had closed as a working site in the early 1990s.

Actually, even that wasn't quite true. A local television news team had accompanied one of the early safety crews and had filmed them placing boards over the wall murals and picture windows. Mandeville had a copy of the footage in his bag; in it, the unseen presenter talked about the glories and controversies of the art deco pieces that adorned the Grand's walls whilst workmen nailed large boards over each piece "to protect it for the few months that the hotel was shut during its refit". The "few months" had turned into almost two hundred, the refit had never occurred and the Grand had remained shut to everyone as it changed owners time and again in the intervening years. Until now.

Behind Mandeville, Parry began to unload the van, dropping their gear onto the cracked surface of the car park and telling a joke to Yeoman, the third member of the self-dubbed "Save Our Shit Crew". Mandeville could already smell the sharp tang of Yeoman's cigarette, and he smiled to himself.

Yeoman had said little on the journey, but his silence had become more pointed as they travelled and Parry refused to pull over for a rest stop, claiming that he was helping to break Yeoman's habit by forcing him into periods of abstinence. Yeoman wouldn't enter the Grand until he had smoked at least three cigarettes in the car park, Mandeville knew. It was an old routine, practised and refined over the previous years until they were all comfortable with it. Leaving them, Mandeville stepped forward into the Grand.

The foyer was large and circular, with the wings branching off through large, arched entrances at his left and right. Opposite Mandeville, the reception desk hugged the curved rear wall, its surface thick with dust. The great staircase rolled around from Mandeville's right, clinging to the wall as it rose before letting onto the floors above the reception. He could just see the dark smears of the doorways leading to the upper bar and the outdoor sun deck.

Under his feet, the original wooden flooring was hidden under heavy linoleum, assuming it still existed at all. The light reaching him was dirty and dank; two storeys above him, the atrium's great glass roof was mostly intact but had been covered from the outside with wooden sheets. Where these had peeled back or broken, allowing the light to enter, he saw a film of dirt and old leaves covering the glass.

Clicking on his torch, he let the beam play across the roof's frame. It looked to be in fairly good condition, all things considered. There were rust patches, not unexpected given the Grand's coastal location, and several of the more delicate sections of the pattern looked to be twisted out of shape. Some of the glass had been removed by the safety team; other panes, he knew, had fallen in long ago, the coloured glass swept up and discarded.

"Can we come in yet?"

"No," said Mandeville. He wanted to savour this; he felt like a time traveller, stepping back into a past placed in storage and only now being brought back to use.

The Ocean Grand had been decaying for years, not just for the fifteen it had been closed and its ownership a fluid thing; even when it had been open, the rising costs of maintaining a building that had so many unique features had led to a legacy of mismanagement, cost-cutting and barely done repairs, of unique fixtures and fittings falling into disuse, of damage, of art lost and stolen and sold. The Ocean Grand was a part of England's industrial and cultural heritage, abused and battered and only now receiving the attention it deserved.

Mandeville and his small team had to find out how bad things were in the Grand, catalogue what remained, and work out what could be saved and what was gone.

Even in the foyer, Mandeville could see evidence of the neglect. There should have been ten balustrade tops in the "primitive figures" style, cast in metal and spaced every five feet up the staircase, but three were missing. Sections of the reception desk's ornate wooden panelling had been replaced with plain wood sheets and, worst of all, the large panels of the Gravette mural that should have faced the guests as they approached the reception desk were gone.

Mandeville knew two were in storage in London; the other two were missing, presumably destroyed or taken when the mural was removed in the early 1980s rather than pay for its professional renovation. There was always someone prepared to buy an original Gravette, even one that was painted on a twenty-foot by six-foot wooden panel and which was only actually a quarter of the whole piece.

To the left of the reception desk was the entrance to the restaurant and, beyond it, the sun corridor. Moving to the doorway, Mandeville saw immediately that sections of the intricate floor designed by Constance Priest were gone. Created by using nearly four thousand handmade tiles, its pattern should have covered the floor, an interlocking swirl of lines and blooms suggesting water, air and life. However, some of the tiles had been replaced by ones that only almost matched and whose colours, size or patterning was just off-kilter. Other tiles had been replaced by plain squares which cut into Priest's patterns clumsily, disrupting its movement.

Mandeville sighed to see it.

Tables, cheap Formica models with spindle legs, were piled against the walls like the skeletons of long-dead animals. In the sunlight, the floor pattern and the shadows from the tables merged at the corners of the room, bleeding together in black clots.

The doors to the sun corridor were open and through them, Mandeville could see the grey ocean churning beyond its glass walls. He walked towards it, his feet crunching on the grit and dirt on the floor, and peered into the glass corridor.

A later addition to the Grand, running the length of its rear, the 1950s structure had suffered badly from neglect during the previous years. Streaks of rust crawled down the glass from metal struts that were losing an uneven battle against the corroding, salt-laden atmosphere. Several of the panes were broken and had been replaced by plywood sheets. More sheets lay piled against the seaward wall, having been removed from the windows at Mandeville's request. Apart from the roof in the foyer, all the windows that had complete glass panes had been uncovered so that the Crew could work in daylight where possible.

Mandeville was about to leave the sun lounge when he noticed something beyond the glass. No, not beyond the glass, on it: swirls of colour, so incredibly pale as to be almost invisible, but present nonetheless. An arc of red and green straddled the pane nearest to him, blue and red in the next pane along.

Stepping close, he ran his fingers across the glass, leaving streaks along the surface. Looking at his fingertips, he saw that the ovals of grime below his nails also contained tiny flashes of colour. Paint? he wondered, sniffing at it. Had someone sprayed or splashed paint on the windows in the past and then tried to wipe it off? Vandalism? He would check with Parry, see if there was a record of that kind of damage; God alone knew what other problems they would come across in here.

Turning, he called for his colleagues.

Setting Up; Working the Hotel; Cataloguing

Parry, the Crew's archivist and researcher, had set up in the foyer. Laid out across the floor were photocopies and typed sheets, indicating precisely what the Crew was to look for and where within the Grand it was, how it was made and the materials used. Where makers were known, this was indicated as well.

Yeoman, the architect, who had less to do in this initial phase, was setting up a base camp in the restaurant.

The Crew was staying in the hotel, sleeping in the open expanse of the empty dining area to save time. There was a lot to do, and they had only a week to do it before the owners wanted an initial report. In seven days, Mandeville had to be able to make recommendations about the order of jobs and which parts of the hotel's original decorations could be preserved or restored and incorporated into the latest developments planned for the hotel. It was a big job, the biggest the Crew had taken on.

Mandeville was re-reading the initial site assessment carried out by the owner's own assessors. There were a couple of areas in the hotel the Crew had been instructed to stay away from (the kitchen; not an issue as there was nothing in there for them to assess according to Parry, and a first floor bathroom whose floor was rotten but which Mandeville did want to check out if he could).

Up or down? he asked himself. Top or bottom first? Finally, he chose bottom simply because the closest of what Parry called his "Interest Lists" dealt with ground floor.

Taking the sheet of paper, Mandeville moved into one of the Grand's lower corridors.

Parry was in the top corridor. Unlike Mandeville, the artist and restorer, or Yeoman the architect, Parry was a historian and he simply wanted to see what remained of the hotel's past. Of course, the great delight in being part of the Save Our Shit Crew was that sometimes they could persuade those designers of the present and the future to save or incorporate the past into their plans.

Take this place, for example; the Ocean Grand. Originally owned by one of Britain's smaller rail companies, the Grand was the crowning glory of the artists Howard Gravette and Marie Priest, and the only hotel they had ever designed. Working with the architect, Edward Manning, they had created a small, opulent establishment, intended for the moneyed classes. Its every element was part of a unified, intelligent whole, creating a unique holiday venue that had been popular in the periods just before and after the First World War.

Manning's architecture and Gravette and Priest's designs incorporated the ideas and principles of the art deco movement, blending them with, in particular, Gravette's ideas of art as a reflection of what he called "the lived life".

Aided by Priest's skills in the use of pattern and intricate textile work, Gravette's intense, layered artwork utilised images from both the natural and industrial worlds, turning the Grand into a building that was, in a review of the time, "simply astonishing" and which celebrated both mankind's move towards an industrialised society and the supremacy of the natural world.

Guests in its heyday found themselves surrounded on the ground floor by designs that were solid, geometric, echoing the patterns found in the factories of the time. On the first and second floors, the designs became more fluid, twisting and losing their angles, and by the third floor, nature had taken over.

Here, every element of the decor and the original furniture had implied a triumphant natural world, burying the industrial world's edges beneath the flows and sweeps of leaf and coastline and animal. The Grand was unique, and strangely subversive.

As he walked up the tattered staircase to the third floor, Parry couldn't help but smile. Gravette and Priest had been lovers at the time of the hotel's design and construction, and throughout the building elements of that sexuality, slipped in below the radar of the rail company executives, were apparent.

It wasn't subtle even; Parry had seen photographs of the missing mural that had adorned the foyer. Across the four sections, a vast and dark locomotive had strained, its windows filled with pale and crammed faces. The train was, in the leftmost panel, erupting from a copse of twisting, stunted trees, and in the rightmost was burying itself into a tunnel whose dark brickwork was surrounded by a collar of white.

Celebrated at the time as a grand depiction of the reach and the power of the rail industry, it was in actuality, a huge cock disappearing into a vagina. The white collar was a not-very-subtle reference to Priest, the stunted trees Gravette's own pubic hair. How had they missed it? mused Parry as he wandered the corridors. How had they not seen?

"So what's left?" asked Mandeville that evening. A small lamp illuminated the three men; takeaway pizza boxes littered the floor between them. Around them, Parry's lists were piled, now covered in notations and scrawled comments.

"The carpets are all gone," said Parry. "I can't find any of the original designs. Most of the rooms have been refitted, so none of the original furniture's left, although rooms 212 and 208 have the lamp fittings in the wall. The bathrooms on the second floor were torn out in the sixties, so we know that all that's gone, but the suites on the third floor still have the original baths with the bath taps."

"Are they the ones shaped like breasts?" asked Yeoman.

"Not breasts, octopuses," said Mandeville, smiling.

"Whatever," said Yeoman, also smiling. "They look like tits to me."

"They're supposed to," said Parry. "The third floor suites are all about sexuality, about sex and it being the driving force in nature. Octopuses suited Gravette because he could mould the taps to look like their bodies and still have it represent the female form. Priest's form, to be precise. His own form was there in the long lines of the taps' stems. It's all over, the male and female, Gravette and Priest. This whole place is a shrine to them, to their love."

"Did they really fuck in every room on the third floor before the hotel opened?" asked Yeoman, which made Parry grin broadly.

"That's the rumour. They called it 'christening the hotel', according to Manning's diary."

"What else?" asked Mandeville, bringing back the discussion to the hotel's current state, knowing that Parry could happily talk about the history of a place for hours, and that Yeoman would encourage him just because he could.

"The first floor sun deck is pretty solid," said Yeoman. "I went up after I got the camp sorted. It's just a reinforced roof space, but the walls have still got designs etched into them. Waves, by the look of it, although I'm fairly sure I made out fish and fins and things like that. It's pretty faded."

"That was Manning," said Parry, checking a sheet. "He worked with Gravette and Priest pretty closely, but he didn't do much in the way of decoration. It's good that the sun deck still exists; it'll probably be the only bit by him left that isn't the actual structure. He was a big believer in the energising power of the sun, though, and the bracing sea atmosphere, and insisted on having his own designs in the area of the sun lounge.

"Can you imagine all those rich men and their wives lying on stripy deckchairs in the chilly British summer? Overlooked by the people on the second and third floor?"

"Was he another mucky one?" asked Yeoman.

"No," said Parry, not hearing the humour in Yeoman's voice; Yeoman knew all this, he just wanted Parry to talk. "He was tightly buttoned by all accounts, but got on surprisingly well with Gravette and Priest. They believed in the same things, ultimately, in the human body and the power of the natural world. They liked fucking, he liked sunbathing."

"So where do we concentrate?"

"We need a full inventory," said Parry, "but the third floor's the least changed. There's panels covering the walls between the room doors, which might mean they were protecting artwork. The contemporary reports aren't very clear about what was actually done to protect the art, and I didn't want to remove a panel without help."

Mandeville made a note on his work plan. Gravette had designed and created two large murals, one for the reception and one for the restaurant, which depicted scenes of men, women, animals and machines existing in verdant landscapes of greens and blues. Both were gone, although his smaller pieces were hopefully still inset into the third floor corridor walls. Mirroring the stations of the cross, the fourteen small panels showed mythological scenes re-imagined so that in every piece the nude figures of gods and people moved around animals and plants. It would be a real bonus if the fourteen still existed and could be restored and incorporated into the new decorative scheme. *Tomorrow,* he thought. *We start finding out tomorrow.*

Mandeville couldn't sleep. It was partly that his camp bed was uncomfortable and that both Parry and Yeoman snored, but it was also excitement; the Grand was the most important job the Crew had ever taken on, and it could make their reputation.

Most of their other work had been in helping homeowners discover the histories of the buildings they lived in and to carry out refits and rebuilds taking this history into account, but the Grand was a step into the next league. The art alone, even if only a part of it could be rescued, would add to their understanding of how art had changed and grown between the wars, and the building itself was, in design and construction, almost unique and certainly one of the few surviving examples of its type.

Restless, he walked through to the sun corridor but could see little through the glass. He heard the sound of the ocean crouched in the darkness, muted and elastic like the breathing of some huge animal at rest. It was cold and he pulled his coat tightly around him, watching as his breath misted on the glass in front of him, bleeding to odd colours because the thin coating of paint smeared across the inside of the panes.

I forgot to ask Parry about that, he thought briefly and made a mental note to do so before they started work tomorrow. When he played the narrow beam of his penlight across the pane, the smears of paint were clearer than they had been in daylight. For a moment, he couldn't tell what the smears reminded him of, and then it came to him; it looked as though the windows were covered in hundreds of handprints.

Yeoman whistled as he worked, and knew that his whistle would reach throughout the building. At some point in the near future, Parry would go and turn on the radio that was sitting on the floor in the middle of the foyer to drown him out, but for now he was enjoying the idea that something of him was filling this place, swooping along the corridors and entering the rooms, tuneless and sharp though it may be.

Parry was somewhere on the first floor, he thought, and Mandeville was recording the art that remained on the ground floor, noting the missing or badly repaired sections of Priest's tiled floor on which they slept at night.

Yeoman himself was in the bar that emerged from the rear of the building over the restaurant. Panels of dark wood, designed but not carved by Gravette, lined the walls, many were warping and sagging, and he was trying to ascertain whether the problem lay with the walls themselves or simply the panels. His initial thought was that it was the panels; each was hanging loose from the walls, the wood twisting and buckled so that the figures carved on their fronts (barely seen workmen, faceless automata, things that might have been gods or giants standing above them and all around the edges animals and fish) seemed hunched and wretched.

As he leaned in to get a better look at the wall, Yeoman placed his hand on one of the panels, holding it steady away from the wall so that he could angle his torch into the space behind it. The concrete seemed fine; dank, certainly, covered mould spores that probably indicated some minor damp problems, but essentially sound and with no sign of cracking.

He started back from the wall, pushing his hand against the panel for leverage, and was alarmed to feel it give around his fingers. The wood, oddly soft, separated and his fingers descended into the warm and damp wood.

Warm? Everything else in the hotel was cold and damp. Yeoman pulled, but his hand didn't come free from the panel and he pulled again, laughing as he thought of Mandeville's face when he told him that he'd accidentally pushed his fingers through a piece of artwork.

The wood felt tight around his fingertips, still warm, but there were splinters in there as well, sharp and needling. He pulled again and then, when his fingers still were not released, he pulled a last, forceful, time.

Mandeville had gridded and completely mapped the floor in the restaurant and was taking a rest. His eyes ached from trying to plot the precise positions of the missing or replaced tiles, almost two hundred of them, on a copy of Priest's original plans. It was a job made more difficult because, in the bright sunlight, the pattern, despite its disruptions, seemed to swirl in a constant half-seen movement, black eyes and mouths forming at the corner of his vision and then breaking up again, only to reform moments later.

Imagine eating with this under your feet, he thought, *it'd be like floating on the surface water in which huge fish swam and kept breaching and peering at you!* He started to laugh and then saw the three camp beds, pushed back against the wall, and had a sudden vision of a vast leviathan emerging from under the floor and swallowing him and Parry and Yeoman whole as they slept.

Something clattered in the foyer.

It was Parry, Mandeville assumed, come to turn the radio on to drown out Yeoman's whistling, although the architect had actually stopped his tuneless noises several minutes earlier.

He waited for the music or inane DJ chatter to begin, but nothing came except another clatter and then the sound of rapid footsteps. Sighing, he got to his feet and went to the doorway, expecting to find some trick or joke being prepared or having already been enacted; Parry and Yeoman were his friends, and were the best men he had ever worked with, but they wound each other up and let the tension out in bickering and jokes and tricks. Sometimes, it was funny; more often, it was childish and irritating.

The foyer, however, was empty.

Well, not empty. The radio was lying in the middle of the floor, no longer standing but on its back, its power cable tangled into a black knot next to it. The floor around it was covered in footprints, scuffed and indistinct in the old dust.

At first, Mandeville thought that the prints were from Parry or Yeoman, but something about them made him reassess. There were lots, overlaying each other, small and with their edges bleeding into each other, making the floor around the small radio into a manic dance chart.

Small?

The prints were small, and neither Parry nor Yeoman was a small man.

These prints were much smaller than any he or his colleagues would make. They were narrow, short, a different shape to their own footwear.

Experimentally, he placed his foot in an unmarked space and pressed it down hard. When he lifted it, he saw a faint impression of the diamond pattern of his boot sole pressed into the grime. The other footprints were far clearer, as though their makers had trodden in something before walking around the radio.

Mandeville pressed his fingers into one of the prints. His fingers came away smeared with dirt that smelled of something familiar, although he couldn't remember precisely what.

Some of the prints appeared to trail back towards the staircase and he went to the bottom step, peering up and wondering. If it wasn't him or Parry or Yeoman, then there was someone, several someones actually, in here with them, and judging by the size of the prints, the someones were probably kids.

Mandeville cursed under his breath. It was to be expected, of course; closed-up buildings like the Ocean Grand attracted different groups of people who wanted to get inside. Aside from historians and urban creepers, kids were the commonest intruders, with drunks and vandals close behind, and they could be a pain. If they had kids breaking in, the likelihood was that they'd damage the place, they'd piss in the corners or set fires, maybe try and steal from the SOS Crew's equipment or belongings.

They'd have to be found and turfed out, he thought. He'd need to pull Parry and Yeoman back from the jobs they were on and they'd need to do a systematic search of the hotel. Damn, damn, *damn.*

Before Mandeville could call his colleagues, however, Yeoman appeared from the bar, holding one hand out in front of him. The hand was dripping blood, bright in the musty surroundings, and in a tone that was almost conversational, he said, "The fucking thing bit me!"

Yeoman refused to go to hospital, despite Parry's insistence that the slash across his fingers needed stitches. Instead, he made Parry bind each of his injured three fingers with gauze from their first aid kit and took painkillers and told Parry to stop nagging him.

The wounds were messy, punctures that had torn sideways, elongating the openings in his flesh into a series of ragged-edged striations between the first and second knuckles of his middle fingers. They bled heavily, slow to clot despite the pressure that Parry put on them, ripping open as soon as Yeoman moved his hand. Fresh blooms of blood soon soaked the bandages covering his fingers and by the time the three men came to eat their evening meal, Yeoman had gone through three sets of dressings.

Food that night was pizza again, collected by Mandeville from one of the seafront takeaways, and over it they assessed their progress.

"There were two sorts of art here," Parry was saying as they finished their food, "what Gravette called 'integral' and 'peripheral'. The integral stuff is the panels, the floors, the stuff that was built in from the beginning. The peripheral is the other stuff, the things that could be moved or changed, like hanging pictures or chairs or the types of plates used.

"From Gravette's perspective, the whole place was art, and everything in the building was supposed to add to the feeling of being inside a piece of living, breathing, functional art, from the taps that looked like octopuses or tits, to the colours they used in the original carpet. The peripheral stuff has mostly gone although we have records of some of it from the original design plans and in photographs, so what we're looking at here is the integral, about fifty per cent of which is still here as far as I can tell.

"The top corridor is the best bet, although a lot of what should be there is hidden at the moment, so tomorrow we'll take the boards off and see what state it's in, but the rooms are mostly intact. The bar and sun deck are pretty much in their original state, although some philistine has replaced the pumps in the bar, probably in the sixties."

"Gravette designed the pumps?" asked Yeoman.

"He designed *everything*. Well, he and Priest did, letting Manning in because they needed his technical skills for the building itself. I keep telling you, this whole place was a testament to Gravette and Priest's belief in the supremacy of the natural world over the things man created.

"The fittings, the art, the colours, all of them were designed to tell people that they were insignificant when faced with the grandeur of God's creation. The richest guests had to caress something that might have been an octopus, that might have been a tit, when they wanted to turn the tap on to run a bath or brush their teeth.

"Think of it, all the rich industrialists whose money came from the mechanical and soulless, come to the seaside for bracing fresh air and views of the North Sea having to rub their great callused hands over brass tits every day and then had their bathwater spurt out of something that could well be Gravette's cock! And when they went into their corridor, they were surrounded by art that only barely hid its message that shagging was the profoundest act a human could engage in behind classical and religious allusions. Even on the sun deck, they were faced with it."

"With what? You said the sun deck was Manning's creation."

"It was, but he couldn't draw for shit apparently, so he had to ask Gravette and Priest to help him. You can't see it when you look at the carvings of the waves straight on, but when the shadows are right, you can."

"See what?"

Instead of replying, Parry got to his feet, lifting the last piece of pizza from one of the boxes. "Come with me," he said, chewing, and led the other two upstairs.

Mandeville followed because Parry had an artist's heart and eye and sometimes saw things that he did not. When he put the final report together, containing his recommendations to the new owners, Parry's suggestions about the art and what could be done with it would be central to the document.

The sun deck was dark and cold, and the sound of the nearby sea was a grey, shifting mass in the night, chilling the air further. "Stand there," said Parry, pointing to the centre of the deck, "and crouch, so that you're the height of someone on a sunlounger. Now, imagine, you're reading a book, maybe having a little drink, and this is what you can see." He pointed his torch beam at the wall, showing the carved indentations of Manning's design; the waves, line etchings of what might have been fish, plants or undersea grottoes.

"Now," said Parry, "watch the shadows." He began to move his torch slowly around in an arc, travelling over the carvings. The shadows caught in the etched lines and then spilled over, stretched, blossoming into black patches like moss on the wall. Mandeville did not see anything unusual and was about to say so when Yeoman said, "Holy shit!"

"No, holy vagina, technically," said Parry and Mandeville was about to ask why when he saw it too. The lengthening shadows reached a point where they combined with the lines of carving and the image changed, danced into something new, a stylised picture of a woman's legs, curved and invitingly open. As Parry kept moving the torch, the image wavered and then vanished, collapsing back in on itself and reforming into waves and sea creatures.

"There," he said triumphantly. "Even out here, this place is about being surrounded by femininity, by procreation. By sex. By *life*."

"We have got to recommend that they re-etch these," said Yeoman, laughing.

"Absolutely," said Parry without pause, "and don't tell them why," and Mandeville could only nod in amused agreement.

Already, a plan was forming for the report, where he would recommend that restoration of the hotel back to its original state, and the use of modern artists to fill in the gaps. He was thinking about how to word and present his proposals as they walked back down to the restaurant, his head filled with the possibilities of this place, and it was only later he remembered about the children.

The thought actually pulled him back to consciousness as he was drifting off to sleep, lying wrapped in his sleeping bag on his travel cot. In all the excitement of Yeoman's fingers, and then eating and catching up, he had completely forgotten the intruders. Now he remembered them, though, the thought that they hadn't checked the hotel for obvious entry points wouldn't leave him alone.

The Grand had survived its locked-up years surprisingly well, with little damage apparently done by vandalism. There was definitely evidence that people had broken in, he had seen it: a pile of old food cartons in the kitchens, a blackened circle in one of the bedrooms that might have meant a small fire had burned there, but there was no real damage. Most of what had broken or collapsed had done so as a result simply of time and the coastal atmosphere, of dampness and neglect and air closed in on itself, trapped and rotting. But still, he should check. Kids, once they found an entrance could be persistent and destructive.

Sighing, he clambered out of his sleeping bag and slipped on his boots and a thick jumper; he was sleeping in his jeans and shirt anyway, to ward of the chill air. His breath misted in front of his face as his tied his laces, and he wondered about waking Yeoman and Parry up to help him, but both were snoring and he decided against it.

Yeoman had been weary by the time he fell asleep, and his fingers clearly causing him pain. Parry, he knew from uncomfortable experience, was terribly grumpy if woken before he thought he ought to be. He would scout around himself and if he found anything, they could call the security service tomorrow and get them to deal with it.

In the almost complete darkness, Priest's flooring seemed to shift and swirl under him in shades of luminal grey as he walked from the makeshift camp to the entrance to the foyer, tracking him. His footsteps were gritty, fractured things, his breathing loud, and there was someone standing in the sun corridor.

They were only a shape in the darkness, pressed against the glass with their arms stretched out as though supplicant to the grey swathe of beach and sea beyond. Surprised, Mandeville stopped. The figure did not move. After a moment, he began to approach it cautiously, listening; they were singing, low and wordless, crooning something that might have been a lament or a lullaby, and they were scratching their fingers against the glass. The sound of it was carrying descant to the song, setting Mandeville's teeth on edge.

The figure was female, he thought, certainly long-haired and curvaceous around the buttocks and thighs, and wearing some kind of long dress or coat that swayed as she moved.

Standing in the entrance to the sun corridor, perhaps fifteen feet from the intruder, Mandeville stopped again and watched her. She was pressed up against the glass, flattened against it, her hair hanging down the sides of her face so that he couldn't make out her features, just a veil of thick tangles that seemed to be catching distant lights from outside and glittering a myriad colours.

Her outstretched arms were fully extended, reaching above her, and her hands were splayed out, hooking against the pane, and she was still singing.

Close to, he could almost hear words in the song, muffled and lost. Her lips and nose had to be pressed hard against the glass as well, he realised. Perhaps that was why her voice was so muffled, seemed to be coming from so far away. This didn't seem like normal vandal behaviour, he thought. Perhaps she was ill? If so, she might need help. "Hello," he said quietly.

The girl fled, spinning away from Mandeville and running down the sun corridor at high speed. Startled, it took him a moment to follow, wondering fleetingly as he did how she had managed to leave an image of herself printed on the glass and why it was so smeared and shot through with wide sweeps of colour.

The girl darted down the sun corridor and Mandeville went after her.

When she reached the far end, she ran through a second doorway into, if Mandeville remembered rightly, a games room off the lower corridor. By the time Mandeville reached it, the girl was nowhere to be seen, but he instinctively ran through the room and out into the corridor, turning back towards the reception area.

Something skittered through the shadows ahead of him, telling him that he had guessed correctly, and then he was into the reception, its floor crossed by the weak light falling through the iron lattice of the glass roof far above him. He expected to find the girl here, but there was no sign of her.

Mandeville slowed, confused. The nearest staircase started at the far side of the reception area, and even if she'd made it there, the girl should have still been visible on the stairs. There was nowhere for her to hide except behind the reception desk, but a quick check told him that she wasn't there. The main door was still shut and locked; he checked it with a shake. Turning, he peered up the stairs and saw movement in the murky depths of the bar.

How did she make it up there without me seeing? he wondered as he started to climb the stairs. *She must have moved like a fucking gazelle!*

Whatever it was he had seen, it wasn't there now. The bar was deserted, the floor space empty of chairs and tables as it had been for years. As he cast his torch beam around, the only movement was the warped wooden panel that hung loose from the wall, rocking slightly as though moved by a breeze.

Mandeville peered behind the bar, but the mirrored walls reflected only dust and empty shelves. The wooden panel swayed again, leaning drunkenly out from the wall, held by two of its fittings, the other two dangling loose, the screw-threads clenching torn shreds of wood and plaster.

It was the panel that Yeoman had caught his fingers on, Mandeville saw, that he had said had bitten him. Parry had ribbed him mercilessly about it after binding his fingers, particularly when they found a torn string of skin caught in the lion's mouth on the front of the panel. Dried blood was still crusted around its wooden teeth, dribbling down its chin and the rest of the panel in long, clotted strings.

Mandeville went back across the bar, flicking the torch around him as he went. Nothing. The girl had either gone further down the corridor, which he doubted as all the doors along it were locked except the very furthest, an exit to the fire stairs which squealed violently as it opened, or she had gone higher, to the second or third floor.

This was becoming annoying and complicated, and he would have to wake the other members of the Crew to help look for her.

As he reached the doorway, a noise came from behind him, a throaty, hoarse growl that stretched for seconds, and as he turned a dark shape came across the floor at him with a rapid, ferocious clatter.

Yeoman woke to find himself staring a warped wooden lion, blood flaking from its mouth in dark red drifts.

"It fell off the wall last night," said Mandeville by way of explanation, "and nearly fucking gave me a heart attack. Maybe it's got it in for us, what do you think? By the way, we've got an intruder, or at least, we did last night. Somewhere there's a place to get in that we don't know about, and first job today is to find it."

It was colder that morning, and even dressed and with coffee and breakfast (cooked on the tiny camping stove) inside him, Yeoman shivered.

Outside the temperature was even lower, and as he walked the perimeter of the Grand smoking and looking for potential entry points, Yeoman tried to see the hotel as it might be in the future.

Architecturally, it was generally sound, so most of his work was done. He had some suggestions to make about the use of the lower floor rooms and about how some of the walls could be altered to make a more open space, but he knew that his role here had become one of support rather than leading. This job would bear Parry's and, especially, Mandeville's stamp rather than his own. He was fine with that, knowing that he would get equal credit anyway; Mandeville was strict about the fact that the Save Our Shit Crew were partners. Whatever fortune they shared, they shared in equal proportion.

There were no obvious entry points that Yeoman could see, and Parry told the same story from his search of the hotel's insides. Mandeville himself didn't look convinced, but didn't argue, telling them instead to keep an eye out and to be alert. He was distracted, Yeoman knew, because once the search was done they could reveal the third floor's secrets.

"The rooms are intact," said Parry, unnecessarily. They had discussed this already, but he looked as nervous as Mandeville. "Whatever other idiocies the various owners inflicted on this places, they knew that keeping the suites on the third floor as close to their original state was important.

"The carpets have gone, of course, but we have the patterns for them in Priest's records so they can be recreated, the wall hangings likewise. The taps, the window latches, the door handles, the bath feet and the fittings for the showers and toilets are all original except for one or two replaced items, but they can be easily sorted out.

"The carpet in the corridor has been replaced as well, and we don't have a pattern for it, but we do have photographs and descriptions, so recreating it might be complex but it's achievable. The theme is all there, waiting for the new owners to agree it, but it only works if the art itself still exists. It's the thing that ties it together, gives the guests the language to understand what their rooms were telling them."

Parry spoke like this when he got excited, Yeoman remembered, talking about art's "language", its "voice", its "pulse" and its "heartbeat".

"If it's survived, we can recommend that the top floor is recreated in its entirety, that the new guests can be as surrounded by Gravette's and Priest's beliefs in God and nature as interchangeable beauties as their predecessors were. If it's damaged, irreparable, then it doesn't matter, the heart will be gone."

As he spoke, Parry was levering the first of the cheap panels from wall. The screws came unwillingly from the wood with a noise like cats in the darkness. The panel, a composite of some sort, bowed out damply, splintering apart as Mandeville took hold of it.

"Shit," said Mandeville quietly; the panel was so damp his fingers were leaving denting grooves in it, "they didn't even use decent fucking wood. In this atmosphere . . ." He voiced tailed off, miserable in the silence, as Parry removed the last screw and then the first of Gravette's pieces was revealed.

It was a picture of a woman standing on the edge of a great sea. She was naked, her back to the canvas, her buttocks and shoulders clearly delineated by Gravette's loving brush, her hair long down her back. Although there was nothing obvious, something in the way the brushstrokes, still visible in the thick paint, formed the sea and the sky hinted at things below the surface or just beyond vision, things that swirled and glided and floated.

Around the woman, by her feet on the sand, pieces of machinery lay glittering with oily life, cogs and levers and panelling and rivets forming a platform that looked like a vast mechanical hand upon whose edge the woman was precariously balanced.

The picture was, despite the damp affecting the panel covering it, in remarkably good condition. Apart from a small amount of blackly-furred moss just creeping along a part of the picture's bottom edge, there was no obvious damage; the colours were bright, vibrant, the detailing astonishing. The woman's muscles were distinct beneath her skin, her outstretched hands seeming to grasp at the whole of the scene beyond her.

"Beautiful," breathed Mandeville, and Parry simply nodded.

Yeoman, less moved by the artwork but still appreciating the skill that had rendered the picture, said, "Is that Priest then? Nice arse."

"It's not Priest," said Parry, ignoring the obvious provocation, "it's *woman*, an archetype, a feminine ideal."

"It's an ideal arse," agreed Yeoman, grinning at Parry.

Parry, shaking his head disgustedly but unable to prevent himself grinning back, said, "Let's do the others."

All fourteen pictures were in similar condition, having survived far better than Mandeville could have hoped. Collectively, the pictures were called *The Stations of the Way*, and if you followed their story, up one side of the corridor and then back down the other, right side along and left back, they told the story of Gravette and Priest's beliefs as surely as any bible or philosophical tract.

Across the pictures, the woman waded into the ocean, leaving the machinery behind, swimming and dancing with vast and unnameable creatures under the green surface before being lifted out and hauled into the sky by flying versions of the same creatures.

The figure of the woman became smaller and smaller in the pictures, surrounded by winged and tentacled and finned creatures with fierce and unforgiving faces, but who robed her and held her as, in the distance, small and insignificant, machines ploughed the surface of the water and left tiny trails across the sky.

Despite her size, the woman remained the absolute focal point in each picture, and every one of the creatures in the picture laid their full attention upon her.

The Inhabitants of the Grand; The End of the Crew

Although they hadn't finished the job of assessing the Grand, Mandeville went out for champagne, and the three men drank it that night from plastic cups after they had finished another take-away meal.

They had spent the evening photographing the pictures, making careful notes of any damage they found, and then had re-covered them, this time with plastic sheeting. As they had covered the last of the pictures, Parry had said, "Sorry, ma'am, but you can come out again soon."

Mandeville had never seen Parry so excited. "Do you understand how important this is, that they've survived? Gravette and Priest, they were both fine artists in their own right, but this was considered by both to be their crowning glory, and it's still here, and we can make it public again!

"As you move up through the levels of the hotel, you pass from the mechanised glories of the man-made world on the ground floor, through human pastimes, hunting and drinking and sunbathing, on the first floor.

"If the second floor had been left alone and not torn apart, we'd have found art that showed men and women abandoning their earthly pursuits, their clothes, work, so that by the time we hit the third floor we're returning to an understanding that all of life is about the worship of nature and a recognition of its power, its *supremacy*.

"Do you know that through most of the 1960s, '70s and '80s, the pictures on the third floor had other pictures hung in front of them? That they were considered 'old-fashioned' and 'outdated'? What a fucking travesty, all that beauty and life trapped behind crappy prints and photographs of misty fucking landscapes and Victorian watercolours, desperate to be free, and we can do it, we can free it, let it out, let it be loved again!"

"Well, the owners can, if that's what they want to do. All we can do is make the suggestion and try to persuade them," said Mandeville.

"Persuade them?" said Parry. "They *have* to. We have to make them! It can't stay hidden any more, it was made to be looked at, created to be seen. They *have* to."

"We'll try," said Mandeville. "Trust me, we'll try."

Mandeville was woken by footsteps. Bleary, champagne-heavy, he forgot he was wrapped in a sleeping bag and on a cot and tried to roll, falling heavily to the floor. The shock jolted him fully alert, and as he struggled to his knees, he listened.

They weren't footsteps, not exactly; they were too rapid, too light, and seemed to come from all around the room, from two or three places at once.

It was dark, the only light the digital glow from the clock and the glimmer from the extension cable's unblinking LED eye. At the edge of the pale illumination, a darkness shifted, bled out into the shadows around it and formed again, low and cautious. Another patch moved on the far side of the room, easing in through the entrance from the sun corridor.

Mandeville freed his arms from his sleeping bag and unzipped it, stepping out and fumbling for his boots. As his hand found them, one of the patches moved again, slinking around the edge of the room.

Now the noise was slower, still light, like pencil tips tapping a wooden desk. Mandeville risked looking down for a second to slip his boots on, Priest's patterned floor turning sinuously beneath his soles, and when he looked up, the two patches had been joined by a third.

Parry's cot was empty, but Yeoman was sleeping soundly on his.

Mandeville hissed at him, leaning over to shake him when he didn't wake. Even as he leaned, the flowing, creeping patches of darkness, somehow blacker than the shadows around them, began to come in closer, still circling.

"What?" mumbled Yeoman.

"Be quiet," said Mandeville softly, "and wake up. *Now*. There's something in here."

"Something?" asked Yeoman loudly. His breath smelled of cigarettes and sour air and tiredness.

"Something," repeated Mandeville. "Three somethings, actually. Look."

Yeoman sat up in bed, rubbing his hands through his beard with a noise like sandpaper rustling. Whatever it was circling the room, they reacted to the noise, coming in closer, still just out of reach of the light, still mere blackness against blackness, moving with an increasingly rapid *tactactactac* sound.

"What the fuck?" said Yeoman, finally seeing them. "What are they?"

"Don't know," said Mandeville. "Have you got the torch?"

"Yeah," said Yeoman and began rooting on the floor. Finally, with a muffled grunt that might have been the words "found it", he emerged holding the large lantern torch they used at night.

The things were moving faster and faster around them, passing each other, getting lower, still impossible to see other than the *movement*, the rapid circling centring in on the two men, purposeful and raw.

There was a click as Yeoman turned the light on, the beam at first glancing into Mandeville's eyes and then upwards, leaving him dazzled, before dropping and gleaming out into the room, catching in its gaze the things that moved about them.

Yeoman screamed.

Mandeville fled as things that could not be, impossible things, came streaking across the space towards Yeoman in a matter of seconds, brown and lithe in the jerking, spastic light from the torch, and fell upon him.

As Mandeville reached the entrance to the sun corridor, Yeoman shrieked, once, the sound cutting off with a noise like tearing paper.

The sun corridor was deserted, silent apart from the frenzied fall of his own feet, and Mandeville ran. The large panes were covered, he saw, in blurred silhouettes, arms outstretched as though trying to embrace the world beyond, overlapping and chaotic, a silent audience for his flight.

Ripping sounds danced around him, roars and snarls and, once, a sharp, heavy *crack*, and he ran faster. Through the empty games room and out, along the corridor and into the foyer towards the door, but he was already too late, one of the shapes was there before him, drained to a grimy sepia by the light from above them except around its mouth, where a rich redness pooled and dripped.

It came from the restaurant, cutting off his passage to the door, forcing him to shift direction, to go towards the stairs.

He hit them at a stumbled run, leaping two or three at a time as the thing streaked towards him, emitting a noise like an escalating fire siren. Its feet *(claws,* he told himself, disbelieving, *they're claws)* skittered as it ran, the nightmarish *tactactactac* getting closer and closer.

At the top of the stairs, Mandeville hesitated briefly. The bar was open ahead of him, but he would be trapped in there. The panel that had nearly fallen on him was leaning in the doorway where he had propped it earlier in the day, its face now blank, the wood smooth and unsullied.

The *tactactactac* was getting louder behind him, closer, the fire-whistle sound of the impossible thing's growling surrounding him, and then there was light from above him.

It wasn't light, though, not really; more a kind of greasy glow that clung to the walls, dripping from above him, from the upper flights of stairs, from above the second floor in the shadows that clung to the opening of the third floor. In the opening, the darkness seemed to close itself up like a fan, solidifying into a figure that emerged from the doorway, waving at him.

He started towards it and then, shrieking, the thing from below was on him.

Despite the champagne, Parry couldn't sleep. Even when Yeoman started snoring (which, oddly, he found a reassuring rather than an irritating sound), he found himself lying awake, teasing at something. He couldn't work out what it was, not exactly; they'd uncovered the pictures that formed *The Stations of the Way* and found them in almost perfect condition, true, so he should be celebrating, yes?

No.

Something about the top corridor, about this whole place, bothered him. Despite what he had said earlier, flushed with success and alcohol, he wasn't sure about recreating Gravette and Priest's masterwork in its entirety.

It seemed too intense, almost extremist in its views; it was *everywhere*, when you looked. From the panels and pictures on all the floors to the design of the taps to the carpeting along the corridors (which no longer existed but which pictures showed had consisted of a complex paisley pattern of interlocking, swirling stems and buds which Priest had called "cunts and pricks" in one of her notebooks), this place wasn't so much a homage to the supremacy of life and procreation over industrialisation as it was a proselytisation of it.

The Stations of the Way was a good example: taken by itself, it was simply a series of pictures that between them formed a narrative, one of returning to recognise the beauty of nature and God's place within it.

The religious allegory was unsubtle, and the pictures themselves beautifully done, some of Gravette's best work. But, read another way, they were something more.

Gravette and Priest had fucked in every room on the third floor once the pictures were set in place, and there were persistent rumours that Gravette had mixed his semen and Priest's menstrual blood into his paints. Early sketches showed that the original ideas for the *Stations* pictures were far more graphic, with the angels of sea and air having sex with the woman, transporting her to God's side in a storm of sexual energy and passion and lust.

The woman. It was the woman in the pictures that bothered him, he suddenly realised. Getting out of his sleeping bag, he pulled on his shoes and went to his untidy pile of folders and photocopies and prints.

The problem was that the art in the Grand hadn't ever been formally catalogued, and most of it wasn't recorded anywhere, so his research had had, by necessity, to travel circuitous routes to find the information they needed.

As well as Gravette's and Priest's notebooks, he had scoured old newspaper articles, private photograph collections and what little television appearances the Grand had made to try to get an accurate picture of its inside.

Leafing through the papers, he came across the screen grabs from the television documentary about the Grand's closure, eight of them that showed in not particularly good details some of the pictures from the third floor. Looking at them by torchlight, prints from a not very high quality source document, he saw what bit it was that had been bothering him.

The pictures were different.

The positioning of the characters within the pictures was the same, their layout and structure unchanged, but the woman and the creatures that surrounded her were definitely altered.

Christ, had someone removed the originals, replacing them with fakes? Only, that didn't feel right either; the boards covering the pictures had looked to be the originals from the documentary, filmed just after the Grand finally closed and the pictures themselves were, he would have sworn, original Gravettes.

This made no sense, none.

Taking the prints and the torch, Parry went out into the Grand.

The pictures were definitely different, every one of them that he could make comparisons for. In the prints he held, the woman and the creatures, both the ones that emerged from the air and the water, were painted as innocents. They had wide eyes, almost perfectly round (*like* anime *characters*, Parry suddenly thought, wondering if there was a research paper there, looking at the shorthand artists of different ages used to depict innocent and vitality), looking back at the observer as they viewed the pictures.

Now, though, that had changed. The woman looked past the viewer, her eyes no longer open wide but narrowed, focused on something over the viewer's shoulder. The undersea creatures, although not completely anthropomorphic, had flickers of recognisable emotion painted across their features, mouths twisting in anger or frustration, arms and fins and tentacles curling around the woman not in support but in possessive twists, as though holding her back and preventing her from escaping.

The later pictures in the series, the ones with the woman being elevated into the sky and surrounded by things that might have been angels, or man's better nature freed from the shackles of the flesh, showed the woman still looking back out of the pictures, still staring at something beyond Parry, beyond the Grand itself.

The angels looked cold, emotionless, their hands taut upon the woman's body but the expressions on their faces supercilious and dismissive.

Parry had reached the end of the corridor, had studied each of the pictures as best he could in torchlight, and he was convinced that they were the work of Gravette. They were technically skilled, full of subtleties and tight, hidden details that only emerged when you looked at them for longer periods, but they weren't the pictures that had been nailed behind cheap boards of wood fifteen or more years back.

Had the owners pulled some kind of switch? But why? What would be the point, when they could have merely taken the pictures? He'd have to tell Mandeville, let the owners know, assuming they weren't already aware of the changes.

He made to go back down the corridor when he stopped. Was something moving down there, in the tar-like shadows that pooled along the edges of the floor? And there? There?

Everywhere?

As Parry watched, something glistening detached from one of the pictures and drifted to the floor in the centre of the corridor. It rippled and swelled as it fell, floated really, dancing in the air as more fell from every picture along the corridor.

Soon the corridor was full of the things, gossamer and glimmering. Some of them moved along the floor after they descended, slithering to the edges of the walls and joining the shadows, thickening them, making them pulse and bulge.

It was oddly beautiful, the descents drifting, slow, tracing gentle parabolas through the corridor before alighting with a touch that appeared as delicate as the spinning of feathers or the kiss of elegant mouths.

Soon, the corridor was full of them, pressing out from the walls, swelled by the arrival of more and more of the things.

In the centre of the corridor, the first shape he had seen was now moving, not to the side but away from him, along the carpeted floor towards the stairway. As it went, it coalesced, drawing in seemingly identical shapes that were standing ahead of it. Parry counted three, four, ten, fourteen, and as they merged the remaining moving shape became more solid, more *real*.

Parry made out the curve of buttocks, the sway of full breasts, the outstretching of arms, and the opening of hands, and then something else was moving.

A long tendril came out of the shadow by Parry's side, solidifying as though it was drawing itself together from the thinner shapes, languidly curling in the air above his head. It tapered down to a delicate point, he saw, trembling as though sniffing the atmosphere. As it broadened, became fatter and more solid, pale discs emerged across its underside, shivering and clenching wetly.

It's a tentacle, he thought to himself, but before he had time to scream, it had dropped onto him and wrapped around his neck.

It *hurt*, crashing into Mandeville's legs and knocking him to the floor. He braced himself for further attack, but whatever it was simply flung him out of the way, growling, and dashed on. It hit the wooden panel leaning just inside the doorway, sending it spinning on one edge before it fell, ending up propped between the two sides of the doorframe, canted at a drunken angle.

Where it had been blank before, the wood now contained a carving of a huge jungle cat, not a tiger or a lion exactly, but a creature that was an amalgam of those and others.

Fierce nature, Mandeville thought wildly, *Gravette's fierce nature, hunted and abused but never cowed.* Would two other panels in the bar be blank if he went in and looked at them? He suspected so.

His legs were bleeding, although the tears in his skin didn't feel deep. Mandeville rolled and then stood, unsteadily, leaning on the wall for support.

The panel in the doorway swayed, making the cat's face emerge and vanish into the bar's darkness, as though it was rocking back and forth and considering him quizzically.

From below, in the foyer, came the sound of a distant train, the noise ascending, dopplering and then muffling within the space of a moment.

Going into the tunnel, he thought as the noise started again. *In and out, in and out.*

The other two cats were there, and God knew what else. He looked back up at the waving figure; it had emerged and was now standing at the top of the stairs, still waving, beckoning him upwards.

It was the woman.

Even in the grey light filtering through the glass ceiling, she seemed to glow all colours, casting her illumination about her the way great art did. And she was great art, he understood suddenly, perhaps the greatest there was.

He began to move to her, wincing as he climbed the stairs. Where else could he go?

As he approached, she moved back, returning to the corridor where her glow danced about her like distant, guttering flames. As he reached the corridor entrance, he saw movement beyond her.

At the far end of the third floor, almost lost to the darkness that pooled there like spilled paint, Parry was sitting against the wall as a myriad tentacles clenched about him. The largest was wrapped around his neck, was pulled so taut that the skin either side of the tentacle bulged, bloody and mottled.

The air around Parry was filled with moving, darting shapes, fins lifting and dropping and mouths open wide. As Mandeville watched, a larger shape emerged, conical, mouth agape, and tore into Parry's side, shaking him like a rag doll, tearing a piece from him and disappearing back into the darkness.

Parry twitched spastically, blood spraying from him but not falling to the floor, instead floating around him, breathed in by the fish and the octopuses and squid and the things without names that scuttled and bobbed and feasted upon him.

Parry managed to twist his head, despite the ever-tightening arm of the octopus that was wrapped around his neck and whose bulbous body was drifting in the air above him. For a moment he was looking directly at Mandeville, his eyes desperate, and then the contact was gone as he was twisted further around.

Mandeville didn't move. After all, what could he do?

There were none of the angels in the corridor, he suddenly realised, and just as quickly the realisation came that they were only metaphors, not alive in the way that the cats, the train that was in fact a prick, the undersea creatures were. They were intellect and spirituality, not flesh and lusts and desires and passions and things to worship. They weren't alive in the way that *she* was, the woman.

She was standing in the centre of the corridor, her arms outstretched as though to show him the things that belonged to her, and they *did* belong to her, he saw; they moved around her, never touching her, always giving her space.

It's how they've been painted, he realised, *to worship her. If she's a female archetype, then those other things are men, sleek and brutal and driven by lust and greed and desire, and between them they make . . . what?*

She was approaching him again now, moving down the corridor as though carried by currents that he could not feel, moving towards him, beautiful and austere and suddenly he wanted her, was hard and sweating despite the pain in his legs and the part of him that even now was calling for his attention, was screeching its fear of this impossible situation.

She came closer still, her features resolving, streaks forming on her skin in a pattern of delicate brushstrokes. Her hair moved in clumps, strands matted together, *painted* together. Her arms were outstretched and suddenly Mandeville thought about her, about her pressing herself against the glass of the sun corridor, about her seeing the outside world at night and spending most of her time trapped under boards, locked inside the paint, alive and claustrophobic and alone except for creatures without mouths or intellects, just cocks made to love her.

How terrible must her life have been these last years, he suddenly thought, trapped here day in night out, with no one to look at her, no one to feast themselves upon her, how awful it must have been.

And what damage had it done to her?

Her face twisted into a snarl as she came, lips drawing back from teeth that seemed suddenly too large and too white and too hard, her arms stretching forward, the skin of her hands broken by paintbrush swirls that reminded Mandeville of the sucking pads of the octopuses and squid that served attendance upon her.

Sharks darted between her legs, and still she came and Mandeville saw the hate in her eyes, the desperation to hold him and own him, to take him from the outside and bring him in and keep him so that he, too, could look at her and worship her, and he turned and ran.

The two cats were waiting for him on the stairs between the foyer and first floor, brown and wooden yet terribly fluid, moving back and forth with a restless energy. Trapped between them and her, Mandeville stopped on the first floor and turned a full circle, looking for an escape route.

The bar was blocked to him; the third cat still stood in its entrance, back on its board but its mouth open in a rictus of teeth and ravenous appetite. He debated running back to the second floor, losing himself in the place where Gravette and Priest's hold had been comprehensively removed, but the woman was already between him and it.

A vast octopus, stretching an impossible height from the floor, moved behind her, its black eyes gleaming, and around it circled the sharks and the smaller fish. She was smiling, possessive, absolute, still coming on, placid and inexorable.

That left only the sun deck.

Mandeville ran to it, crashing against the door and forcing the cheap lock in one stumbled fall of his body weight. One of the cats leaped at him, snagging its teeth into his leg, but its grip was weak and he managed to kick it off. The octopus came past the woman, spreading its arms in an effort to reach him but he ran, dodging past it and out onto the wooden apron of the deck.

He had time to wonder why, if they wanted to get out, the woman and her entourage didn't simply come out here, and then he was at the concrete wall with its pictures that moved as he saw them, writhing and trying to grasp at him, and then he was over the wall and was airborne.

In the moment before he hit the ground, Mandeville suddenly realised: art, true art, has no urge to escape to the outside, it wants instead to bring the outside in, to make itself the centre of a world that it defines.

The last thing he saw as he fell past the sun corridor's floor-length windows were the myriad images that the woman had left of herself across the inside of the glass, and he smiled.

Falling, colliding, escaping, these were human things and he was, at least, human and free to fall.

EVANGELINE WALTON

They That Have Wings

EVANGELINE WALTON (1907–96) WAS the pseudonym used by
Evangeline Wilna Ensley. Born to a Quaker family in Indianapolis,
Indiana, she suffered from chronic respiratory illness as a child.
Treated with silver nitrate tincture, her fair skin absorbed the
pigment and turned blue-grey, which continued to darken as she
aged.

She grew up reading the works of L. Frank Baum, Lord
Dunsany, Algernon Blackwood and James Stephens, and most of
her fiction was written between the 1920s and the early 1950s.

Inspired by the Welsh *Mabinogi*, her first novel, *The Virgin
and the Swine* was published in 1936, but it was not until it was
reissued as *The Island of the Mighty* in 1970, as part of the
Ballantine Adult Fantasy Series, that the subsequent three books
in the series – *The Children of Lyr*, *The Song of Rhiannon* and
Prince of Annwn – saw print. All four novels were collected in an
omnibus volume, *The Mabinogian Tetralogy*, in 2002.

Meanwhile, *Witch House* was published in 1945 as the initial
title in the "Library of Arkham House Novels of Fantasy and
Terror", and her other novels include *The Cross and the Sword*
and *The Sword is Forged*.

More recently, Centipede Press has published a new collection
of the author's work, *Above Ker-Is and Other Stories*, which
includes four previously unpublished tales, and an expanded

re-issue of her second novel, *Witch House*, which again contains bonus material.

During her lifetime, she was honoured with three Mythopoeic Fantasy Awards and two Locus Awards. She also received the World Fantasy Convention Award in 1985 and the World Fantasy Award for Life Achievement in 1989.

At the time of her death, Walton left behind a number of unpublished novels, poems and a verse play. The author's family has been working with Douglas A. Anderson in going through her papers, where they also discovered a handful of unpublished short stories. These include the tale that follows, which originally appeared in *The Magazine of Fantasy & Science Fiction*.

Although the author had one story published in *Weird Tales* ("At the End of the Corridor" in the May 1950 issue), it appears from a letter to her agent, dated 8 May that same year, that "The Unique Magazine" rejected "They That Have Wings" for being "too gory".

So, after more than six decades, it is my great pleasure to present this "lost" *Weird Tales* story of World War II by one of the genre's most meticulous practitioners . . .

TWENTY-NINTH MAY: BERT Madden, Ronnie Lingard and I are in flight through the White Mountains. What will happen to us, God knows; we have become lost from the others, and there is no hope of succour. Nobody will come to look for us unless it is the Germans; nobody can come to look for us. We have known, ever since the attempt to retake the Maleme airdrome failed, that Crete was lost.

We could go faster if it were not for Ronnie. He is British, a flier, who was left behind hospitalized when what remained of our wrecked air force (not over a dozen planes, I think) was ordered out of Crete. He is slight, fair-haired, a boy not yet out of his teens, I am sure, though he casually told us that he is twenty. To say that makes him feel more dignified; I know boys. He has a leg wound that causes him to limp, and Bert and I take turns supporting him. Bert tries to do more than his share; he is a huge man, tough and burly, a stockman from western

Queensland. But although I, John Ogilvy, was only a New Guinea schoolmaster before the war, scrawny and civilised and not used to using my muscles, I am as tough as he. As well able to help the lad.

If and while anybody can help him. There is still snow on the White Mountains. The winds cut like knives, and the barren rocks all about us rise to sharp points. Rocks that a man with two good legs can hardly climb. Not since yesterday have we seen any sign of human habitation, of other living beings. At first we did not mind; it was so good to get out of sight and sound of the Stukas, of the bombs and bullets that had been falling among us like a deadly, fiery hail. Little things that in a moment could change a man to a screaming, mutilated lump of flesh. Or leave no man at all; only a silent, bloody carcass.

But now we are beginning to be afraid. We must rest; we have stopped now; that is how, for the first time in days, I happen to be writing in this diary; it is easier to do that than to keep my hands still. But we cannot stay here; there is not an inch of dryness, of shelter, anywhere. Twice already Bert has helped Ronnie move. The boy does not want to; he wants nothing except to lie still. But if he does so for long at a time the warmth of his body (strange to think of warmth in our bodies!) melts the snow upon the rocks.

He is not strong, as Bert and I are. He will catch pneumonia if we stay here. And he must have food; none of us has eaten in more than forty-eight hours. Before too long we must all have food. A man can go only so long without—

A bird has just flown over us. Queer that the sight of a bird, the dark shadow of its wings upon the snow, should have the power to reduce three grown men to gibbering fear. But we all crouched and covered our faces, and Ronnie screamed; I dropped this book. Anything in the air above us still makes us think of a Stuka. And this was a very large, dark bird.

It has come back. It is circling low above us, as if curious. For a second, its dark, beady eyes met mine; more intelligent, more sinister, than I ever thought a bird's eyes could be. I cannot think what breed it is; I have never seen one like it, either in reality or in photographs. We cannot be frightened now; we know it is no plane; and yet something in the rustling of its wings, in that dark, moving shadow on the snow—

All of a sudden Bert turned over and fired at it, as it wheeled there in the air above us. I saw the revolver flash fire in his hand. The report, reverberating from rocky height to rocky height, was deafening. But the bird did not even seem frightened. It merely turned again, leisurely and lightly, in the air. Not hit; not disturbed.

Bert leaped to his feet, his face was convulsed with rage and fear. "Damn you!" he yelled. "We'll get you! – not you us!" He emptied his revolver into it, it seemed – I have never known a better shot than Bert.

Yet still the bird wheeled on, calm, graceful there, low in the sky. Not a feather fell.

Ronnie laughed. "If there's any eating done, it's going to do it, old man. Not us."

That is what we are afraid of, of course. Why our shot nerves did not quiet when we realised that there was no plane above us. The ancient danger, older than planes. The fate that, through the ages, has come upon unlucky travellers in deserts and upon men left dying upon battlefields. Rustling wings and tearing beaks.

I laughed, but it was not a good laugh. I said, "Shut up, Ronnie. It's not as bad as that, yet. Sit down, Bert."

Bert sat down. His tanned, leathery face looked queerly pale; a kind of yellowish, mottled grey. He licked his lips.

"I can't understand," he said. "I ought to 've hit that thing. I ought to have hit it several times over."

"It must be deaf," I said, frowning. "I never heard of a bird so tame it wouldn't run from gun-fire."

We were all silent a moment, digesting that. The unnatural thing, the thing that has bothered me from the beginning. Then Bert cursed.

"That – thing ain't no pet!" he said feelingly. "I'd hate to think who'd have it for a pet."

And somehow, at those last words, we all shuddered; I do not know why.

"It seems to be watching us," Ronnie said. "Look."

And we did. We are. The bird is staying near us. For the last quarter of an hour it has been flying back and forth, back and forth, between the two great, snow-rimed cliffs that tower above us. Sometimes it flies lower, sometimes higher, yet always I have the feeling that it is edging a little nearer to us, a little closer. I do not think it is healthy to watch it; its movements are like a queer kind of dance; they fascinate. And yet, somehow, I do not like to look away. To turn my back . . .

Soon the sun will be setting. We will not be able to see the creature so well then. To know exactly where it is.

There is already a rim of fire above the western cliffs. And as I noticed that, the bird's small, beady eyes seemed to catch mine again; jewel-bright, night-black, like tiny corridors of polished jet leading down, down, into unfathomable darkness.

Perhaps Bert saw them too, for he caught my arm. "Give me your gun, Johnny! I ain't got no more bullets. And the light'll soon be gone!"

But I shook my head. I said slowly, "What's the use?"

Ronnie spoke dreamily. His eyes have become fixed, staring at the bird. "I wouldn't try to hurt it. I think maybe it wants to help us. To lead us somewhere, like in the old stories."

Bert laughed raucously; I was silent. I know the stories Ronnie means, the fairy tales he must have listened to, not so long ago, at his mother's or his nurse's knee; the old formula of the Helpful Beast or Bird. But I have never believed in those stories; I don't now. And this imperturbable creature of darkness is not my idea of a helper.

But it is true that the pattern of its movements is changing. It flies farther and farther toward the north. And then, every time we hope that it is really leaving, it will stop and turn and hang in the air a moment. Then it will fly back toward us, swift and straight as an arrow, and halt, circling low, just above our heads. The last time that happened Bert cried out and ducked, putting his hands over his eyes.

Twilight: It has happened again. And worse this time. The creature hurtled itself upon us almost as a dive-bomber might. Its flapping wings, its sharp, bright beak, almost raked my face and Bert's. Its beady eyes gleamed red as they glared into ours; demanding, commanding. But it only circled gently above Ronnie's head. Tenderly.

It has flown off to the north again now. But it will be back. It does want us to follow it. And the light is going. Dare we risk a real attack, in the dark? We cannot stay here anyhow; not unless we want Ronnie to freeze. After all, can the bird lead us to a worse place than this may be if we stay?

5th June: I could laugh now, reading that last entry I made here. What queer tricks nerves can play on men who are starving and sick and unbalanced by the shock of events no man ever ought to see! No doubt there was a bird that had been deafened by the din of the Stukas, or by some natural cause. No doubt its failure to be startled by gunshots startled us and set our diseased imaginations off. Certainly it was blessed chance, no bird, that led us to the peace of this little house on the heights. Indeed, only Ronnie claims that he saw any bird during the last half of that terrible night-journey. Bert and I, sick, stumbling, holding him up as best we might, saw only low-hanging clouds about us; mists through which sometimes gleamed two tiny, luminous red points, like eyes.

But all troubles, real and imagined, seem far from us now. We need not fear that the Germans will ever find us, in this little place above the clouds. It is high enough to be a bird's nest, guarded by almost impassable slopes of rock and ice. And the two women here are themselves like birds; they have the same light swiftness of motion, the same high, sweet voices, the same bright, dark eyes.

Aretoúla, the younger, has also a face that might have been carved on some ancient Greek coin. Her grandmother has the same delicate profile, grown beaky now, so that it reminds one a little of a bird of prey. Just as the thinness of her brown, wrinkled old hands sometimes makes one think of claws. But forty years ago I imagine that her body moved and curved with the same singing grace as Aretoúla's.

They are very good to us. They are forever feeding us, continually bringing us tempting little trays because they knew that, at first, our shrunken stomachs could not hold much at a time. Forever apologising for the poor quality of what they have. They do not know how good their bread and honey and olives taste after the days of battle and flight and fear. When we try to tell them how good the old woman only shakes her head and says, almost fiercely, "There is no meat!" a hungry gleam in her black eyes.

It is natural, especially at her age, that she should crave, need meat. When I am a little better I will go out and set traps, as I used to do as a boy in New Guinea. We must give her meat; she has done a great deal for us.

Aretoúla never seems hungry. Aretoúla only holds out her little trays and smiles and says softly: "See the sweet honey, *kyrie*. The honey and the good bread and the strong olives. The *kyrios* must eat, eat all he can, and grow well and strong again. Well and fat and strong."

She has smiles enough for all of us; they bring out the dimples around her lovely mouth just as the sun brings out the unfolding petals of a flower. But the smiles in her eyes are warmest and deepest for Ronnie. Sometimes they make her dark eyes truly soft, take the hardness out of their brightness. I never realised, until this last week, that bright eyes are always hard.

But I am talking like the poet I always wanted to be. The poet very few poor school-teachers get to be. Aretoúla makes a poet of a man. I only hope she is not going to make a lovesick fool of Ronnie. It would be a great pity to repay old Kyra Stamata's hospitality with any kind of hurt. Too bad that the women speak so much English; I am the only one of us three who knows Greek. Perhaps young people do not need a common language.

They are very lonely up here. No neighbours ever seem to visit them; which, perhaps, it not too strange, considering at what an almost inaccessible height their little house is perched. Yet it seems a little queer that nobody ever comes.

Bert said so once, to the old woman; I would not have. And she looked down at her hands and said sadly:

"We are considered unlucky. My man died when we were both young, leaving me with but one child, a girl. And Aretoúla's mother, too, lost Aretoúla's father early. People are afraid to come, lest our ill-luck reach out to them."

A strange thought, that. Of ill-luck as a dark, cloaked presence brooding above the house and ready to stretch out long, invisible arms to clutch anybody who may enter. And how cruel, that such a superstition should isolate two women.

Bert and I were both awkwardly sympathetic. We told old Kyra Stamata that when the war was over she ought to take Aretoúla and go down to some town or village. Where both of them could live nearer other women; where Aretoúla could meet young men.

But she shook her head. "No. In this house I was born, and in this house I will die. As my father and mother died, and my four brothers. My four tall, strong brothers. And after them my husband and my daughter's husband."

Bert said: "That's hard on the girl. Never getting anywhere, never meeting any other young people."

The old woman smiled. A sudden broad smile, so deeply amused that it lit her dark beady eyes, the few yellow teeth still showing under her jutting, beak-like nose, with a red glow oddly like evil. Like a secret, gloating greed.

"If a young man is meant to come to Aretoúla, one will come."

6th June: I am afraid that Aretoúla thinks that young man has already come. And so does Ronnie. Tonight I heard them whispering together, out on the mountainside. Traces of snow still showed beneath their feet, but around them – so clear and fragrant that even a dried-up, prosaic codger like myself could catch it – was the breath of spring. Their arms were round each other, and his head was bent close to her dark one. I heard him saying:

"There must be a priest we can get to come up here, Aretoúla. My friends can go for him, even if I can't, because of this blasted leg; I don't know why it doesn't mend."

It is true that Ronnie's leg is the only one of our ills that this rest here has not mended. He is lamer now than he was when we wandered on the hills. But no doubt the strength of desperation bore him up then.

Aretoúla's voice came, tender, velvety as a caressing hand: "Your leg will be well. All of you will be well. Wait, my Ronnie; only wait. With me."

"I can't wait much longer, Aretoúla. Not for you. The fellows'll be glad to go for a priest. And it'll be safe. Your Cretans are a good sort – they don't betray allies."

She laughed and nuzzled her cheek against his. "Foolish one, my golden love, you do not have to wait! Not for Aretoúla. She is yours. As much so as any priest could make her. We will not ask your comrades to risk their lives among these mountain passes that they do not know. Among, perhaps, the Germans."

He said stubbornly, very low: "I can't do that, Aretoúla. What would your granny think? I can't take advantage of you and her like that; not after all you've both done for us."

She threw back her head then, looked up into his face. Even from where I stood, around the corner of the hut, I could see how the stars shone, reflected in her eyes.

"Listen, my Ronnie. Granny will understand. I see that I must tell you of sad things – things that I had hoped need not yet trouble us. No priest would come here, if your comrades went for him. They hold this place accursed."

"But why – what—"

"You cannot understand, you who are English and so not superstitious. You do not know how the mother of my grandmother died raving mad, after she had tried to kill my grandmother, whom she called a *striga*, the murderess of her brothers. For three of them had died indeed, of some wasting sickness, and grief had turned the old woman's brain, so that she remembered a legend of our people – one that is old, very old, among us. Of how sometimes a girl-child is born with a craving for food that is not meant for man. And with other gifts also – a *striga*.

"Yes, she would have killed my grandmother, her own child. Her husband and her remaining son had all they could do, strong men though they were, to drag her off her only daughter. And that night she died, raving. And soon they themselves died also, of the same sickness that had taken the others. But the words of the poor mother's ravings lived, and my grandmother was left alone. None of the neighbours (for we had neighbours then, here on the mountain) would enter this house; none of her kin would take her in. All hated and feared her; all shunned her. Until my grandfather came climbing this way from another village in another valley – tall and strong and laughing, such a man as her brothers had been. And he laughed at the tales and loved her. All might have been different if he had lived – or if my father had lived. But now the curse has settled here, like a black bird brooding above this house forever. No man will ever marry Aretoúla."

"I will – some day." Ronnie's young face was exalted. "I'll take you away from here. To England, where people are civilised and don't do things like this to women. We'll always be together."

His arms tightened around her, and his head bent to hers. Her mouth plastered itself on his. She pressed herself against him, seemed almost to press herself into him, as if her body might melt, cloud-like, into his.

I came forward then. I said, "Good evening," casually, before I came round the corner, and Ronnie jumped back, out of her arms. I stayed with them until she went in, and later, after he was asleep, I got Bert out of the house and talked with him:

"We'll have to leave, Bert. Things are getting too thick here; the kids are falling in love."

I told him everything; everything, that is, except those fantastic nightmares of old Kyra Stamata's mother's. Bert, like many Queenslanders, has seen a good deal of the aborigines; and although he pretends to scoff at their dark beliefs and practices, they have left their mark upon his mind. I was afraid he might be too much impressed.

As it was, he was not enough impressed. He laughed.

"Me, I'd let the kids have their fun, Johnny. This is wartime; it may be all they'll ever have. But that's the schoolmaster of it, I suppose; you've got to have everything proper and respectable. And maybe it would be just as well to clear out. The longer we stay the less chance we'll have of getting picked up by our own boats; they may be all gone already."

I was so surprised that I was startled into an undiplomatic honesty. Undiplomatic since I wanted, suddenly and desperately, to get away.

"You know very well there's no chance of that, Bert. Any Englishmen that are left on this island are stranded – without a dog's chance of getting out, unless it's on a Cretan fishing-boat."

Bert looked sheepish. "I know. But, nice as they've been to us here and all, I'd just as soon get out, Johnny. The old lady makes me feel funny; I can't help it. She looks like somebody – or something – I've seen somewhere else. And how do she and the girl both come to know English so well when they've never either one been down off this mountain, and when there's not a book – not even a Greek bible – in the house?"

I said testily: "That's nonsense, Bert. You sound as if you suspected them of something. You know Aretoúla's father had been to America – was educated and progressive, quite different from the superstitious peasants around here. Kyra Stamata has talked about that. He must have taught her English."

He said doggedly: "Maybe. But it's queer she learned it so well – and remembered it so well all these years. And it's queer how she knew every last thing that was going on in the war up until we came here – and now she never hears a thing. Nobody ever comes up here; nobody's supposed to have come up here in a long time. How did she get her news then – and what made it stop? If it did stop. I'm not accusing her of anything; I just don't like the whole layout. It's too queer."

I laughed at him; there can be no doubt of these good women's friendliness. But some of his points were shrewd and well made. More shrewd than I would have expected of Bert. I am more glad than ever that I did not tell him the wild parts of that story of Aretoúla's. In the morning we will ask her grandmother about the mountain passes; about the best way to leave.

7th June: They were hurt and grieved, as I was afraid they would be; our two hostesses. They say that Ronnie's leg is not well enough for any journey – too much truth in that, I fear. They ask us if we are not happy with them – safe? If they have not done everything they can for us? They have; the trouble is that I am afraid that if we stay Aretoúla will do too much. Perhaps I can find a chance to talk with Kyra Stamata before the day is over; warn her of that danger. We cannot leave till tomorrow anyway; that is clear.

Midnight: I have had horrible dreams; I could almost think that I am going mad. Perhaps it was my failure to get a chance for private talk with Kyra Stamata that made me restless, unable to sleep soundly. Yet I was very sleepy when we went to bed; we all were, for, in honour of our last night, Kyra Stamata had brought out her last bottle of wine, one that she had brewed with her own hands, according to an ancient recipe of her family. A strange wine, tasting of honey. And of something else, something to which I cannot put a name.

It went to all our heads, and we were glad to go to bed early; I remember thinking hazily that that would be better, anyway, when we men were to start out early in the morning. But in the dead of night I woke; in a sudden sweat of fear, though I did not know what had roused me.

And then I heard it again: the creak of a door, the door of the inner room, where the women slept. They were coming out, into the room where we lay, and as I realised that my heart leapt with relief – and then stood still.

For Aretoúla was carrying a torch, and in her grandmother's hand was a knife. A long, thin knife. The torchlight shone brightly on the blade and redly in both women's eager eyes.

Aretoúla said softly: "All is well, Grandmother. They sleep."

The old woman did not answer at once. She came a little farther into the room, her head thrust forward, slightly bent. Like a bird's, when it hunts food. Her neck looked long; longer than a woman's neck should be; her jutting nose was like a beak, her beady eyes blazed with greed. And in that instant I knew her! Knew her for the bird that had flown above us in the mountains, the bird that had danced and menaced us as the sun set!

She came and stood looking down at us. And though I strained every muscle to rise, though my throat swelled with a shriek, I could not! I lay as if paralysed; even my lips were locked.

Aretoúla said nervously: "You will not touch the young one, Grandmother? You had Grandfather awhile before you ate out his vitals; Mother had Father awhile before you and she ate his out. I, too, want my time of love."

The old woman grunted. "You shall have it, little one; never fear. We will take the big one first; he should be the richest and most savoury. Give me the dish now."

Aretoúla bent and lifted it from its place beside the hearth. A pot that I had often seen them cook in; a fine old copper pot. It gleamed now as the torchlight touched it.

Kyra Stamata came a step nearer; stood squarely above us. Above Bert . . .

I tried to cry out; I tried, as hard as any man ever tried to move. But I might as well have tried to lift a stone wall as my own body.

I saw the knife flash, swift and bright as lightning, as the old woman's arm shot down. I saw it rip Bert's whole chest open; heard him groan and saw his body lift convulsively and then stiffen. There was another hollow groan. And then he lay very still, with a bright red ribbon seeming to stretch between his throat and chest.

But not for long. The old woman still bent over him. She thrust the knife back into the wound, turned it . . . thrust in her whole hand . . . I think I must have swooned.

After that I had only brief glimpses. I saw her straightening up again, with Bert's heart in her hand; Bert's heart, red and dripping. I heard her telling Aretoúla to stir the embers of the fire. Once after that, I was roused from another spell of unconsciousness by the smell of burning flesh.

But I will not tell what I saw after that. I cannot. Only one thing: once Ronnie stirred and moaned in his sleep, and Aretoúla came across to him and laid her hand gently on his face, her own face as tender as a young mother's.

"Sleep, my golden one," she murmured in her soft, singing voice. "Sleep."

And he did sleep. Thank God, he is still asleep.

Before they went back into the inner room they came and leaned over Bert again. They ran their slim hands gently over his body. And they laughed; their sweet, shrill, birdlike laughter.

"Beware! Beware, O squeezed sponge, of running water!"

And then again, I seemed to swoon. And when I awoke, a little while ago, Bert was breathing peacefully. There was no sign of any wound upon his chest. But I dare not try to sleep again; I dare not dream again. I will sit up for what is left of this night.

8th June: I will steal a few minutes to write in this journal before we leave. To write something sane and sensible in it, after last night's vagaries. It was a dream; all a horrible, fantastic dream.

And yet Bert seems a little pale this morning; not quite his hearty, vigorous self. He has not joined in the laughter and talk about the breakfast table as he usually does. And I wish Kyra Stamata were not polishing her copper pot. Polishing it carefully, as if it had been used. And I wonder why Aretoúla is so gay and laughing; I had thought she would be sad for Ronnie's going.

But they are calling me now; Bert himself is calling me. We must start.

Night again: We are back in Kyra Stamata's cottage. That is, two of us are back. Bert is dead.

We walked all morning, down the steep mountain roads that Kyra Stamata had told us of. And he complained of hunger, of a queer feeling of emptiness. "Like as if I was hollow inside," he said once. He, the strong man, was as ready as Ronnie to rest, when we sat down at noon.

We did not dare eat much; we did not know how long the food Kyra Stamata had given us might have to last. And Bert was ravenous. After he had eaten he rose and walked over toward a little mountain stream that foamed about a hundred yards from us.

"Water ain't my choice of a drink, but maybe it'll fill me up some. I don't know what ails me, anyway. The old lady's wine must have given me a funny kind of hangover."

He drank. I was beside him; I saw his throat move as the water went down. And then I heard him gasp; saw the red ribbon spring out again, across his chest. He fell forward, with his face in the torrent. Ronnie and I pulled him out together.

Ronnie thinks it must have been a haemorrhage; some lesion caused by all the fatigue of our wanderings, begun again too soon. There was a little blood on his mouth; Ronnie thinks it must have fallen from there to his chest, that shows no wound. But there was not much blood anywhere. I cannot help thinking of a sponge that has been squeezed . . .

And while we were dragging the body up the bank Ronnie's leg crumpled under him. I had to go back to the cottage and get the women to come and help me. With Ronnie; with Bert's body. So we are back here – back, I had almost said, where it all happened.

But there is no danger. There can be no danger. What I saw last night was a dream. Bert's illness and death were a coincidence. I will not insult, even in thought, women who have been kind to me; who have risked their lives to help me, as all Cretans risk their lives when they help Allied soldiers now. I will not let myself go mad.

I will not remember blood running down the sides of a copper pot . . .

*   *   *

15th Aug: I have let the weeks pass by as in a trance; I have not even written in this journal. I was ill for awhile, and Kyra Stamata nursed me as tenderly as if she had been my mother. And sometimes Ronnie and Aretoúla would tiptoe in, hand in hand, and smile down at me ... They are happy. Perhaps Bert was right, and one should never try to prevent happiness. It may indeed be all that these war-united youngsters will ever have.

I do not sleep well. Kyra Stamata has noticed it, and has brewed potions of herbs for me to drink. I try to throw them out when she is not looking, for somehow at night I am afraid to sleep. Full of fancies; not sane and reasonable as I am by day.

But she watches me too closely; it is becoming harder and harder to get chances to empty the stuff out. I suppose she thinks I do not like the taste of it, and has a womanly determination to help me against my will. So often I have to fall into sleep as a man might fall over a precipice; passing blindly, in blind terror, into oblivion.

16th Aug: Morning again, the good, bright morning, wholesome as fresh bread. It shows one how foolish are night terrors, the grisly shadows childhood leaves in every man's brain. Ronnie and Aretoúla are laughing outside the window; young wholesome laughter. Her laugh is as tender as any woman's could be, and yet it never loses that shrill sweet note that is a little wild; the note that sounds like a bird ...

There! He has caught her, and they are kissing. Their lips are too busy for laughter now. Too sweetly busy. Her arms are tight about his neck, with that hungry, enfolding tightness they seem to have at times. She loves him.

I do not know why I am afraid, even at night. For Bert knew nothing; he did not wake. And I will never see that happen to Ronnie. They will take me before they will take him, because Aretoúla still loves him. And when his turn does come he, too, will know nothing. We will not suffer; men die far worse deaths on the battlefield.

And yet—

I will tear this page out. It is lunacy, madness as great as Aretoúla's great-grandmother's.

*   *   *

17th Aug: Today Kyra Stamata said that she was feeling ill and sent Ronnie and me out onto the mountain to look for more of a certain herb she wanted to dose herself with. Aretoúla, she said, must stay with her. Ronnie and I wandered far afield; we were never able to find any herb to match the sample she had given us.

When we came back there seemed to be tension between the two women. Kyra Stamata looked well enough, but Aretoúla was white and her eyes look red, as if from weeping. All evening she has been very quiet. Ronnie is much concerned; he makes more fuss over a cut finger of Aretoúla's than he would if he broke his own arm. All trivial, no doubt; women's squabbles. The best of them will do it. And yet my nerves respond to any tension now, like race-horses to a cut of the whip. I can feel them tensing; feel fear shooting through them, as electricity shoots through wires.

One good thing: when Kyra Stamata gave me my nightly sleeping-draught, she forgot to look at me. She was staring at Aretoúla, who was staring at Ronnie, and I poured the drug quietly into the embers of the fire.

Kyra Stamata remembered me after a moment. She looked at me and smiled. "An empty cup already? Good. You will sleep well, soldier. You must sleep very well and grow strong again; very strong. We have all been worrying about you long enough, soldier. Long enough."

18th Aug: This may be the last entry I shall ever make in this diary; I think that probably it will be.

I did not sleep last night. I closed my eyes and lay still; I breathed regularly, as I have trained myself to do, when Kyra Stamata bent above me. I could see her through my eyelashes as a shadow, as a black vulture's shadow, when she bent . . .

But then perhaps I did fall asleep. For the next thing I knew I heard Aretoúla's voice:

"See, I have the knife, Grandmother. Let us eat; let us eat and drink tonight."

My eyes opened; saw the flash of the knife in her hand. And shut again; faintness took me. Once more I could not move.

Then I heard the old woman laugh; shrill, cackling laughter.

"As you will, granddaughter. As you will."

I felt the cold chill of steel as Aretoúla set it, ever so gently, against my throat.

"Surely he will be enough for this time, Grandmother. Let us eat of him, let us eat and drink of him tonight. Let me show you how well I can cut his throat. I have never killed before; I have fed – yes, feasted – but I have never killed."

Kyra Stamata laughed again, more loudly; harsh shrill laughter like the screech of a bird.

"You think that will show me your strength, girl? You think I will feed on that weakling, who cannot grow strong again, no matter how well I nurse him? No! He dies only that we may be rid of him. It is your lover that we will feed on, child. Tonight, or tomorrow night, as you choose."

There was silence a moment. Then Aretoúla said eagerly: "He is not so strong, either. He has been hurt; and he is slight – as slightly built as this one." She did not move the knife from my throat.

"But young and healthy, girl; healthy enough to please you. You have made him happy, you have made him strong. And we have kept him long enough; I am hungry."

Aretoúla did not answer at once. For a second the knife pressed closer against my throat. Then she lowered it. Slowly, I could tell; reluctantly. Her grandmother's derisive cackle came again.

"What! Have you lost your taste for your first kill, girl? Will you let him live?"

Aretoúla said sullenly: "You have promised me one more night. And if he should see this man dead tomorrow my Ronnie would grieve. He would not think only of me. Tomorrow night, before the dawn comes, I will kill him; I will kill them both, if you wish it. But not tonight."

She went away then. Back to the inner room that she shares with Ronnie now. Kyra Stamata fell asleep again; I heard her deep, regular breathing; I thought of creeping toward her quietly, there where she lay curled on her pallet by the hearth. Of putting my hands about her skinny old throat.

What a pity that her father and brother did not let her mother kill her – put out of the world the monstrosity she had brought into it! But they saved her – saved her to be their own destroyer, and now ours! No doubt they thought, poor fools, that they were protecting innocence; no doubt she was young and lovely then, like Aretoúla.

Like Aretoúla!

Twice I did creep toward the hag. But each time she woke and stirred; each time I dropped back quickly. Her senses have indeed the sharpness of a bird's.

Through the rest of the night she lay in peaceful sleep, and I lay thinking. Thinking and fearing, hating and shuddering, and trying to plan.

And at last, toward dawn, the idea came. Like white light.

It may not work. I think it very unlikely that it will work. But it may win us death in the open.

At dawn I rose and walked out of the house. I walked on and on. Up the mountain; to its crest and over.

From this high rock where I am writing I can look down upon the little ledge where the hut stands; that vulture's nest that we all thought was salvation, paradise. It lies there black under the red morning light; still in shadow. Shadow less black than what it holds.

If Ronnie does not follow me I will go back tonight. I will watch and try to surprise them; I will do whatever man may do. But Ronnie will follow me. He will be worried and come in search of me. And then, with my two sound legs, it ought not to be hard for me to keep ahead of him. With luck – incredible luck! – I may lead him on such a chase that we will fall into the Germans' hands. A prison camp would seem like heaven now.

But will he follow me so far? Or will he turn back – to Aretoúla? He would only think me mad if I tried to tell him what I know.

He is coming. I see him clearly, down there in the morning sun. Climbing the mountain, shading his eyes with his hand as he looks about him. For me . . .

5 p.m.: I am very tired. All day I have played this ghastly game of hide-and-seek with Ronnie, here in the mountains. Without food, without any more rest than I knew we had to take. For if Ronnie's leg crumples under him again we are done. This game in which our lives are the stakes will be over.

He must think me mad indeed, the boy. Deranged, after our hardships and my long, low fever; by the shock of Bert's death. But he keeps after me with a blind, sweet stubbornness; he will not desert a comrade.

He is resting now, on a ledge some three hundred feet below me. He has not the strength, I think, to climb up to this rock where he must know that I am hiding; I moved once and let him see me. I wish, desperately, that I could see some house, some sign of man. But there is nothing. The peaks press close about us, like enemies; dark and implacable now in this failing light. Great masses of spiky, barren rock at best indifferent, alien to man.

What will happen when night falls? But it was not night before, when—

God, I dare not think of that! If only we can stay alone, in the darkness and among the rocks, meet no dangers but those that nature planned for these terrible, desolate heights!

The sun is setting. The clouds above the peaks are as red as fire, as red as blood. The sky itself gleams like a vast sheet of white light. No speck of darkness on it anywhere.

No, no! There are two specks, far to the north. Two black specks, blotting the shining red-and-whiteness of the heavens. They are coming closer, growing larger – and my heart is tightening into a knot of terror in my breast!

Birds!

Later: It is over. It all happened very quickly after that. They came and flew low and circled over Ronnie's head. I was scrambling down toward him as they came. I do not know what I thought I could even try to do; I knew he would believe nothing that I said.

I was in time to see his face as they circled above him. To see its first puzzled look fade and turn into a smile. A very gentle, very boyish and trusting smile.

"Two of you this time, you little beggars! What is it? Do you want me to go back – to her?"

For a little while he lay watching their weird weaving, the pattern that their black wings seemed to be making in the air above him. And then slowly, his eyes still fixed upon them, he rose – like a man entranced, not moving by his own volition.

He turned back – back the way we had come.

I showed myself then. I sprang up and called to him – loudly, desperately, in anguish.

"Ronnie! Ronnie!"

He hesitated. He turned again, and looked at me, and in his eyes there was a strange struggle – bewilderment and friendliness and recognition, all fighting with a strange charm that moved him as if he had been an automaton, no longer in control of his own limbs.

I called him again: "Ronnie – Ronnie!"

He took an uncertain step toward me; then another and another. He said, "Johnny – old John!"

And then the birds swooped. With a terrible, shrill cry of rage one of them leapt at me, her long bright beak aiming at my eyes. I saw hers as she came, and knew them, for all their red fierceness – the eyes of Aretoúla!

Then my hands were over my face, and I could feel her savage beak tearing them, biting through muscle and flesh and bone. Could feel her claws slashing at my chest like knives, while her great wings beat my shoulders and head.

I heard Ronnie give a cry of horror – and then another cry, a long-drawn, horrible cry of pain. And knew that the other bird's swoop had taken him.

I forgot my own danger. I lowered one hand and looked.

She had him by the chest and throat. Her long claws held him by his shirt-front, and by the flesh beneath it, and her beak was in his throat. He was reeling, staggering, trying to fight her off, but that beak was sawing ever deeper . . .

And then I heard another shriek, the most terrible of all. The fiercest sound of rage and hate, surely, that ever came out of any throat, human or beast's or demon's.

The bird that had been attacking me had left me. Had launched herself through the air, a black, whirling missile, straight for the other's throat!

Her beak closed just beneath that other beak, which was set in Ronnie's throat; sank deep into the black feathers just below that savage, red-eyed little head. And the bird let go of Ronnie. He staggered back, blood streaming from his throat and chest, and fell.

I ran to him. I worked to staunch his wounds while the battle raged above us.

And not only above us. Over the ledge and over the heights above it they fought, sometimes breaking apart and staring at each other, red-eyed, and then springing back upon each other, with mad, savage cries. Sometimes they fought almost over our heads, so that bloody feathers fell on us and I covered Ronnie's face and my own eyes; and sometimes they flew so far away, a whirling, battling black ball of awful, self-destroying oneness, that we lost sight of them, and hoped that they were gone.

But always they came back. Always we heard those shrill, deadly cries again, saw the beating of those black, threshing wings.

They whirled in battle above the depths below the ledge, shrieking and biting, clawing and tearing, pounding each other with their wings.

And there one of them fell. Sank down slowly, softly, like a dropped ball of down, into the depths below.

The other staggered in the air, then turned and flew back toward us, its wide wings black against the shining heavens.

I crouched over Ronnie, shielding his head with my body, peeping through the fingers that I held before my own face.

Which had won – *which*?

The bird reached the ledge. Swung in the air six feet above us. I could see its head quite clearly against the darkness of the great, outspread wings. And the reddish-black little eyes were glazed and queerly glassy; no longer menacing. Its beak was red – red as the wounds that covered its body.

It looked down once, as if seeking something it could not find – Ronnie's face, that my body hid. And then its eyes closed and it fell.

But as it struck the earth it trembled and spread out as water spreads. It quivered and changed and grew in a strange, trans-forming convulsion. And then, where the dying sun had glistened in a bird's black feathers, it glistened on a woman's black hair. Aretoúla lay there, pale and torn and bloody, her mouth redder than the wounds that disfigured her lovely face.

With a great cry Ronnie tore himself away from me. He ran to her. And as he came she lifted slim, dripping fingers and tried to wipe the blood away from her mouth. She seemed ashamed.

When he dropped to his knees beside her she smiled at him, and once again her mouth was lovely and tender, a woman's mouth.

"I – loved you, Ronnie. I could not let her kill you – when the moment came. I was – more woman than *striga*."

He could only gasp, "Aretoúla – Aretoúla!" and hold her close. He could not understand.

I came to them, and she looked up at me. "Is – my mouth all right now, Johnny? Not – ugly? I would like him to remember me as – beautiful. As beautiful as – any of your English girls."

I knelt and wiped the last of her grandmother's blood from her mouth. Ronnie kissed her, sobbing. His grief-stricken eyes were dazed.

She said gently, explaining, "My grandmother would have killed you, Ronnie. She did kill Bert. And now I have killed her – for you. And I – am dying. But there is a village – yonder – beyond that peak – to the west." She tried to raise her hand, but could not. I had to raise it; with a great effort she pointed the shaking fingers.

"They will – hide you there. From the Germans. They are – clean. No *strigas* – there. And no – woman who will love you as much as – I—" And then the words stopped, and the breath rattled in her throat. She never spoke again.

She has been dead since moonrise. Ronnie and I have dug her grave. We will not go down into the abyss and try to find the other; the birds of prey, her kin, may clean her bones. We will rest here tonight, and in the morning we will go on. To the village. To another day.

THANA NIVEAU

White Roses, Bloody Silk

THANA NIVEAU LIVES IN the Victorian seaside town of Clevedon, where she shares her life with fellow writer John Llewellyn Probert in a Gothic library filled with arcane books and curiosities.

This is her second appearance in *The Mammoth Book of Best New Horror*. Other stories have appeared in *Magic: An Anthology of the Esoteric and Arcane*, *Terror Tales of the Cotswolds*, *The Seventh Black Book of Horror*, *The Eighth Black Book of Horror*, *The Ninth Black Book of Horror*, *Death Rattles*, *Delicate Toxins* and the charity anthology *Never Again*, in addition to the final issue of *Necrotic Tissue*.

She is currently working on a short story collection to be titled *From Hell to Eternity*.

"'White Roses, Bloody Silk' was written for the Hanns Heinz Ewers tribute anthology *Delicate Toxins*," explains the author. "A controversial figure, Ewers was fascinated by themes of obsession, transformation, decadence and blood.

"I enjoyed his weird fiction and really wanted to write something Gothic and decadent myself. I'm also a huge fan of the Italian *giallo* films of the 1970s and there's nothing more Gothic or decadent than those *Grand Guignol* sex-and-murder extravaganzas with their strange, evocative titles.

"A single image came to me – that of a girl clutching a bunch of roses in her bleeding hands. I didn't know how or why she had come to be in that situation, but I knew that it wasn't entirely unpleasant for her.

"I hit on the idea of writing her into a Victorian *giallo* and it all fell into place. *Black Static* reviewer Peter Tennant likened it to 'a P. G. Wodehouse story filtered through the lens of Hammer Horror'."

"AND WHO IS your German guest, Elizabeth dear," asked Harriet Dalrymple, narrowing her small piggish eyes at the hand-written list of names, "Wilhelm – Cross, is it?"

Frédérique Cheniere giggled from behind a cloud of face powder at the dressing table. "I believe they pronounce it Krauss," she offered in heavily accented French, "and I hear he is quite the *roué*!"

Cornelia Myler nodded in enthusiastic agreement. "Yes, a positive scoundrel! Why ever did you invite him?"

Their hostess, Lady Elizabeth Rossiter, continued to admire herself in the cheval mirror, turning this way and that as she kept her friends in suspense. At last she finished smoothing down the heavy brocade gown and turned to face them, her crinoline swinging round her like a bell. "He was once a doctor," she said, her birdlike features producing a malicious grin, "but a scandal with a certain lady patient led to his disgrace and exile."

"I hear she was the wife of an archduke," said Cornelia. "Or whatever they call it over there." She waved her hand dismissively. Gossip was always more important than facts.

Frédérique sniffed. "No, she was only the wife of a clergyman," she corrected, "but he was – how do you say? – ex-communicated. And later the church, it burned down."

"It did," Cornelia was quick to confirm, as though she'd seen it with her own eyes. She added in a scandalised whisper, "They say he's in league with the Devil."

Harriet gasped and fluttered a hand to the ample bosom straining beneath the confines of her apricot gown.

"I have it on good authority," said Lady Elizabeth, "that when his lodgings were searched they found the skulls of a dozen maidens in a velvet hatbox beside his bed."

"*Oui!* And hidden inside a big black piano, he kept . . . other parts."

Harriet's face was contorted with both horror and fascination. "Good heavens! And you have invited this man to dine with us? And stay the weekend? Elizabeth, are you quite mad?"

Frédérique laughed and Cornelia immediately joined in with her.

"Now, now," Elizabeth said, placing a hand on Harriet's meaty arm. "My dear, you'll work yourself into a state. Who knows what the truth of it is? But I find the prospect of his company rather stimulating. His manners are impeccable after all even if he is a bit . . . eccentric."

"You haven't paired him with my Jane for dinner, have you?" Harriet asked suddenly. "The child's only sixteen and—"

Elizabeth shook her head. "Of course not, dear. Nor you," she hastened to add, seeing Frédérique's worried expression. "I've put him between Aunt Florence and me. That grizzled old harridan is in no state to complain and she's lucky George and I don't keep her locked in her room all weekend. His little maid can amuse him if he finds Florence too tiresome."

Cornelia's head jerked up immediately, like an animal scenting prey. "Maid?"

"Oh! I quite forgot to tell you. He travels with a female valet. Never lets her out of his sight and he won't allow anyone else to serve him."

"Goodness me," Cornelia said archly. "Where does she sleep – on the floor at the foot of his bed?"

They all giggled at the thought and fancied themselves quite decadent.

Elizabeth dabbed her throat with scent and grinned at the others. "I've given him the room at the end of the east wing. It has an antechamber and Perkins was just able to fit a small bed in for the maid."

Frédérique's eyes glittered as she fingered the black velvet choker at her throat, her mischievous thoughts obvious to everyone.

"Well, perhaps they do things differently in Germany," Harriet conceded.

Cornelia grinned. "He might at least make some concession to decency by disguising her as a boy!"

There came a soft knock at the door and the ladies stifled their giggling as Elizabeth called out "Yes?"

A dull-eyed girl shuffled inside and stood staring sullenly at the floor.

Harriet swooped down on her at once. "Jane darling, I thought we agreed you looked best in the yellow silk! This green is far too sombre for you. I wonder you even brought it!"

"I don't feel very well," Jane moaned, clutching her stomach.

"You'll feel much better out of that dreary green," Harriet insisted. "Now come along and let's find you a nice summery frock."

The remaining three rolled their eyes as the garrulous woman dragged her daughter off down the corridor, prattling incessantly.

Wilhelm Krauss was a man of imposing physique and imperious countenance. His dark hair was combed back and his temples and sideboards were shot through with silver. His eyes were deep pools of black that seemed to reflect no light. He rose from his chair by the fire as three of the ladies entered the library with a rustle of skirts.

"What did I tell you, Krauss?" said Lord George Rossiter, clapping his companion on the shoulder with a hearty laugh. "I believe they call it 'fashionably late'."

"George!" Elizabeth scolded, affecting a debutante's pout that was dramatically at odds with her ageing features.

Captain Charles Myler and James Dalrymple glanced up from a game of chess in the corner. Myler aimed a polite smile at Cornelia and immediately returned his attention to the game while Dalrymple didn't seem particularly bothered by the absence of his own wife and daughter.

"Good evening, my lady," Krauss said with a sharp little bow to Elizabeth. "I want to thank you for your generosity this weekend. I am aware that my company is unwelcome in certain circles."

Elizabeth inclined her head graciously, ignoring his indiscretion despite the flutter it provoked in her friends. "You are indeed very welcome, Mr Krauss," she said, unable to avoid glancing at the maid who stood like a ghost behind him, her hands folded demurely.

Cornelia and Frédérique were sizing her up too. The girl was certainly fetching – a pretty, petite creature with delicate features and wide blue eyes. Her hair was pinned beneath a scrap of lace and she wore a white pinafore over a plain black uniform.

Elizabeth seated herself on the chintz-covered sofa opposite the fireplace and Krauss resumed his seat in the chair beside it. Cornelia and Frédérique arranged themselves on the sofa next to their friend. They each accepted glasses of sherry from the butler in turn.

"I do hope you are enjoying your visit to England," Elizabeth said.

"I find your countryside most invigorating," Krauss replied, his voice deep and resonant. "And you have a most impressive estate. Exquisitely furnished. However, I am not merely visiting."

The lady had just raised her glass to her lips. "Oh?"

"Yes, I intend to make my home here. There is nothing for me back in Germany."

The ladies exchanged glances, recalling their conversation upstairs.

"How delightful," Elizabeth said. "Then perhaps we shall be seeing more of you."

He smiled slyly. "Perhaps you shall." As he drained his sherry glass the maid took it from him and set it on the little mahogany table beside him. The butler was quick to follow with his tray, collecting the glass and hovering beside the maid until Krauss waved him away.

There followed an awkward silence, which grew until it was broken at last by a shrill barking voice. "That machine makes a frightful noise!"

The group turned to regard the elderly lady installed in an armchair by the bay window. She had looked up from her needlepoint and was staring about like someone who'd woken to find herself in strange and disagreeable surroundings.

"No one is using any machine, Aunt Florence," said Elizabeth, miming a long-suffering expression for Krauss' benefit.

George cupped a hand to his mouth and shouted across the room. "Sit tight, old thing! We'll have supper soon!"

The old lady blinked at the sewing needle in her shaky hand as though someone else must have put it there. Then she plucked at the pattern and set to work again, taking a full minute to complete one stitch.

Amused, Krauss watched her efforts for a moment and then turned back to his hostess. "These roses are enchanting," he said, gesturing to the display.

A large crystal vase sat atop a marble table in the centre of the window alcove, holding an extravagant spray of white roses.

Elizabeth beamed. "Why, thank you. They're called 'Purity'. I find them so much more appealing than those garish 'American Beauties' that are all the rage in London at the moment."

"Far more elegant," Frédérique agreed. "But ever so thorny!"

"Do you have roses in Germany?" Cornelia asked.

Frédérique shot her a withering look, as though Cornelia were a crass rival who had nonetheless managed to upstage her.

"Oh yes, we have magnificent flowers. Some brash and colourful, some rather more . . . delicate. Subdued." He turned in his chair just enough to meet the eyes of the maid. "Some requiring, shall we say, very special care."

Elizabeth frowned and glanced at her husband, whose bushy eyebrows had climbed to his hairline. For all their perceived decadence, they were really rather squeamish.

"But appearances can be deceiving," Krauss continued, his voice compelling and seductive. "You would be surprised. Some things are much hardier than they look." The maid blushed and looked down at the floor.

"I've never been to Germany," Elizabeth said, hurriedly changing the subject. "Where is it you are from . . . Mr Krauss?"

If he noticed her slight hesitation over how to address him, he didn't let on. "Hamburg," he said with pride. "It's a lovely and prosperous city in the north, on the River Elbe."

Frédérique made at once for the ornate globe that stood adjacent to the fireplace. "Will you show me where it is?" she said. "I am so hopeless at geography."

The other guests exchanged a knowing look. It was extremely unlikely that Frédérique didn't know where such a famous city was.

"Certainly, my dear," Krauss said. He took her pale hand in his and drew her finger down the length of the painted surface until it rested on Hamburg. "It's just . . . here."

She shuddered girlishly at his touch. "Ah yes, I see it."

"Has it recovered from the epidemic?" George asked suddenly.

Frédérique gave a little squeak of surprise and yanked her hand away as though the globe itself could contaminate her.

"Epidemic?" Cornelia spluttered.

The word was enough even to distract Myler and Dalrymple from their chess game. Elizabeth looked nervously from her husband to her guest.

But Krauss' polite expression did not waver. "Cholera," he said simply. "Two years ago there was an outbreak of the disease."

Captain Myler grunted. "Hmm. Saw plenty of that in India. Nasty bug." With that he picked up his remaining knight and advanced it two paces. "Check."

"Blast!" said Dalrymple.

"Were there very many deaths?" Cornelia asked, her eyes shining with unhealthy interest.

"Oh yes. More than eight thousand people died. They said the Devil had signed his name in Hamburg. Of course, it was mostly the lower classes who succumbed. 'Untouchables', I believe you say in English?"

Frédérique nodded awkwardly as she edged away from him and resumed her seat.

"We say common," Cornelia informed him, wrinkling her nose to emphasise her disgust at such creatures. "Peasants."

Elizabeth grimaced. "Yes, well, I'm not quite sure they deserved to die."

"Bah!" said George. "Bloody vagrants, the lot of 'em!" He lifted his glass as though to toast their demise.

"Disposable in any case," Krauss said offhandedly. "Anna, I seem to have mislaid my glass."

If the little maid was disturbed by the conversation she gave no sign. She scurried to retrieve the glass from the butler who, despite his obvious contempt for Krauss, clearly didn't appreciate being made obsolete. Anna refilled the glass with sherry and returned it to her master.

"Good idea," George said, nodding approval. "Perkins, make the rounds. Er, everyone except Krauss obviously. Incidentally, is it 'Mr' or 'Dr'?"

Elizabeth looked startled. "George!" It was shockingly poor etiquette not to know the correct form of address for one's guests and she quickly covered her embarrassment with a nervous laugh. "You must excuse my husband's directness," she said, "I'm afraid we . . ."

But Krauss raised a hand and offered her a forgiving smile. "It's quite all right. I would be very pleased if you would simply call me Wilhelm."

He had deftly avoided answering the question in everyone's mind (Just how "disgraced" was he?) and the offer of his Christian name imposed the same vulgar familiarity on everyone present. Frédérique in particular looked horrified by the suggestion.

"I suppose they do things differently in Germany," she said, resuming her seat on the sofa.

As if summoned by the echo of her earlier comment, Harriet Dalrymple appeared in the doorway, looking breathless and stricken. "I'm most dreadfully sorry, Elizabeth, but we must make our apologies. Our Jane has suddenly been taken ill."

"Oh dear! I hope it's nothing serious," Elizabeth said. She glanced nervously at Krauss, as though at the same time hopeful and afraid that he might volunteer his services. It was clear he did not have what one would term a "calling".

But Krauss made no offer of assistance. He merely expressed his disappointment at not being able to meet the young lady and wished her the best.

"That's very kind of you," said Harriet. "I'm sure the poor child will be fine, but I fear we must get her home."

James Dalrymple grumbled as he got reluctantly to his feet, glowering at the chess game he was losing. "Sorry, Myler. We'll have to finish this another time."

George and Elizabeth escorted their friends out while an embarrassed lull fell over the remaining guests. Only Krauss seemed unfazed by the events.

"Snick snick snick, all day!"

"No one's using the sewing machine, Aunt Florence," Elizabeth said with patronising exasperation as she returned. Her cheeks were flushed and several strands of hair had come loose from her elaborate bun. She downed her sherry and nodded eagerly at Perkins for a refill.

The old lady was shaking with rage. "Those wicked, wicked fingers!"

"Aunt Florence—"

"It's positively unbearable!" With that she flung her arm out to the side, pointing presumably towards the source of the noise only she could hear. Her hand collided with the crystal vase, knocking it to the floor with a great crash. She screamed and covered her face with her hands, one of which was bleeding.

"Oh, good heavens," Elizabeth cried. "Whatever next?" She leapt to her feet and dragged the old lady up from her chair. "Perhaps it's best if you had a little nap, Aunt Florence. You know the sound doesn't carry as far as your room."

"I'll get a cloth, madam," said Perkins, looking a little flustered himself.

"There was no need to throw it at me," the old lady complained, staring round the room in bewilderment, her wrinkled face smeared with blood.

"Come on, Aunt Florence. I'll have cook send you up some dinner."

Cornelia and Frédérique squirmed like schoolgirls stifling giggles while George and Captain Myler merely looked bored. From the hall they could hear Elizabeth shouting for the cook.

When Frédérique got control of herself she turned to Krauss. "Shall I read the cards for you, *monsieur*?"

The evening was fast becoming a social debacle and a palpable relief flooded the room at the prospect of a diversion.

"My dear lady, what a charming suggestion."

Frédérique placed a small table between herself and Krauss. She had just produced a deck of Tarot cards from a velvet pouch and begun to shuffle them when Elizabeth returned, looking even more dishevelled. She stared forlornly at Perkins, who was mopping up the spilt water and brushing the broken shards of crystal into a dustpan. He picked up one of the roses, intending to deposit it with the rest of the debris, but then dropped it with a sudden hiss of pain. A bead of blood welled from the tip of his finger and he grumbled as he wiped it on his cloth. He grabbed the rose again, this time by the petals, crushing the bloom.

"No," said Krauss firmly, startling the butler, who promptly dropped the flower. "I won't see beautiful things discarded so carelessly."

Elizabeth smiled weakly, as though at a great compliment. "You're quite right. Perhaps, Perkins, another vase . . ."

"Very good, madam," he said, his tone somewhat clipped. Clearly he didn't approve of his mistress's strange guest, but it wasn't his place to say anything.

But Krauss shook his head. "That won't be necessary. After all, that's what the suffering classes are for."

Perkins' eyes widened slightly at the comment, but no one else reacted.

"Anna, would you collect the roses for me?"

She obeyed without hesitation, carefully picking up each thorny stem with her right hand and gathering them loosely together with her left. When she had retrieved all twelve she stood before her master with a shy smile, holding the roses carefully in a bunch with both hands.

He favoured her with an indulgent smile, as though she were a well-trained pet. Then he placed his hands around hers and squeezed them together sharply. Anna uttered a little yelp of pain as he slowly took his hands away, leaving her clutching the thorny stems. Tears shimmered in her eyes, but although the thorns must have been driven into her palms in a dozen places, she made no move to unclench her fingers.

"There," he said, still smiling. "Now why don't you go and stand where the vase was? The roses did look lovely in front of the window. There. Isn't that a pretty sight."

The guests stared, shocked into silence, as blood began to seep from between the girl's fingers and run down the ends of the stems. Bright red droplets soon speckled her pinafore and Perkins spread his cloth on the floor at her feet. He turned away, ashen-faced. Anna stood silently, trembling and drawing quick shallow breaths as she held the torturous bouquet, for all the world like a statue come to life.

Krauss gazed at the spectacle for a few moments, then clapped his hands together, making everyone jump. "Now then. You were going to tell us the future, madame."

Frédérique blinked slowly, as though emerging from a trance. "Future? Oh. Oh, yes." She tore her gaze from the maid's plight and focused on the cards as she fumbled them between fingers suddenly grown clumsy. She shuffled the deck and dealt a row of cards face down, her eyes occasionally flicking back to Anna.

She turned over the first card. It depicted a woman, bound and blindfolded, standing helpless within a cage formed of eight swords that pierced the ground around her bare feet.

"That looks like rather an unhappy state of affairs," Krauss said genially. "For someone."

Frédérique pursed her lips and stared determinedly at the card while everyone else in the room glanced across at Anna, as though compelled by the image to look. "Yes," she said at last. "But perhaps it is not all bad. We must see what the other cards have to tell us."

She hurriedly turned up the next card and gave a little gasp. Nine swords hung menacingly over a figure waking from a nightmare. "The Lord of Cruelty," she whispered.

Krauss smiled. "Indeed? How very interesting."

The next card was even worse. The nightmare had come to fruition. A body lay on the ground beneath a black sky, pierced by ten swords.

Frédérique's hand hung trembling above the card while the others craned their necks to see the strange sequence of doom.

With a strained laugh Elizabeth said, "Freddie dear, are you quite sure you shuffled the cards properly?"

Frédérique bristled. "Of course! You saw me."

"Show us the next one," Cornelia said, entranced.

Frédérique took a deep breath and revealed the next card. The Tower. She stared at it in silence. Two figures were plunging to their deaths from a flaming tower that had been struck by lightning.

"Well, that can't be good," George said with a scowl.

"No," Frédérique whispered. "It is not good at all." She hesitated for a long time before turning over the final card. The Devil. Her eyes widened. Then she swept all the cards together with a violent movement and shoved them back inside the velvet pouch.

Cornelia plucked at Frédérique's sleeve like a child. "Are we in danger?" she asked.

Captain Myler snorted. "Poppycock!"

Frédérique shot him a poisonous look. "Do not mock the cards, *monsieur*," she warned.

Myler spread his hands. "Are there any swords in this room, madame? No. Nor are we in a tower. Why, there isn't even a storm raging outside. You're all a bunch of bloody fools if you believe in any of that rubbish." He tossed back the last of his sherry and made for the door. "I'm going out for some fresh air. If you will excuse me." With a curt little bow he made his exit.

"The cards, they are symbolic," Frédérique said petulantly. "Swords do not necessarily mean real swords."

From the window alcove Anna whimpered softly. Her pinafore was soaked with blood. Krauss went to her and stood regarding her for a moment. Then he gently unlaced her fingers from their cruel burden. She gasped with pain and relief as the roses fell one by one to the floor.

Krauss held her wrists and examined her hands, which had begun to bleed again. Then he positioned his glass beneath her left hand and squeezed her wrist. Several drops of blood splashed into his sherry. Anna closed her eyes in almost beatific surrender. Krauss swirled the liquid in his glass and sipped it, smiling as though tasting a particularly fine vintage.

For several moments no one moved. Then Cornelia pressed a hand to her mouth and ran from the room. They heard her shoes slapping the mosaic tiles of the hall and then for several seconds there was nothing. A piercing scream shattered the silence.

The ladies froze in horror and George ran after Cornelia. The screams ceased abruptly as he reached her, to be replaced by howling sobs.

Frédérique wrapped her arms around herself on the sofa and Elizabeth drifted uncertainly towards the door, glancing back and forth from her guests and then into the hall.

"My poor Charles! How could she? Why did she—?" Cornelia was demanding in a voice choked with tears.

George led her back into the room, looking bewildered. He guided the hysterical woman into a chair near the fire and beckoned his wife over.

Elizabeth hurried across to them and placed her hands on Cornelia's shoulders. "What happened, dear? Who's 'she'?"

"Her!" Cornelia shrieked, gesturing wildly towards the ceiling. "Your 'old harridan'! She killed my husband!"

Elizabeth shook her friend gently as she began to dissolve into sobs again. "What are you talking about? Aunt Florence? She's asleep upstairs. She couldn't have—"

But George was nodding his head solemnly.

"What?" Elizabeth snapped.

"She's right. The captain's dead. Cook too." He shuddered and put a hand across his eyes, recalling the sight. "Their eyes. There were – knitting needles . . ."

"Have you gone mad? Aunt Florence is—"

The sound of breaking glass drew everyone's attention to the doorway. The old lady stood there, clutching two fistfuls of vicious-looking sewing needles of every shape and size, some of them as long as meat skewers. She glanced at the china figurine she had knocked over and then turned her malevolent stare on the occupants of the room.

"He ought to have known better," she said, her voice as unsteady as her hands. "I can still count, you see. Eight, nine, ten!"

Frédérique gasped. "The swords," she whispered.

Perkins was edging slowly towards the old lady, apparently intent on catching her off guard and disarming her. George noticed and moved to distract her.

"Look here, Flo," he said. "Let me have those things. You'll do yourself an injury, old girl."

"I know what the numbers mean," Florence said icily, brandishing the needles at him. As she raised her arms they could see that she was only holding a few of the needles; the rest had been shoved through her palms like crucifixion nails.

Suddenly Perkins rushed her. But he wasn't quick enough. The old lady drove her hands against either side of his head as though crushing a mosquito in mid-air. Some of the needles remained in his face while others were simply forced through the backs of Florence's hands. Perkins shrieked with pain as he fell to the floor, clawing at the pincushion his face had become.

With unbelievable speed Florence went for the next nearest victim. George and Elizabeth had already dodged away but Cornelia was unable to get out of the chair in time. She screamed and flailed helplessly as the old lady fell on her and set about raking the metallic claws across her face and throat.

Frédérique saw her chance and fled. Perkins lay writhing and groaning in a spreading pool of blood as he tried to dig the needles out of his face. George and Elizabeth watched in horror for a few moments before running after Frédérique. Perkins got to his feet and stumbled after them, trailing blood in his wake.

The old lady soon grew bored with Cornelia, whose cries had grown weak and feeble before she finally lost consciousness. Her baleful gaze swept the room and fell for a moment on Krauss and Anna, who stood calmly by the window.

The remaining needles clicked together as the old lady moved her fingers in the air like skewered spiders. "Snick snick snick," she mumbled. Then she turned back to where the butler had been. Seeing he had escaped, she smiled like a child at play and crept after him. From the corridor came the sound of a struggle. There was a shout, then the sound of gurgling, moaning, then silence.

Alone at last, Krauss turned Anna to face him. A slow grin spread over her features and she placed her bloodstained hands on either side of his face.

"Apparently I'm the daughter of a clergyman," she said. "And you're in league with the Devil."

"Is that so?"

"I suspect the Dalrymples have already made his acquaintance."

Krauss nodded. "A few drops in the jug of water by their daughter's bed earlier this afternoon. If she isn't dead by morning she'll wish she was."

From somewhere outside, Frédérique began to scream.

"Let's go somewhere quieter," Krauss said.

He led Anna up the stairs and into the master bedroom. Once there, he undressed her slowly and laid her naked on the four-poster bed. She writhed in anticipation, her hands leaving streaks of blood on the white silk sheets. Krauss kissed her gored palms.

"Does it hurt?" he asked.

"Oh yes," she said, breathless. "But not nearly enough."

He withdrew a knife from his pocket. It gleamed like a smile in the candlelight. "Where shall we begin?" he asked.

She guided him to the soft skin of her abdomen and lifted her hips, pressing herself against the tip of his blade. "Here," she said. "Sign your name."

JOHN AJVIDE LINDQVIST

The Music of Bengt Karlsson, Murderer

Translated by Marlaine Delargy

JOHN AJVIDE LINDQVIST WAS born 1968 and grew up in Blackberg, a suburb of Stockholm. He is probably the only Swedish person who makes his living from writing horror.

A former stand-up comedian and expert at card tricks, Lindqvist's first novel, *Let the Right One In*, has sold over half-a-million copies in a country with nine million inhabitants. The book has been published in thirty countries and been made into two movies, one Swedish and the other American (under the title *Let Me In*).

The author's other novels include *Handling the Undead* and *Harbour*, both of which are in the process of being turned into films, and *Little Star*. A collection of his short fiction, *Let the Old Dreams Die* (which includes sequels to both *Let the Right One In* and *Handling the Undead*), was recently published in the UK by Quercus.

The following novella is Lindqvist's first story written specifically for an English-language market and, as he explains: "The idea for 'The Music of Bengt Karlsson, Murderer' came to me four years ago, when my son was ten years old and started taking piano lessons.

"The disjointed, unharmonic notes coming from his room gave me the thought, *What if he would accidentally hit on a series of notes that . . . summoned something?* I wrote down the idea and waited for that critical second idea that could turn it into a story. It never came by itself, so the original idea just lay slumbering in that special file on my computer.

"When asked for a contribution to an anthology, I opened the file, shook life into the notes-that-summon idea and examined it more closely. Originally I had a vague plan of some Cthulhuesque monster being attracted by the music, but that didn't work out. Then the idea of a father and son being alone and isolated clicked together with the image of *mylingar*, the ghosts of murdered children . . . and the rest was the usual sweat and tears to forge those images into a story.

"It might be the one story I have written that has scared me the most. It plays deeply on my own fears of losing all I love. Especially towards the end, I wrote on in a state of mild but constant horror.

"It was a relief when it was over."

I'M ASHAMED TO admit it, but I bribed my son to get him to start learning to play the piano.

The idea came to me one night when I heard him sitting plinking and plonking away on the toy synthesiser he'd been given for his birthday two years earlier. He'd actually taken a break from playing computer games – imagine that. So I went into his room and asked if he'd like piano lessons.

No, he would not. No way. I hinted that an increase in his pocket money might well be on the cards if he agreed. Eighty kronor a week instead of fifty. Robin must have realised how desperate I was, because he refused even to come and look at the community music school unless we were talking about doubling the amount. A hundred kronor a week.

I gave in. What else could I do? Something had to change. My son was sliding towards unreality, and if a piano lesson now and again could bring him back to the IRL-world to some extent, then fifty kronor a week was a cheap price to pay.

IRL. In real life. I don't know what the other world is called, but that was where Robin spent almost all of his waking hours when he wasn't in school. Online. Wearing a headset and with a control in his hands, he had surfed away to a coastline where I could no longer reach him.

Not too much of a problem, you might think. Completely normal, the youth of today, etc. Well yes. But he was only eleven years old. It just can't be healthy to sit there locked inside an electronic fantasy world for five, six, seven hours a day at that age. So I bribed him.

And what would an eleven-year-old do with the hundred kronor a week he had managed to extort from a father who was completely at a loss? What do you think? *Buy new games*, of course. But I couldn't work out what else to do. Anything that could divert him from slaying monsters and conversing with invisible friends felt like progress.

Now I know better. Now I wish I'd spent the money on a faster Internet connection, a cordless headset, a new computer, anything at all. Perhaps then the darkness wouldn't have got hold of me. I'll never know.

It started well. Robin turned out to have a natural inclination for playing the piano, and after spending a few weeks playing "Frère Jacques" and "Mary Had a Little Lamb" with one finger, he had grasped the basic principles of the notes and was able to play his first chord. His achievement was all the more praiseworthy because there was no help to be had from his father.

I am completely useless when it comes to music. I've never sung, nor played any instrument. Robin must have inherited that gene from his mother, and she should have been the one sitting beside him on the piano stool. But one of the few things we have left of her is in fact her piano. Perhaps that was why I insisted on Robin playing that particular instrument. To maintain some form of . . . contact.

When Robin started piano lessons it was almost two years to the day since Annelie got in the car and never came back. An icy road, a bus coming from the opposite direction. Only a month later they erected a central barrier separating the two carriage-ways. About bloody time. I came to hate that barrier, its wire structure like a wound across my field of vision every time I drove past the spot. Because it hadn't been there *then*.

Six months after Annelie's death, we moved. There were too many rooms in the old house. Rooms meant for more children, for Annelie's loom. Rooms just standing there like empty memorials to a life that might have been. Rooms where I could get trapped, sitting there hour after hour. And on top of all that: rooms which together made up a house that was far too big and far too expensive to run on one income.

I decided to try to come to terms with all the dreams that had died, and got a job 300 kilometres away in Norrtälje. We moved from the house in Linköping to an eighty-square-metre wind-blown shack in the forest. The house was five kilometres from the town, where I didn't know a soul. The property was surrounded by coniferous forest on three sides, and in the winter you hardly ever caught a glimpse of the sun.

But it was cheap. Extremely cheap.

I carried out the move in a state of agitation. After six months, during which my grief had taken on a physical form and squeezed my throat at night, tangled me up in the sheets and thrown me out of bed, I saw the chance to breathe in at least a little light. I would start afresh in a new place. For Robin's sake, if nothing else. It wasn't good for him, living with a father whose only companion in bed was death, and who never slept for longer than an hour at a time.

So I cleared the place out. Anything we didn't need for our new life on the edge of the forest went into a skip. Annelie's clothes, her hand-woven rugs. Piece after piece of furniture that belonged to a life for two, and carried its own memories. Out. I smashed up the loom with an axe and took it out in bits.

The night after the skip had been taken away, I slept well for the first time in six months, only to wake up in absolute terror.

What had I done?

In my feverish enthusiasm I had thrown away not only things that Robin and I could have made use of (but I just couldn't keep the kitchen table where she still sat with her cup of coffee, or the lamp that still illuminated her face, casting dead shadows), but also things that I would have liked to keep. The cushion she used to hug to her stomach. Her hair slides, with a few strands of hair still attached. The odd talisman. But everything had been crushed to bits at some rubbish dump.

The only thing that remained was the piano. The lads who came to pick up the skip had refused to touch it, and I couldn't manage to drag it out on my own. So it stayed where it was, with her fingerprints still lingering on the keys.

That morning . . . oh, that morning. If it hadn't been for the piano I might have lost my mind completely, and Robin would have ended up calling the emergency services instead of being driven to school to say goodbye to his classmates. It's a paradox, but that's just how it was: that piano kept me from sinking.

And so it came with us to our new home, and the only place we could find enough space was in Robin's bedroom, and that's how it came about that Robin started to play the piano, and after six weeks was able to try out his first hesitant chord.

I can't say he practised much, but enough to get by. He liked his piano teacher, a guy who was a few years younger than me but had already settled for a cardigan and Birkenstocks. Robin wanted to please his teacher, so he did his exercises, which meant at least an hour or two away from the games.

Since I had nothing to offer in musical terms, Robin didn't want me in the room when he was practising. Instead I would sit at the kitchen table reading the paper, listening as his plinking became more assured each time he went through "Twinkle, Twinkle Little Star".

Then the roars and explosions of *Halo* or *Gears of War* took over again, and I would move into the living room and the TV, pleased with how things had turned out in spite of everything.

If I remember rightly it happened in the eighth week. I had just driven Robin home from his piano lesson and settled down at the kitchen table with a cup of coffee and the newspaper, while he started practising in his room.

Since I had got used to the sound, I was able to concentrate on my reading without being distracted. But after a while I began to feel uneasy, for some reason. I looked up from the paper and listened.

Robin was playing the piano. But what was he playing?

I listened more carefully and tried to pick out a melody, something I recognised. From time to time I heard a sequence of notes which at a push could be linked to an existing tune, only to fall apart again. I assumed Robin was just messing around on the keyboard, and I should have been pleased that he'd reached this point. If it hadn't been for that strange sense of unease.

The only way I can explain it is to say that I thought I recognised the notes, in spite of the fact that I had no idea what it was, and in spite of the fact that it didn't sound like a melody. It was like knowing that you know something, but at the same time being incapable of expressing it. That feeling. That sense of unease.

I gritted my teeth, put my hands over my ears and tried to concentrate on the newspaper. I mean, I knew I ought to welcome this new development, and it would be completely wrong to go and ask Robin to stop. So I tried to concentrate on an article about the expansion of wind power, but failed to read a single word. The only thing that went into my head was the faint sound of those notes vibrating through the palms of my hands.

I was on the point of getting up and going to knock on Robin's door after all when there was a short pause, followed by a halting version of "Jingle Bells". I let out a long breath and returned to my reading.

That night I had a horrible dream.

I was in a forest, a dense coniferous forest. Only a glimmer of moonlight penetrated down among the dark tree trunks. I could hear singing coming from somewhere, and I stood there motionless as a weight dragged me towards the ground. When I looked down I could just make out a crowbar. A heavy iron crowbar, which I was holding in my hands. The singing turned into a scream, and I woke up with the taste of rust in my mouth.

Even though it was the end of November, we still hadn't had any snow. Robin was practising for the Christmas concert – songs about happy little snowflakes and sleigh rides – while the temperature refused to drop below zero. Dark mornings with the smell of rotting leaves in the damp air, long evenings with the pine trees around the house swaying and creaking in the strong winds.

One evening I was sitting at the table in the living room with my MacBook, trying to write a job application. I was in charge of the greengrocery department at the ICA hypermarket, but for a long time I had dreamed of being in charge of a smaller shop. Such a position had just come up. The work itself would be more varied, plus my journey would be five kilometres shorter each day.

So I polished up my set phrases and tried to present myself in as responsible and creative a light as possible, while the wind howled in the television aerial and Robin began to play the piano.

My fingers stopped, hovering over the keys. It was those notes again. Despite the wind which was making the windows creak and the wooden joints whimper, I could hear the notes as clearly as if the piano had been in the same room.

Dum, di-dum, dum . . .

I couldn't remember whether the notes were exactly the same as the last time, but I always knew exactly which note would come next, even though there was nothing recognisable or logical about the melody. My fingers extended and moved in time with the music, as my thoughts drifted off into space.

I was woken by the sound I made closing the computer. The clock showed that half-an-hour had passed, half-an-hour of which I had no memory whatsoever.

Robin had stopped playing the piano, and from his room I could hear the low murmur of conversation as he spoke to some friend on Skype or Live. As usual I wondered what they actually talked about, given that they had no real lives, if you'll pardon the expression.

I sat down at the kitchen table with a cup of coffee and stared out at the swaying trees; I could vaguely make out the shapes in the glow of the outside light. No real lives. But then again, what would people say about my own life?

My empire during the day was a space measuring some two hundred square metres, where my role was to satisfy people's need for fruit and vegetables in a way that pleased the eye. No empty shelves, fresh goods on display, arranging the trays in

combinations that were dictated by head office, teaching assistants the correct way to handle mushrooms.

On one occasion when we were running a promotion I had
improvised slightly and placed a battery-driven monkey among
the bananas. Naturally it had frightened a child so much that the
kid burst into tears, and I had received a reprimand from up
above, instructing me to stick to the manual issued by head
office. It's like working in an East European dictatorship, but
with brighter colours.

I was sitting at the kitchen table thinking about all this when
the fir trees and pine trees suddenly disappeared. All the tiny
electronic sounds of equipment on standby were gone, and the
house was completely silent.

A power cut. I sat for a while in the darkness, listening to the
silence. As I was just about to get up and find some candles and
oil lamps, I heard something that made me stop dead.

The electricity was off and nothing was working. So how
come Robin was still talking away in his bedroom? I turned my
head towards the sound of his voice and tried to listen more
closely. What I heard made me shudder. Of course it was only a
phenomenon created by the movement of the wind through and
around the house, but I really thought I could hear one or more
voices in addition to Robin's.

It's hardly a father's job to come up with imaginary friends for
his son, but I still couldn't help sitting with my head tilted to one
side, trying to make out what those voices were saying. Faint,
almost inaudible utterances, and then Robin's replies, which I
couldn't make out either. I chewed my nails. Robin wasn't in the
habit of talking to himself, as far as I knew. Perhaps he'd nodded
off, and was talking in his sleep?

I groped my way over to the side of the room to get out the
torch. Just as I pulled open the drawer the power came back on,
and I let out a little scream as all the everyday objects jumped out
of the darkness. The voices in Robin's room fell silent, and the
fridge shuddered as it started up again.

When I knocked on Robin's door it was a couple of seconds
before I heard "Mmm?" from inside. I looked in and saw him
sitting on the piano stool, his body turned away from the
instrument.

"Hi," I said.

I was expecting the usual expression of listless amazement at the fact that I was disturbing him yet again, but the look he gave me was that of someone trying to place a face which is vaguely familiar. He said: "Hi?" as if he were speaking to a stranger.

"There was a power cut," I said, unable to help myself from glancing around his room to see if I could spot the people who had been talking. The scruffy, peeling wallpaper I hadn't had the time or energy to change, the vinyl flooring with its gloomy seventies pattern.

"Yes," said Robin. "I noticed."

I nodded, my eyes still flicking from the bed to the desk, the wardrobe. The wardrobe.

"Were you talking to somebody just now?"

Robin shrugged his shoulders. "Yeah, what about it? On Skype."

"But . . . when we had the power cut."

"When we had the power cut?"

I could hear how stupid it sounded. But I had heard *something*. My gaze was drawn to the wardrobe. It was a basic, recently purchased IKEA wardrobe in white laminate, but I thought there were an unusual number of grubby marks around the doorknob.

"So you weren't talking to anybody then?"

"No."

Before I could stop myself I had taken three strides into the room and pulled open the wardrobe door. Robin's clothes had been shoved carelessly into the wire baskets, with odd tops and shirts that he never wore arranged on hangers. Apart from that, the wardrobe was empty.

"What are you doing?" he asked.

"Just checking that . . . you've got clean T-shirts and stuff."

I couldn't come up with anything better, even though I'd folded and put away the clean laundry that very afternoon. As I pretended to check the stock of underwear I felt a cold draught. The window was slightly ajar, with both catches open.

"Why is the window open?"

Robin rolled his eyes. "Because I forgot to close it, maybe?"

"But why did you open it? It's really windy out there."

Robin was now back to himself, and gave me the look that means: *Have you got any more amazingly interesting questions?* Even I didn't understand what I was getting at, so I closed the window, flicked the catches down and left the room. As I was closing the door I saw Robin start up the computer, and a few minutes later I could hear the one-sided mumbling as he communicated via Skype. I placed a pan on the hob to make our bedtime hot chocolate.

It was a bad habit I couldn't bring myself to give up, that hot chocolate. Because Robin spent so much time sitting still it had begun to show on his body; he had a little belly protruding above the waistband of his trousers. But I still made hot chocolate every night, and we had three pastries each along with it.

Because that's what we used to do when he was little. Ever since he was four years old it had been a little ritual every night: the three of us would gather around the kitchen table before it was time for Robin to go to bed, and we would drink hot chocolate and chat.

I couldn't bring myself to let go, even though there were only two cups on the table and we frequently ended up sitting in mutual silence. At least we were sitting there. When Annelie was alive we used to have a lit candle in the middle of the table, but I decided to skip that particular detail after trying it once following her death. It had felt like keeping vigil beside a corpse.

When the chocolate was ready I placed six pastries in the microwave and shouted for Robin. We munched our way through the pastries and drank our chocolate without saying anything while the wind continued to squeeze the house and nudge its way in through the cracks. I was picking up bits of sugar by pressing my finger down on them when Robin suddenly said: "Did you know a murderer used to live here?"

I stopped with my finger halfway to my mouth. "What are you talking about? A murderer?"

"Yes. His bed used to be where mine is now."

"Who is this murderer, and who's he supposed to have murdered?"

"Children. He murdered children. And his bed used to be where mine is now."

"Where did you get this from?"

Robin finished off his chocolate and an impotent wave of tenderness swept through me as I noticed that he had a chocolate moustache. When I pointed to it he rubbed it off and said: "I heard it."

"Who from?"

Robin gave his trademark shrug and got up from the table, then went and placed his cup in the sink.

"Hang on," I said. "Where are you going with all this?"

"Nowhere. That's just the way it is."

"I don't understand . . . do you want to move your bed or something?"

Robin considered this for a moment with a frown. Then he said: "No, it's fine. He's dead," at which point he left me alone with my empty cup and the wind. I sat there for a long time staring at the streaks of chocolate in the bottom of the cup, as if there were something to be interpreted from the pattern they formed.

He murdered children. His bed used to be where mine is now.

The television aerial began to sing, as it sometimes does when the wind is coming from a certain direction. It sounded as if the house itself was moaning or crying out for help.

I found it difficult to sleep that night. The aerial's lament combined with Robin's strange assertion kept me awake, and I lay tossing and turning in my narrow bed.

The double bed from the years with Annelie had been the first thing I dragged outside for disposal when I was getting ready to move. Night after night I had lain awake in that bed, tormented by the phantom pains of grief just below my collarbone where she used to rest her head when we settled down to go to sleep.

The new single bed went some way towards helping me cope with her searing absence, but I still sometimes reached out to touch her when I was half-asleep, only to find myself fumbling in the empty space beyond the edge of the bed.

"Annelie," I whispered. "What shall I do?"

No reply. Outside the bedroom window sleet had begun to fall; the wind was driving it against the pane, and it sounded like little wet feet scrabbling across the glass. I crawled out of bed and pulled on my dressing gown with the idea of sitting down at the computer and idly surfing the net until I felt tired enough to sleep.

When I opened the screen I was confronted by the document I had left half-finished in the afternoon. I read through the account of my responsibilities in the greengrocery department, my experience in negotiating with suppliers and with quality control, my social skills and—

What the hell?

I had no recollection whatsoever of writing the final section, and it sat badly with the rest of the text, to say the least. I read the whole passage once again.

> During my three years in charge of the fruit and vegetable section my areas of responsibility have included among other things the dead speak through the notes, but how can a person bear it?

There was a cold draught blowing through the house and I shivered as I sat there in my thin dressing gown, staring at the words I had written. *The dead speak through the notes.* I understood which notes it was referring to, of course, but where had I got such an idea?

I'm losing the plot. Soon I'll be singing along with the TV aerial.

I felt a strong desire to smash the computer to pieces, but I pulled myself together and deleted the whole passage instead, then settled down to rewrite it.

The next morning, the previous afternoon and evening felt like a bad dream. The wind had abated, and the sun was peeping through gaps in the cloud cover. When I drove Robin to school he allowed himself a big hug before he got out of the car. On the way to work I switched the radio on and was rewarded with "Viva la Vida" by Coldplay.

I drummed along with the beat on the steering wheel and managed to convince myself that it was loneliness, grief and my anxiety about Robin that made it feel as if reality was slipping through my fingers. That I just needed to pull myself together.

Life *could* work if I could just manage to slough off the old skin and accept things as they were. From now on I would make it work.

I spent the morning inspecting the fruit counters and making some adjustments to Thursday's order, as well as putting up posters announcing this week's promotion: fifty kronor to fill a plastic bucket with your choice of fruit, and you get to keep the bucket into the bargain.

Kalle Granqvist from the deli counter took his lunch break at the same time as me, and we sat in the staff room talking about this and that. Kalle is a permanent fixture at the store; he's been there since it opened in 1989, and is due to retire next year. Since he's also something of a local historian I took the opportunity to tackle the issue that was niggling away at me.

Over coffee I asked: "Apropos of nothing, do you have any idea who used to live in our house? Before, I mean."

Kalle stroked his short grey beard and said: "Benke Karlsson."

"Benke Karlsson?"

"Yes."

He said the name in the way you might say "Olof Palme" or "Jussi Björling". A person everybody is expected to know, with no further explanation needed. Kalle assumed that everyone was as well up on the recent history and characters of the area as he was.

"Should I have heard of Benke Karlsson?" I asked, relieved at the everyday sound of the name.

"I don't know," said Kalle. "I mean, it's a while since he was up to his tricks."

"Up to his tricks? What does that mean, *up to his tricks*?"

Kalle grinned. "Why are you looking so worried? He was a musician. He used to play at parties and such like, until . . ." Kalle jerked his head a few times, which could have meant just about anything.

"Until what?"

"Oh, you don't want to go poking into all that."

"What happened?"

"Well, his wife died. And he took it badly. After a few years he killed himself. That's all it was."

Kalle gathered up his dishes, rinsed them and placed them in the dishwasher. I knew I shouldn't ask, that it was probably better not to know, but I couldn't help myself: "How did he kill himself? And where?"

Kalle sighed and looked at me with a somewhat sorrowful expression. He seemed to be searching for a more sympathetic way of putting it, but the only thing he could come up with was: "He hanged himself. At home."

"In the house where we live now?"

Kalle scratched his beard. "Yes. I assume that's why you got it so cheap. Shall we go?"

I didn't believe in ghost stories, which was just as well, I thought as I tidied up after lunch. But still I felt a tinge of unease and my hands were shaking slightly as I drank a glass of water. I thought I had an idea where Benke Karlsson had chosen to leave this earthly life.

What I called my bedroom was in fact just a part of the living room. Fixed to the ceiling in the centre of the room was a substantial hook that had probably supported a heavy lamp. I went through the rest of the house in my mind and couldn't find any other fixture on a ceiling that would bear the weight of a grown man's body. Benke Karlsson had hanged himself two metres from the spot where I slept.

A suicide, then. That was an unpleasant enough idea. But where had Robin got the idea that Benke Karlsson had also murdered children? And that his bed had stood where Robin's was now?

Regardless of what you believe or don't believe, it was an uncomfortable image. I had cleared out my own past and instead moved straight into another man's dark history. Fortunately there are no direct links between the present and the past, except in our minds.

That's what I thought at the time. Now I think differently.

I could hear the notes as soon as I got out of the car.

It was half-past five and I was worn out after a day at work, during which I had had to make a real effort to concentrate on the task in hand and to stop my thoughts drifting off to the former owner of our house. The outside light was switched off, and apart from the faint glow from Robin's room where he sat playing, only the moonlight made it possible to see my way.

I slammed the car door and the tinkling of the piano stopped. I stood there taking deep breaths as my eyes grew accustomed to the darkness. Then it occurred to me that I ought to go to the tool shed. There was something in there I needed to look at.

As I groped my way towards the blacker darkness that was the old shed, I caught a movement out of the corner of my eye. The light from Robin's room had illuminated something moving on the ground outside his window. I would have investigated the matter if it hadn't seemed more important at the time to go and look at what was in the shed.

Dum, di-dum.

The notes Robin had played were still echoing in my head as I lifted the hasp on the door of the shed, which I hadn't cleared out after the previous owner. Benke Karlsson. *He took it badly*.

The darkness inside was dense, and I couldn't see a thing. However, some time ago I had left a box of matches just inside the door for situations such as this. I stepped into the shed, found the half-full box and struck a match.

Shelves cluttered with extension leads, folded tarpaulins, screws and nails. A carpenter's bench where my own tools lay in a higgledy-piggledy heap with things that had already been there when we moved in. But I was looking for something else. What I wanted to see was right at the back.

I crouched down, blew out the match which was starting to burn my fingers, and struck another. Leaning against the wall was a spade with a wooden handle, and a heavy iron crowbar. I gazed at the two objects. Spade and crowbar. Crowbar and spade.

Dum, di-dum, dum. Di-di-dum.

By the time I had finished looking there was only one match left in the box. I put it back in the right place and stepped out into the pale moonlight. As I lowered the hasp I couldn't understand what I had been doing in the shed. I had a bag full of groceries in the car, I was on my way indoors to cook dinner for Robin and me. What was this detour all about?

Annelie used to say that if there was a complicated way of doing things, I would find it. I smiled to myself, hearing her voice inside me as I walked over to the car. When I had put the key in the lock of the boot, I stopped.

I *had* heard her voice, hadn't I? Just recently, somewhere. I looked around as if I was expecting to see her standing next to the car, her hands pushed down in the pockets of that duffel coat she found at a flea market.

But I had shoved the duffel coat into a rubbish bag myself. It had been incinerated at some dump, and no Annelie would ever put it on again. I was overwhelmed with a sense of loss so strong and physical that I had to lean on the boot for support to stop myself from falling as my knees gave way. Why is the world constructed in such a way that people can be taken away from one another?

Then I picked up the bag of groceries and went inside to make dinner.

As I was boiling the potatoes for mash and frying the sausages, I could hear Robin mumbling into his headset, along with the roar of futuristic weapons and the groans of vanquished enemies. I wondered what Annelie would have said about it all.

She would probably have come up with a way of limiting the amount of time Robin spent gaming, thought of alternatives. I couldn't do that.

Can two people converse or hang out together when they live on different planets? Here was I, frying sausages and adding nutmeg to my mashed potatoes, while Robin battled against mutants with a flame-thrower. If you looked at it like that, could we ever really meet?

I knocked on Robin's door and told him dinner was ready. He asked for five more minutes to finish off the session. I sat down at the kitchen table with my hands resting on my knee, listening to the sounds of the slaughter. I looked at the dish of steaming mashed potato and felt so unbearably lonely.

Robin emerged after five minutes. As we were eating I asked what kind of a day he'd had in school, and he said "Good" with no further comment. I asked how the gaming was going and that was good too. Everything was good. The mash grew in my mouth and I felt as if my throat was closing up. I had to make a real effort in order to swallow.

When we'd finished I asked Robin if he fancied a game of Monopoly. He looked at me as if I'd made a bad joke, then disappeared into his room. I tackled the washing up.

I had just put the last plate in the drying rack when I heard those notes again. I listened more carefully, and thought they reminded me of voices. Had I been mistaken the previous evening, during the power cut? Was it in fact the piano I had heard? There was something about the rise and fall of the notes that sounded like voices. Terrified voices.

My arms dropped, but before I disappeared into the same state as before, I got a grip, strode over to Robin's door and pushed it open.

Robin was sitting at the piano with tears pouring down his cheeks. On the music stand I saw a piece of paper, stained and yellowed. The last note he had played died away, and he looked at me wide-eyed.

"What are you doing?" I asked. "What's that you're playing?"

Robin's eyes were drawn to the piece of paper, which flickered as a gust of wind blew in through the half-open window. When I went over to close it I noticed bits of soil on the windowsill. Behind me Robin played a couple more notes and I yelled: "Stop it! Stop playing!"

He lifted his hands from the keyboard and I slammed the lid shut. Robin jumped and the sharp crash as wood met wood vibrated through my breastbone, through the walls. Robin's eyes met mine. They were the eyes of a child, pure and clear. He whispered: "I don't want to play, Dad. I don't want to play."

I sank to my knees and he fell into my arms, still whispering through his tears: "I don't want to play, Dad. Fix it so I don't have to play any more, Dad."

Over his shaking shoulders I could see the piece of paper on the music stand. It was covered in hand-written notes. Here and there things had been crossed out and something new added; dark brown patches caused by damp made some of the notes illegible. It must have been written over a fairly long period, because several different writing implements – a pencil, a ball-point pen, a fountain pen – had been used.

I stroked Robin's head and sat with him until he had calmed down. Then I took his head between my hands and looked him in the eye. "Robin, my darling boy. Where did you get that piece of paper?"

His voice was muffled from all the tears and he glanced over at his bed. "I found it. Behind the wallpaper."

The wallpaper next to his bed was coming away from the wall and was ripped in a couple of places; Robin had made it worse by lying there picking at it. I nodded in the direction of the torn patch and asked: "There?"

"Yes. He wrote the notes."

"Who?"

"The murderer. Can we have some hot chocolate?"

We didn't bother with the pastries as it wasn't long since we'd eaten. As we sat at the table with our cups, Robin's gaze was more open than it had been for months. He looked me in the eye and didn't waver. This was so unusual that I didn't know what to say; in the midst of everything I was just so happy to feel that contact between us. I sat and revelled in it for a while, but eventually we had to talk about what had happened.

"This murderer," I said. "Do you know his name?"

Robin shook his head.

"So how do you know he was a murderer, then?"

Robin sat there chewing his lips, as if he were considering whether what he wanted to say was permitted or not. With a glance in the direction of his room he whispered, "The children told me."

"Children? What children?"

"The children he murdered."

This was the point at which I should have said: "What on earth are you talking about, that's nonsense" or: "Now you see what happens if you spend too much time playing computer games", but that wasn't what I said because

The dead speak through the notes

because I knew that something was going on in our house that wasn't covered in the *Good Advice for Parents* handbook. Instead I looked at Robin in a way that I hoped would indicate that I was taking him seriously and asked: "Tell me about these children. How many of them are there?"

"Two. Quite small."

"What do they look like?"

"Don't know."

"But you've seen them, haven't you?"

Robin shook his head again and stared down at the table as he said, "You're not allowed to look at them. If you do, they take your eyes." He glanced anxiously at his room. "I don't know if you're allowed to talk about them either."

"But they talk to you?"

"Mm. Can I sleep in your room tonight?"

"Of course you can. But there's something we're going to do first of all."

I went into Robin's room and picked up the hand-written sheet of music from the piano. A horrible feeling had settled in my chest after what Robin had said, and as I stood there with the piece of paper in my hand I had the impression that something was radiating from it. I ran my eyes over the messy notes, the damp patches and the creases and I saw that it was *evil*.

As I said, I can't read music, so it must have been something in the way the notes were written, the hand that had guided the pen, the pens. Or perhaps there is a language that transcends the barriers of reason and goes straight in without passing through the intellect.

Whatever the case may be, there was only one sensible thing to do. I took the piece of paper into the kitchen, screwed it up and dropped it in the stove. Robin sat watching from his chair as I struck a match and brought it towards the paper.

I have to admit that my hand was shaking slightly. My sense of the inherent evil in the piece of paper had been so strong that I was afraid something terrible would happen when I set fire to it. But it began to burn just like any other piece of paper. A little yellow flame took hold, flared up, and after ten seconds all that remained were black flakes, torn apart by the draught from the chimney.

I gave a snort of relief and shook my head at my own fantasies. What had I expected – blue flashes, or a demon flying out of the fireplace and running amok in the kitchen? I flung my hands wide like a magician demonstrating that an object really has disappeared.

"There," I said. "Now you don't have to play those notes any more."

I looked at Robin, but the relief I had hoped to see on his face wasn't there. Instead his eyes filled with tears and he tapped his temples with his fingertips as he whispered: "But I can remember them, Dad. I can *remember* them."

If there's one expression I can't stand, it's *Every cloud has a silver lining*. Take Annelie's death. I can think until my ears bleed without coming up with a single good thing it has brought us. The atomic bombs that were dropped on Japan? They led to Japan's dominance of the electronics market through a complex pattern of cause and effect, but tell that to those who were blown to bits, wave the stock market prices under the noses of the children mutilated as a result of radiation. Good luck with that.

I'm rambling. What I wanted to say was that for once there was a grain of truth in that ugly expression. Later in the evening Robin and I actually played Monopoly. He didn't want to go back to his room; he preferred to sit beneath the safe circle of the kitchen lamp, moving his little car along the unfamiliar streets of Stockholm.

The wind was whistling around the house and I had lit a fire. The roll of the dice across the board, the soft rustle of well-worn bank notes changing hands, our murmured comments or cries of triumph or disappointment. They were good hours, pleasant hours.

It was half-past ten by the time I found myself bankrupt as a result of Robin's ownership of Centrum and Norrmalmstorg, with the requisite hotels. As we gathered up the plastic pieces and various bits of paper, Robin said with amazement in his voice, "That was quite good fun!"

I made myself a bed on a mattress on the floor so that Robin could have my bed. I set the alarm for seven as usual and turned off all the lights apart from the lava lamp; I lay there for a long time watching the viscous, billowing shapes until my eyelids began to feel heavy. Then I heard Robin's voice from the bed.

"Dad?"

I sat up, leaning on my elbow so that I could see him. His eyes were open and in the soft, red light he looked like a small child.

"Yes?"

"I don't want to play the piano any more."

"No. I understand."

"And I don't want us to keep the piano."

"Okay. We'll get rid of it then."

Robin nodded and curled up, closing his eyes. I lay down on my side and looked at my son. For the second time that day the feeling struck me again: things could all work out, in spite of everything. It might all be okay.

The feeling didn't diminish when Robin half-opened his eyes and mumbled sleepily: "We can play Monopoly or something. Or cards. So I don't spend as much time playing computer games."

"We certainly can," I said. "Now go to sleep."

Robin muttered something and after a moment his breathing was deeper. I lay there looking at him, listening to the wind and waiting for it to increase in strength and make the aerial sing. It happened just as my consciousness was about to drift away, and a single long note followed me down into sleep.

Annelie came to me that night.

If it had been a dream, the setting should have been one of the many places where we had actually slept and made love. But she came to me there on the mattress next to the bed. She crept naked under the narrow spare duvet and one thigh slid over mine as she burrowed her nose in the hollow at the base of my throat.

I could smell the scent of her hair as she whispered, "Sorry I went away," and her dry palm caressed my chest. I pulled her close and held her tight. If I had doubted that this was really happening, my doubts dispersed when she said: "Hey, steady!" because I was squeezing her as hard as I could to prevent her from disappearing again.

"I've missed you so much," I murmured, moving one arm so that I could stroke her belly, her breasts, her face. It really was Annelie. The particular curve of her hips, the birthmark beneath her left breast, all the tiny details imprinted on my mind. Only now did I understand how intense the actual physical longing for this woman had been, this woman whose skin I knew better than my own.

She moved her fingers over my lips and said, "I know. I know. But I'm here now."

One part of my body had been sure ever since her thigh slid over mine. I was so hard I felt as if I might burst. I pressed her body to mine and as I pushed inside her I couldn't tell whether the throbbing beats pulsating through me were mine or hers. I followed their rhythm, and the rhythm turned into notes which became a melody that I recognised, and I couldn't hold back. My body contracted in a convulsion so powerful that I slipped out of her and my seed shot out all over the sheets in a single spasm.

I opened my eyes wide.

I was alone on the mattress. My penis was stiff and I could feel the warm stickiness of my ejaculation, the faint aroma of sperm beneath the covers. But that wasn't all. Annelie's scent still lingered in the room. The shampoo she always used, the moisturiser from the Body Shop perfumed with oranges and cinnamon, the one she called her "Christmas moisturiser". Plus the scent of her own body, but I have no words to describe that. They were there in the room. All of them.

I was so preoccupied with trying to drink in that smell and to remain in the moment that it was a long time before I grasped that the notes were real. That they were being played in the house.

I propped myself up on one elbow and saw that the bed was empty. Robin had got up and gone to the piano.

Something moved in my peripheral vision. A faint, swaying movement. Annelie's scent was superseded by another. Sweaty feet. Horrible, stinking, sweaty feet. I turned my head slowly to the side and saw a bare foot swinging to and fro next to me. As my gaze travelled upwards I saw that the foot belonged to an equally naked body. A hairy pot belly and flaccid testicles. A head on a broken neck, eyes staring into mine. The hanged man opened his mouth and said:

"Without her . . . nothing. That's true, isn't it? You can get her back. I did. I am happy now."

I squeezed my eyes tight shut and pressed my wrists against my eyelids so hard that my eyeballs were pushed into my skull and I saw a shower of red stars. I counted to ten, and while I was counting the piano stopped playing. I heard voices coming from Robin's room. And a faint creaking sound.

I opened my eyes. A long, dirty toenail was swaying to and fro centimetres from my face, and from above I heard the gurgling, muffled voice saying, "The door is open. You just have to—"

A strong impulse made me want to curl up, put my hands over my ears and wait until the madness went away. Perhaps I might even have done it if I hadn't heard Robin. In a tearful voice he suddenly yelled: "I can't! I can't!"

I rolled off the mattress, away from the visitation above my head. I got to my feet and ran to Robin's room without looking back.

The window was wide open and the room was freezing cold. Robin was standing by the window dressed only in his underpants, leaning out. When I put my arms around him to pull him inside I saw movement on the lawn outside. Two small, hunched bodies dressed in rags were running erratically towards the forest.

The door is open.

In my despair I pulled too hard and Robin lost his balance. I fell over backwards and he landed on top of me without making a sound.

"Robin? Robin? Are you all right?"

I sat up, holding him in my arms. His expression was distant and he was looking straight through me. I shook him gently.

"Robin? What happened?"

His head moved feebly from side to side, and when I checked him over I saw four long scratches on one forearm, scratches made by fingernails.

I picked him up and carried him into the kitchen. As I approached the door of the living room I let out a sob and held onto him more tightly. I inched forward two steps and peered in through the doorway. Above my mattress and the stained duvet cover there was nothing but an empty hook on the ceiling.

"Robin? It's okay now. They've gone." It was as if another voice was speaking through my mouth as I added, "The door is closed."

Robin didn't respond, and I gently laid him down on my bed and tucked him in. His wide-open eyes were staring at the hook. Could he see something I couldn't? The stale smell of sweaty feet still lingered in the room, and had completely obliterated the scent of Annelie. I looked at the hook with loathing. *Couldn't the bastard have showered before he hanged himself?*

"Dad . . ."

I stroked Robin's hair, his cheeks. "Yes, son?"

"Dad, get rid of it. Get rid of it."

I nodded and licked my lips. They had a sour taste, like sweaty feet. When I got up from the bed I realised I was still naked. I pulled on my dressing gown, went into the kitchen, rummaged in the drawer where I kept tools for indoor use and dug out a pair of heavy pliers.

The first thing I did was to unscrew the hook from the ceiling. I didn't know if it would help, but I didn't want the accursed thing in the house. When I opened the living room window Robin whispered, "No, no, don't open it." I hurled the hook as far as I could, closed the window and said: "It's fine."

"Get rid of it, Dad. You have to get rid of it. I can't."

"What do you mean, son?"

"The piano. Get rid of it. I don't want to."

I was on the point of saying that it would have to wait until tomorrow because I hadn't the strength to carry or even drag the piano on my own, but then I realised there might be a simpler solution.

When I stood in front of the open lid looking at the keyboard, the notes were playing inside my head. By now I had heard them so many times I knew them by heart. I was able to make out a melody, and what's more, when I looked at the keys it was as if some of them glowed, flashed as the notes passed through my mind. *I can play, if I want to.* My hands were irresistibly drawn towards the piano.

Dum, di-dum, daa.

Just once. Or twice. Or as many times as necessary.

When I placed my right hand on the keyboard to begin playing, there was something in the way. A pair of pliers. I was holding a pair of pliers in my hand. A pair of pliers. I worked the handles and saw the sharp jaws opening and closing. *Bite through it. Snip snip.*

I blinked a couple of times and pushed the notes out of my head, concentrating on the pliers. Then I opened the top of the piano and whispered, "Sorry, Annelie."

It took me ten minutes to snip through every single string inside the piano, and when I hit a key to check, the hammer thudded against empty space and the note didn't play. The piano was dead.

Finally I fetched a roll of duct tape and wound it round and round the window catches so that it would be impossible to open them without tools. When I turned away the piano was staring at me; the notes popped into my head and my fingers itched.

I laughed out loud, sat down at the piano and played through the entire melody, but the only sound was the soft, dull thud of the hammers.

"Try that, you bastard," I said, without any idea of who the bastard in question was.

Robin was still awake when I went back into the living room. When I told him what I'd done he nodded and said, "But I don't want to sleep in there."

"You don't have to," I said, lying down beside him on the narrow bed. "You can sleep here for as long as you like."

He reached for my hand and tucked my arm around his chest. I held him and rested my forehead against the back of his head. When five minutes had passed and he still hadn't relaxed, I said: "Do you want to tell me what happened?"

Robin mumbled something into the pillow, but I couldn't make any sense of it.

"What did you say?"

Robin turned his head a fraction to the side; his voice was so faint that I had to put my ear right next to his mouth in order to pick up the words.

"Those children came. They want me to find them. He killed them."

I glanced up at the hole in the ceiling and shuddered as I thought about the pale, shapeless face that had been hanging there. Puffy cheeks covered with stubble. I had no doubt whatsoever that it was the murderer I had seen. The murderer who had spoken to me. Bengt Karlsson. *He took it badly.*

"I don't want to do it, Dad."

"Of course you're not going to do any such thing. How could you?"

"Because they told me. Where they are."

Bearing in mind the insanity in which my son and I found ourselves, perhaps it won't sound too strange if I say that it was a relief to think that here at least was something to hold onto, something I recognised.

While Annelie was still alive we had watched all the *Emil in Lönneberga* films. Robin had been frightened by Krösa-Maja's talk of mylings, the ghosts of murdered children who have not been given a proper burial.

Mylings. If someone had told me a week ago . . . but never mind. I took it seriously. I accepted that this was what we were dealing with, and so I was relieved that it had a name. Something that has a proper designation can probably be dealt with.

I asked: "So where are they, then?"

Robin whispered, "In the forest."

"Did he bury them in the forest?" Robin shook his head. "So what did he do?"

Robin carried on shaking his head as he buried his face in the pillow. I tugged gently at his shoulder.

"Robin? You have to tell me. I don't know what we can do, but . . . you have to tell me. I believe you."

Suddenly he curled himself into a ball with his bottom sticking up in the air, just like he used to do when he was asleep when he was very small. Then he yelled into the pillow, "It's so horrible!"

I stroked his back and said: "I know. I know it's horrible."

Robin shook his head violently and shouted: "You haven't a clue how horrible it is!" He was breathing hard through the pillow, in and out, in and out, and his body kept on heaving those deep, convulsive breaths as I helplessly carried on stroking his back.

I was afraid he was actually going over the edge in some way. It would hardly be surprising. I too felt that I was very close to the edge in terms of what my mind could cope with.

Suddenly Robin's body grew still and he rolled over onto his back. In a thin, expressionless but perfectly clear voice he addressed the ceiling: "The man found a rock. A big rock. He dug a hole next to the rock. Then he tied up the child so that it couldn't move. Then he carried the child to the hole. He had one of those iron bar things. He had it with him so that he could roll the rock down into the hole. On top of the child. But the child's head was sticking out so that the man could listen to the child screaming. And the child screamed because it hurt so much. Lots of bones got broken when the rock rolled on top of the child. The man sat and listened to the child screaming. He sat and listened right up until it died. It might have taken all night. Then he dug a little more and moved the rock so that the child disappeared."

When Robin had uttered the final words he pulled the covers over his head and rolled himself into a secure cocoon. I lay there beside him with his story crawling around inside my head like a mutilated child.

His bed used to be where mine is now.

The man who had done these things had slept in Robin's room. How had he been able to sleep? He had made his coffee on our stove and drunk it in our kitchen. He had looked out of the same windows as us, walked on the same floors, heard the same creaking floorboard just inside the door. And he had hanged himself next to my bed.

My eyes were drawn to the dark spot on the ceiling where the hook had been.

I am happy now.

I lay there looking at the black hole for so long that it started to take on the qualities of its astronomical namesake. Everything in the room was being drawn towards it, waiting to be sucked in; my thoughts moved around it like defenceless planets, orbiting in ever-decreasing circles on their way to destruction. And all the time I could hear the music. Round and round the music went, twelve notes in an incomplete melody.

Incomplete?

If you hum: "Baa baa black sheep, have you any wool, Yes sir, yes sir, three—" and stop there, then you know some notes are missing, even if you've never heard the tune before. It was equally clear to me that notes were missing from the melody which was now so much a part of me that I couldn't get it out of my head. I lay in bed staring at the hole and trying to catch hold of the missing notes.

The pile of bedding next to me had started to move up and down with deep, regular breaths, and I managed to free Robin's sweaty head without waking him up before tucking him in properly. Then I got up and put my clothes on, barely aware of what I was doing, because the notes absorbed all of my attention.

Dum, di-dum, daa.

I sat down at the piano and played the entire melody. The notes were so clear to my inner ear that I had played it twice before I realised there was no sound. I banged a couple of the notes really hard as if violence was the way to entice them out. It was only then I remembered. The pliers. The strings.

I looked around the room, unsure what to do, and I caught sight of the box under Robin's bed. Among cast-off cuddly toys and plastic figures I found the Casio toy synthesiser. It covered only three octaves, but that was enough.

I played the twelve notes, and a dark serenity came over me. Yes, dark serenity. I can't find a better way to express it. It was like getting stuck in the mud and slowly sinking. The moment when you realise it's pointless to struggle, that there is no help to be had, and that the mud is going to win. I imagine you reach a point when you give up, and that this brings with it a certain serenity.

Over and over again I played the twelve notes, trying out different instruments in the synthesiser's repertoire to make them sound good; in the end I settled for "harpsichord". I think it's called *cembalo* in Swedish, and the imitation of its metallic tone was quite convincing.

Dum, di-dum, daa . . .

I went into the hallway, put on my jacket, found the head torch, switched it on and fastened it around my head. The synthesiser had a strap which meant I could hang it around my neck. Fully equipped, I opened the front door and headed for the forest.

A mist hung in the air, and although the head torch was powerful, the light reached no further than about ten metres. As I set off among the damp tree trunks it was like walking through an underground vault where the trunks were pillars, carrying their crowns like a single, immense roof. There wasn't a sound apart from the soft rustle as drops of water fell from the branches onto last year's dead grass.

I hadn't played for several minutes, and the blind determination that had driven me on had begun to falter when I reached the place.

This had to be the place. I had walked in a straight line from the house, I might even have followed an overgrown path, come to think of it. On the way I had passed the odd rock, but none of them would have been suitable for the purpose Robin had described.

In front of me lay a number of large rocks which sprang up out of the darkness when the beam of the head torch swept over them. When I examined the area more closely I found something in the region of fifty large and small erratic blocks which the inland ice had strewn across the ground where pines and fir trees would one day grow. Even without the knowledge I possessed, it didn't take much imagination to compare this place with a graveyard.

With two inhabitants. Two children. Beneath the rocks.

I wandered around aimlessly, directing the beam of the torch at the base of the rocks in the hope of finding some sign that the ground had been disturbed. But everything was overgrown, and every rock looked the same as every other rock. I wrapped my arms around my body and shivered.

What was to say that there weren't dead people, dead children under every single rock? What was to say things would be better if I found the two who had sought out Robin to ask for help, to ask him to find them?

We have to move away from here!

The idea was so obvious I couldn't understand why I hadn't thought of it before. There was nothing to tie me or my son to this haunted place with its gloomy coniferous forest and its brooding rocks. Nothing. It wasn't my responsibility to drive away the ghosts of evil deeds committed in the past.

I breathed out and switched off the torch, closed my eyes and listened to the silence, relaxed. When I had been standing like that for a little while, a faint awareness came over me. It grew into a certainty: diagonally in front of me to the left. Something was drifting towards me from that direction, faint as the draught caused by a fly's wings against the skin, and blacker than the night. When I opened my eyes it was gone.

The darkness felt almost solid, and the only light came from the diode indicating that the toy synthesiser around my neck was on. I switched on the torch and studied the keyboard. Then I played a note. Then another. The twelve notes echoed from the plastic speakers and were swallowed up by the darkness and the mist. I edged forward a few steps and played the melody again.

Something moved in front of me, and I glimpsed a figure disappearing behind a rock. I went over and leaned my back against the rough surface, then crouched down and played the melody once more. When I took my fingers off the keys I could hear scrabbling, the sound of small feet flitting across the moss and needles on the other side of the rock.

You're not allowed to look at them. If you do, they take your eyes.

I directed the beam of the head torch at the trunk of a fir tree five metres in front of me and spoke out into the air: "I am here now."

Feet moved across the ground, rustling, squelching as they came closer. Nails scraped down the rock just a metre or so away, and I closed my eyes so that I wouldn't be tempted to look over my shoulder. Then I said it again: "I am here now. What shall I do?"

At first I thought it was a noise originating from the forest. A broken branch creaking in a gust of wind, or the distant cry of an injured animal. But it was a voice. The faint, mournful voice of an unhappy old man who has lost everything but his memories, who cries at the sight of semolina pudding because it reminds him of his childhood and makes him talk in the voice of a child:

"Find us," said the voice behind my shoulder.

Without opening my eyes I replied, "I have found you. What shall I do now?"

"Fetch us."

I had somehow known that this was my task right from the start, from the moment I stood in front of the spade and crowbar in the tool shed. To find, to fetch, to . . . conclude.

"Why?" I whispered. "Why did he do this to you?"

The only response was the slow breathing of the forest. I pressed my back against the stone, suddenly conscious of its terrible weight and solidity. To have that weight on top of you, to be slowly crushed to pieces beneath its impervious hardness. To be a child.

When the voice spoke again the tone had changed; perhaps it wasn't the same voice. Cutting through the old man's growl there was something that told me this was a younger child.

"The old man had a piece of paper," said the voice. "He was writing."

"What do you mean, writing?" I asked. "When?"

"When I was dying. I screamed. Because it hurt so much. Then he wrote on the piece of paper. He said I would scream a lot. And I screamed. Because it hurt so much."

The voice was faint as it uttered the final words, and I felt the presence behind me disappear. I bent my head so that the beam of the torch shone on the keyboard. Thirty-six innocent pieces of black and white plastic. Now I understood how I had mistaken the notes for terrified voices.

Bengt Karlsson, the musician who *took it badly*, had made musical notes out of the most horrific sound imaginable, the tortured screams of a dying child. And these notes ... opened the door.

How can a person bear it?

I struggled to my feet and pressed my knuckles against my temples as I staggered among the rocks. How can a person bear it? The dampness, the mist, the dark tree trunks, the evil contained within the very warp and weft of existence. How? I watched myself strike the rough surface of a rock with the palms of my hands until the blood flowed.

The pain woke me up. I gazed at my bleeding hands. Then I glanced up. All the rocks looked the same, and I no longer knew where the dead children were.

When I played the first note on the synthesiser, my finger left a dark streak on the white plastic. By the time I had played the whole melody, the keys were soiled with blood and a few of them resisted when I pressed them. Soon it would be impossible to play.

I found the button that said REC and pushed it down, then I played the whole melody again and pressed REC STOP. Then PLAY. I laughed out loud as the toy synthesiser carried on playing the melody all by itself, over and over again.

Dum, di-dum, daa . . .

I slipped the instrument round to the side so that I was comfortable, and it went on playing the melody as I set off for home and the tool shed.

A dirty grey dawn had found its tentative way among the tree trunks by the time my work was finished. The blood from my hands had been absorbed by the spade's wooden handle, spread itself over the dark iron of the crowbar. The synthesiser's batteries were running out, and the sound of the melody was growing ever fainter as I walked back from the forest, opened the front door and went into the hallway.

I picked up the duct tape which was still lying on the piano. The notes from the synthesiser were now so weak that they were drowned out by the creaking of the kitchen floor as I crossed the threshold. But the incomplete melody playing inside my head was all the stronger, and I noticed without surprise that Bengt Karlsson was sitting at the kitchen table with his hands neatly folded on top of one another.

The black line around his neck became visible when he nodded to me, and I nodded back in mutual understanding. We were men who knew what must be done. He had been unable to bear it. Now it was time for me to take over.

Robin didn't wake up until I had secured his hands behind his back with the tape, and I placed a strip over his mouth before he had time to start yelling. I would have to remove it later, of course, but at the moment it would be troublesome to have him screaming. I held his legs firmly so that I could secure his ankles, then slipped my arm beneath the back of his knees and heaved him up over my shoulder.

The melody continued to play as I carried him through the kitchen, softly, softly as a whisper it played, and I hummed along. My body was aching with a feverish longing for the missing notes, desperate to hear the completed melody.

Robin twisted and turned over my shoulder, and his under-pants rubbed against my ear as I carried him across the lawn. The skin on his bare legs turned to gooseflesh in the chill of the winter dawn. I could hear him panting and snuffling behind my back as snot spurted out of his nose, and from the muffled sounds he was making I guessed that he was crying. It didn't matter. Soon it would be over. Concluded.

The pale light of dawn made the tree trunks step forward out of the mist like dark silhouettes, a silently observing group of spectators with no knowledge of right or wrong, good or evil. Only the blind laws of nature and the circle of life and death, life and death. And the door between them.

I laid Robin down in the hollow I had dug next to a rock. I no longer knew whether the music I could hear existed only inside my head. Robin twitched and jerked, his fair skin in sharp contrast to the dark earth. His head moved from side to side and his eyes were wide open as he tried to scream through the duct tape.

"Hush," I said. "Hush . . ."

I ripped off the gag, and without paying attention to his plead-ing sobs I concentrated on the crowbar which I had driven into the ground on the other side of the rock. I calculated that it would take just one decent push forwards to make the rock tip over into the hollow. I rubbed my hands, which were covered in flakes of coagulated blood, and set to work.

As I grabbed hold of the crowbar I was aware of a movement out of the corner of my eye. Instinctively I looked over and saw a child. Its age was difficult to determine, because the face was so sunken that the cheekbones stood out. It was dressed in the remains of silky red pyjamas patterned with yellow teddy bears, and its chest was visible through the torn material. A number of ribs were crushed, and sharp fragments of bone had pierced the skin in several places.

The child raised its hands to its face. The nails were long and broken from scratching at rocks. And behind the fingers, the eyes. I looked into those eyes and they were not eyes at all, but black wells of hatred and pain.

Only then did I realise what I had done.

Before I had time to close my eyes or grab hold of the crowbar again, another small body hurled itself onto my back. I bent over and the child in pyjamas leapt up and seized me around the neck, burying its fingers just above my shoulder blades.

The body on my back ran its hands over my forehead, and then I felt jagged nails moving over my eyelids. I screamed as the sharp edges penetrated the skin on either side of the top of my nose, and blood ran down into my mouth. The child let out a single sharp hiss, then jerked its hands outwards.

Both my eyeballs were ripped out of my skull, and the last thing I heard before I lost consciousness was the viscous, moist sound of the optical nerves tearing, then a grunting, smacking noise as the children chewed on my eyes.

I don't know how long I was out. When I came round I could no longer see any light, and I had no idea of the sun's progress across the sky. There were empty holes in my head where my eyes had been, and my cheeks were sticky with the remains of my eyelids and optical nerves. The pain was like a series of nails being hammered into my face.

I pulled myself up onto my knees. Total darkness. And silence. The synthesiser's batteries had given up. I fumbled around and found the crowbar, traced the surface of the rock until I reached the edge of the hollow, and was rewarded with the only sound that was of any importance now.

"Dad . . . Dad . . ."

I crawled down to Robin. I bit through the tape around his wrists and ankles. I tore off my jacket and shirt and wrapped them around him. I wept without being able to shed any tears, and I fumbled in the darkness until he took my hand and led me back to the house.

Then he made a call. I couldn't use the phone, and had forgotten every number. I was frightened when he spoke to someone whose voice I couldn't hear. I groped my way to bed and sought refuge beneath the covers. That's where they found me.

They say I'm on the road to recovery. I will never regain my sight, but my sanity has begun to return. They say I will be allowed out of here. That I will learn to adapt.

Robin comes to see me less and less often. He says he's happy with his foster family. He says they're nice. He says he doesn't spend so much time playing games these days. He's stopped talking about how things will be when I get out.

And I don't think I will get out, because I don't want to leave.

Food at fixed times and a bed that is made every day. I move blindly through the stations of each day. I have my routines, and the days pass. No, I shouldn't be let out.

Because when I sit in the silence of my room or lie in my bed at night, I can hear the notes. My fingers extend in empty space, moving over an invisible keyboard, and I dream of playing.

Of replaying everything. Getting Annelie to visit me again and embracing her in the darkness, paying no heed to which doors are open or what might emerge through them.

There are no musical instruments in the unit.

RAMSEY CAMPBELL

Passing Through Peacehaven

RAMSEY CAMPBELL'S MOST RECENT books from PS Publishing include the novels *Ghosts Know* and *The Kind Folk*, along with the definitive edition of the author's early Arkham House collection, *Inhabitant of the Lake*, which includes all the first drafts of the stories, along with new illustrations by Randy Broecker.

Forthcoming from the same publisher is a new Lovecraftian novella, *The Last Revelation of Glaaki*.

Now well in to his fifth decade as one of the world's most respected authors of horror fiction, Campbell has won multiple World Fantasy Awards, British Fantasy Awards and Bram Stoker Awards, and is a recipient of the World Horror Convention Grand Master Award, the Horror Writers Association Lifetime Achievement Award, the Howie Award of the H. P. Lovecraft Film Festival for Lifetime Achievement, and the International Horror Guild's Living Legend Award.

He is also President of both the British Fantasy Society and the Society of Fantastic Films.

"Lord, it's so long since I wrote 'Passing Through Peacehaven' – 2006 – that I don't recall much about its genesis," reveals Campbell about his second contribution to this volume.

"It was certainly suggested by overhearing announcements at a railway station, the kind of everyday occurrence that I may have taken for granted for most of my life until it suddenly turns around in my mind to display an unexpected side.

"Ideas are everywhere!"

"WAIT," MARSDEN SHOUTED as he floundered off his seat. His vision was so overcast with sleep that it was little better than opaque, but so far as he could see through the carriages the entire train was deserted. "Terminate" was the only word he retained from the announcement that had wakened him. He blundered to the nearest door and leaned on the window to slide it further open while he groped beyond it for the handle. The door swung wide so readily that he almost sprawled on the platform. In staggering dangerously backwards to compensate he slammed the door, which seemed to be the driver's cue. The train was heading into the night before Marsden realised he had never seen the station in his life.

"Wait," he cried, but it was mostly a cough as the smell of some October fire caught in his throat. His eyes felt blackened by smoke and stung when he blinked, so that he could barely see where he was going as he lurched after the train. He succeeded in clearing his vision just in time to glimpse distance or a bend in the track extinguish the last light of the train like an ember. He panted coughing to a halt and stared red-eyed around him.

Two signs named the station Peacehaven. The grudging glow of half a dozen lamps that put him in mind of streetlights in an old photograph illuminated stretches of both platforms but seemed shy of the interior of the enclosed bridge that led across the pair of tracks. A brick wall twice his height extended into the dark beyond the ends of the platform he was on. The exit from the station was on the far side of the tracks, through a passage where he could just distinguish a pay phone in the gloom. Above the wall of that platform, and at some distance, towered an object that he wasted seconds in identifying as a factory chimney. He should be looking for the times of any trains to Manchester, but the timetable among the vintage posters alongside the platform was blackened by more than the dark. As he squinted at it, someone spoke behind him.

It was the voice that had wakened him. Apart from an apology for a delay, the message was a blur. "I can't hear much at the best of times," Marsden grumbled. At least the station hadn't closed for the night, and a timetable on the other platform was beside a lamp. He made for the bridge and climbed the wooden stairs to the elevated corridor, where narrow grimy windows above head height and criss-crossed by wire mesh admitted virtually no illumination. He needn't shuffle through the dark; his mobile phone could light the way. He reached in his overcoat pocket, and dug deeper to find extra emptiness.

Marjorie wouldn't have approved of the words that escaped his lips. He wasn't fond of them himself, especially when he heard them from children in the street. He and Marjorie would have done their best to keep their grandchildren innocent of such language and of a good deal else that was in vogue, but they would need to have had a son or daughter first. He ran out of curses as he trudged back across the bridge, which felt narrowed by darkness piled against the walls. The platform was utterly bare. Did he remember hearing or perhaps only feeling the faintest thump as he'd left his seat? There was no doubt that he'd left the mobile on the train.

He was repeating himself when he wondered if he could be heard. His outburst helped the passage to muffle the announcer's unctuous voice, which apparently had information about a signal failure. Marsden wasn't going to feel like one. He marched out of darkness into dimness, which lightened somewhat as he reached the platform.

Had vandals tried to set fire to the timetable? A blackened corner was peeling away from the bricks. Marsden pushed his watch higher on his wizened wrist until the strap took hold. Theoretically the last train – for Bury and Oldham and Manchester – was due in less than twenty minutes. "What's the hold-up again? Say it clearly this time," Marsden invited not quite at the top of his voice. When there was no response he made for the phone on the wall.

Was it opposite some kind of memorial? No, the plaque was a ticket window boarded up behind cracked glass. Surely the gap beneath the window couldn't be occupied by a cobweb, since the place was staffed. He stood with his back to the exit from the station and fumbled coins into the slot beside the receiver before groping for the dial that he could barely see in the glimmer from the platform.

"Ray and Marjorie Marsden must be engaged elsewhere. Please don't let us wonder who you were or when you tried to contact us or where we can return the compliment . . ." His answering message had amused them when he recorded it – at least, Marjorie had made the face that meant she appreciated his wit – but now it left him feeling more alone than he liked. "Are you there?" he asked the tape. "You'll have gone up, will you? You'll have gone up, of course. Just to let you know I'm stranded by an unexpected change of trains. If you play me back don't worry, I'll be home as soon as practicable. Oh, and the specialist couldn't find anything wrong. I know, you'll say it shows I can hear when I want to. Not true, and shall I tell you why? I'd give a lot to hear you at this very moment. Never mind. I will soon."

Even saying so much in so many words earned him no response, and yet he didn't feel unheard. His audience could be the station announcer, who was presumably beyond one of the doors that faced each other across the corridor, although neither betrayed the faintest trace of light. "I nearly didn't say I love you," he added in a murmur that sounded trapped inside his skull. "Mind you, you'll know that, won't you? If you don't after all these years you never will. I suppose that had better be it for now as long as you're fast asleep."

He still felt overheard. Once he'd hung up he yielded to a ridiculous urge to poke his head out of the corridor. The platforms were deserted, and the tracks led to unrelieved darkness. He might as well learn where he'd ended up while there was no sign of a train. "Just stepping outside," he informed anyone who should know.

The corridor didn't seem long enough to contain so much blackness. He only just managed to refrain from rubbing his eyes as he emerged onto an unpromising road. The front of the station gave it no light, but the pavements on either side of the cracked weedy tarmac were visibly uneven. Beyond high railings across the road the grounds of the factory bristled with tall grass, which appeared to shift, although he couldn't feel a wind. Here and there a flagstone showed pale through the vegetation. A sign beside the open gates had to do with motors or motor components, and Marsden was considering a closer look to pass the time when the announcer spoke again. "Going to attract effect" might have been part of the proclamation, and all that Marsden was able to catch.

Some delay must be owing to a track defect, of course. Much of the voice had ended up as echoes beyond the railings or simply dissipated in the night, but he also blamed its tone for confusing him. It had grown so oily that it sounded more like a parody of a priest than any kind of railway official. Marsden tramped into the passage and knocked on the door beside the ticket window. "Will you repeat that, please?"

If this sounded like an invitation to an argument, it wasn't taken up. He found the doorknob, which felt flaky with age, but the door refused to budge. He rubbed his finger and thumb together as he crossed to the other door, which tottered open at his knock, revealing only a storeroom. It was scattered with brushes and mops, or rather their remains, just distinguishable in the meagre light through a window so nearly opaque that on the platform he'd mistaken it for an empty poster frame. Vandals must have been in the room; the dimness smelled as ashen as it looked, while the tangles of sticks that would once have been handles seemed blackened by more than the dark. That was all he managed to discern before the voice spoke to him.

Was the fellow too close to the microphone? If he was trying to be clearer, it achieved the opposite. Of course nobody was next to alive; a train was the next to arrive. "Speak clearly, not up," Marsden shouted as he slammed the door and hurried to the bridge, where he did his best to maintain his pace by keeping to the middle of the passage. If an object or objects were being dragged somewhere behind him, he wanted to see what was happening. He clumped breathlessly down the stairs and limped onto the platform. How could he have thought the windows were poster frames? There was one on either side of the exit, and although both rooms were unlit, a figure was peering through the window of the office.

Or was it a shadow? It was thin and black enough. There was no light inside the room to cast it, and yet it must be a shadow, since it had nothing for a face. Marsden was still trying to identify its source when he noticed that the door he'd slammed was wide open. It had felt unsteady on its hinges, and at least he had an explanation for the dragging sound he'd heard. He set about laughing at his own unease, and then the laugh snagged in his throat like another cough. The silhouette was no longer pressed against the window.

Had it left traces of its shape on the discoloured glass? As he paced back and forth, trying either to confirm or shake off the impression, he felt like an animal trapped in a cage and watched by spectators. He'd met with no success by the time the voice that might belong to the owner of the shadow had more to say. "Where's the party?" Marsden was provoked to mutter. "What's departing?" he demanded several times as loud. "It's supposed to arrive first," he pointed out, glaring along the tracks at the unrelieved night. The few words he'd managed to recognise or at least to guess had sounded oilier than ever, close to a joke. Why couldn't the fellow simply come and tell him what to expect? Was he amusing himself by spying on the solitary passenger? "Yes, you've got a customer," Marsden declared. "He's the chap who has to stand out here in the cold because you can't be bothered to provide a waiting-room."

The complaint left him more aware of the storeroom, so that he could have imagined he was being observed from there too. He would much rather fancy his return home to the bed that he hoped Marjorie was keeping warm for him. As he hugged himself to fend off the late October chill he wasn't too far from experiencing how her arms would feel when she turned in her sleep to embrace him. He couldn't help wishing that the tape had brought him her voice.

The only one he was likely to hear was the announcer's, and he needed to ensure he did. He lowered himself onto a bench opposite the exit and planted his hands on his knees. Though the seat felt unwelcomingly moist if not actually rotten, he concentrated on staying alert for the next message. His ears were throbbing with the strain, and his skin felt as if his sense of being watched were gathering on it, by the time his attention was rewarded.

Was someone clinking glasses? Had the staff found an excuse to celebrate? Marsden had begun to wonder if they were deriding his predicament when he identified the noise of bricks knocking together. The factory was more dilapidated than he'd been able to make out, then, and there was movement in the rubble. Perhaps an animal was at large – more than one, by the sound of it – or else people were up to no good. Suppose they were the vandals who'd tried to set fire to the station? Would the announcer deign to emerge from hiding if they or others like them trespassed on railway property, or was he capable of leaving his solitary customer to deal with them? Marsden could hear nothing now except his own heart, amplified by his concentration if not pumped up by stress. He wasn't sure if he glimpsed surreptitious movement at the exit, where he could easily imagine that the dark was growing crowded; indeed, the passage was so nearly lightless that any number of intruders might sneak into it unseen. He was gripping his knees and crouching forward like a competitor at the start of some pensioners' event while he strained to see whether anyone was sidling through the gloom when his heart jumped, and he did.

The voice was louder than ever, and its meaning more blurred. Even the odd relatively clear phrase amid the magnified mumbling left much to be desired. Marsden could have thought he was being warned about some further decay and informed that he had a hearing problem. The latter comment must refer to engineering, but wasn't this unreasonable too? How many hindrances was the train going to encounter? The reports of its progress were beginning to seem little better than jokes. But here was a final one, however inefficiently pronounced. It meant that the train was imminent, not that anything would shortly be alive.

Perhaps the man was slurring his words from drunkenness, and the clinking had indeed been glass, unless the contrivance of equality had reached such a pitch that the station was obliged to employ an announcer with a speech impediment. On that basis Marsden might seek a job as a telephone operator, but he and Marjorie were resigned to leaving the world to the young and aggressive. He peered along the railway, where the view stayed as black as the depths of the corridor opposite. All that his strained senses brought him besides a charred smell and a crawling of the skin was, eventually, another message.

"You won't be burying this old man," he retorted under his clogged breath. While the announcement must have referred to the train to Bury and Oldham, the voice had resembled a priest's more than ever. "And where's this train that's supposed to be arriving?" he demanded loud enough to rouse an echo in the exit corridor.

The next message was no answer. Presumably he was being told that unattended luggage would be removed without warning, but since he had no luggage, what was the point? Couldn't the fellow see him? Perhaps some legislation allowed him to be blind as well as largely incomprehensible. Still, here were another few words Marsden understood, even if he couldn't grasp where passengers were being told to change. "What was that?" he shouted, but the announcer hadn't finished. His tone was so ecclesiastical that for the space of an exaggerated heartbeat Marsden fancied he was being offered some kind of service, and then he recognised the phrase. It was "out of service".

He sucked in a breath that he had to replace once he'd finished coughing. "What's out?" he spluttered. "Where's my train?"

The only reply was an echo, all the more derisive for sounding more like "Where's my Ray?" He levered himself to his feet, muttering an impolite word at having somehow blackened the knee of his trousers, and hobbled to the bridge. An arthritic pang set him staggering like an old drunk, but he succeeded in gaining the top of the stairs without recourse to the banisters. He preferred to keep to the middle of the bridge, especially along the passage over the tracks. It was too easy to imagine that the darkness beneath the obscured windows was peopled with supine figures. Surely the humped mounds consisted simply of litter, despite the marks on a window about halfway along, five elongated trails that might have been left by a sooty hand as its owner tried to haul his body up. That afternoon Marsden had given a few coins to a woman lying in a railway underpass, but he hoped not to encounter anyone of the kind just now. He faltered and then stumbled fast to the end of the passage, mumbling "No change" as he clattered down to the platform.

"Here's your customer," he said at several times the volume, "and what are you going to do about it?" The question trailed away, however, and not only because the office was so thoroughly unlit from within. The imprint on the window had silenced him. He might still have taken it for a shadow if it weren't so incomplete. Just the top half of a face with holes for eyes was recognisable, and the bones of a pair of hands.

Some grimy vandal must have been trying to see into the
room. Of course the marks weren't on the inside of the glass, or
if they were, that was no reason to think that the figure at the
window had stood in the same place. Nevertheless Marsden
wasn't anxious to look closer, although he'd managed to distinguish nothing in the office. He made for the door with all the
confidence he could summon up.

The storeroom distracted him. Even if his stinging eyes had
adjusted to the dimness, he couldn't understand how he'd failed
to see that the room was more than untidy. It was full of burned
sticks and bits of stick, some of which were thin as twigs. One
charred tangle that, to judge by the blackened lump at the nearer
end, consisted partly of a mop or brush came close to blocking
the door. When he lurched to shut away the sight the edge of the
door caught the object, and he glimpsed it crumbling into restless fragments before the slam resounded through the passage.
He limped to the office door and, having rapped on a scaly panel,
shouted "Will you come and tell me to my face what's
happening?"

As far as he could determine, silence was the answer. He could
have fancied that the station and its surroundings were eager for
his next outburst. "You're meant to make yourself plain," he
yelled. "I couldn't understand half of what you said."

If he was hoping to provoke a response, it didn't work. Had
he offended the man? "I need to know where I'm going," he
insisted. "I don't think that's unreasonable, do you?"

Perhaps the fellow thought he could behave as he liked while
he was in charge. Perhaps he felt too important to descend to
meeting the public, an attitude that would explain his tone of
voice. Or might he not be on the premises? If he was beyond the
door, what could he expect to gain by lying low? Surely not even
the worst employee would act that way – and then Marsden
wondered if he'd strayed on the truth. Suppose it wasn't a railway employee who was skulking in the office?

The kind of person who'd tried to set fire to the station would
certainly be amused by Marsden's plight and think it even more
of a joke to confuse him. Perhaps the indistinctness of the
announcements was the result of suppressed mirth. Marsden
shouldn't waste any more time if the information was false. He

hurried to the phone and glared at the dim wall, which didn't bear a single notice.

No doubt vandals had removed any advertisements for taxis. At least the phone wasn't disabled. He fumbled the receiver off its hook and leaned almost close enough to kiss the blackened dial as he clawed at an enquiry number. He could have thought his hearing had improved when the bell began to ring; it sounded close as the next room. The voice it roused was keeping its distance, however. "Can you speak up?" Marsden urged.

"Where are you calling, please?"

This was sharp enough for a warning. Presumably the speaker was ensuring he was heard. "Peacehaven," Marsden said. "Taxis."

"Where is that, please?"

"Peacehaven," Marsden pronounced loud enough for it to grow blurred against his ear before he realised that he wasn't being asked to repeat the name. "Somewhere near Manchester."

In the pause that ensued he might have heard movement outside the passage. His hectic pulse obscured the noise, which must have been the tall grass scraping in a wind, even if he couldn't feel it. He was relieved when the voice returned until he grasped its message. "Not listed," it said.

"Forgive me, I wasn't asking for Peacehaven Taxis. Any cab firm here will do."

"There is no listing."

Was the fellow pleased to say so? He sounded as smug as the worst sort of priest. "The nearest one, then," Marsden persisted. "I think that might be—"

"There are no listings for Peacehaven."

"No, that can't be right. I'm in it. I'm at the railway station. You must have a number for that at least."

"There is none."

Marsden was aware of the dark all around him and how many unheard lurkers it could hide. "Is there anything more I can do for you?" the voice said.

It sounded so fulsome that Marsden was convinced he was being mocked. "You've done quite enough," he blurted and slammed the receiver on its hook.

He could try another enquiry number, or might he call the police? What could he say that would bring them to his aid yet avoid seeming as pathetic as he was determined not to feel? There was one voice he yearned to hear in the midst of all the darkness, but the chance of this at so late an hour seemed little better than infinitesimal. Nevertheless he was groping for change and for the receiver. He scrabbled at the slot with coins and dragged the indistinct holes around the dial. The bell measured the seconds and at last made way for a human voice. It was his own. "Ray and Marjorie Marsden must be engaged elsewhere . . ."

"I am. I wish you weren't," he murmured and felt all the more helpless for failing to interrupt his mechanical self. Then his distant muffled voice fell silent, and Marjorie said "Who is it?"

"It's me, love."

"Is that Ray?" She sounded sleepy enough not to know. "I can hardly hear you," she protested. "Where have you gone?"

"You'd wonder." He was straining to hear another sound besides her voice – a noise that might have been the shuffling of feet in rubble. "I'm stuck somewhere," he said. "I'll be late. I can't say how late."

"Did you call before?"

"That was me. Didn't you get me?"

"The tape must be stuck like you. I'll need to get a new one."

"Not a new husband, I hope." He wouldn't have minded being rewarded with the laugh he'd lived with for the best part of fifty years, even though the joke felt as old as him, but perhaps she was wearied by the hour. "Anyway," he said, "if you didn't hear me last time I'll sign off the same way, which as if you didn't know—"

"What was that?"

For too many seconds he wasn't sure. He'd been talking over it, and then she had. Surely it had said that a train was about to arrive; indeed, wasn't the noise he'd mistaken for thin footsteps the distant clicking of wheels? "It's here now," he tried to tell her through a fit of coughing. By the time he was able to speak clearer, the train might have pulled in. Dropping the receiver on the hook, he dashed for the platform. He hadn't reached it when he heard a scraping behind him.

The storeroom was open again, but that wasn't enough in itself to delay him. His eyes had grown all too equal to the gloom in the passage, so that he was just able to discern marks on the floor, leading from outside the station to the room. Could some-one not be bothered to pick up their dirty feet? The trails looked as if several objects had been dragged into the room. He didn't believe they had just been left; that wasn't why they made him uneasy. He had to squint to see that they were blurred by more than the dark. Whatever had left them – not anybody shuffling along, he hoped, when their feet would have been worse than thin – had crumbled in transit, scattering fragments along the route. He thought he could smell the charred evidence, and swal-lowed in order not to recommence coughing, suddenly fearful of being heard. What was he afraid of? Was he growing senile? Thank heaven Marjorie wasn't there to see him. The only reason for haste was that he had a train to catch. He tramped out of the passage and might have maintained his defiant pace all the way to the bridge if a shape hadn't reared up at the window of the storeroom.

Was the object that surmounted it the misshapen head of a mop? He couldn't distinguish much through the grimy pane, but the idea was almost reassuring until he acknowledged that some-body would still have had to lift up the scrawny excuse for a figure. It hadn't simply risen or been raised, however. A process that the grime couldn't entirely obscure was continuing to take place. The silhouette – the blackened form, rather – was taking on more substance, though it remained alarmingly emaciated. It was putting itself back together.

The spectacle was so nightmarishly fascinating that Marsden might have been unable to stir except for the clatter of wheels along the tracks. He staggered around to see dim lights a few hundred yards short of the station. "Stop," he coughed, terrified that the driver mightn't notice him and speed straight through. Waving his arms wildly, he sprinted for the bridge.

He'd panted up the stairs and was blundering along the middle of the wooden corridor when he thought he heard a noise besides the approach of the train. Was he desperate to hear it or afraid to? He might have tried to persist in mistaking it for wind in the grass if it weren't so close. He did his utmost to fix his shaky gaze on the far end of the corridor as he fled past shadow after crouch-ing shadow. He almost plunged headlong down the further stairs, and only a grab at the slippery discoloured banister saved him. As he dashed onto the platform he saw that both doors in the passage out of the station were open. The sight brought him even closer to panic, and he began to wave his shivering arms once more as he tottered to the edge of the platform. "Don't leave me here," he cried.

The squeal of brakes seemed to slice through the dark. The engine blotted out the view across the tracks, and then a carriage sped past him. Another followed, but the third was slower. Its last door halted almost in front of him. Though the train was by no means the newest he'd ridden that day, and far from the cleanest, it seemed the next thing to paradise. He clutched the rusty handle and heaved the door open and clambered aboard. "You can go now. Go," he pleaded.

Who was the driver waiting for? Did he think the noises on the bridge were promising more passengers? There was such a volume of eager shuffling and scraping that Marsden almost wished his ears would fail him. He hauled at the door, which some obstruction had wedged open. He was practically deaf with his frantic heartbeat by the time the door gave, slamming with such force that it seemed to be echoed in another carriage. At once the train jerked forward, flinging him onto the nearest musty seat. He was attempting to recover his breath when the announcer spoke.

Was a window open in the carriage? The voice sounded close enough to be on the train, yet no more comprehensible. It was no longer simply unctuous; it could have been mocking a priest out of distaste for the vocation. Its only recognisable words were "train now departing", except that the first one was more like Ray – perhaps not just on this occasion, Marsden thought he recalled. He craned towards the window and was able to glimpse that both doors in the exit corridor were shut. Before he had time to ponder any of this, if indeed he wanted to, the train veered off the main line.

"Where are you taking me?" he blurted, but all too soon he knew. The train was heading for the property behind the station, a turn of events celebrated by a short announcement. There was no question that the speaker was on board, though the blurring of the words left Marsden unsure if they were "Ray is shortly alive." The swerve of the train had thrown open the doors between the carriages, allowing him to hear a chorused hiss that might have signified resentment or have been an enthusiastic "Yes" or, possibly even worse, the collapse of many burned objects into the ash he could smell. As the train sped through a gateway in the railings, he read the name on the sign: not Peacehaven Motors at all, or anything to do with cars. Perhaps the route was only a diversion, he tried to think, or a short tour. Perhaps whoever was on the train just wanted somebody to visit the neglected memorials and the crematorium.

DAVID BUCHAN

Holiday Home

DAVID BUCHAN DISCOVERED horror fiction as a teenager and began writing short stories in his early twenties, leading to his first publication on the website *Whispers of Wickedness*.

Since then his work has appeared in a number of small press publications on the both sides of the Atlantic, including the Sam's Dot Publishing magazine *Champagne Shivers*. He is currently working towards an undergraduate degree in Humanities with the Open University.

"I am often struck by the manner in which some killers transport their victims from the scene of the crime," says Buchan, "and the method used in this story is, somewhat inevitably, inspired by real-life cases."

IT WAS LAST week he moved his family into the next cottage. I'd asked him if he needed a hand with the luggage. He shook his head and smiled. Just glad to get some peace and quite, he laughed, hauling the bulging suitcases from the car.

We could see them inside whenever we walked by: the wife and kids slumped in the same chairs, like mannequins; the husband moving about, his form rendered ghostly by the steamed-up window pane and the flies bouncing off its surface.

At the time, it never occurred to me.

STEPHEN JONES & KIM NEWMAN

Necrology: 2011

AS WE ENTER THE second decade of the twenty-first century, we are losing many of the writers, artists, performers and technicians we grew up with and who, during their lifetimes, helped shape the horror, science fiction and fantasy genres . . .

AUTHORS/ARTISTS/COMPOSERS

Best-selling British children's author **Dick King-Smith** OBE (Ronald Gordon King-Smith) died in his sleep on 4 January after a long illness. He was eighty-eight. The former farmer's more than 100 books included the 1983 novel *The Sheep-Pig*, which was filmed as *Babe* (1995), and *The Water Horse* (which was made into a film in 2007). His other titles include *The Invisible Dog* and *The Witch of Blackberry Bottom*.

Ruth Evelyn Kyle, who was married to SF fan/writer/publisher David A. Kyle for fifty-three years, died after a brief illness on 5 January, aged eighty-one. The couple met at a science fiction convention. Ruth Kyle was Secretary of the 14th World Science Fiction Convention held in New York City in 1956.

American author and dealer **Jerry Weist** died of multiple myeloma after a long illness on 7 January, aged sixty-one. Initially inspired by *Famous Monsters of Filmland* in the late 1950s, he began publishing the fanzines *Nightmares* and

Movieland Monsters, and in 1967 he founded the famed EC comics fanzine *Squa Tront*, which ran until 1983. His books include three editions of *The Comic Art Price Guide*, *The R. Crumb Price Guide*, *The Underground Price Guide*, *Bradbury: An Illustrated Life* and *The 100 Greatest Comic Books*, and he contributed (with Robert Weinberg) a bibliographical index to the revised editions of *From the Pen of Paul: The Fantastic Images of Frank R. Paul*. In 1974 Weist opened The Million Year Picnic in Boston, one of the first specialty comic stores in the US.

American SF artist and illustrator **Gene Szafran** (Eugene Szafran) died on 8 January, aged sixty-nine. During the late 1960s and early '70s he painted more than seventy-five covers for books by Robert A. Heinlein, Robert Silverberg, Poul Anderson, Ray Bradbury and others. His work also appeared in numerous magazines, including *Playboy*. Szafran's career was curtailed in the late 1970s when he developed multiple sclerosis.

Prolific American SF, mystery and Western author **Edward [Paul] Wellen** died on 15 January, aged ninety-one. He began contributing to the SF digest magazines in the early 1950s (including *Galaxy*, *Imagination*, *Science Stories*, *Universe* and *Infinity*), while his 1971 novel *Hijack* was described as "The Mafia takes to space".

British occultist **Kenneth Grant**, who claimed to be the "heir" to "the wickedest man in the world", Aleister Crowley (1875–1947), died the same day, aged eighty-six. After Crowley's death, he edited and published many of his mentor's works, but he also became involved in a lengthy controversy over his succession to Outer Head of Crowley's self-styled Order of the Ordo Templi Orientis. Grant liberally borrowed from Crowley and H. P. Lovecraft in his own novels, poems and occult treatises.

American writer, poet and artist **Melissa Mia Hall** died of a heart attack on 29 January, aged fifty-five. A former creative writing teacher at the University of Texas Arlington's Continuing Education programme, she started publishing in 1979, and her more than sixty stories appeared in such magazines and anthologies as *Twilight Zone*, *Shayol*, *Realms of Fantasy*, *Shadows 12*, *100 Hair-Raising Little Horror Stories*, *Masques 3* and *Cross Plains Universe*. Hall also collaborated on stories with Douglas E. Winter and Joe R. Lansdale, edited the 1987 anthology *Wild*

Women, and wrote hundreds of reviews and interviews for *Publishers Weekly*.

John Barry [Prendergast] OBE, perhaps Britain's finest and most influential film composer and arranger, died of a heart attack in New York on 31 January. He was seventy-seven. Among many memorable scores, Barry is perhaps best known for his work on the James Bond movies *Dr No* (uncredited), *From Russia with Love*, *Goldfinger*, *Thunderball*, *You Only Live Twice*, *On Her Majesty's Secret Service*, *Diamonds Are Forever*, *The Man with the Golden Gun*, *Moonraker*, *Octopussy*, *A View to a Kill* and *The Living Daylights*. The four-time Oscar winner's numerous other credits include *They Might Be Giants*, *Alice's Adventures in Wonderland* (1972), *The Day of the Locust*, *King Kong* (1976), *The White Buffalo*, *The Deep*, *Starcrash*, Disney's *The Black Hole*, *Raise the Titanic*, *Somewhere in Time* (based on the novel by Richard Matheson), *The Legend of the Lone Ranger*, *Murder by Phone*, *Svengali* (1983), *Howard the Duck* (aka *Howard: A New Breed of Hero*) and *Peggy Sue Got Married*. He also composed the theme music for the 1973 TV series *Orson Welles' Great Mysteries*. The second of Barry's four wives was actress Jane Birkin.

Children's fantasy writer and radio broadcaster [James] **Brian Jacques** died following emergency heart surgery on 5 February. He was seventy-one. He was best known for his popular "Redwall" animal fantasy series, which began in 1987 and ran for more than twenty books. The series, which sold twenty million copies around the world and was translated into almost thirty languages, was adapted into a Canadian animated TV series in 1999. Jacques also published various picture books, "Redwall" spin-offs, and the "Castaways of the Flying Dutchman" series, while his short fiction was collected in *Seven Strange and Ghostly Tales* and *The Ribbajack & Other Curious Yarns*.

American TV writer **Donald S. Sanford** died on 8 February, aged ninety-two. His many credits include episodes of *Thriller* (including "The Incredible Doctor Markesan" starring Boris Karloff) and *The Outer Limits*, and the 1979 post-apocalyptic movie *Ravagers* (set in 1991).

Joanne Siegel (Jolan Kovacs) died on 12 February, aged ninety-three. As a teenager in the late 1930s she advertised her availability in a local newspaper and became the model for "Lois Lane" in the *Superman* comic book series cartoonists Joe Shuster and Jerry Siegel were hoping to sell. She married Siegel in 1948 and in later years campaigned to reclaim her husband's copyright in the character after he sold all rights to DC Comics in 1937 for just $130.

American children's book editor and publisher **Margaret K. (Knox) McElderry**, who created her own eponymous children's imprint in 1971, died on 14 February, aged ninety-eight. In 1952, while working for Harcourt Brace and Company, she became the first editor to publish both the Newbery and Caldecott award-winning books in the same year. Her authors included Mary Norton, Susan Cooper, Andre Norton, Ursula K. Le Guin and Margaret Mahy.

Sixty-seven-year-old German SF author, editor, translator and literary agent **Hans Joachim Alpers** (aka "Jurgen Andreas") died of hepatic cancer after a short illness on 16 February. He edited around fifty anthologies, published numerous juvenile novels under a variety of pseudonyms, and co-edited several reference works, including *Lexicon der Science Fiction Literatur* (1980).

Comics and animation writer **Dwayne McDuffie** died on 21 February, the day after his forty-ninth birthday, from complications due to a surgical procedure. He was a co-founder of the Milestone Media imprint, a coalition of African-American comics writers and artists, through which he helped create such characters as "Static Shock" and "Icon". He also worked for DC and Marvel on such titles as *Damage Control*, *Fantastic Four*, *Justice League of America*, *Firestorm* and *Beyond*. In the field of animation McDuffie's credits include episodes of *Static Shock*, *Ben 10: Alien Force*, *Justice League Unlimited*, *Teen Titans*, *What's New Scooby-Doo?* and the cartoon features *Justice League: Crisis on Two Earths* and *All-Star Superman*.

American author **Lisa Wolfson** (Lisa Kay Madigan), who published YA novels as "L. K. Madigan", died of pancreatic cancer on 23 February, aged forty-seven. Her books include the 2010 fantasy *The Mermaid's Mirror*.

Brazilian literary fantasy author **Moacyr Scliar**, who had more than seventy books to his credit, died on 27 February following a stroke. He was seventy-three.

Dutch fantasy and SF author **Wim Stolk**, who wrote as "W. J. Maryson", died of heart problems on 9 March, aged sixty. An artist and musician, his books include the six-volume "Master Magician" series and the "Unmagician" trilogy.

Reclusive American writer, editor and collector **Bill Blackbeard** (William Elsworth Blackbeard) died on 10 March, aged eighty-four. Widely credited with having one of the most comprehensive newspaper comic strip collections ever assembled – comprising more than 2.5 million strips published between 1893 and 1996 – he co-edited (with Martin Williams) *The Smithsonian Collection of Newspaper Comics* (1977). His other books include *The Comic Strip Art of Lyonel Feininger, R. F. Outcault's the Yellow Kid* and *Sherlock Holmes in America*. Blackbeard's story "Hammer of Cain" (co-written with James Causey) appeared in the November 1943 issue of *Weird Tales*. His archive was acquired by Ohio State University in 1997.

Hollywood and Broadway songwriter **Hugh Martin** who, with Ralph Blane (who died in 1995), composed the songs "Have Yourself a Merry Little Christmas", "The Boy Next Door" and "The Trolly Song" for the 1944 MGM movie *Meet Me in St. Louis*, died on 11 March, aged ninety-six. In 1964 Martin wrote *High Spirits*, a musical version of Noël Coward's *Blithe Spirit*, and he was a vocal arranger and accompanist for Judy Garland, Lena Horne and Debbie Reynolds.

J. K. Rowling's former school chemistry teacher, **John Nettleship**, who was the original inspiration for "Severus Snape" in the *Harry Potter* books, died on 12 March, aged seventy-one.

Sixty-four-year-old English-born Canadian fanzine editor and mathematics teacher **Mike Glicksohn** (Michael David Glicksohn) died of a stroke on 18 March, following treatment for bladder cancer. A founding member of the Ontario Science Fiction Club, he won the Hugo Award in 1973 for his fanzine *Energumen*, which he co-published with his wife, Susan Wood. Glicksohn also published the fanzine *Xenium* and was Fan Guest of Honour at a number of conventions, including Aussiecon in 1975.

American graphic artist **Jim Roslof** (James Paul Roslof) who was TSR's art director for the role-playing game *Dungeons & Dragons* in the 1980s, died on 19 March, aged sixty-five. He also provided artwork for adventure modules and scripted gaming scenarios. After leaving TSR, Roslof contributed art for Goodman Games' *Dungeon Crawl Classics*.

Publisher **April R.** (Rose) **Derleth**, the daughter of Arkham House co-founder August Derleth (who died in 1971), died on 21 March, aged fifty-six. She was co-owner of the imprint with her brother, Walden.

British fantasy writer **Diana Wynne Jones** died after a long battle with lung cancer on 26 March, aged seventy-six. She published more than forty books, mostly for children and young adults, including *The Ogre Downstairs*, *Dogsbody*, *Power of Three*, *The Time of the Ghost*, *The Homeward Bounders*, *Fire and Hemlock*, *Black Maria*, *A Sudden Wild Magic*, *Hexwood* and *Enchanted Glass*. She was also the author of the "Dalemark", "Chrestomanci", "Howl", "Magids" and "Derkholm" series. Jones' short fiction was collected in *Warlock at the Wheel and Other Stories*, *Everard's Ride*, *Minor Arcana* (aka *Believing is Seeing*), *Mixed Magics* and *Unexpected Magic*; she edited the anthologies *Fantasy Stories* (aka *Spellbound*) and *Hidden Turnings*, and wrote the non-fiction study *The Tough Guide to Fantasyland*. *Archer's Goon* was adapted by the BBC into a six-part TV series in 1992, while *Howl's Moving Castle* was turned into an Oscar-nominated *anime* by Hayao Miyazaki. A winner of the Mythopoeic Award and the British Fantasy Society Special Award, she was a Guest of Honour at the 1988 World Fantasy Convention in London and was a recipient of the 2007 World Fantasy Award for Life Achievement.

Prolific British crime writer and critic **H. R. F. Keating** (Henry Reymond Fitzwalter Keating) died on 27 March, aged eighty-four. Best known for his books featuring Detective Inspector Ghote, he also wrote the SF novels *The Strong Man* and *A Long Walk to Wimbledon*.

Welsh author **Craig Thomas** (aka "David Grant"), whose eighteen novels include the techno-thrillers *Firefox* (filmed by Clint Eastwood in 1982) and *Firefox Down*, died of leukemia on 4 April, aged sixty-nine.

American writer **Larry** [Eugene] **Tritten** died after a long illness on 6 April, aged seventy-two. His first SF story appeared in *The Magazine of Fantasy & Science Fiction* in 1974, and he went on to contribute fiction to numerous magazines and anthologies over the next three decades. Tritten also wrote more than 1,500 reviews, columns and travel articles for newspapers and non-genre periodicals.

American TV scriptwriter and producer **Sol Saks**, who created the pilot episode of *Bewitched* (1964–72), died on 16 April, aged 100.

British TV, radio and film scriptwriter **Ken Taylor** (Kenneth Heywood Taylor) died 17 April, aged eighty-eight. In 1983 he scripted three episodes of the Granada TV series *Shades of Darkness* based on stories by Edith Wharton ("The Lady's Maid's Bell"), C. H. B. Kitchin ("The Maze") and Walter De La Mare ("Seaton's Aunt").

British TV and radio comedy writer **Bob Block** (Timothy Robert William Block) died the same day, aged eighty-ine. He created and scripted such children's TV series as *Pardon My Genie* (1972–73), *Robert's Robots* (1973–74), *Rentaghost* (1976–80) and *Galloping Galaxies!* (1985–86). A *Rentaghost: The Musical* was produced on stage in 2006 starring Joe Pasquale, and a movie version of the series is currently in development.

American artist **Doug** (Douglas) **Chaffee** died on 26 April, aged seventy-five. After leaving his job as head of IBM's Art Department, he became a freelance illustrator, working for NASA and contributing to such TSR role-playing games as *Dungeons & Dragons* and *Magic: The Gathering*.

Wiescka Masterton (Wiescka Walach), the Polish-German wife and literary agent of horror writer Graham Masterton, died on 27 April, aged sixty-five. She had been suffering from a long illness and died of complications from a fall. The couple met when they were both working at *Penthouse* magazine in the early 1970s, and Masterson's first horror novel, *The Manitou*, was inspired by his wife's pregnancy. In 1988 she sold the book to Poland, before the collapse of the Communist regime, and it became the first Western horror novel to be published in the country since World War II.

American feminist SF writer and ground-breaking critic **Joanna** [Ruth] **Russ** died on 29 April, following a series of strokes. She was seventy-four. Russ' first story appeared in *The Magazine of Fantasy & Science Fiction* in 1959, and her short fiction is collected in *Alyx* (aka *The Adventures of Alyx*), *The*

Zanzibar Cat, *Extraordinary People* and *The Hidden Side of the Moon*. Best known for her influential 1975 novel *The Female Man*, her other novels include *Picnic on Paradise*, *And Chaos Died*, *We Who Are About To* . . ., and *The Two of Them*. Her essays and criticism are collected in a number of volumes, and during her career she won the Hugo, Nebula, Tiptree and Pilgrim Awards.

British scriptwriter **Jeremy Paul** [Roche] died of pancreatic cancer on 3 May, aged seventy-one. His credits include Hammer's *Countess Dracula* and episodes of TV's *Out of the Unknown*, *Journey to the Unknown*, *Tales of the Unexpected*, *Play for Today* ("The Flipside of Dominick Hide" and "Another Flick for Dominick"), *The Adventures of Sherlock Holmes*, *The Return of Sherlock Holmes*, *The Case-Book of Sherlock Holmes* ("The Last Vampyre") and *The Memoirs of Sherlock Holmes*. Paul also scripted the 1988 stage production *The Secret of Sherlock Holmes* starring Jeremy Brett.

British SF author and organic chemist **Martin Sherwood**, who published two novels with New English Library in the mid-1970s, *Survival* and *Maxwell's Demon*, died on 10 May, aged sixty-nine.

Simon Heneage (Simon Anthony Helyar Walker-Heneage), co-founder of London's Cartoon Museum and an expert on artist W. Heath Robinson, died on 14 May, aged eighty.

British psychologist, novelist, scriptwriter, engineer and artificial intelligence researcher **Martin** [Charlton] **Woodhouse** died on 15 May, aged seventy-eight. Credited with creating the first ebooks, his novels include the "Giles Yeoman" series of technothrillers: *Tree Frog*, *Bush Baby*, *Mama Doll*, *Blue Bone* and *Moon Hill*. In the 1960s Woodhouse scripted six early episodes of *The Avengers* featuring Honor Blackman and a later show featuring Diana Rigg. He also wrote twenty-two episodes of *Supercar* with his younger brother Hugh, and the children's SF serial *Emerald Soup*.

Iconic fantasy artist **Jeffrey** ["Catherine"] **Jones**, who was once praised by Frank Frazetta as "the greatest living painter", died of complications from emphysema, bronchitis and heart problems on 18 May, aged sixty-seven. He was reportedly severely underweight. A member of the legendary 1970s artists' group The Studio (which also included Michael William Kaluta,

Barry Windsor-Smith and Bernie Wrightson), Jones was one of
the most prolific genre artists of the 1960s and '70s, producing
more than 150 covers for books by Fritz Leiber (notably the
"Fafhrd and the Gray Mouser" series), Jack Vance, Andre
Norton, Robert E. Howard, Karl Edward Wagner, Dean Koontz
and many others, along with magazine and comics work. In
1998 Jones began hormone replacement therapy, and subsequently suffered an apparent nervous breakdown before
returning to painting in the early 2000s. The World Fantasy
Award-winning artist's work is collected in *The Studio*, *Age of
Innocence: The Romantic Art of Jeffrey Jones*, *The Art of Jeffrey
Jones*, *Jeffrey Jones Sketchbook* and *Jeffrey Jones: A Life in Art*.

American author and music composer [Robert] **Mark
Shepherd** committed suicide by a self-inflicted gunshot wound
on 25 May. He was forty-nine. Shepherd was best known for his
collaborations with Mercedes Lackey (whose personal secretary
he was during the 1990s) on such fantasy novels as *Wheels of
Fire* and *Prison of Souls*. His solo books set in the same worlds
include *Elvendude*, *Spiritride*, *Lazerwarz* and *Escape from
Roksamur*, while *Blackrose Avenue* was a dystopian SF novel.

British fan artist, writer and publisher [Byron] **Terry Jeeves**
died on 29 May, aged eighty-eight. A founder of the British
Science Fiction Association in 1958, he edited the group's journal *Vector* from 1958–59. Jeeves also edited the fanzines *Triode*
and *ERG*, and his articles and artwork appeared in numerous
publications, winning him the Rotsler Award in 2007. He was
also a recipient of the Doc Weir Award for services to British
fandom, and he was inducted into the First Fandom Hall of
Fame in 2010. Jeeves' story "Upon Reflection" appeared in *The
25th Pan Book of Horror Stories*, and much of his fanzine writing was collected in the tribute magazine *Wartime Days* (2010).

Fifty-seven-year-old Canadian-born fantasy and SF author
Joel Rosenberg, an outspoken gun advocate, died in Minneapolis
on 2 June after suffering respiratory problems that resulted in a
heart attack, brain damage and major organ failure. He made his
writing debut in *Asimov's* magazine in 1982, and his novels
include *The Sleeping Dragon* (and nine sequels in his "Guardians
of the Flame" series), *Ties of Blood and Silver*, *D'Shai*, *The Fire
Duke*, *The Silver Stone*, *The Crimson Sky*, *Home Front*, the

"Riftwar" novel *Murder in LaMut* (with Raymond E. Feist), *Paladins* and *Knight Moves*. In November 2010, Rosenberg, who also wrote *Everything You Need to Know About (Legally) Carrying a Handgun in Minnesota*, was arrested for carrying a holstered semi-automatic handgun into a meeting at City Hall.

American writer, editor, journalist and book critic **Alan** [Peter] **Ryan** died of pancreatic cancer in Brazil on 3 June, aged sixty-eight. His articles and reviews appeared in the *Washington Post*, *Chicago Tribune*, *USA Today*, *New York Times*, *Los Angeles Times*, *Village Voice* and other periodicals. The author of such superior 1980s horror novels as *Panther!*, *The Kill*, *Dead White* and *Cast a Cold Eye*, he won a World Fantasy Award for his story "The Bone Wizard", and his short fiction is collected in *Quadriphobia* and *The Bone Wizard and Other Stories*. Ryan was also an accomplished editor whose anthologies include *Perpetual Light*, *Night Visions 1*, *Halloween Horrors*, *The Penguin Book of Vampire Stories* (aka *Vampires*) and *Haunting Women*. Following a twenty-year absence from the genre, and after suffering a stroke and a heart attack in recent years, he had begun contributing fiction to magazines and anthologies again.

Sixty-four-year-old British author, editor and journalist **Tim** (Timothy) **Stout** died in County Wexford, Ireland, on 5 June. He had been suffering from Alzheimer's disease for many years. Stout began his career in the genre with contributions to John Carpenter's fanzine *Fantastic Films Illustrated*, and he edited the only two issues of the superior British horror film magazine *Supernatural* (1969). As an author, his short story "The Boy Who Neglected His Grass Snake" appeared in *The 9th Pan Book of Horror Stories* (1968), and during the 1970s and '80s he had fiction published in such anthologies as *Space 2, 5* and *8*, *Armada Sci-Fi 1* and *2*, *The Year's Best Horror Stories: Series III*, *Spectre 2, 3* and *4*, and *The Jon Pertwee Book of Monsters*, all edited by Richard Davis, along with Peter Haining's *Tales of Unknown Horror*. Stout's short fiction was collected in *Hollow Laughter* and *The Doomsdeath Chronicles*, and his only published novel was *The Raging* (1987).

Prolific British SF author, professional research chemist and astronomer **John** [Stephen] **Glasby** died of complications from a fall the same day, aged eighty-three. His first novel appeared in

1952 and, while working for ICI, over the next two decades he produced more than 300 novels and short stories in all genres, most of them published pseudonymously (under such shared bylines as "A.J. Merak", "Victor La Salle", "John E. Muller", etc.) for the legendary Badger Books imprint. More recently, he published a new collection of ghost stories, *The Substance of Shade* (2003), the occult novel *The Dark Destroyer* (2005), and the SF novel *Mystery of the Crater* (2010). Glasby also wrote four novels continuing the late John Russell Fearn's "Golden Amazon" series, and his short fiction was anthologized by, amongst others, Richard Dalby, Robert M. Price, Philip Harbottle and Stephen Jones.

American writer and bookseller **Malcolm M.** (Magoun) **Ferguson** died on 11 June following hip surgery. He was ninety-one. Between 1946 and 1950 he had five stories published in *Weird Tales*, and he was also a regular contributor to *The Arkham Sampler*. Ferguson was also an antiquarian bookseller, and his own collection reportedly contained around 30,000 volumes.

American scriptwriter **David Rayfiel** died of congestive heart failure on 22 June, aged eighty-seven. His credits include the allegorical war film *Castle Keep* (1969), *Lipstick*, *Death Watch* (based on the novel by David Compton) and two episodes of Rod Serling's *Night Gallery* ("She'll Be Company for You" and "Whisper"). Rayfiel was married to actress Maureen Stapleton from 1963–66.

American comics artist **Gene Colon** (Eugene Jules Colan) died of complications from a broken hip and liver disease on 23 June. He was eighty-four. Colan began his career in comics in 1944, but he is best remembered for his work for Marvel Comics on such titles as *Daredevil*, *Captain America*, *Doctor Strange*, *The Avengers*, *Howard the Duck*, *Dracula Lives* and *The Tomb of Dracula*. With Stan Lee he created the "Falcoln", the first African-American superhero in mainstream comics, and also vampire-hunter "Blade", whose exploits were adapted into a series of films and a TV series. During the 1980s the artist also worked at DC Comics on such titles as *Batman* and *Detective Comics*, along with *Wonder Woman*, *Spectre*, *Elvira's House of Mystery* and the movie tie-in of *Little Shop of Horrors*.

American music composer and orchestrator **Fred** (Frederick) **Steiner**, who wrote the memorable theme for TV's *Perry Mason*, died the same day in Mexico, aged eighty-eight. The son of noted film composer George Steiner, he worked (often uncredited) on *Run for the Sun*, *The Colossus of New York*, *Teenagers from Outer Space*, *Snow White and the Three Stooges*, *Robinson Crusoe on Mars*, *The Greatest Story Ever Told*, *Project X*, *Return of the Jedi*, *Cloak & Dagger* and *Gremlins 2: The New Batch*, along with episodes of *The Twilight Zone*, *The Wild Wild West* and the original *Star Trek*.

Prolific anthologist, packager and author **Martin H.** (Harry) **Greenberg** died on 25 June after a long battle with cancer. He was 70. Greenberg – who used his middle initial to differentiate himself from Gnome Press publisher Martin Greenberg – worked on more than 1,000 anthologies in all genres, many of them published through his own Tekno Books business. His first anthology, *Political Science Fiction* (co-edited with Patricia Warrick), appeared in 1974, and his other collaborators included Isaac Asimov, Poul Anderson, Arthur C. Clarke, Peter Crowther, Ed Gorman, Andre Norton, Frederik Pohl, Robert Silverberg, Robert Weinberg and numerous others. Greenberg won the Milford Award for Lifetime Achievement in 1989 and the Life Achievement Award from the Horror Writers Association in 2004.

Belgian SF and crime author, anthology editor and comics historian **Thierry Martens** (aka "Yves Varende") died on 27 June, aged sixty-nine. He also edited the comic *Journal de Spirou*.

British novelist, poet and short story writer **Francis** [Henry] **King** CBE died on 3 July, aged eighty-eight. Three of his early novels were published by Herbert van Thal, who also included King's story "School Crossing" in *The 20th Pan Book of Horror Stories*.

American author **Theodore Roszak**, best known for his 1991 novel *Flicker*, died of liver cancer on 5 July, aged seventy-seven. Among his other novels are *Pontifex*, *Bugs*, *Dreamwatcher*, *The Memoirs of Elizabeth Frankenstein* and *The Devil and Daniel Silverman*. A professor emeritus of history at Cal State East Bay, his scholarly works include the ground-breaking study *The Making of a Counter Culture: Reflections on the Technocratic Society* (1969).

Japanese *anime* artist **Shinji Wada** (Yoshifumi Iwamoto) died of ischaemic heart disease the same day, aged sixty-one. He was best known for creating the *Sukeban Deka* franchise in 1979, which was turned into TV series and movies.

Veteran American comedy TV writer and producer **Sherwood** [Charles] **Schwartz** died on 12 July, aged ninety-four. Best known for creating such shows as *Gilligan's Island*, *It's About Time* and *The Brady Bruch*, he also co-scripted the 1983 TV movie *The Invisible Woman*.

Philip J. Rahman, one half of the publishing imprint Fedogan & Bremer, took his own life on 23 July, aged fifty-nine. He had been in declining health for some years and suffering personal difficulties. F&B was set up in the late 1980s by Rahman and Dennis Weiler (who named the imprint after nicknames they had in college – Weiler was "Fedogan" and Rahman was "Bremer") to produce the kind of books they no longer felt Arkham House was publishing. Following an audio version of H. P. Lovecraft's *Fungi from Yuggoth*, the first F&B book title was *Colossus: The Collected Science Fiction of Donald Wandrei*, and they went on to publish collections and novels by Robert Bloch, Hugh B. Cave, Howard Wandrei, Carl Jacobi, Basil Copper, Karl Edward Wagner, Richard L. Tierney, Brian Lumley, R. Chetwynd-Hayes, Richard A. Lupoff and Adam Niswander, along with anthologies edited by Robert M. Price and Stephen Jones. The imprint won the World Fantasy Award – Non-Professional, and many of the titles it published were also award winners or nominees.

Cryonics advocate **Robert C.** (Chester) **W.** (Wilson) **Ettinger,** who wrote a number of non-fiction books about extending life through cryonic freezing, died the same day, aged ninety-two. He also published some SF stories, beginning with "The Penultimate Trump" in *Startling Stories* (1948). Not surprisingly, his body was cryopreserved at the Cryonics Institute, which he founded in 1976.

Eighty-year-old Japanese SF writer **Sakyo Komatsu** (Minoru Komatsu), best known for his 1973 disaster novel *Nippon Chinbotsu* (*Japan Sinks*, filmed in 1974 and 2006), died of pneumonia on 26 July. He was also a prolific writer of short stories, articles and *anime* scripts.

Best-selling urban fantasy and paranormal romance writer **L. A. Banks** (Leslie Esdaile Banks) died of a rare form of adrenal cancer on 2 August, aged fifty-one. The author of more than forty books since her debut in 1996, her popular "Vampire Huntress Legends" series began in 2003 with *Minion* and continued with *The Awakening*, *The Hunted*, *The Bitten*, *The Forbidden*, *The Damned*, *The Forsaken*, *The Wicked*, *The Cursed*, *The Darkness*, *The Shadows* and *The Thirteenth*. She also wrote the "Crimson Moon" werewolf series, comprising *Bad Blood* (2008), *Bite the Bullet*, *Undead on Arrival*, *Cursed to Death*, *Never Cry Werewolf* and *Left for Dead*. *Surrender the Dark* and *Conquer the Dark* were the first two books in a new series about angels. Banks also wrote romance, crime and media tie-ins under various pseudonyms.

American children's and young adult author **William Sleator** (William Warner Sleator III) died in Thailand the same day, aged sixty-six. His more than thirty books include *The Angry Moon*, *Blackbriar*, *House of Stairs*, *Fingers*, *Interstellar Pig*, *Singularity*, *The Duplicate*, *The Boy Who Reversed Himself*, *Rewind*, *The Boy Who Couldn't Die* and *The Phantom Limb*. Sleator was also an accomplished pianist, playing for a number of ballet schools.

American comics writer and editor **Del Connell** died of complications from Alzheimer's disease on 12 August, aged ninety-three. He started out as a character sculptor for the Walt Disney Studio in 1939, where he worked on the stories for *The Three Caballeros* and *Alice in Wonderland* (1951). After moving to Western Publishing's Dell Comics in 1954, he wrote thousands of comics (usually uncredited), including *Space Family Robinson* (which was turned into the TV series *Lost in Space*) and numerous Disney titles. For more than twenty years Connell also wrote the daily and Sunday *Mickey Mouse* newspaper strip.

Fifty-year-old British fantasy and SF author **Colin Harvey** died on 15 August, having suffered a massive stroke the day before. His novels include *Vengeance*, *Lightning Days*, *The Silk Palace*, *Blind Faith*, *Winter Song* and *Damage Time*, and his stories appeared in such magazines and anthologies as *Albedo One*, *Interzone*, *Apex*, *Daily Science Fiction*, *Fearology* and *Gothic.net*. His short fiction was collected in *Displacement*, and he also edited the anthologies *Killers*, *Future Bristol*, *Dark Spires* and *Transtories*. While working for Unilever, Harvey helped launch Ben & Jerry's Ice Cream in Iceland.

British artist **John Holmes,** best known for his iconic cover for Germaine Greer's *The Female Eunuch* (1970), died on 17 August, aged seventy-six. His other credits include the cover of Peter Benchley's *Jaws*, the Ballentine editions of H. P. Lovecraft, the Peter Haining anthologies *The Evil People* and *The Midnight People*, plus reissues of Pan's two volumes of *The Hammer Horror Omnibus* and various editions of *The Fontana Book of Horror* edited by Mary Danby.

Veteran Hammer scriptwriter, producer and director **Jimmy Sangster** (James Henry Kimmel Sangster, aka "John Sansom") died on 19 August, aged eighty-three. He began his career at the studio as an assistant director on *Man in Black*, *Dick Barton Strikes Back*, *Room to Let*, *Stolen Face* and *Spaceways*. However, starting as a scriptwriter with *X: The Unknown* in 1956, Sangster was responsible (with director Terrence Fisher and others) for ushering the Hammer House of Horror era with *The Curse of Frankenstein*, *Dracula* (aka *Horror of Dracula*), *The Revenge of Frankenstein*, *The Snorkel*, *The Man Who Could Cheat Death*, *The Mummy* (1959), *The Brides of Dracula*, *The Terror of the Tongs*, *Taste of Fear*, *Paranoiac*, *Maniac*, *Nightmare*, *Hysteria*, *The Nanny*, *Dracula Prince of Darkness*, *The Anniversary* and *Crescendo*. For Hammer he also directed *The Horror of Frankenstein*, *Lust for a Vampire* and *Fear in the Night*, and he novelised a number of his screenplays. Sangster worked for other production companies, and his film credits also include *Blood of the Vampire*, *The Trollenberg Terror* (aka *The Crawling Eye*), *Jack the Ripper* (1959), *The Hellfire Club*, *Deadlier Than the Male*, *A Taste of Evil*, *Whoever Slew Auntie Roo?*, *Scream Pretty Peggy*, *Maneater*, *Good Against Evil*, *The Legacy*, *The Billion Dollar Threat*, *Phobia*, *Once Upon a Spy*, Disney's *The Devil and Max Devlin* and *Flashback – Mörderisc Ferien*. During the 1970s he wrote numerous scripts for American TV shows, including *Ghost Story*, *The Six Million Dollar Man*, *Kolchak: The Night Stalker* and *Wonder Woman*. His autobiography, *Do You Want it Good or Tuesday?* was published in 1997.

Sixty-three-year-old American bookseller **Bill Trojan** (William T. Trojan) died of a massive heart attack in his hotel room on 21 August, the final day of Renovation, the 2011 World Science Fiction Convention in Reno, Nevada. He had been suffering with health problems for several years. Trojan was one of the chairs of the 1996 World Horror Convention in Eugene, Oregon, and was a major financial supporter of Pulphouse Publishing in the late 1980s.

Fifty-nine-year-old American SF fan **Dan Hoey**, who chaired the 1995 Disclave convention in Washington DC, committed suicide on 31 August.

American journalist and cartoonist **Bill Kunkel** (William Henry Patrick Kunkel), who co-created *Electronic Games*, the first video and computer game magazine, died of an apparent heart attack on 4 September, aged sixty-one. He also wrote comic books for Marvel and DC Comics and created video games.

Digital publishing pioneer **Michael S.** (Stern) **Heart**, the founder of Project Gutenberg, the world's oldest digital library, died of a heart attack on 6 September, aged sixty-four. He is often credited as the "creator" of the ebook, having made an electronic copy of the American Declaration of Independence available for download at the University of Illinois in Urbana in 1971.

Former US Army soldier and shipyard worker **Charles E. Hickson** died of a heart attack on 9 September, aged eighty. On 11 October, 1973, Hickson and another man were fishing off the west bank of the Pascagoula River, Mississippi, when they claimed they were abducted by aliens. This became known as the "Pascagoula Abduction". Hickson appeared in the 1978 feature documentary, *The Force Beyond*, and in 1983 he wrote a book about his experience, *UFO Contact in Pascagoula*.

American comics artist **Jack Adler** died on 18 September, aged ninety-four. He was a staff member of DC Comics' production department from 1946 to 1981, working as a cover artist and colourist on such titles as *Sea Devils*, *Green Lantern* and *G.I. Combat*.

American horror short fiction writer and editor **Mark W.** (Whitney) **Worthen** died on 19 September, aged forty-nine. He created the online magazine *Blood Rose* (1998–2005) and co-edited *Desolate Souls*, the souvenir anthology of the 2008 World Horror Convention, with his second wife, Jeannie Eddy (aka "J. P. Edwards"). Worthen was closely involved with the Horror Writers Association, as both a webmaster and co-chair of the awards committee. He received the HWA's Richard Laymon President's Award for Services in 2007.

Eighty-nine-year-old British author **John** [Frederick] **Burke** died on 21 September following a fall in his home. He became a SF fan in the 1930s, writing letters to *Weird Tales* and founding the early UK fanzine *The Satellite* with David McIlwain (aka "Charles Eric Maine"). Sam Youd (aka "John Christopher") was also a regular contributor to the magazine. Burke's short stories appeared in *Authentic Science Fiction*, *Science Fantasy*, *Nebula*, *New Worlds*, the *6th* and *9th Pan Book of Horror Stories*, *Tandem Horror Three*, the *6th* and *8th Ghost Book*, *New Terrors 2*, *After Midnight*, *Scare Care*, *The Mammoth Book of Best New Horror Volume Nine*, *Don't Turn Out the Light*, *Brighton Shock!* and many other magazines and anthologies. His first novel, published in 1949, won an Atlantic Award in Literature from the Rockefeller Foundation, and he worked for Museum Press before becoming European story editor for 20th Century-Fox Productions in 1963. Best known for his 1970s trilogy of novels featuring psychic investigator "Dr Caspian" (*The Devil's Footsteps*, *The Black Charade* and *Ladygrove*), he wrote more than 150 books (under his own name and a variety of pseudonyms), many of them film and TV novelisations, including the Beatles' *A Hard Day's Night*, *Dr Terror's House of Horrors*, *The Hammer Horror Film Omnibus*, *The Second Hammer Horror Film Omnibus*, *Chitty Chitty Bang Bang*, *Privilege*, *Moon Zero Two* and two tie-ins to Gerry Anderson's *U.F.O.* (as "Robert Miall"). Burke also edited three anthologies for Pan Books (*Tales of Unease*, *More Tales of Unease* and *New Tales of Unease*), and some of his best short stories are collected in *We've Been Waiting for You*, edited by Nicholas Royle for Ash-Tree Press. A new macabre collection, *Murder, Mystery and Magic*, and a new SF collection, *The Old Man of the Stars*, were published in 2011, and he had completed a new horror novel, *The Nightmare Whisperers*, shortly before he died. Burke also scripted the 1967 Boris Karloff movie *The Sorcerers*, but only received credit for the original idea.

Best-selling Australian fantasy author **Sara Douglass** (Sara Mary Warneke) died of ovarian cancer on 26 September, aged fifty-four. Best known for the "Wayfarer Redemption" series, which began in 1995 with the best-seller *BattleAxe* and continued with *Enchanter*, *Starman*, *Sinner*, *Pilgrim* and *Crusader*, her other series include the "Crucible" trilogy, "Darkglass Mountain" and "Troy Game". Douglass also wrote *Beyond the Hanging Wall*, *Threshold* and *The Devil's Diadem*, and some of her short stories were collected in *The Hall of Lost Footsteps*.

American playwright and screenwriter **David Z.** (Zelag) **Goodman** died of progressive supranuclear palsy the same day, aged eighty-one. His credits include Hammer's *The Stranglers of Bombay*, *Straw Dogs*, *Man on a Swing*, *Logan's Run* and *Eyes of Laura Mars*.

Italian comics writer and publisher **Sergio Bonelli** also died on 26 September, aged seventy-nine. His Sergio Bonelli Editore imprint published the psychic-investigator title *Dylan Dog*.

Italian editor and writer **Vittorio Curtoni** died of a heart attack on 4 October, aged sixty-two. He had been suffering from cancer. Between 1970–75 he co-edited the Galassia paperback line, founded the Italian SF magazine *Robot* in 1976 and translated more than 300 novels. Curtoni's own short stories were collected in *Bianco su nero* (*White on Black*) and he wrote the novel *Dove stiamo volando* (*Where Are We Flying To*).

American lawyer and civil rights activist **Derrick Bell** (Derrick Albert Bell, Jr.) died of carcinoid cancer on 5 October, aged eighty. His SF story "The Space Traders" was adapted by HBO for the 1994 anthology TV show *Cosmic Slop*.

British author **Jack D. Shackleford** died of lung cancer on 13 October, aged seventy-three. A former professional heavyweight boxer, professional cricketer, folk-singer and practising traditional witch, he wrote the novels *Tanith* (1970), *The Strickland Demon* (1977) and *The House of the Magus* (1979), and he had a short story in *The 17th Pan Book of Horror Stories*.

Veteran American comic book writer **Alvin Schwartz**, who is credited for inventing the "Bizarro World" concept in *Superman*, died of heart-related problems in Canada on 28 October, aged ninety-five. He also scripted copies of *Batman*, *Wonder Woman*, *Green Lantern*, *The Flash* and *House of Mystery*. Schwartz wrote the newspaper strips for a number of DC Comics heroes and worked on rival Fawcett's *Captain Marvel*.

Comic book writer, artist and editor **Mick Anglo** (Maurice Anglowitz), the creator of British superhero "Marvelman", died on 31 October, aged ninety-five. Over the years he re-vamped the character (and often the same artwork) as "Captain Universe", "Captain Miracle" and Miracle Man". Anglo produced a 1966 hardcover annual for TV's *The Avengers*; the short-lived mid-1960s comics *Fantasy Stories*, *Macabre Stories*, *Spectre Stories* and *Strange Stories* for John Spencer & Co., and he also illustrated the tie-in strips "Voyage to the Bottom of the Sea" and "Green Hornet" for *TV Tornado*, which he edited.

American author, journalist and musician **Les Daniels** (Leslie Noel Daniels, III) died of a heart attack on 5 November, aged sixty-eight. Best known for his centuries-spanning series of books about the vampire Don Sebastian de Villanueva (*The Black Castle*, *The Silver Skull*, *Citizen Vampire*, *Yellow Fog* and *No Blood Spilled*), he was also the author of the non-fiction study *Living in Fear: A History of Horror in the Mass Media* and edited the anthology *Dying of Fright: Masterpieces of the Macabre*, illustrated by the Lee Brown Coye. Daniels was also an authority on comic books, and he wrote *Comix: A History of Comic Books in America* (1971) and definitive guides to Superman, Batman and Wonder Woman, along with authoritative histories of Marvel and DC Comics. His short fiction appeared in such anthologies as *Best New Horror 4*, *Dark Voices 4* and *5*, and *Dark Terrors 5*.

Hollywood screenwriter, producer and director **Hal Kanter** died of pneumonia on 6 November, aged ninety-two. He was the son of Albert L. Kanter, who founded the Classic Comics (later Classics Illustrated) line in 1941. Kanter wrote the screenplays for such Bob Hope comedies as *My Favorite Spy*, *Road to Bali*, *Here Come the Girls* and *Casanova's Big Night*, and in 1953 he began regularly scripting the Annual Academy Awards show.

American composer, bandleader and trumpeter **Russell Garcia**, who composed the music scores for the George Pal productions *The Time Machine* (1960) and *Atlantis the Lost Continent*, died of cancer in New Zealand on 20 November, aged ninety-five.

American science fiction author **Anne [Inez] McCaffrey** died of a massive stroke at her home in Ireland on 21 November, aged eighty-five. She began her writing career in 1953, and is best known for her best-selling "Pern" series, which began with the "fix-up" novel *Dragonflight* in 1968 and continued for more than twenty further volumes, with later titles co-written with her son, Todd McCaffrey. Her more than 100 books also include the "Talents", "Doona", "Dinosaur Planet", "Killashandra" and "Catteni" series, along with such stand-alone novels as *The Mark of Merlin*, *The Coelura*, *Nimisha's Ship* and *Catalyst*. McCaffrey's short fiction is collected in *The Ship Who Sang* and *Get Off the Unicorn*, she edited two anthologies and wrote two cookbooks, while *Dragonholder* (1999) is a biography written by her son. She was the first woman to win both the Nebula and Hugo Awards, and her "Pern" book *The White Dragon* (1978) was the first SF novel to appear on the *New York Times* best-seller list. She was also a recipient of the British Fantasy Society's Karl Edward Wagner Award, and was named a SFWA Grand Master in 2005.

Robert E. Briney (Robert Edward "Bob" Briney, Jr.), an expert on Sax Rohmer and mystery and supernatural fiction, died on 25 November, aged seventy-seven. A co-founder of the Advent: Publishing imprint in 1956, he edited the 1953 anthology *Shanadu* and also contributed a novella under the pseudonym "Andrew Duane" (written with Brian J. McNaughton). Briney edited the 1972 reference book *SF Bibliographies: An Annotated Bibliography of Bibliographical Works on Science Fiction and Fantasy Fiction* along with eighteen issues of *The Rohmer Review* (1970–83).

Japanese *anime* artist and director **Shingo Araki** died on 1 December, aged seventy-two. Among his credits are *Ulysses 31*, *Inspector Gadget* and *The Mighty Orbots*.

Sixty-three-year-old American fanzine publisher **Bob Sabella** died of an inoperable brain tumour on 3 December. He edited 170 issues of *Visions of Paradise* and wrote the 2000 study *Who Shaped Science Fiction?*

American artist **Darrell K.** (Kinsman) **Sweet** died on 5 December, aged seventy-seven. Best known for his work with such imprints as Ballantine Books and Del Rey in the 1970s, he produced the cover art for Robert Jordan's "Wheels of Time" series, Stephen R. Donaldson's "Chronicles of Thomas Covenant" series, and Piers Anthony's "Xanth" series. His artwork was collected in *Beyond Fantasy: The Art of Darrell K. Sweet* (1997).

American comic book artist and historian **Jerry Robinson** died in his sleep on 7 December, aged eighty-nine. Originally hired as an inker at the age of seventeen by "Batman" creator Bob Kane, Robinson went on to co-create "Robin, the Boy Wonder" and was a primary influence on the creation of the duo's arch-nemesis "The Joker" (modelled after Conrad Veidt in the 1928 movie *The Man Who Laughs*), "Two-Face" and Bruce Wayne's butler, "Alfred Pennyworth". In later years he moved into newspaper comic strips and became an advocate for the rights of artists. Robinson's 1974 book, *The Comics*, was one of the first books about newspaper strips.

Scottish writer, critic and translator **Gilbert Adair** died on 8 December, aged sixty-six. In the 1980s he wrote the children's sequels *Alice Through the Needle's Eye* and *Peter Pan and the Only Children*.

British fantasy author **Euan Harvey** died of cancer on 9 December, aged thirty-eight. He began his writing career in 2007 and sold eight stories to *Realms of Fantasy* magazine.

French SF author **Louis Thirion** died the same day, aged eighty-eight. He published more than thirty novels, starting in 1964 with *Waterloo, morne plaine*. He also contributed several scripts to the radio series *Théâtre de l'Étrange*.

American-born author and illustrator **Russell** [Conwell] **Hoban**, best known for his post-holocaust novel *Riddley Walker* (1980), died of congestive heart failure in London on 13 December, aged eighty-six. He began publishing in 1959, and produced more than twenty titles for children and adults, including *Pilgerman*, *The Medusa Frequency*, *Turtle Diary*, *The Mouse and His Child* and the "Frances the Badger" series.

American SF author and medical doctor **T. J. Bass** (Thomas J. Bassler) died in Honoloulu the same day, aged seventy-nine. Starting in 1968, he had a number of stories published in *If* and *Galaxy* magazines, and his linked novels *Half Past Human* (1971) and *The Godwhale* (1974) were both nominated for Nebula Awards.

Legendary comic book creator **Joe Simon** (Hymie Simon, aka Joseph Henry "Joe" Simon) died after a brief illness on 14 December, aged ninety-eight. He created (with Jack Kirby) such characters as Captain America, the Newsboy Legion, the Boy Commandos, Manhunter, Fighting American and the Fly. The duo also worked on *Adventure Comics*, *Detective Comics*, *Sandman* and numerous other titles in all genres, including the horror comics *Black Magic* and *The Strange World of Your Dreams*. Titan Books recently published the huge retrospective volume of their work, *The Best of Simon and Kirby*, along with the autobiographical work *Joe Simon: My Life in Comics*.

Fifty-year-old Italian fantasy and horror author and magazine editor **Gianluca Casseri**, known for his extreme right-wing views, killed himself the same day after shooting dead two Senegalese street traders and wounding three others in Florence.

French SF and espionage author **Richard Bessiere** died on 22 December, aged eighty-eight. His first science fiction series, "Conquérants de l'universe" (1951–54), was followed by a number of stand-alone SF/horror novels, including *Les maîtres du silence* and *Cette lueur qui venait des ténèbres*, along with a series about a futuristic James Bond named "Dan Seymour".

American SF fan, book dealer and collector **James L. "Rusty" Hevelin** died on 27 December, aged eighty-nine. Instantly recognisable from his Gandalf-style beard, he edited such fanzines as *Aliquot*, *H-1661* and *Badly*, and was Fan Guest of Honour at the 1981 World Science Fiction Convention.

Ninety-one-year-old British illustrator **Ronald** [William Fordham] **Searle** CBE, whose famous *St. Trinian's* cartoons often rivalled those of Charles Addams for macabre humour, died after a short illness at his home in the south of France on 30 December. Besides the *St. Trinian's* titles, his many other books include Charles Dickens' *A Christmas Carol* (1961), James Thurber's *The 13 Clocks and the Wonderful O*, *Scrooge* (1970), *Dick Deadeye* (filmed in 1975), *Marquis de Sade Meets Goody Two-Shoes* and *Something in the Cellar*.

American agent, editor and publisher **Glenn** [Richard] **Lord**, best known for his work as agent for the Robert E. Howard Estate, died on 31 December, aged eighty. He edited *The Howard Collector* magazine from 1961–73, and the 1979 compilation *The Howard Collector: By and About Robert E. Howard*. His non-fiction volumes include the still-indispensable *The Last Celt: A Bio-Bibliography of Robert Ervin Howard* and two volumes of *Robert E. Howard: Selected Letters*. Lord received a World Fantasy Special Convention Award in 1978.

PERFORMERS/PERSONALITIES

Dependable British character actor **Pete Postlethwaite** OBE
(Peter William Postlethwaite) died in his sleep after a long battle
with cancer on 2 January, aged sixty-four. A former drama
teacher, his credits include *Split Second* (1992), *Alien³*, *The
Usual Suspects*, *James and the Giant Peach*, *DragonHeart*, *The
Lost World: Jurassic Park*, *Alice in Wonderland* (1999), *Animal
Farm* (1999), *Dark Water* (2005), *Æon Flux*, *The Omen* (2006),
Lamberto Bava's *Ghost Son*, *Solomon Kane*, *Clash of the Titans*
(2010) and *Inception*.

Hollywood leading lady **Anne [Lloyd] Francis**, who memorably starred as "Altaira" in the SF classic *Forbidden Planet* (1956),
died of pancreatic cancer the same day, aged eighty. A former
child model, she also appeared in the films *Portrait of Jennie*
(uncredited), *The Satan Bug*, *Brainstorm* and the TV movies
Haunts of the Very Rich and *Mazes and Monsters*. From 1965–
66 Francis portrayed the sexy private detective with a pet ocelot
in ABC's *Honey West* (a spin-off series from *Burke's Law*) and
she also appeared in episodes of *Suspense*, *Lights Out*, *Climax!*,
The Twilight Zone, *Alfred Hitchcock Presents*, *The Alfred
Hitchcock Hour*, *The Man from U.N.C.L.E.*, *The Invaders*,
Search Control, *Wonder Woman*, *Fantasy Island* (both the original series and 1990s revival) and *Conan*.

Early American talkies star **Mirian Seegar** also died on
2 January. She was 103 years old. Seegar's credits include RKO's
1929 version of *Seven Keys to Baldpate*. In the early 1930s she
married director Tim Whelan and retired from the screen.

British-born actress **[Valeria] Jill Haworth** died in her sleep
at her apartment in Manhattan on 3 January, aged sixty-five.
The first actress to portray "Sally Bowles" in *Cabaret* on the
Broadway stage, during the late 1960s and early '70s she
appeared in the British horror films *It!*, *The Haunted House
of Horror* (aka *Horror House*), *Tower of Evil* (aka *Horror on
Snape Island/Beyond the Fog*) and *The Mutations* (aka *The
Freakmaker*). Haworth was also in episodes of *The Outer
Limits* ("The Sixth Finger") and *The Most Deadly Game*
("Witches' Sabbath"), along with the TV movie *Home For
the Holidays*.

American actor **Aron Kincaid** (Norman Neale Williams II), who was in a number of "Beach Party" movies during the 1960s, died of heart-related complications on 6 January, aged seventy. He also appeared in Roger Corman's *The Wasp Woman*, *Dr Goldfoot and the Bikini Machine* (with Vincent Price), *The Ghost in the Invisible Bikini* (with Boris Karloff and Basil Rathbone), *Creature of Destruction*, *Planet Earth*, *Brave New World*, *Silent Night Deadly Night* and *The Golden Child*, along with episodes of TV's *Thriller*, *Get Smart*, *The New People*, *The Immortal* and *Mr Merlin*. His voice-work in cartoons included playing "Killer Croc" on *Batman: The Animated Series* and "Sky Lynx" on *Transformers*. In later years Kincaid became a model and artist.

American TV actor **John** [Carroll] **Dye**, who starred as the celestial "Andrew" in CBS' *Touched by an Angel* (1994–2003), died of a heart attack on 10 January, aged forty-seven. He was also in the fantasy TV movies *Once Upon a Christmas* and *Twice Upon a Christmas*.

American actor [Horace] **Paul Picerni**, a regular on TV's *The Untouchables* (1959–63), died of a heart attack on 12 January, aged eighty-eight. He appeared in *House of Wax* (with Vincent Price), only the trailer for *The Beast from 20,000 Fathoms*, the last "Bomba the Jungle Boy" movie, *Lord of the Jungle*, and *Capricorn One*, along with episodes of *Alfred Hitchcock Presents*, *Men Into Space*, *Batman*, *The Immortal*, *The Sixth Sense*, *Ghost Story*, *Kolchak: The Night Stalker*, *Project U.F.O.*, *Fantasy Island*, *The Incredible Hulk* and *The Powers of Matthew Star*.

Susannah York (Susannah Yolande Fletcher) died on 14 January after a long battle with bone marrow cancer. She was seventy-two. The British actress and author starred in *Jane Eyre* (1970), Robert Altman's *Images* (based on her own children's book, *In Search of Unicorns*), *The Shout*, *Superman* (1978) and sequels *II* and *IV* (as the Man of Steel's mother "Lara"), *The Golden Gate Murders*, *The Awakening* (based on *The Jewel of Seven Stars* by Bram Stoker), *A Christmas Carol* (1984), *Daemon*, *Mio in the Land of Faraway* (with Christopher Lee), *Visitors* and *Franklyn*. On TV she appeared in episodes of *ITV Play of the Week* ("The Crucible" with Sean Connery), *Mystery* *and Imagination* ("The Fall of the House of Usher" as "Madeleine Usher"), *Orson Welles' Great Mysteries* (with Peter Cushing) and *The Ray Bradbury Theatre*.

Sixty-nine-year-old TV horror host **Dr Creep** (Barry Lee Hobart, aka "Dr Death") died the same day, following a series of strokes. He hosted *Shock Theater* on Dayton, Ohio's WKEF from 1972–85, and later on public-access TV between 1999–2005. The character also appeared in the shorts *Joe Nosferatu: Homeless Vampire* and *Casting Bruce Campbell*, along with the direct-to-DVD movie *Necrophagia: Through Eyes of the Dead*, and he was featured in the 2006 documentary *American Scary*. Hobart was the nephew of horror film make-up artist and stunt-man Doug Hobart.

American actress **Patti Gilbert** (Patti Friedman) died on 15 January, aged seventy-nine. She played the wife of Victor Buono's villainous "King Tut" in a 1967 episode of TV's *Batman*, appeared in a couple of episodes of *Get Smart* and voiced "Princess of Sweet Rhyme" in *The Phantom Tollbooth* (1970).

Gruff American character actor **Bruce Gordon**, another regular on TV's *The Untouchables*, died on 20 January, aged ninety-four. His credits include Roger Corman's *Curse of the Undead* and *Tower of London* (1962), *Hello Down There*, *Piranha* (1978) and *Timerider: The Adventure of Lyle Swann*, along with episodes of *One Step Beyond*, *The Man from U.N.C.L.E.*, *The Girl from U.N.C.L.E.* ("The Mother Muffin Affair" with Boris Karloff), *The Flying Nun*, *Get Smart* and *Tarzan* (1968). Gordon also appeared alongside Karloff in the long-running Broadway play *Arsenic and Old Lace* (1941–44).

American physical fitness guru **Jack LaLanne** (François Henri LaLanne) died of respiratory failure and pneumonia on 23 January, aged ninety-six. Along with his own TV show (1951–85), he appeared in *More Wild Wild West*, *Repossessed*, *The Year Without Santa Claus* (as "Hercules"), and episodes of such 1960s TV shows as *Mr Ed*, *The Addams Family* and *Batman*.

American comedian **Charlie Callas** (Charles Callias), best remembered for his zany sound effects, died in Las Vegas on 27 January. He was eighty-three. A TV talk show favourite and "Rat Pack" associate, the rubber-faced Callas' credits include such movies as *The Snoop Sisters*, *Silent Movie*, Disney's *Pete's*

Dragon (as the voice of "Elliott", the dragon), *High Anxiety*, *History of the World: Part I*, *Hysterical* (as "Dracula"), *Amazon Women on the Moon*, *Vampire Vixens from Venus*, *Dracula Dead and Loving It* and *Horrorween*, along with episodes of TV's *The Munsters*, *The Monkees*, *Legends of the Superheroes* (as the voice of "Sinestro"), *Silk Stalkings* and *A. J.'s Time Travelers*.

TV character actor **Michael Tolan** (Seymour Tuchow) died of heart disease and kidney failure on 31 January, aged eighty-six. He appeared in episodes of *Inner Sanctum*, *Diagnoses: Unknown* ("The Curse of the Gypsy"), *Play of the Week* ("The Dybbuk"), *The Outer Limits* ("The Zanti Misfits"), *Tarzan*, *The Invaders*, Hammer's *Journey to the Unknown* and *Ghost Story*.

Welsh-born TV character actress **Margaret John** died after a short illness on 2 February, aged eighty-four. She began her career in 1960 and appeared in episodes of *Suspense*, *Mysteries and Miracles*, *Doctor Who* (in 1968 and 2006), *Menace*, *Doomwatch*, *Dead of Night*, *The Rivals of Sherlock Holmes*, *The Ghosts of Motley Hall*, *Blakes 7*, *Shadows*, *The Boy Merlin*, *Tardisodes*, *Being Human*, and *Game of Thrones*. John also portrayed "Mrs Hudson" in the early 1990s TV movies *Sherlock Holmes and the Leading Lady* and *Incident at Victoria Falls*, both starring Christopher Lee as Holmes and Patrick Macnee as Dr Watson.

French actress **Maria Schneider**, best known for her role opposite Marlon Brando in Bernardo Bertolucci's controversial *Last Tango in Paris* (1972), died of cancer on 3 February, aged fifty-eight. Her other film credits include *Mama Dracula* and Franco Zeffirelli's 1996 version of *Jane Eyre*.

Japanese-born American actress, exotic dancer and martial arts expert **Tura Satana** (Tura Luna Pascual Yamaguchi), who starred in Russ Myer's cult classic *Faster, Pussycat! Kill! Kill!* (1965) died of heart failure on 4 February, aged seventy-two. She also appeared in *Our Man Flint* (uncredited), *The Astro-Zombies*, *The Doll Squad*, *Mark of the Astro-Zombies*, *Astro-Zombies M3: Cloned* and an episode each of TV's *The Man from U.N.C.L.E.* and *The Girl from U.N.C.L.E.*. Her life stories included being gang-raped when she was nine years old, first marrying at thirteen, posing for nude for photographs taken by silent screen comic Harold Lloyd, working as a stripper, turning down a marriage proposal from Elvis Presley, being shot by a former lover and breaking her back in a car accident.

American character actress **Peggy Rea** died of complication from congestive heart failure on 5 February, aged eighty-nine. She appeared in *7 Faces of Dr Lao*, *What's the Matter with Helen?*, *Lipstick*, and episodes of TV's *The Man from U.N.C.L.E.*, *The Wild Wild West*, *The Immortal* and *Monsters*.

J. Paul Getty, III, the grandson of oil magnate J. Paul Getty, died after a long illness the same day, aged fifty-four. After being kidnapped and held to ransom in Italy for four months in 1973, he appeared in the Portuguese horror film *The Territory* (aka *O Território*, 1981).

Hollywood character actress **Myrna Dell** (Marilyn Adele Dunlap) died on 11 February, aged eighty-six. While under contract to RKO Pictures she appeared in three *Falcon* movies, along with *The Spiral Staircase* (as an uncredited murder victim). The former showgirl was also in an episode of the *Jungle Jim* TV series and had a small role in an episode of *Batman*. Along with actress Marguerite Chapman, Dell is credited with originating the idea of autograph shows.

American character actor **Kenneth Mars**, best known for his comedy roles in Mel Brooks' *The Producers* and *Young Frankenstein* (as the one-armed "Inspector Kemp"), died of pancreatic cancer on 12 February, aged seventy-five. His other film credits include *Superman* (1975), *Full Moon High*, *Get Smart Again!*, Disney's *The Little Mermaid* and *The Little Mermaid 2: Return to the Sea*, *Shadows and Fog*, *We're Back! A Dinosaur's Story*, and as the voice of "Grandpa Longneck" in *The Land Before Time* sequels. He appeared in episodes of *Get Smart*, *The Ghost & Mrs Muir*, *Wonder Woman*, *Tabitha*, *Project U.F.O.*, *Supertrain*, *Tucker's Witch*, *Misfits of Science*, *The Twilight Zone* (1986), *Shades of LA*, *Star Trek: Deep Space Nine*, *M.A.N.T.I.S.*, *The New Adventures of Superman*, *Weird Science* and *The Pretender*. Mars also supplied voices for numerous cartoon shows, including *The Jetsons*, *Challenge of the GoBots*, *The 13 Ghosts of Scooby-Doo*, *Teen Wolf*, *The Flintstone Kids*, *A Pup Named Scooby-Doo*, *Duck Tales*, *Tiny Toon Adventures*, *Darkwing Duck*, *Captain Planet and the Planeteers*, *Animaniacs*, *The Little Mermaid*, *Batman* (1994–95), *Freakazoid!*, *The Real*

Adventures of Jonny Quest, Godzilla: The Series, The Legend of Tarzan and *The Land Before Time* TV series.

Hollywood actress and singer **Betty Garrett** died the same day, aged ninety-one. Best know for her role as the man-hungry taxi driver in the classic musical *On the Town* (1949), later in her career she also appeared in an episode of the children's TV show *Mr Merlin*, along with Larry Blamire's low budget genre comedies *Trail of the Screaming Forehead* and *Dark and Stormy Night*. Garrett was married to actor Larry Parks from 1944 until his death in 1975. During the 1950s both their careers were derailed by the anti-Communist witch-hunts.

Irish character actor **T.** (Thomas) **P.** (Patrick) **McKenna** died in London after a long illness on 13 February, aged eighty-one. He always brought class to the roles he played in such movies as Tigon's *The Beast in the Cellar*, *Straw Dogs*, *Percy's Progress* (with Vincent Price), *Britannia Hospital*, *The Doctor and the Devils* and *Jack the Ripper* (1988). McKenna's TV credits include *The Avengers*, *Adam Adamant Lives!*, *Randall and Hopkirk (Deceased)*, *BBC Play of the Month* ("Rasputin"), *Thriller*, Nigel Kneale's *Beasts*, *Blakes 7* and *Doctor Who*.

British character actor **Alfred Burke**, who portrayed down-at-heel private eye "Frank Marker" in the popular TV series *Public Eye* (1965–75), died on 16 February, aged ninety-two. Although he appeared in such films as *Children of the Damned*, Hammer's *The Nanny*, *The Night Caller* (aka *Blood Beast from Outer Space*), *A Midsummer Night's Dream* (1996) and *Harry Potter and the Chamber of Secrets*, Burke was much better known for his numerous appearances on TV in shows like *Colonel March of Scotland Yard* (starring Boris Karloff), *Invisible Man* (1959), *One Step Beyond*, *The Indian Tales of Rudyard Kipling*, *The Avengers*, *Randall and Hopkirk (Deceased)*, *Tales of the Unexpected* and *Shades of Darkness*.

American character actor **Len Lesser** (Leonard King Lesser) died of cancer-related pneumonia the same day, aged eighty-eight. Best known for playing "Uncle Leo" on *Seinfeld* (1991–98), Lesser appeared in such movies and TV shows as *How to Stuff a Wild Bikini*, *Blood and Lace*, *Ruby*, *Someone's Watching Me!*, *Through the Magic Pyramid*, *Sorority Girls and the Creature from Hell*, *The Werewolf Reborn!*, *Alfred Hitchcock Presents*,

The Outer Limits, The Wild Wild West, The Munsters, My Favorite Martian, Get Smart, The Monkees, Land of the Giants, Kolchak: The Night Stalker, The Ghost Busters, The Hardy Boys/Nancy Drew Mysteries, The Amazing Spider-Man, Amazing Stories ("Mummy Daddy") and *Sabrina the Teenage Witch*.

British actor **Nicholas Courtney** (William Nicholas Stone Courtney), best known for his recurring role as UNIT leader "Brigadier Alistair Lethbridge-Stewart" in BBC-TV's *Doctor Who*, died on 22 February, aged eighty-one. The Egyptian-born actor first appeared in the show in a 1965 episode entitled "The Dalek's Master Man", but he became a semi-regular when he took over the role of the Brigadier (after actor David Langton pulled out) in the 1968 serial "The Web of Fear". Courtney appeared in 107 episodes of *Doctor Who* and recreated the character of Lethbridge-Stewart in a number of short films, audio dramas, a video game and a 2008 two-part episode of *The Sarah Jane Adventures*. He also appeared in episodes of *The Avengers, The Indian Tales of Rudyard Kipling, The Champions, Randall and Hopkirk (Deceased), Doomwatch* and *The Rivals of Sherlock Holmes*, and had uncredited roles in the films *The Brides of Fu Manchu, Doppelgänger* (aka *Journey to the Far Side of the Sun*) and *Endless Night*. Courtney also portrayed "Inspector Lionhart" in four episodes of the radio drama *The Scarifyers*, broadcast on BBC Radio 7 (2007–10). His 1998 autobiography was entitled *Five Rounds Rapid!* after a line of dialogue he had as the Brigadier in "The Dæmons" (1971). A revised autobiography, *Still Getting Away with It* (co-written with Michael McManus), appeared in 2005.

American character actor **Frank Alesia**, who appeared in the AIP "Beach Party" movies *Bikini Beach, Pajama Party, Beach Blanket Bingo* and *The Ghost in the Invisible Bikini*, died on 27 February, aged sixty-five. He also appeared in episodes of *Bewitched* and *The Flying Nun* before becoming a TV director.

Hollywood star **Jane Russell** (Ernestine Jane Geraldine Russell) died on 28 February, aged eighty-nine. A former dentist receptionist and discovery of Howard Hughes (who orchestrated her screen debut in his controversial 1943 Western *The Outlaw*), she mostly appeared in musical-comedies during the 1950s, including an uncredited cameo appearance in *Road to Bali*. In 1967 she had a small roll in the "Billy Jack" motorcycle exploitation movie *The Born Losers*. With the first of her three husbands, quarterback Bob Waterfield, she formed Russ-Field Productions, who produced *The Most Dangerous Game* remake, *Run for the Sun* (1956). During the 1970s Russell was the TV spokesperson for Playtex bras.

Former beauty queen turned actress **Darlene Lucht** (Darlene Brimmer), who was crowned Miss Wisconsin in 1961, died on 5 March, aged seventy-two. She had small roles in *The Haunted Palace*, *Muscle Beach Party*, *Bikini Beach*, *Beach Blanket Bingo* and Al Adamson's *Five Bloody Graves* (as "Tara Ashton"), which starred her husband, Robert Dix.

Japanese voice actor **Kan Tokumaru** died on 6 March, aged sixty-nine. His many *anime*, TV and game credits include *Vampire Hunter D*, *Legend of the Galactic Heroes* and *Vampire Savior EX Edition*. In the Japanese dub of *Live and Let Die* (1973) he was the voice of "M".

Distinguished British stage actor and iconic horror film star **Michael Gough** died on 17 March, aged ninety-three. Best known to modern audiences for his role as faithful butler "Alfred Pennyworth" in the 1980s–90s Batman films (*Batman*, *Batman Returns*, *Batman Forever* and *Batman & Robin*) and his later collaborations with director Tim Burton (*Sleepy Hollow*, *Corpse Bride* and *Alice in Wonderland*), the Malaysian-born Gough's many other movies also include *The Man in the White Suit*, Hammer's *Dracula* (aka *Horror of Dracula*) and *The Phantom of the Opera* (1962), *Horrors of the Black Museum*, *Konga*, *What a Carve Up!* (aka *No Place Like Homicide!*), *Black Zoo*, *Dr Terror's House of Horrors*, *The Skull*, *They Came from Beyond Space*, *Berserk*, *Curse of the Crimson Altar* (aka *The Crimson Cult*), *Trog*, *The Corpse* (aka *Crucible of Horror*), *Horror Hospital*, *The Legend of Hell House* (uncredited), *Satan's Slave* (aka *Evil Heritage*), *The Boys from Brazil*, *Venom*, *A Christmas Carol* (1984), *Arthur the King* (aka *Merlin and the Sword*), *The Serpent and the Rainbow*, *Nostradamus* and the TV movie *The Haunting of Helen Walker* (based on "Turn of the Screw" by Henry James). He also appeared in episodes of *The Adventures of Sherlock Holmes*, *The Wednesday Play*

("Alice in Wonderland"), *Doctor Who*, *The Avengers* ("The Cybernauts"), Hammer's *Journey to the Unknown*, *The Champions*, *The Rivals of Sherlock Holmes*, *Moonbase 3*, *Blakes 7*, *The Little Vampire* (1986–87) and *The Young Indiana Jones Chronicles*.

American dancer and novelist **Dorothy Young**, who worked as an assistant to stage magician Harry Houdini from 1925–26, died on 20 March, aged 103. She made her debut as the futuristic "Radio Girl of 1950", but left the act two months before the escapologist's death on 31 October, 1926. Young was the last surviving member of Houdini's touring show.

Legendary Hollywood star Dame **Elizabeth** [Rosemond] **Taylor** died of complications from congestive heart failure on 24 March, aged seventy-nine. She had been hospitalised for six weeks. Born to American parents in London, England, Taylor's family relocated to Los Angeles in 1939 where, within a few years, she became a child star at MGM. In later years she developed into one of the screen's most iconic figures, winning two Academy Awards for Best Actress. Her films include *Jane Eyre* (1943), *Suddenly Last Summer*, *Doctor Faustus* (1967), *Hammersmith is Out*, *Night Watch*, *The Blue Bird* (1976) and *The Flintstones* (1994). She also contributed voice work to the animated TV series *Captain Planet and the Planeteers*, *The Simpsons* and *God, the Devil and Bob*, and in later years became a spokesperson for AIDS research. Taylor was almost as well-known for her eight marriages as her movies, and her husbands included Michael Wilding, Michael Todd, Eddie Fisher and, most famously, Richard Burton (twice). It was revealed that the scheduled start time was delayed for almost fifteen minutes, after the actress left instructions that she wanted to be late for her own funeral.

American leading man **Farley** [Earle] **Granger** [II] died on 27 March, aged eighty-five. Best remembered for his roles in Alfred Hitchcock's *Rope* (1948) and *Strangers on a Train* (1951), he also appeared in *Behave Yourself!* (with Lon Chaney, Jr.), *Full House* ("The Gift of the Magi"), *Hans Christian Andersen*, *Something Creeping in the Dark* (aka *Qualcosa striscia nel buio*), *Amuck!* (aka *Hot Bed of Sex*), *So Sweet So Dead* (aka *Penetration*), *Arnold* and *The Prowler* (aka *Rosemary's Killer*), along with episodes of TV's *The United States Steel Hour* ("The Bottle Imp"), *Dow Hour of Great Mysteries* ("The Inn of the Flying Dragon"), *Get Smart*, *Wide World Mystery* ("The Haunting of Penthouse D"), *The Six Million Dollar Man*, *Matt Helm*, *The Invisible Man* (1975), *Tales from the Dark Side* and *Monsters*. In 1980 Granger also starred on Broadway in Ira Levin's *Deathtrap*.

American child actress and singer **Donna Lee** [O'Leary], who appeared in Val Lewton's *The Body Snatcher* and *Bedlam*, both starring Boris Karloff, died on 3 April, aged eighty-one. She also appeared (uncredited) as a member of the Donna Lee Trio in the 1936 mystery thriller *A Face in the Fog*.

Angela [Margaret] **Scoular**, the second wife of actor Leslie Phillips, died on 11 April, aged sixty-five. The bi-polar and alcoholic British actress feared that her bowel cancer would return (despite a successful operation in 2009) and killed herself by drinking drain cleaner. Scoular appeared in two James Bond films, *Casino Royale* (1966) and *On Her Majesty's Secret Service*, an episode of *The Avengers*, and starred as "Cathy" opposite Ian McShane's "Heathcliff" in a 1967 BBC-TV serial of *Wuthering Heights* (the inspiration for the Kate Bush song and video).

British character actor **Trevor** [Gordon] **Bannister**, best known for his role as "Mr Lucas" in the BBC sitcom *Are You Being Served?*, died of a heart attack while repairing his allotment shed on 14 April, aged seventy-six. He also appeared in such TV series as *Object Z*, *Object Z Returns*, *The Man in Room 17* ("The Black Witch"), *The Avengers*, *Doomwatch*, *The Tomorrow People*, *The Young Indiana Jones Chronicles* and *Woof!*.

American actor **Jon Cedar** died the same day, aged eighty. He appeared in episodes of TV's *The Girl from U.N.C.L.E.*, *The Invisible Man* (1975), *The Incredible Hulk*, *The Greatest American Hero* and *Tales from the Darkside*, along with the movies *Stowaway to the Moon* (with John Carradine), *Time Travelers* (1976), *Day of the Animals*, *Capricorn One*, *The Manitou* (based on the novel by Graham Masterton), *By Dawn's Early Light* and *Asteroid*.

Canadian-born leading man **Michael Sarrazin** (Jacques Michel André Sarrazin) died in Montreal of cancer on 17 April, aged seventy. He starred in *Eye of the Cat*, *The Groundstar Conspiracy*, *Frankenstein the True Story* (as "The Creature"), *The Reincarnation of Peter Proud*, *Earthquake in New York*, *The Second Arrival* (aka *Arrival II*) and *FeardotCom*, and appeared in episodes of the 1988 *Alfred Hitchcock Presents*, *The Ray Bradbury Theatre*, *Kung Fu: The Legend Continues*, *Star Trek: Deep Space Nine*, *The Outer Limits*, *Poltergeist: The Legacy*, *Mentors* (as Edgar Allan Poe) and *Earth: Final Conflict*. Sarrazin was in a relationship with actress Jacqueline Bisset for fourteen years.

British actress **Elisabeth** [Claira Heath] **Sladen**, who starred as "Sarah Jane Smith" in the BBC's *Doctor Who* and her own spin-off series, died of cancer on 19 April, aged sixty-five. She first joined John Pertwee's Doctor in the 1973 series "The Time Warrior", and went on to appear alongside Tom Baker's incarnation of the Time Lord until 1976. She recreated the role for the TV specials *K-9 and Company: A Girl's Best Friend* (1981), *Doctor Who*: "The Five Doctors" (1983) and *Doctor Who*: "Dimensions in Time" (1993), along with the independent video, *Downtime* (1995), and various radio serials. She returned to *Doctor Who* as the inquisitive journalist in 2006 and subsequently got her own children's spin-off series, *The Sarah Jane Adventures* (2007–11). Sladen also appeared in the TV movies *Gulliver in Lilliput* (1982) and *Alice in Wonderland* (1986), as well as an episode of *Doomwatch*.

British character actor **Terence Longdon** (Hubert Tuelly Longdon) died of cancer on 23 April, aged eighty-eight. He appeared in the first four *Carry On* films, along with *What a Whopper*, *The Return of Mr Moto*, and episodes of *The Avengers*, *The New Avengers*, *The Martian Chronicles* and *The Return of Sherlock Holmes*. Longdon also starred as the titular charter pilot in the BBC children's adventure series *Garry Halliday* (1959–62). He was married to actress Barbara Jefford from 1953 to 1960.

Sixty-six-year-old French actress, novelist and director **Marie-France Pisier** was found dead in the swimming pool at her home in Saint Cyr sur Mer on 24 April. Born in French Indochina (now Vietnam), her credits include *The Vampire of Dusseldorf* (1965), Luis Buñuel's surreal *The Phantom of Liberty* and *Céline and Julie Go Boating*.

Cult American B-movie star **Yvette Vickers** (Iola Yvette Vedder) was found dead from heart failure in an upstairs room of her dilapidated Bendedict Canyon home in Los Angeles on 27 April. The mummified state of the eighty-one-year-old actress' body indicated that she could have been dead for nearly a year. The July 1959 *Playboy* Playmate appeared in *Sunset Boulevard* (uncredited), *Attack of the 50 Foot Woman* (1958), *Attack of the Giant Leeches* (aka *Demons of the Swamp*), *Beach Party* (uncredited), *What's the Matter with Helen?*, *The Dead Don't Die!* (scripted by Robert Bloch) and *Evil Spirits*, along with an episode of TV's *One Step Beyond*.

William Campbell, who portrayed Klingon commander "Koloth" in the classic *Star Trek* episode "The Trouble with Tribbles", died on 28 April, aged eighty-seven. He appeared in Francis Ford Coppola's *Dementia 13* (aka *The Haunted and the Hunted*), *Hush ... Hush Sweet Charlotte*, *Portrait in Terror*, *Blood Bath* (aka *Track of the Vampire*), *Pretty Maids All in a Row* and *The Return of the Six Million Dollar Man and the Bionic Woman*, along with episodes of TV's *The Wild Wild West*, *Star Trek* ("The Squire of Gothos"), *Shazam!*, *The Hardy Boys/Nancy Drew Mysteries*, *The Next Step Beyond*, *Star Trek: Deep Space Nine* (reprising his role as "Koloth") and *Kung Fu: The Legend Continues*. From 1952 to 1958 he was married to Judith Campbell Exner, a paramour of President John F. Kennedy and Mafia figure Sam Giancana.

Veteran Hollywood character actor and director **Jackie Cooper** (John Copper, Jr.) died after a short illness on 3 May, aged eighty-eight. He began his career as a child actor in 1929, and is best known for portraying *Daily Planet* newspaper editor "Perry White" in *Superman* (1978) and its three sequels. He was nominated for an Oscar in 1931 when he was just nine years old, and his other credits include *Chosen Survivors*, *The Invisible Man* (1975) and episodes of TV's *Tales of Tomorrow*, *Suspense*, *The Twilight Zone* and *Ghost Story*. Cooper was also an Emmy Award-winning director, with the *Holmes and Yo-Yo* pilot and the TV movie *The Night They Saved Christmas* to his credit.

American actress **Mary Murphy**, who co-starred with Marlon Brando in *The Wild One* (1953), died of heart disease on 4 May, aged eighty. A former shop assistant, she began her acting career with uncredited appearances in *When Worlds Collide*, *My Favorite Spy* and *The Atomic City*, before moving on to such films as *The Mad Magician* (with Vincent Price) and episodes of TV's *Alfred Hitchcock Presents*, *The Outer Limits*, *Honey West* and *Ghost Story*. In 1956 she was married to actor Dale Robertson for just three months.

German-born actress **Dana Wynter** (Dagmar Winter), who helped Kevin McCarthy battle the pod people in the original *Invasion of the Body Snatchers* (1956), died of congestive heart failure in California on 5 May, aged seventy-nine. Her other credits include the Gene Roddenberry TV movie *The Questor Tapes* and episodes of *Suspense*, *Colonel March of Scotland Yard* (with Boris Karloff), *The Alfred Hitchcock Hour*, *The Wild Wild West*, *The Invaders*, *Get Smart*, *Orson Welles' Great Mysteries* and *Fantasy Island*.

Rugged American character actor **Ross Hagen** (Leland Lando Lilly) died of prostate cancer on 7 May, aged seventy-two. His films include *Wonder Women*, *Night Creature* (with Donald Pleasence), *Angel*, *Avenging Angel*, *Prison Ship* (aka *Star Slammer*), *Warlords*, *B.O.R.N.* (which he also co-scripted and directed), *The Phantom Empire*, *Alienator*, *Time Wars* (which he also wrote and directed), *Dinosaur Island*, *Attack of the 60 Foot Centerfolds*, *Bikini Drive-In*, *Cyberzone* (aka *Phoenix 2*), *Night Shade*, *The Elf Who Didn't Believe*, *Invisible Dad*, *Jungle Boy*, *The Kid with X-ray Eyes* and *Sideshow*, along with episodes of *Captain Nice*, *The Wild Wild West*, *The Invaders* and *Kung Fu*. Hagen made around twenty films with director Fred Olen Ray, and he also directed *Reel Terror* (1985) featuring footage of John Carradine and Victor Buono.

Dolores Fuller (Dolores Agnes Eble), who was director Edward D. Wood, Jr.'s muse and leading lady in such cult classics as *Glen or Glenda* (aka *I Led Two Lives*), *Jail Bait* and *Bride of the Monster*, died after a long illness on 9 May, aged eighty-eight. Her other films include *Mesa of Lost Women*, *The Ironbound Vampire* and *The Corpse Grinders 2*, along with an episode of TV's *Adventures of Superman*. As a lyricist, Fuller also co-wrote thirteen songs for Elvis Presley, including "Rock-a-Hula Baby" for the film *Blue Hawaii*. Her autobiography, *A Fuller Life: Hollywood, Ed Wood and Me* (co-written with Stone

Wallace and her husband, Philip Chamberlin) was published in 2008. Sarah Jessica Parker portrayed Fuller in Tim Burton's *Ed Wood* (1994).

British character actor **Edward [Cedric] Hardwicke**, the son of actor Sir Cedric Hardwicke, died of cancer on 16 May, aged seventy-eight. Following the departure of David Burke, in 1986 he took over the role of "Dr John Watson" opposite Jeremy Brett's consulting detective in the series *The Return of Sherlock Holmes* (1968–88), *The Case-Book of Sherlock Holmes* (1991–93), *The Memoirs of Sherlock Holmes* (1994) and the TV movies *The Sign of Four* (1987) and *The Hound of the Baskervilles* (1988). He also recreated the role on the West End stage in *The Secret of Sherlock Holmes* in 1989. Hardwicke began his career as a child actor, and his other films include *A Guy Named Joe* (uncredited), *Full Circle* (aka *The Haunting of Julia*), *Venom*, Disney's *Baby: Secret of the Lost Legend*, *Photographing Fairies* (as "Sir Arthur Conan Doyle"), *Shadowlands*, *Appetite*, *The Alchemists* (based on the novel by Peter James) and yet another remake *She* (2001), plus episodes of TV's *Invisible Man* (1959), *Sherlock Holmes* (1968), Hammer's *Journey to the Unknown*, *Wessex Tales*, *Thriller* (1974) and *Supernatural* ("The Werewolf Reunion").

Veteran Australian actor **Bill Hunter** died of cancer on 21 May, aged seventy-one. His credits include *The Return of Captain Invincible* (with Christopher Lee), *Moby Dick* (1998) and *On the Beach* (2000), along with episodes of *Space: Above and Beyond* and *Two Twisted* ("Arkham's Curios and Wonders"). Hunter also contributed voice work to Disney's *Finding Nemo* and *Legends of the Guardians: The Owls of Ga'Hoole*.

American actress **Tallie Cochrane** (Lillian Rose Cochrane) died of cancer the same day, aged sixty-six. Under various pseudonyms, such as "Toni Talley", "Viola Reeves", "Dandy Thomas", "Chic Jones", "Talie Wright" and "Silver Foxx", she appeared in a number of sexploitation films, including *Wam Bang Thank You Spaceman*, *Tarz & Jane Cheeta & Boy* and *Devil's Ecstasy*. She also had small roles in *Slapstick (of Another Kind)* and *Frightmare* (aka *The Horror Star*). Cochrane worked as a make-up artist on *Track of the Moon Beast*.

Sixty-year-old American actor **Jeff Conaway** (Jeffrey Charles William Michael Conaway) died of pneumonia exacerbated by substance abuse on 27 May. Having battled drug and alcohol addiction since he was a teenager, Conaway was found unconscious at his home sixteen days earlier and remained in a medically induced coma until his family terminated his life-support. He appeared in Disney's *Pete's Dragon*, *Bay Coven*, *Elvira: Mistress of the Dark*, *Ghost Writer*, *The Sleeping Car*, *Mirror Images*, *Alien Intruder* and *Curse of the Forty-Niner*. On TV Conaway was a regular on *Wizards and Warriors* (1983) and *Babylon 5* (1994–98), and he also guest-starred in episodes of *Tales from the Darkside* ("My Ghostwriter – the Vampire"), *Monsters*, *Freddy's Nightmares*, *Shades of LA* and three *Babylon 5* spin-off movies.

American actress **Clarice Taylor**, who played Bill Cosby's mother on TV's *The Cosby Show*, died of heart failure on 30 May, aged ninety-three. Her other credits include *Change of Mind* and *Play Misty for Me*. Taylor portrayed "Addaperle, the Good Witch of the North" in the 1970s Broadway musical *The Wiz*.

American leading man **James Arness** (James King Aurness), best remembered for his role as "Marshall Matt Dillon" on the long-running Western series *Gunsmoke* (aka *Gun Law*, 1955–75) and a number of spin-off TV movies, died on 3 June. He was eighty-eight. Arness' film credits include *Two Lost Worlds*, *The Thing from Another World* (as "The Thing") and *Them!*. His younger brother was actor Peter Graves.

British character actress and comedienne **Miriam Karlin** OBE (Miriam Samuels) died after a long battle with cancer the same day, aged eighty-five. She appeared in The Goons' comedy *Down Among the 'Z' Men*, Hammer's *Phantom of the Opera* (1962), *A Clockwork Orange*, *Jekyll & Hyde* (1990) and *Children of Men*. On TV, Karlin starred in the supernatural sitcom *So Haunt Me* (1992–94).

Ninety-year-old **Wally Boag** (Wallace Vincent Boag) and ninety-one-year-old **Betty Taylor**, who co-starred as sweethearts Pecos Bill and Slue-Foot Sue five days a week for nearly three decades in Disneyland's *Golden Horseshoe Revue*, died on 3 and 7 June, respectively. The show is officially the longest-running stage production in entertainment history (1955–86). Boag also appeared in Disney's *The Absent-Minded Professor*, *Son of Flubber* and *The Love Bug* (1968).

British TV actor **Donald** [Marland] **Hewlett** died of pneumonia on 4 June, aged ninety. He had suffered from epilepsy and Alzheimer's disease for many years. Hewlett appeared in episodes of *Sherlock Holmes* (1965), *The Avengers*, *Doctor Who* ("The Claws of Axos") and *The New Avengers*.

Canadian-born actor **Paul Massie** (Arthur Dickinson Massé), best known for playing an ugly Dr Jekyll and a handsome Mr Hyde in Hammer's *The Two Faces of Dr Jekyll* (aka *Jekyll's Inferno*, 1960), died of lung cancer in Nova Scotia on 8 June, aged seventy-eight. He also appeared in an episode of TV's *The Avengers*. He retired from acting at the age of forty to teach drama at the University of South Florida in Tampa.

Seventy-nine-year-old voice and theatre actor **Roy** [William] **Skelton**, who not only voiced the popular British children's TV puppet characters George and Zippy for *Rainbow* (1973–92), but also the Daleks and Cybermen in *Doctor Who*, died of pneumonia the same day. He had suffered a stroke five months earlier. Skelton was also the voice of a robot in an episode of *Out of the Unknown*, the "Mock Turtle" in a BBC version of *Alice in Wonderland* (1986), "Henry Swift" in the two *Ghosts of Albion* animated webseries and George and Zippy again in 2008 for the first episode of *Ashes to Ashes*. He started supplying voices for the various aliens on *Doctor Who* in 1966, and he continued until "Remembrance of the Daleks" in 1988.

Seventy-two-year-old Indian-born British character actor **Badi Uzzaman** (Mohammed Badji Uzzaman Azmi) died of a lung infection on 14 June in Pakistan. He appeared in *The Sign of Four* (1987), Stephen Gallagher's *Chimera*, and *Gulliver's Travels* (1996), along with episodes of *The Singing Detective*, *Screen One* ("Frankenstein's Baby") and *Torchwood*.

Thirty-four-year-old stuntman **Ryan** [Matthew] **Dunn**, best known as one of the moronic *Jackass* team on MTV, died on 20 June when he crashed the Porsche he was driving drunk at 3 a.m., killing himself and his passenger, twenty-nine-year-old Zachary Hartwell. The car had been travelling at speeds of up to 140 mph and the crash turned the vehicle into a fireball. Dunn also had small roles in *Invader* and *Welcome to the Bates Motel*.

Just one more thing . . . veteran Hollywood actor **Peter** [Michael] **Falk**, best known for his Emmy Award-winning role as the wily raincoat-wearing, cigar-smoking police Lieutenant in NBC-TV's *Columbo* (1971–2003), died on 23 June, aged eighty-three. He had been suffering from Alzheimer's disease and dementia. Falk's movie credits include *Brigadoon* (1966), *Castle Keep*, *Murder by Death*, *The Great Muppet Caper*, *Wings of Desire* (1987), *The Princess Bride*, *Vibes*, *The Lost World* (2001), *Shark Tale*, *When Angels Come to Town* and *Next*. He also appeared in episodes of *Alfred Hitchcock Presents*, *The Twilight Zone* and *The Alfred Hitchcock Hour*. Falk's right eye was surgically removed at the age of three because of cancer.

British stage and screen actress **Margaret** [Maud] **Tyzack** CBE died of cancer on 25 June, aged seventy-nine. Her credits include *2001: A Space Odyssey*, *A Clockwork Orange*, *The Legacy*, *Quatermass* (aka *The Quatermass Conclusion*), *Until Death* and *The Thief Lord*, along with episodes of TV's *The Indian Tales of Rudyard Kipling* and *The Young Indiana Jones Chronicles*.

Indian-born British leading man **Michael Latimer**, who starred in Hammer's *Slave Girls* (aka *Prehistoric Women*), died the same day, aged sixty-nine. He also appeared in episodes of the TV series *Sir Arthur Conan Doyle*, *The Avengers* ("A Touch of Brimstone"), *Sexton Blake*, *The New Avengers* and *Hammer House of Horror*, along with Gene Roddenberry's TV pilot movie *Spectre* and the SF film *Project: Alien* (aka *Fatal Sky*).

American child actress **Edith** [Marilyn] **Fellows** died on 26 June, aged eighty-eight. She had made around thirty films by the age of thirteen and was the subject of a high-profile custody case in 1936. Her credits include *Jane Eyre* (1934), *Lilith* and *The Hills Have Eyes Part II* (1985), and she also appeared in four episodes of TV's *Tales of Tomorrow*.

Eighty-one-year-old Hollywood actress **Elaine Stewart** (Elsy H. Steinberg) died after a long illness on 27 June. A former 1950s *Playboy* pin-up turned TV hostess, she starred opposite Gene Kelly in MGM's *Brigadoon* (1954) and her other movie credits include *The Adventures of Hajji Baba* and *Most Dangerous Man Alive*.

British actress **Anna** [Raymond] **Massey** OBE died of cancer on 2 July, aged seventy-three. The daughter of actor Raymond Massey and the younger sister of Daniel Massey, she appeared in *Peeping Tom*, *ITV Play of the Week* ("A Midsummer Night's

Dream"), *Bunny Lake is Missing*, *De Sade*, Alfred Hitchcock's *Frenzy*, *The Vault of Horror* (based on the EC comics), *Rebecca* (1979), *Around the World in 80 Days* (1989) and *Haunted* (based on the novel by James Herbert), as well as episodes of TV's *Dead of Night*, *Tales of the Unexpected*, *Mistress of Suspense*, *The Young Indiana Jones Chronicles* and *Strange*. She was married to actor Jeremy Brett from 1958 to 1962, and her godfather was director John Ford.

American character actor, poet and playwright **Roberts [Scott] Blossom**, who memorably played psychopathic backwoods killer "Ezra Cobb" in *Deranged* (1974), died on 8 July, aged eighty-seven. He was also in *Slaughterhouse-Five*, *Close Encounters of the Third Kind*, *Resurrection*, *Christine* (based on the novel by Stephen King) and *Always*, along with episodes of *Amazing Stories*, *Tales from the Darkside* and the 1980s *The Twilight Zone* series.

Indian-born British actress **Googie Withers** (Georgette Lizette Withers) CBE died in Australia on 15 July, aged ninety-four. Her credits include Alfred Hitchcock's *The Lady Vanishes* (1938), *Dead of Night* (1945) and *Miranda*.

Eighty-nine-year-old British character actress **Sheila [Mary] Burrell** died on 19 July, after a long illness following a serious stroke two years earlier. Sir Laurence Olivier's cousin and a long-standing member of the Royal Shakespeare Company, she appeared in such films as Hammer's *Man in Black* and *Paranoiac*, *Afraid of the Dark* and *Jane Eyre* (1996), plus episodes of *Colonel March of Scotland Yard* (starring Boris Karloff), *Adam Adamant Lives!*, *Out of the Unknown*, *The Avengers*, *Spooky*, *Tales of the Unexpected* and *The Young Indiana Jones Chronicles*. Burrell was married to actor Laurence Payne from 1944 to 1951.

Mexican-born actress **Linda Christian** (Blanca Rosa Welter), described as "The Anatomic Bomb" by *Life* magazine, died of colon cancer on 22 July in California, aged eighty-seven. A former beauty contest winner, her credits include *Tarzan and the Mermaids* and *The Devil's Hand* (with her younger sister Ariadna Welter), along with episodes of *Climax!* ("Casino Royale", the first James Bond adaptation) and *The Alfred Hitchcock Hour*. Best known for her various romantic liaisons with wealthy playboys, racing drivers and bullfighters, she married and divorced actors Tyrone Power and Edmund Purdom.

A former corporate lawyer, independent oil producer, cattle rancher and local politician before he became a character actor, **G. (Gervase) D. (Duan) Spradlin** died on 24 July, aged ninety. He appeared (usually as authority figures) in *Hell's Angels '69*, *Zabriskie Point*, *Maneaters Are Loose!*, *Apocalypse Now*, *The Formula*, *Intruders*, *Ed Wood* (as "Reverend Lemon") and episodes of TV's *Search Control*, *Kung Fu*, *The Greatest American Hero* and *Dark Skies*.

Dukes of Hazzard star **Christopher Mayer** (George Charles Mayer III, aka "Chip Mayer") died the same day, aged fifty-seven. He also appeared in episodes of TV's *Weird Science*, *Xena: Warrior Princess*, *Sliders*, *Silk Stalkings* and *Star Trek: Deep Space Nine*.

Val Warren (Valmore Warren), who won a National Horror Makeup Contest in *Famous Monsters of Filmland* magazine to play a teenage werewolf in the AIP film *Bikini Beach* (1964), died of complications from cancer on 25 July, aged sixty-nine. An author, illustrator and musician, he edited the early 1960s fantasy film fanzine *Kaleidoscope* and wrote the 1979 book *Lost Lands, Mythical Kingdoms and Unknown Worlds*. Warren was also an authority on Buddy Holly and the Crickets.

Welsh-born character actor **Richard [de Pearsall] Pearson** died on 2 August, aged ninety-three. His films include *Scrooge* (1951), *Svengali* (1954), *How I Won the War*, *Macbeth* (1971), *Alice Through the Looking Glass* (1973), Disney's *One of Our Dinosaurs is Missing*, *The Blue Bird* (1976), *Whoops Apocalypse* and *Men in Black II* (as the voice of "Gordy"), and he appeared in episodes of *Stranger from Space*, *The Mystery of Edwin Drood* (1960), *Mystery and Imagination* (M. R. James' "Lost Hearts"), *Sherlock Holmes* (1968), *Out of the Unknown*, *The Rivals of Sherlock Holmes*, *Hammer House of Horror* ("The Thirteenth Reunion") and *Tales of the Unexpected*. Pearson was also the voice of "Mole" in *The Wind in the Willows* (1983–88) and *Oh! Mr Toad* (1989–90).

Former NFL football star-turned-actor **Bubba Smith** (Charles Aaron Smith), best known for his role in the *Police Academy* movies, died on 3 August, aged sixty-six. The six-foot, seven-inch Smith appeared in *Black Moon Rising*, *Blood River*, and episodes of *Wonder Woman* and *Sabrina the Teenage Witch*. He was also a regular on the 1984 TV series *Blue Thunder*.

Forty-eight-year-old **Francesco** [Daniele] **Quinn**, the son of actor Anthony Quinn, died .of an apparent heart attack while jogging in Malibu on 5 August. He portrayed "Vlad Tepes" in the 2003 film *Vlad*, and his other credits include episodes of *The Young Indiana Jones Chronicles* and *The Glades*. Quinn also provided the voice of "Dino" in *Transformers: Dark of the Moon*.

Distinguished British stage and screen actor **John Wood** CBE died on 6 August, aged eighty-one. He made his film debut in the 1952 Hammer thriller *Stolen Face*, directed by Terence Fisher, and he went on to appear in *The Mouse on the Moon*, *One More Time*, *Slaughterhouse-Five*, *WarGames*, *Agentii 009 ja kuoleman kurvit*, *The Purple Rose of Cairo*, *Ladyhawk*, *Shadowlands*, *Citizen X*, *Richard III* (1995), *Jane Eyre* (1996), *Rasputin* (1996), *The Avengers* and *The Little Vampire*. On TV his credits include *The Hooded Terror* and episodes of *Tales of Mystery*, *Saki*, *Out of the Unknown*, *The Avengers*, *Doomwatch*, *The Storyteller: Greek Myths* and *The Young Indiana Jones Chronicles*. In 1974 Wood appeared on stage in the title role of the Royal Shakespeare Company's revival of William Gillette's 1899 melodrama *Sherlock Holmes*.

In early August it was announced that British TV actress **Anne Ridler** had died. She had been suffering from throat cancer for some years. Best remembered for her distinctive voice in the series *Terrahawks* (1983–86), she also appeared in episodes of *One Step Beyond*, *Doctor Who* ("The Wheel in Space"), *Moonbase 3*, *Tom's Midnight Garden*, *Bedtime Stories* and *The Tomorrow People*.

Former British child actor turned TV producer and director **John Howard Davies** died of cancer on 22 August, aged seventy-two. At the age of eight he starred in David Lean's classic *Oliver Twist* (1948), and the following year he was in *The Rocking Horse Winner* (based on the short story by D. H. Lawrence). In later years he produced such comedy series as *Monty Python's Flying Circus*, *The Goodies*, *Fawlty Towers* and *The Good Life*.

Child star **Sybil Jason** (Sybil Jacobson) died of chronic obstructive pulmonary disease on 23 August, aged eighty-three. The South African-born actress was brought to Hollywood from

Britain in the mid-1930s by Warner Bros., who starred her opposite Al Jolson in *The Singing Kid* and several other films. After
the studio let her go in 1938, she appeared with screen rival
Shirley Temple in *The Little Princess* and *The Blue Bird* (from
which many of her scenes were cut, reportedly at the demand of
Temple's mother), before she retired from the screen.

The body of American actor **Michael Showers** was found floating in the Mississippi River, near New Orleans' French Quarter, on
the morning of 25 August. He had been diagnosed with multiple
sclerosis five months earlier and had been suffering from depression and anxiety. The forty-five-year-old Showers had a recurring
role as police Captain John Guidry in the HBO series *Treme*. He
also appeared in *Kiss of the Vampire* (aka *Imortally Yours*, 2009),
The Collector and Hammer's *The Resident* (with Christopher Lee),
along with an episode of TV's *The Vampire Diaries*.

American actress **Eve Brent** (Jean Ann Lewis), who portrayed
"Jane" opposite Gordon Scott's "Tarzan" in the TV fix-up
movies *Tarzan and the Trappers* and *Tarzan's Fight for Life*
(both 1958), died on 27 August, aged eighty-one. Her other films
include *Female Jungle*, *The Bride and the Beast*, *The White
Buffalo*, *Fade to Black*, *BrainWaves*, *Date with an Angel*, *The
Green Mile* and *The Curious Case of Benjamin Button* (uncredited). On TV she appeared in episodes of *Adventures of Superman*,
The Veil (hosted by Boris Karloff), *Highway to Heaven*, *Tales
from the Crypt*, *Twin Peaks*, *Weird Science* and *Roswell High*.

Former model turned actress **Cobina** [Carolyn] **Wright, Jr.**,
who co-starred in *Charlie Chan in Rio* (1941), died on
1 September, aged ninety.

American actress **Annette Charles** (Annette Cardona), who
played "Cha Cha DiGregorio" in *Grease* (1978), died of lung
cancer on 4 August, aged sixty-three. She also appeared in
episodes of *The Flying Nun*, *The Bionic Woman*, *Man from
Atlantis* and *The Incredible Hulk*.

American character actor **John Clark** died on 9 September,
aged ninety-five. He appeared in *The Light at the Edge of the
World*, *Graveyard of Horror* (aka *Necrophagus*), *The Time
Guardian* and *The Lords of Magick*.

Oscar-winning American leading man **Cliff Robertson**
(Clifford Parker Robertson) died on 10 September, the day after

his eighty-eighth birthday. He won an Academy Award for his starring role in *Charley* (1968). Based on the novel by Daniel Keyes, it had previously been filmed for TV in 1965 with Robertson again in the lead role. However, the actor's attempts to get a sequel made some years later only resulted in around fifteen minutes of promotional footage. His other film credits include *Man on a Swing*, Brian De Palma's *Obsession*, *Dominique* (aka *Dominique is Dead*), *Brainstorm* (1983), *Dead Reckoning*, *Escape from L.A.*, *13th Child*, *Riding the Bullet* (based on the novel by Stephen King) and *Spider-Man* (2002) and its two sequels (as "Ben Parker"), along with episodes of *Rod Brown of the Rocket Rangers* (in the title role), *The Twilight Zone*, *The Outer Limits* (1963 and 1999) and *Batman* (as cowboy villain "Shame"). Robertson was instrumental in exposing the major fraud that brought down Columbia Pictures executive David Begelman in the 1970s, but his own career suffered as a result. His marriages to actresses Cynthia Stone and Dina Merrill both ended in divorce.

Thirty-nine-year-old Welsh-born actor **Andy Whitfield**, who portrayed the title character in the Starz TV series *Spartacus: Blood and Sand* (2010), died in his home country of Australia on 11 September. He had been battling non-Hodgkins Lymphoma since being diagnosed in March 2010. A former building inspector and model, he also starred in the horror movies *Gabriel* and *The Clinic*.

Petite Canadian-born character actress **Frances Bay** (Frances Goffman) died in California on 15 September, aged ninety-two. She made her belated screen debut in 1978, and went on to appear in such movies as *Topper* (1979), *The Attic*, *Double Exposure*, *Nomads*, *Blue Velvet*, *Big Top Pee-wee*, *Arachnophobia*, *The Pit and the Pendulum* (1991), *Critters 3*, *Grave Secrets: The Legacy of Hilltop Drive*, *Twin Peaks: Fire Walk with Me*, *Single White Female*, *The Neighbor*, *In the Mouth of Madness*, Disney's *Inspector Gadget*, and *Ring Around the Rosie* (aka *Fear Itself: Dark Memories*). The actress' prolific TV credits include episodes of *Faerie Tale Theatre*, *Amazing Stories*, *Alien Nation*, *ALF*, *Tales from the Crypt*, *Twin Peaks* (as "Mrs Tremond"), *Quantum Leap*, *The X Files*, *Beyond Belief: Fact or Fiction*, *Charmed* and *Cavemen*.

American photographic model-turned-actress **Norma Eberhardt** died of complications from a stroke on 16 September, aged eighty-two. She co-starred in the 1958 film *The Return of Dracula* (aka *The Fantastic Disappearing Man*).

Eton-educated character actor **Jonathan Cecil** (Jonathan Hugh Gascoyne-Cecil), who usually portrayed upper-class English characters in films and on television, died of pneumonia on 22 September, aged seventy-two. Best known for portraying "Captain Arthur Hastings" in three 1980s TV movies starring Peter Ustinov as Hercule Poirot, he also appeared in Hammer's *Lust for a Vampire* and TV versions of *Alice Through the Looking Glass* (1973), *Gulliver in Lilliput* (1982) and *Alice in Wonderland* (1986).

Mexican comedian and singer **Gaspar Henaine** [Perez], better known as "Capulina" to his many fans, died from pneumonia on 30 September, aged eighty-five. In a career spanning five decades, he appeared in numerous films, including *Se los chupó la bruja*, *Los invisibles*, *Santo contra Capulina*, *Capulina contra los vampiros*, *El terror de Guanajuato* and *Capulina contra los monstruos*.

Grizzled American character actor **Charles Napier** died on 5 October, aged seventy-five. He made his full-frontal screen debut in Russ Meyer's sex comedy *Cherry Harry & Raquel!*, and also appeared in the director's *Beyond the Valley of the Dolls*, *The Seven Minutes* and *Supervixens*. Napier went on to appear in *Wacko*, *The Night Stalker* (1987), *Body Count*, *Deep Space*, *The Incredible Hulk Returns*, *Alien from the Deep*, *Dragonfight*, *Future Zone*, *Maniac Cop 2*, *The Silence of the Lambs*, *Frogtown II*, *Eyes of the Beholder*, *Body Bags*, *Skeeter*, *Ripper Man*, *Alien Species*, *The Cable Guy*, *Austin Powers: International Man of Mystery*, *Steel*, *Austin Powers: The Spy Who Shagged Me*, *Pirates of the Plain*, *Nutty Professor II: The Klumps*, *Dinocroc*, *The Manchurian Candidate* (2004) and *One-Eyed Monster*. Along with supplying voices to numerous cartoon series, on TV the actor also appeared in the original *Star Trek*, *Starsky and Hutch* ("Satan's Witches"), *The Incredible Hulk*, *Knight Rider*, *Tales of the Gold Monkey*, *Outlaws*, *The New Adventures of Superman*, *Star Trek: Deep Space Nine*, *Roswell High*, *The Legend of Tarzan* and *The 4400*. He also reportedly supplied the growls for the final two seasons of TV's *The Incredible Hulk*.

Striking Australian actress **Diane Cilento** died after a long illness on 7 October, aged seventy-seven. She left her second husband, James Bond actor Sean Connery, after eleven years for playwright Anthony Shaffer while starring in *The Wicker Man* (1973). After roles in the BBC's *A Tomb with a View* (1951) and the 1952 short *All Hallowe'en*, Cilento appeared in *Meet Mr Lucifer*, *The Angel Who Pawned Her Harp* and *Z.P.G.* (aka *Zero Population Growth*), along with episodes of *Late Night Horror* ("The Kiss of Blood"), *Thriller* ("Spell of Evil") and in a recurring role on the children's series *Halfway Across the Galaxy and Turn Left*. She also reportedly doubled for Mia Hama in a swimming scene in the Bond film *You Only Live Twice*.

Bulgarian-born British character actor and writer **George Baker** MBE, who starred as "Chief Inspector Wexford" in ITV's *The Ruth Rendell Mysteries* (1987–2000), died of pneumonia after a recent stroke the same day. He was eighty. Baker's other credits include such films as *Sword of Lancelot* (aka *Lancelot and Guinevere*), *Curse of the Fly*, the James Bond adventures *On Her Majesty's Secret Service* and *The Spy Who Loved Me*, *The Canterville Ghost* (1987) and *Back to the Secret Garden*, along with episodes of *The Prisoner* (as the "New Number Two"), *Doomwatch*, *Zodiac*, *Survivors* (1975), *Doctor Who* ("Full Circle"), *Robin of Sherwood*, *Johnny and the Dead* (based on the book by Terry Pratchett) and *Randall and Hopkirk {Deceased}* (2001). Creator Ian Fleming had apparently wanted the actor to play James Bond on the screen. Baker's third wife, actress **Louie Ramsay**, died in March at the age of eighty-one.

American actor and musician **David** [Alexander] **Hess**, who starred in and additionally composed the soundtrack for Wes Craven's infamous psycho thriller *The Last House on the Left*, died on 8 October, aged sixty-nine. He also appeared in *The House on the Edge of the Park*, *Swamp Thing*, *Body Count*, *Zombie Nation*, *Zodiac Killer*, *The Absence of Light*, *Fallen Angels* and *Smash Cut*, along with episodes of TV's *Knight Rider* and *Manimal*. Hess also directed the 1980 slasher film *To All a Goodnight*. In the late 1950s he had a music-recording career under the name "David Hill". He wrote a number of songs ¬orded by Elvis Presley, as well as "Speedy Gonzalez", which #1 hit for Pat Boone.

Dependable American actor **Alan Fudge** died of lung and liver cancer on 10 October, aged seventy-seven. His movies include *Bug, Capricorn One, Are You in the House Alone?*, *The Golden Gate Murders, Goliath Awaits, Brainstorm* (1983), *Chiller, My Demon Lover, I Saw What You Did* (1988), *Nightmare on the 13th Floor, Edward Scissorhands, Galaxis* and *Shark Swarm*. Fudge played "C. W. Crawford" on the 1977–78 TV series *Man from Atlantis*, and he also appeared in episodes of *Ghost Story, Wonder Woman, The Greatest American Hero, Knight Rider*, the 1980s *Twilight Zone* and *Alfred Hitchcock Presents* series, *Highway to Heaven, Alien Nation, Quantum Leap, M.A.N.T.I.S.* and *Dark Skies*.

British stage and screen actress **Sheila Allen** died on 13 October, aged seventy-eight. She appeared in the films *Children of the Damned, Venom* (aka *The Legend of Spider Forest*) and *Harry Potter and the Goblet of Fire*, along with an episode of TV's *The Prisoner* (1967).

Michael Cornelison, who starred in Frank Darabont's 1983 short *The Woman in the Room*, based on the story by Stephen King, died of liver complications on 15 October, aged fifty-nine. He also appeared in *Superstition, Timesweep, Mommy* and *Mommy's Day, Haunting Villisca* and *Husk*, along with two episodes of TV's *The Greatest American Hero*.

Glamorous British actress **Sue Lloyd** (Susan Margery Jeaffreson Lloyd) died on 20 October, aged seventy-two. A former chorus girl, showgirl and model, she studied acting with Jeff Corey and appeared in Hammer's *Hysteria, Corruption* (with Peter Cushing), *Go For a Take, No.1 of the Secret Service* and the 1993 Roy "Chubby" Brown comedy *U.F.O.* During the 1960s and '70s, the actress was a regular on British TV in such series as *The Avengers, Journey to the Unknown, Randall and Hopkirk (Deceased), Sherlock Holmes and Doctor Watson* and *Super Gran*. Lloyd starred in a short-lived stage version of *The Avengers* in 1971, and twenty years later she married actor Ronald Allen, six weeks before his death from lung cancer.

American character actor **Leonard Stone** (Leonard Steinbock) died of cancer on 2 November, the day before his eighty-eighth birthday. Best remembered as the father of the gum-chewing Violet Beauregarde in *Willy Wonka & the Chocolate Factory*

(1971), he also appeared in *Shock Treatment* (1964), *Soylent Green* and *Once Upon a Spy* (with Christopher Lee), along with episodes of TV's *The Outer Limits* (1963), the "lost" pilot *The Ghost of Sierra de Cobre, The Invaders, Lost in Space, Land of the Giants, The Six Million Dollar Man, Gemini Man, The Next Step Beyond, Bigfoot and Wildboy* and *The Invisible Man* (2001).

American actor and comedian **Sid Melton** (Sidney Meltzer) died of pneumonia on 3 November, aged ninety-four. His film credits include *Lost Continent* (1951) and *The Atomic Submarine*. Melton portrayed "Ichabod 'Ikky' Mudd" on TV's *Captain Midnight* (1954–56), and he also appeared in episodes of *Adventures of Superman, Alfred Hitchcock Presents, The Munsters* and *I Dream of Jeannie*.

Cynthia [Jeanette] **Myers**, who posed as a *Playboy* "Playmate of the Month" when she was just seventeen, died on 4 November, aged sixty-one. She studied acting with Jeff Corey and was in *Beyond the Valley of the Dolls* as well as playing an uncredited native girl in Hammer's *The Lost Continent* (1968), based on the novel by Dennis Wheatley.

Former World Heavyweight Boxing Champion "Smokin'" **Joe Frazier** (Joseph William Frazier) died of liver cancer on 7 November, aged sixty-seven. He had a role in the 1987 horror-comedy *Ghost Fever*.

British actor **Richard** [Lindon Harvey] **Morant**, the nephew of Bill Travers and son-in-law of Douglas Fairbanks, Jr. by his first marriage, died of an aneurysm on 9 November, aged sixty-six. He appeared in the films *The Hunchback of Notre Dame* (1976) and *The Company of Wolves*, as well as episodes of TV's *The Rivals of Sherlock Holmes, Bedtime Stories, The Mad Death, Jack the Ripper* (1988) and *The Legend of the Lost Keys*. Morant also played the eponymous space hero in the second series of the 1984 children's SF game show *Captain Zep – Space Detective*. As well as being an actor, he also sold bespoke carpets and rugs from his London gallery.

Malaysian-born British stage and screen actress **Dulcie Gray** ¯ (Dulcie Winifred Catherine Bailey) died of bronchial pneu- ɔn 15 November, aged ninety-five. She made her film ɔ early 1940s and appeared in *A Place of One's Own*, *Iurder* (aka *A Voice in the Night*) and an episode of TV's *Tales from the Crypt*. As an author, she wrote twenty-four books (mostly theatrical crime novels) and contributed eight stories to Herbert van Thal's *The Pan Book of Horror Stories* series. Her short fiction was collected in *Stage Door Fright: A Collection of Horror and Other Stories* (1977). Gray was married to fellow actor Michael Denison for fifty-nine years.

Ninety-three-year-old Austrian-Hungarian-born actor **Karl Slover** (Karl "Karchy" Kosiczky), one of the last surviving Munchkins from *The Wizard of Oz* (1939), died the same day from cardiopulmonary arrest. The four-foot, four-inch Slover, whose father sold him to a troupe of vaudeville performers when he was nine, was the smallest Munchkin. He played four parts in the classic movie: the "Munchkin Herald #1", "Sleepyhead", a singing Munchkin and a soldier. He also appeared in *Bringing Up Baby* and *The Terror of Tiny Town*.

Distinguished British actor **John Neville** OBE died of Alzheimer's disease in Toronto on 19 November, aged eighty-six. He emigrated to Canada in 1972, and his film credits include *Unearthly Stranger*, *A Study in Terror* (as "Sherlock Holmes"), *The Adventures of Baron Munchausen* (in the title role), *Journey to the Center of the Earth* (1993), *Shadow Zone: The Teacher Ate My Homework*, *The Fifth Element*, *Johnny 2.0*, *The X Files*, *Urban Legend* and *Spider*. He also appeared in episodes of such TV series as *Shadows of Fear*, *The Rivals of Sherlock Holmes* (as Austin Freeman's "Dr Thorndyke"), *Star Trek: The Next Generation*, *Viper*, *The X Files* (in a recurring role as "The Well-Manicured Man"), *F/X: The Series*, *The Adventures of Shirley Holmes* and the pilot for *Odyssey 5*.

Susan Palermo[-Piscitello] died of brain cancer on 23 November, aged fifty-nine. For many years she was Vice President of Operations for Sandy Frank Productions, and more recently she worked as an actress, musician, producer and/or special effects artist on such low budget horror films as *Zombies! Zombies! Everywhere*, *Post Mortem America 2021* and *Road Hell*.

American character actor **Bill McKinney** (William Denison McKinney), best known for his role as a crazed Mountain Man in *Deliverance*, died of cancer of the oesophagus on 1 December, aged eighty. His many other credits include *She Freak*, *Angel Unchained*, *Cleopatra Jones*, *The Strange and Deadly*

Occurrence, Strange New World, Back to the Future Part III, It Came from Outer Space II, The Green Mile, Hellborn (aka *Asylum of the Damned*), *Looney Tunes: Back in Action, 2001 Maniacs* and *The Devil Wears Spurs*, along with episodes of *I Dream of Jeannie, Galactica 1980* and *The Young Indiana Jones Chronicles*. McKinney also voiced the role of "Jonah Hex" on an episode of the animated *Batman* TV series.

American comedy actor **Alan** [Grigsby] **Sues**, a regular on *Rowan & Martin's Laugh-In* in the late 1960s and early 1970s, died of a heart attack the same day, aged eighty-five. He appeared in the movies *Oh! Heavenly Dog* and *A Bucket of Blood* (aka *The Death Artist*, 1995), while his other TV credits include episodes of *The Twilight Zone, The Wild Wild West, Fantasy Island, Time Express* (with Vincent Price), *Misunderstood Monsters* and *Sabrina the Teenage Witch*. On stage, Sues portrayed "Professor Moriarty" in the 1975 Broadway production of *Sherlock Holmes*.

Dependable American character actor and TV director **Harry Morgan** (Harry Bratsberg, aka "Henry Morgan"), best remembered for his Emmy Award-winning role as "Colonel Sherman T. Potter" in the long-running CBS-TV series *M*A*S*H* (1975–83), died of pneumonia on 7 December, aged ninety-six. During his extensive career, Morgan appeared in *The Loves of Edgar Allan Poe, Dragonwyck* (with Vincent Price), *Crime Doctor's Man Hunt* (scripted by Leigh Brackett), Disney's *Charlie and the Angel* and *The Cat from Outer Space, Exo-Man, Maneaters Are Loose!, The Wild Wild West Revisited* and *More Wild Wild West*, and *Dragnet* (1987), along with episodes of *Alfred Hitchcock Presents, Night Gallery*, the revived *The Twilight Zone* and a recurring role on *3rd Rock from the Sun*.

Child actress **Susan Gordon**, the daughter of producer/director Bert I. Gordon, died of cancer on 11 December, aged sixty-two. She appeared in her father's films *Attack of the Puppet People* (aka *Six Inches Tall*), *The Boy and the Pirates, Tormented* and *̇ture Mommy Dead*. Her other credits include a TV version of *̇le on 34th Street* (1959) and episodes of *Alfred Hitchcock̇ The Alfred Hitchcock Hour* and *The Twilight Zone*.

̇erican character actress **Louise Henry** (Jesse Louise ̇n 12 December, aged 100. She appeared in

Charlie Chan on Broadway and *Charlie Chan in Reno*. She retired from the screen in 1939.

Argentina-born actor **Alberto de Mendoza** (Alberto Manuel Rodríguez Gallego Gonzáles de Mendoza) died of respiratory failure in Spain the same day, aged eighty-eight. He began his film career in 1930, and his many credits include *The Ghost Lady* (1945), *La bestia humana*, *Horror Express* (with Christopher Lee and Peter Cushing) and the 1974 version of *And Then There Were None*.

Jennifer Miro (Jennifer Anderson), vocalist and electric piano player with the 1970s San Francisco punk/new wave/goth band The Nuns, died in New York City on 14 December. She appeared in the movies *Nightmare in Blood* (uncredited), *The Video Dead* and *Dr Caligari* (1989).

Seventy-three-year-old Scottish actor **Nicol Williamson**, who portrayed Sherlock Holmes in *The Seven-Per-Cent Solution* and Merlin in *Excalibur*, died of oesophageal cancer on 16 December. His other film credits include *Hamlet* (1969), *Venom*, *Macbeth* (1983), Disney's *Return to Oz*, *The Exorcist III* and *Spawn*. Williamson also appeared in an episode of the little-seen 1990 anthology TV show *Chillers*, hosted by Anthony Perkins. From 1971–77 he was married to actress Jill Townsend.

American character actor **Robert Easton** (Robert Burke, aka "Bob Easton"), regarded as "the Henry Higgins of Hollywood" for his later career as a respected dialect coach, died the same day, aged eighty-one. He appeared in *The Beast from 20,000 Fathoms* (uncredited), *The Neanderthal Man*, *Voyage to the Bottom of the Sea*, *The Loved One*, *One of Our Spies is Missing*, *Johnny Got His Gun*, *The Touch of Satan*, *The Giant Spider Invasion*, *Mr Sycamore*, Disney's *Pete's Dragon*, *Star Trek VI: The Undiscovered Country*, *Pet Sematary II*, *Needful Things*, *Spiritual Warriors* and *Horrorween*, plus episodes of TV's *Adventures of Superman*, *The Munsters*, *Lost in Space*, *My Mother the Car*, *The Man from U.N.C.L.E.*, *Get Smart*, *The Ghost Busters* (1975), *Kolchak: The Night Stalker* ("Mr R.I.N.G.") and *The Bionic Woman*. Easton was also the voice of co-pilot "Phones" and other characters in Gerry Anderson's "supermarionation" series *Stingray* (1964–65).

A chimpanzee, whose owner claimed was the eighty-year-old **Cheeta** that appeared in the Johnny Weissmuller *Tarzan* films of the 1930s, died of kidney failure at a Florida primate sanctuary on 24 December. However, experts agreed that it was extremely unlikely that it was the original chimp.

Virtuoso violinist **Israel Baker**, who contributed the screeching violin chords to Bernard Herrmann's score for Alfred Hitchcock's *Psycho* (1960), died on Christmas Day, aged ninety-two. A highly paid session musician and acclaimed concert musician, Baker's movie credits also include *Jonathan Livingstone Seagull* and *Indiana Jones and the Temple of Doom*.

Mexican-born character actor **Pedro Armendáriz, Jr.** (Pedro Armendáriz Bohr) died of cancer in New York on 26 December, aged seventy-one. He began his career in the 1960s in such films as *Las vampiras* (with John Carradine), and he continued to work in both his native country and the US. Armendárez's movie credits include *Don't Be Afraid of the Dark* (1973), *Chosen Survivors*, *Earthquake*, *Licence to Kill*, *The Legend of the Mask*, *The Mask of Zorro* (1998) and *The Legend of Zorro*, and he also appeared an episode of TV's *Knight Rider*.

FILM & TV TECHNICIANS/PRODUCERS

American make-up artist and musician **Verne Langdon** died on 1 January, aged sixty-nine. Perhaps best remembered as creator of the Universal Monster "Calendar Masks" for Don Post Studios, he worked on such movies as *The Haunted Palace*, *The Comedy of Terrors*, *Planet of the Apes*, *Beneath the Planet of the Apes*, *Escape from the Planet of the Apes* and *Conquest of the Planet of the Apes*, along with TV's *The Star Wars Holiday Special*. Langdon also created and co-produced the 1967 Decca record album *An Evening with Boris Karloff and His Friends*, and co-created the 1980 "Castle Dracula" show at Universal Studios.

Spanish screenwriter, producer and director **Juan Piquer ʼmón** (aka "J. P. Simon") died of lung cancer on 7 January, ʼeventy-five. His many genre films include *Where Time* ʼased on the novel by Jules Verne), *Satan's Blood*, ʼ*Man*, *Monster Island* (with Peter Cushing and Paul ʼ*Extraterrestrial Visitors*, *Slugs* (based on the novel by Shaun Hutson), *Cthulhu Mansion* (which had absolutely nothing to do with H. P. Lovecraft), *The Rift* and *La isla del diablo*. Simón additionally scripted *Beyond Terror* (as "Alfredo Casado"), *Nexus 2.431* (which was based on his unproduced screenplay) and *El escarabajo de oro* (a 1999 adaptation of Edgar Allan Poe's "The Gold Bug"). In 2008 he was the subject of Nacho Cerdà's documentary *Pieces of Juan (Piquer Simón)*.

Del Reisman, who was associate producer on the original TV series of *The Twilight Zone* and scripted episodes of *Ghost Story* and *The Six Million Dollar Man*, died on 8 January, aged eighty-six.

Peter Yates, the British film director probably best remembered for the iconic car chase movie *Bullitt* (1968) starring Steve McQueen, died after a long illness on 9 January, aged eighty-one. He began his career as a dubbing assistant, working his way up to assistant director on such films as the sleazy *Cover Girl Killer* before getting his break directing the classic Cliff Richard musical *Summer Holiday*. His varied other credits include *The Deep* and *Krull*, along with episodes of TV's *The Saint* and *Danger Man*.

British production designer **Peter** (Edward Sidney Canton) **Phillips**, best known for his BAFTA Award-winning work on TV's *Brideshead Revisited* (1981), died on 10 January, aged eighty-five. He worked as a production design assistant on the 1947 film *Uncle Silas* (aka *The Inheritance*, based on the novel by J. Sheridan Le Fanu) before joining Granada Television, where his credits include three episodes of 1980s series *Shades of Darkness* – "Bewitched", based on the story by Edith Wharton; "The Demon Lover", based on the story by Elizabeth Bowen, and "Agatha Christie's The Last Séance".

David [Oswald] **Nelson**, the real-life son of Ozzie Nelson and Harriet Hilliard, and the older brother of singer/actor Ricky Nelson, died of complications from colon cancer on 11 January, aged seventy-four. He was the last surviving star of the 1952–66 TV show *The Adventures of Ozzie & Harriet*, and in 1982 he directed the horror movie *Death Screams* (aka *House of Death*).

Dan Filie, who wrote and produced the 2009 horror comedy *Frankenhood*, died on 13 January, aged fifty-six. As Senior Vice President for Drama Development for Universal Television in the 1990s, he was instrumental in creating the TV series *Hercules* and *Xena: Warrior Princess*.

American music producer and publisher **Don** (Donald) **Kirshner** died of heart failure on 17 January, aged seventy-six. During the 1960s, Kirshner helped launch the careers of such songwriters as Carole King, Neil Sedaka and Neil Diamond when he became music supervisor on NBC-TV's *The Monkees*, before he was fired when the manufactured group demanded more control. Kirshner went on to work as a music consultant/supervisor on such TV series as *Bewitched*, *I Dream of Jeannie*, the animated *Archie* series ("Sugar Sugar" stayed at #1 in the US for four weeks in 1969), *The Amazing Chan and the Chan Clan* and the 1976 TV movie *The Savage Bees* (which he also executive produced). He also produced the rarely-seen 1970 SF musical *Toomorrow*, directed by Val Guest and starring a young Olivia Newton-John.

Greek-born film and stage costume designer **Theoni V. Aldredge** (Theoni Athanasiou Vachliotis) died of a heart attack in Stamford, Connecticut, on 21 January, aged eighty-eight. Broadway dimmed its lights to mark her death. The Oscar-winning designer created costumes for such movies as *No Way to Treat a Lady*, *The Fury*, *Eyes of Laura Mars*, *The First Deadly Sin*, *Ghostbusters*, *Addams Family Values* and *The Rage: Carrie 2*.

Bernd Eichinger, Germany's most successful movie producer, died of a heart attack while having dinner with family and friends at his home in Los Angeles on 24 January. He was sixty-one. Best known as the producer of *Resident Evil* and the sequels starring Milla Jovovich, his other film credits include *The NeverEnding Story*, *The Name of the Rose*, *The Fantastic Four* (both the 1994 and 2005 versions), *Prince Valiant* (1997), *The Calling*, *The Mists of Avalon* (based on the novel by Marion Zimmer Bradley), *666: In Bed with the Devil*, *Perfume: The Story of a Murderer* (which he also co-scripted from Patrick Süskind's World Fantasy Award-winning novel) and *4: Rise of the Silver Surfer*.

Richard Datin, who headed the team of model-makers that created the Starship USS *Enterprise* for the original *Star Trek* TV series (1966–69), died the same day.

American TV director **Phil Bondelli** died 31 January, aged ~~-three. He directed episodes of *The Bionic Woman*, *The Six Dollar Man*, *Fantasy Island*, *Blue Thunder* and *Outlaws*.

director and author **Charles E. Sellier, Jr.**, founder ~ Grizzly Adams Productions, Inc., died the same day, aged sixty-seven. From the early 1970s onwards he produced a string of paranormal documentaries, including *The Mysterious Monsters*, *In Search of Noah's Ark*, *The Amazing World of Psychic Phenomena*, *Beyond and Back*, *The Bermuda Triangle* and *Beyond Death's Door*, along with the TV series *Encounters with the Unexplained*. Sellier also executive produced *The Time Machine* (1978), *The Fall of the House of Usher* (1979), *Hangar 18*, *The Legend of Sleepy Hollow* (1980), *Earthbound*, *The Boogens* and *Knight Rider 2000*, and he directed the Christmas horror movie *Silent Night Deadly Night* (1984).

Walt Disney animator and director **Bill** (William) **Justice**, who joined the studio in 1937 and stayed there for forty-two years, died on 10 February, aged ninety-seven. He began his career as an "in-betweener" on *Snow White and the Seven Dwarfs* (1937) and went on to work as a full animator on such films as *Pinocchio*, *Fantasia*, *Bambi*, *The Three Caballeros*, *The Adventures of Ichabod and Mr Toad* (uncredited), *Alice in Wonderland* and *Peter Pan*, along with numerous shorts. Although a film of Roald Dahl's first children's story, "The Gremlins", was developed by the studio during World War II, it was eventually abandoned. However, Justice's concept illustrations were used in the book when it was published in 1943. He directed the opening title sequence for TV's *The Mickey Mouse Club*, which premiered in October 1955, and with Disney colleagues T. Hee and Xavier Atencio he created stop-motions scenes for *The Shaggy Dog*, *The Misadventures of Merlin Jones* and *Mary Poppins*. Justice went on to help create the audio-animatronic figures for Disneyland's Pirates of the Caribbean, Mission to Mars and Haunted Mansion attractions, and he also designed parades and costumes for the theme park. Justice retired in 1979, and his 1992 autobiography was entitled *Justice for Disney*. He was named a Disney Legend in 1996.

British TV producer and director **Paul** [Coryn Valentine] **Lucas** died of cancer on 13 February, aged fifty-five. Best known for his work on the award-winning *Prime Suspect* series, he also directed two episodes of the BBC's *Murder Rooms: The Dark Beginnings of Sherlock Holmes* and the 2000 movie *After Alice* (aka *Eye of the Killer*).

American exploitation film producer, director and screen-writer **David F.** (Frank) **Friedman** died of heart failure on 14 February, aged eighty-seven. He had lost his hearing and eyesight almost a decade before. He began his career in the early 1960s with business partner Herschell Gordon Lewis making "nudie-cuties", before the pair moved on to horror with the infamous *Blood Feast* (1963). Made for just $24,500, the "first splatter film" went on to make millions. The pioneering pair followed it up with the equally gory *Two Thousand Maniacs!* and *Color Me Blood Red*, and Friedman's numerous other cult credits include *She Freak, Space-Thing, The Erotic Adventures of Siegfried, The Adult Version of Jekyll & Hyde* and *Ilsa: She-Wolf of the SS*. He was credited as executive producer on the more recent *Blood Feast 2: All U Can Eat, 2001 Maniacs, Crustacean* (featuring writer Peter Atkins) and *2001 Maniacs: Field of Screams*. Friedman's fun 1990 autobiography was titled *A Youth in Babylon: Confessions of a Trash-Film King*.

Thirty-nine-year-old **Perry Moore** (William Perry Moore IV), who was an executive producer on *The Chronicles of Narnia: The Lion, the Witch and the Wardrobe* and its two sequels, *Prince Caspian* and *The Voyage of the Dawn Treader*, died from an apparent drug overdose on 17 February, after being found unconscious in his New York apartment. Moore was also chosen by the C. S. Lewis estate to write the *Official Illustrated Movie Companion* to the first film. In 2009 he produced the TV documentary *Tell Them Anything You Want: A Portrait of Maurice Sendak*. As a response to how gay characters were depicted in the comic book industry, Moore wrote the award-winning YA novel *Hero* (2007), about a teenage superhero struggling with his sexual orientation. He was voted *People Magazine*'s "Sexy Man of the Week" in the 19 November 2007 issue.

Hollywood press agent turned movie producer **Walter Seltzer** died on 18 February, aged ninety-six. His credits include *The War Lord, The Omega Man* and *Soylent Green*, all starring his ˙d Charlton Heston.

˙ican former assistant director and production manager ˙ was killed, along with his wife and another couple, ˙, several days after their yacht had been hijacked ˙n the Gulf of Aden. Adam worked in various capacities on *The Savage Bees*, *Day of the Animals*, *The Evil*, *The Goonies* and episodes of the original *V* TV series before he began sailing around the world performing missionary work.

American film producer and director **Gary Winick** died of a brain tumour on 27 February, aged forty-nine. A pioneer in digital film-making, he found commercial success with such films as *13 Going on 30* and the 2006 remake of *Charlotte's Web*.

British-born film and television director **Charles Jarrott** died of cancer in Los Angeles on 4 March. He was eighty-three. Jarrot's credits include the 1968 TV movie of *The Strange Case of Dr Jekyll and Mr Hyde* starring Jack Palance, the 1973 musical remake of *Lost Horizon*, Disney's *Condorman* and episodes of TV's *The Unforseen*, *Out of This World*, *Haunted* and *Armchair Theatre* ("The Picture of Dorian Gray" and "The Rose Affair").

American director **Sidney Lumet** died of lymphoma on 9 April, aged eighty-six. A former actor, he began his directing career in live television in the 1950s before going on to make a string of acclaimed films. His credits include *Fail-Safe* (1964), *The Wiz* and *Deathtrap* (1982). Lumet had a small role in the 2004 remake of *The Manchurian Candidate*, and he was presented with an honorary Academy Award in 2005.

Japanese *anime* director **Osamu Dezaki** died on 17 April, aged sixty-seven. His TV credits include *The Mighty Orbots* and *Bionic Six*.

American TV director **Charles** [Friedman] **Haas** died on 12 May, aged ninety-seven. He began his career as an extra at Universal in 1935, and his directing credits include *Tarzan and the Trappers* (with Gordon Scott as Tarzan), stitched together from three unsold TV shows, plus episodes of *Dick Tracy* (1951), *The Shadow* (1954), *The New Adventures of Charlie Chan*, *Men Into Space*, *The Alfred Hitchcock Hour*, *The Outer Limits* and *The Man from U.N.C.L.E.*

Harry Redmond, Jr., the son of special effects pioneer Harry Redmond, Sr., died of complications from heart disease on 23 May, aged 101. Redmond worked (often uncredited) with his father – who was head of special effects at RKO Radio – on such films as *The Most Dangerous Game* (aka *Hounds of Zaroff*), *King Kong* (1933), *The Son of Kong* and *She* (1935). He also worked on *Lost Horizon* (1937), *Wonder Man*, *Angel on My*

Shoulder, *The Secret Life of Walter Mitty*, *The Bishop's Wife* (1947), *The Magnetic Monster*, *Donovan's Brain*, *Riders to the Stars* and *Gog*. Redmond's TV credits include *Ten Little Niggers* (1947), *Science Fiction Theatre*, *The Outer Limits* and the 1964 spin-off pilot *The Unknown*.

British film editor (Hitchcock's *The Man Who Knew Too Much*, *The Spy in Black*) turned producer **Hugh** [St. Clair] **Stewart** died on 31 May, aged 100. After working on films with Norman Wisdom and Morecambe and Wise, his later credits as a producer included *Mr Horatio Knibbles* and *The Flying Sorcerer* for the Children's Film Foundation.

British film and TV director **Pat Jackson** (Patrick Douglas Selmes Jackson), reportedly the last surviving director of the 1967–68 TV series *The Prisoner*, died on 3 June, aged ninety-five. He also directed the 1961 crime film *Seven Keys* (which appears to be an uncredited version of the much-filmed *Seven Keys to Baldpate*) and the lively horror comedy *What a Carve Up!* (aka *No Place Like Homicide!*), starring Sidney James and Kenneth Connor.

American writer, producer and director **Leonard B.** (Bernard) **Stone** died of heart failure on 7 June, aged eighty-seven. He began his career scripting Abbott and Costello's later films (including *Africa Screams*), before creating such TV shows as *McMillan & Wife*, and writing and producing episodes of *Get Smart*, *The Snoop Sisters* and *Holmes and Yo-Yo*. Stone's other credits include the *Get Smart* movies, *The Nude Bomb* and *Get Smart Again!*. From 1951–53 he was married to actress Julie Adams.

Swedish cinematographer [Erling] **Gunnar Fischer** died of an infection on 11 June, aged 100. He is best known for his twelve collaborations with director Ingmar Bergman, including *The Seventh Seal*, *The Magician* and *The Devil's Eye*.

American movie producer **Laura** [Ellen] **Ziskin** died on 12 June, aged sixty-one. She had been battling breast cancer for seven years. Responsible for the blockbuster *Spider-Man* (2002) and its two sequels, her other credits include *Eyes of Laura Mars*, *Fail Safe* (2000) and the 2012 franchise re-boot *The Amazing Spider-Man*, plus episodes of the 2003 *Tarzan* TV series.

Film and TV producer **Christopher** [Elwin] **Neame**, the son of director and cinematographer Ronald Neame, died in France of an aneurysm the same day. He was sixty-eight. Starting out as a clapper boy at Hammer on *Dracula Prince of Darkness* and *Rasputin the Mad Monk*, Neame worked as an uncredited assistant director on *Frankenstein Created Woman*, *Quatermass and the Pit* (aka *Five Million Miles to Earth*) and *The Devil Rides Out* and as a production manager on *Frankenstein Must Be Destroyed*, *Blood from the Mummy's Tomb*, *Fear in the Night*, *Demons of the Mind* and *Frankenstein and the Monster from Hell*. He was also an associate producer on Tigon's *The Beast in the Cellar* and production manager/designer on the sexy sci-fi comedy *Zeta One*. The first of his three autobiographies, *Rungs On a Ladder* (2003), was about his time at Hammer. Neame's godfather was Noël Coward.

Michael J. Hein, founder of the New York City Horror Film Festival in 2002, died of a heart attack on 9 July, aged forty-one. He contributed special effects make-up to *Metamorphosis: The Alien Factor*, *Class of Nuke 'Em High Part II: Subhumanoid Meltdown* and *Out of Darkness*, and scripted, produced and directed the 2001 horror film *Biohazardous*.

American TV producer and writer **Sherwood** [Charles] **Schwartz**, who created such series as *It's About Time*, *Gilligan's Island* and *The Brady Bunch*, died on 12 July, aged ninety-four. A former joke writer for Bob Hope's radio show, his other credits include the comedy 1983 TV movie *The Invisible Woman*. Schwartz also created the theme tunes to a number of his shows.

Japanese film and TV animator **Toyoo Ashida**, who directed the 1985 *anime*, *Vampire Hunter D*, died on 23 July, aged sixty-seven. His many other credits include the *Space Battleship Yamato*, *Ulysses 31* and *Fist of the North Star* (1986).

Cyprus-born film director **Mihalis Kakogiannis** (aka Michael Yannis/Michael Cacoyannis), who directed the Oscar-winning *Zorba the Greek* (1964), died in Athens, Greece, on 25 July. He was eighty-nine. Kakogiannis made an uncredited appearance in the 1948 body-swap comedy *Vice Versa* and he also scripted, produced and directed the 1967 counter-culture SF comedy *The Day the Fish Came Out*.

Canadian-born film and TV director **Silvio Narizzano** died in London on 26 July, aged eighty-four. After producing a 1952 series of *20,000 Leagues Under the Sea* for Canadian television, he moved to the UK, where he directed Hammer's *Fanatic* (aka

Die! Die! My Darling) and worked uncredited on an episode of *Space Precinct*. Narizzano's low budget *Las flores del vicio* (aka *Bloodbath*, 1979) starred Dennis Hopper and was filmed in Spain.

Polly Platt (Mary Marr Platt), who was married to director Peter Bogdanovich from 1962 until 1972, died of amyotrophic lateral sclerosis (Lou Gehrig's disease) on 27 July, aged seventy-two. Her various credits in the movie industry include being Nancy Sinatra's stunt double in *The Wild Angels*, production co-ordinator on *Voyage to the Planet of Prehistoric Women*, co-story writer and production designer of Bogdanovich's *Targets* (starring Boris Karloff), production designer on *The Man With Two Brains* and *The Witches of Eastwick*, and executive producer of the 2011 A&E documentary *Corman's World: Exploits of a Hollywood Rebel*.

Italian film director and journalist **Gualtiero Jacopetti**, who created the exploitation "Mondo" genre with his 1962 documentary *Mondo Cane* (A Dog's Life), died on 17 August, aged ninety-one. The film was a huge commercial success and led to a number of similar "shockumentaries" in the mid-1960s. J. G. Ballard incorporated the director's aesthetics into his fragmentary novel *The Atrocity Exhibition* (1970).

Scottish-born BAFTA and Emmy Award-winning TV and film director **Alastair Reid** died the same day, aged seventy-two. His credits include *The Night Digger* (scripted by Roald Dahl), *Dr Jekyll and Mr Hyde* (1980, starring David Hemmings), *Artemis 81*, and two episodes of *Tales of the Unexpected*.

Iranian-born **Reza** [Sayed] **Badiyi**, who holds the Directors Guild of America record for directing more television episodes than anybody else, died in Los Angeles on 21 August, aged eighty-one. He shot the iconic "wave curl" title sequence for *Hawaii Five-0* and the opening sequence for *Get Smart*. His numerous other credits include episodes of *Mission: Impossible*, *The Magician*, *The Six Million Dollar Man*, *Man from Atlantis*, *Holmes and Yo-Yo*, *The Incredible Hulk*, *The Phoenix*, *Superboy*, *Dinosaurs*, *Star Trek: Deep Space Nine*, *Nowhere Man*, *Viper*, *Baywatch Nights*, *Buffy the Vampire Slayer*, *Mortal Combat: Conquest*, *Sliders* and *Early Edition*. Badiyi also directed the 1972 TV movie *The Eyes of Charles*

Sands, and he was assistant director on *Carnival of Souls* (1962), in which he made an uncredited appearance as a bus ticket customer.

Veteran American TV director **Charles S. Durbin** (Charles Samuel Dubronevski) died on 5 September, aged ninety-two. He helmed episodes of such shows as *Tales of Tomorrow* (including an adaptation of Cyril M. Kornbluth's "Little Black Bag"), *Tarzan* (1966), *The New People*, *Ghost Story*, *Kung Fu*, *Man from Atlantis*, *Tabitha*, *Supertrain*, *Herbie the Love Bug* and *Starman*, along with the TV movies *Cinderella* (1965), *Death in Space* and *Topper* (1979). In 1958 Durbin was blacklisted for four years by the House Committee on Un-American Activities.

American underground film-maker, comics artist and teacher **George** (Andrew) **Kuchar**, died of prostate cancer on 6 September, aged sixty-nine. He began making 8mm films in the 1950s with his twin brother Mike, and his numerous experimental and avant-garde short films include such titles as *The Slasher*, *I Was a Teenage Rumpot*, *The Fall of the House of Yasmin*, *Route 666*, *Hush Hush Sweet Harlot*, *Planet of the Vamps*, *Kiss of Frankenstein* and *The Fury of Frau Frankenstein*. In 1975 he published a cartoon biography of H. P. Lovecraft in *Arcade #3*, which offended many fans of the writer.

Highly-respected Hollywood producer and studio executive **John Calley** died of cancer after a long illness on 13 September, aged eighty-one. His film credits include *The Loved One*, *13* (aka *Eye of the Devil*), *Castle Keep* and *Catch-22*. After leaving the movie industry in 1980 for more than a decade, he returned to produce *The Da Vinci Code* and its sequel, *Angels & Demons*. Calley received the Irving G. Thalberg Memorial Award in 2009 from The Academy of Motion Pictures Arts & Sciences. His second wife was actress Meg Tilly.

Canadian film producer **John Dunning** died on 19 September, aged eighty-four. He co-founded Cinepix (later Lions Gate Films) in 1962, and his movie credits include *The Sensual Sorceress*, *Death Weekend*, David Cronenberg's *Shivers* and *Rabid*, *My Bloody Valentine* (1981 and 2009 versions), *Happy Birthday to Me*, *Spacehunter: Adventures in the Forbidden Zone*, *Whispers* and *The Incredible Adventures of Marco Polo and His Journeys to the End of the Earth*.

Fritz Manes, a boyhood school friend of Clint Eastwood who went on to produce a number of the actor's movies, including *Firefox, Tightrope* and *Pale Rider,* died on 27 September, aged seventy-nine. He also produced *Ratboy* (1986), directed by Eastwood's former girlfriend, Sandra Locke.

Fifty-six-year-old technology guru **Steve Jobs** (Steven Paul Jobs), who co-created Apple Computer Inc. in 1977 with Steve Wozniak, died of respiratory arrest stemming from a metastatic pancreatic tumour on 5 October. He had been diagnosed with a rare form pancreatic cancer in 2003. In 1986, Jobs purchased a computer graphics firm from George Lucas and renamed it Pixar Animation Studios. In 1991 the company signed a deal with Disney, and Jobs is credited as an executive producer on *Toy Story* (1995).

Welsh-born TV director and scriptwriter [Alan] **Paul Dickson** died on 6 October, aged ninety-one. An award-winning documentary film-maker, he also helmed episodes of *Colonel March of Scotland Yard* (starring Boris Karloff), *The Avengers, The Champions, Randall and Hopkirk (Deceased)* and *Department S.* In 1956 Dickson directed the low budget SF film *Satellite in the Sky.*

Yugoslavia-born cinematographer **Andrew Laszlo** (András László) died in Montana on 7 October, aged eighty-five. After beginning his career in documentaries (including *The Beatles at Shea Stadium*), he worked on *Miracle on 34th Street* (1973), *The Dain Curse, The Funhouse, Southern Comfort, Streets of Fire, Remo: Unarmed and Dangerous, Poltergeist II: The Other Side, Innerspace, Star Trek V: The Final Frontier* and *Ghost Dad.*

Iranian-born Hollywood costume designer **Ray Aghayan** (Reymond G. Aghayan) died on 10 October, aged eighty-three. His credits include *Our Man Flint, In Like Flint* and *Doctor Dolittle* (1967), along with more than a dozen Academy Awards shows. He won an Emmy Award with his lifetime partner Bob Mackie for the costumes in an all-star TV version of *Alice Through the Looking Glass* (1966).

Prolific British TV director **Peter Hammond** (Peter Charles Hammond Hill) died on 12 October, aged eighty-seven. A former actor (the 1949 *Helter Skelter,* Hammer's *X The Unknown*), he began directing in the early 1960s and his credits include episodes of *Out of This World* (hosted by Boris Karloff), *The Avengers*, *Out of the Unknown*, *Wuthering Heights* (1978), *Tales of the Unexpected*, *Shades of Darkness*, *The Return of Sherlock Holmes*, *The Case-Book of Sherlock Holmes* and *The Memoirs of Sherlock Holmes*. In 1987, Hammond also directed the Holmes TV movie *The Sign of Four* and the BBC mini-series *Dark Angel* (aka *Uncle Silas*), based on the Gothic novel by J. Sheridan Le Fanu.

British-born film producer **Richard Gordon** died in New York City on 1 November, aged eighty-five. Along with his older brother Alex, Gordon moved to the US in 1947, starting up his own distribution company, Gordon Films, on the East Coast. This resulted in him entering into co-production deals with various European companies, and he produced or executive produced such films as *The Haunted Strangler* (aka *Grip of the Strangler*, starring Boris Karloff), *Fiend Without a Face*, *Corridors of Blood* (with Karloff and Christopher Lee), *First Man Into Space*, *The Playgirls and the Vampire*, *Devil Doll* (1964), *Curse of the Voodoo* (aka *Curse of Simba*), *The Projected Man*, *Naked Evil* (aka *Exorcism at Midnight*), *Island of Terror* (starring Peter Cushing), *Secrets of Sex* (aka *Bizarre*), *Tower of Evil* (aka *The Horror of Snape Island/Beyond the Fog*), *Horror Hospital* (with Michael Gough), *The Cat and the Canary* (1978) and *Inseminoid* (aka *Horror Planet*). Gordon also "presented" such films as *Metempsyco* (aks *Tomb of Torture*) and *Cave of the Living Dead* to the American market. He became Bela Lugosi's agent in the 1950s, and after a UK theatrical tour of *Dracula* flopped in 1951, he came up with the story idea for the comedy *Mother Riley Meets the Vampire* (aka *My Son the Vampire*) starring the ailing actor.

Hollywood costume designer **Theadora Van Runkle** (Dorothy Schweppe) died of lung cancer on 4 November, aged eighty-two. Best known for her designs for *Bonnie and Clyde*, *Bullitt* and *The Godfather Part II*, she also worked on *Myra Breckinridge*, *Johnny Got His Gun*, *Peggy Sue Got Married* and *White Dwarf*, along with the TV series *Wizards and Warriors*.

British TV producer and director **Mark [William] Hall** died after a short illness on 17 November, aged seventy-five. With his college friend Brian Cosgrove, Hall formed their own animation company, Cosgrove Hall Productions, in 1976, and together they created such children's shows as *Jamie and the Magic Torch*, *Creepy Crawlies*, *The Wind in the Willows*, *Count Duckula*, *Oh! Mr Toad*, *Danger Mouse*, *Noddy's Toyland Adventures*, *Fantomcat* and *Truckers*, *Soul Music* and *Wyrd Sisters* (all based on novels by Terry Pratchett). Hall also co-produced TV movies of *Cinderella* (1979), *The Pied Piper of Hamelin* (1981), *The Wind in the Willows* (1983), *The Reluctant Dragon* (1987) and Roald Dahl's *The BFG* (1989).

British film production designer **Syd Cain** died on 21 November, aged ninety-three. His credits include *Fahrenheit 451* (based on the novel by Ray Bradbury), *Billion Dollar Brain*, *On Her Majesty's Secret Service*, Alfred Hitchcock's *Frenzy* and TV's *The New Avengers*. As an art director, Cain also contributed to *The Road to Hong Kong*, *Dr No* and *Live and Let Die*, and he worked in various capacities on *Uncle Silas* (1947), *The Gamma People*, *Supergirl*, *Who Framed Roger Rabbit*, *Neverending Story III: The Return to Fantasia*, *GoldenEye* and *Tarzan and the Lost City*.

Eighty-four-year-old maverick British director **Ken Russell** (Henry Kenneth Alfred Russell) died on 27 November, following a series of strokes. After making a string of acclaimed TV documentaries and short films for the BBC in the late 1950s–early '60s, he transferred his talents to the cinema, where he directed a number of flamboyant and often controversial movies, including *Billion Dollar Brain*, *The Devils*, *Tommy*, *Lisztomania*, *Altered States*, *Gothic*, *The Lair of the White Worm*, the home-made comedy-musical *The Fall of the Louse of Usher: A Gothic Tale for the 21st Century*, the "Girl with Golden Breasts" episode of the anthology horror movie *Trapped Ashes*, and the short *Revenge of the Elephant Man*. Russell made cameo appearances in a number of his own films, and had a role in the 2011 zombie comedy *Invasion of the Not Quite Dead*.

The **35mm Motion Picture Camera** officially died in 2011. In an article written by Debra Kaufman for the *Creative Cow* website, it was revealed that ARRI, Panavision and Aaton had all ceased making them, concentrating instead on professional digital cameras.

Maverick American film producer and political activist **Bert Schneider** (Berton Jerome Schneider), who co-produced the

Emmy Award-winning TV series *The Monkees* (1966–68) and the music group's psychedelic spin-off movie *Head* (1968), died on 12 December, aged seventy-eight. Schneider's other credits include *Easy Rider*, *Five Easy Pieces*, *The Last Picture Show* and *Days of Heaven*.

Australian-born scriptwriter and director **Don Sharp** (Donald Herman Sharp), who made six films with Christopher Lee, died in Cornwall, England, on 14 December, aged eighty-nine. A former actor, he moved to the UK after World War II and started directing in the mid-1950s. Although not prolific, Sharp was always a stylish director and his credits include Hammer's *The Kiss of the Vampire*, *The Devil-Ship Pirates* and *Rasputin the Mad Monk*, along with *Witchcraft* (with Lon Chaney, Jr.), *Curse of the Fly*, *The Face of Fu Manchu* and *The Brides of Fu Manchu*, *Rocket to the Moon* (aka *Those Fantastic Flying Fools*), *Dark Places*, *Psychomania* (aka *The Death Wheelers*) and *What Waits Below* (aka *Secrets of the Phantom Caverns*). Sharp also directed three episodes of *The Avengers*, plus an episode each of *The Champions* and *Hammer House of Horror* ("Guardian of the Abyss"). As an actor, he also had a leading role in the 1953 BBC Radio serial *Journey Into Space*.

USEFUL ADDRESSES

THE FOLLOWING LISTING OF organizations, publications, dealers and individuals is designed to present readers and authors with further avenues to explore. Although I can personally recommend many of those listed on the following pages, neither the publisher nor myself can take any responsibility for the services they offer. Please also note that the information below is only a guide and is subject to change without notice.

—The Editor

ORGANIZATIONS

The Australian Horror Writers Association (*www.australianhorror.com*) is a non-profit organization that was formed in 2005 as a way of providing a unified voice and a sense of community for Australian (and New Zealand) writers of horror/dark fiction. AHWA aims to become the first point of reference for writers and fans of the dark side of literature in Australia, to spread the acceptance and improve the understanding of what horror is in literature to a wider audience, and in doing so gain a greater readership for established and new writers alike. Email: *ahwa@australianhorror.com*.

The British Fantasy Society (*www.britishfantasysociety. org*) was founded in 1971 and publishes the newsletter *Prism* and the magazines *Dark Horizons* and *New Horizons* featuring articles, interviews and fiction, along with occasional special booklets. The BFS also enjoys a lively online community – there is an email news-feed, a discussion board with numerous links, and a CyberStore selling various publications. FantasyCon is one of the UK's friendliest conventions and there are social gatherings and meet-the-author events organised around Britain. For yearly membership details, email: *secretary@britishfantasysociety.org*. You can also join online through the Cyberstore.

The Friends of Arthur Machen (*www.machensoc.demon.co.uk*) is a literary society whose objectives include encouraging a wider recognition of Machen's work and providing a focus for critical debate. Members get a hardcover journal, *Faunus*, twice a year, and also the informative newsletter *Machenalia*. For membership details, contact Deputy Treasurer Jon Preece: *machenfoam@yahoo.co.uk*.

The Friends of the Merril Collection (*www.friendsofmerril.org/*) is a volunteer organization that provides support and assistance to the largest public collection of science fiction, fantasy and horror books in North America. Details about annual membership and donations are available from the website or by contacting The Friends of the Merril Collection, c/o Lillian H. Smith Branch, Toronto Public Library, 239 College Street, 3rd Floor, Toronto, Ontario M5T 1R5, Canada. Email: *ltoolis@tpl.toronto.on.ca*.

The Horror Writers Association (*www.horror.org*) is a world-wide organization of writers and publishing professionals dedicated to promoting the interests of writers of Horror and Dark Fantasy. It was formed in the early 1980s. Interested individuals may apply for Active, Affiliate or Associate membership. Active membership is limited to professional writers. HWA publishes a monthly online *Newsletter*, and sponsors the annual Bram Stoker Awards. Apply online or write to HWA Membership, PO Box 50577, Palo Alto, CA 94303, USA.

World Fantasy Convention (*www.worldfantasy.org*) is an annual convention held in a different (usually American) city each year, oriented particularly towards serious readers and genre professionals.

World Horror Convention (*www.worldhorrorsociety.org*) is a smaller, more relaxed, event. It is aimed specifically at horror fans and professionals, and held in a different city (usually American) each year.

SELECTED SMALL PRESS PUBLISHERS

Aeon Press Books (*www.aeonpressbooks.com*).

Atomic Fez Publishing (*www.atomicfez.com*).

Bad Moon Books/Eclipse (*www.badmoonbooks.com*), 1854 W. Chateau Avenue, Anaheim, CA 92804-4527, USA.

B!/Bedabbled (*bedabbled.blogspot.com/*), 24 Whinney Moor Lane, Retford DN22 7AA, UK. Email: *bedabbled@hotmail.co.uk*.

Big Finish Productions Ltd. (*www.bigfinish.com*), PO Box 1127, Maidenhead SL6 3LW, UK.

Books of the Dead Press (*booksofthedead.blogspot.com*). Email: *besthorror@gmail.com*.

Cemetery Dance Publications (*www.cemeterydance.com*), 132-B Industry Lane, Unit #7, Forest Hill, MD 21050, USA. Email: *info@cemeterydance.com*.

ChiZine Publications (*www.chizinepub.com*). Email: *info@chizinepub.com*.

Chômu Press (*www.chomupress.com*), 70 Hill Street, Richmond, Surrey TW9 1TW, UK. Email: *info@chomupress.com*.

Cycatrix Press (*www.jasunni.com*), JaSunni Productions LLC, 16420 SE McGillivray Blvd., Ste 103-1010, Vancouver, WA 98683, USA. Email: *jasunni@jasunni.com*.

Dark Arts Books (*www.darkartsbooks.com*). Email: *emailsales@darkartsbooks.com*.

Dark Continents Publishing (*www.darkcontinentspublishing*).

Dark Minds Press (*www.darkmindspress.com*), 31 Gristmill Close, Cheltenham GL51 0PZ, UK. Email: *mail@darkmindspress.com*.

Dark Regions Press/Ghost House (*www.darkregions.com*), PO Box 1264, Colusa, CA 95932, USA.

Donald M. Grant, Publisher, Inc. (*www.grantbooks.com*), 19 Surrey Lane, PO Box 187, Hampton Falls, NH 03844, USA.

DreamHaven Books (*www.dreamhavenbooks.com*), 2301 East 38th Street, Minneapolis, MN 55406, USA.

Earthling Publications (*www.earthlingpub.com*), PO Box 413, Northborough, MA 01532, USA. Email: *earthlingpub@yahoo.com.*

Edge Science Fiction and Fantasy Publishing/Hades Publications, Inc. (*www.edgewebsite.com/www.hadespublications.com*), PO Box 1714, Calgary, Alberta T2P 2L7, Canada. Email: *publisher@hadespublications.com.*

Guntlet Publications (*www.gauntletpress.com*), 5307 Arroyo Street, Colorado Springs, CO 80922, USA. Email: *info@gauntletpress.com.*

Gray Friar Press (*www.grayfriarpress.com*), 9 Abbey Terrace, Whitby, North Yorkshire Y021 3HQ, UK. Email: *gary.fry@virgin.net.*

Hersham Horror Books (*hershamhorrorbooks.web.com/*). Email: *silenthater@aol.com.*

Hippocampus Press (*www.hippocampuspress.com*), PO Box 641, New York, NY 10156, USA. Email: *info@hippocampuspress.com.*

IDW Publishing (*www.idwpublishing.com*), 5080 Santa Fe Street, San Diego, CA 92109, USA.

Imajiin Books (*www.imajiinbooks.com*).

Jurassic London (*www.pandemonium-fiction.com*), 153 South Lambeth Road, London SW8 1XN, UK. Email: *jared@jurassic-london.com.*

LCR Books (*www.liliesandcannonballs.com*), PO Box 720422, Jackson Heights, NY 11372, USA. Email: *editor@liliesandcannonballs.com.*

McFarland & Company, Inc., Publishers (*www.mcfarlandpub.com*), Box 611, Jefferson, NC 28640, USA.

MHB Press (*www.mhbpress.com*), The White House, 29 Park Lane, Shifnal, Shropshire TF11 9HD, UK.

Miskatonic River Press (*www.miskatonicriverpress.com*), 944 Reynolds Road, Suite 188, Lakeland, Florida 33801, USA. Email: *keeper@miskatonicriverpress.com.*

Mortbury Press (*mortburypress.webs.com/*), Shiloh, Nantglas, Llandrindod Wells, Powys LD1 6PD, UK. Email: *mortburypress@yahoo.com.*

Mythos Books, LLC (*www.mythosbooks.com*), 351 Lake Ridge Road, Poplar Buff, MO 63901, USA.

NewCon Press (*www.newconpress.co.uk*).

Noose and Gibbet Publishing (*www.nooseandgibbetpublishing.com*). Email: *info@nooseandgibbetpublishing.com*.

Nightjar Press (*nightjarpress.wordpress.com*), 38 Belfield Road, Manchester M20 6BH, UK.

Night Shade Books (*www.nightshadebooks.com*), 1661 Tennessee Street, #3H, San Francisco, CA 94107, USA. Email: *night@nightshadebooks.com*.

Obverse Books (*www.obversebooks.co.uk*). Email: *info@obversebooks.co.uk*.

P'rea Press (*www.preapress.com*), 34 Osborne Road, Lane Cove, NSW 2066, Australia. Email: *dannyL58@hotmail.com*.

PS Publishing Ltd/PS Artbooks Ltd (*www.pspublishing.co.uk*), Grosvenor House, 1 New Road, Hornsea HU18 1PG, UK. Email: *editor@pspublishing.co.uk*.

Raven Electrick Ink (*ravenelectrick.com*), 9327 Creemore Drive, Tujunga, CA 91042, USA. Email: *comments@raven electrick.com*.

The Scarecrow Press, Inc. (*www.scarecrowpress.com*), The Rowman & Littlefield Publishing Group, Inc., 4501 Forbes Boulevard, Suite 200, Lanham, Maryland 20706, USA.

Screaming Dreams Publishing (*www.screamingdreams.com*), 25 Heol Evan Wynne, Pontlottyn, Bargoed, Mid Glamorgan CF81 9PQ, UK. Email: *steve@screamingdreams.com*.

Side Real Press (*www.siderealpress.co.uk*), 34 Normanton Terrace, Elswick, Newcastle Upon Tyne NE4 6PP, UK. Email: *siderealpress@hotmail.com*.

Small Beer Press (*www.smallbeerpress.com*), 150 Pleasant Street #306, Easthampton, MA 01027, USA. Email: *info@smallbeerpress.com*.

Spectral Press (*spectralpress.wordpress.com*), 5 Serjeants Green, Milton Keynes, Buckinghamshire MK14 6HA, UK. Email: *spectralpress@gmail.com*.

Stumar Press (*www.stumarpress.co.uk*), 4 Pottery Close, Belper, Derbyshire DE56 0HU, UK. Email: *stumarpress@gmail.com*.

Subterranean Press (*www.subterraneanpress.com*), PO Box 190106, Burton, MI 48519, USA. Email: *subpress@gmail.com*.

Swallowdown Press (*www.swallowdownpress.com*), PO Box 86810, Portland, OR 97286-0810, USA.

Tachyon Publications (*www.tachyonpublications.com*), 1459 18th Street #139, San Francisco, CA 94107, USA.

Tartarus Press (*tartaruspress.com*), Coverley House, Carlton-in-Coverdale, Leyburn, North Yorkshire DL8 4AY, UK. Email: *tartarus@pavilion.co.uk*.

Telos Publishing Ltd (*www.telos.co.uk*), 17 Pendre Avenue, Prestatyn, Denbighshire LL19 9SH, UK. Email: *david@telos.co.uk*.

Ticonderoga Publications (*www.ticonderogapublications.com*), PO Box 29, Greenwood, WA 6924, Australia.

Two Ravens Press Ltd. (*www.tworavenspress.com*), Taigh nam Fitheach, 26 Breanish Uig, Isle of Lewis HS2 9HB, UK.

Undertow Publications (*www.undertowbooks.com*), 1905 Faylee Crescent, Pickering, ON L1V 2T3, Canada. Email: *undertowbooks@gmail.com*.

SELECTED MAGAZINES

Albedo One (*www.albedo1.com*) is Ireland's magazine of science fiction, fantasy and horror. The editorial address is Albedo One, 2 Post Road, Lusk, Co. Dublin, Ireland. Email: *bobn@yellowbrickroad.ie*.

Ansible is a highly entertaining monthly SF and fantasy newsletter/gossip column edited by David Langford. It is available free electronically by sending an email to: *ansible-request@dcs.gla.ac.uk* with a subject line reading "subscribe", or you can receive the print version by sending a stamped and addressed envelope to Ansible, 94 London Road, Reading, Berks RG1 5AU, UK. Back issues, links and book lists are also available online.

Black Gate: Adventures in Fantasy Literature (*www.blackgate.com*) is an attractive pulp-style publication that includes heroic fantasy and horror fiction. Subscriptions are available from: New Epoch Press, 815 Oak Street, St. Charles, IL 60174, USA. Email: *john@blackgate.com*.

Black Static (*www.ttapress.com*) is the UK's premier horror fiction magazine, published bi-monthly. Six- and twelve-issue subscriptions are available, along with a new lifetime subscription, from TTA Press, 5 Martins Lane, Witcham, Ely, Cambs CB6 2LB, UK, or from the secure TTA website. Email: *black static@ttapress.com*.

Cemetery Dance Magazine (*www.cemeterydance.com*) is edited by Richard Chizmar and includes fiction up to 5,000 words, interviews, articles and columns by many of the biggest names in horror. For subscription information contact: Cemetery Dance Publications, PO Box 623, Forest Hill, MD 21050, USA. Email: *info@cemeterydance.com*.

Dark Discoveries (*www.darkdiscoveries.com*) sets out to unsettle, edify and involve with fiction, interviews and non-fiction and is published irregularly. 142 Woodside Drive, Longview, WA 98632, USA. Email: *info@darkdiscoveries. com*.

The Ghosts & Scholars M. R. James Newsletter (*www. pardoes.info/roanddarroll/GS.html*) is a scholarly journal published roughly twice a year. It is dedicated to the classic ghost story and, as the title implies, to M. R. James in particular. Two-issue subscriptions are available from Haunted Library Publications, c/o Flat One, 36 Hamilton Street, Hoole, Chester CH2 3JQ, UK.

The Horror Zine (*www.thehorrorzine.com*) is a monthly online magazine edited by Jeani Rector that features fiction, poetry, interviews and reviews.

Locus (*www.locusmag.com*) is the monthly newspaper of the SF/fantasy/horror field. Contact: Locus Publications, PO Box 13305, Oakland, CA 94661, USA. Subscription information with other rates and order forms are also available on the website. Email: *locus@locusmag.com*. You can also now subscribe to a digital edition at: *weightlessbooks.com/genre/ nonfiction/locus-12-month-subscription*.

Locus Online (*www.locusmag.com/news*) is an excellent online source for the latest news and reviews.

The Magazine of Fantasy & Science Fiction (*www.fandsf. com*) has been publishing some of the best imaginative fiction for more than sixty years. Edited by Gordon Van Gelder, and now published bi-monthly, single copies or an annual subscription are available by US cheques or credit card from: Fantasy & Science Fiction, PO Box 3447, Hoboken, NJ 07030, USA, or you can subscribe via the new website.

Morpheus Tales (*www.morpheustales.com*) is a quarterly magazine of horror, science fiction and fantasy, with reviews appearing on the website and myspace versions (*www.myspace. com/morpheustales*).

Murky Depths: The Quarterly Anthology of Graphically Dark Speculative Fiction (*www.murkydepths.com*) is a glossy magazine devoted to graphic strips and short fiction.

Phantom Drift: A Journal of New Fabulism (*www.word craftoforegon.com/pd.html*) is a literary journal dedicated to building an understanding of and appreciation for New Fabulism and a Literature of the Fantastic. The journal is published annually. Email: *phantomdrifteditor@yahoo.com*.

Rabbit Hole is a semi-regular newsletter about Harlan Ellison® that also offers exclusive signed books by the author. A subscription is available from The Harlan Ellison® Recording Collection, PO Box 55548, Sherman Oaks, CA 91413-0548, USA.

Rue Morgue (*www.rue-morgue.com*), is a glossy monthly magazine edited by Dave Alexander and subtitled "Horror in Culture & Entertainment". Each issue is packed with full colour features and reviews of new films, books, comics, music and game releases. Subscriptions are available from: Marrs Media Inc., 2926 Dundas Street West, Toronto, ON M6P 1Y8, Canada, or by credit card on the website. Email: *info@rue -morgue.com*. *Rue Morgue* also runs the Festival of Fear: Canadian National Horror Expo in Toronto. Every Friday you can log on to a new show at Rue Morgue Radio at *www. ruemorgueradio.com* and your horror shopping online source, The Rue Morgue Marketplace, is at *www.ruemorguemarket place.com*.

Shadows & Tall Trees (*www.undertowbooks.com*) is published annually. Editor Michael Kelly's trade paperback magazine is open to previously unpublished submissions of quiet, literary horror fiction from 1 January to 28 February. Standard manuscript format, up to 7,500 words. Email: *under towbooks@gmail.com*.

Space and Time: The Magazine of Fantasy, Horror, and Science Fiction (*www.spaceandtimemagazine.com*) is published quarterly. Single issues and subscriptions are available from the website or from the new address: Space and Time Magazine, 458 Elizabeth Avenue #5348, Somerset, NJ 08873, USA. In the UK and Europe, copies can be ordered from BBR Distributing, PO Box 625, Sheffield S1 3GY, UK.

Spectral Press (*spectralpress.wordpress.com*), 5 Serjeants Green, Neath Hill, Milton Keynes, Bucks MK14 6HA, UK. Email: *spectralpress@gmail.com*.

Subterranean Press Magazine (*www.supterraneanpress.com/magazine*).

Supernatural Tales (*suptales.blogspot.com*) is a twice-yearly fiction magazine edited by David Longhorn. Three-issue subscriptions are available via post (UK cheques or PayPal only) to: Supernatural Tales, 291 Eastbourne Avenue, Gateshead NE8 4NN, UK. Email: *davidlonghorn@hotmail.com*.

Theaker's Quarterly Fiction (*www.theakersquarterly.blogspot.com*). Email: *theakers@silveragebooks.com*.

Video WatcHDog (*www.videowatchdog.com*) describes itself as "The Perfectionist's Guide to Fantastic Video" and is published bi-monthly. One year (six issues) subscriptions are available from: *orders@videowatchdog.com*.

DEALERS

Bookfellows/Mystery and Imagination Books (*www.mystery-andimagination.com*) is owned and operated by Malcolm and Christine Bell, who have been selling fine and rare books since 1975. This clean and neatly organised store includes SF/fantasy/horror/mystery, along with all other areas of popular literature. Many editions are signed, and catalogues are issued regularly. Credit cards accepted. Open seven days a week at 238 N. Brand Blvd, Glendale, California 91203, USA. Tel: (818) 545-0206. Fax: (818) 545-0094. Email: *bookfellows@gowebway.com*.

Borderlands Books (*www.borderlands-books.com*) is a nicely designed store with friendly staff and an impressive stock of new and used books from both sides of the Atlantic. 866 Valencia

Street (at 19th), San Francisco, CA 94110, USA. Tel: (415) 824-8203 or (888) 893-4008 (toll free in the US). Credit cards accepted. World-wide shipping. Email: *office@borderlands-books.com*.

Cold Tonnage Books (*www.coldtonnage.com*) offers excellent mail order new and used SF/fantasy/horror, art, reference, limited editions, etc. Write to: Andy & Angela Richards, Cold Tonnage Books, 22 Kings Lane, Windlesham, Surrey GU20 6JQ, UK. Credit cards accepted. Tel: +44 (0)1276475388. Email: *andy@coldtonnage.com*.

Ken Cowley issues a bumper catalogue filled with a huge number of titles both old and new, many from his own extensive collection. Write to: Ken Cowley, Trinity Cottage, 153 Old Church Road, Clevedon, North Somerset BS21 7TU, UK. Tel: +44 (0)1275872247. Email: *kencowley@blueyonder.co.uk*.

Richard Dalby issues an annual Christmas catalogue of used Ghost Stories and other supernatural volumes at very reasonable prices. Write to: Richard Dalby, 4 Westbourne Park, Scarborough, North Yorkshire Y012 4AT. Tel: +44 (0)1723 377049.

Dark Delicacies (*www.darkdel.com*) is a Burbank, California, store specialising in horror books, toys, vampire merchandise and signings. They also do mail order and run money-saving book club and membership discount deals. 3512 W. Magnolia Blvd, Burbank, CA 91505, USA. Tel: (818) 556-6660. Credit cards accepted. Email: *darkdel@darkdel.com*.

DreamHaven Books & Comics (*www.dreamhavenbooks.com*) became an online and mail-order outlet only in early 2012, offering new and used SF/fantasy/horror/art and illustrated etc. with regular catalogues (both print and email). Credit cards accepted. Tel: (612) 823-6070. Email: *dream@dreamhaven books.com*.

Fantastic Literature (*www.fantasticliterature.com*) mail order offers the UK's biggest online out-of-print SF/fantasy/horror genre bookshop. Fanzines, pulps and vintage paperbacks as well. Write to: Simon and Laraine Gosden, Fantastic Literature, 35 The Ramparts, Rayleigh, Essex SS6 8PY, UK. Credit cards and PayPal accepted. Tel/Fax: +44 (0)1268747564. Email: *simon@ fantasticliterature.com*.

Horrorbles (*www.horrorbles.com*), 6731 West Roosevelt Road, Berwyn, IL 60402, USA. Small, friendly Chicago store selling horror and sci-fi toys, memorabilia and magazines that has monthly specials and in-store signings. Specialises in exclusive "Basil Gogos" and "Svengoolie" items. Tel: (708) 484-7370. Email: *store@horrorbles.com*.

Kayo Books (*www.kayobooks.com*) is a bright, clean treasure-trove of used SF/fantasy/horror/mystery/pulps spread over two floors. Titles are stacked alphabetically by subject, and there are many bargains to be had. Credit cards accepted. Visit the store (Wednesday–Saturday, 11 a.m. to 6 p.m.) at 814 Post Street, San Francisco, CA 94109, USA or order off their website. Tel: (415) 749 0554. Email: *kayo@kayobooks. com*.

Iliad Bookshop (*www.iliadbooks.com*), 5400 Cahuenga Blvd, North Hollywood, CA 91601, USA. General used bookstore that has a very impressive genre section, reasonable prices and knowledgeable staff. They have recently expanded their fiction section into an adjacent building. Tel: (818) 509-2665.

Porcupine Books offers regular catalogues and extensive mail order lists of used fantasy/horror/SF titles via email *brian@ porcupine.demon.co.uk* or write to: 37 Coventry Road, Ilford, Essex IG1 4QR, UK. Tel: +44 (0)20 85543799.

Kirk Ruebotham (*www.ukbookworld.com/members/kirk*) is a mail-order only dealer, who specializes in mainly out-of-print and second-hand horror/SF/fantasy/crime fiction and related non-fiction at very good prices, with regular catalogues. Write to: 16 Beaconsfield Road, Runcorn, Cheshire WA7 4BX, UK. Tel: +44 (0)1928560540. Email: *kirk.ruebotham@ntlworld. com*.

The Talking Dead is run by Bob and Julie Wardzinski and offers reasonably priced paperbacks, rare pulps and hardcovers, with catalogues issued *very* occasionally. They accept wants lists and are also the exclusive supplier of back issues of *Interzone*. Credit cards accepted. Contact them at: 12 Rosamund Avenue, Merley, Wimborne, Dorset BH21 1TE, UK. Tel: +44 (0)1202 849212 (9 a.m.–9 p.m.). Email: *books@thetalkingdead.fsnet. co.uk*.

Ygor's Books specialises in out of print science fiction, fantasy and horror titles, including British, signed, speciality press and limited editions. They also buy books, letters and original art in these fields. Email: *ygorsbooks@gmail.com.*

ONLINE

All Things Horror (*www.allthingshorror.co.uk*) is a genre interview site run by Johnny Mains that mainly focuses on authors, editors, artists and movie stars of the 1960s, 1970s and 1980s. It also caters to reviews of both films and books, and features a short fiction section that is open to submissions.

Cast Macabre (*www.castmacabre.org*) is the premium horror fiction podcast that is "bringing Fear to your ears", offering a free horror short story every week.

Fantastic Fiction (*www.fantasticfiction.co.uk*) features more than 2,000 best-selling author biographies with all their latest books, covers and descriptions.

FEARnet (*www.fearnet.com*) is a digital cable channel dedicated to all things horror, including news, free movie downloads (sadly not available to those outside North America) and Mick Garris' online talk show *Post Mortem.*

Hellnotes (*www.hellnotes.com*) offers news and reviews of novels, collections, magazines, anthologies, non-fiction works, and chapbooks. Materials for review should be sent to editor and publisher David B. Silva, Hellnotes, 5135 Chapel View Court, North Las Vegas, NV 89031, USA. Email: *news@hell notes.com* or *dbsilva13@gmail.com.*

The Irish Journal of Gothic and Horror Studies (*irishgothich orrorjournal.homestead.com*) features a diverse range of articles and reviews, along with a regular "Lost Souls" feature focusing on overlooked individuals in the genre.

SF Site (*www.sfsite.com*) has been posted twice each month since 1997. Presently, it publishes around thirty to fifty reviews of SF, fantasy and horror from mass-market publishers and some small press. They also maintain link pages for Author and Fan Tribute Sites and other facets including pages for Interviews, Fiction, Science Fact, Bookstores, Small Press, Publishers, E-zines and Magazines, Artists, Audio, Art Galleries, Newsgroups and

Writers' Resources. Periodically, they add features such as author and publisher reading lists.

Vault of Evil (*www.vaultofevil.wordpress.com*) is a site dedicated to celebrating the best in British horror with special emphasis on UK anthologies (although they apparently don't care much for this series!). There is also a lively forum devoted to many different themes at *www.vaultofevil.proboards.com*.